WIZARD
BY TRADE

Books by Jim Butcher

WIZARD BY TRADE

SUMMER KNIGHT

DEATH MASKS

Jim Butcher

SFBC
FANTASY

SUMMER KNIGHT Copyright © 2002 by Jim Butcher
    Publication History: Roc paperback, September 2002
DEATH MASKS Copyright © 2003 by Jim Butcher
    Publication History: Roc paperback, August 2003

First SFBC Science Fiction Printing: April 2006

Published by arrangement with:
NAL Signet
a division of Penguin Group (USA) Inc.
375 Hudson Street
New York, NY 10014

Visit The SFBC online at http://www.sfbc.com

ISBN 10: 0-7394-6581-3
ISBN 13: 978-0-7394-6581-3

Printed in the United States of America.

Contents

Contents

SUMMER KNIGHT

This book is for big sisters everywhere who have enough patience not to strangle their little brothers—and particularly for my own sisters, who had more than most. I owe you both so much.

And for Mom, for reasons that are so obvious that they really don't need to be said—but I thought I would make special mention of candy cane cookies and that rocking chair that creaked me to sleep.

ACKNOWLEDGMENTS

The author (that's me) wishes to thank all the people who should have been thanked in other books—Ricia and A.J., obviously, and the mighty Jen. Thank you to all the folks who have been so supportive of my work all along, including (but not limited to) Wil and Erin (who fed me great Chicago information and who I missed the first time around), Fred and Chris, Martina and Caroline and Debra and Cam and Jess and Monica and April.

Thank you also to you mighty librarians who have tricked people into reading these books, and to the bookstore personnel (and lurkers) who have gone out of their way to help me get noticed. I admit to being somewhat baffled, but I'm very grateful to you all.

I owe thanks to so many people that I probably am incapable of remembering everyone. If I missed someone, let Shannon know. She will club me on the head with a baseball bat and point out the mistake.

(P.S. Shannon and J.J., as always, thank you. I'd promise to be less of a weirdo, but we all know how long *that* one would last.)

Chapter One

❦

It rained toads the day the White Council came to town.

I got out of the Blue Beetle, my beat-up old Volkswagen bug, and squinted against the midsummer sunlight. Lake Meadow Park lies a bit south of Chicago's Loop, a long sprint from Lake Michigan's shores. Even in heat like we'd had lately, the park would normally be crowded with people. Today it was deserted but for an old lady with a shopping cart and a long coat, tottering around the park. It wasn't yet noon, and my sweats and T-shirt were too hot for the weather.

I squinted around the park for a moment, took a couple of steps onto the grass, and got hit on the head by something damp and squishy.

I flinched and slapped at my hair. Something small fell past my face and onto the ground at my feet. A toad. Not a big one, as toads go—it could easily have sat in the palm of my hand. It wobbled for a few moments upon hitting the ground, then let out a bleary croak and started hopping drunkenly away.

I looked around me and saw other toads on the ground. A lot of them. The sound of their croaking grew louder as I walked further into the park. Even as I watched, several more amphibians plopped out of the sky, as though the Almighty had dropped them down a laundry chute. Toads hopped around everywhere. They didn't carpet the ground, but you couldn't possibly miss them. Every moment or so, you would hear the thump of another one landing. Their croaking sounded vaguely like the speech-chatter of a crowded room.

"Weird, huh?" said an eager voice. I looked up to see a short young man with broad shoulders and a confident walk coming toward me. Billy the Werewolf wore sweatpants and a plain dark T-shirt. A year or two ago the outfit would have concealed the forty or fifty extra pounds he'd been carrying. Now they concealed all the muscle he'd traded it in for. He stuck out his hand, smiling. "What did I tell you, Harry?"

"Billy," I responded. He crunched down hard as I shook his hand. Or maybe he was just that much stronger. "How's the werewolf biz?"

"Getting interesting," he said. "We've run into a lot of odd things lately when we've been out patrolling. Like this." He gestured at the park. Another toad fell from the sky several feet away. "That's why we called the wizard."

Patrolling. Holy vigilantes, Batman. "Any of the normals been here?"

"No, except for some meteorological guys from the university. They said that they were having tornadoes in Louisiana or something, that the storms must have thrown the toads here."

I snorted. "You'd think 'it's magic' would be easier to swallow than that."

Billy grinned. "Don't worry. I'm sure someone will come along and declare it a hoax before long."

"Uh-huh." I turned back to the Beetle and popped the hood to rummage in the forward storage compartment. I came out with a nylon backpack and dragged a couple of small cloth sacks out of it. I threw one to Billy. "Grab a couple of toads and pitch them in there for me."

He caught the bag and frowned. "Why?"

"So I can make sure they're real."

Billy lifted his eyebrows. "You think they're not?"

I squinted at him. "Look, Billy, just do it. I haven't slept, I can't remember the last time I ate a hot meal, and I've got a lot to do before tonight."

"But why wouldn't they be real? They look real."

I blew out a breath and tried to keep my temper. It had been short lately. "They could look real and feel real, but it's possible that they're just constructs. Made out of the material of the Nevernever and animated by magic. I hope they are."

"Why?"

"Because all that would mean is that some faerie got bored and played a trick. They do that sometimes."

"Okay. But if they're real?"

"If they're real, then it means something is out of whack."

"What kind of out of whack?"

"The serious kind. Holes in the fabric of reality."

"And that would be bad?"

I eyed him. "Yeah, Billy. That would be bad. It would mean something big was going down."

"But what if—"

My temper flared. "I don't have the time or inclination to teach a class today. Shut the hell up."

He lifted a hand in a pacifying gesture. "Okay, man. Whatever." He fell into step beside me and started picking up toads as we walked across the park. "So, uh, it's good to see you, Harry. Me and the gang were wondering if you wanted to come by this weekend, do some socializing."

I scooped up a toad of my own and eyed him dubiously. "Doing what?"

He grinned at me. "Playing Arcanos, man. The campaign is getting really fun."

Role-playing games. I made a monosyllabic sound. The old lady with the shopping cart wandered past us, the wheels of the cart squeaking and wobbling.

"Seriously, it's great," he insisted. "We're storming the fortress of Lord Malocchio, except we have to do it in disguise in the dead of night, so that the Council of Truth won't know who the vigilantes who brought him down were. There's spells and demons and dragons and everything. Interested?"

"Sounds too much like work."

Billy let out a snort. "Harry, look, I know this whole vampire war thing has you jumpy. And grouchy. But you've been lurking in your basement way too much lately."

"What vampire war?"

Billy rolled his eyes. "Word gets around, Harry. I know that the Red Court of the vampires declared war on the wizards after you burned down Bianca's place last fall. I know that they've tried to kill you a couple of times since then. I even know that the wizards' White Council is coming to town sometime soon to figure out what to do."

I glowered at him. "What White Council?"

He sighed. "It's not a good time for you to be turning into a hermit, Harry. I mean, look at you. When was the last time you shaved? Had a shower? A haircut? Got out to do your laundry?"

I lifted a hand and scratched at the wiry growth of beard on my face. "I've been out. I've been out plenty of times."

Billy snagged another toad. "Like when?"

"I went to that football game with you and the Alphas."

He snorted. "Yeah. In January, Dresden. It's June." Billy glanced up at my face and frowned. "People are worried about you. I mean, I know you've been working on some project or something. But this whole unwashed wild man look just isn't you."

I stooped and grabbed a toad. "You don't know what you're talking about."

"I know better than you think," he said. "It's about Susan, right? Something happened to her last fall. Something you're trying to undo. Maybe something the vampires did. That's why she left town."

I closed my eyes and tried not to crush the toad in my hand. "Drop the subject."

Billy planted his feet and thrust his chin out at me. "No, Harry. Dammit, you vanish from the face of the earth, you're hardly showing up at your office, won't answer your phone, don't often answer your door. We're your friends, and we're worried about you."

"I'm fine," I said.

"You're a lousy liar. Word is that the Reds are bringing more muscle into town. That they're offering their groupies full vampirehood if one of them brings you down."

"Hell's bells," I muttered. My head started to ache.

"It isn't a good time for you to be outside by yourself. Even during daylight."

"I don't need a baby-sitter, Billy."

"Harry, I know you better than most. I know you can do stuff that other people can't—but that doesn't make you Superman. Everyone needs help sometimes."

"Not me. Not now." I stuffed the toad into my sack and picked up another. "I don't have time for it."

"Oh, that reminds me." Billy drew a folded piece of paper out of the pocket of his sweats and read it. "You've got an appointment with a client at three."

I blinked at him. "What?"

"I dropped by your office and checked your messages. A Ms. Sommerset was trying to reach you, so I called her and set up the appointment for you."

I felt my temper rising again. "You did what?"

His expression turned annoyed. "I checked your mail, too. The landlord for the office dropped off your eviction notice. If you don't have him paid off in a week, he's booting you out."

"What the hell gives you the right to go poking around in my office, Billy? Or calling my clients?"

He took a step in front of me, glaring. I had to focus on his nose to avoid the risk of looking at his eyes. "Get off the high horse, Harry. I'm your freaking friend. You've been spending all your time hiding in your apartment. You should be happy I'm helping you save your business."

"You're damned right it's my business," I spat. The shopping cart lady circled past in my peripheral vision, cart wheels squeaking as she walked behind me. "Mine. As in none of yours."

He thrust out his jaw. "Fine. How about you just crawl back into your cave until they evict you from that, too?" He spread his hands. "Good God, man. I don't need to be a wizard to see when someone's in a downward spiral. You're hurting. You need help."

I jabbed a finger into his chest. "No, Billy. I don't need more *help*. I don't need to be baby-sitting a bunch of kids who think that because they've learned one trick they're ready to be the Lone Ranger with fangs and a tail. I don't need to be worrying about the vamps targeting the people around me when they can't get to me. I don't need to be second-guessing myself, wondering who *else* is going to get hurt because I dropped the ball." I reached down and snatched up a toad, jerking the cloth bag from Billy's hands on the way back up. "I don't need *you*."

Naturally, the hit went down right then.

It wasn't subtle, as attempted assassinations go. An engine roared and a black compact pickup truck jumped the curb into the park fifty yards away. It jounced and slewed to one side, tires digging up furrows in the sunbaked grass. A pair of men clung to a roll bar in the back of the truck. They were dressed all in black, complete with black sunglasses over black ski masks, and their guns matched—automatic weapons in the mini-Uzi tradition.

"Get back!" I shouted. With my right hand, I grabbed at Billy and shoved him behind me. With my left, I shook out the bracelet on my wrist, hung with a row of tiny, medieval-style shields. I lifted my left hand toward the truck and drew in my will, focusing it with the bracelet into a sudden, transparent, shimmering half-globe that spread out between me and the oncoming truck.

The truck ground to a halt. The two gunmen didn't wait for it to settle. With all the fire discipline of an action-movie extra, they pointed their guns more or less at me and emptied their clips in one roaring burst.

Sparks flew from the shield in front of me, and bullets whined and hissed in every direction as they ricocheted. My bracelet grew uncomfortably warm within a second or two, the energy of the shield taxing the focus to its limit. I tried to angle the shield to deflect the shots up into the air as much as possible. God only knew where all those bullets were going—I just hoped that they wouldn't bounce through a nearby car or some other passerby.

The guns clicked empty. With jerky, unprofessional motions, both gunmen began to reload.

"Harry!" Billy shouted.

"Not now!"

"But—"

I lowered the shield and lifted my right hand—the side that projects energy. The silver ring I wore on my index finger had been enchanted to save back a little kinetic energy whenever my arm moved. I hadn't used the ring in months, and it had a whale of a kick to it—one I hardly dared to use on the gunmen. That much force could kill one of them, and that would be basically the same as letting them fill me full of bullets. It would just take a little longer to set in. The White Council did not take kindly to anyone violating the First Law of Magic: Thou Shalt Not Kill. I'd slipped it once on a technicality, but it wouldn't happen again.

I gritted my teeth, focused my shot just to one side of the gunmen, and triggered the ring. Raw force, unseen but tangible, lashed through the air and caught the first gunman with a glancing blow across his upper body. His automatic slammed against his chest, and the impact tore the sunglasses off his head and shredded bits of his clothes even as it flung him back and out of the pickup, to land somewhere on the ground on the other side.

The second gunman got less of the blast. What did hit him struck against his shoulder and head. He held on to his gun but lost the sunglasses, and they took the ski mask with them, revealing him to be a plain-looking boy who couldn't have been old enough to vote. He blinked against the sudden light and then resumed his fumbling reload.

"Kids," I snarled, lifting my shield again. "They're sending kids after me. Hell's bells."

And then something made the hairs on the back of my neck

try to lift me off the ground. As the kid with the gun started shooting again, I glanced back over my shoulder.

The old lady with her shopping basket had stopped maybe fifteen feet behind me. I saw now that she wasn't as old as I had thought. I caught a flicker of cool, dark eyes beneath age makeup. Her hands were young and smooth. From the depths of the shopping basket she pulled out a sawed-off shotgun, and swung it toward me.

Bullets from the chattering automatic slammed against my shield, and it was all I could do to hold it in place. If I brought any magic to bear against the third attacker, I would lose my concentration and the shield with it—and inexpert or not, the gunman on the truck was spraying around enough lead that sooner or later he wouldn't miss.

On the other hand, if the disguised assassin got a chance to fire that shotgun from five yards away, no one would bother taking me to the hospital. I'd go straight to the morgue.

Bullets hammered into my shield, and I couldn't do anything but watch the third attacker bring the shotgun to bear. I was screwed, and probably Billy was along with me.

Billy moved. He had already gotten out of his T-shirt, and he had enough muscle to ripple—flat, hard muscle, athlete's muscle, not the carefully sculpted build of weight lifters. He dove forward, toward the woman with the shotgun, and stripped out of his sweatpants on the fly. He was naked beneath.

I felt the surge of magic that Billy used then—sharp, precise, focused. There was no sense of ritual in what he did, no slow gathering of power building to release. He blurred as he moved, and between one breath and the next, Billy-the-Naked was gone and Billy-the-Wolf slammed into the assailant, a dark-furred beast the size of a Great Dane, fangs slashing at the hand that gripped the forward stock of the shotgun.

The woman cried out, jerking her hand back, scarlet blood on her fingers, and swept the gun at Billy like a club. He twisted and caught the blow on his shoulders, a snarl exploding from him. He went after the woman's other hand, faster than I could easily see, and the shotgun tumbled to the ground.

The woman screamed again and drew back her hand.

She wasn't human.

Her hands distended, lengthening, as did her shoulders and her jaw. Her nails became ugly, ragged talons, and she raked them down at Billy, striking him across the jaw, this time eliciting a pained yelp mixed with a snarl. He rolled to one side and came up on his feet, circling in order to force the woman-thing's back to me.

The gunman in the truck clicked on empty again. I dropped the shield and hurled myself forward, diving to grip the shotgun. I came up with it and shouted, "Billy, move!"

The wolf darted to one side, and the woman whipped around to face me, her distorted features furious, mouth drooling around tusklike fangs.

I pointed the gun at her belly and pulled the trigger.

The gun roared and bucked, slamming hard against my shoulder. Ten-gauge, maybe, or slug rounds. The woman doubled over, letting out a shriek, and stumbled backward and to the ground. She wasn't down long. She almost bounced back to her feet, scarlet splashed all over her rag of a dress, her face wholly inhuman now. She sprinted past me to the truck and leapt up into the back. The gunman hauled his partner back into the truck with him, and the driver gunned the engine. The truck threw out some turf before it dug in, jounced back onto the street, and whipped away into traffic.

I stared after it for a second, panting. I lowered the shotgun, realizing as I did that I had somehow managed to keep hold of the toad I had picked up in my left hand. It wriggled and struggled in a fashion that suggested I had been close to crushing it, and I tried to ease up on my grip without losing it.

I turned to look for Billy. The wolf paced back over to his discarded sweatpants, shimmered for a second, and became once more the naked young man. There were two long cuts on his face, parallel with his jaw. Blood ran down over his throat in a fine sheet. He carried himself tensely, but it was the only indication he gave of the pain.

"You all right?" I asked him.

He nodded and jerked on his pants, his shirt. "Yeah. What the hell was that?"

"Ghoul," I told him. "Probably one of the LaChaise clan. They're working with the Red Court, and they don't much like me."

"Why don't they like you?"

"I've given them headaches a few times."

Billy lifted a corner of his shirt to hold against the cuts on his face. "I didn't expect the claws."

"They're sneaky that way."

"Ghoul, huh. Is it dead?"

I shook my head. "They're like cockroaches. They recover from just about anything. Can you walk?"

"Yeah."

"Good. Let's get out of here." We headed toward the Beetle. I picked up the cloth sack of toads on the way and started shaking them back out onto the ground. I put the toad I'd nearly squished down with them, then wiped my hand off on the grass.

Billy squinted at me. "Why are you letting them go?"

"Because they're real."

"How do you know?"

"The one I was holding crapped on my hand."

I let Billy into the Blue Beetle and got in the other side. I fetched the first aid kit from under my seat and passed it over to him. Billy pressed a cloth against his face, looking out at the toads. "So that means things are in a bad way?"

"Yeah," I confirmed, "things are in a bad way." I was silent for a minute, then said, "You saved my life."

He shrugged. He didn't look at me.

"So you set up the appointment for three o'clock, right? What was the name? Sommerset?"

He glanced at me and kept the smile from his mouth—but not from his eyes. "Yeah."

I scratched at my beard and nodded. "I've been distracted lately. Maybe I should clean up first."

"Might be good," Billy agreed.

I sighed. "I'm an ass sometimes."

Billy laughed. "Sometimes. You're human like the rest of us."

I started up the Beetle. It wheezed a little, but I coaxed it to life.

Just then something hit my hood with a hard, heavy thump. Then again. Another heavy blow, on the roof.

A feeling of dizziness swept over me, a nausea that came so suddenly and violently that I clutched the steering wheel in a simple effort not to collapse. Distantly, I could hear Billy asking me if I was all right. I wasn't. Power moved and stirred in the air outside—hectic disruption, the forces of magic, usually moving in smooth and quiet patterns, suddenly cast into tumult, disruptive, maddening chaos.

I tried to push the sensations away from me, and labored to open my eyes. Toads were raining down. Not occasionally plopping, but raining down so thick and hard that they darkened the sky. No gentle laundry-chute drop for these poor things, either. They fell like hailstones, splattering on concrete, on the hood of the Beetle. One of them fell hard enough to send a spiderweb of cracks through my windshield, and I dropped into gear and scooted down the street. After a few hundred yards we got away from the otherworldly rain.

Both of us were breathing too fast. Billy had been right. The rain of toads meant something serious was going on, magically speaking. The White Council was coming to town tonight to discuss the war. I had a client to meet, and the vampires had evidently upped the stakes (no pun intended), striking at me more openly than they had dared to before.

I flipped on the windshield wipers. Amphibian blood left scarlet streaks on the cracked glass.

"Good Lord," Billy breathed.

"Yeah." I said. "It never rains, it pours."

Chapter Two

⋘⊱∞⊰⋙

I dropped Billy off at his apartment near campus. I didn't think the ghoul would be filing a police report, but I wiped down the shotgun anyway. Billy wrapped it in a towel I had in the backseat of the Beetle and took it with him, promising to dispose of the weapon. His girlfriend, Georgia, a willowy girl a foot taller than him, waited on the apartment's balcony in dark shorts and a scarlet bikini top, displaying a generous amount of impressively sunbronzed skin in a manner far more confident and appealing than I would have guessed from her a year before. My, how the kids had grown.

The moment Billy got out of the car, Georgia looked up sharply from her book and her nostrils flared. She headed into the house and met him at the door with a first aid kit. She glanced at the car, her expression worried, and nodded to me. I waved back, trying to look friendly. From Georgia's expression, I hadn't managed better than surly. They went into the apartment, and I pulled away before anyone could come out to socialize with me.

After a minute I pulled over, killed the engine, and squinted up at myself in the rearview mirror of the Beetle.

It came as a shock to me. I know, that sounds stupid, but I don't keep mirrors in my home. Too many things can use mirrors as windows, even doors, and it was a risk I preferred to skip entirely. I hadn't glanced at a mirror in weeks.

I looked like a train wreck.

More so than usual, I mean.

My features are usually kind of long, lean, all sharp angles. I've got almost-black hair to go with the dark eyes. Now I had

grey and purplish circles under them. Deep ones. The lines of my
face, where they weren't covered by several months of untrimmed
beard, looked as sharp as the edges of a business card.

My hair had grown out long and shaggy—not in that sexy-
young-rock-star kind of way but in that time-to-take-Rover-to-
the-groomer kind of way. It didn't even have the advantage of
being symmetrical, since a big chunk had been burned short in
one spot when a small incendiary had been smuggled to me in a
pizza delivery box, back when I could still afford to order pizza.
My skin was pale. Pasty, even. I looked like Death warmed over,
provided someone had made Death run the Boston Marathon. I
looked tired. Burned out. Used up.

I sat back in my seat.

I hate it when I'm wrong. But it looked like maybe Billy and
the werewolves (stars and stones, they sounded like a bad rock
band) had a point. I tried to think of the last time I'd gotten a haircut, a shave. I'd had a shower last week. Hadn't I?

I mopped at my face with my shaking hands. The days and
nights had been blurring lately. I spent my time in the lab under
my apartment, researching twenty-four seven. The lab was in the
subbasement, all damp stone and no windows. Circadian rhythms,
bah. I'd pretty much dispensed with day and night. There was too
much to think about to pay attention to such trivial details.

About nine months before, I'd gotten my girlfriend nearly
killed. Maybe more than killed.

Susan Rodriguez had been a reporter for a yellow journal
called the *Midwestern Arcane* when we met. She was one of the
few people around who were willing to accept the idea of the supernatural as a factual reality. She'd clawed for every detail, every
story, every ounce of proof she could dig up so that she could try
to raise the public consciousness on the matter. To that end, she'd
followed me to a vampire shindig.

And the monsters got her.

Billy had been right about that, too. The vampires, the Red
Court, had changed her. Or maybe it would be more accurate to
say that they infected her. Though she was still human, technically, she'd been given their macabre thirst. If she ever sated it,
she would turn all the way into one of them. Some part of her
would die, and she would be one of the monsters, body and soul.

That's why the research. I'd been looking for some way to
help her. To create a vaccine, or to purge her body. Something.
Anything.

I'd asked her to marry me. She told me no. Then she left town. I read her syndicated column in the *Arcane*. She must have been mailing them in to her editor, so at least I knew she was alive. She'd asked me not to follow her and I hadn't. I wouldn't, until I could figure out a way to get her out of the mess I'd gotten her into. There *had* to be something I could do.

Had to be. There had to be.

I bowed my head, suddenly grimacing so hard that the muscles of my face cramped, ached, and smoldered. My chest felt tight, and my body seemed to burn with useless, impotent flame. I'm a wizard. I should have been able to protect Susan. Should have been able to save her. Should have been able to help her. Should have been smarter, should have been faster, should have been better.

Should have told her you loved her before it was too late. Right, Harry?

I tried not to cry. I willed myself not to with all of my years of training and experience and self-discipline. It would accomplish nothing. It wouldn't put me anywhere closer to finding a cure for Susan.

I was so damned tired.

I left my face in my hands. I didn't want someone walking by to see me bawling.

It took a long time to get myself back under control. I'm not sure how long it was, but the shadows had changed and I was baking in the car, even with the windows down.

It occurred to me that it was stupid to be sitting there on the street for more vampire thugs to come find, plain as day. I was tired and dirty and hungry, but I didn't have the cash to get anything to eat, and by the sun I didn't have the time to go back to the apartment for soup. Not if I was to keep my appointment with Ms. Sommerset.

And I needed that appointment. Billy had been right about that, too. If I didn't start earning my keep again, I would lose the office and the apartment. I wouldn't get much magical research done from a cardboard box in an alley.

Time to get moving, then. I raked my fingers uselessly through my mop of hair and headed for my office. A passing clock told me that I was already a couple of minutes late for the appointment. Between that and my appearance, boy, was I going to wow the client. This day just kept getting better.

My office is in a building in midtown. It isn't much of a building, but it still looked too good for me that day. I got a glare from the aging security guard downstairs and felt lucky that he recognized me from previous encounters. A new guy probably would have given me the bum's rush without blinking. I nodded at the guard and smiled and tried to look businesslike. Heh.

I walked past the elevator on my way to the stairs. There was a sign on it that said it was under repair. The elevator hadn't ever been quite the same since a giant scorpion had torn into one of the cars and someone had thrown the elevator up to the top of its chute with a torrent of wind in order to smash the big bug against the roof. The resulting fall sent the car plummeting all the way back to the ground floor and wreaked havoc with the building in general, raising everyone's rents.

Or that's what I heard, anyway. Don't look at me like that. It could have been someone else. Okay, maybe not the orthodontist on four, or the psychiatrist on six. Probably not the insurance office on seven, or the accountant on nine either. Maybe not the lawyers on the top floor. Maybe. But it isn't always me when something goes catastrophically wrong.

Anyway, no one can prove anything.

I opened the door to the stairwell and headed up the stairs to my office, on the fifth floor. I went down the hall, past the quiet buzz of the consulting firm that took up most of the space on the floor, to my office door.

The lettering on the frosted glass read HARRY DRESDEN— WIZARD. I reached out to open the door. A spark jumped to my finger when my hand got within an inch or three of the doorknob, popping against my skin with a sharp little snap of discomfort.

I paused. Even with the building's AC laboring and wheezing, it wasn't *that* cool and dry. Call me paranoid, but there's nothing like a murder attempt in broad daylight to make a man cautious. I focused on my bracelet again, drawing on my apprehension to ready a shield should I need it.

With the other hand I pushed open the door to my office.

My office is usually pretty tidy. Or in any case, I didn't remember it being quite as sloppy as it looked now. Given how little I'd been there lately, it seemed unfair that it should have gotten quite that bad. The table by the door, where I kept a bunch of flyers with titles like "Magic for Dummies" and "I'm a Wizard— Ask Me How" sat crookedly against the wall. The flyers were scattered carelessly over its surface and onto the floor. I could smell the faintest stink of long-burnt coffee. I must have left it on.

Oops. My desk had a similar fungus coating of loose papers, and several drawers in my filing cabinets stood open, with files stacked on top of the cabinets or thrust sideways into their places, so that they stood up out of the drawers. My ceiling fan whirled woozily, clicking on every rotation.

Someone had evidently tried to straighten things up. My mail sat neatly stacked in three different piles. Both metal trash cans were suspiciously empty. Billy and company, then.

In the ruins of my office stood a woman with the kind of beauty that makes men murder friends and start wars.

She stood by my desk with her arms folded, facing the door, hips cocked to one side, her expression skeptical. She had white hair. Not white-blond, not platinum. White as snow, white as the finest marble, bound up like a captured cloud to bare the lines of her slender throat. I don't know how her skin managed to look pale beside that hair, but it did. Her lips were the color of frozen mulberries, almost shocking in a smooth and lovely face, and her oblique eyes were a deep green that tinted to blue when she tilted her head and looked me over. She wasn't old. Wasn't young. Wasn't anything but stunning.

I tried to keep my jaw from hitting the floor and forced my brain to start doing something by taking stock of her wardrobe. She wore a woman's suit of charcoal grey, the cut immaculate. The skirt showed exactly enough leg to make it hard not to look, and her dark pumps had heels just high enough to give you ideas. She wore a bone-white V-neck beneath her jacket, the neckline dipping just low enough to make me want to be watching if she took a deep breath. Opals set in silver flashed on her ears, at her throat, glittering through an array of colors I wouldn't have expected from opals—too many scarlets and violets and deep blues. Her nails had somehow been lacquered in the same opalescence.

I caught the scent of her perfume, something wild and rich, heavy and sweet, like orchids. My heart sped up, and the testosterone-oriented part of my brain wished that I'd been able to bathe. Or shave. Or at least that I hadn't worn sweatpants.

Her mouth quirked into a smile, and she arched one pale brow, saying nothing, letting me gawk.

One thing was certain—no woman like that would have anything less than money. Lots of money. Money I could use to pay the rent, buy groceries, maybe even splurge a little and get a wheelbarrow to help with cleaning my apartment. I only hesitated for a heartbeat, wondering if it was proper for a full-fledged wizard of the White Council to be that interested in cash. I made up my mind fast.

Phenomenal cosmic powers be damned. I have a lease.

"Uh, Ms. Sommerset, I presume," I managed finally. No one can do suave like me. If I was careful, I should be able to trip over something and complete the image. "I'm Harry Dresden."

"I believe you are late," she replied. Sommerset had a voice like her outfit—rich, suggestive, cultured. Her English had an accent I couldn't place. Maybe European. Definitely interesting. "Your assistant informed me when to arrive. I don't like to be kept waiting, so I let myself in." She glanced at my desk, then back at me. "I almost wish I hadn't."

"Yeah. I didn't hear you were coming until, uh . . ." I looked around at my office, dismayed, and shut the door behind me. "I know this looks pretty unprofessional."

"Quite correct."

I moved to one of the chairs I keep for clients, facing my desk, and hurriedly cleared it off. "Please, sit down. Would you like a cup of coffee or anything?"

"Sounds less than sanitary. Why should I take the risk?" She sat, her back straight, on the edge of the chair, following me with her eyes as I walked around the desk. They were a cool, noticeable weight on me as I moved, and I sat down at my desk, frowning.

"Are you the kind who takes chances?"

"I like to hedge my bets," she murmured. "You, for example, Mister Dresden. I have come here today to decide whether or not I shall gamble a great deal upon your abilities." She paused and then added, "Thus far, you have made less than a sterling impression."

I rested my elbows on my desk and steepled my fingers. "Yeah. I know that all this probably makes me look like—"

"A desperate man?" she suggested. "Someone who is clearly obsessed with other matters." She nodded toward the stacks of envelopes on my desk. "One who is shortly to lose his place of business if he does not pay his debts. I think you need the work." She began to rise. "And if you lack the ability to take care of such minor matters, I doubt you will be of any use to me."

"Wait," I said, rising. "Please. At least let me hear you out. If it turns out that I think I can help you—"

She lifted her chin and interrupted me effortlessly. "But that isn't the question, is it?" she asked. "The question is whether or not *I* think you can help me. You have shown me nothing to make me think that you could." She paused, sitting back down again. "And yet . . ."

I sat back down across from her. "Yet?"

"I have heard things, Mister Dresden, about people with your abilities. About the ability to look into their eyes."

I tilted my head. "I wouldn't call it an ability. It just happens."

"Yet you are able to see within them? You call it a soulgaze, do you not?"

I nodded warily and started adding together lots of small bits and pieces. "Yes."

"Revealing their true nature? Seeing the truth about the person upon whom you look?"

"And they see me back. Yes."

She smiled, cool and lovely. "Then let us look upon one another, Mister Dresden, you and I. Then I will know if you can be of any use to me. Surely it will cost me nothing."

"I wouldn't be so sure. It's the sort of thing that stays with you." Like an appendectomy scar, or baldness. When you look on someone's soul, you don't forget it. Not ever. I didn't like the direction this was going. "I don't think it would be a good idea."

"But why not?" she pressed. "It won't take long, will it, Mister Dresden?"

"That's really not the issue."

Her mouth firmed into a line. "I see. Then, if you will excuse me—"

This time I interrupted her. "Ms. Sommerset, I think you may have made a mistake in your estimations."

Her eyes glittered, anger showing for a moment, cool and far away. "Oh?"

I nodded. I opened the drawer to my desk and took out a pad of paper. "Yeah. I've had a rough time of things lately."

"You can't possibly know how little that matters to me."

I drew out a pen, took off the lid, and set it down beside the pad. "Uh-huh. Then you come in here. Rich, gorgeous—kind of too good to be true."

"And?" she inquired.

"Too good to be true," I repeated. I drew the .44-caliber revolver from the desk drawer, leveled it at her, and thumbed back the hammer. "Call me crazy, but lately I've been thinking that if something's too good to be true, then it probably isn't. Put your hands on the desk, please."

Her eyebrows arched. Those gorgeous eyes widened enough to show the whites all the way around them. She moved her hands, swallowing as she did, and laid her palms on the desk. "What do you think you are doing?" she demanded.

"I'm testing a theory," I said. I kept the gun and my eyes on her and opened another drawer. "See, lately, I've been getting nasty visitors. So it's made me do some thinking about what kind of trouble to expect. And I think I've got you pegged."

"I don't know what you are talking about, Mister Dresden, but I am certain—"

"Save it." I rummaged in a drawer and found what I needed. A moment later I lifted a plain old nail of simple metal out of the drawer and put it on the desk.

"What's that?" she all but whispered.

"Litmus test," I said.

Then I flicked the nail gently with one finger, and sent it rolling across the surface of my desk and toward her perfectly manicured hands.

She didn't move until a split second before the nail touched her—but then she did, a blur of motion that took her two long strides back from my desk and knocked over the chair she'd been sitting on. The nail rolled off the edge of the desk and fell to the floor with a clink.

"Iron," I said. "Cold iron. Faeries don't like it."

The expression drained from her face. One moment, there had been arrogant conceit, haughty superiority, blithe confidence. But that simply vanished, leaving her features cold and lovely and remote and empty of all emotion, of anything recognizably human.

"The bargain with my godmother has months yet to go," I said. "A year and a day, she had to leave me alone. That was the deal. If she's trying to weasel out of it, I'm going to be upset."

She regarded me in that empty silence for long moments more. It was unsettling to see a face so lovely look so wholly alien, as though something lurked behind those features that had little in common with me and did not care to make the effort to understand. That blank mask made my throat tighten, and I had to work not to let the gun in my hand shake. But then she did something that made her look even more alien, more frightening.

She smiled. A slow smile, cruel as a barbed knife. When she spoke, her voice sounded just as beautiful as it had before. But it was empty, quiet, haunting. She spoke, and it made me want to lean closer to her to hear her more clearly. "Clever," she murmured. "Yes. Not too distracted to think. Just what I need."

A cold shiver danced down my spine. "I don't want any trouble," I said. "Just go, and we can both pretend nothing happened."

"But it has," she murmured. Just the sound of her voice made the room feel colder. "You have seen through this veil. Proven your worth. How did you do it?"

"Static on the doorknob," I said. "It should have been locked. You shouldn't have been able to get in here, so you must have gone through it. And you danced around my questions rather than simply answering them."

Still smiling, she nodded. "Go on."

"You don't have a purse. Not many women go out in a three-thousand-dollar suit and no purse."

"Mmmm," she said. "Yes. You'll do perfectly, Mister Dresden."

"I don't know what you're talking about," I said. "I'm having nothing more to do with faeries."

"I don't like being called that, Mister Dresden."

"You'll get over it. Get out of my office."

"You should know, Mister Dresden, that my kind, from great to small, are bound to speak the truth."

"That hasn't slowed your ability to deceive."

Her eyes glittered, and I saw her pupils change, slipping from round mortal orbs to slow feline lengths. Cat-eyed, she regarded me, unblinking. "Yet have I spoken. I plan to gamble. And I will gamble upon you."

"Uh. What?"

"I require your service. Something precious has been stolen. I wish you to recover it."

"Let me get this straight," I said. "You want me to recover stolen goods for you?"

"Not for me," she murmured. "For the rightful owners. I wish you to discover and catch the thief and to vindicate me."

"Do it yourself," I said.

"In this matter I cannot act wholly alone," she murmured. "That is why I have chosen you to be my emissary. My agent."

I laughed at her. That made something else come into those perfect, pale features—anger. Anger, cold and terrible, flashed in her eyes and all but froze the laugh in my throat. "I don't think so," I said. "I'm not making any more bargains with your folk. I don't even know who you are."

"Dear child," she murmured, a slow edge to her voice. "The bargain has already been made. You gave your life, your fortune, your future, in exchange for power."

"Yeah. With my godmother. And that's still being contested."

"No longer," she said. "Even in this world of mortals, the concept of debt passes from one hand to the next. Selling mortgages, yes?"

My belly went cold. "What are you saying?"

Her teeth showed, sharp and white. It wasn't a smile. "Your mortgage, mortal child, has been sold. I have purchased it. You are mine. And you *will* assist me in this matter."

I set the gun down on my desk and opened the top drawer. I took out my letter opener, one of the standard machined jobs with a heavy, flat blade and a screw-grip handle. "You're wrong," I said, and the denial in my voice sounded patently obvious, even to me. "My godmother would never do that. For all I know, you're trying to trick me."

She smiled, watching me, her eyes bright. "Then by all means, let me reassure you of the truth."

My left palm slammed down onto the table. I watched, startled, as I gripped the letter opener in my right hand, slasher-movie style. In a panic, I tried to hold back my hand, to drop the opener, but my arms were running on automatic, like they were someone else's.

"Wait!" I shouted.

She regarded me, cold and distant and interested.

I slammed the letter opener down onto the back of my own hand, hard. My desk is a cheap one. The steel bit cleanly through the meat between my thumb and forefinger and sank into the desk, pinning me there. Pain washed up my arm even as blood started oozing out of the wound. I tried to fight it down, but I was panicked, in no condition to exert a lot of control. A whimper slipped out of me. I tried to pull the steel away, to get it *out* of my hand, but my arm simply twisted, wrenching the letter opener counterclockwise.

The pain flattened me. I wasn't even able to get enough breath to scream.

The woman, the faerie, reached down and took my fingers away from the letter opener. She withdrew it with a sharp, decisive gesture and laid it flat on the desk, my blood gleaming all over it. "Wizard, you know as well as I. Were you not bound to me, I would have no such power over you."

At that moment, most of what I knew was that my hand hurt, but some dim part of me realized she was telling the truth. Faeries don't just get to ride in and play puppet master. You have to let them in. I'd let my godmother, Lea, in years before, when I was younger, dumber. I'd given her the slip last year, forced an abeyance of her claim that should have protected me for a year and a day.

But now she'd passed the reins to someone else. Someone who hadn't been in on the second bargain.

I looked up at her, pain and sudden anger making my voice into a low, harsh growl. "Who are you?"

The woman ran an opalescent fingernail through the blood on my desk. She lifted it to her lips and idly touched it to her tongue. She smiled, slower, more sensual, and every bit as alien. "I have many names," she murmured. "But you may call me Mab. Queen of Air and Darkness. Monarch of the Winter Court of the Sidhe."

Chapter Three

The bottom fell out of my stomach.

A Faerie Queen. A Faerie Queen was standing in my office. I was looking at a Faerie Queen. Talking to a Faerie Queen.

And she had me by the short hairs.

Boy, and I'd thought my life was on the critical list already.

Fear can literally feel like ice water. It can be a cold feeling that you swallow, that rolls down your throat and spreads into your chest. It steals your breath and makes your heart labor when it shouldn't, before expanding into your belly and hips, leaving quivers behind. Then it heads for the thighs, the knees (occasionally with an embarrassing stop on the way), stealing the strength from the long muscles that think you should be using them to run the hell away.

I swallowed a mouthful of fear, my eyes on the poisonously lovely faerie standing on the other side of my desk.

It made Mab smile.

"Yes," she murmured. "Wise enough to be afraid. To understand, at least in part. How does it feel, to know what you know, child?"

My voice came out unsteady, and more quiet than I would have liked. "Sort of like Tokyo when Godzilla comes up on the beach."

Mab tilted her head, watching me with that same smile. Maybe she didn't get the reference. Or maybe she didn't like being compared to a thirty-story lizard. Or maybe she *did* like it. I mean, how should I know? I have enough trouble figuring out human women.

I didn't meet Mab's eyes. I wasn't worried about a soulgaze any longer. Both parties had to have a soul for that to happen. But plenty of things can get to you if you make eye contact too long. It carries all sorts of emotions and metaphors. I stared at Mab's chin, my hand burning with pain, and said nothing because I was afraid.

I hate being afraid. I hate it more than anything in the whole world. I hate being made to feel helpless. I hate being bullied, too, and Mab might as well have been ramming her fist down my throat and demanding my lunch money.

The Faerie Queens were bad news. Big bad news. Short of calling up some hoary old god or squaring off against the White Council itself, I wasn't likely to run into anything else with as much raw power as Mab. I could have thrown a magical sucker punch at her, could have tried to take her out, but even if we'd been on even footing I doubt I would have ruffled her hair. And she had a bond on me, a magical conduit. She could send just about anything right past my defenses, and there wouldn't be anything I could do about it.

Bullies make me mad—and I've been known to do some foolish things when I'm angry.

"Forget it," I said, my voice hot. "No deal. Get it over with and blast me. Lock the door on your way out."

My response didn't seem to ruffle her. She folded her arms and murmured, "Such anger. Such fire. Yes. I watched you stalemate your godmother the Leanansidhe autumn last. Few mortals ever have done as much. Bold. Impertinent. I admire that kind of strength, wizard. I need that kind of strength."

I fumbled around on my desk until I found the tissue dispenser and started packing the wound with the flimsy fabric. "I don't really care what you need," I told her. "I'm not going to be your emissary or anything else unless you want to force me, and I doubt I'd be much good to you then. So do whatever you're going to do or get out of my office."

"You should care, Mister Dresden," Mab told me. "It concerns you explicitly. I purchased your debt in order to make you an offer. To give you the chance to win free of your obligations."

"Yeah, right. Save it. I'm not interested."

"You may serve, wizard, or you may be served. As a meal. Do you not wish to be free?"

I looked up at her, warily, visions of barbecued me on a table with an apple in my mouth dancing in my head. "What do you mean by 'free'?"

"Free," she said, wrapping those frozen-berry lips around the word so that I couldn't help but notice. "Free of Sidhe influence, of the bonds of your obligation first to the Leanansidhe and now to me."

"The whole thing a wash? We go our separate ways?"

"Precisely."

I looked down at my hurting hand and scowled. "I didn't think you were much into freedom as a concept, Mab."

"You should not presume, wizard. I adore freedom. Anyone who doesn't have it wants it."

I took a deep breath and tried to get my heart rate under control. I couldn't let either fear or anger do my thinking for me. My instincts screamed at me to go for the gun again and give it a shot, but I had to think. It was the only thing that could get you clear of the fae.

Mab was on the level about her offer. I could feel that, sense it in a way so primal, so visceral, that there was no room left for doubt. She would cut me loose if I agreed to her bargain. Of course, her price might be too high. She hadn't gotten to that yet. And the fae have a way of making sure that further bargains only get you in deeper, instead of into the clear. Just like credit card companies, or those student loan people. Now there's evil for you.

I could feel Mab watching me, Sylvester to my Tweetie Bird. That thought kind of cheered me up. Generally speaking, Tweetie kicks Sylvester's ass in the end.

"Okay," I told her. "I'm listening."

"Three tasks," Mab murmured, holding up three fingers by way of visual aid. "From time to time, I will make a request of you. When you have fulfilled three requests, your obligation to me ceases."

Silence lay on the room for a moment, and I blinked. "What. That's *it*?"

Mab nodded.

"Any three tasks? Any three requests?"

Mab nodded.

"Just as simple as that? I mean, you say it like that, and I could pass you the salt three times and that would be that."

Her eyes, green-blue like glacial ice, remained on my face, unblinking. "Do you accept?"

I rubbed at my mouth slowly, mulling it over in my head. It was a simple bargain, as these things went. They could get really complicated, with contracts and everything. Mab had offered me a great package, sweet, neat, and tidy as a Halloween candy.

Which meant that I'd be an idiot not to check for razor blades and cyanide.

"I decide which requests I fulfill and which I don't?"

"Even so."

"And if I refuse a request, there will be no reprisals or punishments from you."

She tilted her head and blinked her eyes, slowly. "Agreed. You, not I, will choose which requests you fulfill."

There was one land mine I'd found, at least. "And no more selling my mortgage, either. Or whistling up the lackeys to chastise or harass me by proxy. This remains between the two of us."

She laughed, and it sounded as merry, clear, and lovely as bells—if someone pressed them against my teeth while they were still ringing. "As your godmother did. Fool me twice, shame on me, wizard? Agreed."

I licked my lips, thinking hard. Had I left her any openings? Could she get to me any other way?

"Well, wizard?" Mab asked. "Have we a bargain?"

I gave myself a second to wish I'd been less tired. Or less in pain. The events of the day and the impending Council meeting this evening hadn't exactly left my head in world-class negotiating condition. But I knew one thing for certain. If I didn't get out from under Mab's bond, I would be dead, or worse than dead, in short order. Better to act and be mistaken than not to act and get casually crushed.

"All right," I said. "We have a bargain." When I said the words, a little frisson prickled over the nape of my neck, down the length of my spine. My wounded hand twitched in an aching, painful pang.

Mab closed her eyes, smiling a feline smile with those dark lips, and inclined her head. "Good. Yes."

You know that look on Wile E. Coyote's face, when he runs at full steam off the cliff and then realizes what he's done? He doesn't look down, but he feels around with one toe, and right then, right before he falls, his face becomes drawn with a primal dread.

That's what I must have looked like. I know it was pretty much what I felt like. But there was no help for it. Maybe if I didn't stop to check for the ground underneath my feet, I'd keep going indefinitely. I looked away from Mab and tried to tend to my hand as best I could. It still throbbed, and disinfecting the wound was going to hurt a lot more. I doubted it would need sutures. A small blessing, I guess.

A manila envelope hit my desk. I looked up to see Mab drawing a pair of gloves onto her hands.

"What's this?" I asked.

"My request," she replied. "Within are the details of a man's death. I wish you to vindicate me of it by discovering the identity of his killer and returning what was stolen from him."

I opened the envelope. Inside was an eight-by-ten glossy black-and-white of a body. An old man lay at the bottom of a flight of stairs, his neck at a sharp angle to his shoulders. He had frizzy white hair, a tweed jacket. Accompanying the picture was an article from the *Tribune*, headlined LOCAL ARTIST DIES IN MIDNIGHT ACCIDENT.

"Ronald Reuel," I said, glancing over the article. "I've heard of him. Has a studio in Bucktown, I think."

Mab nodded. "Hailed as a visionary of the American artistic culture. Though I assume they use the term lightly."

"Creator of worlds of imagination, it says. I guess now that he's dead, they'll say all kinds of nice things." I read over the rest of the article. "The police called it an accident."

"It was not," Mab responded.

I looked up at her. "How do you know?"

She smiled.

"And why should you care?" I asked. "It isn't like the cops are after you."

"There are powers of judgement other than mortal law. It is enough for you to know that I wish to see justice done," she said. "Simply that."

"Uh-huh," I said, frowning. "You said something was stolen from him. What?"

"You'll know it."

I put the picture back in the envelope and left it on my desk. "I'll think about it."

Mab assured me, "You will accept this request, Wizard Dresden."

I scowled at her and set my jaw. "I said I'll *think* about it."

Mab's cat-eyes glittered, and I saw a few white, white teeth in her smile. She took a pair of dark sunglasses from the pocket of her jacket. "Is it not polite to show a client to the door?"

I glowered. But I got up out of the chair and walked to the door, the Faerie Queen's heady perfume, the narcotic *scent* of her enough to make me a little dizzy. I fought it away and tried to keep my scowl in place, opening the door for her with a jerky motion.

"Your hand yet pains you?" she asked.

"What do you think?"

Mab placed her gloved hand on my wounded one, and a sudden spike of sheer, vicious cold shot up through the injury like a frozen scalpel before lancing up my arm, straight toward my heart. It took my breath, and I felt my heart skip a beat, two, before it labored into rhythm again. I gasped and swayed, and only leaning against the door kept me from falling down completely.

"Dammit," I muttered, trying to keep my voice down. "We had a deal."

"I agreed not to punish you for refusing me, wizard. I agreed not to punish or harass you by proxy." Mab smiled. "I did that just for spite."

I growled. "That isn't going to make it more likely that I take this case."

"You will take it, emissary," Mab said, her voice confident. "Expect to meet your counterpart this evening."

"What counterpart?"

"As you are Winter's emissary in this matter, Summer, too, has sought out one to represent her interests."

"I got plans tonight," I growled. "And I haven't taken the case."

Mab tilted her dark glasses down, cat eyes on mine. "Wizard. Do you know the story of the Fox and Scorpion?"

I shook my head, looking away.

"Fox and Scorpion came to a brook," Mab murmured, her voice low, sweet. "Wide was the water. Scorpion asked Fox for a ride on his back. Fox said, 'Scorpion, will you not sting me?' Scorpion said, 'If I did, it would mean the death of us both.' Fox agreed, and Scorpion climbed onto his back. Fox swam, but halfway over, Scorpion struck with his deadly sting. Fox gasped, 'Fool, you have doomed us both. Why?' 'I am a scorpion,' said Scorpion. 'It is my nature.' "

"That's the story?" I said. "Don't quit your day job."

Mab laughed, velvet ice, and it sent another shiver through me. "You will accept this case, wizard. It is what you are. It is your nature." Then she turned and walked down the hall, aloof, reserved, cold. I glowered after her for a minute before I shut the door.

Maybe I'd been shut away in my lab too long, but Spenser never mentions that the Faerie Queen has a great ass.

So I notice these things. So sue me.

Chapter Four

I leaned against my door with my eyes closed, trying to think. I was scared. Not in that half-pleasant adrenaline-charged way, but quietly scared. Wait-on-the-results-of-medical-tests scared. It's a rational sort of fear that puts a lawn chair down in the front of your thoughts and brings a cooler of drinks along with it.

I was working for the queen of wicked faeries—well, Queen of Winter, of the Unseelie faeries, at any rate. The Unseelie weren't universally vicious and evil, any more than the Seelie, the Summer fae, were all kind and wise. They were much like the season for which they had been named—cold, beautiful, pitiless, and entirely without remorse. Only a fool would willingly associate with them.

Not that Mab had given me much of a choice, but technically speaking there had been one. I could have turned her down flat and accepted whatever came.

I chewed on my lip. Given the kind of business I was in, I hadn't felt the need to spend too much time hunting for a good retirement plan. Wizards can live a long, long time, but most of the ones that do tend to be the kind that stick at home in their study. Not many tossed their gauntlets into as many faces as I had.

I'd been clever a couple of times, lucky a couple of times, and I'd come out ahead of the game so far—but sooner or later the dice were going to come up snake eyes. It was as simple as that, and I knew it.

Fear. Maybe that was why I'd agreed to Mab's bargain. Susan's life had been twisted horribly, and that was my fault. I wanted to help her before I went down swinging.

But some little voice in the back of my head told me that I was being awfully noble for someone who had flinched when push had come to shove. The little voice told me that I was making excuses. Some part of me that doesn't trust much and believes in even less whispered that I had simply been afraid to say no to a being who could probably make me long for death if I denied her.

Either way, it was too late for questions now. I'd made the bargain, for better or worse. If I didn't want it to end badly, I'd better start figuring out how to get out of it without getting swallowed up in faerie politics. I wouldn't do that by taking the case of Ronald Reuel, I was pretty damn sure. Mab wouldn't have offered it if she hadn't thought it would get me further entangled than I already was. Maybe she had me in a metaphysical armlock, but that didn't mean I was going to jump every time she said "frog." I could figure out something else. And besides, I had other problems on my mind.

There wasn't much time to spare before the Council meeting that evening, so I got my things together and got ready to leave. I paused at the door, with that nagging feeling I get when I'm forgetting something. My eyes settled on my stack of unpaid bills and I remembered.

Money. I'd come here to get a case. To make some cash. To pay my bills. Now I was hip-deep in trouble and heading straight out to sea, and I hadn't gotten a retainer or made one red cent.

I swore at myself and pulled the door shut behind me.

You'd think as long as I was gambling with my soul, I would have thought to get Mab to throw in fifty bucks an hour plus expenses.

I headed out to start taking care of business. Traffic in Chicago can be the usual nightmare of traffic in any large American city, but that afternoon's was particularly bad. Stuck behind a wreck up ahead, the Beetle turned into an oven, and I spent a while sweating and wishing that I wasn't too much of a wizard for a decent modern air conditioner to survive. That was one of the hazards of magical talent. Technology doesn't get along so well when there is a lot of magic flying around. Anything manufactured after World War II or so seemed prone to failure whenever a wizard was nearby. Stuff with microcircuits and electrical components and that kind of paraphernelia seemed to have the most trouble, but even simpler things, like the Beetle's air conditioner, usually couldn't last long.

Running late, I dropped by my apartment and waded through

the wreckage looking for my gear for the meeting. I couldn't find everything, and I didn't have time to get a shower. The refrigerator was empty, and all I could find to eat was a half-wrapped candy bar I'd started and never finished. I stuffed it into my pocket, then headed for the meeting of the White Council of Wizardry.

Where I was sure to cut a devastating swath with my couth, hygiene, and natural grace.

I pulled into the parking lot across the street from McCormick Place Complex, one of the largest convention centers in the world. The White Council had rented one of the smaller buildings for the meeting. The sun hung low in the sky, growing larger and redder as it dropped toward the horizon.

I parked the Beetle in the relative cool of the lowest level of the parking garage, got out of the car, and walked around to the front to open the trunk. I was shrugging into my robe when I heard a car coming in, engine rumbling and rattling. A black '37 Ford pickup, complete with rounded fenders and wooden-slat sides on the bed, pulled into the empty space next to mine. There wasn't any rust on the old machine, and it gleamed with fresh wax. A weathered shotgun rode on top of a wooden rack against the rear wall of the passenger compartment, and in the slot beneath it sat a worn old wizard's staff. The Ford crunched to a halt with a kind of dinosaur solidity, and a moment later the engine died.

The driver, a short, stocky man in a white T-shirt and blue denim overalls, opened the door and hopped down from the truck with the brisk motions of a busy man. His head was bald except for a fringe of downy white tufts, and a bristling white beard covered his mouth and jowls. He slammed the door shut with thoughtless strength, grinned, and boomed, "Hoss! Good to see you again."

"Ebenezar," I responded, if without the same ear-ringing volume. I felt myself answer his grin with my own, and stepped over to him to shake his offered hand. I squeezed hard, purely out of self-defense. He had a grip that could crush a can of spinach. "You'd better take the shotgun down. Chicago PD is picky about people with guns."

Ebenezar snorted and said, "I'm too old to go worrying about every fool thing."

"What are you doing out of Missouri, sir? I didn't think you came to Council meetings."

He let out a barking laugh. "The last time I didn't, they saddled me with this useless teenage apprentice. Now I don't hardly dare miss one. They might make him move in again."

I laughed. "I wasn't that bad, was I?"

He snorted. "You burned down my barn, Hoss. And I never did see that cat again. He just lit out and didn't come back after what you did with the laundry."

I grinned. Way back when, I'd been a stupid sixteen-year-old orphan who had killed his former teacher in what amounted to a magical duel. I'd gotten lucky, or it would have been me that had been burned to a briquette instead of old Justin. The Council has Seven Laws of Magic, and the first one is Thou Shalt Not Kill. When you break it, they execute you, no questions asked.

But some of the other wizards had thought I deserved lenience, and there was a precedent for using lethal magic in self-defense against the black arts. I'd been put on a kind of horrible probation instead, with any further infraction against the Laws punishable by immediate summary judgement. But I'd also been sixteen, and legally a minor, which meant I had to go someplace—preferably where the Council could keep an eye on me and where I could learn better control of my powers.

Ebenezar McCoy had lived in Hog Hollow, Missouri, for as long as anyone could remember—a couple of centuries at least. After my trial, the Council packed me off to his farm and put him in charge of the remainder of my education. Education, to Ebenezar, meant a lot of hard work on the farm during the day, studying in the evening, and getting a good night's sleep.

I didn't learn much magic from him, but I'd gotten some more important stuff. I'd learned more about patience. About creating something, making something worthwhile out of my labor. And I'd found as much peace as a teenager could expect. It had been a good place for me then, and he'd given me the kind of respect and distance I'd needed. I would always be grateful.

Ebenezar frowned past me, squinting at the Beetle. I followed his gaze and realized that my car looked like it had been pounded with bloody hailstones. The toad blood had dried to dark caramel brown, except where my windshield wipers had swept it away. Ebenezar looked back at me, lifting his eyebrows.

"Rain of toads," I explained.

"Ah." He rubbed his jaw and squinted at me and then at the cloth wrapped around my hand. "And that?"

"Accident in the office. It's been a long day."

"Uh-huh. You know, you don't look so good, Hoss." He looked up at me, his eyes steady, frowning. I didn't meet the look. We'd traded a soulgaze, years ago, so I wasn't afraid of it happening again. I just didn't want to look at the old man and see disappointment there. "I hear you been getting into some trouble up here."

"Some," I admitted.

"You all right?"

"I'll make it."

"Uh-*huh*. I'm told the senior Council is pretty upset," he said. "Could mean trouble for you, Hoss."

"Yeah. I figured."

He sighed and shook his head, looking me up and down, nose wrinkling. "You don't exactly look like a shining example of young wizardry. And you're not going to make much of an impression wearing that."

I scowled, defensive, and draped the stole of rich blue silk over my head. "Hey, I'm supposed to wear a robe. We all are."

Ebenezar gave me a wry look and turned to the pickup. He dragged a suit carrier out of the back and pulled out a robe of opulent dark fabric, folding it over one arm. "Somehow I don't think a plaid flannel bathrobe is what they had in mind."

I tied the belt of my old bathrobe and tried to make the stole look like it should go with it. "My cat used my good robe as a litter box. Like I said, it's been a long day, sir."

He grunted and took his stumpy old wizard's staff off the gun rack. Then he drew out his scarlet stole and draped it over the robe. "Too hot to wear this damn thing out here. I'll put it on inside." He looked up, pale blue eyes glittering as he swept his gaze around the parking garage.

I frowned at him and tilted my head. "We're late. Shouldn't we be getting to the meeting?"

"In a minute. Some people want to talk before we close the circle." He glanced aside at me and said more quietly, "Senior Council."

I drew in a sharp breath. "Why do they want to talk to us?"

"Not us. You. Because I asked them to, boy. People are scared. If the Senior Council allows things to come to an open vote of the entire Council, it could go badly for you. So I wanted some of them to get a chance to meet you for themselves before they started making choices that could get you hurt."

Ebenezar leaned back against his truck and folded his arms across his belly, bowing his head with his eyes squinted almost completely shut. He said nothing more. Nothing about him betrayed any tension, from the set of his bull neck and solid shoulders to the stillness of his gnarled, work-hardened hands. But I felt it in him, somewhere.

I said quietly, "You're going out on a limb for me, aren't you?"

He shrugged. "Some, maybe."

I felt the anger run hot in my belly, and I tightened the muscles of my jaw. But I made an effort to keep my voice even. Ebenezar had been more than my teacher. He'd been my mentor at a time when I hadn't had anything else left to me. He'd helped me when a lot of other people wanted to kick me while I was down—or, more accurately, decapitate me while I was down. I owed him my life in more than one sense.

It would be wrong for me to lose my temper, no matter how tired or hurt I was. Besides, the old man could probably kick my ass. So I managed to tone my answer down to, "What the hell do you think you're doing, *sir*? I am not your apprentice anymore. I can look out for myself."

He didn't miss the anger. Guess I'm not much of a poker player. He looked up at me and said, "I'm trying to help you, boy."

"I've got all the help I can stand already," I told him. "I've got vampires breathing down my neck, toads falling from the sky, I'm about to get evicted from everywhere, I'm late to the Council meeting, and I am *not* going to stand around out here and suck up to members of the Senior Council to lobby their vote."

Ebenezar thrust out his jaw, rapping his staff against the ground to emphasize his sentences. "Harry, this is not a game. The Wardens and the Merlin are dead set against you. They *will* move. Without support in the Senior Council you're in trouble, Hoss."

I shook my head and thought of Mab's glacial gaze. "It can't be much more than I'm in already."

"The hell it can't. They could make a sacrificial lamb of you."

"They will or they won't. Either way I'm not going to start brownnosing the Council now, Senior or otherwise."

"Harry, I'm not saying you need to get on your knees and beg, but if you would just—"

I rolled my eyes. "What? Offer a couple of favors? Sell my vote to one of the blocs? Fuck that. Pardon my French. I've got enough problems without—" I broke off abruptly, narrowing my eyes. "You're the last one I would expect to be telling me to get involved in Council politics."

Ebenezar scowled at me. "Oh?"

"Yeah. In fact, the last time I checked, you told me the whole

swill-spouting pack of lollygagging skunkwallows could trans-
form one another into clams, for all you cared."

"I did not say that."

"Did so."

Ebenezar's face turned red. "Boy. I ought to—"

"Save it," I told him. "Go ahead and punch me or whatever,
but threats just aren't hitting me like they used to."

Ebenezar snorted at me and slammed his staff on the concrete
once more before turning and stalking several paces away. He
stood there for a minute, muttering to himself. Or I thought he was
muttering. After a minute, the sound resolved itself into swallowed laughter.

I scowled at his back. "What?" I demanded. "Why are you
laughing at me?"

Ebenezar turned out to an open parking space across the row
and said, "There. Are you satisfied?"

I never felt a whisper of power, not a breath of magic stirring
against me. Whatever veil had been used, it was beyond anything
I could have even attempted. I'm not exactly a neurosurgeon when
it comes to magic. I've had my moments, but mostly I muddle
through by shoving a lot of energy into my spells until it doesn't
matter if half of it is slopping out. Magically speaking, I'm a
brawny thug, and noisy as hell.

This veil was good, almost perfect, completely silent. Way
better than I would be able to do anytime in the next couple of de-
cades. I stared in abrupt shock as it fell and two people I hadn't
sensed at all simply flickered into existence in front of me.

The first was a woman better than six feet tall. She wore her
grey hair coiled in a net at the base of her neck. She had already
put on her robes of office, black silk nearly the same color as her
skin, and her purple stole echoed the gems at her throat. Her eyebrows were still dark, and she had one of them arched as she regarded Ebenezar, then me, with a completely unamused
expression. When she spoke, her voice was a low, rich alto. "Lollygagging skunkwallows?"

"Matty—" Ebenezar began, laughter still flavoring his words.
"You know how I get when I'm talking about Council politics."

"Don't you 'Matty' me, Ebenezar McCoy," she snapped. She
looked past my old mentor to focus on me. "Wizard Dresden, I am
less than amused with your lack of respect toward the White
Council."

I lifted my chin and glared down at the woman without meeting her eyes. It's a tough trick to learn, but if you're motivated enough you can do it. "That's a coincidence. I'm not terribly amused with you spying on me."

The black woman's eyes flashed, but Ebenezar cut in before either of us could gather any more steam. "Harry Dresden," he said dryly, "Meet Martha Liberty."

She shot him a look and said pointedly, "He's arrogant, Ebenezar. Dangerous."

I snorted. "That's every wizard ever."

Martha continued as if I hadn't spoken. "Bitter. Angry. Obsessive."

Ebenezar frowned. "Seems to me he has good reason to be. You and the rest of the Senior Council saw to that."

Martha shook her head. "You know what he was meant to be. He's too great a risk."

I snapped my fingers twice and hooked a thumb at my own chest. "Hey, lady. He's also right here."

Her eyes flashed at me. "Look at him, Ebenezar. He's a wreck. Look at the destruction he has caused."

Ebenezar took two quick, angry steps toward Martha. "By challenging the Red Court when they were going to kill that young woman? No, Matty. Hoss didn't cause what's happened since. They did. I've read his report. He stood up to them when they damn well needed standing up to."

Martha folded her arms, strong and brown against the front of her robes. "The Merlin says—"

"I know what he says," Ebenezar muttered. "By now I don't even need to hear him say it. And as usual, he's half right, half wrong, and all gutless."

Martha frowned at him for a long and silent moment. Then she looked at me and asked, "Do you remember me, Mister Dresden?"

I shook my head. "They had a hood on me all through the trial, and I missed the meeting Warden Morgan called a couple years back. They were taking a bullet out of my hip."

"I know. I never saw your face before today." She moved then, lifting a slender staff of some dark reddish wood, and walked toward me, the staff clicking with each step. I faced her, bracing myself, but she didn't try to meet my gaze. She studied my features for a long moment and then said, very quietly, "You have your mother's eyes."

An old pain rolled through me. I barely managed more than a whisper in response. "I never knew her."

"No. You didn't." She lifted one wide, heavy hand and passed it through the air on either side of my head, as though smoothing my hair without touching it. Then she raked her eyes over me, staring intently at my bandaged hand. "You hurt. You're in great pain."

"It isn't bad. It should heal in a few days."

"I'm not talking about your hand, boy." She closed her eyes and bowed her head. Her voice came heavily, slowly, as though her lips were reluctant to let the words pass them. "Very well, Ebenezar. I will support you."

She stepped back and away from me, back to the side of the second person who had appeared. I'd almost forgotten about him, and looking at him now I began to see why. He contained a quality of stillness I could all but feel around him—easy to sense but difficult to define. His features, his bearing, everything about him blended into his background, swallowed by that stillness, patient and quiet as a stone beneath moon and sun.

He was of innocuous height, five eight, maybe five nine. His dark hair was plaited in a long braid, despite age that seamed his features like bronzed leather under a scarlet sun, warm and worn. His eyes, beneath silver brows, were dark, inscrutable, intense. Eagle feathers adorned his braid, a necklace of bits of bone circled his throat, and he had a beaded bracelet wrapped around one forearm, which poked out from beneath his black robe. One weathered hand gripped a simple, uncarved staff.

"Hoss," Ebenezar said, "this here is Listens to Wind. But that's always been too much of a mouthful for me, even for a genuine Illinois medicine man. I just call him Injun Joe."

"How—" I began. Maybe some kind of irony could be found in the first part of asking how did he do, but something scratched at my foot and I left off the rest. I let out a yelp and jumped away from a flash of fur near my feet without stopping to see what it was. It had been that kind of day.

I tripped over my own staff and fell down. I scrambled over on my back to put my legs between my face and whatever snarling thing might be coming for me, drawing back one foot to kick.

I needn't have bothered. A raccoon, and a fairly young one at that, stood up on its hind legs and chittered at me in annoyance, soft grey fur bristling wildly as though it had been fit for an animal several sizes larger. The raccoon gave me what I swore was an irritated look, eyes glittering within the dark mask of fur around them, then ran over to Injun Joe's feet and neatly scaled the old man's wooden staff. It swarmed up Injun Joe's arm to perch on his shoulder, still chittering and squeaking.

"Uh," I managed, "how do you do."

The raccoon chirruped again, and Injun Joe tilted his head to one side, then nodded. "Good. But Little Brother is irritated with you. He thinks anyone with that much food should share it."

I frowned, then I remembered the half-eaten stale candy bar in my pocket. "Oh, right." I pulled it out, broke it in half, and held it out to the raccoon. "Peace?"

Little Brother let out a pleased squeak and darted back down Injun Joe's arm and staff to my hand. He snatched the candy and then retired a few feet away to eat it.

When I looked up, Injun Joe stood over me, offering his hand. "Little Brother thanks you. He likes you, too. How do you do, Wizard Dresden."

I took his hand and got to my feet. "Thanks, uh, Listens to Wind."

Ebenezar interjected, "Injun Joe."

Injun Joe winked one grave eye at me. "The redneck hillbilly doesn't read. Otherwise he'd know that he can't call me that anymore. Now I'm Native American Joe."

I wasn't sure I was supposed to laugh, but I did. Injun Joe nodded, dark eyes sparkling. Then he murmured, "The one you knew as Tera West sends her respects."

I blinked at him.

Injun Joe turned to Ebenezar and nodded, then walked slowly back to Martha's side.

Ebenezar let out a satisfied grunt. "Fine. Now where is the Russian? We haven't got all day."

Martha's expression became remote. Injun Joe's face didn't change, but he moved his eyes to the tall wizard beside him. No one spoke, and the silence grew thick enough to choke on.

Ebenezar's face went very pale, and he suddenly leaned hard on his staff. "Simon," he whispered. "Oh, no."

I stepped up beside Ebenezar. "What happened?"

Martha shook her head. "Simon Pietrovich. Senior Council member. Our vampire expert. He was killed less than two days ago. The whole compound in Archangel, Ebenezar. All of them. I'm sorry."

Ebenezar shook his head slowly. His voice was a pale shadow of its usual self. "I've been to his tower. It was a fortress. How did they do it?"

"The Wardens said that they couldn't be sure, but it looked like someone let the killers in past the defenses. They didn't get away unscathed. There were the remains of half a dozen nobles of the Red Court. Many of their warriors. But they killed Simon and the rest."

"Let them in?" Ebenezar breathed. "Treachery? But even if it was true, it would have to be someone who knew his defenses inside and out."

Martha glanced at me, then back at Ebenezar. Something passed between them in that look, but I couldn't tell what.

"No," Ebenezar said. "That's insane."

"Master to student. You know what the Wardens will say."

"It's buffalo chips. It wouldn't ever get past the Senior Council."

"Eben," Martha said gently, "Joseph and I are only two votes now. Simon is gone."

Ebenezar took a blue bandanna from the pocket of his overalls and rubbed it over his pate. "Damnation," he muttered. "Guts and damnation."

I looked at Ebenezar and then at Martha. "What?" I asked. "What does this mean?"

She said, "It means, Wizard Dresden, that the Merlin and others on the Council are preparing to bring allegations against you accusing you of precipitating the war with the Red Court and placing the responsibility for a number of deaths on your head. And because Joseph and I no longer have the support of Simon on the Senior Council, it means that we cannot block the Merlin from laying it to general vote."

Injun Joe nodded, fingers absently resting on Little Brother's fur. "Many of the Council are frightened, Hoss Dresden. Your enemies will use this opportunity to strike through them. Fear will drive them to vote against you."

I shot Ebenezar a glance. My old mentor traded a long look with me, and I saw his eyes stir with uncertainty.

"Hell's bells," I whispered. "I'm in trouble."

Chapter Five

A heavy silence followed, until Ebenezar flexed the fingers of one hand and his knuckles popped. "Who is up for Simon's place?"

Martha shook her head. "I suspect the Merlin will want one of the Germans."

Ebenezar growled. "I've got fifty years' seniority on every mother's son of them."

"It won't matter," Martha said. "There are too many Americans on the Senior Council already for the Merlin's tastes."

Injun Joe scratched Little Brother's chest and said, "Typical. Only real American on the Senior Council is me. Not like the rest of you Johnny-come-latelies."

Ebenezar gave Injun Joe a tired smile.

Martha said, "The Merlin won't be happy if you decide to press a claim now."

Ebenezar snorted. "Aye. And I can't tell you how that breaks my heart."

Martha frowned, pressing her lips together. "We'd best get inside, Ebenezar. I'll tell them to wait for you."

"Fine," my old teacher said, his words clipped. "Go on in."

Without a further word, Martha and Injun Joe departed, black robes whispering. Ebenezar slipped into his robe and put on his scarlet stole. Then he took up his staff again and strode determinedly toward the convention center. I kept pace silently, and worried.

Ebenezar surprised me by speaking. "How's your Latin coming, Hoss? You need me to translate?"

I coughed. "No. I think I can manage."

"All right. When we get inside, hang on to your temper. You've got a reputation as a hothead for some reason."

I scowled at him. "I do not."

"And for being stubborn and contrary."

"I am not."

Ebenezar's worn smile appeared for a moment, but by then we had reached the building where the Council was to meet. I stopped walking, and Ebenezar paused, looking back at me.

"I don't want to go in with you," I said. "If this goes bad, maybe it's better if you have some distance from me."

Ebenezar frowned at me, and for a second I thought he was going to argue. Then he shook his head and went into the building. I gave him a couple of minutes, and then walked up the steps and went in.

The building had the look of an old-time theater—high, arched ceilings, floors of polished stone laid with strips of carpet, and several sets of double doors leading into the theater itself. The air conditioning had probably been running full blast earlier, but now there was no sound of fan or vent and the building inside felt warmer than it probably should have. None of the lights were on. You couldn't really expect even basic things like lights and air conditioning to keep running in a building full of wizards.

All the doors leading into what was apparently an actual theater were closed except for one pair, and two men wearing dark Council robes, scarlet stoles, and the grey cloak of the Wardens stood before them.

I didn't recognize one of the men, but the other was Morgan. Morgan stood nearly as tall as I did, only with maybe another hundred pounds of solid, working-man muscle. He had a short beard, patchy with brown and grey, and he wore his hair in a long ponytail. His face was still narrow, sour, and he had a voice to match it. "Finally," he muttered upon seeing me. "I've been waiting for this, Dresden. Finally, you're going to face justice."

"I see someone had a nice big bowl of Fanatic-Os this morning," I said. "I know you don't like it, Morgan, but I was cleared of all those charges. Thanks to you, actually."

His sour face screwed up even more. "I only reported your actions to the Council. I did not think they would be so"—he spat the word like a curse—"lenient."

I stopped in front of the two Wardens and held out my staff. Morgan's partner lifted a crystal pendant from around his neck and ran the crystal over the staff and then over my head, temples, and down the front of my body. The crystal pulsed with a gentle glow of light as it passed over each chakra point. The second Warden nodded to Morgan, and I started to step past him and into the theater.

He put out one broad hand to stop me. "No," he said. "Not yet. Get the dogs."

The other Warden frowned, but that was all the protest he made. He turned and slipped into the theater, and a moment later emerged, leading a pair of Wardhounds behind him.

In spite of myself, I swallowed and took a half step back from them. "Give me a break, Morgan. I'm not enspelled and I'm not toting in a bomb. I'm not the suicidal type."

"Then you won't mind a quick check," Morgan said. He gave me a humorless smile and stepped forward.

The Wardhounds came with him. They weren't actual dogs. I like dogs. They were statues made of some kind of dark grey-green stone, their shoulders as high as my own belt. They had the gaping mouth and too-big eyes of Chinese temple dogs, complete with curling beards and manes. Though they weren't flesh, they moved with a kind of ponderous liquid grace, stone "muscles" shifting beneath the surface of their skins as if they had been living beings. Morgan touched each on the head and muttered something too vague for me to make out. Upon hearing it, both Wardhounds focused upon me and began to prowl in a circle around me, heads down, the floor quivering beneath their weight.

I knew they'd been enchanted to detect any of countless threats that might attempt to approach a Council meeting. But they weren't thinking beings—only devices programmed with a simple set of responses to predetermined stimuli. Though Wardhounds had saved lives often before, there had also been accidents—and I didn't know if my run-in with Mab would leave a residual signature that might set the Wardhounds off.

The dogs stopped, and one of them let out a growl that sounded soothingly akin to bedrock being ripped apart by a backhoe. I tensed and looked down at the dog standing to my right. Its lips had peeled back from gleaming, dark fangs, and its empty eyes were focused on my left hand—the one Mab had wounded by way of demonstration.

I swallowed and held still and tried to think innocent thoughts.

"They don't like something about you, Dresden," Morgan said. I thought I heard an almost eager undertone to his voice. "Maybe I should turn you away, just to be careful."

The other Warden stepped forward, one hand on a short, heavy rod worn on his belt. He murmured, "Could be the injury, if he's hurt. Wizard blood can be pretty potent. Moody, too. Dog could be reacting to anger or fear, through the blood."

"Maybe," Morgan said testily. "Or it could be contraband he's trying to sneak in. Take off the bandage, Dresden."

"I don't want to start bleeding again," I said.

"Fine. I'm denying you entrance, then, in accordance with—"

"Dammit, Morgan," I muttered. I all but tossed my staff at him. He caught it, and held it while I tore at the makeshift bandages I'd put on my hand. It hurt like hell, but I pulled them off and showed him the swollen and oozing wound.

The Wardhound growled again and then appeared to lose interest, pacing back over to sit down beside its mate, suddenly inanimate again.

I turned my eyes to Morgan and stared at him, hard. "Satisfied?" I asked him.

For a second I thought he would meet my gaze. Then he shoved my staff back at me as he turned away. "You're a disgrace, Dresden. Look at yourself. Because of you, good men and women have died. Today you will be called to answer for it."

I tied the bandage back on as best I could and gritted my teeth to keep from telling Morgan to take a long walk off a short cliff. Then I brushed past the Wardens and stalked into the theater.

Morgan watched me go, then said to his partner, "Close the circle." He followed me into the theater, shutting the door behind him, even as I felt the sudden, silent tension of the Wardens closing the circle around the building, shutting it off from any supernatural access.

I hadn't ever actually seen a meeting of the Council—not like this. The sheer variety of it all was staggering, and I stood staring for several moments, taking it in.

The space was a dinner theater of only moderate size, lit by nothing more than a few candles on each table. The room wouldn't have been crowded for a matinee, but as a gathering place for wizards it was positively swamped. The tables on the floor of the theater were almost completely filled with black-robed wizards, variously sporting stoles of blue, gold, and scarlet. Apprentices in their muddy-brown robes lurked at the fringes of the crowd, standing along the walls or crouching on the floor beside their mentors' chairs.

The variety of humanity represented in the theater was startling. Canted Oriental eyes, dark, rich skins of Africa, pale Europeans, men and women, ancient and young, long and short hair, beards long enough to tuck into belts, beards wispy enough to be stirred by a passing breeze. The theater buzzed in dozens of languages, of which I could identify only a fraction. Wizards laughed and scowled, smiled and stared blankly, sipped from flasks and soda cans and cups or sat with eyes closed in meditation. The scents of spices and perfumes and chemicals all blended together into something pervasive, always changing, and the auras of so many practitioners of the Art seemed to be feeling just as social, reaching out around the room to touch upon other auras, to echo or strike dissonance with their energies, tangible enough to feel without even trying. It was like walking through drifting cobwebs that were constantly brushing against my cheeks and eyelashes— not dangerous but disconcerting, each one wildly unique, utterly different from the next.

The only thing the wizards had in common was that none of them looked as scruffy as me.

A roped-off section at the far right of the hall held the envoys of various organizations of allies and supernatural interests, most of whom I had only a vague idea about. Wardens stood here and there where they could overlook the crowd, grey cloaks conspicuous amid the black and scattered brown ones—but somehow I doubted they were as obtrusive as my own faded blue-and-white flannel. I garnered offended looks from nearly everyone I walked past—mostly white-haired old wizard folk. One or two apprentices nearer my own age covered their mouths as I went past, hiding grins. I looked around for an open chair, but I didn't spot one, until I saw Ebenezar wave at me from a table in the front row of the theater, nearest the stage. He nodded at the seat next to him. It was the only place available, and I joined him.

On the theater stage stood seven podiums, and at six of them stood members of the Senior Council, in dark robes with purple stoles Injun Joe Listens to Wind and Martha Liberty stood at two.

At the center podium stood the Merlin of the White Council, a tall man, broad of shoulder and blue of eye, with hair falling past his shoulders in shining, pale waves and a flowing silver beard. The Merlin spoke in a rolling basso voice, Latin phrases gliding as smoothly from his mouth as from any Roman senator's.

". . . et, quae cum ita sint, censeo iam nos dimittere rees cottidianas et de magna re gravi deliberare—id est, illud bellum contra comitatum rubrum." *And given the circumstances, I move to dispense with the usual formalities in order to discuss the most pertinent issue before us—the war with the Red Court.* "Consensum habemus?" *All in favor?*

There was a general murmur of consent from the wizards in the room. I didn't feel any need to add to it. I tried to slip unnoticed into the seat beside Ebenezar, but the Merlin's bright blue eyes spotted me and grew shades colder.

The Merlin spoke, and though I knew he spoke perfectly intelligible English, he addressed me in Latin, quick and liquid—but his own perfect command of the speech worked against him. He was easy to understand. "Ahhh, Magus Dresdenus. Prudenter ades nobis dum de bello quod inceperis diceamus. Ex omni parte ratio tua pro hoc comitatu nobis placet." *Ah, Wizard Dresden. How thoughtful of you to join us in discussions of the war you started. It is good to know that you have such respect for this Council.*

He delivered that last while giving my battered old bathrobe a pointed look, making sure that anyone in the room who hadn't noticed would now. Jerk. He let silence fall afterward and it was left to me to answer him. Also in Latin. Big fat jerk.

Still, it was my first Council meeting as a full wizard, and he *was* the Merlin, after all. And I *did* look pretty bad. Plus, Ebenezar shot me a warning glance. I swallowed a hot answer and took a stab at diplomacy.

"Uh," I said, "ego sum miser, Magus Merlinus. Dolor diei longi me tenet. Opus es mihi altera, uh, vestiplicia." *Sorry, Merlin. It's been a very long day. I meant to have my other robe.*

Or that's what I *tried* to say. I must have conjugated something wrong, because when I finished, the Merlin blinked at me, expression mild. "Quod est?"

Ebenezar winced and asked me in a whisper, "Hoss? You sure you don't want me to translate for you?"

I waved a hand at him. "I can do it." I scowled as I tried to put together the right words, and spoke again. "Excusationem vobis pro vestitu meo atque etiam tarditate facio." *Please excuse my lateness and appearance.*

The Merlin regarded me with passionless, distant features, evidently well content to let my mouth run. Ebenezar put his hand over his eyes.

"What?" I demanded of him in a fierce whisper.

Ebenezar squinted up at me. "Well. First you said, 'I am a sorry excuse, Merlin, a sad long day held me. I need me a different laundress.'"

I blinked. "What?"

"That's what the Merlin said. Then you said 'Excuses to you for my being dressed and I also make lately.'"

I felt my face heat up. Most of the room was still staring at me as though I was some sort of raving lunatic, and it dawned on me that many of the wizards in the room probably did not speak English. As far as they were concerned, I probably sounded like one.

"Goddamned correspondence course. Maybe you should translate for me," I said.

Ebenezar's eyes sparkled, but he nodded with a grave expression. "Happy to."

I slipped into my seat while Ebenezar stood up and made an apology for me, his Latin terse and precise, his voice carrying easily throughout the hall. I saw the gathered wizards' expressions grow more or less mollified as he spoke.

The Merlin nodded and continued in his textbook-perfect Latin. "Thank you, Wizard McCoy, for your assistance. The first order of business in addressing the crisis before us is to restore the Senior Council to its full membership. As some of you have doubtless learned by now, Senior Council member Pietrovich was killed in an attack by the Red Court two days past."

A gasp and a low murmur ran through the theater.

The Merlin allowed a moment to pass. "Past conflicts with the Red Court have not moved with this kind of alacrity, and this may indicate a shift in their usual strategy. As a result, we need to be able to react quickly to further developments—which will require the leadership provided by a full membership on the Senior Council."

The Merlin continued speaking, but I leaned over to Ebenezar. "Let me guess," I whispered. "He wants to fill the opening on the Senior Council so that he'll be able to control the vote?"

Ebenezar nodded. "He'll have three votes for sure, then, and most times four."

"What are we going to do about it?"

"You aren't going to do anything. Not yet." He looked intently at me. "Keep your temper, Hoss. I mean it. The Merlin will have three plans to take you down."

I shook my head. "What? How do you know that?"

"He always does things that way," Ebenezar muttered. His

eyes glittered with something ugly. "A plan, a backup plan, and an ace in the hole. I'll shoot down the first one, and I'll help you with the second. The third is all yours, though."

"What do you mean? What plan?"

"Hush, Hoss. I'm paying attention."

A balding wizard with bristling white eyebrows and a bushy blue beard, his scalp covered in flowing blue tattoos, leaned forward from the far side of the table and glared at me. "Shhhhh."

Ebenezar nodded at the man, and we both turned back to face the stage.

"And it is for this reason," the Merlin continued, "that I now ask Klaus Schneider, as a long-standing senior wizard of impeccable reputation, to take on the responsibility of membership in the Senior Council. All in favor?"

Martha glanced at Ebenezar and murmured, "A moment, honored Merlin. I believe protocol requires that we open the floor to debate."

The Merlin sighed. "Under normal circumstances, Wizard Liberty, of course. But we have little time for the niceties of our usual procedures. Time is of the essence. So, all in—"

Injun Joe interrupted. "Wizard Schneider is a fine enchanter, and he has a reputation for skill and honesty. But he is young for such a responsibility. There are wizards present who are his senior in experience and the Art. They deserve the consideration of the Council."

The Merlin shot Injun Joe a frown. "*Thank* you for your perspective, Wizard Listens to Wind. But though your commentary is welcome, it was not asked for. There is no one present senior to Wizard Schneider who has not already declined a seat upon the Senior Council, and rather than run through meaningless nominations and repeated declinations, I had intended—"

Ebenezar cut in, sotto voce but loud enough for the Merlin to hear him, in English. "You had intended to shove your favorite down everyone's throats while they were too worried to notice."

The Merlin fell abruptly quiet, his eyes falling on Ebenezar in a sudden, pointed silence. He spoke in a low voice, his English carrying a rich British accent. "Go back to your mountain, Ebenezar. Back to your sheep. You are not welcome here, and never have been."

Ebenezar looked up at the Merlin with a toothy smile, Scots creeping back into his vowels. "Aye, Alfred, laddie, I know." He switched back to Latin and raised his voice again. "Every member of the Council has a right to speak his mind on these matters. You all know how important the appointment of one Senior Council member is. How many of you believe this matter too serious to leave to a consensus? Speak now."

The theater rumbled with a general "Aye," to which I added my own voice. Ebenezar looked around the room and then raised an eyebrow at the Merlin.

I could see frustration not quite hidden on the old man's face. I could almost taste his desire to slam his fist down on the podium, but he controlled himself and nodded. "Very well. Then, in accordance with procedure, we will offer the position to the senior-most wizards present." He looked to one side, where a slim-faced, prim-looking wizard sat with a quill, a bottle of ink, and pages and pages of parchment. "Wizard Peabody, will you consult the registry?"

Peabody reached under his table and came out with a bulging satchel. He muttered something to himself and rubbed some ink onto his nose with one finger, then he opened the satchel, which held what looked like a couple of reams of parchment. His eyes glazed over slightly, and he reached into the papers seemingly at random. He drew out a single page, put it on the desk before him, nodded in satisfaction, then read in a reedy voice, "Wizard Montjoy."

"Research trip in the Yucatán," Martha Liberty said.

Peabody nodded. "Wizard Gomez."

"Still sleeping off that potion," provided a grey-cloaked Warden standing by the wall.

Peabody nodded. "Wizard Luciozzi."

"Sabbatical," said the blue-bearded and tattooed wizard behind me. Ebenezar frowned, and one of his cheeks twitched in a nervous tic.

It went on like that for close to a quarter hour. Some of the more interesting reasons for absence included "He got real married," "Living under the polar ice cap," and "Pyramid sitting," whatever that was.

Peabody finally read, with a glance up at the Merlin, "Wizard McCoy." Ebenezar grunted and stood. Peabody read another half-dozen names before stating, "Wizard Schneider."

A small, round-cheeked man with a fringe of gauzy white down over his scalp and a round belly stretching his robes stood up and gave Ebenezar a brief nod. Then he looked up at the Merlin and said, in Latin with a heavy Germanic accent, "While I am grateful for the offer, honored Merlin, I must respectfully decline your nomination, in favor of Wizard McCoy. He will serve the Council more ably than I."

The Merlin looked as though someone had grated slices of lemon against his gums. "Very well," he said. "Do any other senior wizards here wish to present themselves for consideration over Wizard McCoy?"

I was betting no one would, especially given the looks on the faces of the wizards nearby. Ebenezar himself never moved his eyes from the Merlin. He just stood with his feet spread wide apart and planted, his eyes steady, confident. Silence fell over the hall.

The Merlin looked around the hall, his lips pressed tightly together. Finally, he gave his head a very slight shake. "All in favor?"

The room rumbled with a second, more affirmative "Aye."

"Very well," the Merlin said, his upper lip twisting and giving the words an acid edge. "Wizard McCoy, take your place upon the Senior Council."

There was a murmur of what sounded a bit like relief from those in the hall. Ebenezar glanced back and winked at me. "One down. Two to go," he murmured. "Stay sharp." Then he hitched up his robes and stumped onto the stage, to the empty podium between Martha Liberty and Injun Joe. "Less talking, more doing," he said, loudly enough to be heard by the whole hall. "There's a war on."

"Precisely what I was thinking," the Merlin said, and nodded to one side. "Let us address the war. Warden Morgan, would you please stand forward and give the Council the Wardens' tactical assessment of the Red Court?"

An oppressive silence settled over the room, so that I heard every sound of Morgan's boots as he stepped up onto the stage. The Merlin moved aside, and Morgan placed a glittering gem or crystal of some kind upon the podium. Behind that, he set a candle, which he lit with a muttered incantation. Then he framed the candle with his hands and murmured again.

Light streaked from the candle into the crystal in a glowing stream and sprang up out of the crystal again in a large cone stretching up above the stage, several yards across at the top. Within the cone of light appeared a spinning globe of the Earth, its continents vaguely misshapen, like something drawn from a couple of centuries past.

A murmur ran through the room, and Bluebeard, at my table, muttered in Latin, "Impressive."

"Bah," I said in English. "He stole that from *Return of the Jedi*."

Bluebeard blinked at me, uncomprehending. I briefly debated trying to translate *Star Wars* into Latin and decided against it. See, I can have common sense, too.

Morgan's low voice rumbled out in Latin phrases, rough but understandable. Which meant he spoke it better than me. Jerk. "The flashing red spots on the map are the locations of known attacks of the Red Court and their allies. Most of them resulted in casualties of one form or another." As he spoke, widely scattered motes of red color began to form on the globe like the glowing lights of a Christmas tree. "As you can see, most of the activity has taken place in Western Europe."

A mutter went through the room. The Old World was the domain of the Old School of wizardry—the "maintain secrecy and don't attract attention" way of thinking. I guess they have a point, given the Inquisition and all. I don't belong to the Old School. I have an ad in the Yellow Pages, under "Wizards." Big shocker—I'm the only one there. I have to pay the bills somehow, don't I?

Morgan droned on dispassionately. "We have known for a long time that the main power center of the Red Court is somewhere in South America. Our sources there are under pressure, and it has become difficult to get any information out of the area. We have had advance warning of several attacks, and the Wardens have managed to intercede with minimal losses of life, with the exception of the attack at Archangel." The globe paused in its spinning, and my eyes fastened on the glowing point of light on the northwest coast of Russia. "Though it is presumed that Wizard Pietrovich's death curse took a heavy toll on his attackers, no one in his household survived the attack. We don't know how they got past his defenses. It would appear that the Red Court may have access to information or aspects of the Art that they have not before had."

The Merlin stepped back to the podium, and Morgan collected his crystal. The globe vanished. "Thank you, Warden," the Merlin said. "As we expected from Council records, our various retreats and Paths through the Nevernever are threatened. Frankly speaking, ladies and gentlemen, the Red Court holds us at a disadvantage within the mortal world. Modern technology so often disagrees with us that it makes travel difficult under the best of circumstances and unreliable in a time of conflict. We vitally need to secure safe Paths through the Nevernever or else risk being engaged and overwhelmed in detail by an opponent who can move more rapidly than we. To that end, we have dispatched missives to both Queens of the Sidhe. Ancient Mai."

My eyes flickered to the podium to the Merlin's left, where stood another of the Senior Council members, apparently the Ancient Mai. She was a tiny woman of Oriental extraction, her skin fine and pale, her granite-colored hair worn in a long braid curled up at the back of her head and held with a pair of jade combs. She had delicate features only lightly touched by the passage of years, though her dark eyes were rheumy. She unfolded a letter written upon parchment and addressed the Council in a creaky but firm voice. "From Summer, we received this answer. 'Queen Titania does not now, nor will she ever choose sides in the disputes of mortal and anthrophage. She bids both Council and Court alike to keep their war well away from the realms of Summer. She will remain neutral.'"

Ebenezar frowned and leaned forward to ask, "And from Winter?"

I twitched.

The Ancient tilted her head and regarded Ebenezar in perfect silence for a moment, somehow implying her annoyance at his interruption. "Our courier did not return. Upon consulting records of former conflicts, we may confidently assume that Queen Mab will involve herself, if at all, in a time and manner of her own choosing."

I twitched more. There was a pitcher of water on the table, along with some glasses. I poured a drink. The pitcher only rattled against the cup a little. I glanced back at Bluebeard and saw him regarding me with a pensive gaze.

Ebenezar scowled. "Now what is that supposed to mean?"

The Merlin stepped in smoothly. "It means that we must continue whatever diplomacy we may with Winter. At all costs, we must secure the cooperation of one of the Sidhe Queens—or at least prevent the Red Court from accomplishing an alliance of its own until this conflict can be resolved."

Martha Liberty lifted both eyebrows. "Resolved?" she said, her tone pointed. "I would have chosen a word like 'finished' myself."

The Merlin shook his head. "Wizard Liberty, there is no need for this dispute to devolve into an even more destructive conflict. If there exists even a small chance that an armistice can be attained—"

The black woman's voice lashed out at the Merlin, harsh and cold. "Ask Simon Pietrovich how interested the vampires are in reaching a peaceable settlement."

"Contain your emotions, Wizard," the Merlin replied, his

voice calm. "The loss of Pietrovich strikes each of us deeply, but we cannot allow that loss to blind us to potential solutions."

"Simon knew them, Merlin," Martha said, her tone flat. "He knew them better than any of us, and they killed him. Do you really think that they will be inclined to seek a reasonable peace with us, when they have already destroyed the wizard best able to protect himself against them? Why should they seek a peace, Merlin? They're *winning*."

The Merlin waved a hand. "Your anger clouds your judgement. They will seek a peace because even in victory they would pay too high a cost."

"Don't be a fool," Martha said. "They will never sue for peace."

"In point of fact," said the Merlin, "they already have." He gestured to the second podium on his left. "Wizard LaFortier."

LaFortier was an emaciated man of medium height and build. His cheekbones stood out grotesquely from his sunken face, and his bulging eyes looked a couple of sizes too large. He had no hair at all, not even eyebrows, and on the whole it gave him a skeletal look. When he spoke, his voice came out in a resonant basso, deep and warm and smooth. "Thank you, Merlin." He held up an envelope in one thin-fingered hand. "I have here a missive from Duke Ortega, the war leader of the Red Court, received this morning. In it he details the Red Court's motivations in this matter and the terms they desire for peace. He also offers, by token of goodwill, a temporary cessation of hostilities in order to give the Council time to consider, effective this morning."

"Bullshit!" The word burst out of my mouth before my brain realized I had said it. A round of snickers, mostly from brown-robed apprentices, echoed through the theater, and I heard fabric rustle as every wizard in the place turned to look at me. I felt my face heat again, and cleared my throat. "Well, it is," I said to the room. Ebenezar translated for me. "I was attacked by a Red Court hit squad only a few hours ago."

LaFortier smiled at me. It stretched his lips out to show his teeth, like the dried face of a thousand-year-old mummy. "Even if you are not lying, Wizard Dresden, I would hardly expect perfect control of all Red Court forces given your role in precipitating this war."

"*Precipitating* it?" I exclaimed. "Do you have any idea what they *did*?"

LaFortier shrugged. "They defended an assault upon their

sovereignty, Wizard. You, acting in the role of representative of this Council, attacked a noble of their court, damaged her property, and killed members of said noble's household and her as well. In addition, the records of local newspapers and authorities reveal that during the altercation, several young men and women were also killed—burned up in a fire, I think. Does that sound familiar to you, Wizard Dresden?"

I clenched my jaw, the sudden rush of rage spilling through me in such a torrent that I could scarcely see, much less trust myself to speak. I'd been brought before the Council for the first time when I had been put on trial for violating the First Law of Magic: Thou Shalt Not Kill. I'd burned my old mentor, Justin, to death. When I'd clashed with Bianca, lately of the Red Court, the previous year, I'd called up a firestorm when it looked as if my companions and I were going to buy it anyway. A lot of vampires burned. The bodies of some people had been found afterward, too. There was no way to tell which of them had been victims of the vampires and already dead when the fire got to them and which, if any, had been alive before I came along. I still have nightmares about it. I'm a lot of things, but I'm not a willing murderer.

To my shock, I felt myself gathering in power, getting ready to unleash it at LaFortier, with his skeletal smirk. Ebenezar caught my eye, his own a little wide, and shook his head quickly. I clenched my hands into tight fists instead of blasting anybody with magic and forced myself to sit down again before I spoke. Self-disciplined, that's me. "I have already detailed my recollection of the events in my report to the Council. I stand by them. Anyone who tells you differently than what you read there is lying."

LaFortier rolled his eyes. "How comfortable it must be to live in such a clear-cut world, Wizard Dresden. But we are not counting the cost of your actions in coins or hours wasted—we are counting it in blood. Wizards are *dying* because of what *you* did while acting in this Council's name." LaFortier swept his gaze to the rest of the theater, his expression stern, controlled. "Frankly, I think it may be wise for the Council to consider that we may indeed stand in the wrong in this matter and that it might be prudent to give careful considerations to the Red Court's terms for peace."

"What do they want?" I snarled at the man, Ebenezar providing the Latin for the rest of the Council. "A pint of blood a month from each of us? Rights to hunt freely wherever they choose? Amulets to shield them from the light of the sun?"

LaFortier smiled at me and folded his hands atop his podium. "Nothing so dramatic, Dresden. They simply want what any of us would want in this situation. They want justice." He leaned toward me, bulging eyes glittering. "They want you."

Chapter Six

Gulp.

"Me?" I said. *Et la*, LaFortier. Feel the bite of my rapier wit.

"Yes. Duke Ortega writes that you, Wizard Dresden, are considered a criminal by the Red Court. In order to end this conflict they wish to extradite you to an area of their designation for trial. A resolution that is, perhaps, distasteful, but may also be only just."

He didn't get the last word out of his mouth before several dozen wizards around the auditorium rose to their feet with outraged shouts. Others stood up to cry out against them, and still more against them. The room descended into a cacophony of shouts, threats, and cussing (among wizards, cursing is a different matter altogether) in dozens of languages.

The Merlin let people shout for a moment before he called out in a ringing voice, "Order!" No one paid him any attention. He tried once more, then lifted his staff and slammmed it down hard on the stage beside him.

There was a flash of light, a roar of sound, and a concussion that slopped the water in my glass up over the brim, spilling it on my flannel bathrobe. A couple of the wispier wizards were knocked down by the force of it—but in any case, the shouting ceased.

"Order!" the Merlin demanded again, in exactly the same tone. "I am well aware of the implications of this situation. But lives are at stake. Your lives and my own. We must consider our options with the utmost gravity."

"What options?" Ebenezar demanded. "We are wizards, not a

herd of frightened sheep. Will we give one of our own to the vampires now and pretend that none of this has happened?"

LaFortier snapped, "You read Dresden's report. By his own admission, what the Red Court accuses him of is true. They have a just grievance."

"The situation was clearly a manipulation, a scheme to force Dresden to those actions in hopes of killing him."

"Then he should have been smarter," LaFortier said, his tone flat. "Politics is not a game for children. Dresden played and was beaten. It is time for him to pay the price so that the rest of us may live in peace."

Injun Joe put a hand on Ebenezar's arm and spoke quietly. "Peace cannot be bought, Aleron," he murmured to LaFortier. "History teaches that lesson. I learned it. You should have, too."

LaFortier sneered at Injun Joe. "I don't know what you are babbling about, but—"

I rolled my eyes and stood up again. "He's talking about the American tribes losing their land to white settlers, dolt." I figured Ebenezar would leave the insult out of the translation, but there were more stifled snorts from brown robes around the room. "And about Europe's attempts to appease Hitler before the Second World War. Both attempted to purchase peace with compromise, and both got swallowed up bit by bit."

The Merlin glared at me. "I did not recognize you, Wizard Dresden. Until you have the floor, you will refrain from such outbursts or I will have you removed from this meeting."

I clenched my jaw and sat down. "Sorry. Here I was, figuring we had a responsibility to protect people. What was I thinking?"

"We will protect no one, Wizard Dresden, if we are dead," the Merlin snapped. "Be silent or be removed."

Martha Liberty shook her head. "Merlin, it seems clear that we cannot simply hand one of our own over to the Red Court because of their demands. Despite past differences with Council policy, Dresden *is* a fully ranked wizard—and given his performance in recent years, he seems well deserving of the title."

"I do not question his ability with the Art," LaFortier put in. "I question his judgement, his choices. He has played loose and reckless with his status as a wizard since Justin's death." The bald man turned his bulging eyes to the wizards in the theater. "Wizard Harry Dresden. Apprentice to the Wizard Justin DuMorne. Apprentice to the Wizard Simon Pietrovich. I wonder how the Red

Court learned enough of Pietrovich's defenses to bypass them so completely, Dresden."

I stared at LaFortier for a second, shocked. Did the man actually believe that I had learned about this Pietrovich's defenses through Justin? Then sold a Senior Council member of the White Council to the vampires? Justin hadn't exactly taken me around much. Before I'd been put on trial, I hadn't even known that there *was* a White Council—or other wizards at all, for that matter. I gave him the only answer I could. I laughed at him. Wheezy, quiet laughter. I shook my head.

LaFortier's expression grew outraged. "You see?" he demanded to the room. "You see in what contempt he holds this Council? His position as a wizard? Dresden has constantly endangered us all with his obtuse indiscretion, his reckless disregard for secrecy and security. Even if it was someone else who betrayed Pietrovich and his students to the Red Court, Dresden is as guilty of their murder as if he himself had cut their throats. Let the consequences of his decisions fall upon him."

I rose and faced LaFortier, but glanced at the Merlin for permission to speak. He gave the floor to me with a grudging nod. "Impossible," I said. "Or at least impractical. I have violated none of the Laws of Magic in this matter, which rules out a summary trial. I am a full wizard. By Council law, I am therefore entitled to an in-depth investigation and trial—neither of which would provide any kind of workable solution anytime soon."

The room rumbled with agreement when Ebenezar finished translating for me. That was hardly a surprise. If the Council jammed a trial down my throat and then threw me to the wolves, it would set a deadly precedent—one that could haunt any wizard in the room, and they knew it.

LaFortier jabbed a forefinger at me and said, "Quite true. Provided that you are, in fact, a full wizard. I move that the Council vote, immediately, to determine whether or not Dresden's status as a wizard is valid. I remind the Council that his appointment to his stole was a de facto decision based upon circumstantial evidence. He has never stood Trial, never been judged worthy by his peers."

"Like hell I haven't," I answered him. "I beat Justin DuMorne in a duel to the death. Is that not Trial enough for you?"

"Wizard DuMorne died, yes," LaFortier said. "Whether he was defeated in an open duel or burned in his sleep is another matter entirely. Merlin, you have heard my motion. Let the Council vote upon the status of this madman. Let us end this foolishness and return to our lives."

Ouch. An angle I hadn't thought of. If I was stripped of my stole, it would be like a medieval noble having his title taken away. I would no longer be a wizard, politically speaking, and according to Council law and to the Accords between the various supernatural factions, the Council would be obligated to turn over a fugitive murderer to the Red Court. Which would mean, if I was fortunate, a horrible death. If I wasn't fortunate, it could be considerably worse.

Given the kind of day I'd been having, my heart started skittering in my chest.

The Merlin frowned and nodded. "Very well, then. We vote upon the issue of the status of one Harry Dresden. Let those who would have him keep his stole vote for, and those who favor that his status be restored to that of apprentice vote against. All those in fav—"

"Wait," Ebenezar interjected. "I invoke my right as a member of the Senior Council to reduce the vote to the Senior Council alone."

The Merlin glared at Ebenezar. "On what grounds?"

"On the grounds that there exists a great deal of information about this matter of which the Council at large is unaware. It would be impractical to attempt to explain it all."

"Seconded," Injun Joe murmured.

"Accord," Martha Liberty added. "Three votes yea, honored Merlin. Let the Senior Council make this decision."

My heart started beating again. Ebenezar had made the right call. In a room full of frightened men and women, I wouldn't have had a prayer of keeping my stole. With the vote reduced to the Senior Council, maybe I had a fighting chance.

I could almost see the Merlin trying to figure a way out of it, but Council law is pretty clear on that point. The Senior Council members can always take a matter to a closed vote with three supporters.

"Very well," the Merlin said. The room rustled with whispers. "My interests lie in preserving the health and safety of those upon this Council, and of the communities of mankind in general. I vote against Dresden's validity as an initiate wizard of this Council."

LaFortier jumped in, bulging eyes narrowed. "As do I, and for the same reasons."

Ebenezar spoke next. "I've lived with this young man. I know him. He's a wizard. I vote to preserve his status."

Little Brother chittered from his perch on Injun Joe's shoulder, and the old wizard stroked the raccoon's tail with one hand. "My instincts about this man tell me that he comports himself as a wizard should." He gave a very mild glance to LaFortier. "I vote in favor of his status."

"As do I," Martha Liberty added. "This is not a solution. It is merely an action."

Harry three, bad guys two. I turned my eyes to Ancient Mai.

The tiny woman stood with her eyes closed for a moment, her head bowed. Then she murmured, "No wizard should so blatantly misuse his status as a member of this Council. Nor should he be as irresponsible as Harry Dresden has been with his use of the Art. I vote against his retention of wizard status."

Three to three. I licked my lips, and realized at just that moment that I had been too nervous and involved with events to take note of the seventh member of the Senior Council. He was standing at the far left of the stage. Like the other wizards, he wore a black robe, but his dark purple, almost black stole had a deep cowl upon it as well, which covered his face entirely. The candlelit dimness masked in shadow whatever the cowl didn't cover. He was tall. Taller than me. Seven feet, and thin. His arms were folded, hands hidden inside the voluminous sleeves of his robe. Every eye in the place turned to the seventh member of the Council, and a silence deeper than that of the nearby Great Lake enveloped the room.

It lasted for long moments, then the Merlin prompted, quietly, "Gatekeeper. What say you?"

I leaned forward in my chair, my mouth dry. If he voted against me, I was betting a Warden would zap me unconscious before the sound of his voice died away.

After several of my frantic heartbeats, the Gatekeeper spoke in a resonant, gentle voice. "It rained toads this morning."

A baffled silence followed. It became, a moment later, a baffled mutter.

"Gatekeeper," the Merlin said, his voice more urgent, "how do you vote?"

"With deliberation," the Gatekeeper said. "It rained toads this morning. That bears consideration. And for that, I must hear what word returns with the messenger."

LaFortier eyed the Gatekeeper and said impatiently, "What messenger? What are you talking about?"

The back doors of the theater burst open, hard, and a pair of grey-cloaked Wardens entered the theater. They each had a shoulder under one of the arms of a brown-robed young man. His face was puffy and swollen, and his hands looked like rotten sausages about to burst. Frost clung to his hair in a thick coating, and his robe looked like it had been dipped in water and then dragged behind a sled team from Anchorage to Nome. His lips were blue, and his eyes fluttered and rolled semicoherently. The Wardens dragged him to the foot of the stage, and the Senior Council gathered at its edge, looking down.

"This is my courier to the Winter Queen," Ancient Mai stated.

"He insisted," one of the Wardens said. "We tried to take him for treatment, but he got so worked up about it I was afraid he would hurt himself, so we brought him to you, Ancient."

"Where did you find him?" the Merlin asked.

"Outside. Someone drove up in a car and pushed him out of it. We didn't see who it was."

"You get the license number?" I asked. Both Wardens turned to eye me. Then they both turned back to the Merlin. Neither of them had gotten it. Maybe license plates were too new a concept. They weren't yet a whole century old, after all. "Hell's bells," I muttered. "I would have gotten it."

Ancient Mai carefully descended from the stage and moved to the young man. She touched his forehead and spoke to him gently in what I presumed to be Chinese. The boy opened his eyes and babbled something broken and halting back at her.

Ancient Mai frowned. She asked something else, which the boy struggled to answer, but it was apparently too much for him. He sagged, his eyes rolling back, and went completely limp.

The Ancient touched his hair and said in Latin, "Take him. Care for him."

The Wardens laid the boy on a cloak, and then four of them carried him out, moving quickly.

"What did he say?" Ebenezar asked. He beat me to it.

"He said that Queen Mab bade him tell the Council she will permit them travel through her realm, provided one request is fulfilled."

The Merlin arched a brow, fingers touching his beard thoughtfully. "What does she request?"

Ancient Mai murmured, "She did not tell him. She said only that she had already made her desires known to one of the Council." The Senior Council withdrew together to one side, speaking in low voices.

I didn't pay them any mind. The Ancient's translation of the messenger's words shocked me enough to keep me from so much as breathing, much less speaking. When I could move, I turned back to my table, leaned forward, and banged my head gently on the wooden surface. Several times.

"Dammit," I muttered, in time with the thumps. "Dammit, dammit, dammit."

A hand touched my shoulder, and I looked up to see the shadowed cowl of the Gatekeeper, standing apart from the rest of the Senior Council. His hand was covered by a black leather glove. I couldn't see any skin showing on him, anywhere.

"You know what the rain of toads means," he said, his voice very quiet. His English had a gentle accent, something part British and part something else. Indian? Middle Eastern?

I nodded. "Trouble."

"Trouble." Though I could not see his face, I suspected a very slight smile had colored the word. The cowl turned toward the other Senior Council members, and he whispered, "There isn't much time. Will you answer me one question honestly, Dresden?"

I checked Bluebeard to see if he was listening in. He had leaned way over toward a round-faced grandma-looking wizardess at another table and appeared to be listening intently to her. I nodded to the Gatekeeper.

He waved his hand. No words, no pause to prepare, nothing. He waved his hand, and the sounds of the room suddenly seemed to blur together, robbed of any coherence at all. "I understand you know how to Listen, too. I would rather no one else heard us." The sound of his voice came to me warped, parts pitched high and others low, oddly reverberating.

I gave him a wary nod. "What is the question?"

He reached up to his cowl, black leather against twilight purple, and drew back the hood a little, enough that I could see the gleam of one dark eye and a rough, thin grey beard against bronzed skin. I couldn't see his other eye. His face seemed to ripple and contort in the shadows, and I had an idea that he was disfigured, maybe burned. In the socket of the missing eye, I saw something silver and reflective.

He leaned down closer and whispered near my ear, "Has Mab chosen an Emissary?"

I struggled not to let the surprise show in my face, but I'm not always good at hiding my feelings. I saw comprehension flicker in the Gatekeeper's shadowed eye.

Dammit. Now I understood why Mab had been so confident. She'd known all along that she had set me up for a deal I couldn't refuse. She'd done it without breaking our bargain, either. Mab wanted me to take up her case, and she seemed perfectly happy to meddle in a supernatural war to get what she wanted.

She'd just been toying with me in my office, and I'd fallen for it. I wanted to kick myself. Somewhere out there was a village I'd deprived of its idiot.

In any case, there was no sense lying to the guy whose vote would decide my fate. I nodded to him. "Yes."

He shook his head. "Precarious balance. The Council can afford neither to keep you nor to cast you out."

"I don't understand."

"You will." He drew the cowl back down and murmured, "I cannot prevent your fate, wizard. I can only give you a chance to avoid it on your own."

"What do you mean?"

"Cannot you see what is happening?"

I frowned at him. "A dangerous imbalance of forces. The White Council in town. Mab meddling in our affairs."

"Or perhaps we are meddling in hers. Why has she appointed a mortal Emissary, young wizard?"

"Because someone up there takes a malevolent amusement in my suffering?"

"Balance," the Gatekeeper corrected me. "It is all about balance. Redress the imbalance, young wizard. Resolve the situation. Prove your worth beyond doubt."

"Are you telling me I *should* work for Mab?" My voice sounded hollow, tinny, as though it was trapped in a coffee can.

"What is the date?" the Gatekeeper asked.

"June eighteenth," I said.

"Ah. Of course." The Gatekeeper turned away, and sounds returned to normal. The Gatekeeper joined the rest of the Senior Council, and they trooped back up to their podiums. Podii. Podia. Whatever. Goddamned correspondence course.

"Order," called the Merlin again, and the room grew quiet after a reluctant moment.

"Gatekeeper," the Merlin said, "what is your vote?"

The silent figure of the Gatekeeper silently lifted one hand.

"We have set our feet upon a darkling path," he murmured. "A road that will only grow more dangerous. Our first steps are critical. We must make them with caution."

The cowl turned toward Ebenezar, and the Gatekeeper said, "You love the boy, Wizard McCoy. You would fight to defend him. Your own dedication to our cause is not inconsiderable. I respect your choice."

He turned toward LaFortier. "You question Dresden's loyalty and his ability. You imply that only a bad seed can grow from bad soil. Your concerns are understandable—and if correct, then Dresden poses a major threat to the Council."

He turned to Ancient Mai and inclined the cowl forward a few degrees. The Ancient responded with a slight bow of her own. "Ancient Mai," the Gatekeeper said. "You question his ability to use his power wisely. To judge between right and wrong. You fear that DuMorne's teaching may have twisted him in ways even he cannot yet see. Your fears, too, are justified."

He turned to the Merlin. "Honored Merlin. You know that Dresden has drawn death and danger down upon the Council. You believe that if he is removed, so will be that danger. Your fears are understandable, but not reasonable. Regardless of what happens to Dresden, the Red Court has struck a blow against the Council too deep to be ignored. A cessation of current hostilities would only be the calm before the storm."

"Enough, man," Ebenezar demanded. "Vote, for or against."

"I choose to base my vote upon a Trial. A test that will lay to rest the fears of one side of the issue, or prove falsely placed the faith of the other."

"What Trial?" the Merlin asked.

"Mab," the Gatekeeper said. "Let Dresden address Queen Mab's request. Let him secure the assistance of Winter. If he does, that should lay to rest your concerns regarding his ability, LaFortier."

LaFortier frowned, but then nodded at the Gatekeeper.

He turned next to Ancient Mai. "Should he accomplish this, it should show that he is willing to accept responsibility for his mistake and to work against his own best interests for the greater good of the Council. It should satisfy your concerns as to his judgement—to make the mistakes of youth is no crime, but not to learn from them is. Agreed?"

Ancient Mai narrowed her rheumy eyes, but gave the Gatekeeper a precise nod.

"And you, honored Merlin. Such a success may do much to alleviate the pressure of the coming war. If securing routes through the Nevernever places the Red Court at a severe enough disadvantage, it may even enable us to avoid it entirely. Surely it would prove Dresden's dedication to the Council beyond a doubt."

"That's all well and good," Ebenezar said. "But what happens if he fails?"

The Gatekeeper shrugged. "Then perhaps their fears are more justified than your affection, Wizard McCoy. We may indeed conclude that his appointment to full Wizard Initiate may have been premature."

"All or nothing?" Ebenezar demanded. "Is that it? You expect the youngest wizard in the Council to get the best of Queen Mab somehow? *Mab?* That's not a Trial. It's a goddamned execution. How is he even supposed to know what her request was to begin with?"

I stood up, my legs shaking a little. "Ebenezar," I said.

"How the hell is the boy supposed to know what she wants?"

"Ebenezar—"

"I'm not going to stand by while you—" He abruptly blinked and looked at me. So did everyone else.

"I know what Mab wants," I said. "She approached me earlier today, sir. She asked me to investigate something for her. I turned her down."

"Hell's bells," Ebenezar breathed. He took the blue bandanna from his pocket and mopped at his gleaming forehead. "Hoss, this is out of your depth."

"Looks like it's sink or swim, then," I said.

The Gatekeeper murmured to me in English, "Will you accept this, Wizard Dresden?"

I nodded my head. My throat had gone dry. I swallowed and tried to remind myself that there wasn't much choice. If I didn't play with the faeries and come out on top, the Council would serve me up to the vampires on a silver platter. The former might get me really, really killed. The latter would certainly kill me as well—and probably more than that.

As deals went, it blew. But some little part of me that hadn't let me forget all the destruction, maybe even the deaths I'd caused last year, danced gleefully at my apparent comeuppance. Besides, it was the only game in town. I tightened my grip on my staff and spoke as clearly as I could manage.

"Yeah. I accept."

Chapter Seven

The rest of the Council meeting was somewhat anticlimactic—for me, anyway.

The Merlin ordered the wizards to disperse immediately after the meeting via preplanned, secure routes. He also distributed a list to everyone, noting the Wardens near them to call upon if help was needed, and told them to check in with the Wardens every few days, as a safety precaution.

Next, a grizzled old dame Warden went over the theories to a couple of newly developed wards meant to work especially well against vampires. Representatives of the White Council's allies—secret occult brotherhoods, mostly—each gave a brief speech, declaring his or her group's support of the Council in the war.

Toward the end of the meeting, Wardens showed up in force to escort wizards to the beginnings of their routes home. The Senior Council, I presumed, would loiter around for a few days in order to see if I got killed trying to prove that I was one of the good guys. Sometimes I feel like no one appreciates me.

I stood up about three seconds before the Merlin said, "Meeting adjourned," and headed for the door. Ebenezar tried to catch my eye, but I didn't feel like talking to anyone. I slammed the doors open a little harder than I needed to, stalked out to the Blue Beetle, and drove away with all the raging power the ancient four-cylinder engine could muster. Behold the angry wizard puttputtputting away.

My brain felt like something made out of stale cereal, coffee grounds, and cold pizza. Thoughts trudged around in aimless depression, mostly about how I was going to get myself killed playing private eye for Mab. If things got really bad, I might even drag down a few innocent bystanders with me.

I growled at myself. "Stop whining, Harry," I said in a firm, loud voice. "So what if you're tired? So what if you're hurt? So what if you smell like you're already dead? You're a wizard. You've got a job to do. This war is mostly your own fault, and if you don't stay on the ball, more people are going to get hurt. So stiff upper lip, chin up, whatever. Get your ass in gear."

I nodded at that advice, and glanced aside, to the envelope Mab had given me, which lay on the passenger seat. I had a name, an address, a crime. I needed to get on the trail of the killer. That meant I would need information—and the people who would have the most information, a couple of days after the fact, would be the Chicago PD.

I drove to Murphy's place.

Lieutenant Karrin Murphy was the head of Chicago PD's Special Investigations team. SI was the city's answer to weirdness in general. They got all of the unusual crimes, the ones that didn't fall neatly into the department's other categories. SI has handled everything from sightings of sewer alligators to grave robbing in one of the city's many cemeteries. What fun. They also got to take care of the genuine supernatural stuff, the things that no one talks about in official reports but that manage to happen anyway. Trolls, vampires, demon-summoning sorcerers—you name it. The city had appointed SI to make sure the paperwork stayed nice and neat, with no mention of preposterous fantasies that could not possibly exist. It was a thankless job, and the directors of SI typically blew it after about a month by refusing to believe that they were dealing with genuine weirdness. Then they got shuffled out of Chicago PD.

Murphy hadn't. She'd lasted. She'd taken things seriously and employed the services of Chicago's only professional wizard (guess who) as a consultant on the tougher jobs. Murphy and I have seen some very upsetting things together. We're friends. She would help.

Murphy lives in a house in Bucktown, near a lot of other cops. It's a tiny place, but she owns it. Grandma Murphy left it to her. The house is surrounded by a neat little lawn.

I pulled up in the Beetle sometime well after summertime dark but before midnight. I knew she'd be home, though I wasn't certain she'd be awake. I made sure that I didn't sound like I was trying to sneak up anywhere. I shut the door of the Beetle hard and walked with firm footsteps to her door, then knocked lightly.

A moment later the curtains on the barred windows beside the door twitched and then fell back into place. A lock disengaged, then another, then a door chain. I noted, as I waited, that Murphy had a steel-reinforced door just like I did. Though I doubted she'd had as many demons or assassins showing up at it.

Murphy opened the door partway and peered out at me. The woman didn't look like the chief of Chicago PD's monster hunters. Her bright blue eyes were heavy, weary, and underscored with dark bags. She stood five feet nothing in her bare feet. Her golden hair was longer on top than in back, with bangs hanging down to her eyes. She wore a pale peach terry-cloth bathrobe that fell most of the way to her feet.

In her right hand she held her automatic, and a small crucifix dangled on a chain wrapped around her wrist. She looked at me.

"Heya, Murph," I said. I looked at the gun and the holy symbol and kept my voice calm. "Sorry to drop in on you this late. I need your help."

Murphy regarded me in silence for more than a minute. Then she said, "Wait here." She shut the door, returned a minute later, and opened it again, all the way. Then, gun still in hand, she stepped back from the doorway and faced me.

"Uh," I said, "Murph, are you all right?"

She nodded.

"Okay," I said. "Can I come in?"

"We'll know in a minute," Murphy said.

I got it then. Murphy wasn't going to ask me in. There are plenty of monsters running around in the dark that can't violate the threshold of a home if they aren't invited in. One of them had caught up to Murphy last year, nearly killing her, and it had been wearing my face when it did it. No wonder she didn't look exactly overjoyed to see me.

"Murph," I said, "relax. It's me. Hell's bells, there isn't anything that I can think of that would mimic me looking like this. Even demonic fiends from the nether regions of hell have *some* taste."

I stepped across her threshold. Something tugged at me as I did, an intangible, invisible energy. It slowed me down a little, and I had to make an effort to push through it. That's what a threshold is like. One like it surrounds only my home, a field of energy that keeps out unwanted magical forces. Some places have more of a threshold than others. My apartment, for example, didn't have much of a threshold—it's a bachelor pad, and whatever domestic energy is responsible for such things doesn't seem to settle down as well in rental spaces and lone dwellings. Murphy's house had a heavy field surrounding it. It had a life of its own; it had history. It was a home, not just a place to live.

I crossed her threshold uninvited, and I left a lot of my power at the door as I did. I would have to really push to make even the simplest of spells work within. I stepped inside and spread my hands. "Do I pass inspection?"

Murphy didn't say anything. She crossed the room and put her gun back into its holster, setting it down on an end table.

Murphy's place was . . . dare I say it, *cute*. The room was done in soft yellows and greens. And there were ruffles. The curtains had ruffles, and the couch had more, plus those little knitted things (aren't they called doilies?) were draped over the arms of the two recliners, the couch, the coffee table, and just about every other surface that seemed capable of supporting lacy bits of froo-fra. They looked old and beautiful and well cared for. I was betting Murphy's grandma had picked them out.

Murphy's own decorating was limited to the gun-cleaning kit sitting on the end table beside the holster for her automatic and a wooden rack over the fireplace that bore a pair of Japanese swords, long and short, one over the other. That was the Murphy I knew and loved. Practical violence ready at hand. Next to the swords was a small row of photographs in holders—maybe her family. A thick picture album with what looked like a real leather cover sat open on the coffee table, next to a prescription bottle and a decanter of some kind of liquor—gin? The decanter was half empty. The glass next to it was completely empty.

I watched her settle down in the corner of the couch in her oversized bathrobe, her expression remote. She didn't look at me. I got more worried by the moment. Murphy wasn't acting like Murphy. She'd never passed up a chance to trade banter with me. I'd never seen her this silent and withdrawn.

Dammit, just when I needed some quick and decisive help. Something was wrong with Murphy, and I hardly had time to play dime-store psychologist, trying to help her. I needed whatever information she could get me. I also needed to help her with whatever it was that had hurt her so badly. I was fairly sure I wouldn't be able to do either if I didn't get her talking.

"Nice place, Murph," I told her. "I haven't seen it before."

She twitched one shoulder in what might have been a shrug.

I frowned. "You know, if conversation is too much for you we could play charades. I'll go first." I held up my hand with my fingers spread. Murphy didn't say anything, so I provided her end of the dialogue. "Five words." I tugged on my ear. "Sounds like . . . What Is Wrong with You?"

She shook her head. I saw her eyes flicker toward the album.

I leaned forward and turned the album toward me. It had been opened on a cluster of wedding pictures. The girl in them must have been Murphy, back when. She had longer, sunnier hair and a kind of adolescent slenderness that showed around her neck and wrists. She wore a white wedding gown, and stood next to a tuxedo-clad man who had to have been ten years older than she was. In other pictures she was shoving cake into his mouth, drinking through linked arms, the usual wedding fare. He had carried her to the getaway car, and the photo-Murphy's face had been caught in a moment of laughter and joy.

"First husband?" I asked.

That got through to her. She glanced up at me for just a second. Then nodded.

"You were a kid in this. Maybe eighteen?"

She shook her head.

"Seventeen?"

She nodded. At least I was getting some kind of response out of her.

"How long were you married to him?"

Silence.

I frowned. "Murph, I'm not like a genius about this stuff or anything. But if you're feeling guilty about something, maybe you're being a little hard on yourself."

Without a word, she leaned forward and picked up the album, moving it aside to reveal a copy of the *Tribune*. It had been folded open to the obituaries page. She picked it up and handed it to me.

I read the first one out loud. "Gregory Taggart, age forty-three, died last night after a long bout with cancer . . ." I paused and looked at the photograph of the deceased and then at Murphy's album. It was the same man, give or take several years of wear and tear. I winced and lowered the paper. "Oh, God, Murph. I'm sorry. I'm so sorry."

She blinked her eyes several times. Her voice came out thready, quiet. "He didn't even tell me that he was sick."

Talk about your nasty surprises. "Murph, look. I'm sure that . . . that things will work out. I know how you're hurting, how you must feel, but—"

"Do you?" she said, still very quiet. "Do you know how I feel? Did you lose your first love?"

I sat quietly for a full minute before I said, "Yeah. I did."

"What was her name?"

It hurt to think the name, much less to say it. But if it helped me get through to Murphy, I couldn't afford to be touchy. "Elaine. We were . . . both of us were orphans. We got adopted by the same man when we were ten."

Murphy blinked and looked up at me. "She was your sister?"

"I don't have any relatives. We were both adopted by the same guy, that's all. We lived together, drove one another nuts, hit puberty together. Do the math."

She nodded. "How long were you together?"

"Oh. Until we were about sixteen."

"What happened? How did she . . ."

I shrugged. "My adoptive father tried to get me into black magic. Human sacrifice."

Murphy frowned. "He was a wizard?"

I nodded. "Strong one. So was she."

"Didn't he try to get Elaine, too?"

"Did get her," I said. "She was helping him."

"What happened?" she asked quietly.

I tried to keep my voice even and calm, but I wasn't sure how well I managed it. "I ran away. He sent a demon after me. I beat it, then went back to save Elaine. She hit me with a binding spell when I wasn't looking, and he tried a spell that would break into my head. Make me do what he wanted. I slipped out of the spell Elaine had on me and took on Justin. I got lucky. He lost. Everything burned."

Murphy swallowed. "What happened to Elaine?"

"Burned," I said quietly, my throat tightening. "She's dead."

"God, Harry." Murphy was quiet for a moment. "Greg left me. We tried to talk a few times, but it always ended in a fight." Her eyes welled up with tears. "Dammit, I should have at least gotten to tell him good-bye."

I put the paper back on the table and closed the album, studiously not looking at Murphy. I knew she wouldn't want me to see her crying. She inhaled sharply. "I'm sorry, Harry," she said.

"I'm flaking out on you here. I shouldn't. I don't know why this is getting to me so hard."

I glanced at the booze and the pills on the table. "It's okay. Everyone has an off day sometimes."

"I can't afford it." She drew the bathrobe a little closer around herself and said, "Sorry, Harry. About the gun." Her words sounded heavy, maybe a little slurred. "I had to be sure it was really you."

"I understand," I said.

She looked at me and something like gratitude touched her eyes. She got up from the couch abruptly and walked down a hallway, out of the living room, and said over her shoulder, "Let me put something else on."

"Sure, okay," I said after her, frowning. I leaned over to the table and picked up the prescription bottle behind the booze, next to the empty tumbler. A medium-sized dose of Valium. No wonder Murphy had been slurring her words. Valium and gin. Hell's bells.

I was still holding the pills when she came back in, wearing baggy shorts and a T-shirt. She'd raked a brush through her hair and splashed water on her face, so that I could barely tell that she'd been crying. She stopped short and looked at me. I didn't say anything. She chewed on her lip.

"Murph," I said, finally, "Are you okay? Is there . . . I mean, do you need—"

"Relax, Dresden," she said, folding her arms. "I'm not suicidal."

"Funny you say that. Mixing drinks with drugs is a great way to get it done."

She walked over to me, jerked the pill bottle out of my hands, and picked up the bottle of booze. "It isn't any of your business," she said. She walked into the kitchen, dropped things off, and came back out again. "I'm fine. I'll be fine."

"Murph, I've never seen you with a drink in your life. And Valium? It makes me worry about you."

"Dresden, if you came over here to lecture me, you can leave right now."

I shoved my fingers through my shaggy hair. "Karrin, I swear I'm not lecturing. I'm just trying to understand."

She looked away from me for a minute, one foot rubbing at the opposite calf. It hit me how small she looked. How frail. Her eyes were not only weary, I saw now. They were haunted. I walked over to her and put a hand on her shoulder. Her skin was warm underneath the cotton of her T-shirt. "Talk to me, Murph. Please."

She pulled her shoulder out from under my hand. "It isn't a big deal. It's the only way I can get any sleep."

"What do you mean?"

She took a deep breath. "I mean, I can't sleep without help. The drinks didn't help. The drugs didn't, either. I have to use both or I won't get any rest."

"I still don't get it. Why can't you sleep? Is it because of Greg?"

Murphy shook her head, then moved over to the couch, away from me, and curled up in the corner of it, clasping her hands over her knees. "I've been having nightmares. Night terrors, the doctors say. They say it's different from just bad dreams."

I felt my cheek twitch with tension. "And you can't stay asleep?"

She shook her head. "I wake myself up screaming." I saw her clench her fists. "God dammit, Dresden. There's no reason for it. I shouldn't get rattled by a few bad dreams. I shouldn't fall to pieces hearing about a man I haven't spoken to in years. I don't know what the fuck is wrong with me."

I closed my eyes. "You're dreaming about last year, aren't you? About what Kravos did to you."

She shivered at the mention of the name and nodded. "I couldn't stop thinking about it for a long time. Trying to figure out what I did wrong. Why he was able to get to me."

I ached inside. "Murph, there wasn't anything you could have done."

"Don't you think I know that?" she said, her voice quiet. "I couldn't have known that it wasn't you. I couldn't have stopped him even if I had. I couldn't have done anything to defend myself. To stop wh-what he did to me, once he was inside my head." Her eyes clouded with tears, but she blinked them away, her jaw setting. "There wasn't anything I could have done. That's what scares me, Harry. That's why I'm afraid."

"Murph, he's dead. He's dead and gone. We watched them put him in the ground."

Murphy snarled, "I *know* that. I know it, Harry. I know he's gone, I know he can't hurt me anymore, I know he's never going to hurt anyone again." She looked up at me for a moment, chancing a look at my eyes. Hers were clouded with tears. "But I still have the dreams. I know it, but it doesn't make any difference."

God. Poor Murphy. She'd taken a spiritual mauling before I'd shown up to save her. The thing that attacked her had been a spirit being, and it had torn her apart on the inside without leaving a mark on her skin. In a way, she'd been raped. All of her power had been taken away, and she'd been used for the amusement of another. No wonder it had left her with scars. Adding an unpleasant shock of bad news had been like tossing a spark onto a pile of tinder soaked in jet fuel.

"Harry," she continued, her voice quiet, soft, "you know me. God, I'm not a whiner. I hate that. But what that thing did to me. The things it made me see. Made me feel." She looked up at me, pain in the lines at the corners of her eyes, which threatened tears. "It won't go away. I try to leave it behind me, but it won't go. And it's eating up every part of my life."

She turned away, grabbing irritably at a box of tissues. I walked over to the fireplace and studied the swords on the mantel, so she wouldn't feel my eyes on her.

After a moment she spoke, her tone changing, growing more focused. "What are you doing here so late?"

I turned back to face her. "I need a favor. Information." I passed over the envelope Mab had given me. Murphy opened it, looked at the pair of pictures, and frowned.

"These are shots from the report of Ronald Reuel's death. How did you get them?"

"I didn't," I said. "A client gave them to me. I don't know where she got them."

She rubbed her eyes and asked, "What did she want from you?"

"She wants me to find the person who killed him."

Murphy shook her head. "I thought this was an accidental death."

"I hear it isn't."

"Where'd you hear that?"

I sighed. "A magic faerie told me."

That got me a suspicious glare, which dissolved into a frown. "God, you're being literal, aren't you?"

"Yeah."

Murphy shook her head, a tired smile at the corners of her mouth. "How can I help?"

"I'd like to look at the file on Ronald Reuel's death. I can't look at the scene, but maybe CPD caught something they didn't know was a clue. It would give me a place to start, at least."

Murphy nodded without looking at me. "All right. One condition."

"Sure. What?"

"If this is a murder, you bring me in on it."

"Murph," I protested, "come on. I don't want to pull you into anything that—"

"Dammit, Harry," Murphy snapped, "if someone's killing people in Chicago, I'm going to deal with them. It's my job. What's been happening to me doesn't change that."

"It's your job to stop the bad guys," I said. "But this might not be a guy. Maybe not even human. I just think you'd be safer if—"

"Fuck safe," Murphy muttered. "My job, Harry. If you turn up a killing, you will bring me in."

I hesitated, trying not to let my frustration show. I didn't want Murphy involved with Mab and company. Murphy had earned too many scars already. The faeries had a way of insinuating themselves into your life. I didn't want Murphy exposed to that, especially as vulnerable as she was.

But at the same time, I couldn't lie to her. I owed her a lot more than that.

Bottom line, Murphy had been hurt. She was afraid, and if she didn't force herself to face that fear, it might swallow her whole. She knew it. As terrified as she was, she knew that she had to keep going or she would never recover.

As much as I wanted to keep her safe, especially now, it wouldn't help her. Not in the long run. In a sense, her life was at stake.

"Deal," I said quietly.

She nodded and rose. "Stay out here. I need to get on the computer, see what I can pull up for you."

"I can wait if it's better."

She shook her head. "I've already taken the Valium. If I wait any longer I'll be too zonked to think straight. Just sit down. Have a drink. Try not to blow up anything." She padded out of the room on silent feet.

I sat down in one of the armchairs, stretched out my legs, let my head fall forward, and dropped into a light doze. It had been a long day, and it looked like it was just going to get longer. I woke up when Murphy came back into the room, her eyes heavy. She had a manila folder with her. "Okay," she said, "this is everything I could print out. The pictures aren't as clear as they could be, but they aren't horrible."

I sat up, took the folder from her and opened it. Murphy sat down in an armchair, facing me, her legs tucked beneath her. I started going over the details in the folder, though my brain felt like some kind of gelatin dessert topped with mush.

"What happened to your hand?" she asked.

"Magic faerie," I said. "Magic faerie with a letter opener."

"It doesn't look good. The dressing isn't right either. You have anyone look at it?"

I shook my head. "No time."

"Harry, you idiot." She got up, disappeared into the kitchen, and came back out with a first aid kit. I decided not to argue with her. She pulled up a chair from the kitchen next to mine, and rested my arm in her lap.

"I'm trying to read here, Murph."

"You're still bleeding. Puncture wounds will ooze forever if you don't keep them covered."

"Yeah, I tried to explain that, but they made me take the bandage off anyway."

"Who did?"

"Long story. So the security guard on the building didn't see anyone come in?"

She peeled off the bandage with brisk motions. It hurt. She fished out some disinfectant. "Cameras didn't pick up anything, either, and there aren't any bursts of static to indicate someone using magic. I checked."

I whistled. "Not bad, Murph."

"Yeah, sometimes I use my head instead of my gun. This will hurt."

She sprayed disinfectant liberally on my hand. It stung.

"Ow!"

"Wimp."

"Any other ways in and out of the building?"

"Not unless they could fly and walk through walls. The other doors are all fire exits, with alarms that would trip if someone opened them."

I kept paging through the file. " 'Broken neck due to fall,' it says. They found him at the bottom of the stairs."

"Right." Murphy used a wipe to clean both sides of my hand, and then she put more disinfectant on. It hurt a bit less. "He had contusions consistent with a fall, and he was an old man. No one seen entering or leaving an apartment building with a high-security system, so naturally—"

"—no one looked for a killer," I finished. "Or reported anything that might have indicated one. Or, wait, did they? Says here that the first officer on the scene found 'slippery goo' on the landing above where Reuel fell."

"But none of the detectives on the scene later found any such thing," Murphy said. She pressed a gauze pad against the wound from either side and began wrapping medical tape around to hold the pads on. "The first officer was a rookie. They figured he was seeing a killing where there wasn't one so he could get in on a murder investigation."

I frowned, turning the printouts of the photographs around. "See here? The sleeves of Reuel's coat are wet. You can see the discoloration."

She looked and admitted, "Maybe. There's no mention of it, though."

"Slippery goo. It could have been ectoplasm."

"Is that too tight? Ecto-what?"

I flexed my fingers a little, testing the bandage. "It's fine. Ectoplasm. Matter from the Nevernever."

"That's the spirit world, right? Faerieland?"

"Among other things."

"And stuff from there is goo?"

"It turns into goo when there's not any magic animating it. As long as the magic is there, it's as good as real. Like when Kravos made a body that looked like mine and came gunning for you."

Murphy shivered and started putting things back into her kit. "So when whatever it is that has made this ecto goo into matter has gone, it turns back into . . . ?"

"Slime," I said. "It's clear and slippery, and it evaporates in a few minutes."

"So something from the Nevernever could have killed Reuel," Murphy said.

"Yeah," I said. "Or someone could have opened up a portal into the apartment building. There's usually some gunk left when you open a portal. Dust drifting out from the Nevernever. So they could have opened a portal, then gotten out the same way."

"Whoa! Hold it. I thought Faerieland was monsters only. People can go into the Nevernever?"

"If you know the right magic, yeah. It's full of things that are fairly dangerous, though. You don't just cruise through on a Sunday stroll."

"Jesus Christ," Murphy muttered. "So someone—"

"Or something," I interjected.

"—or something could have gotten into the building and out again. Just like that. Past all the locks and guards and cameras. How scary is that?"

"Could have, yeah. Stepped in, pitched grampa down the stairs, stepped out again."

"God. That poor old man."

"I don't think he was helpless, Murph. Reuel was mixed up with the faeries. I kind of doubt his hands were squeaky clean."

She nodded. "Okay. Had he made any supernatural enemies?"

I held up the picture of the body. "Looks like it."

Murphy shook her head. She swayed a little bit, and then sat down next to me, leaning her head against the corner of the couch. "So what's the next step?"

"I go digging. Pound the proverbial pavement."

"You don't look so good. Get some rest first. A shower. Some food. Maybe a haircut."

I rubbed my eyes with my good hand. "Yeah," I said.

"And you tell me, when you know something."

"Murph, if this was something from the Nevernever, it's going to be out of your"—I almost said "league,"—"jurisdiction."

She shrugged. "If it came into my town and hurt someone I'm responsible for protecting, I want to make it answer for that." She closed her eyes. "Same as you. Besides. You promised."

Well, she had me there. "Yeah. Okay, Murph. When I find something out, I'll call."

"All right," she said. She curled up in the corner of the couch again, heavy eyes closing. She leaned her head back, baring the lines of her throat. After a moment, she asked, "Have you heard from Susan?"

I shook my head. "No."

"But her articles are still coming into the *Arcane*. She's all right."

I nodded. "I guess so."

"Have you found anything that will help her yet?"

I sighed and shook my head. "No, not yet. It's like pounding my head against a wall."

She halfway smiled. "With your head, the wall breaks first. You're the most stubborn man I've ever met."

"You say the sweetest things."

Murphy nodded. "You're a good man, Harry. If anyone can help her, it's you."

I looked down so she wouldn't see the tears that made my eyes swim a little, and started putting the file back together. "Thanks, Murph. That means a lot to me."

She didn't answer. I looked up and saw that her mouth had fallen slightly open and her body was totally relaxed, a cheek resting on the arm of the couch.

"Murph?" I asked. She didn't stir. I got up and left the file on the chair. I found a blanket and draped it lightly over her, tucking it in around her. She made a soft sound in the back of her throat and nuzzled her cheek closer to the couch.

"Sleep well, Murph," I said. Then I headed for the door. I locked what I could behind me, made my way back to the Beetle, and drove toward home.

I ached everywhere. Not from sore muscles, but from simple exhaustion. My wounded hand felt like a big throbbing knot of cramping muscle, doused in gasoline and set on fire.

I hurt even more on the inside. Poor Murph had been torn up badly. She was terrified of the things she might have to face, but that made her no less determined to face them. That was courage, and more than I had. I at least was sure that I could hit back if one of the monsters came after me. Murphy didn't have any such certainty.

Murphy was my friend. She'd saved my life before. We'd fought side by side. She needed my help again. She had to face her fear. I understood that. She needed me to help make it happen, but I didn't have to like it. In her condition, she would be extra vulnerable to any kind of attack like the one by Kravos the year before. And if she got hit again before she had a chance to piece herself back together, it might not simply wound her—it might break her entirely.

I wasn't sure I could live with myself if that happened.

"Dammit," I muttered. "So help me, Murph, I'm going to make sure you come out of this okay."

I shoved my worries about Murphy to the back of my mind. The best way to protect her would be to focus on this case, to get cracking. But my brain felt like something had crawled into it and died. The only cracking it was going to be doing was the kind that would land me in a rubber room and a sleeveless coat.

I wanted food. Sleep. A shower. If I didn't take some time to put myself back together, I might walk right into something that would kill me and not notice it until it was too late.

I drove back to my apartment, which is the basement of a

rooming house more than a century old. I parked the Beetle outside and got my rod and staff out of the car to take with me. It wasn't much of a walk between my apartment and the car, but I'd been accosted before. Vampires can be really inconsiderate that way.

I thumped down the stairs to my apartment, unlocked the door, and murmured the phrase that would disarm my wards long enough to let me get inside. I slipped in, and my instincts screamed at me that I was not alone.

I lifted the blasting rod, gathering my power and sending it humming through the focus so that the tip burst into brilliant crimson light that flooded my apartment.

And then there she was, a slender woman standing by my cold fireplace, all graceful curves and poised reserve. She wore a pair of blue jeans over long, coltish legs, with a simple scarlet cotton T-shirt. A silver pentacle hung outside the shirt, resting on the curve of modest breasts, and it gleamed in the light from my readied blasting rod. Her skin was pale, like the inner bark of an oak, the living part of the tree, her hair the brown-gold of ripe wheat, her eyes the grey of storm clouds. Her fine mouth twitched, first into a smile and then into a frown, and she lifted elegant, long-fingered hands to show me empty palms.

"I let myself in," she murmured. "I hope you don't mind. You should change your wards more often."

I lowered the blasting rod, too stunned to speak, my heart lurching in my chest. She lowered her hands and closed the distance between us. She lifted herself onto her toes, but she was tall enough that it wasn't much of an effort for her to kiss my cheek. She smelled like wildflowers and sun-drenched summer afternoons. She drew back enough to focus on my face and my eyes, her own expression gentle and concerned. "Hello, Harry."

And I said, in a bare whisper, fighting through the shock, "Hello, Elaine."

Chapter Eight

Elaine walked past me, making a circuit around my apartment. It wasn't much of a tour. The place consists of a living room and a tiny bedroom. The kitchen is pretty much just an alcove with a sink and a fridge. The floor is smooth grey stone, but I'd covered a lot of it with a few dozen rugs. My furniture is all secondhand and comfortable. It doesn't even come close to matching. Bookshelves fill up most of the wall space, and where they don't, I have several tapestries, plus a *Star Wars* movie poster Billy gave me for Christmas. It's the old poster, the one with Princess Leia clinging to Luke's leg.

Anyway, that was my apartment on a normal day. Lately it had suffered from disrepair. It didn't smell so great, and pizza boxes and empty Coke cans had overflowed the trash can and spilled over a significant portion of the kitchen floor. You could barely walk without stepping on clothing that needed to be washed. My furniture was covered with scribbled-on papers and discarded pens and pencils.

Elaine walked through it all like a Red Cross worker through a war zone and shook her head. "I know you weren't expecting me, Harry, but I didn't think I'd be overdressed. You live in this?"

"Elaine," I choked out. "You're alive."

"A little less of a compliment than I would have hoped for, but I guess it could have been worse." She regarded me from near the kitchen. "I'm alive, Harry." Her face flickered with a trace of apprehension. "How are you feeling?"

I lowered myself onto the couch, papers crunching beneath me. I released the power held ready to strike, and the glowing tip of the blasting rod went out, leaving the apartment in darkness. I kept staring at her afterimage on my vision. "Shocked," I said finally. "This isn't happening. Hell's bells, this has got to be some sort of trick."

"No. It's me. If I was something out of the Nevernever, could I have crossed your threshold uninvited? Do you know anyone else who knows how you set up your wards?"

"Anyone could figure it out eventually," I said.

"All right. Does anyone else know that you failed your driver's test five times in one week? Or that you sprained your shoulder trying to impress me going out for football our freshman year? That we soulgazed on our first night together? I think I can still remember our locker combination, if you like."

"My God, Elaine." I shook my head. Elaine, alive. My brain could not wrap itself around the idea. "Why didn't you contact me?"

I saw her, dimly, lean against the wall. She was quiet for a while, as though she had to shape her words carefully. "At first because I didn't even know if you had survived. And after that . . ." She shook her head. "I wasn't sure I wanted to. Wasn't sure you'd want me to. So much happened."

My shock and disbelief faded before a sudden aching pain, and an old, old anger. "That's putting it mildly," I said. "You tried to destroy me."

"No," she said. "God, no, Harry. You don't understand. I never wanted that."

My voice gained a hard edge. "Which is why you hit me with that binding. Why you held me down while Justin tried to destroy me."

"He never wanted you dead—"

"No, he just wanted to break into my head. Wanted to control me. Make me into some kind of . . . of . . ." Words failed me in the face of my frustration.

"Thrall," Elaine said quietly. "He'd have wrapped you in enough spells to guarantee your loyalty. To make you his thrall."

"And that's worse than dead. And you *helped* him."

Her voice crackled with anger of its own. "Yes, Harry. I helped him. That's what thralls *do*."

My rising ire abruptly quieted. "What . . . what are you saying?"

I saw her dim shape bow its head. "Justin caught me about two weeks before he sent that demon to capture you. That day I stayed home sick, remember? By the time you got home from school, he had me. I tried to fight him, but I was a child. I didn't have enough experience to resist him. And after he had enthralled me, I didn't see why I should fight anymore."

I stared at her for a long minute. "So you're telling me that you didn't have any choice," I breathed. "He forced you to do it. He made you help him."

"Yes."

"Why the hell should I believe you?"

"I don't expect you to."

I rose and paced back and forth restlessly. "I can't believe you're trying to tell me that the devil made you do it. Do you have any idea how lame that excuse sounds?"

Elaine watched me carefully, her grey eyes pensive and sad. "It wasn't an excuse, Harry. Nothing can excuse the kind of pain I put you through."

I stopped and frowned at her. "Then why are you telling me?"

"Because it needs to be said," she murmured. "Because that's what happened. You deserve to know that."

It was quiet for a long time, then I asked, "He really had enthralled you?"

Elaine shivered and nodded.

"What was it like?"

She fretted at her lower lip. "I didn't know it was happening. Not at the time. I didn't have the ability to think clearly. Justin told me that you just needed to be shown what to do and that if I would hold you still long enough to let him explain things to you it would all work out. I believed him. Trusted him." She shook her head. "I never wanted to hurt you, Harry. Never. I'm sorry."

I sat down and rubbed my face with my hands, my emotions running high and out of control again. Without the anger to support me, all that was left inside was pain. I thought I had gotten over Elaine's loss, her betrayal. I thought I had forgotten it and moved on. I was wrong. The wounds burst open again, as painful as they had ever been. Maybe more so. I had to fight to control my breathing, my tone.

I had loved her. I wanted very badly to believe her.

"I . . . I looked for you," I said quietly. "In fire and water. I had spirits combing the Earth for any trace of you. Hoping that you'd survived."

She pushed away from the wall and walked to the fireplace. I heard her putting in wood, and then she murmured something soft and low. Flame licked up over the logs easily, smoothly, low and blue, then settled into a dark golden light. I watched her profile as she stared down at the fire. "I got out of the house before you and Justin were finished," she said finally. "His spells had begun to unravel, and I was struggling against them. Confused, terrified. I must have run. I don't even remember doing it."

"But where have you been?" I asked. "Elaine, I looked for you for years. Years."

"Where you couldn't have found me, Harry. You or anyone else. I found sanctuary. A place to hide. But there was a price, and that's why I'm here." She looked up at me, and though her features were calm and smooth, I could see the fear in her eyes, hear it coloring her voice. "I'm in trouble."

My answer came out at once. For me, chivalry isn't dead; it's an involuntary reflex. It could have been any woman asking for help, and I'd have said the same thing. It might have taken me a second or two longer, but I would have. For Elaine, there was no need to think about it for even that long. "I'll help."

Her shoulders sagged and she nodded, pressing her lips together and bowing her head. "Thank you. Thank you, Harry. I hate doing this, I hate bringing this to you after all this time. But I don't know where else to turn."

"No," I said, "it's all right. Really. What's going on? Why do you think you're in trouble? What do you mean, you're paying a price?"

"It's complicated," she said. "But the short version is that I was granted asylum by the Summer Court of the Sidhe."

My stomach dropped about twenty feet.

"I built up a debt to Titania, the Summer Queen, in exchange for her protection. And now it's time to pay it off." She took a deep breath. "There's been a murder within the realms of the Sidhe."

I rubbed at my eyes. "And Titania wants you to be her Emissary. She wants you to find the killer and prove that the Winter Court is to blame. She told you that you would be contacted tonight by Mab's Emissary, but she didn't tell you who it was going to be."

Elaine's eyes widened in shock, and she fell silent. We stared at one another for a long moment before she whispered, "Stars and stones." She pushed her hair back from her face with one hand, in what I knew to be a nervous gesture, even if it didn't look it. "Harry, if I don't succeed, if I don't fulfill my debt to her, I'm . . . it's going to be very bad for me."

"Hooboy," I muttered, "tell me about it. Mab's more or less got me over the same barrel."

Elaine swore quietly. "What are we going to do?"

"Uh," I said.

She looked at me expectantly.

I scowled. "I'm thinking, I'm thinking. Uh."

She rose and took a few long-legged strides across the living room and back, agitated. "There must be something . . . some way out of this. God, sometimes their sense of humor makes me sick. Mab and Titania are laughing right now."

If I'd had the energy, I'd have been pacing, too. I closed my eyes and tried to think. If I didn't succeed on Mab's behalf, she wouldn't grant rights of passage to the Council. The Council would judge that I had failed my trial, and they'd wrap me up and deliver me to the vampires. I didn't know the specifics of Elaine's situation, but I doubted she had a deal that was any less fatal. My head hurt.

Elaine continued pacing, exasperated. "Come on, Harry. What are you thinking?"

"I'm thinking that if this dilemma grows any more horns I'm going to shoot it and put it up on the wall."

"I know this will never sink into your head, but this isn't a time for jokes. We need to come up with something."

"Okay. I've got it," I said. "Get your stuff and come with me."

Elaine reached back to the shadows beside the fireplace and withdrew a slender staff of pale wood, carved with swirling, abstract shapes. "Where are we going?"

I pushed myself up. "To talk to the Council and get their help."

Elaine lifted her eyebrows. "Don't take this the wrong way, Harry, but are you crazy?"

"Hear me out."

She pressed her lips together, but gave me a quick nod.

"It's simple. We're in way over our heads. We need help. You've got to come out to the Council in any case."

"Says who?"

"Oh, come on. You're human, Elaine, and a wizard. That's what is really important to them. They'll side with us against the faeries, help us figure a way out of this mess."

Elaine twitched at my use of the word, flicking a look around her as if by reflex. "That doesn't sound like the Council I've heard of."

"Could be that you've heard a skewed point of view," I said.

Elaine nodded. "Could be. The Council I've heard of nearly executed you for defending yourself against Justin."

"Well, yeah, but—"

"They put you on probation under threat of summary execution, and you all but had to kill yourself to get cleared."

"Well, I was all but killing myself anyway. I mean, I didn't do it so that the Council would—"

She shook her head. "God, Harry. You just can't see it, can you? The Council doesn't *care* about you. They don't want to protect you. They will only put up with you as long as you toe the line and don't become an inconvenience."

"I'm already inconvenient."

"A liability, then," Elaine said.

"Look, some of the Council have their heads up their rear ends, sure. But there are good people there, too."

Elaine folded her arms and shook her head. "And how many of those good people don't want a thing to do with the Council?"

"Elaine—"

"No, Harry. I mean it. I don't want anything to do with them. I've lived this long without the Council's so-called protection. I think I can muddle through a little longer."

"Elaine, when they find out about you, it needs to be from you. If you come forward, it's going to cut down on any uneasiness or suspicion they might feel."

"Suspicion?" Elaine exclaimed. "Harry, I am not a criminal."

"You're just asking for trouble, Elaine."

"And how are they going to find out about me? Hmmm? Were you planning on running off to tattle?"

"Of course not," I said. But I was thinking how much trouble I was going to be in if one of the Wardens heard I was associating with someone who might be a violator of the First Law, and one of Justin DuMorne's apprentices at that. With the cloud of disfavor I was already under, adding that kind of suspicion to it might be enough to sink me, regardless of how the investigation turned out. Do I have a great life or what?

"I won't say anything," I said finally. "It has to be your choice, Elaine. But please believe me. Trust me. I have friends in the Council, too. They'll help."

Elaine's expression softened and became less certain. "You're sure?"

"Yeah," I said. "Cross my heart."

She leaned on her oddly carved staff and frowned. She was

opening her mouth to speak when my reinforced door rattled under the rapping of a heavy fist.

"Dresden," Morgan growled from the other side of the door. "Open up, traitor. There are questions I need you to answer."

Chapter Nine

⊰≫∘≪⊱

Elaine shot me a wide-eyed look and mouthed the word "Council?"

I nodded and pointed to my staff, in the corner along with my sword cane. Elaine picked it up without a word and tossed it to me. Then she moved silently through the door of my darkened bedroom and vanished inside.

The door rattled again. "Dresden," Morgan growled, "I know you're in there. Open the door."

I swung it open before he could go on. "Or you'll huff and you'll puff and so on?"

Morgan glowered at me, tall, sour, and dour as ever. He'd traded his robes and cloak for dark slacks, a grey silk shirt, and a sport coat. He carried a golf bag on one shoulder, and most people wouldn't have noticed the hilt of a sword nestled among the golf clubs. He leaned forward, cool eyes looking past me and into my apartment. "Dresden. Am I interrupting anything?"

"Well, I was going to settle down with a porn video and a bottle of baby oil, but I really don't have enough for two."

Morgan's expression twisted in revulsion, and I felt an absurd little burst of vindictive satisfaction. "You disgust me, Dresden."

"Yeah, I'm bad. I'm a bad, bad, bad man. I'm glad we got that settled. Good-bye, Morgan."

I started to shut my door in his face. He slammed his palm against it. Morgan was a lot stronger than me. The door stayed open.

"I'm not finished, Dresden."

"I am. It's been one hell of a day. If you've got something to say, say it."

Morgan's mouth set in a hard smile. "Normally I appreciate that kind of directness. Not with you."

"Gee, you don't appreciate me. I'll cry myself to sleep."

Morgan stroked his thumb over the strap to the golf bag. "I want to know how it is, Dresden, that Mab just happened to come to you about this problem. The one thing that can preserve your status with the Council, and it just happened to fall to you."

"Clean living," I said. "Plus my mondo wheels and killer bachelor pad."

Morgan looked at me with flat eyes. "You think you're funny."

"Oh, I *know* I'm funny. Unappreciated, but funny."

Morgan shook his head. "Do you know what I think, Dresden?"

"You think?" Morgan didn't smile. Like I said, unappreciated.

"I think that you've planned all of this. I think you are in with the vampires and the Winter Court. I think this is part of a deeper scheme."

I just stared at him. I tried not to laugh. I really did.

Well. Maybe I didn't try all that hard.

The laughter must have gotten to Morgan. He balled up his fist and slammed a stiff jab into my belly that took the wind out of my sails and half dropped me to my knees.

"No," he said. "You aren't going to laugh this off, traitor." He stepped into my apartment. The threshold didn't make him blink. The wards I had up caught him six inches later, but they weren't designed to be too much of an impediment to human beings. Morgan grunted, spoke a harsh word in a guttural tongue, maybe Old German, and slashed his hand in front of him. The air hissed and popped with static electricity, sparks flashing from his fingertips. He shook his fingers briefly, then walked in.

He looked around the place and shook his head again. "Dresden, you might not be a bad person, all in all. But I think that you're compromised. If you aren't working with the Red Court, then I am certain that they are using you. Either way, the threat to the Council is the same. And it's best removed by removing you."

I tried to suck in a breath and finally managed to say, "What the hell are you talking about?"

"Susan Rodriguez," Morgan said. "Your lover, the vampire."

Anger made bright lights flash behind my eyes. "She's *not* a vampire," I snarled.

"They turned her, Dresden. No one goes back. That's all there is to it."

"They haven't. She's not."

Morgan shrugged. "That's what you would say if she'd addicted you to the venom. You'd say or do just about anything for them by now."

I looked up at him, teeth bared. "Get the fuck out of my house."

He walked over to the fireplace and picked up a dustcovered gift card I'd left sitting on the mantel. He read it and snorted. Then he picked up a picture I had of Susan. "Pretty," he said. "But that's easy to come by. Odds are she was their pawn from the first day she met you."

I clenched my hands into fists. "You shut your mouth," I said. "You just shut your mouth about her. That's not how it was."

"You're a fool, Dresden. A young fool. Do you really think that a normal mortal woman would want anything to do with you or your life? You can't accept that she was just a tool. One of their whores."

I spun to the corner, letting go of my staff, and picked up my sword cane. I drew the blade free with a steely rasp and turned toward Morgan. He saw it coming and had already drawn the bright silver blade of the Wardens from the golf bag.

Every tired, aching, angry bone in my body wanted to lunge at him. I'm not heavy with muscle, but I'm not slow, and I've got arms and legs miles long. My lunge is quick, and I can do it from a long way back. Morgan was a seasoned soldier, but in such close quarters it would be a question of reflexes. Advantage to the guy with the sword weighed in ounces instead of stones.

In that moment, I was sure that I could have killed him. He might have taken me with him, but I could have done it. And I wanted to, badly. Not in any sort of intellectual sense, but in the part of the brain that does all of its thinking after the fact. My temper had frayed to bloody tatters, and I wanted to vent it on Morgan.

But a thought snuck in past the testosterone and spoiled my rage. I stopped myself. Shaking, and with my knuckles white on my sword cane, I drew myself up straight. And I said, very quietly, "That's number three."

Morgan's brow furrowed, and he stared at me, his own weapon steadily extended toward me. "What are you talking about, Dresden?"

"The third plan. The Merlin's ace in the hole. He sent you here to pick a fight with me. With my door still standing open. There's another Warden outside, listening, isn't there? A witness, so that you have a clean kill. Hand the body over to the vampires. End of problem, right?"

Morgan's eyes widened. He stammered over the first word. "I don't know what you're talking about."

I picked up the sheath half of the sword cane and slipped the blade back into it. "Sure, you don't. Get out, Morgan. Unless you'd prefer to stab an unarmed man who isn't offering you violence."

Morgan stared at me for a moment more. Then he shoved the sword back into the golf bag, swung it onto his shoulder, and headed for the door.

He was almost out when there was a clunk from my bedroom. I shot a look at the doorway.

Morgan stopped. He looked at me and then at my bedroom. Something ugly sparkled in his gaze. "Who is in the bedroom, Dresden? The vampire girl, perhaps?"

"No one," I said. "Get out."

"We'll see," Morgan said. He turned and walked to my bedroom door, one hand still on the sword. "You and those who consort with your like will be brought to task very soon. I'm looking forward to it."

My heart started pounding again. If Morgan found Elaine, there were about a million things that might happen, and none of them were good. There seemed little I could do, though. I couldn't warn her, and I couldn't think of a way to get Morgan out of my apartment any faster.

Morgan peered through the doorway and looked around, then abruptly let out a hoarse cry and jumped back. At the same time, there was a harsh feline yowl, and Mister, my bobtailed grey cat, came zooming out of the bedroom. He darted between Morgan's legs and then streaked past him, out of the apartment and up the stairs into the summer evening.

"Gosh, Morgan," I said, "my cat might be a dangerous subversive. Maybe you'd better interrogate him."

Morgan straightened, his face slightly red. He coughed and then stalked to the door. "The Senior Council members wish me to tell you that they will be nearby but that they will not interfere in this Trial or aid you in any way." He took a business card out of his shirt pocket and let it fall to the floor. "That's the contact number for the Senior Council. Use it when you have failed the Trial."

"Don't let the door hit you on the brain on the way out," I responded.

Morgan glared at me as he left. He slammed the door behind him and stomped up the stairs.

I started trembling maybe half a minute after he left—reaction to the stress. At least I hadn't done it in front of him. I turned around, leaned back against the door with my eyes closed, and folded my arms over my chest. It was easier not to feel myself shaking that way.

Another minute or two passed before I heard Elaine move quietly out of my bedroom. The fire popped and crackled.

"Are they gone?" Elaine asked. Her voice was very carefully steady.

"Yeah. Though I wouldn't put it past them to watch my place."

I felt her fingers touch my shoulder. "You're shaking, Harry."

"I'll be all right."

"You could have killed him," Elaine said. "When you first drew."

"Yeah."

"Was he really setting you up like you said?"

I looked at her. Her expression was worried. "Yeah," I said.

"God, Harry." She shook her head. "That's way past paranoia. And you want me to give myself to those people?"

I covered her hand with mine. "Not to them," I said. "Not everyone on the Council is like that."

She looked at my eyes for a moment. Then, carefully, she drew her hand out from under mine. "No. I'm not going to make myself vulnerable to men like that. Not again."

"Elaine," I protested.

She shook her head. "I'm leaving, Harry." She brushed her hair back from her face. "Are you going to tell them?"

I took a deep breath. If the Wardens found out that Elaine was still alive and avoiding them, there would be a literal witch-hunt. The Wardens weren't exactly known for their tolerance and understanding. Morgan was walking, talking proof of that. Anyone who helped shield her from the Wardens would get the same treatment. Didn't I already have enough problems?

"No," I said. "Of course not."

Elaine gave me a strained smile. "Thank you, Harry." She lifted her staff closer to her, holding it with both hands. "Can you get the door for me?"

"They're going to be out there watching."

"I'll veil. They won't see me."

"They're good."

She shrugged and said without emphasis, "I'm better. I've had practice."

I shook my head. "What are we going to do about the faeries?"

"I don't know," she said. "I'll be in touch."

"How can I contact you?"

She nodded toward the door. I opened it. She stepped up beside me and kissed my cheek again, her lips warm. "You're the one with the office and the answering service. I'll contact you." Then she stepped to the door, murmuring quietly under her breath. There was a glitter of sudden silver light around her that made me blink. When I opened my eyes again, she was gone.

I left the door open for a moment, and it was just as well that I did. Mister came padding back down the stairs a moment later and looked up at me with a plaintive meow. He prowled back into the apartment, curling around my legs and purring like a diesel engine. Mister is thirty pounds or so of tomcat. I figure one of his parents must have been a saber-toothed tiger. "Good timing, by the way," I told him, and shut the door, locking it.

I stood in the dim, warm firelight of the room. My cheek still tingled where Elaine had kissed it. I could smell her lingering perfume, and it brought with it a pang of almost tangible memories, a flood of things I thought I had forgotten. It made me feel old, and tired, and very alone.

I walked to the mantel and straightened the card Susan had sent me the previous Christmas. I looked at her picture, next to the card. She'd been in a park that weekend, wearing a blue tank top and cutoff shorts. Her teeth were impossibly white against her darkly tanned skin and coal-black hair. I'd taken the picture while she was laughing, and her dark eyes shone.

I shook my head. "I am tired, Mister," I said. "I am ridiculously tired."

Mister meowed at me.

"Well, resting would be the sane thing to do, but who am I to throw stones, right? I mean, I'm talking to my cat." I scratched at my beard and nodded to myself. "Just a minute on the couch. Then to work."

I remember sitting down on the couch, and after that everything went blissfully black.

Which was just as well. The next day things got complicated.

Chapter Ten

I wasn't too tired to dream. Evidently, my subconscious—we've met, and he's kind of a jerk—had something on his mind, because the dream was a variation on the theme that had taken up most of my sleeping hours since I'd last seen Susan.

The dream began with a kiss.

Susan has a gorgeous mouth. Not too thin and not too full. Always soft, always warm. When she kissed me, it was like the world went away. Nothing mattered but the touch of her lips on mine. I kissed the dream-Susan, and she melted against me with a soft sound, the length of her body pliant, eager. Her fingers reached up and trailed over my chest, nails lightly raking.

I leaned back from the kiss after a long moment, and my eyes felt almost too heavy to open. My lips quivered and tingled with sensation, a feeling that begged for more kisses to make it cease. She looked up at me, dark eyes smoldering. Her hair had been pulled back into a long, silken tail that fell between her shoulder blades. It had grown longer, in the dreams. Her lovely aquiline face tilted up toward mine.

"Are you all right?" I asked her. I always did. And, as always, she gave me a small, sad smile and did not answer. I bit my lip. "I'm still looking. I haven't given up."

She shook her head and drew back from me. I had the presence of mind to look around. A dark alley this time, with the heavy, pounding music of a dance club making the nearest wall vibrate. Susan wore dark tights and a sleeveless blouse, and my black-leather duster had been draped over her shoulders and fell to brush her feet. She looked at me intently and then turned toward the entrance to the club.

"Wait," I said.

She walked to the door and turned back to me, extending her hand. The door opened, and dim, reddish light flooded out over her, doing odd things to the shadows over her face. Her dark eyes grew larger.

No, that wasn't right. The black of her pupils simply expanded, until the whites were gone, until there was nothing but darkness where her eyes should have been. They were vampire eyes, huge and inhuman.

"I can't," I said. "We can't go in there, Susan."

Her features grew frustrated, angry. She extended her hand to me again, more forcefully.

Hands came out of the darkness in the doorway, slim, pale, androgynous. They slipped over Susan, slowly, caressingly. Tugging at her clothing, her hair. Her eyes fluttered closed for a moment, her body growing stiff, before her weight shifted slowly toward the doorway.

Longing shot through me, sudden, mindless, and sharp as a scalpel's blade. Hunger, a simple and nearly violent need to touch, to be touched, followed it into me, and I suddenly could not think. "Don't," I said, and stepped toward her.

I felt her hand take mine. I felt her press herself to me with another moan, and her lips, her mouth, devoured mine with ravenous kisses, kisses I answered with my own, harder and more demanding as my doubts faded. I felt it when her kiss turned poisonous, when the sudden narcotic numbness swept through my mouth and began to spread through my body. It didn't make any difference. I kissed her, tore at her clothes, and she tore at mine. The hands helped, but I didn't pay any attention to them anymore. They were an unimportant background sensation in comparison to Susan's mouth, her hands, her skin velvet and warm beneath my fingers.

There was no romance, nothing but need, animal, carnal. I pushed her against a wall in the dim scarlet light, and she wrapped herself around me, frantic, her body urging me on. I pressed into her, sudden sensation of silk and honey, and had to fight for control, throwing my head back.

She quivered then, and as always, she struck. Her mouth closed on my throat, a flash of heat and agony that melted into a narcotic bliss like that of her kiss—but more complete. Languid delight spread through me, and I felt my body reacting, all traces of control gone, thrusting against her, into her. The motion slowly died as sheer, shivering ecstasy spread through me. I began to lose control of my limbs, muscles turning to gelatin. I sank slowly to the floor. Susan rode me down, her mouth hot and eager on my throat, her body, her hips moving now, taking over the rhythm.

The pleasure of the venom melted my thoughts, and they slid free of my flesh, floating over the ground. I looked down on my body, beneath Susan, pale and still on the floor, eyes empty. I saw the change take her. I saw her body twist and buck, saw her skin split and rip open. I saw something dark and horrible tear its way out, all gaping dark eyes and slippery black hide. Blood, my blood, smeared its mouth.

The creature froze in shock, staring down at my corpse. And as I began to drift away, the creature threw back its head, its body rubbery and sinuous as a snake's, and let out an inhuman, screeching yowl full of rage, pain, and need.

I bolted up out of sleep with a short cry, my skin sheathed in a cold sweat, my muscles aching and stiff.

I panted for a moment, looking around my apartment. My lips tingled with remembered kisses, my skin with dreamed caresses.

I forced myself to my feet with a groan and staggered toward my shower. There were times when it was just as well that I had disconnected the water heater to head off magically inspired mishaps. It made bathing sheer torture in the winter, but sometimes there's no substitute for a cold shower.

I stripped and stood under chilly water for a while, shaking. Not necessarily from cold, either. I shook with a lot of things. First with raw and mindless lust. The shower took the edge off of that in a few moments. Don't get me wrong. I didn't have any particular death-sex fixation. But I had been used to a certain amount of friendly tension relieving with Susan. Her absence had killed that for me, completely—except for rare moments during the damned dreams when my hormones came raging back to the front of my thoughts again as though making up for lost time.

Second, I trembled with fear. My nightmares might be one part lusty dream, but they were also a warning. Susan's curse could kill me and destroy her. I couldn't forget that.

And finally, I shook with guilt. If I hadn't let her down, maybe she wouldn't be in this mess. She was gone, and I didn't have the vaguest idea where she was. I should have been doing more.

I stuck my head in the water, and shoved those thoughts away, washing myself off with a ton of soap and the last shampoo in the bottle. I scrubbed at my beard and finally reached out and got my straight razor, then spent a few minutes and a lot of care removing it. Dark, wiry black hair fell in clumps to the shower floor, and my face tingled as it breathed its first air for a couple of months. But it felt good, and as I went through the routine of grooming, my thoughts cleared.

I dug some clean clothes out of my closet, padded out into the living room, and pulled back the rug that covered the trapdoor leading to the subbasement. I swung the door open, lit a candle, and descended the stepladder staircase into my lab.

My lab, in contrast to the havoc upstairs, looked like something run by a particularly anal-retentive military clerk. A long table ran down the middle of the room, between a pair of other tables, one on either wall, leaving only narrow walkways. White steel wire shelves on the walls held the host of magical components I used in research. They resided in a variety of jars, bottles, boxes, and plastic containers, most with labels listing the contents, how much was left, and when I had acquired the item. The tables were clean except for stacks of notes, a jar of pens and pencils, and myriad candles. I lit a few of them and walked down to the other end of the lab, checking the copper summoning circle set into the floor and making sure that nothing lay across it. You never knew when a magic circle would come in handy.

One area of the lab had retained the casual chaos that had been its major theme before I'd taken up nearly full-time residence last year. One shelf, still battered old wood, hadn't been changed or updated. Candleholders, covered in multiple shades of melted wax that had spilled down over them, sat at either end of the shelf. Between them was a scattering of various articles—a number of battered paperback romances, several Victoria's Secret catalogs, a scarlet scrap of a silk ribbon that had been tied into a bow on a naked young woman named Justine, one bracelet from a broken set of handcuffs, and a bleached old human skull.

"Bob, wake up," I said, lighting candles. "I need to pick your brain."

Lights, orange and nebulous, kindled deep in the shadows of the skull's eye sockets. The skull quivered a little bit on its shelf and then stretched its toothy mouth open in an approximation of a yawn. "So was the kid right? Was there some portent-type action going on?"

"Rain of toads," I said.

"Real ones?"

"Yeah."

"Ouch," said Bob the Skull. Bob wasn't really a skull. The skull was just a vessel for the spirit of intellect that resided inside and helped me keep track of the constantly evolving metaphysical laws that govern the use of magic. But "Bob the Skull" is a lot easier to say than "Bob the Spirit of Intellect and Lab Assistant."

I nodded, breaking out my Bunsen burners and beakers. "Tell me about it. Look, Bob, I've got kind of a difficult situation here and—"

"Harry, you aren't going to be able to do this. There *is* no cure for vampirism. I like Susan too, but it can't be done. You think people haven't looked for a cure before now?"

"*I* haven't looked for one before now," I said. "And I've had a couple of ideas I want to look at."

"Aye, Cap'n Ahab, arr har har har! We'll get that white devil, sir!"

"Damn right we will. But we've got something else to do first."

Bob's eyelights brightened. "You mean something other than hopeless, pointless vampire research? I'm already interested. Does it have to do with the rain of toads?"

I frowned, got out a pad of paper and a pencil, and started scratching things down. Sometimes that helped me sort things out. "Maybe. It's a murder investigation."

"Gotcha. Who's the corpse?"

"Artist. Ronald Reuel."

Bob's eyelights burned down to twin points. "Ah. Who is asking you to find the killer?"

"We don't know he was killed. Cops say it was an accident."

"But you think differently."

I shook my head. "I don't know a thing about it, but Mab says he was killed. She wants me to find the killer and prove that it wasn't her."

Bob fell into a shocked silence nearly a minute long. My pen scratched on the paper until Bob blurted, "Mab? *The* Mab, Harry?"

"Yeah."

"Queen of Air and Darkness? *That* Mab?"

"Yeah," I said, impatient.

"And she's your *client*?"

"Yes, Bob."

"Here's where I ask why don't you spend your time doing

something safer and more boring. Like maybe administering suppositories to rabid gorillas."

"I live for challenge," I said.

"Or you *don't*, as the case may be," Bob said brightly. "Harry, if I've told you once, I've told you a thousand times. You don't get tangled up with the Sidhe. It's always more complicated than you thought it would be."

"Thanks for the advice, skull boy. It wasn't like I had a choice. Lea sold her my debt."

"Then you should have traded her something for your freedom," Bob said. "You know, stolen an extra baby or something and given it to her—"

"Stolen a *baby*? I'm in enough trouble already."

"Well, if you weren't such a Goody Two-shoes all the time . . ."

I pushed at the bridge of my nose with my thumb. This was going to be one of those conversations that gave me a headache, I could tell already. "Look, Bob, can we stick to the subject, please? Time is important, so let's get to work. I need to know why Reuel would have been knocked off."

"Gee whiz, Harry," Bob said. "Maybe because he was the Summer Knight?"

My pencil fell out of my fingers and rolled on the table. "Whoa," I said. "Are you sure?"

"What do you think?" Bob replied, somehow putting a sneer into the words.

"Uh," I said. "This means trouble. It means . . ."

"It means that things with the Sidhe are more complicated than you thought. Gee, if only someone had warned you at some point not to be an idiot and go making deals."

I gave the skull a sour look and recovered my pencil. "How much trouble am I in?"

"A lot," Bob said. "The Knights are entrusted with power by the Sidhe Courts. They're tough."

"I don't know much about them," I confessed. "They're some kind of representative of the faeries, right?"

"Don't call them that to their faces, Harry. They don't like it any more than you'd like being called an ape."

"Just tell me what I'm dealing with."

Bob's eyelights narrowed until they almost went out, then brightened again after a moment, as the skull began to speak. "A Sidhe Knight is mortal," Bob said. "A champion of one of the

Sidhe Courts. He gets powers in line with his Court, and he's the only one who is allowed to act in affairs not directly related to the Sidhe."

"Meaning?"

"Meaning that if one of the Queens wants an outsider dead, her Knight is the trigger man."

I frowned. "Hang on a minute. You mean that the Queens can't personally gun down anyone who isn't in their Court?"

"Not unless the target does something stupid like make an open-ended bargain without even trying to trade a baby for—"

"Off topic, Bob. Do I or don't I have to worry about getting killed this time around?"

"Of course you do," Bob said in a cheerful tone. "It just means that the Queen isn't allowed to actually, personally end your life. They could, however, trick you into walking into quicksand and watch you drown, turn you into a stag and set the hounds after you, bind you into an enchanted sleep for a few hundred years, that kind of thing."

"I guess it was too good to be true. But my point is that if Reuel was the Summer Knight, Mab couldn't have killed him. Right? So why should she be under suspicion?"

"Because she could have done it indirectly. And Harry, odds are the Sidhe don't really care about Reuel's murder. Knights come and go like paper cups. I'd guess that they were upset about something else. The only thing they really care about."

"Power," I guessed.

"See, you can use your brain when you want to."

I shook my head. "Mab said something had been taken, and that I'd know what it was," I muttered. "I guess that's it. How much power are we talking about?"

"A Knight of the Sidhe is no pushover, Harry," Bob said, his tone earnest.

"So we're talking about a lot of magic going AWOL. Grand theft mojo." I drummed my pen on the table. "Where does the power come from originally?"

"The Queens."

I frowned. "Tell me if I'm off track here. If it comes from the Queens, it's a part of them, right? If a Knight dies, the power should snap back to the Queen like it was on a rubber band."

"Exactly."

"But this time it didn't. So the Summer Queen is missing a load of power. She's been weakened."

"If everything you've told me is true, yes," Bob said.

"There's no more balance between Summer and Winter. Hell, that could explain the toads. That's a serious play of forces, isn't it?"

Bob rolled his eyelights. "The turning of the seasons? Duh, Harry. The Sidhe are closer to the mortal world than any other beings of the Nevernever. Summer's had a slight edge for a while now, but it looks like they've lost it."

"And here I thought global warming was due to cow farts." I shook my head. "So, Titania loses a bunch of juice, and naturally suspicion falls on her archenemy, Mab."

"Yeah. It *is* kind of an archenemy-ish thing to do, you have to admit."

"I guess." I frowned down at my notes. "Bob, what happens if this imbalance between the Courts continues?"

"Bad things," Bob said. "It will mess around with weather patterns, cause aberrant behavior in plants and animals, and sooner or later the Sidhe Courts will go to war with one another."

"Why?"

"Because, Harry. When the balance is destroyed, the only thing the Queens can do is to blow everything to flinders and let it settle out into a natural distribution again."

"What does that mean to me?" I asked.

"Depends on who has the edge when everything is settled," Bob said. "A war could start the next ice age, or set off an era of rampant growth."

"That last one doesn't sound so bad."

"No. Not if you're an Ebola virus. You'll have lots of friends."

"Oh. Bad, then."

"Yeah," Bob said. "Keep in mind that this is theory, though. I've never seen it happen. I haven't existed that long. But it's something the Queens will want to avoid if they can."

"Which explains Mab's interest in this, if she didn't do it."

"Even if she did," Bob corrected me. "Did she ever actually tell you she was innocent?"

I mulled it over for a moment. "No," I said finally. "She twisted things around a lot."

"So it's possible that she *did* do it. Or had it done, at any rate."

"Right," I said. "So to find out if it was one of the Queens, we'd need to find her hitter. How tough would it be to kill one of these Knights?"

"A flight of stairs wouldn't do it. A couple of flights of stairs wouldn't do it. Maybe if he went on an elevator ride with you—"

"Very funny." I frowned, drumming my pen on the table. "So it would have taken that little something extra to take out Reuel. Who could manage it?"

"Regular folks could do it. But they wouldn't be able to do it without burning buildings and smoking craters and so on. To kill him so that it looked like an accident? Maybe another Knight could. Among the Sidhe, it was either the Winter Knight or one of the Queens."

"Could a wizard do it?"

"That goes without saying. But you'd have to be a pretty brawny wizard, have plenty of preparation and a good channel to him. Even then, smoking craters would be easier than an accident."

"The wizards have all been in duck-and-cover mode lately. And there are too many of them to make a practical suspect pool. Let's assume that it was probably internal faerie stuff. That cuts it down to three suspects."

"Three?"

"The three people who could have managed it. Summer Queen, Winter Queen, Winter Knight. One, two, three."

"Harry, I said it could have been one of the Queens."

I blinked up at the skull. "There are more than two?"

"Yeah, technically there are three."

"Three?"

"In each Court."

"Three Queens in each *Court*? *Six*? That's just silly."

"Not if you think about it. Each Court has three Queens: The Queen Who Was, the Queen Who Is, and the Queen Who Is to Come."

"Great. Which one does the Knight work for?"

"All of them. It's kind of a group thing. He has different duties to each Queen."

I felt the headache start at the base of my neck and creep toward the crown of my head. "Okay, Bob. I need to know about these Queens."

"Which ones? The ones Who Are, Who Were, or Who Are to Come?"

I stared at the skull for a second, while the headache settled comfortably in. "There's got to be a simpler parlance than that."

"That's so typical You won't steal a baby, but you're too lazy to conjugate."

"Hey," I said, "my sex life has nothing to do with—"

"Conjugate, Harry. Conju—oh, why do I even bother? The

Queen is just the Queen. Queen Titania, Queen Mab. The Queen Who Was is called the Mother. The Queen Who Is to Come is known as the Lady. Right now, the Winter Lady is Maeve. The Summer Lady is Aurora."

"Lady, Queen, Mother, gotcha." I got a pencil and wrote it down, just to help me keep it straight, including the names. "So six people who might have managed it?"

"Plus the Winter Knight," Bob said. "In theory."

"Right," I said. "Seven." I wrote down the titles and then tapped the notebook thoughtfully and said, "Eight."

"Eight?" Bob asked.

I took a deep breath and said, "Elaine's alive. She's on the investigation for Summer."

"Wow," Bob said. "Wow. And I told you so."

"I know, I know."

"You think she might have gacked Reuel?"

"No," I said. "But I never saw it coming when she and Justin came after me, either. I only need to think about if she had the means to do it. I mean, if you think it would have been tough for me, maybe she wasn't capable of taking down Reuel. I was always a lot stronger than her."

"Yeah," Bob said, "but she was better than you. She had a lot going for her that you didn't. Grace. Style. Elegance. Breasts."

I rolled my eyes. "So she's on the list, until I find some reason she shouldn't be."

"How jaded and logical of you, Harry. I'm almost proud."

I turned to the folder Mab had given me and went through the newspaper clippings inside. "Any idea who the Winter Knight is?"

"Nope. Sorry," Bob said. "My contacts on the Winter side are kinda sketchy."

"Okay, then," I sighed and picked up the notebook. "I know what I need to do."

"This should be good," Bob said dryly.

"Bite me. I have to find out more about Reuel. Who was close to him. Maybe someone saw something. If the police assumed an accident, I doubt there was an investigation."

Bob nodded, somehow managing to look thoughtful. "So are you going to take out an ad in the paper or what?"

I went around the lab and started snuffing candles. "I thought I'd try a little breaking and entering. Then I'll go to his funeral, see who shows."

"Gosh. Can I do fun things like you when I grow up?"

I snorted and turned to the stepladder, taking my last lit candle with me.

"Harry?" Bob said, just before I left.

I stopped and looked back at him.

"For what it's worth, be careful." If I hadn't known any better, I'd have said Bob the Skull was almost shaking. "You're an idiot about women. And you have no idea what Mab is capable of."

I looked at him for a moment, his orange eyes the only light in the dimness of my frenetically neat lab. It sent a little shiver through me.

Then I clomped back up the stepladder and went out to borrow trouble.

Chapter Eleven

I made a couple of phone calls, slapped a few things into a nylon backpack, and sallied forth to break into Ronald Reuel's apartment.

Reuel had lived at the south edge of the Loop, in a building that looked like it had once been a theater. The lobby yawned up to a high ceiling and was spacious and pretty enough, but it left me looking for the velvet ropes and listening for the disorganized squawking of an orchestra warming up its instruments.

I walked in wearing a hat with an FTD logo and carrying a long white flower box under one arm. I nodded to an aging security guard at a desk and went on past him to the stairs, my steps purposeful. You'd be surprised how far a hat, a box, and a confident stride can get you.

I took the stairs up to Reuel's apartment, on the third floor. I went up them slowly, my wizard's senses open, on the lookout for any energies that might yet be lingering around the site of the old man's death. I paused for a moment, over the spot where Reuel's body had been found, to be sure, but there was nothing. If a lot of magic had been put to use in Reuel's murder, someone had covered its tracks impressively.

I went the rest of the way up to the third floor, but it wasn't until I opened the door to the third-floor hallway that my instincts warned me I was not alone. I froze with the door from the stairway only half open, and Listened.

Listening isn't particularly hard. I'm not even sure it's all that magical. I can't explain it well, other than to say that I'm able to block out everything but what I hear and to pick up things I would normally miss. It's a skill that not many people have these days, and one that has been useful to me more than once.

This time, I was able to Listen to a half-whispered basso curse and the rustle of papers from somewhere down the hall.

I opened the flower box and drew out my blasting rod, then checked my shield bracelet. All in all, in close quarters like this, I would have preferred a gun to my blasting rod, but I'd have a hell of a time explaining it to security or the police if they caught me snooping around a dead man's apartment. I tightened my grip on the rod and slid quietly down the hall, hoping I wouldn't need to use it. Believe it or not, my first instinct isn't always to set things on fire.

The door to Reuel's apartment stood half open, and its pale wood glared where it had been freshly splintered. My heart sped up. It looked like someone had beaten me to Reuel's place. It meant that I must have been on the right track.

It also meant that whoever it was would probably not be thrilled to see me.

I crept to the door and peered inside.

What I could see of the apartment could have been imported from 429-B Baker Street. Dark woods, fancy scrollwork, and patterns of cloth busier than the makeup girl at a Kiss concert filled every available inch of space with Victorian splendor. Or rather, it once had. Now the place looked wrecked. A sideboard stood denuded of its drawers, which lay upturned on the floor. An old steamer chest lay on its side, its lid torn off, its contents scattered onto the carpet. An open door showed me that the bedroom hadn't been spared the rough stuff either. Clothes and broken bits of finery lay strewn about everywhere.

The man inside Reuel's apartment looked like a catalog model for Thugs-R-Us. He stood a hand taller than me, and I couldn't tell where his shoulders left off and his neck began. He wore old frayed breeches, a sweater with worn elbows, and a hat that looked like an import from the Depression-era Bowery, a round bowler decorated with a dark grey band. He carried a worn leather satchel in one meat-slab hand, and with the other he scooped up pieces of paper, maybe index cards, from a shoe box on an old writing desk, depositing them in the bag. The satchel bulged, but he kept adding more to it with rapid, sharp motions. He muttered something else, emitted a low rumble, and snatched up a Rolodex from the desk, cramming it into the satchel.

I drew back from the door and put my back against the wall. There wasn't any time to waste, but I had to figure out what to do. If someone had shown up at Reuel's place to start swiping papers, it meant that Reuel had been hiding evidence of one kind or another. Therefore, I needed to see whatever it was Kong had in that satchel.

Somehow, I doubted he would show me if I asked him pretty please, but I didn't like my other option, either. In such tight quarters, and with other residents nearby, I didn't dare resort to any of my kaboom magic. Kaboom magic, or evocation, is difficult to master, and I'm not very good at it. Even with my blasting rod as a focus, I had accidentally dealt out structural damage to a number of buildings. So far, I'd been lucky enough not to kill myself. I didn't want to push it if I didn't have to.

Of course, I could always just jump the thug and try to take his bag away. I had a feeling I'd be introduced to whole new realms of physical discomfort, but I could try it.

I took another peek at the thug. With one hand, he casually lifted a sofa that had to weigh a couple of hundred pounds and peered under it. I drew back from the door again. Fisticuffs, bad idea. Definitely a bad idea.

I chewed on my lip a moment more. Then I slipped the blasting rod back into the flower box, squared up my FTD hat, stepped around the corner, and knocked on the half-open door.

The thug's head snapped around toward me, along with most of his shoulders. He bared his teeth, anger in his eyes.

"FTD," I said, trying to keep my voice bland. "I got a delivery here for a Mr. Reuel. You want to sign for it?"

The thug glowered at me from beneath the shelter of his overhanging brow. "Flowers?" he rumbled a minute later.

"Yeah, buddy," I said. "Flowers." I came into the apartment and thrust the clipboard at him, idly wishing I had some gum to chomp. "Sign there at the bottom."

He glowered at me for a moment longer before accepting the clipboard. "Reuel ain't here."

"Like I care." I pushed a pen at him with the other hand. "Just sign it and I'll get going."

This time he glared at the pen, then at me. Then he set the satchel on the coffee table. "Whatever."

"Great." I stepped past him and put the flower box down on the table. He clutched the pen in his fist and scrawled on the bottom of the paper. I reached down with one hand as he did, plucked a piece of paper a little bigger than a playing card from the satchel, and palmed it. I got my hand back to my side just before he finished, growled, and shoved the clipboard at me.

"Now," he said, "leave."

"You bet," I told him. "Thanks."

I turned to go, but his hand shot out and his fingers clamped on to my arm like a steel band. I looked back. He narrowed his eyes, nostrils flared, and then growled, "I don't smell flowers."

The bottom fell out of my stomach, but I tried to keep the bluff going. "What are you talking about, Mr., uh"—I glanced down at the clipboard—"Grum."

Mr. Grum?

He leaned down closer to me, and his nostrils flared again, this time with a low snuffling sound. "I smell magic. Smell wizard."

My smile must have turned green to go with my face. "Uh."

Grum took my throat in one hand and lifted me straight up off the ground with a strength no human could duplicate. My vision reduced itself to a hazy tunnel, and the clipboard fell from my fingers. I struggled against him uselessly. His eyes narrowed, and he bared more teeth in a slow smile. "Should have minded your own business. Whoever you are." His fingers started tightening, and I thought I heard something crackle and pop. I had to hope it was his knuckles instead of my trachea. "Whoever you were."

It was too late by far to use my shield bracelet, and my blasting rod lay out of reach on the coffee table. I fumbled in my pocket, as my vision started to go black, for the only weapon I had left. I had to pray that I was right in my guess.

I found the old iron nail, gripped it as best I could, and shoved it hard at Grum's beefy forearm. The nail bit into his flesh.

He screamed, a throaty, basso bellow that shook the walls. He flinched and spun, hurling me away from him. I hit the door to Reuel's bedroom, slamming it all the way open, and got lucky. I landed on the bed rather than on one of the wooden pillars at its corners. If I'd hit one of those, I'd have broken my back. Instead, I hit the bed, bounced, fetched up hard against the wall, then tumbled back to the bed again.

I glanced up to see that Grum looked very different than he had a moment before.

Rather than the film noir tough-guy getup, he wore a loincloth of some kind of pale leather—and nothing more. His skin was a dark russet, layered with muscle and curling dark hair. His ears stood out from the sides of his head like satellite dishes, and his features had flattened, becoming more bestial, nearly like those of a gorilla. He was also better than twelve feet tall. He had to hunch over to stand, and even so his shoulders pressed against the ten-foot ceiling.

With another roar, Grum tore the nail from his arm and flung it to one side. It went completely through the wall, leaving a hole the size of my thumb. Then he spun back to me, baring teeth now huge and jagged, and took a stalking step toward me, the floor creaking beneath his feet.

"Ogre," I wheezed. "Crap!" I extended my hand toward the blasting rod and focused my will. *"Ventas servitas!"*

A sharp and sudden torrent of air caught up the flower box and hurled it straight toward me. It hit me in the chest hard enough to hurt, but I snatched it, brought out my blasting rod, and trained it on Grum as he closed on me. I slammed more will through the rod, its tip bursting into scarlet incandescence.

"Fuego!" I barked as I released the energy. Fire in a column the size of my clenched fist flashed out at Grum and splashed against his chest.

It didn't slow him down, not by a second. His skin didn't burn—his hair didn't even singe. The fire of my magic spilled over him and did absolutely nothing.

Grum shouldered his way through the bedroom door, cracking the frame as he did, and raised his fist. He slammed it down at the bed, but I didn't wait around to meet it. I flopped over to the far side of the bed and tumbled down to the space between the bed and the wall. He reached for me, but I rolled underneath the bed, bumped against his feet, and scrambled toward the door.

I almost made it. But something heavy and hard slammed against my legs, taking them out from under me and knocking me down. I only had time to realize, dimly, that Grum had picked up an antique Victorian chair that resembled, more than anything else, a throne, and hurled it at me.

The pain kicked in a second later, but I crawled toward the door. The ogre's feet pounded in rapid succession, and the floor shook as he grew closer and closer to me.

From the hall, a querulous female voice demanded, "What's all that racket? I have already called the police, I have! You fruits get out of our hall, or they'll lock you away!"

Grum stopped. I saw frustration and rage flicker over his ape-like features. Then he snarled, stepped over me, and picked up the satchel. When he headed for the door, I rolled out of his way. He was big enough to simply crush my chest if he stepped on me, and I didn't want to make it easy for him.

"You got lucky," the ogre growled. "But this is not over." Then his form blurred and shifted, growing smaller, until he wore the same appearance he had a few moments before. He settled his bowler with one hand, then stalked out the door, aiming a kick at me in passing. I cringed away from it, and he was gone.

"Well?" demanded that same voice. "What's it going to be, you fruit? Get out!"

Police sirens wailed somewhere outside. I got up, wobbled for a moment, and put my hand against the wall to help myself stay up. I turned the other hand over to look at the piece of paper I'd stolen from Grum's satchel.

It wasn't paper. It was a photograph. Nothing fancy—just an instant-camera shot. It showed old white-haired Reuel, standing in front of the Magic Castle at one of the Disney parks.

Several young people stood beside him and around him, smiling, sunburned, and apparently happy. One was a tall, bull-necked young woman in faded jeans, with her hair dyed a shade of muddy green. She had a wide smile and a blunt, ugly face. Standing beside her was a girl who should have been in a lingerie catalog, all curves and long limbs in her brief shorts and bikini top, her hair also green, but the color of summer grass rather than that of pond scum. On the other side of Reuel was a pair of young men. One of them, a short, stocky fellow with a goatee and sunglasses, had his fingers lifted into a V behind the head of his companion, a small, slender man with his skin sunburned to the color of copper and his blond hair bleached out to nearly white.

Who were they? Why had Reuel been with them? And why had Grum seemed so intent on removing their picture from Reuel's apartment?

The sirens grew closer, and if I didn't want to get locked up by some well-meaning member of Chicago's finest, I needed to leave. I rubbed at my aching throat, winced at the wrenching, cramping pain in my back, wondered about the photograph, and stumbled out of the building.

Chapter Twelve

I got out of the old apartment building and back to the Blue Beetle without being mugged by any attackers, inhuman or otherwise. As I pulled out, a patrol car rolled up, blue bubbles flashing. I drove away at a sedate pace and tried to keep my shaking hands from making the car bob or swerve. No one pulled me over, so I must have done all right. Score one for the good guys.

I had time to think, though I wasn't sure I wanted to. I'd gone to Reuel's apartment on a simple snoop, not really expecting to find much, if anything. But I'd gotten lucky. Not only had I shown up at the right place, I'd done it at the right time. Someone obviously wanted to hide something there—either more pictures like the one I'd found or other papers from somewhere in the place. What I needed to determine now was what Grum had been trying to collect or—nearly as good—why he was trying to make some kind of evidence vanish. Failing that, knowing who he was working for would do almost as well—ogres aren't exactly known for their independent initiative. And given what was going on, it would be ludicrous to assume that one of the heavyweight thugs of the lands of Faerie just happened to be doing an independent contract in the home of the recently deceased.

Ogres were wyldfae—they could work for either Winter or Summer, and they could have a range of personalities and temperaments running the gamut from jovially violent to maliciously violent. Grum hadn't seemed to be on the cheerful end of that particular scale, but he *had* been both decisive and restrained. The average walking mountain of muscle from Faerie wouldn't have held back from beating me to a pulp, regardless of what the neighbors shouted. That meant that Grum had more savvy than the average bear, that he was dangerous—even if I didn't take into account how easily he had ignored the spells I'd hurled at him.

All ogres have an innate capacity for neutralizing magical forces to one degree or another. Grum had grounded out my spells like I'd been scuffing my feet on the carpet to give him a little static electricity zap. That meant that he was an old faerie, and a strong one. The quick and thorough shapeshifting supported that assessment as well. Your average club-swinging thewmonger couldn't have taken human form, complete with clothing, so ably.

Smart plus strong plus quick equals badass. Most likely he was a trusted personal guard or a highly placed enforcer.

But for whom?

At a stop light I stared at the photograph I'd taken from Grum. "Damn," I muttered, "who are these people?"

I added it to the list of questions still growing like fungus in a locker room.

Ronald Reuel's funeral had already begun by the time I arrived. Flannery's Funeral Home in the River North area had been a family-run business until a few years before. It was an old place, but had always been well kept. Now the carefully landscaped shrubbery had been replaced with big rocks, which were no doubt easier to maintain. The parking lot had a lot of cracks in it, and only about half of the outdoor lights were burning. The sign, an illuminated glass-and-plastic number that read QUIET ACRES FUNERAL HOME, glared in garish green and blue above the front door.

I parked the Beetle, tucked the photo into my pocket, and got out of the car. I couldn't casually take my staff or my blasting rod into the funeral home. People who don't believe in magic look at you oddly when you walk in toting a big stick covered with carvings of runes and sigils. The people who know what I am would react in much the same way as if I had walked in draped in belts of ammo and carrying a heavy-caliber machine gun in each hand, John Wayne–style. There could be plenty of each sort inside, so I carried only the low-profile stuff: my ring, mostly depleted, my shield bracelet, and my mother's silver pentacle amulet. My reflection in the glass door reminded me that I had underdressed for the evening, but I wasn't there to make the social column. I slipped into the building and headed for the room where they'd laid out Ronald Reuel.

The old man had been dressed up in a grey silk suit with a metallic sheen to it. It was a younger man's suit, and it looked too big for him. He would have looked more comfortable in tweed. The mortician had done only a so-so job of fixing Reuel up. His cheeks were too red and his lips too blue. You could see the dimples on his lips where thin lines of thread had been stitched through them to hold his mouth closed. No one would have mistaken this for an old man in the midst of his nap—it was a corpse, plain and simple. The room was about half full, people standing in little knots talking and passing back and forth in front of the casket.

No one was standing in the shadows smoking a cigarette or looking about with a shifty-eyed gaze. I couldn't see anyone quickly hiding a bloody knife behind his back or twirling a moustache, either. That ruled out the Dudley Do-Right approach to finding the killer. Maybe he, she, or they weren't here.

Of course, I supposed it would be possible for faeries to throw a veil or a glamour over themselves before they came in, but even experienced faeries have trouble passing for mortal. Mab had looked good, sure, but she hadn't really looked *normal*. Grum had been much the same. I mean, he'd looked human, sure, but also like an extra on the set of *The Untouchables*. Faeries can do a lot of things really well, but blending in with a crowd generally isn't one of them.

In any case, the crowd struck me as mostly relatives and business associates. No one matched the pictures, no one seemed to be a faerie in a bad mortal costume, and either my instincts had the night off or no one was using any kind of veil or glamour. Bad guys one, Harry zero.

I slipped out of the viewing room and back into the hallway in time to hear a low whisper somewhere down the hall. That grabbed my attention. I made the effort to move quietly and crept a bit closer, Listening as I went.

"I don't *know*," hissed a male voice. "I looked for her all day. She's never been gone this long."

"Just my point," growled a female voice. "She doesn't stay gone this long. You know how she gets by herself."

"God," said a third voice, the light tenor of a young man. "He did it. He really did it this time."

"We don't know that," the first man said. "Maybe she finally used her head and got out of town."

The woman's voice sounded tired. "No, Ace. She wouldn't just leave. Not on her own. We have to do something."

"What can we do?" the second male said.

"Something," the woman said. "Anything."

"Wow, that's specific," the first male, apparently Ace, said with his voice dry and edgy. "Whatever you're going to do, you'd better do it fast. The wizard is here."

I felt the muscles in my neck grow tense. There was a short, perhaps shocked silence in the room down the hall.

"Here?" the second male echoed in a panicky tone. "Now? Why didn't you tell us?"

"I just did, dimwit," Ace said.

"What do we do?" the second male asked. "What do we do, what do we do?"

"Shut up," snapped the female voice. "Shut *up*, Fix."

"He's in Mab's pocket," said Ace. "You know he is. She crossed over from Faerie today."

"No way," said the second voice, presumably Fix. "He's supposed to be a decent sort, right?"

"Depends on who you hear it from," said Ace. "People who get in his way have had a habit of getting real dead."

"God," said Fix, panting. "Oh God, oh God."

"Look," said the woman, "if he's here, we shouldn't be. Not until we know what it means." Furniture, maybe a wooden chair, creaked. "Come on."

I slipped back down the hall and around the corner into the lobby as I heard footsteps leaving the small side room. They didn't come toward me. Instead, they moved further down the hall, away from the lobby. They had to be heading for a back door. I chewed on my lip and weighed my options. Three very apprehensive folks, maybe human, maybe not, heading down a darkened hall toward a back door that doubtless led into an equally dark alley. It sounded like a recipe for more trouble.

But I didn't think I had any options. I counted to five and then followed the footsteps.

I saw only a retreating shadow at the far end of the hall. I looked into the room the three had been in as I went past it and found a small lounge with several upholstered chairs. I hesitated for a moment at the corner and heard the soft click of a metal door opening, then closing again. As I rounded the corner, I saw a door with a faded sticker spelling EXIT.

I went to the door and opened it as quietly as I could, then poked my head out into the alley it opened into and rubbernecked around.

They were standing not five feet away—three of the young

people from Reuel's photo. The small, skinny man with the blond-white hair and dark tan was facing me. He was dressed in what looked like a secondhand brown suit and a yellow polyester clip-on tie. His eyes widened almost comically, and his mouth dropped open in shock. He squeaked, and it was enough to let me identify him as Fix.

Beside him was the other young man, Ace. He was the one with the dark curly hair and goatee, wearing a grey sport coat with a white shirt and dark slacks. He still had his sunglasses on when he turned to look at me, and he clawed at the pocket of his jacket upon seeing me.

The third was the brawny, homely young woman with the muddy green hair and heavy brow. She had on a pair of jeans tight enough to show the muscles in her thighs and a khaki blouse. She didn't hesitate. She didn't even look. She just turned, her arm sweeping out as she did, and fetched me a blow to my cheek with the back of one shovel-size hand. I managed to move with it a bit at the last second, but even so the impact threw me out of the doorway and into the alley. Stars and cartoon birdies danced in my vision, and I rolled, trying to get clear before she could hit me again.

Ace pulled a small-caliber semiautomatic from his jacket pocket, but the woman growled at him, "Don't be stupid! They'd kill us all."

"Hebbity bedda," I said, by way of attempting a greeting. My mouth had gone rather numb, and my tongue felt like a lead weight. "Jussa hangonna sayke hee."

Fix jumped up and down, pointing at me, his voice shrill. "He's casting on us!"

The woman kicked me in the ribs hard enough to knock the wind out of me. Then she picked me up by the back of my pants, grunting with the effort, and threw me into the air. I came down ten feet away in an open Dumpster and crunched down amid cardboard boxes and stinking refuse.

"Go," the woman barked. "Go, go, go!"

I lay in the garbage for a minute, trying to catch my breath. The sound of three sets of running feet receded down the alley.

I had just sat up when a head popped into view over me, vague in the shadows. I flinched and threw up my left arm, willing power through the shield bracelet. I accidentally made the shield too big, and sparks kicked up where the shield intersected the metal of the Dumpster, but by their light I saw whose head it was.

"Harry?" Billy the Werewolf asked. "What are you doing in there?"

I let the shield drop and extended a hand to him, "Looking for suspects."

He frowned and hauled me out of the trash. I wobbled for a second or two, until my head stopped spinning quite so quickly. Billy steadied me with one hand. "You find any?"

"I'd say so, yeah."

Billy nodded and peered up at me. "Did you decide that before or after they hit you in the face and threw you in the garbage?"

I brushed coffee grounds off my jeans. "Do I tell you how to do your job?"

"Actually, yeah. All the time."

"Okay, okay," I muttered. "Did you bring the pizza?"

"Yeah," Billy said. "Got it back in the car. Why?"

I brushed at my shaggy hair. What I hoped were more coffee grounds fell out. I started walking down the alley toward the front of the building. "Because I need to make a few bribes," I said, looking back over my shoulder at Billy. "Do you believe in faeries?"

Chapter Thirteen

Billy held the pizza while I drew the chalk circle on the ground, back in the alley. "Harry," he said, "how is this supposed to work exactly?"

"Hang on," I said. I didn't quite complete the circle, but took the pizza box from him. I opened it, took out one piece, and put it down in the middle of the circle on a napkin. Then I dabbed a bit of blood from the corner of my mouth where the girl had slugged me onto the bottom of the piece of pizza, stepped back, and completed the circle without willing it closed.

"Pretty simple," I said. "I'll call the faerie in close to the pizza there. He'll smell it, jump on it, eat it. When he does, he'll get the bit of my blood, and it will be enough energy to close the circle around him."

"Uh-huh," Billy said, his expression skeptical. He took out a second piece and started to take a bite. "And then you beat the information out of him?"

I took the piece out of his hand, put it back in the box, and closed it. "And then I bribe the information out of him. Save the pizza."

Billy scowled at me, but he left the pizza alone. "So what do I do?"

"Sit tight and make sure no one else tries to pop me while I'm talking to Toot-toot."

"Toot-toot?" Billy asked, lifting an eyebrow.

"Hell's bells, Billy, I didn't pick the name. Just be quiet. If he thinks there are mortals around he'll get nervous and leave before I can snare him."

"If you say so," Billy said. "I was just hoping to do more good than to deliver pizza."

I raked my fingers through my hair. "I don't know what you could do yet."

"I could track those three in the picture you showed me."

I shook my head. "Odds are they just got into a car and left."

"Yeah," he said, some forced patience in his voice. "But if I get their scent now, it might help me find them later on."

"Oh," I said, feeling a bit stupid. Okay, so I hadn't considered the whole shapeshifting angle. "Fine, if you want to. Just be careful, all right? I don't know what all might be prowling around."

"Okay, Mom," Billy said. He set the pizza box on top of a closed trash can, fell back down the alley, and vanished.

I waited until Billy had gone to find a nice patch of shadows to step into. Then I closed my eyes for a moment, drawing up my concentration, and began to whisper the faerie's Name.

Every intelligent being has a Name, a specific series of spoken sounds linked to its very being. If a practitioner knows the Name of something, knows it in every nuance and detail of pronunciation, then he can use that Name to open a magical conduit to that being. That's how demons get summoned to the mortal world. Call something's Name and you make contact with it—and if you're a wizard, that means that you can then exercise power over it, no matter where in the world it is.

Controlling an inhuman being via its Name is a shady area of magic, only one step removed from taking over the will of another mortal. According to the White Council's Seven Laws of Magic, that's a capital crime—and they make zero-tolerance policies look positively lenient.

Given how much the Council loves me, I'm a tad paranoid about breaking any of the Laws of Magic, so while I was calling the faerie's Name, I put only the tiniest trickle of compulsion into it, just enough to attract his unconscious attention, to make him curious about what might be down this particular alley. I whispered the faerie's Name and stood in the shadows, waiting.

Maybe ten minutes later, something made from a hummingbird and a falling star spiraled down from overhead, a flickering ball of blue-white light. It alighted on the ground, the light dimming to a luminous sheen over the form of a tiny faerie, Toot-toot.

Toot stood about six inches tall. He had a mane of dandelion-fluff hair the color of lilacs and a pair of translucent dragonfly wings rising from his shoulders. Otherwise he looked almost human, his beauty a distant echo of the lords of Faerie, the Sidhe. On his head he wore what looked like a plastic Coke bottle cap. It was tied into place with a piece of string that ran under his chin, and his lilac hair squeezed out from beneath it all the way around, all but hiding his eyes. In one hand he carried a spear fashioned from a battered old yellow Number 2 pencil, some twine, and what must have been a straight pin, and he wore a little blue plastic cocktail sword through another piece of twine on his belt.

Toot landed in a cautious crouch near the pizza, as though streaking in like an errant shot from a Roman candle might not have alerted anyone watching to his presence. He tiptoed in a big circle around the piece of pizza, and made a show of looking all around, one hand lifted to shade his eyes. Then he raised his arm into the air, balled up a tiny fist, and pumped it up and down a few times.

Immediately, half a dozen similar streaks of glowing color darted down out of the air, each one a different color, each one containing a tiny faerie at its center. They alighted more or less together, and every one of them was armed with a weapon that might have been cobbled together from the contents of a child's school box.

"Caption!" Toot-toot piped in a shrill, voice. "Report!"

A green-lit faerie beside Toot snapped to attention and slapped herself on the forehead with one hand, then turned sharply to her left and barked, "Loo Tender, report!"

A purple-hued faerie came to attention as well and smacked himself in the head with one hand, then turned to the next faerie beside him and snapped, "Star Jump, report!"

And so it went down the line, through the "Corpse Oral," the "First Class Privy," and finally to the "Second Class Privy," who marched up to Toot-toot and said, "Everyone's here, Generous, and we're hungry!"

"All right," Toot-toot barked. "Everyone fall apart for messy!"

And with that, the faeries let out shrill hoots of glee, tossed aside their weapons and armaments, and threw themselves upon the piece of pizza.

As soon as the little faeries started eating, the magic circle snapped closed around them with a hardly audible *pop* as it sprang into place. The effect was immediate. The faeries let out half a dozen piercing shrieks of alarm and buzzed into the air, smacking into the invisible wall of the circle here and there, sending out puffs of glowing dust motes when they did. They fell into a panicked spiral, around the inside of the circle, until Toot-toot landed on the ground, looked up at the other faeries, and started shouting, "Ten Huts! Ten Huts!"

The other faeries abruptly came to a complete stop in the air, standing rigidly straight. Evidently, they couldn't do that and keep their little wings going at the same time, because they promptly fell to the alley floor, landing with a half-dozen separate "ouches" and as many puffs of glowing faerie dust.

Toot-toot recovered his pencil spear and stood at the very edge of the closed circle, peering out at the alley. "Harry Dresden? Is that you?"

I stepped out from my hiding spot and nodded. "It's me. How you doing, Toot?"

I expected a torrent of outraged but empty threats. That was Toot-toot's usual procedure. Instead, he let out a hiss and crouched down in the circle, spear at the ready. The other tiny faeries took up their own weapons and rushed to Toot-toot's side. "You can't make us," Toot said. "We haven't been Called and until we are, we belong to ourselves."

I blinked down at them. "Called? Toot, what are you talking about?"

"We're not stupid, Emissary," Toot-toot said. "I know what you are. I can smell the Cold Queen all over you."

I wondered if they made a deodorant for that. I lifted my hand in a placating gesture. "Toot, I'm working for Mab right now, but it's just another client, okay? I'm not here to take you anywhere or make you do anything."

Toot planted the eraser end of his spear on the ground, scowling suspiciously up at me. "Really?" he demanded.

"Really," I said.

"Promise?"

"Promise."

"Super duper double dog promise spit swear?"

I nodded. "Super duper double dog promise spit swear," I repeated gravely.

"Spit!" Toot demanded.

I spat on the ground.

"Oh. Well, then," Toot said. He dropped his spear and darted over to the pizza, much to the consternation of the other little faeries, who let out piping shrills of protest and then followed him. The piece of pizza didn't last long. It was like watching one of those nature shows, where the piranha devour some luckless thing that falls in the water—except here there were glittering wings and motes and puffs of glowing, colorful dust everywhere.

I watched, frowning, until Toot-toot flopped onto his back, his tummy slightly distended. He let out a contented sigh, and the other faeries followed suit.

"So, Harry," Toot said, "who do you think is going to win the war?"

"The White Council," I said. "The Red Court's got no depth on the bench and nothing in the bullpen."

Toot snorted and flipped his plastic bottle-cap helm off his head. His hair waved around in the breeze. "Just because they don't have any cows doesn't mean that they won't win. But I don't mean *that* war."

I frowned. "You mean between the Courts."

Toot nodded. "Yeah."

"Okay. What's with the armor and weapons, Toot?"

The faerie beamed. "Neat, huh?"

"Highly scary," I said gravely. "But why do you have them?"

Toot folded his arms and said, with all the gravity that six inches of fluff and pixie dust can muster, "Trouble's coming."

"Uh-huh. I hear the Courts are upset."

"More than just upset, Harry Dresden. The drawing of the wyldfae is beginning. I saw some dryads walking with a Sidhe Knight from Summer, and a canal nereid climbed up out of the water a couple of blocks over and went into a Winter building."

"Drawing of the wyldfae. Like you guys?"

Toot nodded and propped his feet up on the legs of the Star Jump, who let out a surprisingly basso belch. "Not everyone plays with the Courts. We mostly just do our jobs and don't pay much attention. But when there's a war on, the wyldfae get Called to one side or another."

"Who picks which way you go?"

Toot shrugged. "Mostly the nice wyldfae go to the Warm Queen and the mean ones go to Cold. I think it's got something to do with what you've been doing."

"Uh-huh. So have you been doing Warm or Cold things?"

Toot let out a sparkling laugh. "How should I remember all those things?" He patted his stomach and then rose to his feet again, eyes calculating. "Is that a pizza box you have there, Harry?"

I held the box out and opened it, showing the rest of the pizza.

There was a collective "Ooooo" from the faeries, and they all pressed to the very edge of the circle, until it flattened their little noses, staring at the pizza in fascinated lust.

"You've sure given us a lot of pizza the past couple of years, Harry," Toot said, with a swallow. He didn't look away from the box in my hands.

"Hey, you gave me a hand when I needed it," I said. "It's only fair, right?"

"Only fair?" Toot spat, outraged. "It's . . . it's . . . it's *pizza*, Harry."

"I'm wanting some more work done," I said. "I need information."

"And you're paying in pizza?" Toot asked, his tone hopeful.

"Yes," I said.

"Wah-hoo!" Toot shouted and buzzed into the air in an excited spiral. The other faeries followed him with similar carols of happiness, and the blur of colors was dizzying.

"Give us the pizza!" Toot shouted.

"Pizza, pizza, pizza!" the other faeries shrilled.

"First," I said, "I want some questions answered."

"Right, right, right!" Toot screamed. "Ask already!"

"I need to talk to the Winter Lady," I said. "Where can I find her, Toot?"

Toot tore at his lavender hair. "Is *that* all you need to know? Down in the city! Down where the shops are underground, and the sidewalks."

I frowned. "In the commuter tunnels?"

"Yes, yes, yes. Back in the part the mortals can't see, you can find your way into Undertown. The Cold Lady came to Undertown. Her court is in Undertown."

"What?" I sputtered. "Since when?"

Toot whirled around in impatient loops in the air. "Since the last autumn!"

I scratched at my hair. It made sense, I supposed. Last autumn, a vengeful vampire and her allies had stirred up all sorts of supernatural mischief, creating turbulence in the border between the real world and the Nevernever, the world of spirit. Shortly after, the war between the wizards and the vampires had begun.

Those events had probably attracted the attention of all sorts of things.

I shook my head. "And what about the Summer Lady? Is she in town?"

Toot put his fists on his hips. "Well, *obviously*, Harry. If Winter came here, Summer had to come too, didn't it?"

"Obviously," I said, feeling a little slow on the uptake. Man, was I off my game. "Where can I find her?"

"She's on top of one of those big buildings."

I sighed. "Toot, this is Chicago. There are a lot of big buildings."

Toot blinked at me, then frowned for a minute before brightening. "It's the one with the pizza shop right by it."

My head hurt some more. "Tell you what. How about you guide me to it?"

Toot thrust out his little chin and scowled. "And miss pizza? No way."

I gritted my teeth. "Then get me someone else to guide me. You've got to know someone."

Toot scrunched up his face. He tugged at one earlobe, but it evidently didn't help him remember, because he had to rub one foot against the opposite calf and spin around in vacant circles for ten whole seconds before he whirled back to face me, the nimbus of light around him brightening. "Aha!" he sang. "Yes! I can give you a guide!" He jabbed a finger at me. "But only if that's all the questions, Harry. Pizza, pizza, pizza!"

"Guide first," I insisted. "Then pizza."

Toot shook his arms and legs as though he would fly apart. "Yes, yes, yes!"

"Done," I said. I opened the pizza box and set it on top of a discarded crate nearby. Then I stepped over to the circle, leaned down, and with a smudge of my hand and an effort of will broke it, freeing the energies inside.

The faeries chorused several pitches and variants of "Yahoo!" and streaked past me so quickly that they left a cone of wild air behind them, tossing my unruly hair and scattering lighter pieces of garbage around the alley. They tore into the pizza with much the same gusto they'd used on the one piece earlier, but there was enough of it now to keep them from mangling it in mere seconds.

Toot zipped over to hover in front of my face and held out his little palm. A moment later, something that looked like an errant spark from a campfire whirled down and lighted on his palm. Toot said something in a language I couldn't understand, and the tiny light pulsed and flickered as though in response.

"Right," Toot said, nodding to the light. I peered more closely at it, and could just barely make out a tiny, tiny form inside, no larger than an ant. Another faerie. The light pulsed and flickered, and Toot nodded to it before turning to me.

"Harry Dresden," Toot-toot said, holding out his palm, "this is Elidee. She's going to pay me back a favor and guide you to the Winter Lady and then to the Summer Lady. Good enough?"

I frowned at the tiny faerie. "Does she understand me?"

I barely saw Elidee stamp a tiny foot. The scarlet light around her flickered sharply, twice.

"Yes," Toot-toot translated. "Two lights for yes, and one light for no."

"Two for yes, one for no," I muttered.

Toot frowned. "Or is that one for yes and two for no? I can never keep it straight." And with that, the little faerie blurred and zipped past me and away to join the swarm of softly flashing lights demolishing the pizza.

Elidee, for her part, recovered from the miniature cyclone that Toot-toot left in his wake, whirled around dizzily for a few moments, then spiraled down to me and settled on the bridge of my nose. My eyes crossed trying to look at her. "Hey," I said, "Do I look like a couch to you?"

Two flashes.

I sighed. "Okay, Elidee. Do you want any pizza before we go?"

Two flashes again, brighter. The tiny faerie leapt up into the air again and zoomed over to the cloud around the pizza.

Footsteps came down the alley, then Billy stepped out of the shadows, pulling his sweatshirt down over his muscular stomach. I felt a brief and irrational surge of jealousy. I don't have a muscular stomach. I'm not overlapping my belt or anything, but I don't have abs of steel. I don't even have abs of bronze. Maybe abs of plastic.

Billy blinked at the pizza for a moment and said, "Wow. That's sort of pretty. In a *Jaws* kind of way."

"Yeah," I said. "Don't look at it for too long. Faerie lights can be disorienting to mortals."

"Gotcha," Billy said. He glanced back at me. "How'd it go? You get what you needed?"

"Yeah," I said. "You?"

He shrugged. "Alley isn't the best place to pick up scents, but I should be able to recognize them again if I'm in my other suit. They didn't smell quite normal."

"Gee, what are the odds."

Billy's teeth showed in the dark. "Heh. So what are we waiting for?"

Elidee picked just then to glide back over to me and settle once more on the bridge of my nose. Billy blinked at her and said, "What the hell?"

"This is our guide," I said. "Elidee, this is Billy."

Elidee flashed twice.

Billy blinked again. "Uh, charmed." He shook his head. "So? What's the plan?"

"We go confront the Winter Lady in her underground lair. I do the talking. You stay alert and watch my back."

He nodded. "Okay. You got it."

I looked over to see the last piece of pizza lifted up into the air by greedy faerie hands. They clustered around it, tearing and ripping, and it was gone in seconds. With that, the faeries swarmed away like a squadron of potbellied comets and vanished from view.

Elidee fluttered off my nose and started drifting down the alley in the other direction. I followed her.

"Harry?" Billy asked, his voice a touch hopeful. "Are you expecting trouble?"

I sighed and rubbed at the space between my eyebrows.

Definitely getting a headache. It was going to be a long night.

Chapter Fourteen

Elidee led Billy and me through alleys, up a fire escape to the roof of a building and then down on the other side, and through a junk-cluttered abandoned lot on the way to the Pedway. It took us better than half an hour of scrambling after the tiny faerie through the muggy heat, and by the end of it I wished I'd told Toot-toot that we wanted someone who could read a street map and guide us there in a car.

Chicago's commuter tunnels are fairly recent construction, compared to much of the rest of the city. The tunnels are a maze if you don't know them—long stretches of identical overhead lights, drab, clean walls dotted with advertising posters, and intersections bearing plain and not always helpful directional signs. The tunnels closed after the workday and wouldn't open up again until around six the next morning, but Elidee led us to an unfinished building at Randolph and Wabash. She flitted around in front of a service access door that proved to be unlocked and that led down to a similar door that opened onto a darkened section of the Pedway that looked as though it had been under construction but was abandoned when the building had shut down.

It was completely dark, so I slipped the silver pentacle off my neck, lifting it in my hand and focusing a quiet effort of will upon it. The five-pointed star has been a symbol of magic for centuries, representing the four elements and the power of spirit bound within the circle of will—primal power under the control of human thought. I held the pentacle before me, and as I concentrated it began to glow with a gentle blue light, illuminating enough of our surroundings that we could navigate through the dark, silent tunnels. The little faerie drifted in front of us down the tunnel, and we followed her without speaking. She took us to the intersection with the main tunnels of the Pedway and on a brief walk down another tunnel, to a section shut behind a rusting metal gate with a sign that read, DANGER KEEP OUT. The gate proved to be unlocked, and we went down the tunnel, into a damper section of tunnels, rife with the smell of mold, that was clearly not a part of the Pedway proper.

After another fifty or sixty feet we reached a place where the walls became rough and uneven and shadows lay thick and heavy, despite the glow of my wizard's light.

Elidee drifted over to an especially dark section of wall and flew in a little circle in front of it.

"Okay," I said. "I guess this is where we get in."

"What is where we get in?" Billy asked, his voice skeptical. "Get into where?"

"Undertown," I said. I ran my hands over the wall. To the casual touch it appeared to be bare, unfinished concrete, but I felt a slight unsteadiness when I pressed against it. It couldn't have been solid stone. "Must be a panel here somewhere. Trigger of some kind."

"What do you mean, 'Undertown'? I've never heard of it before."

"I was probably working here for five or six years before I did," I said. "You have to understand the history of Chicago. How they did things here."

Billy folded his arms. "I'm listening."

"The city is a swamp," I said, still searching for a means of opening the door with my fingertips. "We're darn near level with Lake Michigan. When they first built the place, the town kept sinking into the muck. I mean, every year it sank lower. They used to build streets, then build a latticework of wood over them, and then *another* street on top of that, planning on them slowly sinking. They planned houses the same way. Built the front door on the second floor and called it a 'Chicago entry,' so when the house sank, the front door would be at ground level."

"What about when the street sank?"

"Built another one on top of it. So you wound up with a whole city existing under the street level. They used to have a huge problem with rats and criminals holing up under the streets."

"But not anymore?" Billy asked.

"The rats and thugs mostly got crowded out by other things.

Became a whole miniature civilization down here. And it was out of sight of the sun, which made it friendly space for all the night-crawling critters around."

"Hence, Undertown," Billy said.

I nodded. "Undertown. There are a lot of tunnels around Chicago. The Manhattan Project was housed in them for a while during World War Two. Did all that atomic bomb research."

"That's cheerful. You come down here a lot?"

I shook my head. "Hell, no. All kinds of nastiness lives down here."

Billy frowned at me. "Like what?"

"Lots of things. Stuff you don't often see on the surface. Things even wizards know almost nothing about. Goblins, spirits of the earth, wyrms, things that have no name. Plus the usual riffraff. Vampires sometimes find lairs down here during the day. Trolls can hide here too. Molds and fungi you don't get in most of the natural world. You name it."

Billy pursed his lips thoughtfully. "So you're taking us into a maze of lightless, rotting, precarious tunnels full of evil faeries and monsters."

I nodded. "Maybe leftover radiation, too."

"God, you're a fun guy, Harry."

"You're the one who wanted in on the action." My fingers found a tiny groove in the wall, and when I pressed against it a small, flat section of stone clicked and retracted. The switch had to have triggered some kind of release, because the section of wall pivoted in the center, turning outward, and forming a door that led into still more dank darkness. "Hah," I said with some satisfaction. "There we go."

Billy pressed forward and tried to step through the door, but I put a hand on his shoulder and stopped him. "Hang on. There are some things you need to know."

Billy frowned, but he stopped, listening.

"These are faeries. We'll probably run into a lot of the Sidhe, their nobles, hanging out with the Winter Lady. That means that they're going to be dangerous and will probably try to entrap you."

"What do you mean, entrap me?" Billy said.

"Bargains," I said. "Deals. They'll try to offer you things, get you to trade one thing for another."

"Why?"

I shook my head. "I don't know. It's in their nature. The concept of debt and obligation is a huge factor in how they behave."

Billy lifted his eyebrows. "That's why that little guy worked for you, right? Because he owed you for the pizza and he had a debt to you."

"Right," I said. "But it can work both ways. If you owe *them* something, they have a conduit to you and can use magic against you. The basic rule is not to accept any gifts from them—and for God's sake, don't *offer* them any gifts. They find anything other than an equal exchange to be either enticing or insulting. It isn't a big deal with little guys like Toot, but if you get into it with a Sidhe Lord you might not live through it."

Billy shrugged. "Okay. No gifts. Dangerous faeries. Got it."

"I'm not finished. They aren't going to be offering you wrapped packages, man. These are the Sidhe. They're some of the most beautiful creatures there are. And they'll try to put you off balance and tempt you."

"Tempt me? Like with sex, is that what you're saying?"

"Like any kind of sensual indulgence. Sex, food, beauty, music, perfume. When they offer, don't accept it, or you'll be opening yourself up to a world of hurt."

Billy nodded. "Okay, got it. Let's go already."

I eyed the younger man, and he gave me an impatient look. I shook my head. I don't think I could have adequately conveyed the kind of danger we might be walking into with mere words in any case. I took a deep breath and then nodded to Elidee. "All right, Tinkerbell. Let's go."

The tiny scarlet light gave an irritated bob and then darted through the concealed doorway and into the darkness beyond. Billy narrowed his eyes and followed it, and I went after him. We found ourselves in a tunnel where one wall seemed to be made of ancient, moldering brick and the other of a mixture of rotting wooden beams, loose earth, and winding roots. The tunnel ran on out of the circle of light from my amulet. Our guide drifted forward, and we set out to follow her, walking close together.

The tunnel gave way to a sort of low-roofed cavern, supported here and there by pillars, mounds of collapsed earth, and beams that looked like they'd been added in afterward by the dwellers in Undertown. Elidee circled in place a bit uncertainly, then started floating to the right.

I hadn't been following the little faerie for five seconds before the skin on the back of my neck tried to crawl up over my head and hide in my mouth. I drew up short, and I must have made some kind of noise, because Billy shot a look back at me and asked, "Harry? What is it?"

I lifted a hand to silence him and peered at the darkness around me. "Keep your eyes open," I said. "I don't think we are alone."

From the shadows outside the light came a low hissing sound. The rest of my skin erupted in gooseflesh, and I shook my shield bracelet clear. I lifted my voice and said clearly, "I am the Wizard Dresden, Emissary of the Winter Court, bound to pay a call upon the Winter Lady. I've no time or desire for a fight. Stand clear and let me pass."

A voice—a voice that sounded like a tortured cat might, if some demented being gave it the gift of speech—mewled out of the shadows, grating on my ears. "We know who you are, wizard," the voice said. Its inflections were all wrong, and the tone seemed to come from not far above the ground, somewhere off to my right. Elidee let out a high-pitched shriek of terror and zipped back to me, diving into my hair. I felt the warmth of the light around the tiny faerie like a patch of sunlight on my scalp.

I traded a look with Billy and turned toward the source of the voice. "Who are you?"

"A servant of the Winter Lady," the voice replied from directly behind me. "Sent here to guide you safely through this realm and to her court."

I turned in the other direction and peered more closely toward the sound of the voice. The werelight from my amulet suddenly gleamed off a pair of animal eyes, twenty feet away and a few inches from the floor. I looked back at Billy. He'd already noted the eyes and turned to put his back to mine, watching the darkness behind us.

I turned back to the speaker and said, "I ask again. Who are you?"

The eyes shifted in place, the voice letting out an angry, growling sound. "Many names am I called, and many paths have I trod. Hunter I have been, and watcher, and guide. My Lady sent me to bring you thither, safe and whole and well."

"Don't get mad at me, Charlie," I snapped. "You know the drill as well as I do. Thrice I ask and done. Who are you?"

The voice came out harsh and sullen, barely intelligible. "Grimalkin am I called by the Cold Lady, who bids me guide her mother's Emissary with safe conduct to her court and her throne."

I let out a breath. "All right," I said. "So lead us."

The eyes bobbed in place, as though in a small bow, and Grimalkin mewled again. There was a faint motion in the shadows outside my light, and then a dull greenish glow appeared upon the ground. I stepped toward it and found a faint, luminous footprint upon the ground, a vague paw, feline but too spread out and too thin to be an actual cat's. Just as I reached it, another light appeared on the floor several feet away.

"Make haste, wizard," mewled Grimalkin's voice. "Make haste. The Lady waits. The season passes. Time is short."

I moved toward the second footprint, and as I reached it a third appeared before us, in the dark, and so on.

"What was that all about?" Billy murmured. "Asking it the same thing three times, I mean."

"It's a binding," I murmured in reply. "Faeries aren't allowed to speak a lie, and if a faerie says something three times, it has to make sure that it is true. It's bound to fulfill a promise spoken thrice."

"Ah," Billy said. "So even if this thing hadn't actually been sent to guide us safely, you made him say so three times would mean that he'd be obligated to do it. Got it."

I shook my head. "I wanted to make sure Grimalkin was on the level. But they hate being bound like that."

From ahead of us, the faintly glowing eyes appeared briefly, accompanied by another mewling growl that sent a chill down my spine.

"Oh," Billy said. He didn't look any too calm himself. His face had gone a little pale, and he walked with his hands clenched into fists. "So if Grimalkin had good intentions to begin with, wouldn't that make him angry that you needlessly bound him?"

I shrugged. "I'm not here to make friends, Billy. I'm here to find a killer."

"You've never even heard of diplomacy, have you?"

We followed the trail of footprints on the ground for another twenty minutes or so, through damp tunnels, sometimes only a few feet high. More sections of the tunnel showed evidence of recent construction—if you could call swirling layers of stone that seemed to have been smoothed into place like soft-serve ice cream "construction." We passed several tunnels that seemed entirely new. Whatever beings lived down here, they didn't seem too shy about expanding. "How much further?" I asked.

Grimalkin let out a *mrowl*ing sound from somewhere

nearby—not in the direction of the next footprint, either. "Very near, noble Emissary. Very near now."

The unseen faerie guide was good to its word. At the next glowing footprint, no other appeared. Instead, we came to a large, elaborately carved double doorway. Made of some black wood I could not identify, the doors were eight or nine feet high, and carved in rich bas-relief. At first I thought the carvings were of a garden theme—leaves, vines, flowers, fruit, that kind of thing. But as I walked closer to the door, I could see more detail in the light of my glowing amulet. The forms of people lay among the vines. Some sprawled amorously together, while others were nothing more than skeletons wrapped in creeping roses or corpses staring with sightless eyes from within a bed of poppies. Here and there in the garden one could see evidence of the Sidhe—a pair of eyes, a veiled figure, and their hangers-on, little faeries like Toot-toot, leaf-clad dryads, pipe-wielding satyrs, and many, many others hiding from the mortals' views, dancing.

"Nice digs," Billy commented. "Is this the place?"

I glanced around for our guide, but I didn't see any more footprints or any feline eyes. "I guess it must be."

"They aren't exactly subtle, are they?"

"Summer's better at it than Winter. But they all can be when it suits them."

"Uh-huh. You know what bothers me, Harry?"

"What?"

"Grimalkin never said he'd guide us out again."

I glanced back at Billy. Quiet, hissing laughter came out of the darkness, directionless. I took a deep breath. Steady, Harry. Don't let the kid see you get nervous. Then I turned to the door and struck it solidly with my fist, three times.

The blows rang out, hollow and booming. Silence fell on the tunnels for a long moment, until the doors split down the middle, and let out from behind them a flood of light and sound and color.

I don't know what I'd expected from the Winter Court, but it wasn't big-band music. A large brass section blared from somewhere behind the doors, and drums rattled and pounded with the rough, genuine sound of actual skins. The lights were colored and muted, as if the whole place was lit by Christmas strands, and I could see shadows whirling and moving inside—dancers.

"Careful," I muttered. "Don't let the music get to you." I stepped up to the great doors and passed through them.

The room could have come from a Roaring Twenties hotel.

Hell, it might have been, if the hotel had sunk into the earth, turned slightly upon its side, and been decorated by things with no concept of human values. Whatever it had once been, it had always been meant for dancing. The dance floor was made of blocks of rose-colored marble, and even though the floor was tilted, the blocks had been slipped to the level, here and there, creating something that looked almost like a flight of low, shallow stairs. Over the treacherous blocks danced the Winter Sidhe.

Beautiful didn't come close. It didn't start to come close. Men and women danced together, dressed in regalia of the 1940s. Stockings, knee-length skirts, dress uniforms of both the army and the navy that looked authentic to the month and year. The hairstyles in evidence corresponded as well, though the color didn't always match the setting. One Sidhe girl I saw wore hers dyed sapphire-blue, and others wore braids of silver and gold, or of other colors. Here and there, light gleamed from metal or gems set into ears, brows, or lips, and the riot of subtle colors gathered around each and every dancer in its own distinct, fascinating nimbus, a corona of energy, of power manifesting itself as the Sidhe danced.

Even without the whirling auras, the way they moved was something hypnotic in itself, and I had to force my eyes away from it after only a few seconds of lovely legs being displayed as a woman spun, body arched back underneath a strong man's hands, throats bared and breasts offered out, as hair caught the gleam of the colored lights and threw it back in waves of color. I couldn't look anywhere on the dance floor without seeing someone who should have been making fun of people on the covers of magazines for being too ugly.

Billy hadn't been as paranoid as me, and he stood staring at the dance floor, his eyes wide. I nudged him with my hip, hard enough to make his teeth clack together, and he jerked and gave me a guilty look.

I forced my eyes away from the dancers, maybe twenty couples all told, to check out the rest of the ballroom.

To one side of the room stood a bandstand, and the musicians on it all wore tuxes. They were mortals, human. They looked normal, which was to say almost deformed in comparison to the dancers they performed for. Both men and women played, and none of them looked well rested or well fed. Their tuxes were stained with sweat, their hair hung lank and unwashed, and a closer look showed a silver manacle bound around the ankle of each of them, attached to a chain that ran through the bandstand, winding back and forth among them. They didn't look upset, though—far from it. Every one of them was bent to the music, faces locked in intensity and concentration. And they were *good*, playing with the unity of tone and timing that you only see from bands who have really honed their art.

That didn't change the fact that they were prisoners of the fae. But they evidently had no particular problems with the notion. The music rattled the great stone room, shaking dust from the ceiling hidden in the darkness overhead while the Sidhe danced.

Opposite the bandstand, the dance floor descended directly into a pool of water—or what I presumed was water, at any rate. It looked black and unnaturally still. Even as I watched, the waters stirred, moved by something out of sight beneath the surface. Color rolled and rippled over the dark surface, and I got the distinct impression that the pool wasn't water. Or not just water. I fought down another shiver.

Beyond the dance floor, on the side of the room opposite me, stood raised tiers of platforms, each one set with a separate little table, one that could sit three or four at the most, each one with its own dim, green-shaded lamp. The tables all stood at different relative heights to one another, staggered back and forth—until the tiers reached a pinnacle, a single chair made out of what looked like silver, its flaring back carved into a sigil, a snowflake the size of a dinner table. The great chair stood empty.

The drummer on the bandstand went into a brief solo, and then the instruments cut off altogether—but for one. The other band members sagged into their seats, a couple of them simply collapsing onto the floor, but the lead trumpet stayed standing, belting out a solo while the Winter Lords danced. He was a middle-aged man, a little overweight, and his face flushed scarlet, then purple as his trumpet rang out through the solo.

Then, all at once, the Sidhe stopped dancing. Dozens of beautiful faces turned to watch the soloist, eyes glittering in the muted light.

The man continued to play, but I could see that something was wrong. The flush of his face deepened even more, and veins began to throb in his forehead and throat. His eyes widened and began to bulge, and he started shaking. A moment later the music began to falter. The man tore his face away from the trumpet, and I could see him gasping for breath. He couldn't get it. A second later he jerked, then stiffened, and his eyes rolled up in his head. The trumpet slipped from his fingers, and he fell, first to his knees and then limply over onto his side, to the floor of the bandstand. He hit with finality, his eyes open but not focused. He twitched once more, and then his throat rattled and he was still.

A murmur went through the Sidhe, and I looked back to see them parting, stepping aside with deep bows and curtseys for someone emerging from their midst. A tall girl walked slowly toward the fallen musician. Her features were pale, radiant, perfect—and looked like an adolescent copy of Mab's. That was where the resemblance ended.

She looked young. Young enough to make a man feel guilty for thinking the wrong thoughts, but old enough to make it difficult not to. Her hair had been bound into long dreadlocks, each of them dyed a different shade, ranging from a deep lavender to pale blues and greens to pure white, so that it almost seemed that her hair had been formed from glacial ice. She wore leather pants of dark, dark blue, laced and open up the outside seams from calf to hip. Her boots matched the pants. She wore a white T-shirt tight enough to show the tips of her breasts straining against the fabric, framing the words OFF WITH HIS HEAD. She had hacked the shirt off at the top of her rib cage, leaving pale flesh exposed, along with a glitter of silver flashing at her navel.

She moved to the downed musician with a liquid grace, a thoughtless, casual sensuality that made a quiver of arousal slip down my spine. She settled down over him, throwing a leg over his hips, straddling him, and idly raked long, opalescent fingernails over his chest. He didn't move. Didn't breathe.

The girl licked her lips, her mouth spreading into a lazy smile, before she leaned down and kissed the corpse's dead lips. I saw her shiver with what was unmistakably pleasure. "There," she murmured. "There, you see? Never let it be said the Lady Maeve does not fulfill her promises. You said you'd die to play that well, poor creature. And now you have."

A collective sigh went up from the assembled Sidhe, and then they began applauding enthusiastically. Maeve looked back over her shoulder at them all with a lifted chin and a lazy smile before she stood up and bowed, left and right, to the sound of applause. The applause died off when Maeve stalked away from the corpse and to the rising tiers of dinner seats, stepping lithely up them until she reached the great silver throne at the top. She dropped into it, turned sideways, and idly threw her legs over one arm, arching her back and stretching with that same lazy smile. "My lords and ladies, let us give our poor musical brutes a little time to recover their strength. We have a visitor."

The Sidhe began drifting toward the tables on the tiers, stepping into place one by one. I stood where I was and said nothing, though as they settled down I became increasingly conscious of their attention, of the glittering intensity of immortal eyes upon me.

Once they were all settled in, I stepped forward and walked across the dance floor until I stood at the foot of the tier. I looked up at Maeve and inclined my head to her. "Lady Winter, I presume."

Maeve smiled at me, showing a dimple, and gave one foot a girlish bounce. "Indeed."

"You know in what capacity I am here, Lady?"

"Naturally."

I nodded. Nothing like a frontal assault, then. "Did you arrange the murder of the Summer Knight?"

Silence fell on the room. The regard of the Winter Sidhe grew more intent, more uncomfortable.

Maeve's mouth spread into a slow smile, which in turn became a quiet, rolling laugh. She let her head fall back with it, and the Sidhe joined in with her. They sat there laughing at me for a good thirty seconds, and I felt my face begin to heat up with irrational embarrassment before Meave waved one hand in a negligent gesture and the laughter obediently died away.

"Stars," she murmured, "I adore mortals."

I clenched my jaw. "That's swell," I said. "Did you arrange the murder of the Summer Knight?"

"If I had, do you really think I would tell you?"

"You're evading," I growled. "Answer the question."

Maeve lifted a fingertip to her lips as though she needed it to hold in more laughter. Then she smiled and said, "I can't just give you that kind of information, Wizard Dresden. It's too powerful."

"What is that supposed to mean?"

She sat up, crossing her legs with a squeak of leather, and settled back on the throne. "It means that if you want me to answer that question, you're going to have to pay for it. What is the answer worth to you?"

I folded my arms. "I assume you have something in mind. That's why you sent someone to give us safe passage here."

"Quick," she murmured. "I like that. Yes, I do, wizard." She extended a hand to me and gestured to an open seat at the table to the right and a little beneath the level of her throne. "Please sit down," she said. Her teeth shone white. "Let's make a deal."

Chapter Fifteen

"You want me to cut another deal with the Sidhe," I said. I didn't bother to hide my disbelief. "When I burst out laughing at you, do you think you'll be offended?"

"And why should you find the notion amusing?"

I rolled my eyes. "Christ, lady, that's what got me into this crap to begin with."

Maeve's lips slithered into a quiet smile, and she left her hand extended, toward the seat beside her. "Remember, wizard, that you came to seek something from me. Surely it would not harm you to listen to my offer."

"I've heard that before. Usually right before I get screwed."

Maeve touched the tip of her tongue to her lips. "One thing at a time, Mister Dresden."

I snorted. "Suppose I don't want to listen."

Something in her eyes suddenly made her face cold and unpleasant. "I think it might be wise for you to indulge me. I simply go mad when someone ruins a good party mood."

"Harry," Billy muttered, "these people are giving me the creeps. If she's playing games with you, maybe we should go."

I grimaced. "Yeah, that would be the smart thing. But it wouldn't get me any answers. Come on."

I stepped forward and started climbing up to the table Maeve had indicated. Billy followed closely. Maeve watched me the whole time, her eyes sparkling.

"There," she said, once I'd been seated. "Not so untamable as he claimed."

I felt my jaw get a little tighter as Billy took a seat beside me.

A trio of brightly colored lights zipped in, bearing a silver tray holding a crystalline ewer of water and two glasses. "As who said?"

Maeve waved a hand airily. "No matter."

I glared at her, but she didn't seem bothered. "All right, Lady," I said. "Talk."

Maeve idly stretched out a hand. A goblet of some golden liquid appeared in her fingers and rimed over with frost as I watched. She took a sip of the drink, whatever it was, and then said, "First, I will name my price."

"There'd better be a blue light special. I don't have much to trade, all things considered."

"True. I cannot ask for a claim over you, because Queen Mab has that already. But let me see." She tapped a fingernail to her lips again and then said, "Your issue."

"Eh?" I said, glibly.

"Your issue, wizard," she said, toying with a violet dreadlock. "Your offspring. Your firstborn. And in exchange I will give you the knowledge you seek."

"News flash, Coldilocks. I don't have any children."

Maeve laughed. "Naturally not. But the details could be arranged."

Evidently that was a cue. The dark pool of maybe-water stirred, drawing my eye. Ripples whispered as they lapped at the edges of the pool.

"What's that?" Billy whispered to me.

The waters parted, and a Sidhe girl rose out of the pool. She was tall, slender, water sliding down over pale, naked, supple curves. Her hair was a deep shade of emerald green, and as she kept on coming up out of the water, walking up what were apparently submerged stairs, I could tell that it wasn't dyed. Her face was sweetly angelic, sort of girl-next-door pretty. Her hair clung to her head, her throat, her shoulders, as did beads of water that glistened and threw back the fae-lights in dozens of colors. She extended her arms, and immediately half a dozen little lights, pixies, zipped out of nowhere, bearing a swath of emerald silk. They draped it over her extended arms, but the cloth served to emphasize, rather than conceal, her nakedness. She looked up at the tables with her feline fae-eyes and inclined her head to Maeve. Then she focused upon me.

There was an abrupt pulling sensation, something as simple and as difficult to resist as gravity. I felt a sudden urge to get up and go down to her, to remove the silk cloth and to carry her into the water. I wanted to see her hair fan out beneath the surface, feel her naked limbs sliding around me. I wanted to feel that slender waist beneath my hands, twist and writhe with her in the warm, weightless darkness of the pool.

Beside me, Billy gulped. "Is it just me, or is it getting a little warm in here?"

"She's pushing it on you," I said quietly. My lips felt a little numb. "It's glamour. It isn't real."

"Okay," Billy said without conviction. "It isn't real."

He reached for a glass and the ewer of water, but I grabbed his hand. "No. No food. No drink. It's dangerous."

Billy cleared his throat and settled back in his seat. "Oh. Right. Sorry."

The girl glided up the tiers of tables, glittering pixies in darting attendance around her, gathering her hair back with ornate combs, fastening gleaming jewels to her ears, lacing more about her throat, wrist, ankle. I couldn't help but follow the motion of the lights, which took my eyes on a thorough tour of her body. The urge to go to her became even stronger as she neared, as I smelled her perfume, a scent like that of the mist hovering over a still lake beneath a harvest moon.

The green-haired woman smiled, lips closed, then drew up in a deep curtsey to Maeve, and murmured "My Lady."

Maeve reached out and took her hand, warmly. "Jen," she murmured. "Are you acquainted with the infamous Harry Dresden?"

Jen smiled, and her teeth gleamed between her lips. They were as green as seaweed, spinach, and fresh-steamed broccoli. "Only by reputation." She turned to me and extended her hand, arching one verdant brow.

I gave Billy a self-conscious glance and rose to take the Sidhe-lady's hand. I nudged Billy's foot with mine and he stood up too.

I bowed politely over Jen's hand. Her fingers were cool, damp. I got the impression that her flawless skin should have been prune-wrinkled, but it wasn't. I had to fight an urge to kiss the back of her hand, to taste her cool flesh. I managed to keep a neutral tone to my voice and said, "Good evening."

The Sidhe-lady smiled at me, showing her green teeth again, and said, "Something of a gentleman. I wouldn' have expected it." She withdrew her hand and said. "And tall." Her eyes roamed over me in idle speculation. "I like tall men."

I felt my cheeks flush and grow warmer. Other part suffered from similar inflammation.

Maeve asked, "Is she lovely enough to suit you, wizard? You've no idea how many mortal men have longer for her. And how few have known her embrace."

Jen let out a quiet laugh. "For more than about three minutes, at any rate."

Maeve drew Jen down until the nearly nude Sidhe lady knelt beside the throne. Maeve toyed with a strand of her curling, leaf-green hair with one hand. "Why not agree to my offer, wizard? Spend a night in the company of my maiden. Is it not a pleasant price?"

My voice came out more quietly than I'd intended. "You want me to get a child on her. A child you would keep."

Maeve's eyes glittered. She leaned toward me and said, very quietly, "Do not let that concern you. I can feel your hunger, mortal man. The needs in you. Hot as a fever. Let go for a time. No mortal could sate you as she will."

I felt my eyes drawn to the Sidhe woman, trailing down the length of pale flesh left bared between the idle drapes of emerald silk, following the length of her legs. That hunger rose again in me, a raw and unthinking need. Scent flooded over me—a perfume of wind and mist, of heated flesh. Scent evoked more phantom sensations of the silken caress of delicate fae-hands, sweetly hot rake of nails, winding strength of limbs tangled with mine.

Maeve's eyes brightened. "Perhaps she is not enough for you? Perhaps you would wish another. Even myself." As I watched, Jen leaned her cheek against Maeve's thigh and placed a soft kiss upon the tight leather. Maeve shifted, a slow, sensual motion of her hips and back, and murmured, "Mmmm. Or more, if your thirst runs deep enough. Drive a hard bargain, wizard. All of us would enjoy that."

The longing, an aching force of naked need, redoubled. The two faeries were lovely. More than lovely. Sensuous. Willing. Perfectly unrestrained, perfectly passionate. I could feel that in them, radiating from them. If I made the bargain, they *would* make the evening one of nothing but indulgence, sensation, satiation, delight. Maeve and her handmaiden would do things to me that you only read about in magazines.

"Dear *Penthouse*," I muttered, "I never thought something like this would happen to me . . ."

"Wizard," Maeve murmured, "I see you weighing the conse-quences in your eyes. You think too much. It weakens you. Stop thinking. Come down into the earth with us."

Some mathematical and uncaring part of my brain way the hell in the back of my head reminded me that I *did* need that in-formation. A simple statement from Maeve would tell me if she was the killer or not. *Go ahead*, it told me. *It isn't as though it's going to be painful for you to pay her price. Don't you deserve to have something pleasant happen to you for a change? Make the bargain. Get the information. Get wasted on kisses and pleasure and soft skin. Live a little—before that borrowed time you're on runs out.*

I reached out with a shaking hand to the crystal ewer on the table. I clenched it. It clinked and rattled against the glass as I poured cool, sparkling water into it.

Maeve's smile grew sharper.

"Harry," Billy said, his voice uncertain. "Didn't you just say something bad about—you know, taking food or drink from fa—uh, from these people?"

I put the pitcher down and picked up the glass of water.

Jen rubbed her cheek against Maeve's thigh and murmured, "They never really change, do they?"

"No," Maeve said. "The males all fall to the same thing. Isn't it delicious?"

I unbuttoned the fly in my jeans, undid the zipper a little, and dumped the cold water directly down my pants.

Some shocks of sensation are pleasant. This one wasn't. The water was so cold that tiny chips of ice had formed in it, as though it was trying to freeze itself from the inside out. That cold went right down where I had intended it to go, and everything in my jeans tried to contract into my abdomen in sheer, hypothermic horror. I let out a little yelp, and my skin promptly crawled with gooseflesh.

The gesture had its intended effect. That overwhelming, al-most feral hunger withered and vanished. I was able to take my eyes off the Winter Lady and her handmaiden, to clear my thoughts into something resembling a sane line of reason. I shook my head a bit to be sure and then looked up at Maeve. Anger surged through me, and my jaw clenched tight, but I made an ef-fort to keep my words at least marginally polite. "Sorry, sweetie, but I have a couple problems with that offer."

Maeve's lips tightened. "And those would be?"

"One. I'm not handing over a child to you. Not mine, not anyone's, not now, and not ever. If you had a brain in your head, you'd have known that."

Maeve's already pale face blanched even more, and she sat bolt upright on her throne. "You *dare*—"

"Shut up," I snarled, and it came out loud enough to ring off the walls of the ballroom. "I'm not finished."

Maeve jerked as though I'd slapped her. Her mouth dropped open, and she blinked at me.

"I came here under your invitation and protection. I am your *guest*. But in spite of that you've thrown glamour at me anyway." I stood up, my hands spread on the table, leaning toward her for emphasis. "I don't have time for this crap. You don't scare me, lady," I said. "I only came here for answers—but if you keep pushing me, I'm going to push back. Hard."

Maeve's evident anger evaporated. She leaned back on her throne, lips pursed, her expression placid and enigmatic. "Well, well, well. Not so easily captured, it would seem."

A new voice, a relaxed, masculine drawl, slid into the silence. "I told you, Maeve. You should have been polite. Anyone who declares war on the Red Court isn't going to be the sort to take kindly to pressure." The speaker stepped into the ballroom through the double doors and walked casually to the banquet tables and toward Maeve's throne.

It was a man, maybe in his early thirties, medium build, maybe half an inch shy of six feet tall. He wore dark jeans, a white tee, and a leather jacket. Droplets of dark reddish brown stained the shirt and one side of his face. His scalp was bald but for a stubble of dark hair.

As he approached, I picked out more details. He had a brand on his throat. A snowflake made of white scar tissue stood out sharply against his skin. The skin on one side of his face was red and a little swollen, and he was missing half of the eyebrow and a crescent of the stubble on his scalp on that side—he'd been burned, and recently. He reached the throne and dropped to one knee before it, somehow conveying a certain relaxed insolence with the gesture, and extended the box to Maeve.

"It is done?" Maeve asked, an almost childlike eagerness in her voice. "What took you so long?"

"It wasn't as easy as you said it would be. But I did it."

The Winter Lady all but snatched the carved box from his hands, avarice lighting her eyes. "Wizard, this is my Knight, Lloyd of the family Slate."

Slate nodded to me. "How are you?"

"Impatient," I responded, but I nodded back to him warily. "You're the Winter Knight?"

"So far, yeah. I guess you're the Winter Emissary. Asking questions and investigating and so on."

"Yep. Did you kill Ronald Reuel?"

Slate burst out laughing. "Christ, Dresden. You don't waste time, do you?"

"I've filled my insincere courtesy quota for the day," I said. "Did you kill him?"

Slate shrugged and said, "No. To be honest with you, I'm not sure I *could* have killed him. He's been at this a lot longer than me."

"He was an old man," I said.

"So are a lot of wizards," Slate pointed out. "I could have bench-pressed him, sure. Killing him is something else altogether."

Maeve let out a sudden hiss of anger, the sound eerily loud. She lifted her foot and kicked Slate in the shoulder. Something popped when she did, and the force of the kick drove the Winter Knight down a tier, into the table and the Sidhe seated there. The table toppled, and Sidhe, chairs, and Knight went sprawling.

Maeve rose to her feet, sending the green-toothed Jen scooting away from her. She drew what looked like a military-issue combat knife from the carved box. It was crusted with some kind of black gelatinous substance, like burned barbecue sauce. "You stupid animal," she snarled. "Useless. This is useless to me."

She hurled the knife at Slate. The handle hit him in the biceps of his left arm just as he sat up again. His face twisted in sudden fury. He took up the knife, rose to his feet, and stalked toward Maeve with murder in his eye.

Maeve drew herself up, her face shining with a sudden terrible beauty. She lifted her right hand, ring finger and thumb both bent, and murmured something in a liquid, alien tongue. Sudden blue light gathered around her fingers, and the temperature in the room dropped by about forty degrees. She spoke again, and flicked her wrist, sending glowing motes of azure flickering toward Slate.

The snowflake brand flared into sudden light, and Slate's advance halted, his body going rigid. The skin around the brand turned blue, then purple, then black, spreading like a stop-motion enhanced film of gangrene. A quiet snarl slipped from Slate's lips, and I could see his body trembling with the effort to continue toward Maeve. He shuddered and took another step forward.

Maeve lifted her other hand, her index finger extended while the others curled, and a sudden wind whipped past me, cold enough that it stole the breath from my lungs. The wind whipped madly around Slate, making his leather coat flap. Bits of white frost started forming on his eyelashes and eyebrows. His expression, now anguished as well as full of rage, faltered, and his advance halted again.

"Calm him," Maeve murmured.

Jen slipped behind Slate, wrapping her arms around his neck, leaning her mouth down close to his ear. Slate's eyes flickered with hot, violent hate for a moment, and then began to grow heavier. Jen ran her hand slowly down the sleeve of his jacket, fingers caressing his wrist. His arm lowered as I watched. A moment later, Jen slid the jacket from his shoulders. The tee was sleeveless, and Slate's arms were hard with muscle—and tracked with needle marks. Jen held out a hand, and another darting pixie handed her a hypodermic needle. Jen slipped it into the bend of his arm, still whispering to him, sliding the plunger slowly down.

Slate's eyes rolled back in his head, and he sank to his knees. Jen went down with him, wrapped around him like kelp on a swimmer, her mouth next to his ear.

Maeve lowered her hands, and the wind and the cold died away. She lifted a shaking hand to her face and stepped back to the throne, settling stiffly onto it, narrowed eyes locked on Slate's increasingly malleable form. Her cheekbones stood out more sharply than before, her eyes looked more sunken. She gripped the arms of the throne, her fingers twitching.

"What the hell was that?" Billy whispered.

"Probably what passes for a polite disagreement," I muttered. "Get up. We're leaving."

I stood up. Maeve's eyes darted to me. Her voice came out dry, harsh. "Our bargain is not complete, wizard."

"This talk is."

"But I have not answered your question."

"Keep your answer. I don't need it anymore."

"You don't?" Maeve asked.

"We don't?" Billy said.

I nodded toward Slate and Jen. "You had to push yourself to make him stand still. Look at you. You're just about out of gas right now from going up against your own Knight." I started down the tiers, Billy coming with me. "Besides that, you're sloppy, sweetheart. Reckless. A clean killing like Reuel's takes a plan, and that isn't you."

I could feel her eyes pressing against my back like frozen thorns. I ignored her.

"I did not give you leave to go, wizard," she said, her voice chilly.

"I didn't ask."

"I won't forget this insolence."

"I probably will," I said. "It's nothing special. Come on, Billy."

I walked to the double doors and out. As soon as we were both outside, the doors swung shut with a huge, hollow boom that made me jump. Darkness fell, sudden and complete, and I fumbled for my amulet as my heart lurched in panic.

The spectral light from my amulet showed me Billy's strained face first, and then the area immediately around us. The double doors were gone. Only a blank stone wall remained where they had been.

"Gulp," Billy said. He shook his head for a moment, dazed. "Where did they go?"

I rested my fingers against the stone wall, reaching out for it with my wizard's senses. Nothing. It was rock, not illusion. "Beats the hell out of me. The doors here must have been a way to some other location."

"Like some kind of teleport?"

"More like a temporary entrance into the Nevernever," I said. "Or a shortcut through the Nevernever to another place on Earth."

"Kind of intense in there. When she made it get all cold. I've never seen anything like that before."

"Sloppy," I said. "She was laying a binding on Slate. Her power was sloshing over into changing the temperature. A child could do better."

Billy let out a short, quiet laugh. "After what we just saw, anyone else would still be shaking. You're giving her the rating from the Russian judge."

"So sue me." I shrugged. "She's strong. Strong isn't everything."

Billy glanced up at me. "Could you do what she did?"

"I'd probably use fire."

His eyebrows went up, his expression impressed. "Do you really think Maeve's not the killer?"

"I do," I said. "This murder was clean enough to look like an accident. Maeve's obviously got impulse-control issues. Doesn't make for much of a methodical murderer."

"What about Slate?"

I shook my head, my brow tightening. "Not sure about him. He's mortal. There's nothing that says he couldn't lie to us. But I got what I was looking for, and I found out a couple of things on top of that."

"So why are you frowning?"

"Because all I got was more questions. Everyone's been telling me to hurry. Faeries don't do that. They're practically immortal and they're not in a rush. But Mab and Grimalkin both have tried to rush me now. Maeve went for the high-pressure sales tactic too, like she didn't have time for anything more subtle."

"Why would they do that?"

I sighed. "Something's in motion. If I don't run down the killer, the Courts could go to war with one another."

"That would explain the whole World War Two dress motif back there."

"Yeah, but not why time would be so pressing." I shook my head. "If we could have stayed longer, I might have been able to work out more, but it was getting too nervous in there."

"Discretion, valor," Billy said by way of agreement. "We leave now, right?"

"Elidee?" I asked. I felt a stirring in my hair, and then the tiny pixie popped out to hover in the air in front of me. "Can you lead us back to my car?"

The pixie flashed in the affirmative and zipped away. I lifted my amulet and followed.

Billy and I didn't speak until our guide had led us out of the underground complex not far from where I'd parked the Blue Beetle. We cut through an alley.

About halfway down it, Billy grabbed my arm and jerked me bodily behind him, snapping, "Harry, get back!"

In the same motion he swung out one foot and kicked a metal trash can. It went flying, crashing into something I hadn't seen behind it. Someone let out a short, harsh gasp of pain. Billy stepped forward and picked up the metal lid that had fallen to the ground. He swung it down at the shape. It struck with a noisy crash.

I took a couple of steps back to make sure I was clear of the action, and reached for my amulet again. "Billy," I said, "what the hell?"

I felt the sudden presence at my back half a second too late to get out of the way. A hand the size of a dinner plate closed on the back of my neck like a vice and lifted. I felt my heels rise until my toes were just barely touching the ground.

A voice, a feminine contralto, growled, "Let go of the amulet and call him off, wizard. Call him off before I break your neck."

Chapter Sixteen

❖❖ ❖❖

Being held up by your neck hurts. Trust me on this one. I lifted my hands by way of attempting to convey compliance and said, "Billy, get off him."

Billy took a step back from the pale-haired young man he'd knocked down. Fix whimpered and scuttled away on his hands and butt. His borrowed brown suit was soiled and torn, and his yellow polyester tie hung from his collar by only one of its clips. He put his back against the alley wall, eyes wide beneath his shock of white dandelion hair.

Billy's eyes flicked from my assailant to Fix and back. He squinted at her for a moment, then set his jaw in an expression of casual determination. "Harry? You want me to take her?"

"Wait a minute," I managed to say. "Okay, he's off. Put me down."

The grip on the back of my neck relaxed, and as I touched ground again I took a step toward Billy, turning to face the woman who had held me.

As I expected, it was the tall, muscular young woman from the funeral home, her muddy green hair hanging lankly over her eyes and one cheek. She folded her arms and shifted her weight from one foot to the other. "Fix? Are you okay?"

The smaller man panted, "My lip is cut. It isn't bad."

The woman nodded and faced me again.

"All right," I said. "Who the hell are you?"

"My name's Meryl," she said. Her voice was surprisingly quiet, contrasting with her size. "I wanted to apologize to you, Mr. Dresden. For hitting you and throwing you into the Dumpster."

I raised my eyebrows. "Are you sure you got the right guy, Meryl? No one ever apologizes to me for anything."

She pushed at her hair with one hand. It fell right back over her face. "I'm sorry. I was scared earlier, and I acted without thinking."

I traded a glance with Billy. "Uh, okay. I'm pretty sure lurking in a dark alley to mug me with your apology isn't the usual way to go about saying you're sorry. But I didn't read that Mars-Venus book, so who knows."

Her mouth twitched, and she relaxed her stance by a tiny degree. "I didn't know how else to find you, so I was just waiting near your car."

"Okay," I said. My neck still throbbed where her fingers had clamped on. Five to one I would have wonderful stripy bruises the next day. I nodded and turned away. "Apology accepted. Now if you'll excuse me, I have things I need to do."

A note of panic crept into her voice. "Wait. Please."

I stopped and looked back at her.

"I need to talk to you. Just for a minute." She took a deep breath. "I need your help."

Of course she did.

"It's very important."

Of course it was.

The headache started coming back. "Look, Meryl, I've got a lot on my plate already."

"I know," she said. "Investigating Ron's death. I think I can help you."

I pursed my lips. "You were close to Reuel?"

She nodded. "Me. Fix. Ace. And Lily."

I flashed back on the photo of Reuel and the four young people. "Green-haired girl? Very cute?"

"Yes."

"Where's Ace?"

"He had to go to work right after the funeral. But Lily's why I need to talk to you. She's missing. I think she's in trouble."

I started filling in context on the conversation I'd overheard between them. "Who are you?"

"I told you. My name is Meryl."

"Okay, fine. *What* are you, Meryl?"

She flinched at the question. "Oh. I'm sorry, I didn't know what you meant." She raked at her hair again. "I'm a changeling. We all are."

"A what?" Billy asked.

I nodded, getting it. "Changeling," I said to Billy. "She's half mortal and half fae."

"Aha," Billy said. "Which means what?"

I shrugged. "It means that she has to choose whether to remain a mortal or become wholly fae."

"Yes," she said. "And until then I'm under the rule of the Court of my fae father. Winter. The others too. That's why the four of us stuck together. It was safer."

Billy nodded. "Oh."

"Meryl," I said, "what makes you think your friend is in trouble?"

"She's not very independent, Mister Dresden. We share an apartment. She doesn't have a very good idea of how to take care of herself, and she gets nervous if she's out of the apartment for too long."

"And what do you think happened to her?"

"The Winter Knight."

Billy frowned. "Why would he hurt people in his own Court?"

Meryl let out a brief, hard laugh. "Because he can. He had a thing for Lily. He would hurt her, frighten her. He got off on it. He was furious when Maeve told him to back off. And once Ron was gone . . ." Her voice trailed off and she turned her head to one side.

"How does Reuel fit into this?" I asked.

"He was protecting us. Maeve had been torturing us for fun, and we didn't know where to turn. Ron took us in. He put us under his protection, and no one in Winter was willing to cross him."

"What about your fae dad?" Billy asked. "Didn't he do anything to look out for you?"

Meryl gave Billy a flat look. "My mother was raped by a troll. Even if he'd been strong enough to do anything about Maeve hurting us, he wouldn't have. He thinks he's already done enough by not devouring my mom on the spot."

"Oh," Billy said. "Sorry."

I frowned. "And with the Summer Knight gone, you think Slate grabbed the girl."

Meryl said, "Someone broke into the apartment. It looked like there had been a struggle."

I let out a sigh. "Have you contacted the police?"

She eyed me. "Oh, yeah, of course. I called them and told them that a mortal champion of the fae came and spirited away a half-mortal, half-nixie professional nude model to Faerieland. They were all over it."

I had to admire the well-placed sarcasm. "It doesn't take a supernatural studmuffin to cause something very bad to happen to a cute girl in this town. Your plain old mortal kidnappers and murderers can manage just fine."

She shook her head. "Either way, she's still in trouble."

I lifted a hand. "What do you want from me?"

"Help me find her. Please, Mister Dresden."

I closed my eyes. I didn't have time, energy, or brain power to spare for this. The smart thing would be to blow her off entirely, or to promise her I'd do it and promptly forget about it. "This just isn't a good time." I felt like crap the second I said it. I didn't look at the changeling's face. I couldn't. "There's too much trouble already, and I don't even know if I can help myself, much less your friend. I'm sorry."

I turned to go, but Meryl stepped in front of me. "Wait."

"I told you," I said. "There's nothing I can—"

"I'll pay you," Meryl said.

Oh, right. Money.

I was about to lose the office and the apartment, and this faerie work only paid in misery. I needed to pay some bills. Go to the grocery store. My mouth didn't actually water, but it was close.

I shook my head again. "Look, Meryl, I wish I could—"

"Double your fee," she said, her voice urgent.

Double. My. Fee. I hesitated some more.

"Triple," she said. She reached for her back pocket and produced an envelope. "Plus one thousand cash, up front, right now."

I looked back at Fix, still trembling and leaning against the alley wall, a handkerchief pressed to his mouth. Meryl continued to rock from one foot to the other, her eyes on the ground, waiting.

I tried to look at things objectively. A thousand bucks wouldn't spend if I got myself killed while distracted by the additional workload. On the other hand, if I lived through this thing the money would be necessary. My stomach growled, and a sharp pang of hunger made me clench the muscles of my belly.

I needed the work—but more to the point, I needed to be able to live with myself. I wasn't sure I was comfortable with the idea of looking back on this particular patch of memory and seeing myself leave some helpless girl, changeling or not, to the metaphoric wolves. People don't ask me for help if they're anything less than desperate. The changelings had been terrified of me only a few hours before. If they had turned to me for help now, it was because they were out of options.

And they also had money.

"Dammit, dammit, dammit," I muttered. I snatched the envelope. "All right. I'll look into it and do what I can—but I can't make you any promises."

Meryl let out a shuddering breath. "Thank you. Thank you, Mr. Dresden."

"Yeah," I sighed. I reached into my pocket and pulled out a slightly crumpled business card. "Here's my office number. Call and leave a message to let me know how I can reach you."

She took the card and nodded. "I don't know if I can pay your fees all at once. But I'll be good for it, even if it takes a while."

"We can worry about that later, when we're all safe and sound," I said. I nodded to her, then to Fix, and started walking down the alley again. Billy kept an eye on the pair of them and followed me.

We reached the parking lot of the funeral home a few minutes later. The lights were all out, and the Blue Beetle was the only car left in the lot. No one had bothered to steal it. What a shock.

"So what's next?" Billy asked.

"I'll call Murphy. See what she can tell me about Lloyd Slate."

Billy nodded. "Anything I can do to help?"

"Actually, yeah," I said. "Get out the phone book and call the hospitals. See if the morgues have a green-haired Jane Doe."

"You think she's dead, then?"

"I think it would be a lot simpler if she was."

He grimaced. "Calling morgues? There must be about a million of them in Chicagoland. Isn't there anything else I could do?"

"Welcome to the glamorous world of private investigation. You want to help or not?"

"Okay, okay," Billy said. "My car's a block over. I'll get back to you as soon as I'm done making calls."

"All right. I'll probably be at my place, but if not you know the drill."

Billy nodded. "Be careful." Then he walked quickly down the street without looking back.

I fumbled my keys out and walked to the Beetle.

I didn't smell the blood until I was close enough to touch the car. Through the window I saw a form, more or less human-shaped, curled up on my passenger seat. I circled cautiously to the other side of the car, then abruptly opened the door.

Elaine fell out of the car onto the pavement of the parking lot. She was drenched in blood that had soaked through her T-shirt, matted her golden-brown hair on one side, and run down her flanks to saturate her jeans to mid thigh. Her silver pentacle shone with liquid scarlet. The bare skin of her forearms was covered with long slashes and blood, and her face looked white. Dead.

My heart hammered in my chest, and I leaned down to her, fumbling at her throat. She still had a very slow pulse, but her skin felt cool and waxy. She started shuddering and whispered, "Harry?"

"I'm here. I'm here, Elaine."

"Please," she whispered. "Oh, God, please help me."

Chapter Seventeen

I laid Elaine out, first thing, and tried to determine the extent of her injuries. Her forearms had been laced open in several places, but the worst injury was on her back, just inside of her left clavicle—a nasty puncture wound. The edges of it had puckered closed, but it hadn't stopped the bleeding completely, and if she was bleeding internally she could be done for.

I would need both hands to put pressure on the wound. No help was on the way. There was little I could do for her, so I picked her up and put her back into the Beetle, then jumped in myself and started the ignition.

"Hang in there, Elaine," I said. "I'm getting you to a hospital. You're going to be all right."

She shook her head. "No. No, too dangerous."

"You're hurt too badly for me to take care of it," I said. "Relax. I'll be with you."

She opened her eyes and said with sudden, surprising insistence, "No hospitals. They'll find me there."

I started up the car. "Dammit, Elaine. What else am I supposed to do?"

She closed her eyes again. Her voice grew fainter by the word. "Aurora. Summer. Rothchild Hotel. There's an elevator in back. She'll help."

"The Summer Lady?" I demanded. "You're joking, right?"

She didn't answer me. I looked over at her, and my heart all but stopped as I saw her head lolling, her body slumped. I jammed the Beetle into gear and jounced out onto the road.

"Rothchild Hotel," I muttered. "More faeries. Keen."

I got us to the hotel, one of the nice places along the shores of Lake Michigan. I skipped the huge valet-littered front drive and zipped the Beetle into the back parking lot, looking for some kind of service drive, or freight elevator, or maybe just a door with a sign on it that said, SUMMER COURT OF THE FAERIES THIS WAY.

I felt a slight warmth on my ear, and then Elidee zoomed out in front of my face and bumped up against the window. I rolled the window down a bit, and the tiny faerie streaked out ahead of my car, guiding me to the back of the lot. She stopped, circling an unobtrusive, unlit breezeway. Then she sped away, her task evidently completed.

I quickly parked the car and set the brake. Elaine may have been slender, but she had too much muscle to be light. She'd always had the build of a long-distance runner, long and lean and strong. She was only just conscious enough to make it a little easier for me to carry her, wrapping her arms around my neck and leaning her head on my shoulder. She trembled and felt cold. Doubt gnawed at me as I took her down the breezeway. Maybe I should have ignored her and gone to the hospital.

I kept going until it became too dark to see, and I started to put Elaine down so that I could take out my amulet to make some light. Just as I did, a pair of elevator doors swept open, spilling light and canned music onto the breezeway.

A girl stood in the doors. She was five nothing, a hundred and nothing, her sunny hair pulled back into a braid. She wore a blue T-shirt with white painter's overalls, and she was liberally splattered with flecks of what looked like clay. Her rosy mouth opened in dismay as she saw me standing there with Elaine.

"Oh, no!" she exclaimed. She beckoned me urgently. "Come on, get her inside. The Lady can see to her."

My arms and shoulders had begun to burn with the effort of supporting Elaine, so I didn't waste time talking. I shuffled forward into the elevator and leaned against the back wall with a wheeze. The girl closed the elevator doors, took a key from her overalls pocket, and inserted it into a solitary keyhole where you would expect a bunch of buttons to be. The elevator gave a little lurch and started up.

"What happened to Ela?" the girl asked me. She looked from me to Elaine and chewed on one lip.

Ela? "Beats me. I found her like this in my car. She told me to bring her here."

"Oh. Oh, God," the girl said. She looked at me again. "You're with Winter, aren't you?"

I frowned. "How did you know?"

She shrugged. "It shows."

"I'm with Winter for now. But it's a one-shot deal. Think of me as a free agent."

"Perhaps. But an agent of Winter all the same. Are you sure you want to be here?"

"No," I said. "But I'm sure I'm not leaving Elaine until I'm convinced she's in good hands."

The girl frowned. "Oh."

"Can't this thing go any faster?" My shoulders burned, my back ached, my bruises were complaining, and I could feel Elaine's breathing growing weaker. I had to fight not to scream in sheer frustration. I wished there had been a bank of buttons to push, just so that I could have slammed the right button a bunch of times in a senseless effort to speed up the elevator.

The doors opened a geological epoch later, onto a scene as incongruous as a gorilla in a garter belt.

The elevator had taken us to what could only have been the roof of the hotel, assuming the roof opened up onto a section of rain forest in Borneo. Trees and greenery grew so thick that I couldn't see the edge of the roof, and though I could hear the nighttime noises of Chicago, the sounds were vague in the distance and could almost not be heard over the buzz of locusts and the chittering of some kind of animal I did not recognize. Wind rustled the forest around me, and silver moonlight, brighter than I would have thought possible, gave everything an eerie, surreal beauty.

"I'm so glad I was going out for more clay just then. This way," the girl said, and started off on a trail through the forest. I followed as quickly as I could, puffing hard to keep holding Elaine. It wasn't a long walk. The trail wound back and forth and then opened onto a grassy glade.

I stopped and looked around. No, not a glade. More like a garden. A pool rested at its center, still water reflecting the moon overhead. Benches and stones of a good size for sitting on were strewn around the landscape. Statuary, most of it marble and of human subjects, stood here and there, often framed by flowers or placed between young trees. On the far side of the pool stood what at first glance I took to be a gnarled tree. It wasn't. It was a throne, a throne of living wood, its trunk grown into the correct shape, branches and leaves spreading above it in stately elegance, roots spreading and anchoring it in the earth.

People stood here and there. A paint-spattered young man worked furiously on some sort of portrait, his face set in concentration. A tall man, his ageless beauty and pale hair marking him as one of the Sidhe, stood in the posture of a teacher beside a slender girl, who was drawing back a bow, aiming at a target of bundled branches. On the far side of the glade, smoke rose from stones piled into the shape of an oven or a forge, and a broad-chested man, shirtless, bearded, heavy-browed and fierce-looking, stood on the other side of it, wielding a smith's hammer in regular rhythm. He stepped away from the forge, a glowing-hot blade gripped in a set of tongs, and dunked it into a trough of silvery water.

When I got a better look at him, I understood what he was. Steam rose in a cloud over his heavy, equine forelegs, then over his human belly and broad chest, and the centaur stamped a rear hoof impatiently, muttering under his breath, while colored lights played back and forth in the water of the trough. Haunting pipe music, sad and lovely, drifted through the glade from a young woman, mortal, sitting with a set of reed pipes, playing with her eyes closed.

"Where is she?" I demanded. "Where is the Lady?"

The centaur's head snapped around, and he snarled in a sudden, harsh basso. He took up his hammer again, whipped it in a quick circle, and started toward me at a slow canter, Clydesdale-sized hooves striking the ground with dull thumps. "Winter-bound? Here? It cannot be borne."

I tensed, holding Elaine a little closer, and my heart lurched into a higher gear. The centaur was huge and looked ready to kill. "Whoa, there, big fella. I'm not looking for trouble."

The centaur bared his teeth at me and spoke, his deep voice filled with outrage. "There you stand with our Emissary's blood on your hands and expect us to believe you?"

The tall Sidhe man barked, "Korrick, hold."

The centaur drew up short, rearing onto his hind legs and kicking at the air with heavy hooves. "My lord Talos," he growled in frustration. "This arrogance cannot be tolerated."

"Peace," the Sidhe lord said.

"But my *lord*—"

The Sidhe lord stepped between me and the centaur, his back to me. He wore close-fit trousers of dark green and a loose shirt of white linen. The Sidhe lord said nothing, and I couldn't see his expression, but the centaur's face reddened, then blanched. He bowed his head, a stiff gesture, and then walked back over to his forge, hooves striking the ground in sharp, angry motions.

The Sidhe—Talos, I presumed—turned back to me and regarded me with calm, feline eyes the color of a summer sky. He had the pale hair of the Sidhe, hanging in a straight, fine sheet to brush his shoulders. There was a quality of quiet confidence in his features, of relaxed strength, and the sense of him was somehow less alien than that of most of the Sidhe I had encountered. "I hope you will not judge Korrick too harshly, sir. You are, I take it, Harry Dresden?"

"If I'm not, he's going to be upset with me when he catches me running around in his underpants."

Talos smiled. The expression came easily to his features. "Then I grant you passport and license in agreement with the Accords. I am Talos, Lord Marshal of the Summer Court."

"Yeah, that's great, nice to meet you," I said. "Hey, do you think you could help me save this woman's *life* now?"

The Sidhe's smile faded. "I will do what I can." He glanced to the side and gestured with a roll of his wrist.

The garden flew into activity. A cloud of pixies darted through the air, bearing stalks of green plants and broad, soft leaves. They piled them into a soft-looking mound near the side of the pool. Talos looked at me for permission and then gently took Elaine's weight into his arms. My shoulders and biceps all but screamed in relief. The Sidhe lord carried Elaine to the bed of leaves and laid her down upon it. He touched her throat and then her brow with one hand, his eyes closing.

"Weak," he said quietly. "And cold. But she has strength left in her. She will be all right for a little while."

"No offense, but your people have some odd notions about time. Go get your Lady. She needs to see to Elaine now."

Talos regarded me with that same quiet, opaque expression. "She will be here when she will be here. I cannot hurry the sunrise, nor the Lady."

I started to tell him where he could stick his sunrise, but I bit back the words and tried to take out some frustration by clenching my fists. My knuckles popped.

A hand touched my arm, and the girl, the sculptor from the elevator, said, "Please, sir. Let me get you something to drink, or some food. Mortal food, I mean. I wouldn't offer the other kind."

"Like hell," I said. "Not until Elaine is taken care of."

From where he knelt beside Elaine, Talos lifted both eyebrows, but he shrugged his shoulders. "As you wish." He rested his fingertips lightly on either side of her face and bowed his head. "My skills are rather limited. I can at least assure that she loses no ground."

There was a quiet surge of energy, something as gentle and strong as the weight of a wave lifting you off your feet. Elaine suddenly took a deep breath, and color came back into her cheeks. She blinked her eyes open for a moment, then sighed and closed them again.

"Talos can sustain her for a time," the girl said. "Until the Lady decides. He has been Ela's guardian and friend for several years." She tugged at my arm. "Please, take something to eat. You'll make us poor hosts if you do not."

My stomach growled again, and my throat started to complain after all the hard breathing I'd been doing. I exhaled through my nose and nodded to the girl, who led me to one of the benches not far away and pulled a plastic Coleman cooler from underneath it. She rummaged inside, then tossed me a cold can of Coke, a small bag of potato chips, and a long hoagie. None of them held any of the subtle, quivering lure of faerie fare.

"Best I can do for now," she said. "Turkey sub sound all right?"

"Marry me," I responded, tore into the food with fervor, and spent a couple of minutes indulging in one of the purest primal pleasures. Eating. Food never tastes so good as when you are starving, and Talos had granted me safe passport under the Accords, so I wasn't worried about any drugs in it.

While I ate, the girl drew a short stand over to her, on which was a clay bust of a young woman, parts of it still rough, still marked with the tracks of her fingers. She dipped them into a bowl of water attached to the stand and started working on the bust.

"What happened to her?" she asked.

"Hell if I know," I said between bites. "She was in my car like that. Wanted me to bring her here."

"Why did you?" She flushed. "I mean, you're working for Summer's enemies. Right?"

"Yeah. But it doesn't mean I'm friendly with them." I shook

my head, washed down a half-chewed bite with a long drink of Coke. Heaven. I ate for a moment more and then frowned at the bust she was working on. The face seemed familiar. I studied it a bit, then asked, "Is that Lily?"

The girl blinked at me. "You know her?"

"Of her," I said. "She's a changeling, isn't she?"

The girl nodded. "Winter, but she hasn't chosen to go over to them. She was under Ronald's protection, and she models for us sometimes." She gestured vaguely toward the young man who was painting intently. "See, there are a few other pieces she modeled for around here."

I looked around the garden and picked out a pair of statues among all the rest. Both were nudes of white marble. One of them depicted the girl in a tiptoe stretch, arms over her head, body arched prettily. The other showed her kneeling, looking at something cupped in her hands, her expression one of quiet sadness. "Seems like she's well liked."

The girl nodded. "She's very gentle, very sweet."

"Very missing," I said.

She frowned. "Missing?"

"Yeah. Her roommate asked me to see if I could find her. Have you seen her in the past couple of days?"

"She hasn't been here to model, and I've never seen her anywhere but here. I'm sorry."

"Worth a shot," I said.

"Why are you looking for her?"

"I told you. Her roommate asked for my help. I gave it." Which was mostly true. Technically, I suppose, I'd sold it. I got the uneasy feeling that I might start feeling too guilty over the cash Meryl had given me to spend it. "I'm a tad busy this week, but I'll do what I can."

The girl's brow furrowed as she worked at the bust. "You're not like anyone else I've ever met who was working for Winter. Mab usually likes her agents . . . colder, I think. Hungrier. More cruel."

I shrugged. "She wanted someone to find a killer. I've had some experience."

She nodded. "Still, you seem like a decent enough person. It makes me sad to think that you've gotten entangled in Winter's snares."

I stopped chewing and looked up at her, hard. "Oh, Hell's bells."

She looked at me and lifted an eyebrow. "Hmm?"

I put the sandwich down and said, "You're her. You're the Summer Lady."

The shadow of a smile touched the girl's lips, and she bowed her head toward me. Her blond hair cleared out to Sidhe white, her fingers and limbs suddenly seemed slightly longer, and her features became almost identical to Maeve's, eyes vertically slitted and almost violently green. She still wore the coveralls and blue T-shirt, and was still liberally covered in flecks of clay, though. They stood out in sharp contrast to her fair skin and pale hair.

"Call me Aurora," she said. "It's a little easier for everyone."

"Uh, right," I said. I finished the bite I was on and said, "So are you going to stop playing games with me and help Elaine, Aurora?"

She glanced over at Elaine, lying on the ground, and her expression grew troubled. "That depends."

My teeth clenched, and I said in a falsely pleasant voice, "On what?"

She turned her calm, inhuman eyes to me. "On you."

"Don't go getting specific on me, now," I said. "I wouldn't know how to handle it."

"Do you think this is a joke, Mr. Dresden? A game?"

"I know damn well it isn't a game."

She shook her head. "And that is where you are wrong. It is a game, but unlike the ones you know. You aren't allowed to know the rules to this game, and it was never intended to be fair. Do you know why Mab chose *you*, wizard?"

I glared at her. "No."

"Neither do I," she said. "And that is my part of the game. Why choose you? It must be because she expects something of you that she would get from no one else. Perhaps bringing Ela here is what she expected."

"What's the difference?" I demanded. "Elaine is hurt. Your Emissary has been wounded in the line of duty. Don't you think you should get her moving again?"

"But if that is what Winter expects, it could be used against me. I am the least Queen of Summer, but even so I must be cautious in the use of my power."

I snorted. "Maeve sure as hell doesn't think that way."

"Of course not," she said. "She's Winter. She's violent, vicious, merciless."

"And your centaur is just the soul of gentleness and understanding."

Aurora sighed and lowered her clay-crusted fingers. "I hope you will forgive Korrick's temper. He is usually a merrier sort. Everyone's been edgy because of matters here."

"Uh-huh," I said. "Just so we're clear, that was really mortal food, wasn't it?"

"Yes," she said. "I have no desire to threaten your freedom, Mister Dresden, or to bind you in any way."

"Good." I knew she couldn't lie to me, so I took another bite of the sandwich and some more chips. "Look, I'm not here to try to undermine your power or sabotage Summer, Aurora. I just want you to help Elaine."

"I know," she said. "I believe you. But I don't trust you."

"What reason do you have not to trust me?"

"I've watched you," she responded. "You're a mercenary. You work for hire."

"Yeah. To pay the bills and—"

She lifted a hand. "You've made bargains with demons."

"Nickel-and-dime stuff, nothing huge or—"

"You traded yourself to the Leanansidhe for power."

"When I was younger, and a hell of a lot stupider, and in trouble—"

Her inhuman eyes met mine, penetrating. "You've *killed*."

I looked away from her. There wasn't much to say to that. My stomach turned, and I pushed the food a bit away from me.

Aurora nodded, slowly. "From the beginning, you have been meant to be a destroyer. A killer. Do you know the original purpose of a godparent, Mr. Dresden?"

"Yeah," I said. I felt tired. "A godparent was chosen to ensure that a child had religious and moral guidance and teaching."

"Indeed," she said. "And your godmother, your teacher and guide, is the most vicious creature of Mab's Court, more than Maeve's equal, second in strength only to Mab herself."

I let out a harsh laugh. "Teacher? Guide? Is that what you think Lea is to me?"

"Isn't she?"

"Lea barely noticed me except when she thought she could get something from me," I spat. "The rest of the time she couldn't care less. The only thing she taught me was that if I didn't want to get walked on I had to be smarter than her, stronger than her, and willing to do something about it."

Aurora turned her lovely face fully toward me and regarded me with deep, quiet eyes. "Yes." Unease gnawed at my belly as she continued. "The strong conquer and the weak are conquered. That is Winter. That is what you have learned." She leaned closer and said, quietly emphatic, "That is what makes you dangerous. Do you see?"

I stood up and walked a few paces away. Aurora didn't say anything. I heard drips of water as she washed her hands in the little bowl.

"If you aren't going to help Elaine, tell me. I'll take her to the hospital."

"Do you think I should help her?"

"I don't give a damn if you do or not," I said. "But one way or another I'm going to make sure she's taken care of. Make up your mind."

"I already have. What remains is for you to make up yours."

I took a wary breath before asking, "Meaning?"

"Of the two people who entered this garden, Mister Dresden, Elaine is not the most grievously wounded. You are."

"Like hell. I've just got some cuts and bruises."

She rose and walked toward me. "Those aren't the wounds I mean." She reached out and laid a slender hand over my heart. Her skin was warm, even through my shirt, and the simple fact of her touch brought me a small but noticeable sense of comfort. Susan had been gone for months, and with the exception of the occasional assault, no one had actually touched me.

She looked up at me and nodded. "You see. You've been badly wounded, Mister Dresden, and you have found neither rest nor respite from your pains."

"I'll live."

"True," she said. "But this is where it always begins. Monsters are born of pain and grief and loss and anger. Your heart is full of them."

I shrugged. "And?"

"And it makes you vulnerable. Vulnerable to Mab's influence, to temptations that would normally be unthinkable."

"I'm handling temptation pretty damned well, thank you."

"But for how long? You need to *heal*, wizard. Let me help you."

I frowned at her, and at her hand. "How?"

Aurora gave me a small, sad smile. "I'll show you. Here."

Her palm pressed a bit closer to me, and somewhere inside me a dam broke open. Emotions welled up like a riotous rainbow. Scarlet rage, indigo fear, pale blue sadness, aching yellow loneliness, putrid green guilt. The tide flooded through me, coursed over me like a bolt of lightning, searing and painful and beautiful all at once.

And after the tide receded, a deep, quiet stillness followed. A sensation of warmth suffused me, gently easing away my aches and bruises. It spread over my skin, like sunlight on a lazy afternoon outside, and with the warmth my cares began to evaporate. My fear vanished, and I began to relax muscles I hadn't realized were stretched tight as the warmth spread. I floated in warmth for a time, the release from pain an ecstasy in itself.

When I came back to my senses, I was lying on my back on the grass, staring up at leaves and silver-starred sky. My head lay in Aurora's lap. She knelt behind me, and her hands rested lightly, warm and soft, along the sides of my face. The pain began to return to my body, thoughts, and heart, like some quiet and odious tide washing in garbage from a polluted sea. I heard myself make a small sound of protest.

Aurora looked down at me, her eyes concerned. "Worse even than I suspected. You didn't even realize how much pain you were in, did you?"

My chest heaved and I let out a quiet sob. The warmth faded entirely, and the sheer weight of the difficulties I had to face pressed down on me, suffocating me.

Aurora said, "Please, let me help you. We'll make it a bargain, Mr. Dresden. Desist. Relax your efforts to help Winter. Stay here for a time and let me grant you a measure of peace."

Real tears formed, making my vision blur. I mopped at my face with my hands, struggling to think clearly. If I took the deal, it would probably mean my ass. Backing off from Mab's offer would mean that I didn't get a good outcome for the White Council, which meant that they would buy peace with the Red Court of Vampires for the low, low price of one Harry Dresden, slightly damaged.

"Forget it," I said, my voice weak. "I've got a job to do."

Aurora closed her eyes for a moment and nodded. "At least you are true to your word, Mister Dresden. Your honor is admirable. Even if it is misguided."

I forced myself to sit up, away from Aurora. "Go on," I said. "Help Elaine."

"I will," she assured me. "But she is in no danger for the moment, and it will take me some time. There is something I wish to say to you first."

"Okay. Talk."

"How much did Mab tell you about Ronald's death?"

I shook my head. "That he was dead. That the mantle of power he wore went missing. That the killer had to be found."

"Did she tell you why?"

I frowned. "Not exactly."

Aurora nodded and folded her hands in her lap. "Summer readies to go to war against Winter."

I frowned. "You mean it's not just a theoretical possibility anymore. It's real."

"I know no other kind of war. The loss of the Summer Knight has forced Summer's hand."

"I'm not sure I follow."

Her pale brow knit into a soft frown. "The power of our Knights is considerable. It carries a sort of weight that only a free mortal will can possess. That power, that influence, is a critical element of the balance between our Courts."

"Except now yours is gone."

"Exactly."

"Which makes Summer weaker."

"Yes."

I nodded. "Then why the hell are you planning an attack?"

"The seasons are changing," Aurora said. "In two days' time, Midsummer will be upon us. The height of Summer's strength."

She said nothing more, letting me do the math. "You think Winter has taken away your Knight," I said. "And if you wait, you're only going to grow more and more weak, while Winter gets stronger. Right?"

"Correct. If we are to have any chance of victory, we must strike while at the peak of our strength. It will be the only time when our Court might be near equal to Winter's strength. Otherwise, the seasons will change, and at Midwinter Mab and her creatures will come for us. And they *will* destroy us, and with us the balances of the mortal world." She lifted her green eyes from her hands to my face. "Winter, Mister Dresden. Endless Winter. Unending and vicious cycles of predator and prey. Such a world would not be kind to mortals."

I shook my head. "Why would Winter pull this now? I mean, if they had waited another couple of days, they could have held all the cards. Why leave you enough space to wriggle out?"

"I cannot even pretend to know the mind of Winter," Aurora said. "But I know that they must not be allowed to destroy us. For your sake as well as ours."

"Boy, everybody's looking out for my best interests."

"Wizard, please. Promise me that you will do what you can to stop them."

"I'm finished making promises." I stood up and started for the path that led back to the elevator and out, but part of me wanted to do nothing but return to the comfort Aurora had offered. I paused and squeezed my eyes shut, focusing my resolve. "But I will say this. I'm going to find the killer and straighten this out, and I'm going to do it before Midsummer."

I didn't bother to add, "Because I'm as good as dead if I don't."

No need to belabor the obvious.

Chapter Eighteen

❖❖ ❖❖

I got the hell away from the Rothchild and found a pay phone. Murphy picked up on the first ring. "Dresden?"

"Yeah."

"Finally. You all right?"

"I need to talk to you."

There was a short pause, then her voice softened. "Where?"

I rubbed at my head with the heel of one hand, trying to nudge my brain into gear. My thoughts stumbled around sluggishly and in no particular order. "Dunno. Someplace public, bunch of people, quiet enough to talk."

"In Chicago. At this time of night."

"Yeah."

"Okay," Murph said. "I guess I know a place." She told me, we agreed to meet in twenty minutes, and hung up.

As I pulled into the parking lot, I reflected that odds were that not a lot of clandestine meetings involving mystical assassination, theft of arcane power, and the balance of power in the realms of the supernatural had taken place in a Wal-Mart Super Center. But then again, maybe they had. Hell, for all I knew, the Mole Men used the changing rooms as a place to discuss plans for world domination with the Psychic Jellyfish from Planet X and the Disembodied Brains-in-a-Jar from the Klaatuu Nebula. I know I wouldn't have looked for them there.

After midnight the Wal-Mart wasn't crowded, but it wasn't the usual deserted parking lot you'd expect after hours around Wrigleyville, either. The store was open all night, and there were plenty of people in a town like Chicago who would do their shopping late. I had to park about halfway down a row and walk through the cool of the evening before stepping into the refrigerator-cold of the enormous store, whose massive air conditioners had too much momentum to slow down for a few paltry hours of darkness.

A greeter nodded sleepily to me as I came in, and I passed up his offer of a shopping cart. Before I'd gotten all the way into the store, Murphy fell into step beside me. She was wearing a Cubs jacket, jeans, and sneakers, and she had her blond hair tucked up underneath an undecorated black ball cap. She walked with her hands in her pockets, and her expression, one of belligerent annoyance, didn't seem to fit on someone that short. Wordlessly, we walked past all the little hole-in-the-wall franchise businesses, closed and locked up behind their grills, and settled down at the generic cafe near the deli section of the grocery store.

Murphy chose a booth where she could watch the door, and I sat across from her, where I could watch her back. She picked up a couple of cups of coffee, bless her noble heart. I dumped sugar and creamer into mine until bits floated on the surface, stirred it up, and took a slow sip that nearly scalded my tongue.

"You don't look so good," Murphy said.

I nodded.

"You want to talk about it?"

To my own surprise, I did. I set the coffee down and said without preamble, "I'm furious, Murph. I can't think straight, I'm so mad."

"Why?"

"Because I'm screwed. That's why. No matter what I do, I'm going to take it up the ass."

Lines appeared between her eyebrows. "What do you mean?"

"It's this job," I said. "Investigating Reuel's death. There's a lot of resistance and I don't know if I can beat it. And if I don't beat it before tomorrow night, things are really going to go to hell."

"The client isn't being helpful?"

I let out a bitter laugh. "Hell, for all I know the client is doing this to me just so I can get myself horribly killed."

"You don't trust them, then."

"Not as far as I could kick her. And the people who are supposed to be working with me are driving me nuts." I shook my head. "I feel like some guy in a magician's box, just before he starts pushing all those swords through it. Only it's not a trick, and the swords are real, and they're going to start skewering me any second. The bad guys are doing their best to get me wiped out or screwed up. The good guys think I'm some kind of ticking psycho, just waiting to go off, and it's like pulling teeth to try to get a straight answer out of any of them."

"You think you're in danger."

"I know it," I said. "And it's just too damned big." I fell quiet for a moment, and sipped my coffee.

"So," Murph said. "Why did you want to see me?"

"Because the people who should be backing me up are about to throw me to the wolves. And because the only person actually helping me is green enough to get himself killed without a baby-sitter." I set the empty cup down. "And because when I asked myself who I could trust, I came up with a damned short list. You're it."

She settled back in her seat with a slow, long exhalation. "You're going to tell me what's going on?"

"If you're willing," I said. "I know I've kept things from you. But I've done it because I thought it was how I could protect you best. Because I didn't want you to get hurt."

"Yeah," she said. "I know. It's annoying as hell."

I tried to smile. "In this case, ignorance is bliss. If I tell you this stuff, it's going to be serious. Just knowing it could be dangerous for you. And you aren't going to be able to get away from it, Murph. Not ever."

She regarded me soberly. "Then why tell me now?"

"Because you deserve to know, long since. Because you've risked your life for me, and to protect people from all the supernatural crud that's out there. Because being around me has bought you trouble, and knowing more about it might help you if it comes your way again." My cheeks flushed, and I admitted, "And because I need your help. This is a bad one. I'm afraid."

"I'm not going anywhere, Harry."

I gave her a tired smile. "One last thing. If you come in on this, you have to understand something. You have to promise me that you won't haul SI and the rest of the police in on everything. You can dig up information, use them discretely, but you can't round up a posse and go gunning for demons."

Her eyes narrowed. "Why the hell not?"

"Because bringing mortal authorities into a conflict is the nuclear assault of the supernatural world. No one wants to see it happen, and if they thought you might do it, they'd kill you. Or they'd pull strings higher up and get you fired, or framed for something.

They would never allow it to pass. You'd get yourself ruined or hurt or killed and it's likely a lot of people would go down with you." I paused to let the words sink in, then asked, "Still want me to tell you?"

She closed her eyes for a moment and then nodded, once. "Hit me."

"You're sure?"

"Yeah."

"All right," I said. And I told Murphy all of it. It took a while. I told her about Justin and about Elaine. I told her about the supernatural forces and politics at play in and around the city. I told her about the war I'd started because of what the Red Court had done to Susan. I told her about the faeries and Reuel's murder.

And most of all, I told her about the White Council.

"Those spineless, arrogant, egomaniacal sons of bitches," Murphy growled. "Who the hell do they think they are, selling out their own people like that?"

Some silent, delighted part of me let out a mental cheer at her reaction.

She made a disgusted noise and shook her head. "So let me get this straight," she said. "You started a war between the Council and the Red Court. The Council needs the support of the faeries in order to have a chance at victory. But they can't get that support unless you find this killer and restore the stolen magical power thingie—"

"Mantle," I interjected.

"Whatever," Murphy said. "And if you don't get the magic whatsit, the Council fixes you up in a carryout box for the vampires."

"Yeah," I said.

"And if you don't find the killer before Midsummer, the faeries slug it out with each other."

"Which could be bad no matter who won. It would make El Niño look as mild as an early spring thaw."

"And you want my help."

"You've worked homicide before. You're better at it than me."

"That goes without saying," she said, a trace of a smile on her mouth. "Look, Harry. If you want to find out who did the killing, the best way to start is to figure out why."

"Why what?"

"Why the murder. Why Reuel got bumped off."

"Oh, right," I said.

"And why would someone try to take you out in the park yesterday?"

"It could have been almost anyone," I said. "It wasn't like it was a brilliant attempt, as far as they go."

"Wrong," Murphy said. "Not neat, but not stupid either. After you called earlier tonight, I snooped around."

I frowned at her. "You found something?"

"Yeah. Turns out that there have been two armed robberies in the past three days, first outside of Cleveland and then at a gas station just this side of Indianapolis, coming toward Chicago."

"That doesn't sound out of the ordinary."

"No," Murphy said. "Not unless you throw in that in both cases, someone was grabbed at the scene and abducted, and both times the video security broke down just as the robbery started. Eyewitnesses in Indiana identified the perpetrator as a woman."

I whistled. "Sounds like our ghoul, then."

Murph nodded, her lips pressed together. "Any chance those people she grabbed are alive?"

I shook my head. "Not likely. She probably ate them. A ghoul can go through forty or fifty pounds of meat a day. She'll put whatever's left someplace where animals can get to it, cover her tracks."

She nodded. "I figured. The pattern matches several incidents over the past twenty years. It took me a while to piece it together, but something similar has happened three times in connection with the operations of a contract killer who calls herself the Tigress. A friend at the FBI told me that they suspect her of a number of killings in the New Orleans area and that Interpol thinks she's pulled jobs in Europe and Africa, too."

"Hired gun," I said. "So who did the hiring?"

"From what you've said, my money's on the vampires. They're the ones who benefit most from you being dead. If they punch your ticket, the Council will probably sue for peace, right?"

"Maybe," I said, but I doubted it. "If that's what they had in mind, it's stupid timing. They Pearl-Harbored a bunch of wizards somewhere in Russia two nights ago, and the Council was pretty angry about it."

"Okay. So maybe they figure that if your investigation finds Reuel's killer and gets the Council brownie points with the faeries, they're in for a real fight. Killing you before that happens makes sense."

"Except that when it went down, I wasn't involved in the investigation yet."

Murphy shook her head. "I wish we could get you together with a sketch artist, describe her."

"Doubt it would help much. She was in makeup at first, and I didn't give her a second look. By the time I was paying attention, she mostly looked like something out of a Japanese horror cartoon."

She glanced down at her now cold coffee. "Not much we can do but wait, then. I've got a couple of sources trying to turn up more, but I wouldn't bet anything on them. I'll let you know."

I nodded. "Even if we find her, it might not help with the faerie stuff."

"Right," she said. "Mind if I ask you a few questions? Maybe I'll see something you don't."

"Okay."

"This dreadlock chick. Maeve, you said her name was?"

"Yeah."

"How sure are you in your instinct about her? That she couldn't have done the murder, I mean."

"Pretty close to certain."

"But not completely."

I frowned thoughtfully. "No. Faeries are tricky that way. Not completely."

Murphy nodded. "What about Mab?"

I rubbed at my chin, feeling the beginnings of stubble. "She never out and out denied responsibility for Reuel's death, but I don't think she's the killer."

"What makes you say that?"

"I don't know."

"I do. She could have picked anyone she wanted to represent her interests, and she chose you. If she wanted to cover her tracks, it would make more sense for her to choose someone less capable and with less experience. She wouldn't have picked someone as stupidly stubborn as you."

I scowled. "Not stupidly," I said. "I just don't like to leave things undone."

Murphy snorted. "You don't know the meaning of 'give up,' dolt. You see my point."

"Yeah. I guess it's reasonable."

"So what about this Summer girl?"

I blew out a breath. "It doesn't seem to hang on her very well. She was kinder than any faerie I ever met. She could have been pretty darned unpleasant to me, but she wasn't."

"How about the other mortal, then? The Winter Knight."

"He's a violent, vicious heroin addict. I could see him tossing Reuel down those stairs, sure. But I'm not sure he's savvy enough to have worked enough magic to steal the mantle. He was more of a plunder-now-and-think-later sort of guy." I shook my head. "I've got three more faeries to talk to, though."

"Summer Queen and both Mothers," Murphy nodded. "When will you see them?"

"As soon as I can work out how. The Ladies are the closest to the mortal world. They aren't hard to find. The Queens and the Mothers, though, will live in Faerie proper. I'll have to go there to find a guide."

Murphy lifted her eyebrows. "A guide?"

I grimaced. "Yeah. I don't want to, but it's looking like I'm going to have to pay my godmother a visit."

Murphy quirked an eyebrow. "Seriously? You have a faerie godmother?"

"Long story," I said. "Okay, I want to get moving. If you could—"

The store lights went out, all at once.

My heart all but stopped. A second later, battery-powered emergency lights came up and revealed a roiling cloud of silver-grey mist spreading into the store from the doors. The mist rolled over a startled cashier, and the woman slumped, her mouth slightly open and her eyes unfocused, staring.

"Good Lord," Murphy said softly. "Harry, what's happening?"

I had already gotten out of the booth and grabbed the salt shaker from our table, and the one next to it. "Trouble. Come with me."

Chapter Nineteen

At first I tried to circle around to the exit doors, but the mist proved to be flowing in through them as well. "Curse it! We can't get out that way."

Murphy's face went more pale as a young man flung himself at the exit doors. The moment he hit the mist, his running steps faltered. He came to a halt, a puzzled expression on his face, and stared around him blankly, as his shoulders slumped.

"Dear God," she whispered. "Harry, what is that?"

"Come on, to the back of the store," I said, and started running that way. "I think it's a mind fog."

"You *think*?"

I scowled over my shoulder at Murphy. "I've never seen one before, just heard about them. They shut down your head, flatline your ability to remember things, scramble your thoughts. They're illegal."

"Illegal?" Murphy yelled. "Says who?"

"Says the Laws of Magic," I muttered.

"You didn't say anything about any Laws of Magic," Murphy said.

"If we get out of here alive, I'll explain it to you sometime." We ran down a long aisle toward the back of the store, passing housewares, then seasonal goods on our left, while grocery aisles stretched out on our right. Murphy stopped abruptly, broke open the covering over a fire alarm, and jerked it down.

I looked around hopefully, but nothing happened.

"Damn," Murphy muttered.

"Worth a try. Look, the people in the fog should be all right once it's gone, and whoever this is, they won't have any reason to hurt them once we're not around. We'll get out the back door and get away from here."

"Where are we going to go?"

"I don't know," I confessed, as I started moving again. "But anywhere is better than where the bad guys chose to attack and have their pick of a hundred hostages, right?"

"Okay," Murphy said. "Getting out of here is good."

"I bet the bad guys are counting on that, trying to flush us out into a dark alley. You carrying?"

Murphy was already drawing her gun from under her jacket, a well-used military-issue Colt 1911. "Are you kidding?"

I noticed that her hands were shaking. "New gun?"

"Old reliable," she said. "You told me magic can jam a flaky gun."

"Revolver would be even better."

"Why don't I just throw rocks and sharp sticks while I'm at it, Tex?"

"Auto bigot." I spotted an EMPLOYEES ONLY sign. "There," I said, and went that way. "Out the back."

We headed for the swinging doors under the sign. I hit them first, shoving them open. A grey wall of mist lay in front of me and I leaned back, trying to stumble to a halt. If I let myself touch the mist, I might not have enough of my wits left to regret it. I stumbled a foot short of it and almost fell forward, but Murphy grabbed my shirt and jerked me sharply back.

We both backed out into the store. "Can't get out that way," Murphy said. "Maybe they don't want to herd you anywhere. Maybe they just want to gas you and kill you while you're down."

I swept my gaze around the store. Cold grey mist rolled forward, slow and steady, in every direction. "Looks like," I said. I nodded down a tall, narrow aisle containing auto parts. "Down there, quick."

"What's down here?" Murphy asked.

"Cover. I have to get us a defense against that mist." We reached the open space at the end of the aisle, and I nodded to Murphy. "Here, stop here and stand close to me."

She did it, but I could still see her shaking as she asked, "Why?"

I looked up. The mist had reached the far end of the aisle and was gliding slowly down it. "I'm going to put up a circle that should keep it off us. Don't step out of it or let any part of you cross outside."

Murphy's voice took on a higher, more tense pitch. "Harry, it's coming."

I twisted open both salt shakers and started pouring them out in a circle around us, maybe three feet across. As I finished the circle, I invested it with the slightest effort of will, of intent, and it closed with a sudden snap of silent, invisible energies. I stood up again, holding my breath, until the mist touched it a moment later.

It roiled up against the circle and stopped, as though a cylinder of Plexiglas stood between it and us. Murphy and I both let out our breath in slow exhalations. "Wow," she said quietly. "Is that like a force field or something?"

"Only against magical energies," I said, squinting around us. "If someone comes along with a gun, we're in trouble."

"What do we do?"

"I think I can protect myself if I'm ready to do it," I said. "But I need to set up a charm on you."

"A what?"

"Charm, short-term magic." I fumbled at my shirt until I found a frayed thread and started pulling it out. "I need a hair."

Murphy gave me a suspicious frown, but she reached under her hat and unceremoniously jerked out several dark gold hairs. I plucked them up and twisted them together with the strand of thread. "Give me your left hand."

She did. Her fingers shook so hard that I could feel it when I put my own around them. "Murph," I said. She kept looking up and down the aisle, her eyes a little wild. "Karrin."

She looked up at me. She looked very young, somehow.

"Remember what I said yesterday," I said. "You're hurt. But you'll get through it. You'll be okay."

She closed her eyes tightly. "I'm scared. So scared I'm sick."

"You'll get through it."

"What if I don't?"

I squeezed her fingers. "Then I will personally make fun of you every day for the rest of your life," I said. "I will call you a sissy girl in front of everyone you know, tie frilly aprons on your car, and lurk in the parking lot at CPD and whistle and tell you to shake it, baby. Every. Single. Day."

Murphy's breath escaped in something like a hiccup. She opened her eyes, a mix of anger and wary amusement easing into them in place of the fear. "You do realize I'm holding a gun, right?"

"You're fine. Hold your hand still." Though her fingers still trembled a little, the wild, panicked spasms had ceased. I wrapped the twist of hair and thread around her finger.

Murphy kept on peering through the mist, her gun steady. "What are you doing?"

"Enchantment like that mist is invasive," I said. "It touches you, gets inside you. So I'm setting you up with a defense. Left side is the side that takes in energy. I'm going to block that mist's spell from going into you. Tie a string around your finger so you won't forget."

I tied the string in an almost complete knot, so that it would need only a single tug to finish. Then I fumbled my penknife out of my pocket and pricked the pad of my right thumb. I looked up at Murphy, trying to clear my thoughts for the spell.

She regarded me, her face pale and uncertain. "I've never really seen you, you know. Do it. Before."

"It's okay," I told her. I met her eyes for a dangerous second. "I won't hurt you. I know what I'm doing."

She lifted the corner of her mouth in a quick smile that made her eyes sparkle. She nodded and returned to peering out through the mist.

I closed my eyes for a moment and then began gathering my focus for the spell. We were already within a circle, so it happened fast. The air tightened on my skin, and I felt the hairs along my arms rise as the power grew. *"Memoratum,"* I murmured. I tied off the improvised string and touched the bead of blood on my thumb to the knot. *"Defendre memorarius."*

The energy rushed out of me and into the spell, wrapping tight around the string and pressing against Murphy. A wave of goose bumps rippled up her arm, and she drew in a sudden sharp breath. "Whoa."

I looked at her sharply. "Murph? You okay?"

She blinked down at her hand, and then up at me. "Wow. Yeah."

I nodded, and took my pentacle out of my shirt. I wrapped it around my left hand, leaving the five-pointed star lying against my knuckles. "Okay, we're pushing our luck enough. Let's hope this works and get the hell out of here."

"Wait, you don't know if it will work?"

"It should work. It ought to. In theory."

"Great. Would it be better to stay here?"

"Heh, that's a joke, right?"

Murphy nodded. "Okay. How will we know if it works?"

"We step outside the circle and if we don't drift into Lala Land," I said, "we'll know it worked."

She braced her charmed hand on the butt of her gun. "That's what I love about working with you, Dresden. The certainty."

I broke the circle with a shuffle of my foot and an effort of will. It scattered with a pressured sigh, and the grey mist slid forward and over us.

It glided over my skin like a cold and greasy oil, something foul and cloying and vaguely familiar that made me want to start brushing it off. It writhed up over my arms, prickles of distraction and disorientation crawling over my limbs. I focused on the pentacle on my left hand, the solid, cool weight of it, the years of discipline and practice that it represented. I pushed the clinging mist away from my sensations, deliberately excluded it from my perception by sheer determination. A ripple of azure static flickered along the chain of my amulet, flashed around the pentacle, then faded, taking with it the distraction of the mind fog.

Murphy glanced back at me and said, voice low, "You okay? You looked shaky for a second."

I nodded. "I got it now. You okay?"

"Yeah. Doesn't feel like anything."

Damn, I'm good—sometimes. "Go. Out through the garden center."

Murphy had the gun—she walked in front. I kept my eyes open on our flanks as she headed down an aisle. We passed a customer and an employee, down a side aisle, pressed against a wall where they'd apparently tried to avoid the mist. Now they stood with faintly puzzled expressions on their faces, eyes not focused. Another shopper, an old man, stood in an aisle, swaying precariously on his feet. I stopped beside him and said quietly, "Sir, here, sit down for a minute," and helped him sit down before he fell.

We went past another slackly staring employee, her blue smock marked with dirt stains and smelling of fertilizer, and headed for the doors leading out to the garden center.

My memory screamed a sudden alarm at me, and I lurched forward, diving past Murphy and out into the mist-shrouded evening within the chain-link boundaries of the garden center. A hard, sudden weight hit me, driving my thighs and hips down to the floor. My head whiplashed against it a moment later, complete with a burst of phantom light and very real pain.

I rolled, as the employee we'd just passed reversed her grip on a wickedly sharp set of pruners and stabbed them down at me. I oozed to one side in a sluggish dodge. The steel tips of the tool tore through my shirt and some of my skin before biting into the concrete. I kept rolling and kicked at the woman's ankles. She avoided me with a kind of liquid agility, and I looked up into the human face of the ghoul assassin from the rain of toads. The Tigress.

She didn't look particularly pretty, or particularly exotic, or particularly anything. She looked like no one in particular—medium height, medium build, no flattering curves, no outrageous flaws, no nothing. Medium-brown hair, of unremarkable cut and length. She wore jeans, a polo top, the Wal-Mart smock, all very normal.

The gun she started drawing from under the smock commanded attention, though—a revolver, snub-nosed, but it moved with the kind of weight that made me think high-caliber. I started trying to pull a shield together, but the defense I'd been holding against the mist and the blow to my head tangled up the process, slowed me down—not much, but enough to get me really dead.

Murphy saved me. As the Tigress brought the gun to bear on me, Murphy closed with her, trapping the ghoul's gun arm with her own and doing something with her left hand as she twisted her body at the hips, her strong legs spread wide.

Murphy was a faithful practitioner of Aikido, and she knew about grappling. The Tigress let out a shriek. Not a girly wow-does-that-hurt shriek, but the kind of furious, almost whistling sound you expect from a bird of prey. There was a snapping, popping sound, then a clap of thunder, the roar of a discharged gun at close quarters, the sudden sharp smell of burnt powder, and the revolver went skittering free.

The ghoul stabbed the pruners at Murphy, but she was already on the way out, grunting with effort, her entire attack one circle that sent the Tigress stumbling away into a stand of large potted ferns.

Murphy spun to face the ghoul. She took a shooting stance and snarled, "Get on your face on the floor. You are under arrest. You have the right to remain silent."

The ghoul changed. Skin tore at the corners of her mouth as it dropped open and gaped nightmarishly wide, canines lengthening as her lips peeled away from her teeth. Her shoulders jerked and twisted, hunching up and growing wider at the same time, her clothes stretching out while her body grew more hunched. Her fingers lengthened, talons extending from the tips until her hands were spread as wide as the lawn rakes on a display behind her, and a fetid smell of decay and worse flooded out.

Murphy's face went bloodless as she stared at the transformation. If she'd been dealing with an armed thug, I think she would have been fine. But the ghoul wasn't and she wasn't. I saw the fear come surging up through her, winding its way into her through the scars a maddened ghost had left on her spirit the year before. Panic hit her, and her breath came in strangled gasps as a demon from a madman's nightmare clawed its way free of the bushes, spread its talons, and let out a rasping, quivering hiss. Murphy's gun started quivering, the barrel jerking erratically left and right. I struggled to get on my feet and back into the game, but my ears still rang and the constant pressure of the mist slowed me down.

The Tigress must have seen the terror that held Murphy. "A cop, eh?" the ghoul rasped, drool foaming between its teeth, dribbling down its chin. It started slowly toward Murphy, claw tips dragging along the floor. "Aren't you going to tell me that I have the right to an attorney?"

Murphy let out a small, terrified sound, frozen in place, her eyes wide.

It laughed at her. "Such a big gun for a sweet girl. You smell sweet. It makes me hungry." It continued forward, laughter still kissing every word, its distorted, inhuman voice continuing in a steady murmur, "Maybe I should let you arrest me. Wait until we're in the car. If you smell that good, I wonder how good you taste."

I guess the ghoul shouldn't have laughed. Murphy's eyes cleared and hardened. The gun steadied, and she said, "Taste this, bitch."

Murphy started shooting.

The ghoul let out another shriek, this one full of surprise and pain. The bullets didn't drive her back. That's for comic books and TV. Real bullets just rip through you like lead weights through cheesecloth. No gaping, bloody holes appeared in the ghoul's chest, but sudden flowers of scarlet sprayed out from her back, covering the potted ferns with bloody dewdrops.

The ghoul threw her arms up and recoiled, turning, screaming, and threw herself at the ferns.

Murphy kept shooting.

The ghoul stumbled and dropped down amid the ferns, still kicking and struggling wildly, knocking pots over, breaking others, scattering vegetable matter and dirt all over the floor.

Murphy kept shooting.

The gun clicked empty, and the ghoul half-rolled onto her ruined back, the stolen blue smock now ripped with huge holes and soaked through with blood. The ghoul choked and gagged, scarlet trickling out of her mouth. She let out another hiss, this one bubbling, and held up her hands in supplication. "Wait," she rasped. "Wait, please. You win, I give up."

Murphy ejected the clip, put in a fresh one, and worked the slide on the gun. Then she took a shooting stance again and sighted down the barrel, her blue eyes calculating, passionless, merciless.

She didn't see the sudden shadow against the mist to her right, huge and hulking, backlit by emergency lights at the other end of the garden center. I did, and finally shoved my dazed self back to my feet. "Murph!" I shouted. "To your right!"

Murphy's head snapped around, and she darted to her left, even as a garden hoe swept down and shattered against the concrete where she'd been standing. The ghoul scrambled back through the ferns and vanished into the mist, leaving blood smeared everywhere. Murphy backpedaled and shot at the form in the mist, then ducked as another arm swept a shovel in a scything arc that just missed her head.

Grum the Ogre rolled forward out of the mist, in his scarlet-skinned, twelve-foot-tall hulking form, a shovel clenched in one fist. Without slowing a step, he scooped up a twenty-gallon ceramic pot and threw it at Murphy like a snowball. She scooted behind a stack of empty loading palettes, and the pot exploded against them.

Magic would be useless against the ogre. I looked wildly around me, then seized a jumbo-sized plastic bag of round, tinted-glass potting marbles. "Hey!" I shouted. "Tall, red, and ugly!"

Grum's head spun around further than I would have thought possible with a neck that thick, and his already beady eyes narrowed even more. He let out a bellowing roar and turned toward me, his huge feet slamming down on the concrete.

I tore open the bag and dumped it out toward him. Blue-green marbles spread over the floor in a wave. Grum's foot slammed down on several as he advanced, and I hoped for the best. Grum continued toward me unslowed, and when his great foot lifted, I saw small circles of powdered glass on the ground.

I snarled a curse and ran deeper into the garden center, Grum's footsteps heavy behind me. I heard Murphy shoot again, a pair of shots, and tried to keep a mental count of her rounds. Four, in the new clip? Did she have another reload? And how many rounds did that Colt hold anyway?

A sharper, more piercing report cracked through the area—rifle fire. Murphy's Colt barked twice more, and she called, "Harry, someone's covering the exit with gunfire!"

"Kinda busy here, Murph!" I shouted.

"What the hell is that thing?"

"Faerie!" I shouted. Grum was already trying to kill me, so there was no point in being diplomatic. "It's a big, ugly faerie!" I started swiping things off of shelves to crash in the aisle behind me. I'd gained some distance on Grum, but it could be that he just needed time to gather momentum. I heard him snarl again, and he took a swing with the shovel in his hand. He was short of me, but it whooshed loudly enough to make me flinch.

I looked wildly for something made of steel to throw at the ogre or to defend myself with. The mist kept me from seeing more than a couple of yards ahead of me, and from what I could see, I was just heading deeper and deeper into the plant-vending area. The smell of summer-heated greenery, of fertilizer and mild rot, filled my nose and mouth. I rounded the end of the aisle and ducked through a narrow gate and out from under the canopy top that gave shade to this part of the garden center, into a roofless area bounded by a high chain-link fence and filled with young trees and greenery standing in silent rows.

I looked around wildly for a way out into the parking lot at large, and checked how close the ogre was, flicking a glance back over my shoulder.

Grum stopped at the gate to the fenced area and, with a small smile on his lips, swung the gate shut. As I watched, he covered his hand with a plastic trash bag, and bent the latch like soft clay. Metal squealed and the gate fastened shut with no more effort than I would need to close a twist-tie.

My heart fell down through my stomach, and I looked around me.

The chain-link fence was at least nine feet high, with a strand of barbed wire at the top, meant to stop incursions of baby-tree nappers, I guessed. A second gate, much bigger, stood closed—

and the latch had been twisted exactly like the other, warped closed. It was a neat little trap, and I'd been chased right into it.

"Dammit," I said.

Grum let out a grating laugh, though I could barely see anything but his outline, several yards away in the mist. "You lose, wizard."

"Why are you doing this?" I demanded. "Who the hell are you working for?"

"You got no guess?" Grum said. There was a note of casual arrogance to his voice. "Gee. That's too bad. Guess you go to your grave not knowing."

"If I had a nickel for every time I'd heard that," I muttered, looking around me. I had a few options. None of them were good. I could open a way into the Nevernever and try to find my way through the spirit realm and back into the real world somewhere else—but if I did that, not only might I run into something even worse than I already had in front of me, but if I got unlucky I might hit a patch of slower time and not emerge back into my Chicago for hours, even days. I might also be able to melt myself a hole in the fence with conjured flame, providing I didn't burn myself to a cinder doing it. I didn't have my blasting rod with me, and without it my control could be shaky enough to manage just that.

I could probably pile a bunch of baby trees, loading palettes, sacks of potting soil, and so on against the outer wall of chain-link fence and climb out. I might get cut up on the barbed wire, but hell, that would be better than staying here. Either way, there was no time to waste standing around deciding. I turned toward the nearest set of young trees, picked up a couple, and tossed them against the fence. "Murphy! I'm stuck, but I think I can get clear! Get out of here now!"

Murphy's voice floated to me, directionless in the fog. "Where are you?"

"Hell's bells, Murph! Get out!"

Her gun barked twice more. "Not without you!"

I threw more stuff on the pile. "I'm a big boy! I can take care of myself!" I took a long step up onto the pile, and tested my grip. It was enough to let me reach the top. I figured I could pull myself up and worry about the barbed wire when I got there. I started climbing out.

I was looking at a faceful of barbed wire and pushing at the fence with my toes when I felt something wrap around my ankles.

I looked down and saw a branch wrapped around my legs. I kicked at it irritably.

And then as I watched, another branch lifted from the pile and joined the first. Then a third. And a fourth. The branches beneath my feet heaved and I suddenly found myself hauled up into the air, swinging upside down from my heels.

It was an awkward vantage point, but I watched as the trees and plants and soil I'd thrown into a pile surged and writhed together. The young trees tangled their limbs together, growing before my eyes as they did, lengthening and growing thicker to become part of a larger whole. Other bits of greenery, clumps of dirt, and writhing vines and leaves joined the trees, whipping through the air apparently of their own volition and adding to the mass of the thing that held me.

It took shape and stood up, an enormous creature of vaguely human shape made all of earth and root and bough, twin points of brilliant emerald-green light burning in its vine-writhing, leaf-strewn head. It had to have been nine or ten feet tall, and nearly that far across. Its legs were thicker than me, and branches spread out above its head like vast horns against the background of luminous mind fog. The creature lifted its head and screamed, a sound of tortured wood and creaking limb and howling wind.

"Stars and stones, Harry," I muttered, my heart pounding, "when will you learn to keep your mouth shut?"

Chapter Twenty

"Murphy!" I screamed. "Get clear!"

The plant monster—No, wait. I couldn't possibly refer to that thing as a "plant monster." I'd be a laughingstock. It's hard to give a monster a cool name on the spur of the moment, but I used a name I'd heard Bob throw out before.

The chlorofiend lifted me up and shook me like a set of maracas. I focused on my shield bracelet, running my will, bolstered by sudden fear, through the focus. My skin tingled as the shield formed around me, and I shaped it into a full sphere. I was barely in time. The chlorofiend threw me at a post in the chain-link fence. Without the shield, it would have broken my back. I slammed into it, feeling the energy of the shield tighten around me, spreading the impact over the whole of my body instead of solely at the point of impact. The shield transferred a portion of the kinetic energy of impact into heat and light, while the rest came through as an abrupt pressure. The result was like a sudden suit of oven-warmed elastic closing on me, and it felt about three sizes too small. It knocked the wind out of my lungs. Azure and argent light flashed in a vague sphere around me.

I didn't bounce much, just fell to the concrete. The shield gave out a more feeble flash when I hit. I got up off the ground and dodged away from the chlorofiend, but it followed me, slapping aside a stand of wooden tomato stakes with one leafy arm. Its glowing green eyes blazed as it came. I ran up against the fence at the back end of the lot, and the chlorofiend's huge fist smashed down at me again.

I lifted my shield bracelet against it, but the blow tossed me a dozen feet, down the length of fence and into a set of huge steel partitioned shelves holding hundreds of fifty-pound bags of mulch, potting soil, and fertilizer. I lay there dazed for a second, staring at an empty aisle display proclaiming in huge scarlet letters WEED-B-GONE ONLY 2.99!!! I clutched at the display and got to my feet again in time to duck under the chlorofiend's fist as it punched at my head.

It hit one of the metal shelves instead of me, and there was a shriek of warping metal, a creaking yowl of pain from the fiend, and a burst of sizzling smoke. The creature drew its smoking fist back and screeched again, eyes blazing even brighter, angrier.

"Steel," I muttered. "So you're a faerie somethingorother too." I looked up at the enormous shelves as I ran down the length of them, and a second later I heard the chlorofiend turn and begin pacing after me. I started gathering in my will as I ran, and I allowed the physical shield to fall, leaving me only enough defense to keep the mist from blitzing my head. I would need every bit of strength I could muster to pull off my sudden and desperate plan—and if it didn't work, my shield wouldn't protect me for long in any case. Sooner or later, the chlorofiend would batter its way through my defenses and pound me into plant food.

I pulled ahead of it, but it started gaining momentum, catching up to me. As I reached the end of the row, the end of the steel shelves, I turned to face it.

Hell's bells, that thing was big. Bigger than Grum. I could see through it in places, where twists of branches and leaves were not too closely clumped with earth, but that didn't make it seem any less massive or dangerous.

If this didn't work, I wasn't going to last long enough to regret it.

Most magic is pretty time-consuming, what with drawing circles and gathering energies and aligning forces. Quick and dirty magic, evocation, is drawn directly from a wizard's will and turned loose without benefit of guide or limit. It's difficult and it's dangerous. I suck at evocation. I only knew a couple that I could do reliably, and even they required a focus, such as my shield bracelet or blasting rod, to be properly controlled.

But for doing big dumb things that require a lot of energy and not much finesse, I'm usually fine.

I lifted my arms, and the mist was stirred by a sudden rush of moving air. The chlorofiend pounded closer, and I closed my eyes, pouring more energy out, reaching for the wind. *"Vento,"* I muttered, feeling more power stir. The chlorofiend bellowed again, sending a jolt of fear through me, and the winds rose even more. *"Vento! Vento, ventas servitas!"*

Power, magic, coursed through my outstretched arms and lashed out at the night. The wind rose in a sudden roar, a screaming cyclone that whirled into being just in front of me and then whirled out toward the heavy metal shelving.

The chlorofiend screamed again, nearly drowned out by the windstorm I'd called, only a few yards away.

The enormous, heavy shelves, loaded with tons of materials, let out a groan of protest and then fell, toppled over onto the chlorofiend with a deafening din that ripped at my ears and shook the concrete floor.

The chlorofiend was strong, but it wasn't that strong. It went down like a bush under a bulldozer, shrieking again as the steel shelves crushed it and burned into its substance. A foul greyish smoke rose from the wreckage, and the chlorofiend continued to scream and thrash, the shelves jerking and moving.

Exhaustion swept over me with the effort of the spell, and I glowered down at the fallen shelves. "Down," I panted, "but not out. Dammit." I watched the shelves for a moment and decided that the chlorofiend probably wouldn't shrug it off for a few minutes. I shook my head and headed for the gate into the enclosure. Hopefully, Grum hadn't twisted things up so badly that I couldn't get out.

He had. The metal latch on the gate had been pinched into a mess by his talons. They had scored the metal in sharp notches, like an industrial cutter. Note to self: Don't think steel can stop Grum's fingernails. I checked above and decided to risk climbing the fence and getting through the barbed wire.

I had gotten maybe halfway up the chain-link fence when Murphy limped out of the mist on the other side, her gun pointed right at me.

"Whoa, whoa, Murph," I said. I showed her my hands and promptly fell off the fence. "It's me."

She lowered the gun and let out her breath. "Christ, Harry. What are you doing?"

"Texas cage match. I won." From behind me, the chlorofiend let out another shriek and the shelving groaned as it shifted. I gulped and looked back. "Rematch doesn't look promising, though. Where have you been?"

She rolled her eyes. "Shopping."

"Where's Grum and the ghoul?"

"Don't know. The ghoul's blood trail went out, but someone shot at me when I followed it. Haven't seen the ogre." She blinked at the gate's latch. "Damn. Guess he shut you in here, huh?"

"Pretty much. You get shot?"

"No, why?"

"You're limping."

Murphy grimaced. "Yeah. One of those bastards must have thrown a bunch of marbles on the floor. I slipped on one. It's my knee."

"Oh," I said. "Uh."

Murphy blinked at me. "*You* did that?"

"Well, it was a plan at the time."

"Harry, that's not a plan, it's a Looney Tune."

"Kill me later. Help me out of here now." I squinted up at the barbed wire. "Maybe if you get a rake, you can push it up for me so that I can slide between it and the fence."

"We're twenty feet from the hardware department, genius," Murphy said. She limped back into the mist, and returned half a minute later carrying a pair of bolt cutters. She cut a slit in the chain-link fence and I squeezed through it while the chlorofiend thrashed, still pinned.

"I could kiss you," I said.

Murphy grinned. "You smell like manure, Harry." The smile faded. "What now?"

The trapped monster's thrashing sent several smaller shelves toppling over, and I rubbernecked nervously. "Getting out is still first priority. That thing is down, but it'll be coming before long."

"What is it?"

"Chlorofiend," I said.

"A what?"

"Plant monster."

"Oh, right."

"We need to get out."

Murphy shook her head. "Whoever was covering the exit out front can probably see the other doors too. A silhouette in a doorway is a great target. It's just like a shooting range."

"How the blazes did they see you through the mist?"

"Is that really important right now? They can, and it means we can't go out the front."

"Yeah," I said. "You're right. The main exits are covered, that thing is in the garden center, and ten to one Ogre Grum is watching the back."

"Ogre, check. What's his deal?"

"Bullets bounce off him, and he shakes off magic like a duck does water. He's strong and pretty quick and smarter than he looks."

Murphy let out a soft curse. "You can't blast him like you did the loup-garou?"

I shook my head. "I gave him a hard shot once already. I may as well have been spitting on him."

"Doesn't look like we have much choice for getting out."

"And even if we do, Grum or that plant thing could run us down, so we'll need wheels."

"We have to go through one of them."

"I know," I said, and headed back into the store.

"Where are you going?" Murphy demanded.

"I have a plan."

She limped after me. "Better than the Looney Tune one, I hope."

I grunted in reply. No need to agree with her.

We both realized that if this plan wasn't better than the last one, then, as Porky Pig would say, That's all, folks.

Chapter Twenty-one

❧❦ ❧❦

Three minutes later Murphy and I went out the back door, and Grum was waiting for us.

He rose up out of the shadows by the large trash bins with a bull elephant's bellow and stomped toward us. Murphy, dragging a leg and wrapped somewhat desperately in a plaid auto blanket, let out a shrill cry and turned to run, but tripped and fell to the ground before the ogre.

I kept my left hand behind my back and lifted my right. Flame danced up from my cupped fingers, and I thundered, "Grum!"

The ogre's beady eyes turned to me, glittering. He let out another rumbling snarl.

"Stand thee from my path!" I called in that same overdramatic voice, "lest I grow weary of thee and bereft thee of thy life!"

The ogre focused wholly on me now, striding forward, past the whimpering form of Murphy. "I do not fear thy power, mortal," he snarled.

I lifted my chin and waved my fire-holding hand around a bit. "This is thy last warning, faerie dog!"

Grum's beady eyes grew angrier. He let out a harsh laugh and did not slow down. "Feeble mortal trickster. Thy spellfire means nothing to me. Do thy worst."

Behind Grum, Murphy threw the auto blanket off of her shoulders, and with one rip of the starting cord fired up her shiny new Coleman chain saw. She engaged the blade with a hissing whirr of air and without preamble swung it in an arc that ended precisely at the back of Grum's thick, hairy knee. The steel blade chewed through the ogre's hide as if it was made of Styrofoam. Blood and bits of meat flew up in a gruesome cloud.

The ogre screamed, his body contorting in agony. The scarlet skin around the injury immediately swelled, darkening to black, and tendrils of infectious-looking darkness spread from the wound up over the ogre's leg and hip within the space of a breath. He swept one huge fist at Murphy, but she was already getting out of his reach. The ogre's weight came down on the injured leg, and Grum fell to earth with a heavy thud.

I started forward to help, but everything was happening fast, and my movements felt nightmarishly slow. The ogre rolled to his belly at once, maddened at the touch of the iron in the chain saw's blade, and started dragging himself toward Murphy faster than I would have believed with just his arms, talons gouging into the concrete. She hurried away from him, limping, but Grum slammed one fist down on the concrete so hard that half a dozen feet away, she was jarred off balance and fell.

Grum got hold of Murphy's foot and started dragging her back toward him. She let out a hollow gasp, then twisted and wriggled. She slipped out of her sneaker and hauled herself away from the ogre, her face gone white and drawn.

I ran up behind Grum, pulling my left hand out from behind my back, the fingers of my right hand still curled around the flickering flame I'd shown the ogre. A large yellow-and-green pump-pressure water gun sloshed a little in my left fist. I lowered it and squeezed the trigger. A stream of gasoline sprayed out all over Grum's back, soaking the ogre's skin. Grum whirled toward me halfway through, and I shot the gasoline into his eyes and nose, eliciting another scream. He bared his fangs and glared at me through eyes swollen almost shut.

"Wizard," he said, hardly understandable through the fangs and the drool, "your spellflame will not stop me."

I turned my right hand slowly, and showed Grum the burning can of Sterno I'd been palming. "Good thing I've got this plain old vanilla fire, then, huh?"

And I tossed the lit can of Sterno onto the gasoline-soaked ogre.

Hamstrung and blazing like a birthday candle, Grum screamed and thrashed. I skipped back and around him, helping Murphy up to her feet as the ogre slammed himself against the ground and then against the back wall of the Wal-Mart. He did that in a frenzy for maybe twenty seconds, before uttering an odd, ululating cry and hurling himself at a deep shadow behind a trash bin—and vanished, the light from the flames simply disappearing.

Murphy got up only with my help, her face pale with pain. She could put no weight at all on her wounded leg. "What happened?"

"We whipped him," I said. "He packed up and headed back to Faerie."

"For good?"

I shook my head. "For now. How's your leg?"

"Hurts. Think I broke something. I can hop on the other one."

"Lean on me," I said. We went a few paces, and she swayed dangerously. I caught her before she toppled. "Murph?"

"Sorry, sorry," she gasped. "Hopping, bad idea."

I helped her back down to the ground. "Look, stay here, against the wall. I'll get the Beetle and pull it around here to you."

Murphy was in enough pain to keep her from arguing. She did draw her gun, switch the safety on, and offer it to me. I shook my head. "Keep it. You might need it."

"Dresden," Murphy said, "my gun has been about as useful as fabric softener in a steel mill tonight. But someone out there has a rifle. If they're using one, it's because they're a human, and you don't have most of your magic stuff with you. Take the gun."

She was right, but I argued anyway. "I can't leave you defenseless, Murph."

Murphy hauled up the leg of her jeans and pulled a tiny automatic from an ankle holster. She worked the slide, checked the safety, and said, "I'm covered."

I took the Colt, checked the chamber and the safety, more or less by reflex. "That's a *cute* little gun there, Murph."

She scowled at me. "I have small ankles. It's the only one I can hide there."

I chanted, teasing, "Murphy's got a girl gun, Murphy's got a girl gun."

Murphy glowered at me and hauled the chain saw to within easy reach. "Come a little closer and say that."

I snorted at her. "Give me a couple minutes," I said. "I'll tell you it's me. Some of these bad guys can play dress up—so if you aren't sure who it is . . ."

Murphy nodded, pale and resolved, and rested her hand on the gun.

I drew a deep breath and walked through the mist around the side of the building and toward the front parking lot. I kept close to the wall and moved as quietly as I could, Listening as I went. I gathered up energy for the shield bracelet and held my left hand ready. I held the gun in my right. Holding a pair of defenses focused around my left hand, I would have to do all my shooting with my right. I'm not a very good shot even when I can use both hands, so I just had to hope that no sharpshooting would be required.

I got to the front of the building before I heard something click in the fenced area of the garden center. I swallowed and pointed the Colt at it, noting that I wasn't sure how many rounds the gun had left.

As I came closer, through the mist, I saw the chain fence around the ruined area where I'd been trapped with the chlorofiend. It had been torn down in a swath ten feet wide, and from what I could see of the inside, the tree-thing wasn't there anymore. Great. I took a few steps closer to the break in the fence to stare at the ruined chain link. I'd expected bent and stretched wire, still hot enough to burn where it had torn. Instead, I found edges cut off as neatly as with a set of clippers and coated with frost.

I checked around on the ground and found sections of wire, none of them longer than two or three inches. Steam curled up from them, and the cold in the air near the fence made me shiver. The fence had been frozen, chilled until the steel had become brittle and then shattered.

"Winter," I muttered. "I guess that wasn't much of a stretch."

I swept my eyes around through the mist, left my ears open, and paced as quietly as I could toward the dim, flickering lights that lay somewhere ahead in the parking lot. I'd parked the Beetle in an aisle almost even with the front doors, but I didn't have a reference point through the mist. I just headed out, picked the first row of cars, and started prowling silently along them, looking for the Beetle.

My car wasn't in the first row, but a thin stream of some kind of yellowish fluid was. I traced it to the next row, and found the Beetle sitting there in its motley colors. Another leak. They weren't exactly unheard of in a wizard's car, but this would be a hell of a time for the Beetle to get hospitalized.

I got in and set the gun down long enough to shove my keys in the ignition. My trusty steed wheezed and groaned a few times, but the engine turned over with an apologetic cough and the car rattled to life. I put it in gear, pulled through the empty space in front of me, and headed for the back of the building to get Murphy.

I had just passed the garden center with its ruined fence when my windows abruptly frosted over. It happened in the space of a breath, ice crystals forming and growing like plants on a stop-motion film until my view was completely cut off. The temperature dropped maybe fifty degrees, and the car sputtered. If I hadn't given it a bunch of gas, it would have stalled. The Beetle lurched forward, and I rolled down the window, sticking my head out the side in an effort to see what was going on.

The chlorofiend loomed up out of the mist and brought one huge, knobby fist down on the Beetle like an organic wrecking ball. The force of it crumpled the hood like tin foil and drove the shocks down so that the frame smushed up against the tires. The impact threw me forward against the steering wheel and drove the breath out of me with a shock of pain.

The impact would have rolled any car with an engine under the hood. Most of the mass of the car would have been driven down, the lighter rear end would have flipped up, and me without my seat belt would have been bounced around like a piece of popcorn.

The old Volkswagens, though, have their engine in the back. Most of the weight of the car got bounced up a little in the air, then came back down to the ground with a jolt.

I slammed my foot on the gas harder, and the Beetle's engine sputtered gamely in response. As big and strong as the chlorofiend might be, it wasn't solid and it wasn't as heavy as a living mass of the same size. The Beetle bounced up from the blow that had crumpled the empty storage compartment under the hood and slammed into the chlorofiend without losing much of its momentum.

The beast let out a shriek of what might have been surprise, and was definitely pain. My car hammered into it with a flickering of scarlet static and a cloud of smoke from the substance of the faerie creature, swept under its legs, and drove the cholorofiend atop its hood.

I kept my foot on the gas, held the wheel as steadily as I could with one hand, and stuck my head out the window so I could see. The chlorofiend screamed again, the magic around it gathering in a cloud that made the hairs on my neck stand up, but the Beetle rattled through the attempt to hex it down, carrying the chlorofiend the length of the Wal-Mart garden center and to the back of the building.

"Think of it as payback for all those telephone poles," I muttered to the Beetle, and slammed on the brakes.

The chlorofiend rolled off of my car, skidded on the asphalt, and slammed into the side of a metal trash bin with a yowl of pain and an exploding cloud of dirt clods. Only one of my headlights appeared to have survived the attack, and even it flickered woozily through the mist and the cloud of dust and dirt rising from the chlorofiend.

I slammed the car into reverse, backed up a few more feet, then put it back into neutral. I raced the engine, then popped the clutch and sent the Beetle hurtling at the monster. I braced myself for the impact this time, and pulled my head in before I hit. The impact felt violent, shockingly loud, and viscerally satisfying. The chlorofiend let out a broken-sounding creak, but until I backed the car up and whipped the wheel around so that I could see out the side window, I couldn't tell what had happened.

I'd torn the thing in half at about the middle, pinching it between the battered, frost-coated Beetle and the metal trash bin. Thank the stars it hadn't been a Fiberglas job. The legs lay against the trash bin, now only a pile of twisted saplings and earth, while the arms flailed toward me, a dozen long paces away, uselessly pounding the asphalt.

I spat out my window, put the car into gear again, and went to get Murphy.

I jumped out of the car and had to wrench the passenger door hard to get it to open. Murphy pushed herself up, using the wall for support, and stared at the frost-covered Beetle with wide eyes. "What the hell happened?"

"The plant monster."

"A plant monster and Frosty the Snowman?"

I got on her wounded side to support her. "I took care of it. Let's go."

Murphy let out another small sound of pain, but she didn't let it stop her from hobbling along toward the car. I was just about to help her in when she shouted, "Harry!" and threw her weight against me.

The chlorofiend, the upper half, had somehow clawed its way out of the mist, and one long, viny limb was reaching for me. I fell back, away from it, and tried to shield Murphy with my body.

It got me. I felt fingers the size of young tree trunks wrap around my throat and jerk me away from Murphy like I was a puppy. More branch-fingers got one of my thighs, and I felt myself suspended in the air and pulled slowly apart.

"Meddler," hissed an alien voice from somewhere near the

chlorofiend's glowing green eyes. "You should never have involved yourself in these affairs. You have no concept of what is at stake. Die for your arrogance."

I tried for a witty riposte, but my vision blacked out and my head felt like it was trapped in a slowly tightening vise. I tried gathering forces, attempting to push them through my shield bracelet, but the moment I did there was a rustle of wood and leaves, and the bracelet snapped off of my wrist, broken. I tried to gather another spell—and realized as I did that my concentration had wavered too much and that my defense against the insidious enchantment of the mist had begun to fail. My thoughts broke apart into irregular pieces, and I struggled to reach for them and put them together again as the pressure on my body increased, became a red-hot agony.

I only dimly heard the chain saw start up again, and Murphy's scream of challenge. The charm she wore wasn't relying on my concentration. It wouldn't last long, but it would keep the mist away from her for a few more minutes. The chlorofiend let out a shriek, and I heard the saw biting into wood, felt wood chips hitting my face.

I tumbled free, sapling branches tangled all around my head and shoulders, leaves and dirt scratching my face. My leg was still in the chlorofiend's grip, but I could breathe again.

The mist pressed close to me, giving me a sense of detachment and disinterest. It was hard to make any sense of what happened next. Murphy hopped closer, her weight on the one leg, and swept the chain saw through the chlorofiend's other arm. I fell to the ground, more inert tree parts around me.

The chlorofiend waved its arms at Murphy, but they didn't have the crippling force I'd seen it use before. They merely jostled her and knocked her down. Murphy snarled, crawling on her hands and knees, dragging the chain saw with her. She lifted it again and drove it at the creature's head, engine racing, blade singing through the air. The chlorofiend screamed in protest and frustration, lifting the stumps (hah hah, get it, stumps?) of its arms in feeble defense. Murphy tore through them with the chain saw, snicker-snack, and then drove the blade directly between the chlorofiend's glowing green eyes.

The monster shrieked again, writhing, but its arms never managed to do more than shove Murphy around a bit. Then it let out a final groan, and the eyes winked out. Murphy suddenly sat atop a mound of dirt and leaves and gnarled branches.

I lay there, staring stupidly at her, then heard a gunshot, the sharp, cracking report of a rifle. Murphy threw herself down and rolled toward me. A second shot rang out, and a puff of leaves a foot to Murphy's right leapt into the air.

Another sound cut through the night—police sirens, getting closer. Murphy dragged me and herself over the ground toward the car. I heard a harsh curse somewhere in the mist, and then a pair of footsteps retreating. A moment later, I thought the mist was starting to thin out.

"Harry," Murphy said, shaking me. I blinked at her, and the relief showed in her worried expression. "Harry, can you hear me?"

I nodded. My mouth felt dry and my body ached. I fought to clear my head.

"Get us in the car," she said, enunciating the words. "Get us in the car and get us out of here."

The car. Right. I hauled Murphy into the Beetle, got in myself, and stared at the frosted windshield. The heat of the summer night was already melting the frost away, and I could see through it in spots.

"Harry," Murphy said, exasperated, her voice thin and shaky. "Drive!"

Oh, right. Drive. Get out. I put the Beetle in gear, more or less, and we lurched out of the parking lot and out of the mist.

Chapter Twenty-two

"You're *kidding*," Billy said, his voice touched with disbelief. "A chain saw? Where did you get the gasoline?"

Murphy looked up from her wounded leg and the willowy Georgia, who had cut her jeans away and was cleaning out the long gashes she'd acquired from ankle to mid calf. "Gas generator, backup power supply for all the food freezers. They had a ten-gallon plastic jug of it."

Billy's apartment was not a large one, and with a dozen people in it, even with the air-conditioning running full blast, it was too hot and too crowded. The Alphas, Billy's werewolf accomplices, were out in force. We'd been challenged by a tall, thin young man in the parking lot and shadowed to the door by a pair of wolves who kept just far enough away to make it difficult to see them in the shadows.

When I'd first seen them, the Alphas had been a collection of misfits with bad hair, acne, and wanna-be tough guy leather outfits. In the year and a half since, they'd changed. None of them had that pale look anymore, none of them looked wheezy, and like Billy, the kids who'd been carrying baby fat had swapped it for lean, fit muscle. They hadn't become a gang of Hollywood soap opera stars or anything, but they looked more relaxed, more confident, more happy—and I saw some scars, some of them quite vicious, showing on bare limbs. Most of the kids wore sweats, or those pullover knit dresses, garments that could be gotten out of in a hurry.

Pizza boxes were stacked three deep on the table, and a cooler of soft drinks sat on the floor nearby. I piled a plate with half-warm pizza, picked up a Coke, and found a comparatively empty stretch of wall to lean against.

Billy shook his head and said, "Look, Harry, some of this doesn't make sense. I mean, if they could really run around doing this mind fog thing, shouldn't we have heard about it by now?"

I snorted and said around a mouthful of pizza, "It's pretty rare, even in my circles. No one who got hit with it will remember it. Check the paper tomorrow. Ten to one, emergency services showed up after we left, put out the fires, pulled a bunch of confused people out of the building, and the official explanation is a leaky gas line."

Billy snorted. "That doesn't make any sense. There's not going to be evidence of an exploding line, no leak is going to show up at the gas company, no continuing fire of leaking gas—"

I kept eating. "Get real, Billy," I said. "You think people are going to be taken seriously by City Hall if they tell them, 'We really don't know what messed up all these people, we don't know what caused all the damage, we don't know why no one heard or saw anything, and we don't know what the reports of gunshots at the scene were about?' Hell, no. People would be accused of incompetence, publicly embarrassed, fired. No one wants that. So, gas leak."

"But it's stupid!"

"It's life. The last thing the twenty-first century wants to admit is that it might not know everything." I popped open the Coke and guzzled some. "How's the leg, Murph?"

"It hurts," Murphy reported, considerately leaving out the implied "you idiot."

Georgia stood up from attending Murphy's leg and shook her head. She was nearly a foot taller than Billy, and had bound her blond hair back into a tight braid. It emphasized the gauntness of her features. "The cuts and bruises are nothing major, but your knee could be seriously damaged. You should have it checked out by a real doctor, Lieutenant Murphy."

"Karrin," Murphy said. "Anyone who mops up my blood can call me Karrin." I tossed Murphy a Coke. She caught it and said, "Except you, Dresden. Any diet?"

I put several slices of pizza on a paper plate and passed them over. "Live a little."

"All right, Karrin," Georgia said, folding her arms. "If you don't want a twenty-five-thousand-dollar surgery along with seven or eight months of rehab, we need to get you to the hospital."

Murphy frowned, then nodded and said, "Let me eat something first. I'm starving."

"I'll get the car," Georgia said. She turned to Billy. "Make sure she doesn't put any weight on her leg when you bring her down. Keep it straight if you can."

"Got it," Billy said. "Phil, Greg. Get that blanket. We'll make a litter out of it."

"I'm not an infant," Murphy said.

I put my hand on her shoulder. "Easy," I said in a quiet voice. "They can handle themselves."

"So can I."

"You're hurt, Murph," I said. "If you were one of your people, you'd be telling you to shut up and stop being part of the problem."

Murphy shot me a glower, but its edge was blunted by the big mouthful of pizza she took. "Yeah. I know. I just hate being sidelined."

I grunted.

"What are you going to do?" she asked.

I shook my head. "Finish this Coke. I haven't planned much past that."

She sighed. "All right, Harry. Look, I'll be home in a few hours. I'll keep digging, see if I can turn up anything about Lloyd Slate. If you need information on anything else, get in touch."

"You should rest," I told her.

She grimaced at her leg. Her knee was swollen to a couple of times its normal size. "Looks like I'm going to have plenty of time for that."

I grunted again and looked away.

"Hey, Harry," Murphy said. When I didn't look at her, she continued, "What happened to me wasn't your fault. I knew the risks and I took them."

"You shouldn't have had to."

"No one should. We live in an imperfect world, Dresden. In case that hasn't yet become obvious enough for you." She nudged my leg with her elbow. "Besides. You were lucky I was there. The way I count it, I'm the one who put on the boots."

A smile threatened my expression. "You did what?"

"Put on the boots," Murphy said. "I put on the boots and kicked some monster ass. I dropped the ghoul, and I'm the one

who rammed a chain saw through the head of that plant monster
thing. Crippled the ogre, too. What did you do? You threw a can of
Sterno at him. That's barely an assist."

"Yeah, but I soaked him in gasoline first."

She snorted at me, around more pizza. "Shutout."

"Whatever."

"Murphy three, Dresden zero."

"You didn't do all of it."

"I put on the boots."

I raised my hands. "Okay, okay. You've . . . got boots,
Murph."

She sniffed and took an almost dainty sip of Coke. "Lucky I
was there."

I squeezed her shoulder and said, with no particular inflection,
"Yes. Thank you."

Murphy smiled up at me. From the window, one of the Alphas
reported, "Car's ready."

Billy and a couple more laid out a blanket and then carefully
lifted Murphy onto it. She tolerated them with a roll of her eyes,
but hissed with discomfort even at the gentle motion.

"Call," she said.

"Will."

"Watch your back, Harry." Then they carried her out.

I picked up some more pizza, exchanged some more or less
polite chitchat with some of the Alphas, and made my escape
from the crowded living room of the apartment to the balcony. I
shut the sliding glass door behind me. Only one light in the parking lot provided any illumination, so the balcony was mostly covered in sheltering shadows. The night was a close one, humidity
cooking along at a lazy summer broil, but even so it felt less claus-
trophobic than the crowded apartment.

I watched Billy and the Alphas load Murphy into a minivan
and drive off. Then there was as much silence as you ever get in
Chicago. The hiss of tires on asphalt was a constant, liquid background, punctuated with occasional sirens, horns, mechanical
squeaks and squeals, and the buzzing of one lost locust that must
have been perched on a building nearby.

I put my paper plate on the wooden balcony railing, closed my
eyes, and took a deep breath, trying to clear my head.

"Penny for your thoughts," said a quiet female voice.

I nearly jumped off the balcony in sheer reaction. My hand
brushed the paper plate, and the pizza fell to the parking lot below.

I whirled around and found Meryl sitting in a chair at the other side of the balcony, deep in shadows, her large form nothing more than a more solid piece of darkness—but her eyes gleamed in the half-light, reflecting traces of red. She watched the plate fall and then said, "Sorry."

"S'okay," I said. "Just a little nervous tonight."

She nodded. "I was listening."

I nodded back to her and returned to looking at nothing, listening to night sounds. After a while, she asked me, "Does it hurt?"

I waved my bandaged hand idly. "Sort of."

"Not that," she said. "I meant watching your friend get hurt."

Some of my racing thoughts coalesced into irritated anger. "What kind of question is that?"

"A simple one."

I took an angry hit from my can of Coke. "Of course it hurts."

"You're different than I thought you'd be."

I squinted over my shoulder at her.

"They tell stories about you, Mister Dresden."

"It's all a lie."

Her teeth gleamed. "Not all of them are bad."

"Mostly good or mostly bad?"

"Depends on who's talking. The Sidhe crowd thinks you're an interesting mortal pet of Mab's. The vampire wanna-be crowd thinks you're some kind of psychotic vigilante with a penchant for vengeance and mayhem. Sort of a one-man Spanish Inquisition. Most of the magical crowd thinks you're distant, dangerous, but smart and honorable. Crooks think you're a hit man for the outfit, or maybe one of the families back East. Straights think you're a fraud trying to bilk people out of their hard-won cash, except for Larry Fowler, who probably wants you on the show again."

I regarded her, frowning. "And what do you think?"

"I think you need a haircut." She lifted a can to her mouth and I caught a whiff of beer. "Bill called all the morgues and hospitals. No Jane Doe with green hair."

"Didn't figure there would be. I talked to Aurora. She seemed concerned."

"She would. She's everyone's big sister. Thinks she needs to take care of the whole world."

"She didn't know anything."

Meryl shook her head and was quiet for a while before she asked, "What's it like being a wizard?"

I shrugged. "Mostly it's like being a watch fob repairman. It's both difficult and not in demand. The rest of the time . . ."

More emotion rose in me, threatening my self-control. Meryl waited.

"The rest of the time," I picked up, "it's scary as hell. You start learning the kinds of things that go bump in the night and you figure out that 'ignorance is bliss' is more than just a quotable quote. And it's—" I clenched my hands. "It's so damned *frustrating*. You see people getting hurt. Innocents. Friends. I try to make a difference, but I usually don't know what the hell is going on until someone is already dead. Doesn't matter what kind of job I do—I can't help those folks."

"Sounds hard," Meryl said.

I shrugged. "I guess it isn't any different than what anyone else goes through. The names just get changed." I finished off the Coke and stomped the dead soldier flat. "What about you? What's it like being a changeling?"

Meryl rolled the beer can between her broad hands. "About like anyone, until you hit puberty. Then you start feeling things."

"What kinds of things?"

"Different, depending on your Sidhe half. For me it was anger, hunger. I gained a lot of weight. I kept losing my temper over the most idiotic things." She took a drink. "And strength. I grew up on a farm. My older brother rolled a tractor and it pinned him, broke his hip, and caught on fire. I picked it up and threw it off him, then dragged him back to the house. More than a mile. I was twelve. My hair had turned this color by the next morning."

"Troll," I said quietly.

She nodded. "Yeah. I don't know the details about what happened, but yeah. And every time I let those feelings get loose, the more I lost my temper and used my strength, the bigger and stronger I got. And the worse I felt about what I did." She shook her head. "Sometimes I think it would be easier to just choose the Sidhe half. To stop being human, stop hurting. If it wasn't for the others needing me . . ."

"It would turn you into a monster."

"But a happy monster." She finished her beer. "I should go check on Fix—he's sleeping now—and try to call Ace. What are you going to do?"

"Try to add up some facts. Meet some contacts. Interview more Queens. Maybe get a haircut."

Her teeth showed again in a smile, and she rose. "Good luck." She went back into the noisy apartment and shut the door.

I closed my eyes and tried to think. Whoever had sent the Tigress, Grum, the chlorofiend, and the lone gunman after me had been trying to kill me. It was a reasonable assumption, then, that I was on the right track. Generally speaking, the bad guys don't try to bump off an investigator unless they're worried he's actually about to find something.

But if that was true, then why had the Tigress taken a shot at me the day before I'd gotten the case? She could have been working for the Red Court and taken a new contract that just happened to be me, but it didn't sound likely. If the ghoul had been on the same contract, it meant that I'd been judged a threat to the killer's plans from day one, if not sooner.

The frost on my car's windows had probably been the doing of someone from Winter. I mean, a wizard could do the same thing, but as devastating spells go, that one seemed to be kinda limited. The ghoul, presumably, would work for anyone who paid. The chlorofiend, though . . . I hadn't expected it to talk, or to be intelligent.

The more I thought about the plant monster, the more things didn't add up. It had picked a spot and had its allies herd me to it. That wasn't the behavior of your average thug, even of the magical variety. It had a sense of personal conflict about it, as if the chlorofiend had a particular bone to pick with me.

And how the hell had Murphy killed it? It was stronger than your average bulldozer, for crying out loud. It had socked me once when I had my full shield going, and it still hurt. It had clipped me a couple of times and nearly broken bones.

The chlorofiend should have flattened Murphy into a puddle of slurry. It had hit her at least a dozen times, yet it seemed like it had only tapped her, as though unable to risk doing more damage. Then a lightbulb flashed on somewhere in my musty brain. The chlorofiend hadn't been a being, as such. It had been a construct— a magical vessel for an outside awareness. An awareness both intelligent and commanding, but one who could not, for some reason, kill Murphy when she attacked it. Why?

"Because, Harry, you idiot, Murphy isn't attached to either of the Faerie Courts," I told myself. Out loud.

"What's that got to do with it?" I asked myself. Again out loud. And people think I'm crazy.

"Remember. The Queens can't kill anyone who isn't attached to the Courts through birthright or bargain. She couldn't kill Murphy. Neither could the construct she was guiding."

"Damn," I muttered. "You're right."

A Queen seemed reasonable, then—probably from Winter. Or, more realistically, the frosted windshield could have been a decoy. Either way, I couldn't figure who would have had a reason to come after me with something as elaborate as a mind fog and a veritable army of assassins.

Which reminded me. The mind fog had to have come from somewhere. I wasn't sure if the Queens could have managed something like that outside of Faerie. If they couldn't, it meant that the killer had a hired gun, someone who could pull off a delicate and dangerous spell like that.

I started running down that line of thought, but only a moment later the wind picked up into a stiff, whistling breeze that roared through the air and swept down through the city. I frowned at the sudden shift in the weather and looked around.

I didn't find anything obvious, but when I glanced up, I saw the lights going out. A vast cloud bank was racing north, fast enough that I could see it eating the stars. A second wall of clouds was sailing south, toward the first bank. They met in only moments, and as they did, light flashed from cloud to cloud, brighter than daylight, and thunder shook the balcony beneath my feet. Not long after that, a drop of freezing-cold water landed on my head, quickly followed by a mounting torrent of chilly rain. The still-rising wind whipped it into a miserable downpour.

I turned and pulled open the door into the apartment with a frown. The Alphas were peering out windows, speaking quietly with one another. Across the room, Billy finished messing around with a television, and a rather rumpled-looking weatherman appeared, the image flickering with interference lines and bursts of snow.

"Guys, guys," Billy said. "Hush, let me listen." He turned up the volume.

". . . a truly unprecedented event, an enormous Arctic blast that came charging like a freight train through Canada and across Lake Michigan to Chicagoland. And if that wasn't enough, a tropical front, settled quietly in the Gulf of Mexico, has responded in kind, rushing up the Mississippi River in a sudden heat wave. They've met right over Lake Michigan, and we have received several reports of rain and bursts of hail. Thunderstorm warnings have been issued all through the Lake Michigan area, and a tornado watch is in progress for the next hour in Cook Country. National Weather Service has also issued a flash flood warning and a travel advisory for the eastern half of Illinois. This is some beautiful but very violent weather, ladies and gentlemen, and we urge you to remain in shelter until this storm has time to . . ."

Billy turned the volume down. I looked around the room and found nearly a dozen sets of eyes focused on me, patient and trusting. Bah.

"Harry," Billy said at last, "that isn't a natural storm, is it?"

I shook my head, got another Coke out of the cooler, and headed tiredly for the door. "Side effect. Like the toads."

"What does it mean?"

I opened the door and said, without looking back, "It means we're running out of time."

Chapter Twenty-three

❄❄❄❄

I took the Beetle a ways north of town, keeping to the lake shore. Rain sheeted down, and lightning made the clouds dance with shadow and flame. Maybe ten miles from the center of town, the downpour eased up, and the air became noticeably colder—enough so that in jeans and a tee, I was shivering. I pulled the car off Sheridan Road a couple miles north of Northwestern University, out toward Winnetka, set the parking brake and locked it up, and trudged toward the shore of the lake.

It was a dark night, but I called no lights to guide me, and I didn't carry a flashlight. It took my eyes a while, but I finally managed to start making out shapes in the darkness and found my way through the light woods around this part of the lake shore to a long, naked promontory of rock thrusting itself a dozen yards into the water. I walked to the end of the stone and stood there for a moment, listening to the thunder rolling over the lake, the wind stirring the water into waves nearly like those of the sea. The air itself felt restless, charged with violence, and the light rain that still fell was uncomfortably cold.

I closed my eyes, pulling together energy from the elements around me, where water met stone, air met water, stone met air, and drawing as well from my own determination. The power coursed into me, dancing and seething with a quivering life of its own. I focused it with my thoughts, shaped it, and then opened my eyes and lifted my arms, wrists out so that the old pale round scars on either side of the big blue veins there felt the rain falling on them.

I pushed out the power I'd gathered and called into the thunder and rain, "Godmother! *Vente*, Leanansidhe!"

A sudden presence appeared beside me, and a woman's voice said, "Honestly, child, it isn't as though I'm far away. There's no reason to shout."

I jerked in surprise and nearly fell into the lake. I turned to my left to face my faerie godmother, who stood calmly upon the surface of the water, bobbing up and down a bit as waves passed under her feet.

Lea stood nearly my own height, but instead of dark contrasts and harsh angles, she was a creature of gliding curves and gentle shades. Hair the color of flame coursed in curls and ringlets to below her hips, and tonight she wore with it a gown of flowing emerald silk, laced through with veins of ochre and aquamarine. A belt made from a twisted braid of silken threads of gold wound around her waist, and a dark-handled knife rested on a slant at her hip through a loop in the belt.

She was one of the high Sidhe, and her beauty went without saying. The perfection of her form was complemented by features of feminine loveliness, a full mouth, skin like cream, and oblong, feline eyes of gold, cat-slitted like those of most fae. She took in my surprise with a certain reserved mirth, her mouth set with a tiny smile.

"Good evening, Godmother," I said, trying for a proper degree of politeness. "You look lovely as the stars tonight."

She let out a pleased sigh. "Such a flatterer. I'm already enjoying this conversation so much more than the last."

"I'm not dying this time," I said.

The smile faded. "That is a matter of opinion," she responded. "You are in great danger, child."

"Thinking about it, I realize I generally have been whenever you were around."

She clucked reprovingly. "Nonsense. I've never had anything but your best interests at heart."

I barked out a harsh laugh. "My best interests. That's rich."

Lea arched a brow. "What reason have you to think otherwise?"

"For starters, because you tricked me out of a big evil slaying magic sword and sold me to Mab."

"Tut," Lea said. "The sword was just business, child. And as for selling your debt to Mab . . . I had no choice in the matter."

"Yeah, right."

She arched her brows. "You should know better, dear god-child. You know I cannot speak what is untrue. During our last encounter I returned to Faerie with great power and upset vital balances. Those balances had to be redressed, and your debt was the mechanism that the Queen chose to employ."

I frowned at her for a minute. "Returned with great power." My eyes fell to the knife at her waist. "That thing the vampires gave you?"

She rested her fingers lightly on the knife's hilt. "Don't cheapen it. This athame was no creation of theirs. And it was less a gift than a trade."

"*Amoracchius* and that thing are in the same league? Is that what you're saying?" Gulp. My faerie godmother was dangerous enough without a big-time artifact of magic. "What is it?"

"Not what, but whose," Lea corrected me. "And in any case, you may be assured that surrendering my claim on you to Mab was in no way an attempt to do you harm. I have never meant you lasting ill."

I scowled at her. "You tried to turn me into one of your hounds and keep me in a kennel, Godmother."

"You'd have been perfectly safe there," she pointed out. "And very happy. I only wanted what was best for you because I care for you, child."

My stomach did a neat little rollover, and I swallowed. "Yeah. Uh. It's very . . . you. I guess. In a demented, insane way, I can understand that."

Lea smiled. "I knew you would. To business, then. Why have you called to me this night?"

I took a deep breath and braced myself a little. "Look, I know we haven't gotten along really well lately. Or ever. And I don't have a lot to trade with, but I had hoped you'd be willing to work out a bargain with me."

She arched a red-gold brow. "To what ends?"

"I need to speak to them," I said. "To Mab and Titania."

Her expression grew distant, pensive. "You must understand that I cannot protect you from them, should they strike at you. My power has grown, poppet, but not to those heights."

"I understand. But if I don't get to the bottom of this and find the killer, I'm as good as dead."

"So I have heard," my godmother said. She lifted her right hand and extended it to me. "Then give me your hand."

"I *need* my hand, Godmother. Both of them."

She let out a peal of laughter. "No, silly child. Simply put your hand in mine. I will convey you."

I gave her a sidelong look and asked warily, "At what price?"

"None."

"*None?* You never do anything without a price."

She rolled her eyes and clarified, "None to you, child."

"Who, then?"

"No one you know, or knew," Lea said.

An intuition hit me. "My mother. That's who you're talking about."

Lea left her hand extended. She smiled, but only said, "Perhaps."

I regarded her hand quietly for a moment, then said, "I'm not sure I can believe that you're really going to protect me."

"But I already have."

I folded my arms. "When?"

"If you will remember that night in the boneyard, I healed a wound to your head that may well have killed you."

"You only did it to sucker me into getting you the sword!"

Lea's tone became wounded. "Not *only* for that. And if you consider further, I also freed you of a crippling binding and rescued you from a blazing inferno not twenty-four hours later."

"You charged my girlfriend all her memories of me to do it! And you only saved me from the fire so that you could put me in a doghouse."

"That does not change the fact that I was, after all, protecting you."

I stared at her in frustration for a minute and then scowled. "What have you done for me lately?"

Lea closed her eyes for a moment, then opened her mouth and spoke. Her voice came out aged and querulous. "What's all that racket! I have already called the police, I have! You fruits get out of our hall or they'll lock you away!"

I blinked. "Reuel's apartment. That was you?"

"Obviously, child. And at the market, earlier this eve." She lifted her hand in the air, made an intricate motion with long, pale fingers, and opened her mouth again, as if singing a note of music. Instead, the sound of police sirens emerged, somewhat muted and indistinguishable from the real thing.

I shook my head. "I don't get it."

She moved her fingers again, and the sirens blended into another silver-sweet laugh, her expression amused, almost fond. "I am sure you do not, poppet." She offered her hand again. "Come. Time is pressing."

She had that part right at least. And I knew she was telling me the truth. Her words had left her little room for evasion. I'd never gotten anything but burned when making deals with the faeries, and if Lea was offering to help me for free, there had to be a catch somewhere.

Lea's expression told me that she either knew what I'd been thinking or knew me well enough to guess, and she laughed again. "Harry, Harry," she said. "If it is of any consequence to you, remember that our bargain is still in effect. I am bound to do you no harm for several weeks more."

I'd forgotten about that. Of course, I couldn't fully trust to that, either. Even if she had sworn to do me no harm, if I asked her to take me somewhere she could drop me off in a forest full of Unseelie nasties without breaking her word. She'd done something very similar to me last year.

Thunder rumbled again, and the light flared even more brightly in the clouds. Tick, tick, tick, the clock was running, and I wasn't going to get anything done standing here waffling. Either I trusted myself to my godmother or I went back home and waited for something to come along and squash me.

Going with Lea wasn't the best way to get what I wanted—it was just the only way. I took a breath and took her hand. Her skin felt like cool silk, untouched by the rain. "All right. And after them, I need to see the Mothers."

Lea gave me an oblique glance and said, "Survive the flood before hurling yourself into the fire, child. Close your eyes."

"Why?"

Annoyance flickered over her eyebrows. "Child, stop wasting time with questions. You have given me your hand. Close your eyes."

I muttered a curse to myself and did it. My godmother spoke something, a string of liquid syllables in a tongue I could not understand—but it made my knees turn rubbery and my fingers suddenly feel weak. A wave of disorientation, dizzying but not unpleasantly so, scrambled my sense of direction. I felt a breeze on my face, a sense of movement, but I couldn't have said whether I was falling or rising or moving forward.

The movement stopped, and the whirling sensations passed. Thunder rumbled again, very loudly, and the surface I stood on shook with it. Light played against my closed eyelids.

"We are here," Lea said, her voice hushed.

I opened my eyes.

I stood on a solid surface among grey and drifting mist. The mist covered whatever ground I was on, and though I poked at it with my foot, I couldn't tell if it was earth, wood, or concrete. The landscape around me rolled in hills and shallow valleys, all of it covered in ground fog. I frowned up at the skies. They were clear. Stars glittered impossibly bright against the velvet curtain of night, sparkling in dozens of colors, instead of in the usual pale silver, jewels against the blackness of the void. Thunder rumbled again, and the ground shook beneath the mist. Lightning flashed along with it, and the ground all around us lit with a sudden angry blue fire that slowly faded away.

The truth dawned on me slowly. I pushed my foot at the ground again, and then in a circle around me. "We're . . ." I choked. "We're on . . . we're on . . ."

"The clouds," my godmother said, nodding. "Or so it would seem to you. We are no longer in the mortal world."

"The Nevernever, then. Faerie?"

She shook her head and spoke, her voice still hushed, almost reverent. "No. This is the world between, the sometimes place. Where Chicago and Faerie meet, overlap. Chicago-Over-Chicago, if you will. This is the place the Queens call forth when the Sidhe desire to spill blood."

"They call it forth?" I asked in a quiet voice. "They create it?"

"Even so," Lea said, her voice similarly low. "They prepare for war."

I turned slowly, taking it in. We stood on a rise of ground in a broad, shallow valley. I could make out what looked like a mist-shrouded lake shore not far away. A river cut through the cloudscape.

"Wait a minute," I said. "This is . . . familiar." Chicago-Over-Chicago, she had said. I started adding in mental images of buildings, streets, lights, cars, people. "This *is* Chicago. The land."

"A model of it," Lea agreed. "Crafted from clouds and mist."

I kept turning and found behind me a stone, grey and ominous and enormous, startlingly solid amid all the drifting white. I took a step back from it and saw the shape of it—a table, made of a massive slab of rock, the legs made of more stones as thick as the pillars at Stonehenge. Writing writhed across the surface of the stone, runes that looked a little familiar. Norse, maybe? Some of them looked more like Egyptian. They seemed to take something from several different sources, leaving them unreadable. Lightning flashed again through the ground, and a wave of blue-white light flooded over the table, through the runes, lighting them like Las Vegas neon for a moment.

"I've heard of this," I said after a moment. "A long time ago. Ebenezar called it the Stone Table."

"Yes," my godmother whispered. "Blood is power, child. Blood spilled upon that stone forever becomes a part of who holds it."

"Who holds it?"

She nodded, her green eyes luminous. "For half of the year, the Table lies within Winter. For half, within Summer."

"It changes hands," I said, understanding. "Midsummer and Midwinter."

"Yes. Summer holds the Table now. But not for much longer."

I stepped toward the Table and extended a hand. The air around it literally shook, pressing against my fingers, making my skin ripple visibly as though against a strong wind—but I felt nothing. I touched the surface of the Table itself, and could feel the power in it, buzzing through the flowing runes like electricity through high-voltage cables. The sensation engulfed my hand with sudden heat and violence, and I jerked my fingers back. They were numb, and the nails of the two that had touched the table were blackened at the edges. Wisps of smoke rose from them.

I shook my fingers and looked at my godmother. "Let me get this straight. Blood spilled onto the Table turns into power for whoever holds it. Summer now. But Winter, after tomorrow night."

Lea inclined her head, silent.

"I don't understand what makes that so important."

She frowned at the Table, then began pacing around it, slowly, clockwise, her eyes never leaving me. "The Table is not merely a repository for energy, child. It is a conduit. Blood spilled upon its surface takes more than merely life with it."

"Power," I said. I frowned and folded my arms, watching her. "So if, for instance, a wizard's blood spilled there . . ."

She smiled. "Great power would come of it. Mortal life, mortal magic, drawn into the hands of whichever Queen ruled the Table."

I swallowed and took a step back. "Oh."

Lea completed her circuit of the table and stopped beside me. She glanced furtively around her, then looked me in the eyes and said, her voice barely audible, "Child. Should you survive this conflict, do not let Mab bring you here. Never."

A chill crawled down my spine. "Yeah. Okay." I shook my head. "Godmother, I still don't get what you're trying to tell me. Why is the Table so important?"

She gestured, left and right, toward a pair of hilltops facing one another across the broad valley. I looked at one, squinting at a sudden blur in my vision. I tried looking at the other, and the same thing happened. "I can't see," I said. "It's a veil or something."

"You must see if you are to understand."

I drew in a slow breath. Wizards can see things most people can't. It's called the Sight, the Third Eye, a lot of other names. If a wizard uses his Sight, he can see the forces of magic themselves at work, spells like braids of neon lights, veils pierced like projections on a screen. A wizard's Sight shows things as they truly are, and it's always an unsettling experience, one way or the other. What you see with the Sight stays with you. Good or bad, it's always just as fresh in your mind as if you'd just seen it. I'd looked on a little tree-spirit being with my Sight when I'd been about fourteen, the first time it had happened to me, and I still had a perfect picture of it in my head, as though I was *still* looking at it, a little cartoonish being that was part lawn gnome and part squirrel.

I'd seen worse since. Much worse. Demons. Mangled souls. Tormented spirits. All of that was still there too. But I'd also seen better. One or two glimpses of beings of such beauty and purity and light that it could make me weep. But each time it got a little harder to live with, a little harder to bear, a cumulative weight.

I gritted my teeth, closed my eyes, and with careful deliberation unlocked my Sight.

Opening my eyes again made me stagger as I was hit with a sudden rush of impressions. The cloudy landscape absolutely seethed with magical energies. From the southern hilltop, wild green and golden light spilled, falling over the landscape like a translucent garden, vines of green, golden flowers, flashes of other colors spread through them, clawing at the gentle ground, anchored here and there at points of light so vibrant and bright that I couldn't look directly at them.

From the other side, cold blue and purple and greenish power spread like crystals of ice, with the slow and relentless power of a glacier, pressing ahead in some places, melted back in others, especially strong around the valley's winding rivers.

The conflict of energies both wound back to the hilltops themselves, to points of light as bright as small suns. I could, just barely, see the shadow of solid beings within those lights, and even the shadow of each was an overwhelming presence upon my senses. One was a sense of warmth, choking heat, so much that I couldn't breathe, that it pressed into me and set me aflame. The other was of cold, horrible and absolute, winding cold limbs around me, stealing away my strength. Those presences flooded through me, sudden beauty, power so terrifying and exhilarating and awesome that I fell to my knees and sobbed.

Those powers played against one another—I could sense that, though not the exact nature of their conflict. Energies wound about one another, subtle pressures of darkness and light, leaving the landscape vaguely lit in squares of cold and warm color. Fields of red and gold and bright green stood against empty, dead blocks of blue, purple, pale white. A pattern had formed in them, a structure to the conflict that was not wholly complete. Most of a chessboard. Only at the center, at the Table, was the pattern broken, a solid area of Summer's power in green and gold around the Stone Table, while Winter's dark, crystalline ice slowly pressed closer, somehow in time with the almost undetectable motion of the stars overhead.

So I saw it. I got a look at what I was up against, at the naked strength of the two Queens of Faerie, and it was bigger than me. Every ounce of strength I could have summoned would have been no more than a flickering spark beside either of those blazing fountains of light and magic. It was power that had existed since the dawn of life, and would until its end. It was power that had cowed mortals into abject worship and terror before—and I finally understood why. I wasn't a pawn of that kind of strength. I was an insect beside giants, a blade of grass before towering trees.

And there was a dreadful attraction in seeing that power, something in it that called to the magic in me, like to like, made me want to hurl myself into those flames, into that endless, icy cold. Moths look at bug zappers like I looked at the Queens of Faerie.

I tore my eyes away by hiding my face in my arms. I fell to my side on the ground and curled up, trying to shut the Sight, to force those images to stop flooding over me. I shook and tried to say something. I'm not sure what. It came out as stuttering, gibbering sounds. After that, I don't remember much until cold rain started slapping me on the cheek.

I opened my eyes and found myself lying on the cold, wet

ground on the shores of Lake Michigan, where I'd first called out to my godmother. My head was on something soft that turned out to be her lap. I sat up and away from her quickly. My head hurt, and the images the Sight had showed me made me feel particularly small and vulnerable. I sat shivering in the rain for a minute before I glanced back at my godmother.

"You should have warned me."

Her face showed no remorse, and little concern. "It would have changed nothing. You needed to see." She paused and then added, "I regret that it was the only way. Do you yet understand?"

"The war," I said. "They'll fight for control of the area around the Table. If Summer holds the space, it won't matter if it's Winter's time or not. Mab won't be able to reach the table, spill blood on it, and add the power of the Summer Knight to Winter." I took a breath. "There was a sense to what they were doing. As though it was a ritual. Something they'd done before."

"Of course," Lea said. "They exist in opposition. Each wields vast power, wizard—power to rival the archangels and lesser gods. But they cancel one another flawlessly. And in the end, the board will be evenly divided. The lesser pieces will emerge and do battle to decide the balance."

"The Ladies," I said. "The Knights."

"And," Lea added, lifting a finger, "the Emissaries."

"Like hell. I'm not fighting in some kind of fucked-up faerie battle in the clouds."

"Perhaps. Perhaps not."

I snorted. "But you didn't help me. I needed to speak to them. Find out if one of them was responsible."

"And so you did. More truly than if you'd exchanged words."

I frowned at her and thought through what I knew, and what I'd learned on my trip to the Stone Table. "Mab shouldn't be in any hurry. If Summer is missing her Knight, Winter has the edge if they wait. There's no need to take the Table."

"Yes."

"But Summer is moving to protect the Table. That means Titania thinks someone in Winter did it. But if Mab is responding instead of waiting, it means . . ." I frowned. "It means she isn't sure why Summer is moving. She's just checking Titania's advance. And *that* means that she isn't sure whodunit, either."

"Simplistic," Lea said. "But accurate enough reasoning, poppet. Such are the thoughts of the Queens of the Sidhe." She looked out across the lake. "Your sun will rise in some little time. When once again it sets, the war will begin. In a balanced Court, it would mean, perhaps, little of great consequence to the mortal world. But that balance is gone. If it is not restored, child, imagine what might happen."

I did. I mean, I'd had an idea what might go wrong before, but now I *knew* the scale of the forces involved. The powers of Winter and Summer weren't simply a bunch of electricity in a battery. They were like vast coiled springs, pressing against one another. As long as that pressure was equal, the energies were held in control. But an imbalance in one side or the other could cause them to slip, and the release of energies from either side would be vast and violent, and sure to inflict horrible consequences on anything nearby—in this case, Chicago, North America, and probably a good chunk of the rest of the world with it.

"I need to see the Mothers. Get me to them."

Lea rose, all grace and opaque expression, impossible to read. "That, too, is beyond me, child."

"I *need* to speak to the Mothers."

"I agree," Lea said. "But I cannot take you to them. The power is not mine. Perhaps Mab or Titania could, but they are otherwise occupied now. Committed."

"Great," I muttered. "How do I get to them?"

"One does not get to the Mothers, child. One can only answer an invitation." She frowned faintly. "I can do no more to help you. The lesser powers must take their places with the Queens, and I am needed shortly."

"You're going?"

She nodded, stepped forward, and kissed my brow. It was just a kiss, a press of soft lips against my skin. Then she stepped back, one hand on the hilt of the knife at her belt. "Be careful, child. And be swift. Remember—sundown." She paused and looked at me askance. "And consider a haircut. You look like a dandelion."

And with that, she stepped out onto the lake, and her form melted into water that fell back into the storm-tossed waters with a splash.

"Great," I muttered. I kicked a rock into the water. "Just great. Sundown. I know nothing. And the people I need to talk to screen all of their calls." I picked up another rock and threw it as hard as I could over the lake. The sound of rain swallowed up the splash.

I turned and trudged back toward the Beetle through the thunder and the rain. I could see the shapes of the trees a bit better now. Dawn must be coming on, somewhere behind the clouds.

I sat down behind the wheel of the trusty Beetle, put the key in, and started the car.

The battered old Volkswagen wheezed once, lurched without being put into gear, and then started to fill with smoke. I choked and scrambled out of the car. I hit the release on the engine cover and opened it. Black smoke billowed out, and I could dimly see fire behind it, chewing up some part of the engine. I went back to the front storage compartment, got out the fire extinguisher, and put out the fire. Then I stood there in the rain, tired and aching and staring at my burnt engine.

Dawn. At Midsummer, that meant I had maybe fifteen hours to figure out how to get to the Mothers. Somehow, I doubted that their number was listed. Even if it had been, my visit to the battle-ground around the Stone Table had shown me that the Queens possessed far more power than I could have believed. Their sheer presence had nearly blown the top off my head from a mile away—and the Mothers were an order of magnitude above even Mab and Titania.

I had fifteen hours to find the killer and restore the Summer Knight's mantle to the Summer Court. And *then* to stop a war happening in some wild nether-place between here and the spirit world that I had no idea how to reach.

And my car had died. Again.

"Over your head," I muttered. "Harry, this is too big for you to handle alone."

The Council. I should contact Ebenezar, tell him what was happening. The situation was too big, too volatile, to risk screwing it up over a matter of Council protocol. Maybe I'd get lucky and the Council would A, believe me, and B, decide to help.

Yeah. And maybe if I glued enough feathers to my arms, I'd be able to fly.

Chapter Twenty-four

less❦❦

I examined my car for a few minutes more, took a couple of things off it, and walked to the nearest gas station. I called a wrecker, then got a cab back to my apartment, paying for everything with Meryl's advance.

Once there, I got a Coke out of the icebox, put out fresh food and water for Mister, and changed his kitty litter. It wasn't until I had dug around under the kitchen sink, gotten out the bottle of dishwashing soap, and blown the dust off of it that I realized I was stalling.

I glowered at the phone and told myself, "Pride goeth before a fall, Harry. Pride can be bad. It can make you do stupid things."

I took a deep breath and shotgunned the Coke. Then I picked up the phone and dialed the number Morgan had left me.

It barely rang once before someone picked up and a male voice said, "Who is calling, please?"

"Dresden. I need to speak to Ebenezar McCoy."

"One moment." Sound cut off, and I figured whoever answered must have put their hand over the mouthpiece. Then there was a rustle as the phone changed hands.

"You've failed, then, Dresden," Morgan stated. His tone gave me a good mental picture of the smile on his smug face. "Stay where you are until the Wardens arrive to escort you to the Senior Council for judgement."

I bit down on a creative expletive. "I haven't failed, Morgan. But I've turned up some information that the Senior Council should have." Pride goeth, Harry. "And I need help. This is getting too hot for one person to handle. I need some information and some backup if I'm going to sort this out."

"It's always all about you, isn't it?" Morgan said, his voice bitter. "You're the exception to every rule. You can break the Laws and mock the Council, you can ignore the trial set for you because you are too important to abide by their authority."

"It's got nothing to do with that," I said. "Hell's bells, Morgan, pull your head out of your ass. The faeries' power structure has become unstable, and it looks like it might hit critical mass if something isn't done. That's bigger than me, and a hell of a lot more important than Council protocol."

Morgan screamed at me, his voice so vicious that it made me flinch. "Who are *you* to judge that? You are no one, Dresden! You are nothing!" He took a seething breath. "For too long you have flouted the Council's rule. No more. No more exceptions, no more delays, no more second chances."

"Morgan," I began, "I just need to speak to Ebenezar. Let him decide if—"

"No," Morgan said.

"What?"

"No. You won't evade justice this time, snake. This is your Trial. You will see it through without attempting to influence the Senior Council's judgement."

"Morgan, this is insane—"

"No. The insanity was in letting you live when you were a boy. DuMorne's murderous apprentice. Insanity was pulling you from that burning house two years ago." His voice dropped to an even more quiet register, the contrast to his previous tone unsettling. "Someone I dearly cared for was at Archangel, Dresden. And this time your lies aren't going to get your out of what's coming to you."

Then he hung up the phone.

I stared at the receiver for a second before snarling with rage and slamming it down on the end table, over and over, until the plastic broke in my hands. It hurt. I picked up the phone and threw it against the stone of the fireplace. It shattered, its bell chiming drunkenly. I kicked at the heaped mess of my living room, scattering old boxes, empty cans of Coke, books, papers, and startled cockroaches. After a few minutes of that, I was panting, and some of the blind, frustrated anger had begun to recede.

"Bastard," I growled. "That pigheaded, bigoted, self-righteous bastard."

I needed to cool off, and the shower seemed as good a place as any. I got under the cold water and tried to wash off the sweat and fear of the past day. I half expected the water to burst into steam on contact with my skin, but instead I was able to let the anger slip away while focusing on the old shower routine—water, soap, rinse, shampoo, rinse. By the time I finished and stepped out shivering, I felt almost completely nonpsychotic.

I had no idea how to contact Ebenezar. If he was under Warden security, and I'm sure he and the rest of the Senior Council were, there would be no easy way. The best magical countermeasures in the world would create a maze of misleading results for any spell or supernatural being that tried to find him.

For a moment, I debated asking Murphy for help. The Council tended to overlook any method that didn't involve the use of one kind of spell or another. Murphy's contacts in the force might be able to find them by purely old-fashioned methods. I decided against it. Even if Murphy traced the phone number down, Ebenezar might not be at it, and if I showed up there trying to get past the Wardens to get to him, it would be just the excuse Morgan needed to chop my head off.

I mussed up my hair with the towel and threw it on my narrow bed. Fine. I would do it without the Council's help.

I dressed again, putting on a pair of jeans and a white dress shirt still hanging in my closet. I rolled the sleeves up over my elbows. My sneakers were covered in muck, so I dragged my cowboy boots out of the closet and put them on. What the hell. Putting on the boots. Maybe it would do some good.

I got out my big sports bag, the kind you haul hockey gear around in. Into it went my blasting rod, my staff, and my sword cane, along with a backpack stocked with some candles, matches, a cup, a knife, a cardboard cylinder of salt, a canteen of blessed water, and various other bits of magical equipment I could use as needed. I threw in a box of old iron nails and a solid-steel Craftsman claw hammer with a black rubber grip, and put a couple of pieces of chalk in my pocket.

Then I slid the bag over my shoulder, went into the living room, and wrought the spell that would lead me to one of the very few only people who might help.

Half an hour later, I paid the cabbie and walked into one of the hotels surrounding O'Hare International Airport. The subtle tug of the spell led me to the hotel's restaurant, open for breakfast and half full of mostly business types. I found Elaine at a corner table, a couple of buffet plates scattered with the remains of her breakfast. Her rich brown hair had been pulled back into a tight braid and coiled at the base of her neck. Her face looked pale, tired, with deep circles under her eyes. She was sipping coffee and reading a paperback novel. She wore a different pair of jeans, these a lot looser, and a billowy white shirt open over a dark tank top. She stiffened a beat after my eyes landed on her, and looked up warily.

I walked to her table, pulled out the chair next to her, and sat down. "Morning."

She watched me, her expression opaque. "Harry. How did you find me?"

"I got to thinking that same thing last night," I said. "How did you find me, that is. And I realized that you hadn't found me—you'd found my car. You were inside it and nearly unconscious when I got back to it. So I looked around the car." I pulled the cap to a tire's air valve out of my pocket and showed it to her. "And I found that one of these was missing. I figured you were probably the one who took it, and used it to home in on the Blue Beetle. So I took one of its mates from the other tires and used it to home in on the missing one."

"You named your car after a superhero on the *Electric Company*?" Elaine reached into a brown leather purse on the chair beside her and drew out an identical valve cap. "Clever."

I looked at the purse. What looked like airline tickets was sticking out of it. "You're running."

"You are a veritable wizard of the obvious, Harry." She started to shrug, and her face became ashen, her expression twisting with pain. She took a slow breath and then resumed the motion with her unwounded shoulder. "I feel well motivated to run."

"Do you really think a plane ticket will get you away from the Queens?"

"It will get me away from ground zero. That's enough. There's no way to find out who did it in time—and I don't feel like running up against another assassin. I barely got away from the first one."

I shook my head. "We're close," I said. "We have to be. They took a shot at me last night too. And I think I know who did both."

She looked up at me, sharply. "You do?"

I picked up a crust of toast she'd discarded, mopped it through some leftover eggs, and ate it. "Yeah. But you probably have to catch a flight."

Elaine rolled her eyes. "Tell you what. You stay here and feel smug. I'll get another plate and be back when you're done." She got up, rather stiffly, and walked over to the buffet. She loaded her plate up with eggs and bacon and sausage mixed in with some French toast, and came back to the table. My mouth watered.

She pushed the plate at me. "Eat."

I did, but between bites I asked, "Can you tell me what happened to you?"

She shook her head. "Not much to tell. I spoke with Mab and then with Maeve. I was on my way back to my hotel and someone jumped me in the parking lot. I was able to slip most of his first strike and called up enough fire to drive him away. Then I found your car."

"Why did you come to me?" I asked.

"Because I didn't know who did it, Harry. And I don't trust anyone else in this town."

My throat got a little tight. I borrowed her coffee to wash down the bacon. "It was Lloyd Slate."

Elaine's eyes widened. "The Winter Knight. How do you know?"

"While I was with Maeve, he came in carrying a knife in a box, and he'd been burned. It was coated in dried blood. Maeve was pretty furious that it wasn't any good to her."

Lines appeared between her eyebrows. "Slate . . . he was fetching my blood for her so that she could work a spell on me." She tried to cover it, but I saw her shiver. "He probably tailed me out of that party. Thank the stars I used fire."

I nodded. "Yeah. Dried out the blood, made it useless for whatever she wanted." I shoveled down some more food. "Then last night I got jumped by a hired gun and a couple of faerie beasties." I gave her the summary of the attack at Wal-Mart, leaving Murphy out of it.

"Maeve," Elaine said.

"It's about all I've got," I said. "It doesn't fit her very well, but—"

"Of course it fits her," Elaine said absently. "Don't tell me you fell for that psychotic dilettante nymphomaniac act she put on."

I blinked and then said through a mouthful of French toast, "No. 'Course not."

"She's smart, Harry. She's playing on your expectations."

I chewed the next bite more slowly. "It's a good theory. But that's all it is. We need to know more."

Elaine frowned at me. "You mean you want to talk to the Mothers."

I nodded. "I figure they might let a few things slip about how things work. But I don't know how to get there. I thought you might be able to ask someone in Summer."

She closed her paperback. "No."

"No, they won't help?"

"No, I'm not going to see the Mothers. Harry, it's insane. They're too strong. They could kill you—worse than kill you—with a stray thought."

"At this point I'm already in over my head. It doesn't matter how deep the water gets from here." I grimaced. "Besides, I don't really have a choice."

"You're wrong," she said with quiet emphasis. "You don't have to stay here. You don't have to play their game. Leave."

"Like you are?"

"Like I am," Elaine said. "You can't stop what's been set in motion, Harry, but you can kill yourself trying. It's probably what Mab wanted to begin with."

"No. I can stop it."

She gave me a small smile. "Because you're in the right? Harry, it doesn't work like that."

"Don't I know it. But that's not why I think so."

"Then why?"

"You don't try to kill someone who isn't a threat to you. They took shots at both of us. They must think we can stop them."

"They, them," Elaine said. "Even if we are close, we don't know who 'they' is."

"That's why we talk to the Mothers," I told her. "They're the strongest of the Queens. They know the most. If we're smart, and lucky, we can get information from them."

Elaine reached up to tug at her braid, her expression uncertain. "Harry, look. I'm not . . . I don't want to . . ." She closed her eyes for a moment and then said in a voice, pained, "Please, don't ask me to do this."

"You don't have to go," I said. "Just find me the way to them. Just try."

"You don't understand the kind of trouble you're asking for," she said.

I looked down at my empty plate and said quietly, "Yeah. I do. I hate it, Elaine, and I'm afraid, and I must be half insane not to just dig myself a hole and pull it in after me. But I understand." I reached across the table and put my hand over hers. Her skin was soft, warm, and she shivered at the touch. "Please."

Her hand turned up, fingers curling briefly against mine. My turn to shiver. Elaine sighed. "You're an imbecile, Harry. You're such a fool."

"I guess some things don't change."

She let out a subdued laugh before withdrawing her hand and standing. "I've got a favor left to me. I'll call it in. Wait here."

Five minutes later, she was back. "All right. Outside."

I stood. "Thank you, Elaine. You going to make your plane?"

She opened her purse and tossed the airline tickets onto the table along with a pair of twenties. "I guess not." Then she took a couple of other items out of the purse: a slave-ring of ivory carved in the shape of a ring of oak leaves and attached to a similar bracelet by a silver chain. An earring fashioned of what might have been copper and a teardrop-shaped black stone. Then an anklet dangling with bangles shaped like bird wings. She put them all on, then looked at my gym bag. "Still going with the phallic foci, eh? Staff and rod?"

"They make me feel all manly."

Her mouth twitched, and she started for the exit. I followed her and found myself opening doors for her out of habit. She didn't seem to be too horribly upset by it.

Outside, cars pulled up into a circle drive at the front of the hotel, airport shuttles disgorging and swallowing travelers, taxis picking up men and women in business suits. Elaine slipped the strap of her purse over her good shoulder and stood there quietly.

Maybe thirty seconds later, I heard the clopping of hooves on blacktop. A carriage rolled into sight, drawn by a pair of horses. One of them was the blue-white color of a drowned corpse, and its breath steamed in the air. The other was grass-green, its mane sown with wildflowers. The carriage itself looked like something from Victorian London, all dark wood and brass filigree—and no one was driving it. The horses came to a halt directly before us and stood there, stamping their feet and tossing their manes. The door to the carriage swung open in silence. No one was inside.

I took a surreptitious look around me. None of the straights seemed to have noticed the carriage or the unworldly horses pulling it. A taxi heading for the space the carriage occupied abruptly veered to one side and found another spot. I made an effort and could sense the whisper of enchantment around the carriage, subtle and strong, probably encouraging the straights not to notice it.

"I guess this is our ride," I said.

"You think?" Elaine flipped her braid back over one shoulder and climbed in. "This will take us there, but we won't have any protection on the other side. Just remember, Harry, I told you this was a bad idea."

"Preemptive I-told-you-sos," I said. "Now I've seen everything."

Chapter Twenty-five

The carriage took off so smoothly that I almost didn't feel it. I leaned over the window and twitched the shade aside. We pulled away from the hotel and into traffic with no one the wiser, cars giving us a wide berth even while not noting us. That was one hell of a veil. The carriage didn't jounce at all, and after about a minute wisps of mist began to brush up against the windows. Not long after, the mists blocked out the view of the city entirely. The street sounds faded, and all that was left was silver-grey mist and the clop of horse hooves.

The carriage stopped perhaps five minutes later, and the door swung open. I opened my gym bag and took out my rod and staff. I slipped the sword cane through my belt and drew out my amulet to lie openly on my chest. Elaine did the same with hers. Then we got out of the carriage.

I took a slow look at my surroundings. We stood on some kind of spongy grass, on a low, rolling hill surrounded by other low, rolling hills. The mist lay over the land like a crippled storm cloud, sluggish and thick in some places, thinner in others. The landscape was dotted with the occasional tree, boles thick and twisted, branches scrawny and long. A tattered-looking raven crouched on a nearby branch, its bead-black eyes gleaming.

"Cheery," Elaine said.

"Yeah. Very Baskerville." The carriage started up again, and I looked back to see it vanishing into the mist. "Okay. Where to now?"

At my words the raven let out a croaking caw. It shook itself, bits of moldy feather drifting down, and then beat its wings a few times and settled on another branch, almost out of sight.

"Harry," Elaine said.

"Yeah?"

"If you make any corny joke using the word 'nevermore,' I'm going to punch you. Do you understand me?"

"Never more," I confirmed. Elaine rolled her eyes. Then we both started off after the raven.

It led us through the cloudy landscape, flitting silently from tree to tree. We trudged behind it until more trees began to rise in the mist ahead of us, thickening. The ground grew softer, the air more wet, cloying. The raven let out another caw, then vanished into the trees and out of sight.

I peered after it and said, "Do you see a light back there in the trees?"

"Yes. This must be the place."

"Fine." I started forward. Elaine caught my wrist and said in a sharp and warning tone, "Harry."

She nodded toward a thick patch of shadows where two trees had fallen against one another. I had just begun to pick out a shape when it moved and came forward, close enough that I could make it out clearly.

The unicorn looked like a Budweiser horse, one of the huge draft beasts used for heavy labor. It had to have been eighteen hands high, maybe more. It had a broad chest, four heavy hooves, forward-pricked ears, and a long equine face.

That was where its resemblance to a Clydesdale ended.

It didn't have a coat. It just had a smooth and slick-looking carapace, all chitinous scales and plates, mixing colors of dark green and midnight black. Its hooves were cloven and stained with old blood. One spiraling horn rose from its forehead, at least three feet long and wickedly pointed. The spirals were serrated on the edges, some of them covered with rust-brown stains. A pair of curling horns, like those of a bighorn sheep, curved around the sides of its head from the base of the horn. It didn't have any eyes—just smooth, leathery chitin where they should have been. It tossed its head, and a mane of rotted cobwebs danced around its neck and forelegs, long and tattered as a burial shroud.

A large moth fluttered through the mist near the unicorn. The beast whirled, impossibly nimble, and lunged. Its spiral skewered the moth, and with a savage shake of its head, the unicorn threw the moth to the earth and pulverized the ground it landed on with sledgehammer blows of the blades of its hooves. It snorted after that, and then turned to pace silently back into the mist-covered trees.

Elaine's eyes widened and she looked at me.

I glanced at her. "Unicorns," I said. "Very dangerous. You go first."

She arched an eyebrow.

"Maybe not," I relented. "A guardian?"

"Obviously," Elaine said. "How do we get past it?"

"Blow it up?"

"Tempting," Elaine said. "But I don't think it will make much of an impression on the Mothers if we kill their watchdog. A veil?"

I shook my head. "I don't think unicorns rely on the normal senses. If I remember right, they sense thoughts."

"In that case it shouldn't notice you."

"Hah," I said in a monotone. "Hah-hah, ho-ho, oh my ribs. I have a better plan. I go through while you distract it."

"With what? I'm fresh out of virginity. And that thing doesn't look much like the unicorns I saw in Summer. It's a lot less . . . prancy."

"With thoughts," I said. "They sense thoughts, and they're attracted to purity. Your concentration was always better than mine. Theoretically, if you can keep an image in your head, it should focus on it and not you."

"Think of a wonderful thought. Great plan, Peter Pan."

"You have a better one?"

Elaine shook her head. "Okay. I'll try to lead him down there." She gestured down the line of trees. "Once I do, get moving."

I nodded, and Elaine closed her eyes for a moment before her features smoothed over into relaxation. She started forward and into the trees, walking at a slow and measured pace.

The unicorn appeared again, ten feet in front of Elaine. The beast snorted and pawed at the earth and reared up on its hind legs, tossing its mane. Then it started forward at a slow and cautious walk.

Elaine held out her hand to it. It let out a gurgling whicker and nuzzled her palm. Still moving with dream-like slowness, Elaine turned and began walking down the length of the lines of trees. The unicorn followed a pace or two behind her, the tip of its horn bobbing several inches above Elaine's right shoulder.

They'd gone several paces before I saw that the plan wasn't working. The unicorn's body language changed. Its ears flattened back to its skull, and its feet shifted restlessly before it finally rose up on its hind hooves, preparing to lunge, with the deadly horn centered on Elaine's back.

There wasn't time to shout a warning. I lifted my blasting rod in my right hand, summoned the force of my will, and pushed it through the focus with a shout of *"Fuego!"*

Fire erupted from the tip of the rod, a scarlet ribbon of heat and flame and force that lanced out toward the unicorn. After having seen how spectacularly useful my magic wasn't on the Ogre Grum, I didn't want to chance another faerie beast shrugging it off. So I wasn't shooting for the unicorn itself—but for the ground at its feet.

The blast ripped a three-foot trench in the earth, and the unicorn screamed and thrashed its head, trying to keep its balance. A normal horse would have toppled, but the unicorn somehow managed to get a couple of feet onto solid ground and hurled itself away in a forty-foot standing leap. It landed on its feet, already running, body sweeping in a circle to bring it charging toward me.

I ran for the nearest tree. The unicorn was faster, but I didn't have far to go, and I put the trunk between us.

It didn't slow down. Its horn slammed into the trunk of the dead tree and came through it as though it hadn't been there. I flinched away, but not fast enough to avoid catching several flying splinters in the chest and belly, and not fast enough to avoid a nasty cut on my left arm where one of those serrated edges of the horn ripped through my shirt. The pain of the injuries registered, but only as background data. I stepped around the bole of the tree, taking my staff in both hands, and swung it as hard as I could at the delicate bones of the unicorn's rear ankle.

Well, on a horse they're delicate. Evidently on unicorns, they're just a bit tender. The faerie beast let out a furious scream and twisted its body, tearing through the tree, shredding it as it whipped its horn free and whirled to orient on me. It lunged, the horn spearing toward me. I swept my staff up, a simple parry *quatre*, and shoved the tip out past my body while darting a pair of steps to my right, avoiding the beast's oncoming weight. I kept going, ducking a beat before the unicorn planted its forequarters, lifted its hind, and twisted, lashing out toward my head with both rear hooves. I rolled, came up running, and ducked behind the next tree. The unicorn turned and began stalking toward me, circling the tree, foam pattering from its open mouth.

Elaine cried out, and I whipped my head around to see her lifting her right hand, the ring on it releasing a cloud of glowing motes that burst around her in a swarm. The little lights streaked toward the unicorn and gathered around it, swirling and flashing in a dazzling cloud. One of them brushed against me, and my senses abruptly went into whiteout, overwhelmed with a simple image of walking down a sidewalk in worn shoes, the sun bright overhead, a purse bumping on my hip, stomach twinging with pleasant hunger pangs, the scent of hot asphalt in my nose, children laughing and splashing somewhere nearby. A memory, something from Elaine. I staggered and pushed it away from me, regaining my senses.

The motes crowded around the unicorn, darting in to brush against it one at a time, and at each touch the faerie beast went wild. It spun and kicked and screamed and lashed out with its horn, lunging at insubstantial adversaries in wild frenzy, but all to no avail.

I looked past them to see Elaine standing in place, her hand extended, her face set in an expression of concentration and strain. "Harry," she shouted. "Go. I'll hold it."

I rose, heart pounding. "You got it?"

"For a little while. Just get to the Mothers," Elaine responded. *"Hurry!"*

"I don't want to leave you alone."

A bead of sweat trickled down the side of her face. "You won't be. When it gets loose, I'm not waiting around for it to skewer me."

I gritted my teeth. I didn't want to leave Elaine, but to be fair, she'd done better than I had. She stood against the unicorn still, only a dozen long strides away, her hand extended, the creature as contained as if she'd wrapped it in a net. My slender and straight and beautiful Elaine.

Memories, images washed through me, dozens of little things I'd forgotten coming back to me all at once; her laugh, quiet and wicked in the darkness; the feeling of her slender fingers slipping through mine; her face, asleep on the pillow beside me, gentle and peaceful in the morning sun.

There were many more, but I pushed them away. That had been a long time ago, and they wouldn't mean a thing if neither of us survived the next few minutes and hours.

I turned my back on her, left her struggling against the strength of that nightmarish unicorn, and ran toward the lights in the mist.

Chapter Twenty-six

The Nevernever is a big place. In fact, it's the biggest place. The Nevernever is what the wizards call the entirety of the realm of spirit. It isn't a physical place, with geography and weather patterns and so on. It's a shadow world, a magical realm, and its substance is as mutable as thought. It has a lot of names, like the Other Side and the Next World, and it contains within it just about any kind of spirit realm you can imagine, somewhere. Heaven, Hell, Olympus, Elysium, Tartarus, Gehenna—you name it, and it's in the Nevernever somewhere. In theory, at any rate.

The parts of the Nevernever closest to the mortal world are almost completely controlled by the Sidhe. This part of the spirit realm is called Faerie, and has close ties with our own natural world. As a result, Faerie resembles the real world in a lot of ways. It is fairly permanent and unchanging, for example, and has several versions of weather. But make no mistake—it isn't Earth. The rules of reality don't apply as tightly as they do in our world, so Faerie can be viciously treacherous. Most who go into it never come back.

And I had a gut feeling that I was running through the heart of Faerie.

The ground sloped down and grew wetter, softer. The mist swallowed sound quickly behind me, until all I could hear was my own labored breathing. The run made my heart pound, and my wounded hand throbbed painfully. There was a certain amount of exhilaration to the movement, my limbs and muscles stretching and feeling alive after several months of disuse. I couldn't have kept up the pace for long, but luckily I didn't have far to go.

The lights turned out to be a pair of lit windows in a cottage that stood by itself on a slight rise of ground. Stone obelisks the size of coffins, some fallen and cracked and others still upright, stood scattered in loose rings around the mound. The raven rested on one of them, its beady eyes gleaming. It let out another croaking sound and flew through an open window of the cottage.

I stood there panting for a minute, trying to get my breath, before I walked up to the door. My flesh began to crawl with a shivering sensation. I took a step back and looked at the house. Stone walls. A thatch roof. I could smell mildew beneath an odor of fresh-baked bread. The door was made of some kind of heavy, weathered wood, and the snowflake symbol I'd seen before had been carved into it. Mother Winter, then. If she was anything like Mab, she would have the kind of power that would give any wizard the creeps. It would just hang in the air around her, like body warmth. Except that it would take a lot of body to feel its warmth through stone walls and a heavy door. Gulp.

I lifted my hand to knock, and the door swung open of its own accord, complete with a melodramatic Hammer Films whimper of rusting hinges.

A voice, little more than a creaking whisper, said, "Come in, boy. We have been expecting you."

Double gulp. I wiped my palms on my jeans and made sure I had a good grip on both staff and rod before I stepped across the threshold and into the dim cottage.

The place was all one room. The floor was wooden, though the boards looked weathered and dry. Shelves stood against the stone walls. A loom rested in the far corner, near the fireplace, a spinning wheel beside it. Before the fireplace sat a rocking chair, occupied, squeaking as it moved. A figure sat in it, shrouded in a shawl, a hood, as though someone had animated a bundle of blankets and cloth. On the hearth above the fireplace sat several sets of teeth, more or less human-sized. One looked simple enough, all white and even. The next was rotted-looking, with chipped incisors and a broken molar. The next set had all pointed teeth, stained with bits of rusty brown and what looked like rotten bits of flesh stuck between them. The last was made out of some kind of silvery metal, shining like a sword.

"Interesting," came the creaking voice from the creaking chair. "Most interesting. Can you feel it?"

"Uh," I said.

From the other side of the cottage, a brisk voice tsked, and I spun to face the newcomer. Another woman, stooped with age, blew dust from a shelf and ran a cloth over it before replacing the bottles and jars. She turned and eyed me with glittering green eyes from within a weathered but rosy face. "Of course I do. The poor child. He's walked a thorny path." The elderly lady came to me and put her hands firmly on either side of my head, peering at either eye. "Scars here, some. Stick out your tongue, boy."

I blinked. "Uh?"

"Stick out your tongue," she repeated in a crisp tone. I did. She peered at my tongue and my throat and said, "Strength, though. And he can be clever, at times. It would seem your daughter chose ably."

I closed my mouth and she released my head. "Mother Summer, I presume?"

She beamed up at me. "Yes, dear. And this is Mother Winter." She gestured vaguely at the chair by the fire. "Don't be offended if she doesn't get up. It's the wrong season, you know. Hand me that broom."

I blinked, then reached over to pick up the ramshackle old broom with a gnarled handle and passed it to Mother Summer. The old lady took it and immediately began sweeping the dusty floor of the old cottage.

"Bah," whispered Mother Winter. "The dust is just going to come back."

"It's the principle of the thing," Summer said. "Isn't that right, boy?"

I sneezed and mumbled something noncommittal. "Uh, pardon me, ladies. But I wondered if you could answer a few questions for me."

Winter's head seemed to turn slightly toward me from within her hood. Mother Summer stopped and eyed me, her grass-green eyes sparkling. "You wish answers?"

"Yes," I said.

"How can you expect to get them," Winter wheezed, "when you do not yet know the proper questions?"

"Uh," I said again. Brilliance incarnate, that's me.

Summer shook her head and said, "An exchange, then," she said. "We will ask you a question. And for your answer, we will each give you an answer to what you seek."

"No offense, but I didn't come here so that you could ask me questions."

"Are you sure?" Mother Summer asked. She swept a pile of dust past me and out the door. "How do you know you didn't?"

Mother Winter's rasping whisper came to me, disgusted. "She'll prattle on all day. Answer us the questions, boy. Or get out."

I took a deep breath. "All right," I said. "Ask."

Mother Winter turned back to face the fire. "Simply tell us, boy. Which is more important. The body—"

"—or the soul," Mother Summer picked up. They both fell silent, and I felt their focus on me like the tip of a knife resting against my skin.

"I suppose that would depend on who was asking whom," I said, finally.

"We ask," Winter whispered.

Summer nodded. "And we ask *you*."

I thought about my words for a moment before I spoke.

I know, it shocked me too.

"Then I would say that were I old, sick, and dying, I would believe that the soul is more important. And if I was a man about to be burned at the stake in order to preserve his soul, I would believe that the body is more important."

The words fell on a long moment of silence. I found myself shifting my feet restlessly.

"Fairly said," Mother Winter rasped at last.

"Wise enough," Summer agreed. "Why did you give that answer, boy?"

"Because it's a stupid question. The answer isn't as simple as one or the other."

"Precisely," Summer said. She walked to the fire and withdrew a baking sheet on a long handle. A roundish loaf of bread was on it. She set it on a rack to cool. "This child sees what she does not."

"It is not in her nature," Winter murmured. "She is what she is."

Mother Summer sighed and nodded. "These are strange times."

"Hold on," I said. "What she are you talking about, here? It's Maeve, isn't it?"

Mother Winter made a quiet wheezing sound that might have been a laugh.

"I answered your questions," I said. "So pay up."

"Patience, boy," Mother Summer said. She took a kettle from a hook by the fireplace and poured tea into a pair of cups. She dipped what looked like honey into each, then cream, and gave one to Mother Winter.

I waited until each of them had sipped before I said, "Right, patience expired. I can't afford to wait. Tonight is Midsummer.

Tonight the balance begins to tilt back to Winter, and Maeve is going to try to use the Stone Table to steal the Summer Knight's mantle for keeps."

"Indeed. Something to be prevented at all costs." Mother Summer arched an eyebrow. "Then what is your question?"

"Who killed the Summer Knight? Who stole his mantle?"

Mother Summer gave me a disappointed glance and sipped her tea.

Mother Winter lifted her tea to her hood. I still couldn't see her face—but her hand looked withered, the fingers tinged with blue. She lowered her cup and said, "You ask a foolish question, boy. You are more clever than this."

I folded my arms. "What is that supposed to mean?"

Mother Summer frowned at Winter, but said, "It means that who is not as important as *why*."

"And *how*," Mother Winter added.

"Think, boy," Summer said. "What has the theft of the mantle accomplished?"

I frowned. War between the Courts, for one. Odd activity in the magical and natural world alike. But mostly the coming war, Winter and Summer gathering to battle at the Stone Table.

"Exactly," Winter whispered. The skin on the back of my neck rippled with a cold and unpleasant sensation. Hell's bells, she'd heard me *thinking*. "But think, wizard. How was it done? Theft is theft, whether the prize is food, or riches, or beauty or power."

Since it didn't seem to matter either way, I did my thinking out loud. "When something is stolen a couple of things can happen to it. It can be carried away where it cannot be reached."

"Hoarded," Summer put in. "Such as the dragons do."

"Yeah, okay. Uh, it can be destroyed."

"No, it can't," Mother Winter said. "Your own sage tells you that. The German fellow with the wild hair."

"Einstein," I muttered. "Okay, then, but it can be rendered valueless. Or it can be sold to someone else."

Mother Summer nodded. "Both of which are *change*."

I held up a hand. "Hold it, hold it. Look, as I understand it, this power of the Summer Knight, his mantle, it can't just exist on its own. It has to be inside a vessel."

"Yes," Winter murmured. "Within one of the Queens, or within the Knight."

"And it isn't with one of the Queens."

"True," Summer said. "We would sense it, were it so."

"So it's already in another Knight," I said. "But if that was true, there'd be no imbalance." I scratched at my head, and as I did it slowly dawned on me. "Unless it had been changed. Unless the new Knight had been changed. Transformed into something else. Something that left the power trapped, inert, useless."

Both of them regarded me steadily, silently.

"All right," I said. "I have my question."

"Ask it," they said together.

"How does the mantle pass on from one Knight to the next?"

Mother Summer smiled, but the expression was a grim one. "It returns to the nearest reflection of itself. To the nearest vessel of Summer. She, in turn, chooses the next Knight."

That meant that only one of the Queens of Summer could be behind it. Titania was out already—she had begun the war against Mab because she didn't know where the mantle was. Mother Summer would not have been telling me this information if she'd been the one to do it. That left only one person.

"Stars and stones," I muttered. "Aurora."

The two Mothers set down their teacups together. "Time presses," Summer said.

"That which must not be may be," Winter continued.

"You, we judge, are the one who may set things aright once more—"

"—if you are strong enough."

"Brave enough."

"Whoa, hold your horses," I said. "Can't I just bring this out to Mab and Titania?"

"Beyond talk now," Mother Winter said. "They go to war."

"Stop them," I said. "You two have to be stronger than Mab and Titania. Make them shut up and listen to you."

"Not that simple," Winter said.

Summer nodded. "We have power, but bound within certain limits. We cannot interfere with the Queens or Ladies. Not even on a matter so dire as this."

"What *can* you do?"

"I?" Summer said. "Nothing."

I frowned and looked from her to Mother Winter.

One aged, cracked hand lifted and beckoned me. "Come closer, boy."

I started to say no. But my feet moved without asking the rest of me, and I knelt in front of Mother Winter's rocking chair. I couldn't see her, even from here. Even her feet were covered by layers of dark cloth. But on her lap rested a pair of knitting needles, and a simple square of cloth, trailing thick threads of grey, undyed wool. Mother Winter reached down with her withered hands, and took up a pair of rusted shears. She cut the trailing threads and passed me the cloth.

I took it, again without thinking. It felt soft, cold as if it had been in a refrigerator, and it tingled with a subtle, dangerous energy.

"It isn't tied off," I said quietly.

"Nor should it be," Winter said. "It is an Unraveling."

"A what?"

"An unmaking, boy. I am the unmaker, the destroyer. It is what I am. Bound within those threads is the power to undo any enchantment done. Touch the cloth to that which must be undone. Unravel the threads. It will be so."

I stared at the square cloth for a moment, Then asked quietly, "*Any* enchantment? Any transformation?"

"Any."

My hands started shaking. "You mean . . . I could use this to undo what the vampires did to Susan. Just wipe it away. Make her mortal again."

"You could, Emissary." Mother Winter's tone held a bone-dry amusement.

I swallowed and rose, folding up the cloth. I slipped it into my pocket, careful not to let any threads trail out. "Is this a gift?"

"No," Winter rasped. "But a necessity."

"What am I supposed to do with it?"

Mother Summer shook her head. "It is yours now, and yours to employ. We have reached the limits of how we may act. The rest is yours."

"Make haste," Winter whispered.

Mother Summer nodded. "No time remains. Be swift and wise, mortal child. Go with our blessings."

Winter withdrew her frail hands into the sleeves of her robe. "Do not fail, boy."

"Hell's bells, no pressure," I muttered. I gave each of them a short bow and turned for the door. I stepped over the threshold of the cottage and said, "Oh, by the way. I apologize if we did any harm to your unicorn on the way in."

I looked back to see Mother Summer arch a brow. Winter's head shifted, and I could see the gleam of light on yellow teeth. Her voice rasped, "What unicorn?"

The door shut, again of its own accord. I glowered at the wood for a moment and then muttered, "Freaking weirdo faerie biddies." I turned and started back the way I had come. The Unraveling was a cool weight in my pocket, and promised to get uncomfortably chilly if I left it there too long.

The thought of the Unraveling made me walk faster, excitement skipping through me. If what the Mothers said was true, I'd be able to use the cloth to help Susan, which was something just this side of divine intervention. All I had to do was to finish up this case, and then I could go find her.

Of course, I thought sourly, finishing up this case was likely to kill me. The Mothers may have given me some insight, and a magic doily, but they sure as hell hadn't given me a freaking clue as to how to resolve this—and, I realized, they hadn't really *said*, "Aurora did it." I knew they had to speak the truth to me, and their statements had led me to that conclusion—but how much of it was this mysterious prohibition from direct involvement and how much of it had been another fistful of faerie trickery?

"Make haste," I rasped, trying to impersonate Winter's voice. "We have reached the limits," I said, mimicking Summer. I quickened my pace, and frowned over that last little comment Winter had made. She had taken an almost palpable glee in making it, as though it had given her an opening she wouldn't otherwise have had.

What unicorn?

I gnawed over the question. If it was indeed a statement of importance, not just a passing mutter, then it had to mean something.

I frowned. It meant that there hadn't *been* a guardian around the little cottage. Or at least not one Mother Winter had put there.

So who had?

The answer hit me low in the gut, a sensation of physical sickness coming along with the realization. I stopped and clawed for my Sight.

I didn't get to it before Grum came out from under a veil, Elaine standing close behind him. He caught me flat-footed. The ogre drove a sledgehammer fist toward my face. There was a flash of impact, a sensation of falling, and cool earth beneath my cheek.

Then the scent of Elaine's subtle perfume.

Then blackness.

Chapter Twenty-seven

✧❦✧❦

I came to on the ground of that dark Nevernever wood. Spirit realm or not, I felt cold and started shivering uncontrollably. That made playing possum pretty much impossible, so I sat up and tried to take stock.

I didn't feel any new bruises or breaks, so I hadn't been pounded while I was out. It probably hadn't been long. Mother Winter's Unraveling was no longer in my pocket. My bag was gone, as was my ring and my bracelet. My staff and rod, needless to say, had been taken as well. I could still feel my mother's pentacle amulet against my chest, though, which came as something of a surprise. My hand throbbed, where Mab had driven the freaking letter opener through it.

Other than that, I felt more or less whole. Huzzah.

I squinted at my surroundings next and found a ring of toadstools grown up around me. They weren't huge, tentacular, horribly fanged toadstools or anything, but it put a little chill in me all the same. I lifted my hand and reached out for them tentatively, extending my wizard's senses along with the gesture. I hit a wall. I couldn't think of another way to describe it. Where the ring began, my ability to reach, move, and perceive with my supernatural senses simply ended.

Trapped. Double huzzah.

Only after I'd gotten an idea of my predicament did I stand up and face my captors.

There were five of them, which seemed less than fair. I recognized the nearest right away—Aurora, the Summer Lady, now dressed in what I could only describe as a battle gown, made out of some kind of silver mail as fine and light as cloth. It clung closely to her, from the top of her throat down to her wrists and ankles, and shone with its own dim radiance in the forest's gloom. She wore a sword at her hip, and upon her pale hair rested a garland of living leaves. She turned green eyes to me, heartbreakingly lovely, and regarded me with an expression both sad and resolved.

"Wizard," Aurora said, "I regret that it has come to this. But you have come too close to interfering. Once you had served your purpose, I could not allow you to continue your involvement."

I grimaced and looked past her, at the ogre Grum, huge and scarlet-skinned and silent, and the horrific unicorn that had apparently been guarding the way to Mother Winter's cottage.

"What do you intend to do with me?"

"Kill you," Aurora said, her voice gentle. "I regret the necessity. But you're too dangerous to be allowed to live."

I squinted at her. "Then why haven't you?"

"Good question," said the fourth person present—Lloyd Slate, the Winter Knight. He still wore his biker leathers, but he'd added bits of mail and a few metal plates to the ensemble. He wore a sword at his hip, another on his back, and bore a heavy pistol on his belt. The gaunt, tense hunger of his expression hadn't changed. He looked nervous and angry. "If it had been up to me, I'd have cut your throat when Grum first dropped you."

"Why call him Grum?" I said, scowling at the ogre. "You might as well drop the glamour, Lord Marshal. There's not much point to it now."

The ogre's face twisted with surprise.

I glared spitefully at the dark unicorn and spat, "You too, Korrick."

Both ogre and unicorn glanced at Aurora. The Faerie Queen never took her eyes off me, but nodded. The ogre's form blurred and twisted, and resolved itself into the form of Talos, the Sidhe lord from Aurora's penthouse at the Rothchild. His pale hair had been drawn back into a fighting braid, and he wore close-fit mail of some glittering black metal that made him look rail-thin and deadly.

At the same time the unicorn shook itself and rose up into the hulking form of Korrick, the centaur, also dressed in mail and bearing weapons of faerie make. He stamped one huge hoof and said nothing.

Aurora walked in a circle around me, frowning. "How long have you known, wizard?"

I shrugged. "Not long. I started getting it on the way out of Mother Winter's cottage. Once I knew where to start, it wasn't hard to start adding up the numbers."

"We don't have time for this," Slate said and spat on the ground to one side.

"If he puzzled it out, others may have as well," Aurora said, her voice patient. "We should know if any other opposition is coming. Tell me, wizard. How did you piece it together?"

"Go to hell," I snapped.

Aurora turned to the last person there and asked, "Can he be reasoned with?"

Elaine stood a little apart from the others, her back to them. My bag rested on the ground near her feet, and my rod and staff lay there too. She'd added a cloak of emerald green to her outfit, somehow making it look natural. She glanced at Aurora and then at me. She averted her eyes quickly, "You've already told him you're going to kill him. He won't cooperate."

Aurora shook her head. "More sacrifices. I am sorry you pushed me to this, wizard."

Her hand moved. Some unseen force jerked my chin up, my eyes to hers. They flashed, a ripple of colors, and I felt the force of her mind, her will, glide past my defenses and into me. I lost my balance and staggered, leaning helplessly against the invisible solidity of the circle she'd imprisoned me in. I tried to fight it, but it was like trying to push water up a hill—nothing for me to strain against, nothing for me to focus upon. I was on her turf, trapped in a circle of her power. She flowed into me, down through my eyes, and all I could do was watch the pretty colors.

"Now," she said, and her voice was the gentlest, sweetest thing I'd ever heard. "What did you learn of the Summer Knight's death?"

"You were behind it," I heard myself saying, my voice slow and heavy. "You had him killed."

"How?"

"Lloyd Slate. He hates Maeve. You recruited him to help you. Elaine took him inside Reuel's building, through the Nevernever. He fought Reuel. That's why there was ooze on the stairs. The water on Reuel's arms and legs was where Summer fire met Winter ice. Slate threw him down the stairs and broke his neck."

"And his mantle of power?"

"Redirected," I mumbled. "You gathered it in and placed it into another person."

"Who?"

"The changeling girl," I said. "Lily. You gave her the mantle and then you turned her to stone. That statue in your garden. It was right in front of me."

"Very good," Aurora said, and the gentle praise rippled through me. I fought to regain my senses, to escape the glittering green prison of her eyes. "What else?"

"You hired the ghoul. The Tigress. You sent her after me before Mab even spoke to me."

"I do not know this ghoul. You are incorrect, wizard. I do not hire killers. Continue."

"You set me up before I came to interview you."

"In what way?" Aurora pressed.

"Maeve must have ordered Slate to take Elaine out. He made it look like he tried and missed, but Elaine played it for more. You helped her fake the injury."

"Why did I do that?"

"To keep me upset, worried, so that when I spoke to you I wouldn't have the presence of mind to corner you with a question. That's why you attacked me, too. Telling me what a monster I'd become. To keep me off balance, keep me from asking the right questions."

"Yes," Aurora said. "And after that?"

"You decided to take me out. You sent Talos, Elaine, and Slate to kill me. And you created that construct in the garden center."

Slate stepped closer. "Spooky," he said. "He doesn't *look* all that smart."

"Yet he used only reason. Plus knowledge doubtless gained from the Queens and Mothers. He put it together for himself, rather than being told." At that, her gaze slanted past me, to Elaine. I tried to pull away and couldn't.

"Great," Slate said. "No one squealed. Can we kill the great Kreskin now?"

Aurora held up a hand to Slate, and asked me, "Do you know my next objective?"

"You knew that if you bound up the Summer Knight's mantle, Mother Winter would provide an Unraveling to free it and restore the balance. You waited for her to give it to me. Now you're going to take it and the statue of Lily. You're going to take her to the

Stone Table during the battle. You'll use the Unraveling, free Lily from being stone, and kill her on the table after midnight. The Summer Knight's power will go to Winter permanently. You want to destroy the balance of power in Faerie. I don't know why."

Aurora's eyes flashed dangerously. She removed her gaze from mine, and it was like suddenly falling back *up* a flight of stairs. I staggered back, tearing my eyes from her and focusing on the ground.

"*Why?* It should be obvious to you why, wizard. You of all people." She spun in a glitter of silvery mail, pacing restlessly back and forth. "The cycle must be broken. Summer and Winter, constantly chasing each other, wounding what the other heals and healing what the other wounds. Our war, our senseless contest, waged for no reason other than that it has always been so—and mortals trapped between us, crushed by the struggle, made pawns and toys." She took a shuddering, angry breath. "It must end. And I will end it."

I ground my teeth, shivering. "You'll end it by sending the natural world into chaos?"

"I did not set the price," Aurora hissed. I caught sight of her eyes out of the corner of my vision and started tracking up to her face. I forced my gaze down again, barely in time. She continued speaking, in a low, impassioned voice. "I hate it. I hate every moment of the things I've had to do to accomplish this—but it should have been done long since, wizard. Delay is just as deadly. How many have died or been tormented to madness by Maeve, and those like her? You yourself have been tortured, abused, nearly enslaved by them. I do what *must* be done."

I swallowed and said, "Harming and endangering mortal kind in order to help them. That's insane."

"Perhaps," Aurora said. "But it is the only way." She faced me again and asked, her voice cold, "Does the White Council know what you have discovered?"

"Bite me, faerie fruitcake."

Slate stifled a laugh, hiding it under a cough. I felt more than saw Aurora's sudden surge of rage, sparked by the Winter Knight but directed at me. A flare of light erupted from her, and I felt a sudden heat against the side of my body nearest her. The hairs on my arm rose straight up. Her voice rang out, hot and violent and strong. "What did you say, ape?"

"They don't," Elaine said, her voice tense. She put herself between me and Aurora, her back to me. "He told me before we left for the Mothers'. The Council doesn't realize the depth of what's happening. By the time they do, it will be too late for them to act."

"Fine," Slate said. "He's the last loose end, then. Kill him and let's get on with it."

"Dammit, Slate," I said. "Use your head, man. What do you think you're going to get out of helping her like this?"

Slate gave me a cold smile. "That old bastard Reuel's power, for one thing. I'll be twice the Knight I was before—and then I'm going to settle some accounts with that little bitch Maeve." He licked his lips. "After that, Aurora and I will decide what to do next."

I let out a harsh bray of laughter. "I hope you got that in writing, dimwit. Do you really think she would let a man, and a mortal at that, have that much power over her?" Slate's eyes became wary, and I pressed him. "Think about it. Has she ever given it to you straight, a statement, not a question or a dodge, or something she's led you to assume?"

Suspicion grew in his gaze, but Aurora laid a hand on his shoulder. Slate's eyes grew a little cloudy at her touch, and he closed them. "Peace, my Knight," the Summer Lady murmured. "The wizard is a trickster, and desperate. He would say anything he thought might save him. Nothing has changed between us."

I ground my teeth at the meaningless words, but Aurora had Slate's number, whatever it was. Maybe all that time in Maeve's company had softened him, the drugs and pleasures she fed him making him more open to suggestion. Maybe Aurora had just found a hole in his psychology. Either way, he wasn't going to listen to me.

I looked around, but Korrick and Talos ignored me. Aurora kept on whispering to Slate. That left only one person to talk to, and the thought of it felt like someone driving nails into my chest. "Elaine," I said. "This is crazy. Why are you doing this?"

She didn't look up at me. "Survival, Harry. I promised to help Aurora or to give up my own life as forfeit in payment for all the years she protected me. I didn't know when I made the promise that you were going to be involved." She fell quiet for a moment, then swallowed before she said, her voice forced a little louder, "I didn't know."

"If Aurora isn't stopped, someone is going to get hurt."

"Someone gets hurt every day," Elaine answered. "When you get right down to it, does it matter who? How? Or why?"

"People are going to *die*, Elaine."

That stung her, and she looked up at me, sharp anger warring with a sheen of tears in her grey eyes. "Better them than me."

I faced her, without looking away. "Better me than you, too, huh?"

She broke first, turning to regard Aurora and Slate. "Looks that way."

I folded my arms and leaned against the back of my toadstool cell. I went over my options, but they were awfully limited. If Aurora wanted me dead, she would be able to see to it quite handily, and unless the cavalry came riding over the hill, there wasn't diddly I could do about it.

Call me a pessimist, but my life has been marked with a notable lack of cavalry. Checkmate.

Which left me with one last spell to throw. I closed my eyes for a moment, reaching inside, gathering up the magic, the life force within me. Any wizard has a reservoir of power inherent in him, power drawn from the core of his self rather than from his surroundings. Aurora's circle could cut me off from drawing upon ambient magic to fuel a spell—but it couldn't stop me from using the energy within me.

Granted, once used, there wouldn't be anything left to keep me breathing, my heart pumping, and electricity going through my brain. But then, that's why they call it a death curse, isn't it?

It was only a moment later that I opened my eyes, to see Aurora draw back from Lloyd Slate. The Winter Knight focused his eyes on me, scary eyes empty of anything like reason, and drew the sword from his belt.

"A grim business," Aurora said. "Good-bye, Mister Dresden."

Chapter Twenty-eight

I faced Slate head-on. I figured as long as I was going to take one of those swords, it might as well have a shot of killing me pretty quick. No sense in dragging it out. But I left my eyes on Aurora and held whatever power I had gathered up and ready.

"I am sorry, wizard," Aurora said.

"You're about to be," I muttered.

Slate drew back his blade, an Oriental job without enough class to be an actual katana, and tensed, preparing to strike. The blade glittered and looked really, really sharp.

Elaine caught Slate's wrist and said, "Wait."

Aurora gave Elaine a sharp and angry look. "What are you doing?"

"Protecting you," Elaine said. "If you let Slate kill him, he'll break the circle around Dresden."

Aurora looked from Elaine to me and back. "And?"

"Elaine!" I snarled.

She regarded me with flat eyes. "And you'll leave yourself open to his death curse. He'll take you with him. Or make you wish he had."

Aurora lifted her chin. "He isn't that strong."

"Don't be so sure," Elaine said. "He's the strongest wizard I've ever met. Strong enough to make the White Council nervous. Why take a pointless risk so close to the end?"

"You treacherous bitch," I said. "God damn you, Elaine."

Aurora frowned at me and then gestured to Slate. He lowered the sword and put it away. "Yet he is too dangerous to leave alive."

"Yes," Elaine agreed.

"What would you suggest?"

"We're in the Nevernever," Elaine said. "Arrange his death and leave. Once you are back in mortal lands, he won't be able to reach you. Let him spend his curse on Mab if he wishes, or on his godmother. But it won't be on you."

"But when I leave, my power will go with me. He won't be held by the circle. What do you suggest?"

Elaine regarded me passionlessly. "Drown him," she said finally. "Call water and let the earth drink him. I'll lock him into place with a binding of my own. Mortal magic will last, even after I've left."

Aurora nodded. "Are you capable of holding him?"

"I know his defenses," Elaine responded. "I'll hold him as long as necessary."

Aurora regarded me in silence for a moment. "So much rage," she said. "Very well, Elaine. Hold him."

It didn't take her long. Elaine had always been smoother at magic than me, more graceful. She murmured something in the language she'd chosen for her magic, some variant on Old Egyptian, adding a roll of her wrist, a graceful ripple of her fingers, and I felt her spell lock around me like a full-body straitjacket, paralyzing me from chin to toes, wrapping me in silent, unseen force. It pressed against my clothes, flattening them, and made it hard to take a deep breath.

At the same time, Aurora closed her eyes, her hands spread at her side. Then she leveled her palms and slowly raised them. From within the circle, I couldn't sense what she was doing, but there wasn't anything wrong with my eyes and ears. The ground gurgled, and there was a sudden scent of rotten eggs. I felt the earth beneath me shift and sag, and then a slow "bloop bloop" of earth settling as water began rising up beneath me. It took maybe five seconds for the ground to become so soft that my feet sank into the warm mud, up to my ankles. Hell's bells.

"Mortal time is racing," Aurora said, and opened her eyes. "The day grows short. Come."

Without so much as glancing at me, she swept away into the mist. Slate fell into place at her heels, and Talos followed several paces behind, slim and dangerous in his dark armor. Korrick the centaur spared me a sneer and a satisfied snort before he gripped a short, heavy spear in his broad fist and turned to follow the Summer Lady, hooves striking down in decisive clops.

That left Elaine. She came forward until she stood almost

close enough to touch me. Slender and pretty, she regarded me steadily while she took a band from her jeans pocket, and bound her hair back into a tail.

"Why, Elaine?" I asked. I struggled furiously against the spell, but it was stronger than me. "Why the hell did you stop her?"

"You're an idiot, Harry," she said. "A melodramatic fool. You always were."

I kept sinking into the earth and came level with her eyes. "I could have stopped her."

"I couldn't be sure you wouldn't have thrown the curse at me, too." She looked over her shoulder. Aurora had paused, a dim shape in the mist, and was waiting.

The watery earth kept drawing me down, and I looked up at her now, at the soft skin on the underside of her chin. She looked down at me and said, "Good-bye, Harry." She turned and walked after Aurora. Then she paused, one leg bent, and turned enough so that I could see her profile. She said in that same casually neutral tone, "It's just like old times."

After that, they left me there to die.

It's hard not to panic in that kind of situation. I mean, I've been in trouble before, but not in that kind of ticktock-here-it-comes way. The problem in front of me was simple, steady, and inescapable. The ground kept getting softer and I kept on sliding down into it. The sensation of it was warm and not entirely unpleasant. I mean, people pay money for hot mud baths. But mine would be lethal if I didn't find a way out of it, and the mud was already creeping up over my thighs.

I closed my eyes and tried to focus. I reached out to feel the fabric of Elaine's spell around me, and pushed, trying to break through it. I didn't have enough strength. Once Aurora's circle dropped, I would be able to reach out for more power, but I'd be running short on time—and even so, brute strength wasn't the answer. If I just randomly hammered at the spell around me, it would be like trying to escape from a set of shackles using dynamite. I would tear myself apart along with the binding.

Still, that dangerous option seemed to be my only hope. I tried to hang on, to stay calm and focused, and to wait for Aurora's circle to give out. I got the giggles. Don't ask me why, but under the pressure of the moment, it seemed damned funny. I tried not to, but I cackled and chortled as the warm mud slid up over my hips, my belly, my chest.

"Just like old times," I wheezed. "Yeah, just like old times, Elaine. You backbiting, poisonous, treacherous . . ."

And then a thought hit me. Just like old times.

". . . deceitful, wicked, *clever* girl. If this works I'll buy you a pony."

I put the studied indifference of her words together with her whole bloodless attitude. That wasn't the Elaine I remembered. I could buy that she would murder me in a fit of rage, poison me out of flaming jealousy, or bomb my car out of sheer, stubborn pique. But she would never do it and feel *nothing*.

The mud covered my chest, and still Aurora's circle hadn't faded. My heart pounded wildly, but I struggled to remain calm. I started hyperventilating. I might need every spare second I could get. The mud covered my throat and slid up over my chin. I wasn't fighting it any more. I got a good, deep breath just before my nose went under.

Then darkness pressed over my eyes, and I was left floating in thick, gooey warmth, the only sound the beating of my own heart thudding in my ears. I waited, and my lungs began to burn. I waited, not moving, fire spreading over my chest. I kept everything as relaxed as I could and counted the heartbeats.

Somewhere between seventy-four and seventy-five, Aurora's circle vanished. I reached out for power, gathering it in, shaping it in my mind. I didn't want to rush it, but it was hard not to. I took all the time I could without panicking, before I reached out again for the fabric of Elaine's spell.

I'd been right. It was the same binding she'd used when we were kids, when she'd been holding me down while my old master, Justin DuMorne, prepared to enthrall me. I'd found the way out as a kid, because Elaine and I had shared a certain impatience for our magical studies. Besides schoolwork, we'd been forced to pursue an entirely different regimen of spells and mental disciplines as well. Some nights, we would have homework until dinner, then head right for the magical stuff until well after midnight, working out spells and formulae until our eyes ached.

Toward the end, that got to be rough when all we really wanted was to be in bed, doing things much less scholarly and much more hormonal, until other parts ached. Ahem. To that end, we'd split the work. One of us would work out the spell while the other did the homework, then a quick round of copying and straight to . . . bed.

I'd been the one who worked out that binding. And it sucked.

It sucked because it had no flexibility to it, no subtlety, no class. It dropped a cocoon of hardened air around the target and locked it there, period. End of story. As teenagers, we had thought it impressively effective and simple. As a desperate man about to die, I realized that it was a brittle spell, like a diamond that was simultaneously the hardest substance on earth and easily fractured if struck at the correct angle.

Now that I knew what I was doing, I found the clumsy center of the spell, where I'd located it all those years ago, tying all the strands of energy together at the small of the back like a Christmas bow. There in the mud and darkness, I focused on the weak spot of the spell, gathered my will, and muttered, with my mouth clenched closed, "Tappitytaptap." It came out, "Mmphitymm-phmph," but that didn't make any difference on the practical side. The spell was clear in my head. A spike of energy lashed into the binding, and I felt it loosen.

My heart pounded with excitement and I reached out with the spell again. The third time I tried it, the binding slipped, and I flexed my arms and legs, pulling them slowly free.

I'd done it. I'd escaped the binding.

Now I was merely drowning in what amounted to quicksand.

The clock was running against me as I started to feel dizzy, as my lungs struggled against my will, trying to force out what little air remained and suck in a deep breath of nice, cleansing muck. I reached for more power, gathered it in, and hoped I hadn't spun around without noticing. I pushed my palms toward my feet, just as my lungs forced me to exhale, and shouted with it, *"Forzare!"*

Naked force lashed out toward my feet, bruising one leg as it swept past. Even in magic, you can't totally ignore physics, and my action of exerting force down against the earth had the predictable equal and opposite reaction. The earth exerted force up toward me, and I flew out of the mud, muck and water flying up with me in a cloud of spray. I had a wild impression of mist and dreary ground and then a tree, and then it was replaced with a teeth-rattling impact.

By the time I'd coughed out a mouthful of mud and choked air back into my lungs, I had the presence of mind to wipe mud out of my eyes. I found myself twenty feet off the ground, dangling from the branches of one of the skeletal trees. My arms and legs hung loosely beneath me, and my jeans felt tight at the waist. I tried to see how I'd gotten hung up that way, but I couldn't. I could possibly get a hand and a foot on different branches, but I could barely wiggle, and I couldn't get loose.

"You foil a Faerie Queen," I panted to myself. "Survive your own execution. Get away from certain death. And get stuck up a freaking tree." I struggled some more, just as uselessly. One mud-covered boot fell off and hit the ground with a soggy plop. "God, I hope no one sees you like this."

The sound of footsteps drifted out of the mist, coming closer.

I pushed the heel of my hand against my right eyebrow. Some days you just can't win.

I folded my arms and had them sternly crossed over my chest when a tall, shrouded form emerged from the mist below. Dark robes swirled, a deep hood concealed, and a gloved hand gripped a wooden staff.

The Gatekeeper turned his head toward me and became still for a moment. Then he reached his other gloved hand into his hood. He made a strangled, muffled sound.

"Hi," I said. King of wit, that's me.

The Gatekeeper sounded as though he had to swallow half a gallon of laughter as he responded, "Greetings, Wizard Dresden. Am I interrupting anything?"

My other boot fell off and plopped to the ground. I regarded my dangling, muddy sock-feet with pursed lips. "Nothing all that important."

"That is good," he said. He paced around a bit, peering up at me, and then said, "There's a broken branch through your belt. Get your right foot on the branch below you, your left hand on the one above you, and loosen your belt. You should be able to climb down."

I did as he said and got my muddy self down from the tree and to earth. "Thank you," I said. I privately thought to myself that I'd have been a hell of a lot more grateful about five minutes earlier. "What are you doing here?"

"Looking for you," he said.

"You've been watching?"

He shook his head. "Call it listening. But I have had glimpses of you. And matters are worsening in Chicago."

"Stars and stones," I muttered and picked up my boots. "I don't have time to chat."

The Gatekeeper put a gloved hand on my arm. "But you do," he said. "My vision is limited, but I know that you have accomplished your mission for the Winter Queen. She will keep her end of the bargain, grant us safe passage through her realm. So far as the Council is concerned, that will be enough. You would be safe."

I hesitated.

"Wizard Dresden, you could end your involvement in the matter. You could choose to step clear of it, right now. It would end the trial."

My aching, weary, half-smothered, and dirty self liked that idea. End it. Go home. Get a hot shower. A bunch of hot food. Sleep.

It was impossible, anyway. I was only one tired, beat-up, strung-out guy, wizard or not. The faeries had way too many powers and tricks to deal with on a good day, let alone on this one. I knew what Aurora was up to now, but, hell, she was getting set to charge into the middle of a battlefield. A battlefield, furthermore, that I had no idea how to even *find*, much less survive. The Stone Table had been in some weird pocket of the Nevernever like nothing I'd ever felt before. I had no idea how to reach it.

Impossible. Painful. Way too dangerous. I could call it a day, get some sleep, and hope I did better the next time I came up to the plate.

Meryl's face came to mind, ugly and tired and resolute. I also saw the statue of Lily. And Elaine, trapped by her situation but fighting things in her own way despite the odds against her. I thought of taking the Unraveling from Mother Winter, able to think of nothing but using it for my own goals, for helping Susan. Now it would be used for something else entirely, and as much as I wanted to forget about it and go home, I would bear a measure of the responsibility for the consequences of its use if I did.

I shook my head and looked around until I spotted my bag, jewelry, staff, and rod on the ground several yards away from the muddy bog Aurora had created. I recovered all of them. "No," I said. "It isn't over."

"No?" the Gatekeeper said, surprise in the tone. "Why not?"

"Because I'm an idiot." I sighed. "And there are people in trouble."

"Wizard, no one expects you to stop a war between the Sidhe Courts. The Council would assign no such responsibility to any one person."

"To hell with the Sidhe Courts," I said. "And to hell with the Council too. There are people I know in trouble. And I'm the one who turned some of this loose. I'll clean it up."

"You're sure?" the Gatekeeper said. "You won't step out of the Trial now?"

My mud-crusted fingers fumbled with the clasp of my bracelet. "I won't."

The Gatekeeper regarded me in silence for a moment and said, "Then I will not vote against you."

A little chill went through me. "Oh. You would have?"

"Had you walked away, I would kill you myself."

I stared at him for a second and then asked, "Why?"

His voice came out soft and resolute, but not unkind. "Because voting against you would have been the same thing in any case. It seems meet to me that I should take full responsibility for that choice rather than hiding behind Council protocol."

I got the bracelet on, then shoved my feet back into my boots. "Well, thanks for not killing me, then. If you'll excuse me, I've got somewhere to be."

"Yes," the Gatekeeper said. He held out his hand, a small velvet bag in it. "Take these. You may find a use for them."

I frowned at him and took the bag. Inside, I found a little glass jar of some kind of brownish gel and a chip of greyish stone on a piece of fine, silvery thread. "What's this?"

"An ointment for the eyes," he said. His tone became somewhat dry. "Easier on the nerves than using the Sight to see through the veils and glamours of the Sidhe."

I lifted my eyebrows. Bits of drying mud fell into my eyes and made me blink. "Okay. And this rock?"

"A piece from the Stone Table," he said. "It will show you the way to get there."

I blinked some more, this time in surprise. "You're helping me?"

"That would constitute interfering in the Trial," he corrected me. "So far as anyone else is concerned, I am merely seeing to it that the Trial can reach its full conclusion."

I frowned at him. "If you'd just given me the rock, maybe," I said. "The ointment is something else. You're interfering. The Council would have a fit."

The Gatekeeper sighed. "Wizard Dresden, this is something I have never said before and do not anticipate saying again." He leaned closer to me, and I could see the shadows of his features, gaunt and vague, inside his hood. One dark eye sparkled with something like humor as he offered his hand and whispered, "Sometimes what the Council does not know does not hurt it."

I found myself grinning. I shook his hand.

He nodded. "Hurry. The Council dare not interfere with internal affairs of the Sidhe, but we will do what we can." He stretched out his staff and drew it in a circle in the air. With barely a whisper of disturbance, he opened the fabric between the Nevernever and the mortal world, as though his staff had simply drawn a circle of Chicago to step into—the street outside my basement apartment, specifically. "Allah and good fortune go with you."

I nodded to him, encouraged. Then I turned to the portal and stepped through it, from that dark moor in Faerie to my usual parking space at home. Hot summer air hit my face, steamy and crackling with tension. Rain sleeted down, and thunder shook the ground. The light was already fading and dark was coming on.

I ignored them all and headed for my apartment. The mud, substance of the Nevernever, melted into a viscous goo that began evaporating at once, assisted by the driving, cleansing rain.

I had calls to make, and I wanted to change into nonslimy clothes. My fashion sense is somewhat stunted, but I still had to wonder.

What do you wear to a war?

Chapter Twenty-nine

I went with basic black.

I made my calls, set an old doctor's valise outside the front door, got a quick shower, and dressed in black. A pair of old black military-style boots, black jeans (mostly clean), a black tee, black ball cap with a scarlet Coca-Cola emblem on it, and on top of everything my leather duster. Susan had given me the coat a while back, complete with a mantle that falls to my elbows and an extra large portion of billow. The weather was stormy enough, both figuratively and literally, to make me want the reassurance of the heavy coat.

I loaded up on the gear, too—everything I'd brought with me that morning plus the Gatekeeper's gifts and my home-defense cannon, a heavy-caliber, long-barreled, Dirty Harry Magnum. I debated carrying the gun on me and decided against it. I'd have to go through Chicago to get to whatever point would lead me to the Stone Table, and I didn't need to get arrested for a concealed carry. I popped the gun, case and all, into my bag, and hoped I wouldn't have to get to it in a hurry.

Billy and the werewolves arrived maybe ten minutes later, the minivan pulling up outside and beeping the horn. I checked the doctor bag, closed it, and went out to the van, my gym bag bumping against my side. The side door rolled open, and I stepped up to toss my gear in.

I hesitated upon seeing the van, packed shoulder to shoulder with young people. There were ten or eleven of them in there.

Billy leaned over from the driver's seat and asked, "Problem?"

"I said only volunteers," I said. "I don't know how much trouble we're going into."

"Right," Billy said. "I told them that."

The kids in the van murmured their agreement.

I blew out my breath. "Okay, people. Same rules as last time. I'm calling the shots, and if I give you an order, you take it, no arguments. Deal?"

There was a round of solemn nods. I nodded in reply and peered to the back of the dim van, at a head of dull green hair. "Meryl? Is that you?"

The changeling girl gave me a solemn nod. "I want to help. So does Fix."

I caught a flash of white hair and dark, nervous eyes from beside Meryl. The little man lifted a hand and gave me a twitching wave.

"If you go along," I said, "same rules as everyone else. Otherwise you stay here."

"All right," Meryl said with a laconic nod.

"Yeah," Fix said. "Okay."

I looked around at all of them and grimaced. They looked so damned *young*. Or maybe it was just me feeling old. I reminded myself that Billy and the Alphas had already had their baptism by fire, and they'd had almost two years to hone their skills against some of the low-intensity riffraff of the Chicago underground scene. But I knew that they were getting in way over their heads on this one.

I needed them, and they'd volunteered. The trick was to make sure that I didn't lead them to a horrible death.

"Okay," I said. "Let's go."

Billy pushed open the passenger door, and Georgia moved back to the crowded rear seats. I got in beside Billy and asked, "Did you get them?"

Billy passed me a plastic bag from Wal-Mart. "Yeah, that's why it took so long to get here. There was police tape all over and cops standing around."

"Thanks," I said. I tore open a package of orange plastic box knives and put them into the doctor's valise, then snapped it closed again. Then I took the grey stone from my pocket, wrapped the thread it hung by around my hand, and held my hand out in front of me, palm down and level with my eyes. "Let's go."

"Okay," Billy said, giving me a skeptical look. "Go where?"

The grey stone quivered and twitched. Then it swung very

definitely to the east, drawing the string with it, so that it hung at a slight angle rather than straight down.

I pointed the way the stone leaned and said, "Thataway. Toward the lake."

"Got it," Billy said. He pulled the van onto the street. "So where are we heading?"

I grunted and stuck an index finger up.

"Up," Billy said, his voice skeptical. "We're going up."

I watched the stone. It wobbled, and I focused on it as I might on my own amulet. It stabilized and leaned toward the lake without wavering or swaying on its string. "Up there," I clarified.

"Where up there?"

Lightning flashed and I pointed toward it. "There up there."

Billy glanced at someone in the back and pursed his lips thoughtfully. "I hope you know a couple of streets I don't, then." He drove for a while more, with me telling him to bear right or left. At a stoplight, the rain still pounding on the windshield, wipers flicking steadily, he asked, "So what's the score?"

"Well-Intentioned But Dangerously Insane Bad Guys are ahead coming down the stretch," I said. "The Faerie Courts are duking it out up there, and it's probably going to be very hairy. The Summer Lady is our baddie, and the Winter Knight is her bitch. She has a magic hankie. She's going to use it to change a statue into a girl and kill her on a big Flintstones table at midnight."

There were a couple of grunts as Meryl pushed her way toward the front of the van. "A girl? Lily?"

I glanced from the stone back to her and nodded. "We have to find Aurora and stop her. Save the girl."

"Or what happens?" Billy asked.

"Badness."

"Kaboom badness?"

I shook my head. "Mostly longer term than that."

"Like what?"

"How do you feel about ice ages?"

Billy whistled. "Uh. Do you mind if I ask a few questions?"

I kept my eyes on the chip of stone. "Go ahead."

"Right," Billy said. "As I understand it, Aurora is trying to tear apart *both* of the Faerie Courts, right?"

"Yeah."

"Why? I mean, why not shoot for just Winter so her side wins?"

"Because she can't," I said. "She's limited in her power. She knows she doesn't have the strength it would take to force things on her own. The Queens and the Mothers could stop her easily. So she's using the only method she has open to her."

"Screwing up the balance of power," Billy said. "But she's doing it by giving a bunch of mojo to Winter?"

"Limits," I said. "She can't move Winter's power around at all, the way she can Summer's. That's why she had to kill her own Knight. She knew she could pour his power out into a vessel of her choosing."

"Lily," growled Meryl.

I glanced over my shoulder at her and nodded. "Someone who would trust her. Who wouldn't be able to protect herself against Aurora's enchantment."

"So why'd she turn the girl to stone?" Billy asked.

"It was her cover," I said. "The Queens could have found an active Knight. But once Lily was turned to stone, the Knight's mantle was stuck in limbo. Aurora knew that everyone would suspect Mab of doing something clever and that Titania would be forced to prepare to fight. Mab would have to move in response, and the pair of them would create the battleground around the Stone Table."

"What's the Table for?"

"Pouring power into one of the Courts," I said. "It belongs to Summer until midnight tonight. After that, any power that gets poured in goes to Winter."

"Which is where we're going now," Billy said.

"Uh-huh," I said. "Turn left at that light."

Billy nodded. "So Aurora steals the power and hides it, which forces the Queens to bring out the battleground with the big table."

"Right. Now Aurora plans to take Lily there and use the Unraveling to free her of the stone curse she's under. Then she kills her and touches off Faerie-geddon. She's got to get to the table after midnight, but before Mab's forces actually take the ground around it. That means she's only got a small window of opportunity, and we need to stop her from using it."

"I still don't get it," Billy said. "What the hell is she hoping to accomplish?"

"Probably she thinks she can ride out the big war. Then she'll put it all together again from the ashes just the way she wants it."

"Thank God she's not too arrogant or anything," Billy muttered. "It seems to me that Mab is going to be handed a huge advantage in this. Why didn't Aurora just work together with Mab?"

"It probably never occurred to her to try it that way. She's Summer. Mab is Winter. The two don't work together."

"Small favors," Billy said. "So what do we do to help?"

"I'm going to have to move around through a battleground. I need muscle to do it. I don't want to stop to fight. We just keep moving until I can get to the Stone Table and stop Aurora. And I want all of you changed before we go up there. Faeries are vindictive as hell and you're going to piss some of them off. Better if they never get to see your faces."

"Right," Billy said. "How many faeries are we talking about?"

I squinted up at a particularly violent burst of lightning. "All of them."

The stone the Gatekeeper had given me led us to the waterfront along Burnham Harbor. Billy parked the van on the street outside the wharves that had once been the lifeblood of the city and that still received an enormous amount of shipping every year. Halogen floodlights every couple of hundred feet made the docks into a silent still life behind a grid of chain-link fence.

I turned to the Alphas and said, "All right, folks. Before we go up, I've got to put some ointment on your eyes. It stinks, but it will keep you from being taken in by most faerie glamours."

"Me first," Billy said at once. I opened the little jar and smeared the dark ointment on under his eyes, little half-moons of dark, greasy brown. He checked his eyes in the mirror and said, "And I used to sneer at the football team."

"Get your game face on," I said. Billy slipped out of the car and pitched his sweats and T-shirt back in. I got out of the van and opened the side door. Billy, in his wolf-shape, came trotting around the side of the van and sat nearby as I smeared the greasy ointment on the eyes of all the Alphas.

It was a little unnerving, to me anyway. They were all naked as I did it, shimmering into wolf-form as soon as I had finished, and joining Billy outside. One of the girls, a redhead who had been daintily plump, now looked like something from a men's magazine. She gave me a somewhat satisfied smile as I noticed, and the next, a petite girl with mousy brown hair and a long scar on her shoulder, held her dress against her front and confided, "She's been impossible this year," as I smeared ointment on her.

Half a dozen young men and another half a dozen young women, all told, made for a lot of wolf. They waited patiently as I slapped the ointment on Fix, then Meryl, and finally myself. I used the very last of it, and blew out a deep breath. I put on my gun, on a hip rig instead of a shoulder holster, and hoped that the rain and my duster would conceal it from any passing observation. Then I drew my pentacle out to lie on my shirt, gathered up my staff and rod, slipping the latter through the straps on the doctor's bag, and picked it up. I juggled things around for a moment, until I could get the grey stone on its thread out and into my hand, and thought that maybe Elaine had the right idea when it came to going with smaller magical foci.

I had just gotten out into the rain when the wolves all looked out into the night at once. One of them, I think Billy, let out a bark and they scattered, leaving me and Meryl and Fix standing there alone in the rain.

"W-what?" Fix stammered. "What happened? Where did they go?"

Meryl said, "They must have heard something." She reached back into the minivan and came out with a machete and a wood axe. Then she pulled out a heavy denim jacket that had been festooned in layers of what looked like silverware. It rattled as she put it on.

"No chain mail?" I asked.

Fix fussed with a fork that was sticking out too far and said in an apologetic tone, "Best I could do on short notice. It's steel, though. So, you know, it will be harder for anything to bite her." He hopped back into the minivan and came out with a bulky toolbox that looked heavy as hell. The little guy lifted it to his shoulder as though he did it all the time and licked his lips. "What do we do?"

I checked the stone, which still pointed at the lake. "We move forward. If there's something out there, Billy will let us know."

Fix gulped, his frizzy white hair slowly being plastered to his head by the rain. "Are you sure?"

"Stay close to me, Fix," Meryl said. "How are we going to go that way, Dresden? There's a fence. Harbor security, too."

I had no idea, but I didn't want to say that. I headed for the nearest gate instead. "Come on."

We got to the gate and found it open. A broken chain dangled from one edge. Part of the shattered link lay on the ground nearby. The ends had been twisted, not cut, and steam curled up from them in a little hissing cloud where raindrops touched.

"Broken," I said. "And not long ago. This rain would cool the metal down fast."

"Not by a faerie, either," Meryl said quietly. "They don't like to come close to a fence like this."

"Silly," Fix sniffed. "A cheap set of bolt cutters would have been better than just breaking a perfectly good chain."

"Yeah, nasties can be irrational that way," I said. The stone continued to lean out toward the end of one of the long wharves thrusting into the lake. "Out that way."

We went through the gate and had gone maybe twenty feet before the halogen floodlights went out, leaving us in storm-drenched blackness.

I fumbled for my amulet with cold fingers, but Fix and Meryl both beat me to it. Fix's toolbox thunked down, and a moment later he stood up with a heavy-duty flashlight. At almost the same time, there was a crackle of plastic, and Meryl shook the tube of a chemical light into eerie green luminescence.

A gunshot barked, sharp and loud, and Meryl jerked and staggered to one side. She looked down at blood spreading over her jeans, her expression one of startled shock.

"Down!" I said, and hit her at the waist, bearing her to the ground as the gun barked again. I grabbed at the glow stick and shoved it into my coat. "Put out those lights!"

Fix fumbled with the flashlight as another shot rang out, sending a sputter of sparks from his toolbox. Fix yelped and dropped the light. It rolled over to one side, slewing a cone of illumination out behind us.

The light spilled over the form of the Tigress, the ghoul assassin, not even bothering to try a human shape now. In her natural form, she was a hunch-shouldered, grey-skinned fiend, something blending the worst features of mankind, hyena, and baboon. Short, wiry red hairs prickled over her whole body. Her legs were stunted and strong, her arms too long, and her hands tipped in spurs of bone that replaced nails. Her hair hung about her head in a soggy, matted lump, and her eyes, furious as she came running forward, glared with malice. Pink and grey scars stood out against her skin, swollen areas where she'd healed all the damage Murphy had inflicted on her the night before. She flew toward us over the ground, running with all four limbs, mouth gaping wide.

She didn't see the Alphas closing in behind her.

The first wolf, black grease still in half-circles under its eyes, hit her right leg, a quick snapping, jerking motion of its jaws. The ghoul shrieked in surprise and fell, tumbling. She regained her feet quickly and struck out at the wolf who had bloodied her, but the big grey beast rolled aside as a taller, tawnier wolf leapt over him. The second wolf took the ghoul's other leg, bounding away when the ghoul turned on it, while a third wolf darted in at the Tigress's back.

The ghoul screamed and tried to run again. The wolves didn't let her. I watched as another wolf slammed into her, knocking her down. She rolled to her front, but she'd been hamstrung, and her legs were now useless weight. Claws flashed out and drew flecks of blood, but the wolf she'd hit scrambled onto her back, jaws closing in on the back of the ghoul's neck. She let out a last frantic, gurgling scream.

Then the werewolves buried her in a tide of fur and flashing fangs. When they drew away half a minute later, I couldn't have recognized the remains for what they were. My stomach curled up on itself, and I forced myself to look away before I started throwing up.

I grabbed Meryl underneath her arms and started tugging her toward the nearest warehouse. I snarled, "Help me," at Fix, and he pitched in, surprisingly strong.

"Oh, God," Fix whimpered. "Oh, God, Meryl, oh, God."

"It's not bad," Meryl panted, as we dragged her around a corner of the building. "It isn't too bad, Fix."

I got out the glow stick and checked. Her jeans were stained with blood, black in the green light, but not as badly as they should have been. I found a long tear along the fabric of one leg, and whistled. "Lucky," I said. "Grazed you. Doesn't look like it's bleeding too bad." I poked at her leg. "Can you feel that?"

She winced.

"Good," I said. "Stay here. Fix, stay with her."

I left my bag there and unlimbered my gun. I kept it pointed at the ground and made sure my shield bracelet was ready to go, gathering energy into it in order to shield myself from any more rifle shots. I didn't raise the gun to level. I didn't want it to go off accidentally and bounce a bullet off my own shield and into my head.

As I stepped around the corner, I heard a short scream and then a series of sharp barks. One of the wolves appeared in the cone of Fix's fallen light, picked it up in his mouth, and trotted toward me.

"All clear?" I asked.

The wolf ducked his head in a couple of quick nods and dropped the flashlight on my foot. I picked it up. The wolf barked again and started off toward the wharf. I frowned at him and said, "You want me to follow you?"

He rolled his eyes and nodded again.

I started off after him. "If it turns out that Timmy's stuck down the well, I'm going home."

The wolf led me to the wharf the stone had pointed to, and there I found a young man in dark slacks and a white jacket on the ground in a circle of wolves. He held one bleeding hand against his belly and was panting. A rifle lay on the ground nearby, next to a broken pair of sunglasses. He looked up at me and grimaced, his face pale behind his goatee.

"Ace," I said. I shook my head. "You were the one who hired the ghoul."

"I don't know what you're talking about," he lied. "Get these things away from me, Dresden. Let me go."

"I'm running late, Ace, or I'd have the patience for more chitchat." I nodded at the nearest wolf and said, "Tear his nose off."

Ace screamed and fell back, covering his face with both arms. I winked at the wolf and stepped forward to stand over the changeling. "Or maybe his ears. Or toes. What do you think, Ace? What's going to make you talk fastest? Or should I just try them all one at a time?"

"Go to hell," Ace gasped. "You can do whatever you want, but I'm not talking. Go to hell, Dresden."

Footsteps came up behind us. Meryl limped close enough to see Ace, and then just stood there for a minute, staring at him. Fix followed her, staring.

"Ace," Fix said. "You? You shot Meryl?"

The bearded changeling swallowed and lowered his arms, looking at Meryl and Fix. "I'm sorry. Meryl, it was an accident. I wasn't aiming at you."

The green-haired changeling stared at Ace and said, "You were trying to kill Dresden. The only one besides Ron who has ever taken a step out of his way to help us. The only one who can help Lily."

"I didn't *want* to. But that was their price."

"Whose price?" Meryl asked in a monotone.

Ace licked his lips, eyes flicking around nervously. "I can't tell you. They'll kill me."

Meryl stepped forward and kicked him in the belly. Hard. Ace doubled over and threw up, gasping and twitching and sobbing. He couldn't get enough breath to cry out.

"Whose price?" Meryl asked again. When Ace didn't speak, she shifted her weight as though to repeat the kick and he cried out.

"Wait," he whimpered. "Wait."

"I'm done waiting," Meryl said.

"God, I'll tell you, I'll tell you, Meryl. It was the vampires. The Reds. I was trying to get protection from Slate, from that bitch Maeve. They said if I got rid of the wizard, they'd fix it."

"Bastards," I muttered. "So you hired the Tigress."

"I didn't have a choice," Ace whined. "If I hadn't done it, they'd have taken me themselves."

"You had a choice, Ace," Fix said quietly.

I shook my head. "How did you know we'd be coming here?"

"The Reds," Ace said. "They told me where you'd show up. They didn't say you wouldn't be alone. Meryl, please. I'm sorry."

She faced him without expression. "Shut up, Ace."

"Look," he said. "Look, let's get out of here. All right? The three of us, we can get clear of this. We need to before we can't help it anymore."

"I don't know what you're talking about," Meryl said.

"You do," Ace said, leaning up toward Meryl, his eyes intent. "You feel it. You hear her Calling us. You feel it just like I do. The Queen Calls us. All of Winter's blood."

"She Calls," Meryl said. "But I'm not answering."

"If you don't want to run, then we should think about what we're going to do. After this battle is over, Maeve and Slate are just going to come for us again. But if we declare a loyalty, if we Choose—"

Meryl kicked Ace in the stomach again. "You worthless trash. All you ever think of is yourself. Get out of my sight before I kill you."

Ace gagged and tried to protest. "But—"

Meryl snarled, "Now!"

The force of the word made Ace flinch away, and he turned it into a scramble before rising to run. The wolves all looked at me, but I shook my head. "Let him go."

Meryl shrugged her shoulders and lifted her face to the rain.

"You okay?" Fix asked her.

"Have to be," she said. Maybe it was just me, but her voice sounded a little lower, rougher. Trollier. Gulp. "Let's move, wizard."

"Yeah," I said. "Uh, yeah." I lifted the Gatekeeper's stone and followed it down the wharf to the last pier, then down to the end of the last pier, empty of any ships or boats. A dozen wolves and two changelings followed me. Nothing but the cold waters of Lake Michigan and a rolling thunderstorm surrounded me at the end of the pier, and the stone twitched, swinging almost to the horizontal on its pale thread.

"No kidding," I muttered. "I know it's up." I reached out a hand and felt something, a tingle of energy, dancing and swirling in front of me. I reached a bit further, and it became more tangible, solid. I drew up a little of my will and sent it out, toward that force, a gentle surge of energy.

Brilliant light flickering through opalescent shades rose up in front of me, as bright as the full moon and as solid as ice. The light resolved itself into the starry outline of stairs, stairs that began at the end of the pier and climbed into the storm above. I stepped forward and put one foot on the lowest step. It bore my weight, leaving me standing on a block of translucent moonlight over the wind-tossed waters of Lake Michigan.

"Wow," Fix breathed.

"We go up that?" Meryl asked.

"Woof," said Billy the Werewolf.

"While we're young," I said, and took the next step. "Come on."

Chapter Thirty

Sometimes the most remarkable things seem commonplace. I mean, when you think about it, jet travel is pretty freaking remarkable. You get in a plane, it defies the gravity of an entire planet by exploiting a loophole with air pressure, and it flies across distances that would take months or years to cross by any means of travel that has been significant for more than a century or three. You hurtle above the earth at enough speed to kill you instantly should you bump into something, and you can only breathe because someone built you a really good tin can that has seams tight enough to hold in a decent amount of air. Hundreds of millions of man-hours of work and struggle and research, blood, sweat, tears, and lives have gone into the history of air travel, and it has totally revolutionized the face of our planet and societies.

But get on any flight in the country, and I absolutely promise you that you will find someone who, in the face of all that incredible achievement, will be willing to complain about the drinks.

The *drinks*, people.

That was me on the staircase to Chicago-Over-Chicago. Yes, I was standing on nothing but congealed starlight. Yes, I was walking up through a savage storm, the wind threatening to tear me off and throw me into the freezing waters of Lake Michigan far below. Yes, I was using a legendary and enchanted means of travel to transcend the border between one dimension and the next, and on my way to an epic struggle between ancient and elemental forces.

But all I could think to say, between panting breaths, was, "Yeah. Sure. They couldn't possibly have made this an *escalator*."

Long story short: we climbed about a mile of stairs and came out in the land my godmother had shown me before, standing on the storm clouds over Chicago.

But it didn't look like it had before the opening curtain.

What had once been rolling and silent terrain sculpted of cloud, smooth and naked as a dressing dummy, had now been filled with sound, color, and violence. The storm below that battle-field was a pale reflection of the one raging upon it.

We emerged on one of the hills looking down into the valley of the Stone Table, and the hillside around us, lit with flashes of lightning in the clouds beneath, was covered in faeries of all sizes and descriptions. Sounds rang through the air—the crackling snap of lightning and the roar of thunder following. Trumpets, high and sweet, deep and brassy. Drums beat to a dozen different cadences that both clashed and rumbled in time with one another. Shouts and cries rang out in time with those drums, shrieks that might have come from human throats, together with bellows and roars that couldn't have. Taken as a whole, it was its own wild storm of music, huge, teeth-rattling, overwhelming, and charged with adrenaline. Wagner wished he could have had it so good.

Not twenty feet away stood a crowd of short, brown-skinned, white-haired little guys, their hands and feet twice as large as they should have been, bulbous noses the size of lightbulbs behind helmets made out of what looked like some kind of bone. They wore bone armor, and bore shields and weaponry, and stood in rank and file. Their eyes widened as I came up out of the clouds in my billowing black duster, leather slick with rain. Billy and the were-wolves surrounded me in a loose ring as they emerged, and Fix and Meryl pressed up close behind me.

On the other side of us stood a troll a good eight feet tall, its skin upholstered in knobby, hairy warts, lank hair hanging greasily past its massive shoulders, tiny red eyes glaring from beneath its single craggy brow. Its nostrils flared out and it turned toward me, drool dribbling from its lips, but the wolves crouched down around me, snarling. The troll blinked at them for a long moment while it processed a thought, and then turned away as though disinterested. More creatures stood within a long stone's throw, including a group of Sidhe knights, completely encased in faerie armor and mounted on long-legged warhorses of deep blue, violet, and black. A wounded sylph crouched nearby and would have looked like a lovely, winged girl from fifty yards away—but from there I could see her bloodied claws and the glittering razor edge of her wings.

I couldn't see the whole of the valley below. Some kind of mist or haze lay over it, and only gave me the occasional glimpse of whirling masses of troops and beings, ranks of somewhat human things massed together against one another, while other beings, some of which could only be called "monsters," rose up above the rest, slamming together in titanic conflicts that crushed those around them as mere circumstantial casualties.

More important, I couldn't see the Stone Table, and I couldn't even make a decent guess as to where I was standing in relation to where it should have been. The stone the Gatekeeper had given me leaned steadily in one direction, but that led straight down into the madness below us.

"What next?" Meryl yelled at me. She had to shout, though she was only a few feet away—and we were standing above the real fury of the battle below.

I shook my head and started to answer, but Fix tugged on my sleeve and piped something that got swallowed by the sounds of battle. I looked to where he was pointing, and saw one of the mounted Sidhe knights leave the others and come riding toward us.

He raised the visor of his helmet, an oddly decorated piece that somehow seemed insectoid. Pale faerie skin and golden cat-eyes regarded us from atop the steed for a moment, before he inclined his head to me and lifted a hand. The sounds of battle immediately cut off, boom, like someone had turned off a radio, and the silence threatened to put me off balance.

"Emissary," the Sidhe knight said. "I greet thee and thy companions."

"Greetings, warrior," I said in response. "I needs must speak with Queen Mab posthaste."

He nodded and said, "I will guide thee. Follow. And bid thy companions put away their weapons ere we approach her Majesty."

I nodded and said to those with me, "Put the teeth and cutlery away, folks. We need to play nice a while longer."

We followed the knight up the slope of the hill to its top, where the air grew cold enough to sting. I gathered my coat a little closer around me and could almost see the crystals of ice forming on my eyelashes. I just had to hope that my hair wouldn't freeze and break off.

Mab sat upon a white horse at the top of the hill, her hair down, rolling in silken waves to blend in with the mane and tail of her horse. She was clothed in a gown of white silk, the sleeves and trains falling in gentle sweeps to brush the cloudy ground at her steed's feet. Her lips and eyelashes were blue, her eyes as white as moonlight clouds. The sheer, cold, cruel beauty of her made my heart falter and my stomach flutter nervously. The air around her vibrated with power and shone with cold white and blue light.

"Oh, my God," Fix whispered.

I glanced back. The werewolves were simply staring at Mab, much as Fix was. Meryl regarded her from behind a forced mask of neutrality, but her eyes were alight with something wild and eager. "Steady, folks," I said, and stepped forward.

The Faerie Queen turned her regard to me and murmured, "My Emissary. You have found the thief?"

I inclined my head to her. "Yes, Queen Mab. The Summer Lady, Aurora."

Mab's eyes widened, enough that I got the impression that she understood the whole of the matter from that one fact. "Indeed. And can you bring proof of this to us?"

"If I move swiftly," I said. "I must reach the Stone Table before midnight."

Mab's empty eyes flickered to the stars above, and I thought I saw a hint of worry in them. "They move swiftly this night, wizard." She paused and then breathed out, almost to herself, "Time himself runs against thee."

"What can be done to get me there?"

Mab shook her head and regarded the field below us again. One entire swath of the battlefield flooded with a sudden golden radiance. Mab lifted her hand, and the aura around her flashed with a cerulean fire, the air thickening. That flame lashed out against the gold, and the two clashed in a shower of emerald energy, canceling one another out. Mab lowered her hand and turned to look at me again. Her eyes fell on the chip of stone on its pale thread and widened again. "Rashid. What is his interest in this matter?"

"Uh," I said. "Certainly he isn't, uh, you know, it isn't like he's representing the Council and they're interfering."

Mab took her eyes from the battle long enough to give me a look that said, quite clearly, that I was an idiot. "I know that. And your ointment. It's his recipe. I recognize the smell."

"He helped me find this place, yes."

Mab's lips twitched at the corners. "So. What does the old desert fox have in mind this time?" She shook her head and said, "No matter. The stone cannot lead you to the table. The direct route would place you in the path of battle enough to destroy any mortal. You must go another way."

"I'm listening."

She looked up and said, "Queen of the Air I may be, but these skies are still contested. Titania is at the height of her powers and I at the ebb of mine. Not that way." She pointed to the field, all weirdly lighted mist in gold and blue, green mist swirling with violence where they met. "And Summer gains ground despite all. Our Knight has not taken the field with us. He has been seduced, I presume."

"Yes," I said. "He's with Aurora."

Mab murmured, "That's the last time I let Maeve hire the help. I indulge her too much." She lifted her hand, evidently a signal, and scores of bats the size of hang gliders swarmed up from somewhere behind her, launching themselves in a web-winged cloud into the skies above. "We yet hold the river, wizard, though we lose ground on both sides now. Thy godmother and my daughter have concentrated upon it. But reach the river, and it will take thee through the battle to the hill of the Stone Table."

"Get to the river," I said. "Right. I can do that."

"Those who are mine know of thee, wizard," Mab said. "Give them no cause and they will not hamper thee." She turned away from me, her attention back upon the battle, and the sound of it came crashing back in like a pent-up tide.

I turned from her and went back to the werewolves and the changelings. "We get to the river," I shouted to them. "Try to stay in the blue mist, and don't start a fight with anything."

I started downhill, which as far as I know is the easiest way to find water. We passed through hundreds more troops, most of them units evidently recovering from the first shock of battle: scarlet- and blue-skinned ogres in faerie mail towered over me, their blood almost dull compared to their skin and armor. Another unit of brown-skinned gnomes tended to their wounded with bandages of some kind of moss. A group of sylphs crouched over a mound of bloody, stinking carrion, squabbling like vultures, blood all over their faces, breasts, and dragonfly wings. Another troop of battered, lantern-jawed, burly humanoids with wide, bat-like ears, goblins, dragged their dead and some of their wounded over to the sylphs, tossing them onto the carrion pile with businesslike efficiency despite their fellows' feeble screeches and yowls.

My stomach heaved. I fought down both fear and revulsion,

and struggled to block out the images of nightmarish carnage around me.

I kept moving ahead, driving my steps with a sense of purpose I didn't wholly feel, and kept the werewolves moving. I could only imagine that it all was worse for Billy and Georgia and the rest—whatever I saw and heard and smelled, they were getting it a lot worse, through their enhanced senses. I called encouragement to them, though I had no idea if they could hear me through the din, and no idea if it did them any good, but it seemed like something I should do, since I'd dragged them here with me. I tried to walk on one side of Fix, screen out some of the worst sights around me. Meryl gave me a grateful nod.

Ahead of us, the bluish mists began to give way to murky shades of green, faerie steel chimed and rasped on faerie steel, and the shrieks and cries of battle grew even louder. More important, amid the screams and shouts I could hear water splashing. We were near the river.

"Okay, folks!" I shouted. "We run forward and get to the river! Don't stop to slug it out with anyone! Don't stop until you're standing in the water!"

Or, I thought, *until some faerie soldier rips your legs off.*

And I ran forward into the proverbial fray.

Chapter Thirty-one

An angry buzzing sound arose from the musical din of battle ahead of us, and grew louder as we moved forward. I saw another group of goblin soldiers crouched in a ragged square formation. The goblins on the outside of the square tried to hold up shields against whistling arrows that came flickering through the mist over the water, while those within wielded spears against the source of the buzzing sound—about fifty bumblebees as big as park benches, hovering and darting. I could see a dozen goblins on the ground, wracked with the spasms of poison or simply dead, white- and green-feathered arrows protruding from throats and eyes.

A dozen of the jumbo bees peeled off from the goblins and came toward us, wings singing like a shop class of band saws.

"Holy moly!" Fix shouted.

Billy the Werewolf let out a shocked "Woof?"

"Get behind me!" I shouted and dropped everything but my staff and rod. The bees oriented on me and came zipping toward me, the wind stirred up by their wings tearing at the misty ground like the downblast of a helicopter.

I held my staff out in front of me, gathering my will and push-ing it into the focus. I hardened my will into a shield, sending it through the staff, focusing on building a wall of naked force to re-pel the oncoming bees. I held the strike until they were close enough to see the facets of their eyes, swept my staff from right to left, and cried, *"Forzare!"*

A curtain of blazing scarlet energy whirled into place in front of me, and it slammed into the oncoming bees like a giant wind-shield. They went bouncing off of it with heavy thuds of impact.

Several of the bees crash-landed and lay on the ground stunned, but two or three veered off at the last second, circling for another attack.

I lifted my blasting rod, tracking the nearest. I gathered up more of my will and snarled, *"Fuego!"* A lance of crimson energy, white at the core, leapt out from the tip of the blasting rod and scythed across the giant bee's path. My fire caught it across the wings and burned them to vapor. The bee dropped, part of one wing making it spin in a fluttering spiral that slammed into the ground on the bank of the river. The other two retreated, and their fellows attacking the goblins followed suit. The green tones faded from the mist at the edge of the river, which deepened to blue. The goblins let out a rasping, snarling cheer.

I looked around me and found Fix and Meryl staring at me with wide eyes. Fix swallowed, and I saw his mouth form the word "Wow."

I all but tore my hair out in frustration. "Go!" I shouted and started running for the water, pushing and tugging at them to get them moving. "Go, go, go!"

We were ten feet from shore when I heard hoofbeats sweeping toward the river from the far side. I looked up to see horses sailing through the mist—not flying horses but long-legged faerie steeds, coats and manes shining golden and green, that had simply leapt from the far side of the river, bearing their riders with them.

On the lead horse, the first whose hooves touched the ground on our side of the river, was the Winter Knight. Lloyd Slate was spattered in liquids of various colors that could only be blood. He bore a sword in one hand, the reins to his mount in the other, and he was laughing. Even as he landed, the nearby goblins mounted a charge.

Slate turned toward them, sword whirling and gathering with it a howl of freezing winds, its blade riming with ice. He met the first goblin's sword with his own, and the squat faerie soldier's blade shattered. Slate shifted his shoulders and sent his horse leaping a few feet to one side. Behind him, the goblin's head toppled from its shoulders, which spouted greenish blood for a few seconds before the body fell beside the head on the misty ground. The remaining goblins retreated, and Slate whirled his steed around to face me.

"Wizard!" he shouted, laughing. "Still alive!"

More faerie steeds leapt the river, Summer Sidhe warriors touching down behind Slate in helmets and mail in a riot of wildflower colors. One of them was Talos, in his dark mail, also stained with blood and bearing a slender sword spattered in so many colors of liquid that it looked as if it had cut the throat of a baby rainbow. Aurora landed as well, her battlegown shining, and a moment later there was a thunder of bigger hooves and a grunt of effort, and Korrick landed on our side of the river, his hooves driving deep into the ground.

Strapped onto the centaur's shoulders, both human and equine, was the stone statue of the kneeling girl—Lily, now the Summer Knight.

Aurora drew up short and her eyes widened. Her horse must have sensed her disturbance, because it half-reared and danced nervously left and right. The Summer Lady lifted her hand, and once more the roar of battle abruptly ceased.

"You," she half whispered.

"Give me the Unraveling and let the girl go, Aurora. It's over."

The Summer Lady's eyes glittered, green and too bright. She looked up at the stars and then back to me, with that same, too-intense pressure to her gaze, and I began to understand. Bad enough that she was one of the Sidhe, already alien to mortal kind. Bad enough that she was a Faerie Queen, driven by goals I didn't fully understand, following rules I could only just begin to grasp.

She was also mad. Loopy as a crochet convention.

"The hour is here, wizard," she hissed. "Winter's rebirth—and the end of this pointless cycle. Over, indeed!"

"Mab knows, Aurora," I said. "Titania will soon know. There's no point to this anymore. They won't let you do it."

Aurora let her head fall back as she laughed, the sound piercingly sweet. It set my nerves to jangling, and I had to push it back from my thoughts with an effort of will. The werewolves and the changelings didn't do so well. The wolves flinched back with high-pitched whimpers and frightened growls, and Fix and Meryl actually fell to their knees, clutching at their ears.

"They cannot stop me, wizard," Aurora said, that mad laughter still bubbling through her words. "And neither can you." Her eyes blazed, and she pointed her finger at me. "Korrick, with me. The rest of you. Kill Harry Dresden. Kill them all."

She turned and started down the river, golden light burning through the blue mist in a twenty-foot circle around her, and the centaur followed, leaving the battle roar, the horns and the drums, the screams and the shrieks, the music and the terror to come thundering back over us. The Sidhe warriors, a score of them, focused on me and drew swords or lifted long spears in their hands. Talos, in his spell-repelling mail that had enabled him to impersonate an ogre, shook colors from his blade and focused on me with deadly feline intensity. Slate let out another laugh, spinning his sword arrogantly in his hand.

Around me, I heard the werewolves crouch down, growls bubbling up in their throats. Meryl gathered herself to her feet, blood running from her ears, and took her axe in one big hand, drawing her machete into the other. Fix, his ears bleeding, his face pale and resolved, opened his toolbox with shaking hands and drew out a great big old grease-stained monkey wrench.

I gripped my staff and blasting rod and planted my feet. I called my power to me, lifted my staff, and smote it against the ground. Power crackled along its length and rumbled like thunder through the ground, frightening the faerie mounts into restlessness.

Slate leveled his sword at me and let out a cry, taking the panicked animal from a frightened rear to a full frontal charge. Around him, the warriors of the Summer Court followed, the light of stars and moon glittering on their swords and armor, horses screaming, surging toward us like a deadly, bejeweled tide.

The werewolves let out a full-throated howl, eerie and savage. Meryl screamed, wild and loud, and even Fix let out a tinny battle shriek.

The noise was deafening, and no one could have heard me anyway as I let out my own battle cry, which I figured was worth a shot. What the hell.

"I don't believe in faeries!"

Chapter Thirty-two

Cavalry charges are all about momentum. You get a ton of furious horse and warrior going in one direction and flatten everything in your way. As the Sidhe cavalry came thundering toward us along the banks of the river, and as my heart pounded in my chest and my legs started shaking in naked fear, I knew that if I wanted to survive the next few seconds, I had to find a way to steal that momentum and use it for myself.

I dropped my blasting rod to grip my staff in both hand, and extend it before me. The moment I did, Sidhe riders began making swift warding gestures, accompanied by staccato bursts of magical pressure, separate protective charms rising up before each of them to block whatever magic I was about to throw.

The horses, however, didn't do any such thing.

I raised a shield, but not in a wall in front of me. Such a warding would have brought the faerie nobles into contact with it, and no one wizard could hold a spell against the wills of a score of faerie lords. I brought up a shield only a couple of feet high, and stretched it in a ribbon across the ground at the feet of Slate's mount.

The Winter Knight's steed, a giant grey-green beast, never knew what hit it. The low wall I'd called up clipped it at the knees, and it came crashing down to the misty earth with a scream, dragging Slate down with it. Talos, on Slate's right, could not react in time to stop his mount or to avoid the wall, but he threw himself clear as his horse went down, dropped into a roll as nimble and precise as any martial arts movie aficionado could desire, and came up on his feet. He spun, a dance-like step somehow in time with the vast song of the battlefield, and his sword came whipping at my head.

Dimly, I heard other horses screaming, tripping not only on my wall but on one another now, but I had no idea how well the spell had worked on the rest of the Sidhe warriors. I was too busy ducking Talos's first swing and backing out of range of the next.

Meryl stepped between us and caught Talos's sword in the X formed by her axe and machete. She strained against Summer's Lord Marshal, leaning her whole body into the effort, muscles quivering. I'd felt exactly how strong the changeling girl was, but Talos simply pressed against that strength, his face composed, slowly overcoming her.

"Why do you do this, changeling child?" Talos called. "You who have struggled against Winter so long. It is useless. Stand aside. I wish no harm to thee."

"Like you wish no harm to Lily?" Meryl shouted. "How can you do that to her?"

"It does not please me, child, but it is not for me to decide," Talos answered. "She is my Queen."

"She's not mine," Meryl snarled, and drove her forehead forward, into Talos's nose. She struck him hard enough that I heard the impact, and it drove the faerie lord back several staggered paces.

She didn't see Slate come up from the ground a few feet away and make a quick, squatting lunge at her flank.

"Meryl!" I shouted into the tumult. "Look out!"

She didn't hear me. The Winter Knight's sword bit into her just below her lowest rib, and she took more than a foot of frost-covered steel, thrusting up and back. Slate's sword tore through her and came out through her jacket and the flatware coating it, emerging like some bloody blade of grass. She faltered, her mouth opening in a gasp. Both axe and machete fell from her hands.

"Meryl!" Fix screamed nearby.

Slate laughed and said something I couldn't hear. Then he twisted the blade with a wrenching pop and whipped it back out. Meryl stared at him and reached out a hand. Slate slapped it contemptuously aside and turned his back on her. She fell limply down.

I felt the rage rising and climbed back to my feet, gripping my staff in both hands. Slate reached down and dragged Talos up from the ground with one hand.

"Slate!" I shouted. "Slate, you murdering bastard!"

The Winter Knight's head whipped around toward me. His

sword came up to guard. Talos's eyes widened, and his fingers made a series of swift warding gestures.

I gathered my rage together and reached down into the ground beneath me, found the fury of the storm within it that matched my own. I thrust the end of my staff down into the misty cloud-ground as if I'd been driving a hole through a frozen lake, then extended my right hand toward the Winter Knight. *"Ventas!"* I shouted. *"Ventas fulmino!"*

The fury of the storm beneath us reared up through the wood of my staff, electricity rising in a buzzing roar of light and energy coming up from the ground and spiraling around the staff and across my body. It whirled down my extended right arm, a serpent of blue-white lightning, hesitated for a second, and then lashed across the space between me and the tip of Lloyd Slate's sword, fastening onto the blade, and bathing Slate in a writhing coruscation of azure sparks.

Slate's body jerked, his back arching violently. Thunder tore the air apart as the bolt of lightning struck home, throwing Slate into the air and hurling him violently to the ground. The shock wave of the thunder knocked me down, together with everyone else in the immediate area.

Everyone except Talos.

The Lord Marshal of Summer braced himself against the concussion, lifting one hand before his eyes as if it had been a stiff breeze. Then, in the deafening silence that came after, he lifted his sword and came straight toward me.

I reached for my blasting rod, on the ground not far away, lifted it, and threw a quick lash of fire at Talos. The Sidhe lord didn't even bother to gesture it aside. It splashed against him and away, and with a sweep of his sword he sent my blasting rod spinning from my grasp. I lifted my staff as a feeble shield with my left hand, and he struck that away as well.

Some of my hearing returned, enough for me to hear him say, "And so it ends."

"You're damned right," I muttered. "Look down."

He did.

I'd drawn my .357 in my right hand while he'd knocked the staff out of my left. I braced my right elbow against the ground and pulled the trigger.

A second roar of thunder, sharper than the first, blossomed out from the end of the gun. I don't think the bullet penetrated the dark faerie mail, because it didn't tear through Talos like it should have.

It hit him like a sledgehammer instead, driving him back and toppling him to the ground. He lay there for a moment, stunned.

It was cheap, but I was in a freaking war and I was more than a little angry. I kicked him in the face with the heel of my boot, and then I leaned down and clubbed him with the heavy barrel of the .357 until his stunned attempts to defend himself ceased and he lay still, the skin of his face burned and blistered where the steel of the gun's barrel stuck him.

I looked up in time to see Lloyd Slate, his right arm dangling uselessly, swing the broken haft of a spear at my head. There was a flash of light and pain, and I fell back on the ground, too stunned to know how badly I'd been hit. I tried to bring the gun to bear again, but Slate took it from my hand, spun it around a finger, and lowered the barrel toward my head, already thumbing the hammer back. I saw the gun coming down and saw as well that Slate wasn't going to pause for dramatic dialogue. The second I saw the dark circle of the barrel, I threw myself to one side, lifting my arms. The gun roared, and I waited for a light at the end of what I was pretty sure would be a downward sloping tunnel.

Slate missed. A ferocious, high-pitched shriek of fury made him whip his head to one side as a new attacker entered the fray.

Fix brought his monkey wrench down in a two-handed swing that ended at Lloyd Slate's wrist. There was a crunch of impact, of the delicate bones there snapping, and my gun went flying into the water. Slate let out a snarl and swung his broken arm at Fix, but the little guy was quick. He met the blow with the monkey wrench held in both hands, and it was Slate who screamed and reeled from the blow.

"You hurt her!" Fix screamed. His next swing hit Slate in the side of his left kneecap, and dropped the Winter Knight to the ground. "You hurt Meryl!"

Slate tried to roll away, but Fix rained two-handed blows of the monkey wrench down on his back. Evidently, whatever power it was that let Slate shrug off a bolt of lightning had been expended, or else it couldn't stand up to the cold steel of Fix's weapon. The little changeling pounded on Slate's back, screaming at him, until one of the blows landed on the back of his neck. The Winter Knight went limp and lay utterly still.

Fix came over to me and helped me up. As he did, wolves surrounded us, several of them bloodied, all of them with teeth bared. I looked blearily over them, to see the Sidhe warriors regrouping, dragging a couple of wounded. One horse lay on the ground screaming, the others had scattered, and only one warrior was still mounted, another slender Sidhe in green armor and a masked helm. Weapons still in hand, the Sidhe prepared to charge us again.

"Help me," Fix pleaded, hauling desperately at Meryl's shoulder. I stepped up on wobbly legs, but someone brushed past me. Billy, naked and stained with bright faerie blood, took Meryl under the shoulders, and dragged her back behind what protection the pack of werewolves offered.

"This is going to be bad," he said. "We had an edge—their horses were terrified of us. On foot, I don't know how well we'll do. Almost everyone's hurt. How's Harry?"

"Dammit," Meryl growled thickly. "Let me go. It isn't all that bad. See to the wizard. If he goes down none of us are going home."

"Meryl!" Fix said. "I thought you were hurt bad."

The changeling girl sat up, her face pale, her clothing drenched in blood. "Most of it isn't mine," she said, and I knew she was lying. "How is he?"

Billy had sat me down on the ground at some point, and I felt him poking at my head. I flinched when it got painful. Sitting down helped, and I started to put things together again.

"His skull isn't broken," Billy said. "Maybe a concussion, I don't know."

"Give me a minute," I said. "I'll make it."

Billy gripped my shoulder, relief in the gesture. "Right. We're going to have to run for it, Harry. There's more fight coming toward us."

Billy was right. I could hear the sounds of more horses, somewhere nearby in the mist, and the hammering of hundreds of goblin boots striking the ground in step.

"We can't run," Meryl said. "Aurora still has Lily."

Billy said, "Talk later. Here they come!" He blurred and dropped to all fours, taking his wolf-form again as we looked up and saw the Sidhe warriors coming toward us.

The waters behind them abruptly erupted, the still surface of the river boiling up, and cavalry, all dark blue, sea green, deep purple, rose up from under the waves. The riders were more Sidhe warriors, clad in warped-looking armor decorated in stylized snowflakes. There were only a dozen of them to the Summer warriors' score, but they were mounted and attacking from behind. They cut into the ranks of the Summer warriors, blades flickering, led by a warrior in mail of purest white, bearing a pale and cold-looking blade. The Summer warriors turned to fight, but they'd been taken off guard and they knew it.

The leader of the Winter attack cut down one warrior, then turned to another, hand spinning through a series of gestures. Cold power surged around that gesture, and one of the Summer warriors simply stopped moving, the crackling in the air around him growing louder as crystals of ice seemed simply to erupt from the surface of his body and armor, frozen from the inside out. In seconds, he was nothing but a slowly growing block of ice around a gold-and-green figure inside, and the pale rider almost negligently nudged the horse into a solid kick.

The ice shattered into pieces and fell to the ground in a jumbled pile.

The pale rider took off her helmet and flashed me a brilliant, girlish smile. It was Maeve, the Winter Lady, her green eyes bright with bloodlust, dreadlocks bound close to her head. She almost idly licked blood from her sword, as another Summer warrior fell to one knee, his back to the water, sword raised desperately against the riders confronting him.

The waters surged again, and pale, lovely arms reached out, wrapping around his throat from behind. I caught a glimpse of golden eyes and a green-toothed smile, and then the warrior's scream was cut off as he was dragged under the surface. The Summer warriors retreated, swift and in concert. The rest of the mounted Winter warriors set out in pursuit.

"Your godmother sends her greetings," Maeve called to me. "I'd have acted sooner, but it would have been a fair fight, and I avoid them."

"I need to get to the Table," I called to her.

"So I have been told," Maeve said. She rode her horse over to Lloyd Slate's unmoving form, and her lovely young face opened into another brilliant smile. "My riders are attacking further down the river, drawing Summer forces that way. You should be able to run upstream." She leaned down and purred, "Hello, Lloyd. We should have a talk."

"Come on, then," grunted Meryl. "Can you walk, wizard?"

In answer, I pushed myself to my feet. Meryl stood too, though I saw her face twist with pain as she did. Fix hefted his bloodied monkey wrench. I recovered my staff, but my blasting rod was nowhere to be seen. The black doctor bag lay nearby, and I recovered it, taking time to check its contents before closing it again. "All right, people, let's go."

We started along the stream at a jog. I didn't know how far we had to go. Everything around us was chaos and confusion. Once a cloud of pixies flew past us, and I found another stretch over the river where spiders as big as footballs had spun webs, trapping dozens of pixies in their strands. A group of faerie hounds, green and grey and savage, went past hot on the heels of a long panther like being headed for the water. Arrows whistled past, and everywhere lay the faerie dead and dying.

Finally, I felt the ground begin to rise, and looked up to see the hill of the Stone Table before us. I could even see Korrick's hulking form at the top, as the centaur backed away from the stone figure of Lily, evidently just set upon the table. Aurora, dismounted, was a slender, gleaming form, looking down upon us with anger.

"Lily!" Meryl called, though her voice had gone thready. Fix whirled to look at her, his eyes alarmed, and Meryl dropped to one knee, her ugly, honest face twisting in pain. "Get her, Fix. Save her and get her home." She looked around, focusing on me. "You'll help him?"

"You paid for it," I said. "Stay here. Stay down. You've done enough."

She shook her head and said, "One thing more." But she settled down on the ground, hand pressed to her wounded side, panting.

Aurora said something sharp to Korrick. The centaur bowed his head to her and, spear gripped in his hand, came down the hill toward us.

"Crap," I said. "Billy, this guy is a heavy hitter. Don't close with him. See if you can keep him distracted."

Billy barked in acknowledgment, and the werewolves shot forward as the centaur descended, fanning out around him and harrying his flanks and rear while their companions dodged his hooves and spear.

"Stay with Meryl," I told Fix, and scooted around the werewolves' flanks, heading up the hill toward the Stone Table.

I got close enough to the top to see Aurora standing over the statue of Lily. She held Mother Winter's Unraveling in her fingers, pressed against the statue, and she was tugging sharply at the strands, beginning to pull it to pieces. I felt something as she did, a kind of dark gravity that jerked at my wizard's senses with sharp, raking fingers. The Unraveling began to come apart, strand by strand and line by line, under Aurora's slender hands.

I stretched out my hand, adrenaline and pain giving me plenty of fuel for the magic, and called, *"Ventas servitas!"* Wind leapt out in a sudden spurt, seizing the Unraveling and tearing it from Aurora's fingers, sending it spinning through the air toward me. I caught it, stuck my tongue out at Aurora, yelled, "Meep, meep!" and ran like hell.

"Damn thee, wizard!" screamed Aurora, and the sound raked at me with jagged talons. She lifted her hands and shouted something else, and the ground itself shook, throwing me off my feet. I landed and rolled as best I could down the hill until I reached the bottom. It took me a second to drag in a breath, then I rolled to my back to sit up.

Sudden wind slashed at me, slamming me back down to the earth, and tore the Unraveling from my hands. I looked up to see Aurora take the bit of cloth from the air with casual contempt, and start back up the hill. I struggled to sit up and follow, but the wind kept me pinned there, unable to rise from the ground.

"No more interruptions," Aurora spat, and gestured with one hand.

The ground screamed. From it, writhing up with whipping, ferocious motion, came a thick hedge of thorns as long as my hand. It rose into place in a ring around the waist of the hill, so dense that I couldn't see Aurora behind it.

I fought against Aurora's spell, but couldn't overcome it physically, and I didn't even bother to try to rip it to shreds with sheer main magical strength. I stopped struggling and closed my eyes to begin to feel my way through it, to take it apart from the inside. But even as I did, Fix started screaming, "Harry? Harry! Help!"

One of the werewolves let loose a high-pitched scream of agony, and then another. My concentration wavered, and I struggled to regain it. Those people were here because of me, and I would be damned if I would let anything more happen to them. I tried to hang on to the focus, the detachment I would need to concentrate, to unravel Aurora's spell, but my fear and my anger and my worry made it all but impossible. They would have lent strength to a spell, but this was delicate work, and now my emotions, so often a source of strength, only got in the way.

Then hooves galloped up, striking the ground near me. I looked up to see the warrior in green armor, the only rider of those original Sidhe cavalry to stay mounted, standing over me, horse stamping, spear leveled at my head.

"Don't!" I said. "Wait!"

But the rider ignored me, lifted the spear, its tip gleaming in the silver light, and drove it down at my unprotected throat.

Chapter Thirty-three

❧~~❧

The spear drove into the earth beside my neck, and the rider hissed in an impatient female voice, "Hold still."

She swung down from the faerie steed, reached up, and took off the masked helm. Elaine's wheat-brown hair spilled down, escaping from the bun it had been tied in, and she jerked it all the way down irritably. "Hold still. I'll get that off you."

"Elaine," I said. I went through a bunch of heated emotions, and I didn't have time for any of them. "I'd say I was glad to see you, but I'm not sure."

"That's because you always were a little dense, Harry," she said, her voice tart. Then she smoothed her features over, her eyes falling half closed, and spread her gloved hands over my chest. She muttered something to herself and then said, "Here. *Samanyana.*"

There was a surge of gentle power, and the wind pinning me to the ground abruptly vanished. I pushed myself back to my feet.

"All right," she said. "Let's get out of here."

"No," I said. "I'm not done." I recovered my valise and my staff. "I need to get through those thorns."

"You can't," Elaine said. "Harry, I know this spell. Those thorns aren't just pointy, they're poisonous. If one of them scratches you, you'll be paralyzed in a couple of minutes. Two or three will kill you."

I scowled at the barrier and settled my grip on my staff.

"And they won't burn, either," Elaine added.

"Oh." I ground my teeth. "I'll just force them aside, then."

"That'll be like holding open a screen door, Harry. They'll just fall back into place when your concentration wavers."

"Then it won't waver."

"You can't do it, Harry," Elaine said. "If you start pushing through, Aurora will sense it and she'll tear you apart. If you're holding the thorns off you, you won't be able to defend yourself."

I lowered my staff and looked from the thorns back to Elaine. "All right," I said. "Then you'll have to hold them off me."

Elaine's eyes widened. "What?"

"You hold the thorns back. I'll go through."

"You're going to go up against Aurora? *Alone?*"

"And you're going to help me," I said.

Elaine bit her lip, looking away from me.

"Come on, Elaine," I said. "You've already betrayed her. And I am going through those thorns, with your help or without it."

"I don't know."

"Yeah, you do," I said. "If you were going to kill me, you've already had your chance. And if Aurora finishes what she's doing, I'm dead anyway."

"You don't understand—"

"I know I don't," I snapped. "I don't understand why you're helping her. I don't understand how you can stand by and let her do the things she's done. I don't understand how you can stand here and let that girl die." I let that sink in for a second before I added, quietly, "And I don't understand how you could betray me like that. Again."

"For all you know," Elaine said, "it will happen a third time. I'll let those thorns close on you halfway through and kill you for her."

"Maybe so," I said. "But I don't want to believe that, Elaine. We loved each other once upon a time. I know you aren't a coward and you aren't a killer. I want to believe that what we had really meant something, even now. That I can trust you with my life the way you can trust me with yours."

She let out a bitter little laugh and said, "You don't know what I am anymore, Harry." She looked at me. "But I believe you. I know I can trust you."

"Then help me."

She nodded and said, "You'll have to run. I'm not as strong as you, and this is brute work. I won't be able to lift it for long."

I nodded at her. Doubt nagged at me as I did. What if she did it again? Elaine hadn't exactly been sterling in the up-front-honesty department. I watched as she focused, her lovely face going blank, and felt her draw in her power, folding her arms over her chest, palms over either shoulder like an Egyptian sarcophagus.

Hell, I had ten million ways to die all around me. What was one over another? At least this way, if I went out, I'd go out doing something worthwhile. I turned and crouched, bag and staff in hand.

Elaine murmured something, and a wind stirred around her, lifting her hair around her head. She opened her eyes, though they remained distant, unfocused, and spread both hands to her sides.

Wind lashed out in a column five feet around and drove into the wall of thorns. The thorns shuddered and then began to give, bending away from Elaine's spell.

"Go!" she gasped. "Go, hurry!"

I ran.

The wind almost blinded me, and I had to run crouched down, hoping that none of my exposed skin would brush against any thorns. I felt one sharp tug along my jacket, but it didn't pierce the leather. Elaine didn't let me down. After a few seconds, I burst through the wall and came out in the clear on top of the hill of the Stone Table.

The Table stood where it had been before, but the runes and sigils scrawled over its surface now blazed with golden light. Aurora stood at the Table, fingers flying over the Unraveling, its threads pressed against the head of the statue of the kneeling girl, still upon the table. I circled a bit to one side to stay out of her peripheral vision and ran toward her.

When I was only a few feet away, the Unraveling suddenly exploded in a wash of cold white light. The light washed over the statue in a wave, and as it passed, cold white marble warmed into flesh, her stone waves of hair becoming emerald-green tresses. Lily opened her eyes and let out a gasp, looking around dazedly.

Aurora took Lily by the throat, drove the changeling down to the surface of the Stone Table with her hand, and drew the knife from her belt.

It wasn't all that gentlemanly, but I slugged the Summer Lady in the back with a two-handed swing of my staff.

As I did, the stars evidently reached the right position, and we reached midnight, the end of the height of summer, and the glowing runes on the Table flared from golden light to cold, cold blue.

The blow jarred the knife from Aurora's hand, and it fell to the surface of the table. Lily let out a scream and got out from under Aurora's hand, rolling across the table's surface and away from her.

Aurora turned to me, as fast as any of the other Sidhe, leaning back on the table and planting both feet against my chest. She kicked hard and drove me back, and before I was done rolling she had called a gout of fire and sent it roaring toward me. I got to my knees and lifted my staff, calling together my will in time to parry the strike, deflecting the flame into the misty sky.

The red light of it fell on a green faerie steed leaping in the air above the thorns. It didn't make it over the wall but fall twenty feet short, screaming horribly as it landed on the poisoned thorns. Its rider didn't go down with it, though. Talos, his face bloodied, leapt off the horse's back, did a neat flip in the air, and came down inside the circle of thorns unscathed.

Aurora let out a wild laugh and said, "Kill him, Lord Marshal!"

Talos drew his sword and came for me. I thought the first blow was a thrust for my belly, but he'd suckered me, and the sword darted to one side to send my staff spinning off into the thorns. As he stalked me, I gripped my valise and backed away, looking around me for a weapon, for something to buy me a few seconds, for options.

Then a basso bellow shook the hilltop and froze even Aurora for a second. The wall of thorns shook and quivered, and something massive bellowed again and tore through it, into the open. The troll was huge, and green, and hideous, and strong. It wielded an axe in one hand like a plastic picnic knife and was covered in swelling welts, poisoned wounds, and its own dark-green blood. It had a horrible wound in its side, ichor flowing openly from it. It was dragging itself along despite the wounds, but it was dying.

And it was Meryl. She'd Chosen.

I could only stare as I recognized her features, inside the insane fury of the troll's face. It reached for Talos, and the Lord Marshal of Summer whirled, his bright sword taking off one of the troll's hands. She got the other on his leg, though, and dragged him beneath her even as she fell, the weight of her pinning him down, crushing him to the ground with a choked, gurgling cry of rage and triumph.

I looked back, to see Aurora catch Lily by her green hair, and drag her back toward the Table. I ran to it, and beat her to the knife, a curved number of chipped stone, dragging it across the Table and to me.

"Fool," Aurora hissed. "I will tear out her throat with my bare hands."

I threw the knife away and said, "No, you won't."

Aurora laughed and asked, eyes mad and enticing, "And why not?"

I undid the clasp of the valise. "Because I know something you don't."

"What?" she laughed. "What could you possibly know that matters now?"

I gave her a cold smile and said, "The phone number to Pizza Spress." I opened the bag and snarled, "Get her, Toot!"

There was a shrill, piping blast from inside the valise and Toot-toot sailed up out of it, leaving a trail of crimson sparkles in his wake. The little faerie still wore his makeshift armor, but his weapons had been replaced with what I'd had Billy pick up from Wal-Mart—an orange plastic box knife, its slender blade extended from its handle.

Aurora let out another laugh, uglier, and said, "And what can this little thing do?"

Toot blew another little blast on his trumpet and shouted, voice shrill, "In the name of the Pizza Lord! Charge!"

And the valise exploded in a cloud of crimson sparkles as a swarm of pixies, all armed with cold steel blades sheathed in orange plastic, rose up and streaked toward Aurora in a cloud of red sparkles and glinting knives.

She met my eyes as the pixies came for her, and I saw the sudden fear, the recognition of what was coming for her. She lifted a hand, golden power gathering there, but one of the pixies reached her, box knife flashing, and ripped across her hand with its blade. She screamed, blood flowing, and the golden light dimmed.

"No!" she howled. "No! Not now!"

The pixies swarmed her, and it wasn't pretty. The bright faerie mail of her gown gave her no protection against the steel blades, and they sheared through it like cardboard. From all directions, in a whirling cloud around her, Toot-toot and his companions struck dozens of times in only a few seconds, the bright steel splashing scarlet blood into the air.

I saw her eyes open, burning brightly, even as zipping, darting death opened up more cuts, flaying her pale skin. She hauled herself toward the Table.

If she died there, bled to death on the table, she would accomplish her goal. She would hurl vast power to the Winter Courts and destroy the balance between the faerie Courts. I threw myself up onto the Table and into her, bearing her back down and to the ground.

She screamed in frustration and struggled against me—but she didn't have any strength. We rolled down the hill a few times, and then wound up on the ground, me pinning her down, holding her there.

Aurora looked up at me, green eyes faded of color, unfocused. "Wait," she said, her voice weak and somehow very young. She didn't look like a mad faerie sorceress now. She looked like a frightened girl. "Wait. You don't understand. I just wanted it to stop. Wanted the hurting to stop."

I smoothed a bloodied lock of hair from her eyes and felt very tired as I said, "The only people who never hurt are dead."

The light died out of her eyes, her breath slowing. She whispered, barely audible, "I don't understand."

I answered, "I don't either."

A tear slid from her eye and mixed with the blood.

Then she died.

Chapter Thirty-four

⤙⤚

I'd done it. I'd saved the girl, stopped the thief, proved Mab's innocence, and won her support for the White Council, thereby saving my own ass.

Huzzah.

I lay there with Aurora's empty body, too tired to move. The Queens found me maybe a quarter of an hour later. I was only dimly aware of them, of radiant light of gold and blue meeting over me. Gold light gathered over the body for a moment and then flowed away, taking the dead flesh with it. I was left cold and tired on the ground.

The gold light's departure left only cold blue. A moment later, I felt Mab's fingers touch my head, and she murmured, "Wizard. I am well pleased with thee."

"Go away, Mab," I said, my voice tired.

She laughed and said, "Nay, mortal. It is you who must now depart. You and your companions."

"What about Toot-toot?" I asked.

"It is unusual for a mortal to be able to Call any of Faerie, even the lowest, into service, but it has been done before. Fear not for your little warriors. They were your weapon, and the only one accountable for their actions will be you. Take their steel with you, and it will be enough."

I looked up at her and said, "You're going to live up to your side of the bargain?"

"Of course. The wizards will have safe passport."

"Not that bargain. Ours."

Mab's lovely, dangerous mouth curled up in a smile. "First, let me make you an offer."

She gestured, and the thorns parted. Maeve stood there in her white armor, and Mother Winter stood behind her, all shrouded in black cloth. Before them on the ground knelt Lloyd Slate, broken, obviously in pain, his hands manacled to a collar around his throat, the whole made of something that looked like cloudy ice.

"We have a traitor among us," Mab purred. "And he will be dealt with accordingly. After which there will be an opening for a new Knight." She watched me and said, "I would have someone worthy of more trust as his successor. Accept that power and all debts between us are canceled."

"Not just no," I muttered. "Hell, no."

Mab's smile widened. "Very well, then. I'm sure we can find some way to amuse ourselves with this one until time enough has passed to offer again."

Slate looked up, blearily, his voice slurred and panicky. "No. No, Dresden. Dresden, don't let them. Don't let them take me. Take it, please, don't let them keep me waiting."

Mab touched my head again and said, "Only twice more, then, and you will be free of me."

And they left.

Lloyd Slate's screams lingered behind them.

I sat there, too tired to move, until the lights began to dim. I vaguely remember feeling Ebenezar heft me off the ground and get my arm across his shoulders. The Gatekeeper murmured something, and Billy answered him.

I woke up back at my place, in bed.

Billy, who had been dozing in a chair next to the bed, woke up with a snort and said, "Hey, there you are. You thirsty?"

I nodded, throat too dry to speak, and he handed me a glass of cool water.

"What happened?" I asked, when I could speak.

He shook his head. "Meryl died. She told me to tell you that she'd made her Choice and didn't regret it. Then she just changed. We found her on the ground near you."

I closed my eyes and nodded.

"Ebenezar said to tell you that you'd made a lot of people see red, but that you shouldn't worry about them for a while."

"Heh," I said. "The Alphas?"

"Banged up," Billy said, a hint of pride in his voice. "One

hundred and fifty-five stitches all together, but we all came out of it more or less in one piece. Pizza party and gaming at my place tonight."

My stomach growled at the word "pizza."

I took a shower, dried off, and dressed in clean clothes. That made me blink. I looked around the bathroom, then peeked out at my bedroom, and said to Billy, "You cleaned up? Did laundry?"

He shook his head. "Not me." There was a knock at the door and he said, "Just a minute." I heard him go out and say something through the door before he came back in. "Visitors."

I put some socks on, then my sneakers. "Who is it?"

"The new Summer Lady and Knight," Billy said.

"They looking for trouble?"

Billy grinned and said, "Just come talk to them."

I glowered at him and followed him out to the main room. It was spotless. My furniture is mostly secondhand, sturdy old stuff with a lot of wood and a lot of textured fabrics. It all looked clean too, and there were no stains in it. My rugs, everything from something that could have flown in the skies of mythic Araby to tourist-trap faux Navajo, had also been cleaned and aired out. I checked the floor underneath the rugs. Mopped and scoured clean. The hod had fresh wood in it, and the fireplace had been not only emptied out but swept clean to boot.

My staff and blasting rod were in the corner, gleaming as if they'd been polished, and my gun hung in its holster, freshly oiled. The gun had been polished too.

I went over to the alcove with the stove, sink, and icebox. The icebox was an old-fashioned one that stocked actual ice, given my problems with electricity. It had been cleaned, and new ice put in it. It was packed with neat rows of food—fresh fruits and veggies, juice, Cokes—and there was ice cream in the freezer. My pantry was full of dry foods, canned foods, pasta, sauces. And Mister had a new litterbox, made of wood, lined with plastic, and full of fresh litter. He had a carved wooden bowl as well, and a mate for water, and he had emptied it of food. Mister himself sprawled on the floor, batting idly at a cloth sack of catnip hanging from a string on the pantry door.

"I died," I said. "I died and someone made a clerical error and this is heaven."

I looked around to find Billy grinning at me like a fool. He hooked a thumb at the door. "Visiting dignitaries?"

I went to the door and opened it warily, peeking around it.

Fix stood there in a set of mechanic's coveralls. His frizzy white hair floated around his head and complemented his smile. He had grease on his hands and face, and his old toolbox sat on the ground next to him. Beside him stood Lily, shapely figure showing off simple dark slacks and a green blouse. Her hair had been pulled back into a ponytail.

And it had turned snow white.

"Harry," Fix said. "How you doing?"

I blinked at them and said, "You? The new Summer Lady?"

Lily flushed prettily and nodded. "I know. I didn't want it, but when—when Aurora died, her power flowed into the nearest Summer vessel. Usually it would be one of the other Queens, but I had the Knight's power and it just sort of . . . plopped in there."

I lifted my eyebrows and said, "Are you okay?"

She frowned. "I'm not sure. It's a lot to think about. And it's the first time this kind of power has fallen to a mortal."

"You mean you're not, uh. You haven't?"

"Chosen?" Lily asked. She shook her head. "It's just me. I don't know what I'm going to do, but Titania said she'd teach me."

I glanced aside. "And you chose Fix as your Knight, huh."

She smiled at Fix. "I trust him."

"Suits me," I said. "Fix kicked the Winter Knight's ass once already."

Lily blinked and looked at Fix. The little guy flushed, and I swear to God, he dragged one foot over the ground.

Lily smiled and offered me her hand. "I wanted to meet you. And to thank you, Mister Dresden. I owe you my life."

I shook her hand but said, "You don't owe me anything. I'm apparently saving damsels on reflex now." My smile faded and I said, "Besides. I was just the hired help. Thank Meryl."

Lily frowned and said, "Don't blame yourself for what happened. You did what you did because you have a good heart, Mister Dresden. Just like Meryl. I can't repay a kindness like that, and it's going to be years before I can make much use of my . . . my . . ." she fumbled for a word.

"Power?"

"Okay, power. But if you need help, or a safe place, you can come to me. Whatever I can do, I will."

"She had some brownies come clean up your place for you, Harry," Fix said. "And I just finished up with your car, so it should run for you now. I hope you don't mind."

I had to blink my eyes a few times, before I said, "I don't mind. Come on in, I'll get you a drink."

We had a nice visit. They seemed like decent kids.

After everyone left, it was dark, and there was another knock at the door. I answered it, and Elaine stood there, in a T-shirt and jeans shorts that showed off her pretty legs. She had her hair up under a Cubs baseball hat, and she said without preamble, "I wanted to see you before I left."

I leaned against the doorway close to her. "You got out okay, I guess."

"So did you. Did Mab pay up?"

I nodded. "Yeah. What about you? Are you still beholden to Summer?"

Elaine shrugged. "I owed everything to Aurora. Even if she'd wanted to quibble about whether or not I'd paid her back in full, it's a moot point now."

"Where are you going?"

She shrugged. "I don't know. Somewhere with a lot of people. Maybe go to school for a while." She took a deep breath and then said, "Harry, I'm sorry things went like that. I was afraid to tell you about Aurora. I guess I should have known better. I'm glad you came through it all right. Really glad."

I had a lot of answers to that, but the one I picked was, "She thought she was doing something good. I guess I can see how you'd . . . Look, it's done."

She nodded. Then she said, "I saw the pictures on your mantel. Of Susan. Those letters. And that engagement ring."

I glanced back at the mantel and felt bad in all kinds of ways. "Yeah."

"You love her," Elaine said.

I nodded.

She let out a breath and looked down, so that the bill of her hat hid her eyes. "Then can I give you some advice?"

"Why not."

She looked up and said, "Stop feeling sorry for yourself, Harry."

I blinked and said, "What?"

She gestured at my apartment. "You were living in a sewer, Harry. I understand that there's something you're blaming yourself for. I'm just guessing at the details, but it's pretty clear you were driving yourself into the ground because of it. Get over it. You aren't going to do her any good as a living mildew collection. Stop thinking about how bad you feel—because if she cares about you at all, it would tear her up to see you like I saw you a few days ago."

I stared at her for a moment and then said, "Romantic advice. From you."

She flashed me half of a smile and said, "Yeah. The irony. I'll see you around."

I nodded and said, "Good-bye, Elaine."

She leaned up and kissed my cheek again, then turned and left. I watched her go. And illegal mind fog or not, I never mentioned her to the Council.

Later that night I showed up at Billy's apartment. Laughter drifted out under the door, along with music and the smell of delivered pizza. I knocked and Billy answered the door. Conversation ceased inside.

I came into the apartment. A dozen wounded, bruised, cut, and happy werewolves watched me from around a long table scattered with drinks, Pizza Spress boxes, dice, pencils, pads of paper, and little inch-tall models on a big sheet of graph paper.

"Billy," I said. "And the rest of you guys. I just wanted to say that you really handled yourselves up there. A lot better than I expected or hoped. I should have given you more credit. Thank you."

Billy nodded and said, "It was worth it. Right?"

There was a murmur of agreement from the room.

I nodded. "Okay, then. Someone get me a pizza and a Coke and some dice, but I want it understood that I'm going to need thews."

Billy blinked at me. "What?"

"Thews," I said. "I want big, bulging thews, and I don't want to have to think too much."

His face split in a grin. "Georgia, do we have a barbarian character sheet left?"

"Sure," Georgia said, and went to a file cabinet.

I took a seat at the table and got handed pizza and Coke, and listened to the voices and chatter start up again, and thought to myself that it was a whole hell of a lot better than spending another night crucifying myself in the lab.

"You know what disappoints me?" Billy asked me after a while.

"No, what?"

"All of those faeries and duels and mad queens and so on, and no one quoted old Billy Shakespeare. Not even once."

I stared at Billy for a minute and started to laugh. My own aches and bruises and cuts and wounds pained me, but it was an honest, stretchy pain, something that was healing. I got myself some dice and some paper and some pencils and settled down with friends to pretend to be Thorg the Barbarian, to eat, drink, and be merry.

Lord, what fools these mortals be.

DEATH
MASKS

DEATH
MASKS

In memory of Plumicon and Ersha, fallen heroes

Chapter One

Some things just aren't meant to go together. Things like oil and water. Orange juice and toothpaste.

Wizards and television.

Spotlights glared into my eyes. The heat of them threatened to make me sweat streaks through the pancake makeup some harried stagehand had slapped on me a few minutes before. Lights on top of cameras started winking on, the talk-show theme song began to play, and the studio audience began to chant, "Lah-REE, Lah-REE, Lah-REE!"

Larry Fowler, a short man in an immaculate suit, appeared from the doors at the rear of the studio and began walking to the stage, flashing his porcelain smile and shaking the hands of a dozen people seated at the ends of their rows as he passed them. The audience whistled and cheered as he did. The noise made me flinch in my seat up on the stage, and I felt a trickle of sweat slide down over my ribs, beneath my white dress shirt and my jacket. I briefly considered running away screaming.

It isn't like I have stage fright or anything, see. Because I don't. It was just really hot up there. I licked my lips and checked all the fire exits, just to be safe. No telling when you might need to make a speedy exit. The lights and noise made it a little difficult to keep up my concentration, and I felt the spell I'd woven around me wobble. I closed my eyes for a second, until I had stabilized it again.

In the chair beside me sat a dumpy, balding man in his late forties, dressed in a suit that looked a lot better than mine. Mortimer

Lindquist waited calmly, a polite smile on his face, but muttered out of the corner of his mouth, "You okay?"

"I've been in house fires I liked better than this."

"You asked for this meeting, not me," Mortimer said. He frowned as Fowler lingered over shaking a young woman's hand. "Showboat."

"Think this will take long?" I asked Morty.

He glanced beside him at an empty chair, and at another beside me. "Two mystery guests. I guess this one could go for a while. They shoot extra material and edit it down to the best parts."

I sighed. I'd been on *The Larry Fowler Show* just after I'd gone into business as an investigator, and it had been a mistake. I'd had to fight my way uphill against the tide of infamy I'd received from association with the show. "What did you find out?" I asked.

Mort flicked a nervous glance at me and said, "Not much."

"Come on, Mort."

He opened his mouth to answer, then glanced up as Larry Fowler trotted up the stairs and onto the stage. "Not now. Wait for a commercial break."

Larry Fowler pranced up to us and pumped my hand, then Mort's with equally exaggerated enthusiasm. "Welcome to the show," he said into a handheld microphone, then turned to face the nearest camera. "Our topic for today is 'Witchcraft and Wizardry—Phony or Fabulous?' With us in order to share their views are local medium and psychic counselor Mortimer Lindquist."

The crowd applauded politely.

"And beside him, Harry Dresden, Chicago's only professional wizard."

There was a round of snickering laughter to go with the applause this time. I couldn't say I was shocked. People don't believe in the supernatural these days. Supernatural things are scary. It's much more comfortable to rest secure in the knowledge that no one can reach out with magic and quietly kill you, that vampires exist only in movies, and that demons are mere psychological dysfunctions.

Completely inaccurate but much more comfortable.

Despite the relative levels of denial, my face heated up. I hate it when people laugh at me. An old, quiet hurt mixed in with my nervousness and I struggled to maintain the suppression spell.

Yeah, I said spell. See, I really am a wizard. I do magic. I've run into vampires and demons and a lot of things in between, and I've got the scars to show for it. The problem was that technology doesn't seem to enjoy coexisting with magic. When I'm around, computers crash, lightbulbs burn out, and car alarms start screaming in warbling, drunken voices for no good reason. I'd worked out a spell to suppress the magic I carried with me, at least temporarily, so that I might at least have a chance to keep from blowing out the studio lights and cameras, or setting off the fire alarms.

It was delicate stuff by its very nature, and extremely difficult for me to hold in place. So far so good, but I saw the nearest cameraman wince and jerk his headset away from his ear. Whining feedback sounded tinnily from the headset.

I closed my eyes and reined in my discomfort and embarrassment, focusing on the spell. The feedback died away.

"Well, then," Larry said, after half a minute of happy talk. "Morty, you've been a guest on the show several times now. Would you care to tell us a little bit about what you do?"

Mortimer widened his eyes and whispered, "I see dead people."

The audience laughed.

"But seriously. Mostly I conduct séances, Larry," Mortimer said. "I do what I can to help those who have lost a loved one or who need to contact them in the beyond in order to resolve issues left undone back here on earth. I also offer a predictions service in order to help clients make decisions on upcoming issues, and to try to warn them against possible danger."

"Really," Larry said. "Could you give us a demonstration?"

Mortimer closed his eyes and rested the fingertips of his right hand on the spot between his eyes. Then in a hollow voice he said, "The spirits tell me . . . that two more guests will soon arrive."

The audience laughed, and Mortimer nodded at them with an easy grin. He knew how to play a crowd.

Larry gave Mortimer a tolerant smile. "And why are you here today?"

"Larry, I just want to try to raise public awareness about the realm of the psychic and paranormal. Nearly eighty percent of a recent survey of American adults stated that they believed in the existence of the spirits of the dead, in ghosts. I just want to help people understand that they do exist, and that there are other people out there who have had strange and inexplicable encounters with them."

"Thank you, Morty. And Harry—may I call you Harry?"

"Sure. It's your nickel," I responded.

Larry's smile got a shade brittle. "Can you tell us a little bit about what you do?"

"I'm a wizard," I said. "I find lost articles, investigate paranormal occurrences, and train people who find themselves struggling with a sudden development of their own abilities."

"Isn't it true that you also consult for the Special Investigations department at Chicago PD?"

"Occasionally," I said. I wanted to avoid talking about SI if I could. The last thing CPD would want was to be advertised on *The Larry Fowler Show.* "Many police departments across the country employ such consultants when all other leads have failed."

"And why are you here today?"

"Because I'm broke and your producer is paying double my standard fee."

The crowd laughed again, more warmly. Larry Fowler's eyes flashed with an impatient look behind his glasses, and his smile turned into a gnashing of teeth. "No, really, Harry. Why?"

"For the same reasons as Mort—uh, as Morty here," I answered. Which was true. I'd come here to meet Mort and get some information from him. He'd come here to meet me, because he refused to be seen near me on the street. I guess you could say I don't have the safest reputation in the world.

"And you claim to be able to do magic," Larry said.

"Yeah."

"Could you show us?" Larry prompted.

"I could, Larry, but I don't think it's practical."

Larry nodded, and gave the audience a wise look. "And why is that?"

"Because it would probably wreck your studio equipment."

"Of course," Larry said. He winked at the audience. "Well, we wouldn't want that, would we?"

There was more laughter and a few catcalls from the crowd. Passages from *Carrie* and *Firestarter* sprang to mind, but I restrained myself and maintained the suppression spell. Master of self-discipline, that's me. But I gave the fire door beside the stage another longing look.

Larry carried on the talk part of the talk show, discussing crystals and ESP and tarot cards. Mort did most of the talking. I chimed in with monosyllables from time to time.

After several minutes of this, Larry said, "We'll be right back after these announcements." Stagehands help up signs that read

APPLAUSE, and cameras panned and zoomed over the audience as they whistled and hooted.

Larry gave me an annoyed look and strode offstage. In the wings, he started tearing into a makeup girl about his hair.

I leaned over to Mort and said, "Okay. What did you find out?"

The dumpy ectomancer shook his head. "Nothing concrete. I'm still getting back into the swing of things in contacting the dead."

"Even so, you've got more contacts in this area than I do," I said. "My sources don't keep close track of who has or hasn't died lately, so I'll take whatever I can get. Is she at least alive?"

He nodded. "She's alive. That much I know. She's in Peru."

"Peru?" It came as a vast relief to hear that she wasn't dead, but what the hell was Susan doing in Peru? "That's Red Court territory."

"Some," Mort agreed. "Though most of them are in Brazil and the Yucatán. I tried to find out exactly where she was, but I was blocked."

"By who?"

Mort shrugged. "No way for me to tell. I'm sorry."

I shook my head. "No, it's okay. Thanks, Mort."

I settled back in my seat, mulling over the news.

Susan Rodriguez was a reporter for a regional yellow paper called the *Midwestern Arcane*. She'd grown interested in me just after I opened up my practice, hounding me relentlessly to find out more about all the things that go bump in the night. We'd gotten involved, and on our first date she wound up lying naked on the ground in a thunderstorm while lightning cooked a toadlike demon to gooey bits. After that, she parlayed a couple of encounters with things from my cases into a widespread syndicated column.

A couple of years later, she wound up following me into a nest of vampires holding a big to-do, despite all my warnings to the contrary. A noble of the Red Court of Vampires had grabbed her and begun the transformation from mortal to vampire on her. It was payback for something I'd done. The vampire noble in question thought that her standing in the Red Court made her untouchable, that I wouldn't want to start trouble with the entire Court. She told me that if I fought to take Susan back, I would be starting a worldwide war between the White Council of wizards and the vampires' Red Court.

Which I did.

The vampires hadn't forgiven me for taking Susan back from

them, probably because a bunch of them, including one of their nobility, had been incinerated in the process. That's why Mort didn't want to be seen with me. He wasn't involved in the war, and he intended to keep it that way.

In any case, Susan hadn't gone all the way through her transformation, but the vamps had given her their blood thirst, and if she ever gave in to it, she'd become one of the Red Court. I asked her to marry me, promising her that I'd find a way to restore her humanity. She turned me down and left town, trying to sort things out on her own, I guess. I still kept trying to find a way to remove her affliction, but I'd received only a card and a postcard or three from her since she'd left.

Two weeks ago, her editor had called to say that the columns she usually sent in for the *Arcane* were late, and asked if I knew how to get in touch with her. I hadn't, but I started looking. I got zip, and went to Mort Lindquist to see if his contacts in the spirit world would pay off better than mine.

I hadn't gotten much, but at least she was alive. Muscles in my back unclenched a little.

I looked up to see Larry come back onstage to his theme music. Speakers squealed and squelched when he started to talk, and I realized I'd let my control slip again. The suppression spell was a hell of a lot harder than I thought it would be, and getting harder by the minute. I tried to focus, and the speakers quieted to the occasional fitful pop.

"Welcome back to the show," Larry told a camera. "Today we are speaking with practitioners of the paranormal, who are here to share their views with the studio audience and our viewers at home. In order to explore these issues further, I have asked a couple of experts with opposing viewpoints to join us today, and here they are."

The audience applauded as a pair of men emerged from either side of the stage.

The first man sat down in the chair by Morty. He was a little over average height and thin, his skin burned into tanned leather by the sun. He might have been anywhere between forty and sixty. His hair was greying and neatly cut, and he wore a black suit with a white clerical collar sharing space with a rosary and crucifix at his throat. He smiled and nodded to Mort and me and shook hands with Larry.

Larry said, "Allow me to introduce Father Vincent, who has come all the way from the Vatican to be with us today. He is a leading scholar and researcher within the Catholic Church on the subject of witchcraft and magic, both historically and from a psychological perspective. Father, welcome to the show."

Vincent's voice was a little rough, but he spoke English with the kind of cultured accent that seemed to indicate an expensive education. "Thank you, Larry. I'm very pleased to be here."

I looked from Father Vincent to the second man, who had settled in the chair beside me, just as Larry said, "And from the University of Brazil at Rio de Janeiro, please welcome Dr. Paolo Ortega, world-renowned researcher and debunker of the supernatural."

Larry started saying something else, but I didn't hear him. I just stared at the man beside me as recognition dawned. He was of average height and slightly heavy build, with broad shoulders and a deep chest. He was dark-complected, his black hair neatly brushed, his grey-and-silver suit stylish and tasteful.

And he was a duke of the Red Court—an ancient and deadly vampire, smiling at me from less than an arm's length away. My heart rate went from sixty to a hundred and fifty million, fear sending silver lightning racing down my limbs.

Emotions have power. They fuel a lot of my magic. The fear hit me, and the pressure on the suppression spell redoubled. There was a flash of light and a puff of smoke from the nearest camera, and the operator staggered back from it, tearing off his headphones with one of the curses they have to edit out of daytime TV. Smoke began to rise steadily from the camera, along with the smell of burning rubber, and the studio monitors shrieked with feedback.

"Well," Ortega said, under his breath. "Nice to see you again, Mister Dresden."

I swallowed and fumbled at my pocket, where I had a couple of wizard gadgets I used for self-defense. Ortega put his hand on my arm. It didn't look as if he was exerting himself, but his fingers closed on my wrist like manacles, hard enough to send flashes of pain up through my elbow and shoulder. I looked around, but everyone was staring at the malfunctioning camera.

"Relax," Ortega said, his accent thick and vaguely Latinate. "I'm not going to kill you on television, wizard. I'm here to talk to you."

"Get off me," I said. My voice was thin, shaky. Goddamned stage fright.

He released me, and I jerked my arm away. The crew rolled

the smoking camera back, and a director type with a set of headphones made a rolling motion with the fingers of one hand. Larry
nodded to him, and turned to Ortega.

"Sorry about that. We'll edit that part out later."

"It's no trouble," Ortega assured him.

Larry paused for a moment, and then said, "Dr. Ortega, welcome to the show. You have a reputation as one of the premier an-
alysts of paranormal phenomena in the world. You have proven
that a wide variety of so-called supernatural occurrences were actually clever hoaxes. Can you tell us a little about that?"

"Certainly. I have investigated these events for a number of
years, and I have yet to find one that cannot be adequately explained. Alleged alien crop circles proved to be nothing more than
a favorite pastime of a small group of British farmers, for example. Other odd events are certainly unusual, but by no means supernatural. Even here in Chicago, you had a rain of toads in one of
your local parks witnessed by dozens if not hundreds of people.
And it turned out, later, that a freak windstorm had scooped them
up from elsewhere and deposited them here."

Larry nodded, his expression serious. "Then you don't believe
in these events."

Ortega gave Larry a patronizing smile. "I would love to believe
that such things are true, Larry. There is little enough magic in the
world. But I am afraid that even though we each have a part of us
that wishes to believe in wondrous beings and fantastic powers, the
fact of the matter is that it is simple, primitive superstition."

"Then in your opinion, practitioners of the supernatural—"

"Frauds," Ortega said with certainty. "With no offense meant
to your guests, of course. All of these so-called mediums, presum-
ing they aren't self-deluded, are simply skilled actors who have
acquired a fundamental grasp of human psychology and know
how to exploit it. They are easily able to deceive the gullible into
believing that they can contact the dead or read thoughts or that
they are in fact supernatural beings. Why, with a few minutes' effort and the right setting, I am certain that I could convince anyone in this room that I was a vampire myself."

People laughed again. I scowled at Ortega, frustration growing
once more, putting more pressure on the suppression spell. The air
around me started to feel warmer.

A second cameraman yelped and jerked off his squealing earphones, while his camera started spinning about slowly on its
stand, winding power cables around the steel frame it rested on.

The on-air lights went out. Larry stepped to the edge of the stage, yelling at the poor cameraman. The apologetic-looking director appeared from the wings, and Larry turned his attention to him. The man bore the scolding with a kind of oxenlike patience, and then examined the camera. He muttered something into his headset, and he and the shaken cameraman began to wheel the dead camera away.

Larry folded his arms impatiently, then turned to the guests and said, "I'm sorry. Give us a couple of minutes to get a spare camera in. It won't take long."

"No problem, Larry," Ortega assured him. "We can just chat for a moment."

Larry peered at me. "Are you all right, Mister Dresden?" he asked. "You look a little pale. Could you use a drink or something?"

"I know I could," Ortega said, his eyes on me.

"I'll have someone bring them out," Larry said, and strode offstage toward his hairstylist.

Mort had engaged Father Vincent in quiet conversation, his back very firmly turned toward me. I turned back to Ortega, warily, my back stiff, and fought down the anger and fear. Usually being scared out of my mind is kind of useful. Magic comes from emotions, and terror is handy fuel. But this wasn't the place to start calling up gales of wind or flashes of fire. There were too many people around, and it would be too easy to get someone hurt, even killed.

Besides which, Ortega was right. This wasn't the place to fight. If he was here, he wanted to talk. Otherwise, he would have simply jumped me in the parking garage.

"Okay," I said, finally. "What do you want to say?"

He leaned a little closer so that he wouldn't have to raise his voice. I cringed inwardly, but I didn't flinch away. "I've come to Chicago to kill you, Mister Dresden. But I have a proposal for you that I want you to hear, first."

"You really need to work on your opening technique," I said. "I read a book about negotiations. I could loan it to you."

He gave me a humorless smile. "The war, Dresden. The war between your people and mine is too costly, for both of us."

"War's a pretty stupid option to take, generally speaking," I said. "I never wanted it."

"But you began it," Ortega said. "You began it over a point of principle."

"I began it over a human life."

"And how many more would you save by ending it now?" Ortega asked. "Not merely wizards suffer from this. Our attention to the war leaves us less able to control the wilder elements of our own Court. We frown upon reckless killings, but wounded or leaderless members of our Courts often kill when they do not truly need to. Ending the war now would save hundreds, perhaps thousands of lives."

"So would killing every vampire on the planet. What's your point?"

Ortega smiled, showing teeth. Just regular teeth, no long canines or anything. The vampires of the Red Court look human—right up until they turn into something out of a nightmare. "The point, Dresden, is that the war is unprofitable, undesirable. You are the symbolic cause of it to my people, and the point of contention between us and your own White Council. Once you are slain, the Council will accept peace overtures, as will the Court."

"So you're asking me to lay down and die? That's not much of an offer. You really need to read that book."

"I'm making you an offer. Face me in single combat, Dresden."

I didn't quite laugh at him. "Why the hell should I do that?"

His eyes were expressionless. "Because if you do it would mean that the warriors I have brought to town with me will not be forced to target your friends and allies. That the mortal assassins we have retained will not need to receive their final confirmations to kill a number of clients who have hired you in the past five years. I'm sure I need not mention names."

Fear and anger had been about to settle down, but they came surging back again. "There's no reason for that," I said. "If your war is with me, keep it with me."

"Gladly," Ortega said. "I do not approve of such tactics. Face me under the dueling laws in the Accords."

"And after I kill you, what?" I said. I didn't know if I could kill him, but there was no reason to let him think I wasn't confident about it. "The next hotshot Red Duke does the same thing?"

"Defeat me, and the Court has agreed that this city will become neutral territory. That those living in it, including yourself and your friends and associates, will be free of the threat of attack so long as they are in it."

I stared hard at him for a moment. "Chicago-blanca, eh?"

He quirked a puzzled eyebrow at me.

"Never mind. After your time." I looked away from him, and licked sweat from my upper lip. A stagehand came by with a couple of bottled waters, and passed them to Ortega and to me. I took a drink. The pressure of the spell made flickering colored dots float across my vision.

"You're stupid to fight me," I said. "Even if you kill me, my death curse would fall on you."

He shrugged. "I am not as important as the whole of the Court. I will take that risk."

Hell's bells. Dedicated, honorable, courageous, self-sacrificial loonies are absolutely the worst people in the world to go up against. I tried one last dodge, hoping it might pay off. "I'd have to have it in writing. The Council gets a copy too. I want this all recognized, official under the Accords."

"That done, you will agree to the duel?"

I took a deep breath. The last thing I wanted to do was square off against another supernatural nasty. Vampires scared me. They were strong and way too fast, and had an enormous yuck factor. Their saliva was an addictive narcotic, and I'd been exposed to it enough to make me twitch once in a while, wondering what it would be like to get another hit.

I barely went outside after dark these days, specifically because I didn't want to encounter any more vampires. A duel would mean a fair fight, and I hate fair fights. In the words of a murderous Faerie Queen, they're too easy to lose.

Of course, if I didn't agree to Ortega's offer, I'd be fighting him anyway, probably at a time and place of his choosing—and I had the feeling that Ortega wasn't going to show the arrogance and overconfidence I'd seen in other vampires. Something about him said that so long as I wasn't breathing, he wouldn't care much how it happened. Not only that, but I believed that he would start in on the people I cared about if he couldn't have me.

I mean, come on. It was clichéd villainy at its worst.

And an undeniably effective lever.

I'd like to say that I carefully weighed all the factors, reasoned my way to a levelheaded conclusion, and made a rational decision to take a calculated risk, but I didn't. The truth is, I thought of Ortega and company doing harm to some of the people I cared about, and suddenly felt angry enough to start in on him right there. I faced him, eyes narrowed, and didn't bother to hold the anger in check. The suppression spell began to crack, and I didn't bother to keep it going. The spell shattered, and the buildup of wild energy rushed silently and invisibly over the studio.

There was a cough of static from the speakers on the stage before they died with loud pops. The floodlights overhead suddenly burst with flashes of brilliance and clouds of sparks that fell down over everyone on the stage. One of the two surviving cameras exploded into fire, bluish flames rising up from out of the casing, and heavy power outlets along the walls started spitting orange and green sparks. Larry Fowler yelped and leapt up into the air, batting at his belt before pitching a smoldering cell phone to the floor. The lights died, and people started screaming in startled panic.

Ortega, lit only by the falling sparks, looked grim and somehow eager, shadows dancing over his features, his eyes huge and dark.

"Fine," I said. "Get it to me in writing and you've got a deal."

The emergency lights came up, fire alarms started whooping, and people started stumbling toward exits. Ortega smiled, all teeth, and glided off the stage, vanishing into the wings.

I stood up, shaking a little. A piece of something had apparently fallen and hit Mort's head. There was a small gash on his scalp, already brimming with blood, and he wobbled precariously when he tried to stand. I helped him up, and so did Father Vincent on the other side of him. We lugged the little ectomancer toward the fire doors.

We got Mort down some stairs and outside the building. Chicago PD was on the scene already, blue and white lights flashing. Fire crews and an ambulance or three were just then rolling up on the street. We settled Mort down among a row of people with minor injuries, and stood back. We were both panting a little as the emergency medtechs started triage on the wounded.

"Actually, Mister Dresden," Father Vincent said, "I must confess something to you."

"Heh," I said. "Don't think I missed the irony on that one, padre."

Vincent's leathery mouth creased into a strained smile. "I did not really come to Chicago merely to appear on the show."

"No?" I said.

"No. I really came here to—"

"To talk to me," I interjected.

He lifted his eyebrows. "How did you know?"

I sighed, and got my car keys out of my pocket. "It's just been that kind of day."

Chapter Two

I started walking for my car, and beckoned Father Vincent to follow. He did, and I walked fast enough to make him work to keep up with me. "You must understand," he said, "that I must insist upon strict confidentiality if I am to divulge details of my problem to you."

I frowned at him and said, "You think I'm a crackpot at best, or a charlatan at worst. So why would you want me to take your case?"

Not that I would turn him down. I wanted to take his case. Well, more accurately, I wanted to take his money. I wasn't in the bad fiscal shape of the year before, but that meant only that I had to fend the creditors off with a baseball bat rather than a cattle prod.

"I am told you are the best investigator in the city for it," Father Vincent said.

I arched an eyebrow at him. "You've got something supernatural going on?"

He rolled his eyes. "No, naturally not. I am not naive, Mister Dresden. But I am told that you know more about the occult community than any private investigator in the city."

"Oh," I said. "That."

I thought about it for a minute, and figured it was probably true. The occult community he had in mind was the usual New Age, crystal-gazing, tarot-turning, palm-reading crowd you see in any large city. Most of them were harmless, and many had at least a little ability at magic. Add in a dash of feng-shui artists, season liberally with Wiccans of a variety of flavors and sincerities, blend in a few modestly gifted practitioners who liked mixing religion with their magic, some followers of voodoo, a few Santerians and a sprinkling of Satanists, all garnished with a crowd of young people who liked to wear a lot of black, and you get what most folks think of as the "occult community."

Of course, hiding in there you found the occasional sorcerer, necromancer, monster, or demon. The real players, the nasty ones, regarded that crowd the same way a ten-year-old would a gingerbread amusement park. My mental early-warning system set off an imaginary klaxon.

"Who referred you to me, padre?"

"Oh, a local priest," Vincent said. He took a small notebook from his pocket, opened it, and read, "Father Forthill, of Saint Mary of the Angels."

I blinked. Father Forthill didn't see eye-to-eye with me on the whole religion thing, but he was a decent guy. A little stuffy, maybe, but I liked him—and I owed him for favors past. "You should have said that in the first place."

"You'll take the case?" Father Vincent asked, as we headed into the parking garage.

"I want to hear the details first, but if Forthill thinks I can help, I will." I added, hastily, "My standard fees apply."

"Naturally," Father Vincent said. He toyed with the crucifix at his throat. "May I assume that you will spare me the magician rigmarole?"

"Wizard," I said.

"There's a difference?"

"Magicians do stage magic. Wizards do real magic."

He sighed. "I don't need an entertainer, Mister Dresden. Just an investigator."

"And I don't need you to believe me, padre. Just to pay me. We'll get along fine."

He gave me an uncertain look and said, "Ah."

We reached my car, a battered old Volkswagen Bug named the Blue Beetle. It has what some people would call "character" and what I would call lots of mismatched replacement parts. The original car may have been blue, but now it had pieces of green, white, and red VWs grafted onto it in place of the originals as they got damaged in one way or another. The hood had to be held down with a piece of hanger wire to keep it from flipping up when the car jounced, and the front bumper was still smashed out of shape from last summer's attempt at vehicular monsterslaughter. Maybe if Vincent's job paid well, I'd be able to get it fixed.

Father Vincent blinked at the Beetle and asked, "What happened?"

"I hit trees."

"You drove your car into a tree?"

"No. Trees, plural. And then a Dumpster." I glanced at him self-consciously and added, "They were little trees."

His uncertain look deepened to actual worry. "Ah."

I unlocked my door. Not that I was worried about anyone stealing my car. I once had a car thief offer to get me something better for a sweetheart rate. "I guess you want to give me the details somewhere a little more private?"

Father Vincent nodded. "Yes, of course. If you could take me to my hotel, I have some photographs and—"

I heard the scuff of shoes on concrete in time for me to catch the gunman in my peripheral vision as he rose from between a pair of parked cars one row over. Dim lights gleamed on the gun, and I threw myself across the hood of the Beetle, away from him. I crashed into Father Vincent, who let out a squeak of startled surprise, and the pair of us tumbled to the ground as the man started shooting.

The gun didn't split the air with thunder when it fired. Typically, guns do that. They're a hell of a lot louder than anything most folks run into on a day-to-day basis. This gun didn't roar, or bark, or even bang. It made a kind of loud noise. Maybe as loud as someone slamming an unabridged dictionary down on a table. The gunman was using a silencer.

One shot hit my car and caromed off the curve of the hood. Another went by my head as I struggled with Father Vincent, and a third shattered the safety glass of a ritzy sports car parked beside me.

"What's happening?" Father Vincent stammered.

"Shut up," I snarled. The gunman was moving, his feet scuffing on the concrete as he skirted around my car. I reached around the Beetle's headlight and fumbled at the wire holding the hood down while the man came closer. It gave way and the hood wobbled up as I reached into the storage compartment.

I looked up in time to see a man, medium height and build, mid thirties, dark pants and jacket, lift a small-caliber pistol, its end heavy with a manufactured silencer. He fired, but he hadn't taken time to aim at me. He wasn't twenty feet away, but he missed.

I drew the shotgun out of the car's trunk and flicked off the safety as I chambered a round. The gunman's eyes widened and he turned to run. He shot at me again on the way, shattering one of the Beetle's headlights, and he kept shooting toward me as he skittered back the way he came.

I jerked back behind the car and kept my head down, trying to count his shots. He got to eleven or twelve and the gun went silent. I stood up, the shotgun already at my shoulder, and sighted down the barrel. The gunman ducked behind a concrete column and kept running.

"Dammit," I hissed. "Get in the car."

"But—" Father Vincent stammered.

"Get in the car!" I shouted. I got up, twisted the hanger wire on the hood back into place, and got in. Vincent got in the passenger side and I shoved the shotgun at him. "Hold this."

He fumbled with it, his eyes wide, as I brought the Beetle to life with a roar. Well. Not really a roar. A Volkswagen Bug doesn't roar. But it sort of growled, and I mashed it into gear before the priest had managed to completely shut the door.

I headed for the parking garage's exit, whipping around the ramps and turns.

"What are you doing?" Father Vincent demanded.

"He's an outfit hitter," I spat. "They'll have the exit covered."

We screeched around the final corner and toward the parking garage's exit. I heard someone yelling in a breathless voice, and a couple of large and unfriendly-looking men in a car parked across the street were just getting out. One of them held a shotgun, and the other had a heavy-duty semiautomatic, maybe a Desert Eagle.

I didn't recognize the thug with the shotgun, but Thug Number Three was an enormous man with reddish hair, no neck, and a cheap suit—Cujo Hendricks, right hand enforcer to the crime lord of Chicago, Gentleman Johnny Marcone.

I had to bounce the Beetle up onto the sidewalk at the parking-garage exit to get around the security bar, and I mowed down some landscaped bushes on the way. I jounced over the curb and into the street, hauling the wheel to the right, and mashed the accelerator to the floor.

I glanced back and saw the original gunman standing at a fire-exit door, pointing the silenced pistol at us. He snapped off several more shots, though I only heard the last few, as the silencer started to give out. He didn't have a prayer of a clean shot, but he got lucky and my back window shattered inward. I gulped and took the first corner against the light, nearly colliding with a U-Haul moving truck, and kept accelerating away.

A couple of blocks later, my heart slowed down enough that I could think. I slowed the car down to something approaching the speed limit, thanked my lucky stars the suppression spell had fallen apart in the studio and not in the car, and rolled down my window. I stuck my head out for a second to see if Hendricks and his goons were following us, but I didn't see anyone coming along behind us, and took it on faith.

I pulled my head in and found the barrel of the shotgun pointed at my chin, while Father Vincent, his face pale, muttered to himself under his breath in Italian.

"Hey!" I said, and pushed the gun's barrel away. "Careful with that thing. You wanna kill me?" I reached down and flicked the safety on. "Put it down. A patrolman sees that and we're in trouble."

Father Vincent gulped, and tried to lower the gun below the level of the dash. "This weapon is illegal?"

"Illegal is such a strong word," I muttered.

"Oh, my," Father Vincent said with a gulp. "Those men," he said. "They tried to kill you."

"That's what hitters for the outfit do," I agreed.

"How do you know who they are?"

"First guy had a silenced weapon. A good silencer, metal and glass, not a cheapo plastic bottle." I checked out the window again. "He was using a small-caliber weapon, too, and he was trying to get real close before he started shooting."

"Why does that matter?"

It looked clear. My hands trembled and felt a little weak. "Because it means he was using light ammunition. Subsonic. If the bullet breaks the sound barrier, it sort of defeats the point of a silenced weapon. When he saw I was armed, he ran. Covered himself doing it, and went for help. He's a pro."

"Oh, my," Father Vincent said again. He looked a little pale.

"Plus I recognized one of the men waiting at the exit."

"Someone was at the exit?" Father Vincent said.

"Yeah. Some of Marcone's rent-a-thugs." I glanced back at the shattered window and sighed. "Dammit. So where are we going?"

Father Vincent gave me directions in a numb voice, and I concentrated on driving, trying to ignore the quivering in my stomach and the continued trembling of my hands. Getting shot at is not something I handle very well.

Hendricks. Why the hell was Marcone sending goons after me? Marcone was the lord of the mean streets of Second City, but generally he didn't like to use that kind of violence. He thought it was bad for business. I had believed Marcone and I had an understanding—or at least an agreement to stay out of each other's way. So why would he make a move like this?

Maybe I had already stepped over a line somewhere, that I didn't know existed.

I glanced at the shaken Father Vincent.

He hadn't told me yet what he wanted, but whatever it was, it was important enough to covertly drag one of the Vatican's staff all the way to Chicago. Maybe it was important enough to kill a nosy wizard over, too.

Hoo-boy.

It was turning into one hell of a day.

Chapter Three

Father Vincent directed me to a motel a little ways north of O'Hare. It was a national chain, cheap but clean, with rows of doors facing the parking lot. I drove around to the back of the motel, away from the street, frowning. It didn't look like the kind of place someone like Vincent would stay in. The priest left my car almost before I'd set the parking break, hurried to the nearest door, and ducked inside as quickly as he could open the lock.

I followed him. Vincent shut the door behind us, locked it, and then fiddled with the blinds until they closed. He nodded at the room's little table and said, "Please, sit down."

I did, and stretched out my legs. Father Vincent pulled open a drawer on the plain dresser, and drew out a file folder, held closed with a wide rubber band. He sat down across from me, took off the rubber band, and said, "The Church is interested in recovering some stolen property."

I shrugged and said, "Sounds like a job for the police."

"An investigation is under way and I am giving your police department my full cooperation. But . . . How to phrase this politely." He frowned. "History is an able teacher."

"You don't trust the police," I said. "Gotcha."

He grimaced. "It is only that there have been a number of associations between Chicago police and various underworld figures in the past."

"That's mostly movies now, padre. You may not have heard, but the whole Al Capone thing has been over for a while."

"Perhaps," he said. "Perhaps not. I simply seek to do everything within my power to recover the stolen article. That includes involving an independent and discreet investigator."

Aha. So he didn't trust the police and wanted me to work for him on the sly. That's why we were meeting at a cheap motel rather than wherever he was really staying. "What do you want me to find for you?"

"A relic," he said.

"A what?"

"An artifact, Mister Dresden. An antique possessed by the Church for several centuries."

"Oh, that," I said.

"Yes. The article is fragile and of great age, and we believe that it is not being adequately preserved. It is imperative that we recover it as quickly as possible."

"What happened to it?"

"It was stolen three days ago."

"From?"

"The Cathedral of Saint John the Baptist in northern Italy."

"Long ways off."

"We believe that the artifact was brought here, to Chicago, to be sold."

"Why?"

He took an eight-by-ten glossy black and white from the folder and passed it to me. It featured a fairly messy corpse lying on cobblestones. Blood had run into the spaces between the stones, as well as pooling a little on the ground around the body. I think it had been a man, but it was hard to tell for certain. Whoever it was had been slashed to almost literal ribbons across the face and neck—sharp, neat, straight cuts. Professional knife work. Yuck.

"This man is Gaston LaRouche. He is the ringleader of a group of organized thieves who call themselves the Churchmice. They specialize in robbing sanctuaries and cathedrals. He was found dead the morning after the robbery near a small airfield. His briefcase contained several falsified pieces of American identification and plane tickets that would carry him here."

"But no whatsit."

"Ah. Exactly." Father Vincent removed another pair of photos. These were also black-and-white, but they looked rougher, as if they had been magnified several times. Both were of women of average height and build, dark hair, dark sunglasses.

"Surveillance photos?" I asked.

He nodded. "Interpol. Anna Valmont and Francisca Garcia.

We believe they helped LaRouche with the theft, then murdered him and left the country. Interpol received a tip that Valmont had been seen at the airport here."

"Do you know who the buyer is?"

Vincent shook his head. "No. But this is the case. I want you to find the remaining Churchmice and recover the artifact."

I frowned, looking at the photos. "Yeah. That's what they want you to do too."

Vincent blinked at me. "What do you mean?"

I shook my head impatiently. "Someone. Look at this photo. LaRouche wasn't murdered there."

Vincent frowned. "Why would you say that?"

"Not enough blood. I've seen men who were torn up and bled out. There's a hell of a lot more blood." I paused and then said, "Pardon my French."

Father Vincent crossed himself. "Why would his body be found there?"

I shrugged. "A professional did him. Look at the cuts. They're methodical. He was probably unconscious or drugged, because you can't hold a man still very easily when you're taking a knife to his face."

Father Vincent pressed one hand to his stomach. "Oh."

"So you've got a corpse found out in the middle of a street somewhere, basically wearing a sign around his neck that says, 'The goods are in Chicago.' Either someone was incredibly stupid, or someone was trying to lead you here. It's a professional killing. Someone meant his corpse to be a clue."

"But who would do such a thing?"

I shrugged. "Probably a good thing to find out. Do you have any better pictures of these two women?"

He shook his head. "No. And they've never been arrested. No criminal record."

"They're good at what they do then." I took the photos. There were little dossiers paper-clipped to the back of the pictures, listing known aliases, locations, but nothing terribly useful. "This one isn't going to be quick."

"Worthwhile goals rarely are. What do you need from me, Mister Dresden?"

"A retainer," I said. "A thousand will do. And I need a description of this artifact, the more detailed the better."

Father Vincent gave me a matter-of-fact nod, and drew a plain steel money clip from his pocket. He counted off ten portraits of

Ben Franklin, and passed them to me. "The artifact is an oblong length of linen cloth, fourteen feet, three inches long by three feet, seven inches wide made of a handwoven three-to-one herringbone twill. There are a number of patches and stains on the cloth, and—"

I held up my hand, frowning. "Wait a minute. Where did you say this thing was stolen from?"

"The Cathedral of Saint John the Baptist," Father Vincent said.

"In northern Italy," I said.

He nodded.

"In Turin, to be exact," I said.

He nodded again, his expression reserved.

"Someone stole the freaking *Shroud* of *Turin*?" I demanded.

"Yes."

I settled back into the chair, looking down at the photos again. This changed things. This changed things a lot.

The Shroud. Supposedly the burial cloth used by Joseph of Aramithea to wrap the body of Christ after the Crucifixion. Capital Cs. The cloth supposedly wrapped around Christ when he was resurrected, with his image, his blood, imprinted upon it.

"Wow," I said.

"What do you know about the Shroud, Mister Dresden?"

"Not much. Christ's burial cloth. They did a bunch of tests in the seventies, and no one was able to conclusively disprove it. It almost got burned a few years back when the cathedral caught fire. There are stories that it has healing powers, or that a couple of angels still attend it. A bunch of others I can't remember right now."

Father Vincent rested his hands on the table and leaned toward me. "Mister Dresden. The Shroud is perhaps the single most vital artifact of the Church. It is a powerful symbol of the faith, and one in which many people believe. It is also politically significant. It is absolutely vital to Rome that it be restored to the Church's custody as expediently as possible."

I stared at him for a second, and tried to pick out my words carefully. "Are you going to be insulted if I suggest that it's very possible that the Shroud is, uh . . . *significant,* magically speaking?"

Vincent pressed his lips together. "I have no illusions about it, Mister Dresden. It is a piece of cloth, not a magic carpet. Its value derives solely from its historical and symbolic significance."

"Uh-huh," I said. Hell's bells, that's where plenty of magical power came from. The Shroud was old, and regarded as special, and people believed in it. That could be enough to give it a kind of power, all by itself.

"Some people might believe otherwise," I said.

"Of course," he agreed. "That is why your knowledge of the local occult may prove invaluable."

I nodded, thinking. This could be something completely mundane. Someone could have stolen a moldy old piece of cloth to sell it to a crackpot who believed it was a magic bedsheet. It could be that the Shroud was nothing more than a symbol, an antique, a historical Pop-Tart—nifty, but ultimately not very significant.

Of course, there was also the possibility that the Shroud was genuine. That it actually *had* been in contact with the Son of God when he had been brought back from the dead. I pushed that thought aside.

Regardless of why or how, if the Shroud *was* something special, magically speaking, then it could mean a whole new—and nastier—ball game. Of all the various weird, dark, or wicked powers who might abscond with the Shroud, I couldn't think of any who would do anything cheerful with it. All sorts of supernatural interests might be at play.

Even discounting that possibility, mortal pursuit of the Shroud seemed to be deadly enough. John Marcone might already be involved, as well as the Chicago police—probably Interpol and the FBI, too. Even sans supernatural powers, when it came to finding people the cops were damned good at what they did. Odds were good that they'd locate the thieves and haul in the Shroud within a few days.

I looked from the photos to the cash, and thought about how many of my bills I could pay off with a nice, fat fee courtesy of Father Vincent. If I got lucky, maybe I wouldn't have to put myself in harm's way to do it.

Sure.

I believed that.

I put the money in my pocket. Then I picked up the photos too. "How can I get in touch with you?"

Father Vincent wrote a phone number on the motel's stationary and passed it to me. "Here. It's my answering service while I'm in town."

"All right. I can't promise you anything concrete, but I'll see what I can do."

Father Vincent stood up and said, "Thank you, Mister Dresden. Father Forthill spoke most highly of you, you know."

"He's a sport," I agreed, rising.

"If you will excuse me, I have appointments to keep."

"I'll bet. Here's my card, if you need to get in touch."

I gave him a business card, shook hands, and left. At the Beetle, I stopped to open the trunk and put the shotgun back in it, after taking the shell from the chamber and making sure the safety was on. Then I pulled out a length of wood a little longer than my forearm, carved over with runes and sigils that helped me focus my magic a lot more precisely. I tossed my suit jacket in over the gun, and dug out a silver bracelet dangling a dozen tiny, medieval-style shields from my pocket. I fastened that to my left arm, slipped a silver ring onto my right hand, then took my blasting rod and set it beside me on the car seat as I got in.

Between the new case, the outfit hitter, and Duke Ortega's challenge, I wanted to make damn sure that I wasn't going to get caught with my eldritch britches down again.

I took the Beetle home, to my apartment. I rent the basement apartment of a huge, creaking old boarding-house. By the time I got back, it was after midnight and the late-February air was speckled with occasional flakes of wet snow that wouldn't last once they hit the ground. The adrenaline rush of *The Larry Fowler Show* and then the hired-goon attack had faded, and left me aching, tired, and worried. I got out of the car, determined to head for bed, then get up early and start to work on Vincent's case.

A sudden sensation of cold, rippling energy and a pair of muffled thumps from the stairs leading down to my apartment changed my mind.

I drew out my blasting rod and readied the shield bracelet on my left wrist, but before I could step over to the stairs, a pair of figures flew up them and landed heavily on the half-frozen ground beside the gravel parking lot. They struggled, rolling, until one of the shadowy figures got a leg underneath the form on top of it, and pushed.

The second figure flew twenty feet through the air, landed on the gravel with a thump and a cough of expelled air, then got up and sprinted away.

Shield readied, I stepped forward before the remaining intruder could rise. I forced an effort of will through the blasting rod, setting the runes along its length alight with scarlet. Fire coalesced at the tip of the rod, bright as a road flare, but I held the strike as I stepped forward, shoving the tip of the blasting rod down at the intruder. "Make a move and I'll fry you."

Red light fell over a woman.

She was dressed in jeans, a black leather jacket, a white

T-shirt, and gloves. She had her long, midnight hair tied back in a tail. Dark, oblique eyes smoldered up at me from beneath long lashes. Her beautiful face held an expression of wary amusement.

My heart thudded in sudden pain and excitement.

"Well," Susan said, looking from the sizzling blasting rod up to my face. "I've heard of running into an old flame, but this is ridiculous."

Chapter Four

Susan.

My brain locked up for a good ten seconds as I stared down at my former lover. I could smell the scent of her hair, the subtle perfume she wore, mixing with the new-leather scent of her jacket and another, new smell—new soap, maybe. Her dark eyes regarded me, uncertain and nervous. She had a small cut on the side of her mouth, beading with drops of blood that looked black in the red light of the blasting rod's fire.

"Harry," Susan said, her voice quiet and steady. "Harry. You're scaring me."

I shook myself out of my surprise and lowered the blasting rod, stepping over to her. "Stars and stones, Susan. Are you all right?"

I offered her my hand and she took it, rising easily to her feet. Her fingers were feverishly warm, and wisps of winter steam curled from her skin. "Bruises," she said. "I'll be fine."

"Who was that?"

Susan glanced the way her attacker had run and shook her head. "Red Court. I couldn't see his face."

I blinked at her. "You ran off a vampire? By yourself?"

She flashed me a smile that mixed weariness with a sense of pleasure. She still hadn't taken her hand from mine. "I've been working out."

I looked around a bit more, and tried to reach out with my senses, to detect any trace of the unsettling energy that hovered around the Reds. Nothing. "Gone now," I reported. "But we shouldn't hang around out here."

"Inside then?"

I started to agree, and then paused. A horrible suspicion hit me. I let go of her hand and took a step back.

A line appeared between her eyebrows. "Harry?"

"It's been a rough year," I said. "I want to talk, but I'm not inviting you in."

Susan's expression flickered with comprehension and pain. She folded her arms over her stomach and nodded. "No. I understand. And you're right to be careful."

I took another step back and started walking toward my reinforced-steel door. She walked a few feet away, and at my side, where I could see her. I went down the stairs and unlocked the door. Then I pushed out an effort of will to temporarily disable the protective spells laid over my house that amounted to the magical equivalent of a land mine and burglar alarm all in one.

I went in, glanced at the candleholder on the wall by the door, and muttered, *"Flickum bicus."* I felt a tiny surge of energy flowing out of me, and the candle danced to life, lighting my apartment in dim, soft orange.

My place is basically a cave with two chambers. The larger one was my living area. Bookshelves lined most of the walls, and where they didn't I had hung a couple of tapestries and an original *Star Wars* movie poster. I'd scattered rugs all over my floor. I had laid down everything from handmade Navajo rugs to a black area rug with Elvis's face, fully two feet across, dominating the piece. Like the Beetle, I figured some people would call my ragtag assembly of floor coverings eclectic. I just thought of them as something to walk on besides freezing-cold stone floor.

My furniture is much the same. I got most of it secondhand. None of it matches, but it's all comfortable to sprawl on, and my lights are dim enough to let me ignore it. A small alcove held a sink, an icebox, and a pantry for food. A fireplace rested against one wall, the wood all burned down to black and grey, but I knew it would still be glowing under the ash. A door led to my tiny bedroom and the apartment's three-quarters bath. The whole place may have been ragged, but it was very tidy and clean.

I turned to face Susan, and didn't put down my blasting rod. Supernatural creatures cannot lightly step across the threshold of a home unless one of the rightful residents invites them in. Plenty of nasties can put on a false face, and it wasn't inconceivable that one of them had decided to try to get close to me by pretending to be Susan.

A supernatural being would have a hell of a time getting over a threshold without being invited in. If that was some kind of shapeshifter rather than Susan or, God help me, if Susan had gone all the way over to the vampires, she wouldn't be able to enter. If it was the real Susan, she'd be fine. Or at least, the threshold wouldn't hurt her. Getting paranoid suspicion from her ex-boyfriend might do its own kind of damage.

On the other hand, there was a war on, and Susan probably wouldn't be happy to hear I'd gotten myself killed. Better safe than exsanguinated.

Susan didn't pause at the door. She stepped inside, turned around to close and lock it, and asked, "Good enough?"

It was. Relief, coupled with a sudden explosion of naked emotion, roared through me. It was like waking up after days of anguish to find that the pain was gone. Where there had been only hurt, there was suddenly nothing, and other feelings rushed in to fill the sudden void. Excitement, for one, that quivering teenage nervousness that accompanies expectation. A surge of warm emotion, joy and happiness rolled together with a chittering glee.

And in the shadows of those, a few things darker but no less vibrant. Sheer, sensual pleasure in the scent of her, in looking at her face, her dark hair again. I needed to feel her skin under my hands, to feel her pressed to me.

It was more than mere need—it was hunger. Now that she was standing there in front of me, I needed her, all of her, as much as I needed food or water or air, and possibly more. I wanted to tell her, to let her know what it meant to me that she was there. But I'd never been very good at expressing myself verbally.

By the time Susan turned around again, I was already pressed up against her. She let out a quiet gasp of surprise, but I leaned gently into her, pressing her shoulders to the door.

I lowered my mouth to hers, and her lips were soft, sweet, fever-hot. She went rigid for a second, then let out a low sound and wound her arms around my neck and shoulders, kissing me back. I could feel her, the slender, too-warm strength and softness of her body. My hunger deepened, and so did the kiss, my tongue touching hers, lightly teasing. She responded as ardently as I did, her lips almost desperate, low whimpers vibrating through her mouth and into mine. I started to feel a little dizzy and disoriented, and though some part of me warned against it, I only pressed harder against her.

I slid one hand over her hip, beneath the jacket, and slipped up under the T-shirt she wore to curl around the naked sweetness of her waist. I pulled her hard against me, and she responded, her breath hot and quick, lifting one leg to press against mine, winding around my calf a little, pulling me nearer. I lowered my mouth to her throat, tongue tasting her skin, and she arched against me, baring more of her skin. I drew a line of kisses up to her ear, gently biting, sending quivering shock waves through her as she shook against me, her throat letting out quiet sounds of deepening need. I found her eager lips again, and her fingers tightened in my hair, drawing me hard against her.

My dizziness grew. Some kind of coherent thought did a quick flyby of my forebrain. I struggled to take notice of it, but the kiss made it impossible. Lust and need murdered my reason.

A sudden, shrieking hiss startled me, and I jerked back from Susan, looking wildly around.

Mister, my bobtailed, battle-scarred tomcat, had leapt up onto the stones before the fireplace, his luminous green eyes wide and fixed on Susan. Mister weighs about thirty pounds, and thirty pounds of cat can make an absolutely impossible amount of noise.

Susan shuddered and pressed her palm against my chest, turning her face away from me. She pushed, something gentle rather than insistent. My lips burned to touch hers again, but I closed my eyes and took slow, shuddering breaths. Then I backed away from her. I had meant to go stir up the fire—not *that* fire, the literal one—but the room tilted wildly and it was all I could do to stumble into an easy chair.

Mister leapt up into my lap, more daintily than he had any right to be able to do, and rubbed his face against my chest, rumbling out a purr. I fumbled up one hand to pet him, and after a couple of minutes the room stopped spinning.

"What the hell just happened?" I muttered.

Susan emerged from the shadows and crossed the candlelit room to take up the fireplace poker. She stirred through the ashes until she found some glowing orange-red, and then began adding wood to the fire from the old iron hod beside the fireplace. "I could feel you," she said, after a minute. "I could feel you going under. It . . ." She shivered. "It felt nice."

Boy, did it. And I bet it would feel even nicer if all those clothes hadn't been in the way. Aloud, all I said was, "Under?"

She looked over her shoulder at me, her expression hard to read. "The venom," she said quietly. "They call it their Kiss."

"I guess I can't blame them. It sounds a lot more romantic

than 'narcotic drool.' " Some parts of me lobbied for a cessation of meaningless chat and an immediate resumption of any line of thought that would lead to discarded clothing upon the floor. I ignored them. "I remember. When . . . when we kissed before you left. I thought I'd imagined it."

Susan shook her head, and sat down on the stones before the fireplace, her back straight, her hands folded sedately in her lap. The fire began to grow, catching onto the new wood, and though the light of it curled around her with golden fingers, it left her face veiled in shadow. "No. What Bianca did to me has changed me already, in some ways. Physically. I'm stronger now. My senses are sharper. And there's . . ." She faltered.

"The Kiss," I mumbled. My lips didn't find the word to their liking. They liked the real thing a lot better. I ignored them, too.

"Yes," she said. "Not like one of them can do. Less. But still there."

I mopped at my face with my hand. "You know what I need?" Either a naked, writhing, eager Susan or else a liquid-nitrogen shower. "A beer. You want one?"

"Pass," she said. "I don't think lowering my inhibitions would be healthy right now."

I nodded, got up, and went to my icebox. It's an actual icebox, the kind that runs on honest-to-goodness ice rather than Freon. I got out a dark brown bottle of Mac's home-brewed ale and opened it, taking a long drink. Mac would be horrified that I drank his beer cold, since he prided himself on an old-world brew, but I always kept a couple in there, for when I wanted it cold. What can I say. I'm an unlettered, barbaric American wizard. I drank off maybe half of it and put the cold bottle against my forehead afterward.

"Well," I said. "I guess you didn't come over to, uh. . . ."

"Tear your clothes off and use you shamelessly?" Susan suggested. Her voice sounded calm again, but I could sense the underlying tone of her own hunger. I wasn't sure whether I should be unsettled by it or encouraged. "No, Harry. It isn't . . . that isn't something I can afford to do with you. No matter how much either of us wants it."

"Why not?" I asked. I knew why not already, but the words jumped from my brain to my mouth before I could stop them. I peered suspiciously at the beer.

"I don't want to lose control," Susan said. "Not ever. Not with anyone. But especially not with you." There was a silence in which only the fire made any noise. "Harry, it would kill me to hurt you."

More to the point, I thought, *it would probably kill me too. Think about her instead of yourself, Harry. Get a grip. It's just a kiss. Let it go.*

I drank the rest of my beer, which wasn't anywhere near as nice as other things I'd done with my mouth that night. I checked the fridge and asked Susan, "Coke?"

She nodded, looking around. Her gaze hesitated on the fireplace mantel, where I kept the card and three postcards I'd received from her, along with the little grey jewelry box that held the dinky little ring she'd turned down. "Is someone else living here now?"

"No." I got out a couple of cans, and took one over to her. She took it from me without touching my fingers. "Why do you ask?"

"The place looks so nice," she said. "And your clothes smell like fabric softener. You've never used fabric softener in your life."

"Oh. That." You can't tell people about it when faeries are doing your housework, or they get ticked off and leave. "I sort of have a cleaning service."

"I hear you've been too busy to clean up," Susan said.

"Just making a living."

Susan smiled. "I heard you saved the world from some kind of doom. Is it true?"

I fiddled with my drink. "Sort of."

Susan laughed. "How do you sort of save the world?"

"I only saved it in a Greenpeace kind of way. If I'd blown it, there might have been a historically bad storm, but I don't think anyone would have noticed the real damage for thirty or forty years—climate change takes time."

"Sounds scary," Susan said.

I shrugged. "Mostly I was just trying to save my own ass. The world was a twofer. Maybe I'm getting cynical. I suspect the only thing I accomplished was to keep the faeries from screwing up the place so that we could screw it up ourselves."

I sat down on the chair again, and we opened the Cokes and drank in silence for a bit. My heart eventually stopped pounding quite so loudly.

"I miss you," I said finally. "So does your editor. She called me a couple of weeks ago. Said your articles had quit coming in."

Susan nodded. "That's one reason I'm here. I owe her more than a letter or a phone call."

"You're quitting?" I asked.

She nodded.

"You find something else?"

"Sort of," she said. She brushed her hair back from her face with one hand. "I can't tell you everything right now."

I frowned. For as long as I'd known her, Susan had been driven by a passion for discovering the truth and sharing it with other people. Her work at the *Arcane* had arisen from her stubborn refusal to deny things she saw as the truth, even if they had seemed insane. She was one of the rare people who stopped and thought about things, even weird and supernatural things, instead of dismissing them out of hand. That's how she'd begun work at the *Arcane*. That was how she had originally met me.

"Are you all right?" I asked. "Are you in trouble?"

"Relatively speaking, no," she said. "But you are. That's why I'm here, Harry."

"What do you mean?"

"I came to warn you. The Red Court—"

"Sent Paolo Ortega to call me out. I know."

She sighed. "But you don't know what you're getting into. Harry, Ortega is one of the most dangerous nobles of their Court. He's a warlord. He's killed half a dozen of the White Council's Wardens in South America since the war started, and he's the one who planned and executed the attack on Archangel last year."

I sat straight up at that, the blood draining from my face. "How do you know about that?"

"I'm an investigative reporter, Harry. I investigated."

I toyed with the Coke can, frowning down at it. "All the same. He came here asking for a duel. A fair fight. If he's serious, I'll take him on."

"There's more that you need to know," Susan said.

"Like what?"

"Ortega's opinion on the war is not the popular one within the Red Court. A few of the upper crust of the vampires support his way of thinking. But most of them like the idea of a lot of constant bloodshed. They also like the idea of a war to wipe out the White Council. They figure that if they get rid of the wizards once and for all, they won't have to worry about keeping a low profile in the future."

"What's that got to do with anything?"

"Think about it," Susan said. "Harry, the White Council is

fighting this war reluctantly. If they had a decent excuse, they'd end it. That's Ortega's whole plan. He fights you, kills you, and then the White Council sues for peace. They'll pay some kind of concession that doesn't involve the death of one of their members, and that will be that. War over."

I blinked. "How did you find out—"

"Hello, Earth to Harry. I told you, I investigated."

I frowned until the lines between my eyebrows ached. "Right, right. Well, as plans go, I guess it sounds good," I said. "Except for that middle part where I die."

She gave me a small smile. "Much of the rest of the Red Court would rather you kept on breathing. As long as you're alive, they have a reason to keep the war going."

"Swell," I said.

"They'll try to interfere with any duel. I just thought you should know."

I nodded. "Thanks," I said. "I'll—"

Just then, someone knocked firmly at my door. Susan stiffened and rose, poker in hand. I got up a lot more slowly, opened a drawer in the night table beside the chair, and drew out the gun I kept at home, a great big old Dirty Harry Callahan number that weighed about seventy-five thousand pounds. I also took out a length of silk rope about a yard long, and draped it over my neck so that I could get it off in a hurry if need be.

I took the gun in both hands, pointed it at the floor, drew back the hammer, and asked the door, "Who is it?"

There was a moment's silence and then a calm, male voice asked, "Is Susan Rodriguez there?"

I glanced at Susan. She straightened more, her eyes flashing with anger, but she put the poker back in its stand beside the fireplace. Then she motioned to me and said, "Put it away. I know him."

I uncocked the revolver, but I didn't put it away as Susan crossed to the door and opened it.

The most bland-looking human being I had ever seen stood on the other side. He was maybe five nine, maybe one seventy-five. He had hair of medium brown, and eyes of the same ambiguous shade. He wore jeans, a medium-weight brown jacket, and worn tennis shoes. His face was unmemorable, neither appealing nor ugly. He didn't look particularly strong, or craven, or smart, or particularly anything else.

"What are you doing here?" he asked Susan without preamble. His voice was like the rest of him—about as exciting as a W-2.

Susan said, "I told you I was going to talk to him."

"You could have used the phone," the man pointed out. "There's no point to this."

"Hi," I said in a loud voice, and stepped up to my door. I towered over Blandman. And I had a great big gun in my hand, even if I did keep it pointed down at the floor. "I'm Harry Dresden."

He looked me up and down and then looked at Susan.

Susan sighed. "Harry, this is Martin."

"Hi, Martin," I said. I switched my sidearm to my other hand and thrust mine at him. "Nice to meet you."

Martin regarded my hand and then said, "I don't shake hands." That was evidently all the verbal interaction I merited, because he looked back at Susan and said, "We have to be up early."

We? *We?*

I looked at Susan, who flushed with embarrassment. She glared at Martin and then said to me, "I need to go, Harry. I wish I could have stayed longer."

"Wait," I said.

"I wish I could," she said. "I'll try to call you before we go."

There was that *we* again. "Go? Susan—"

"I'm sorry." She stood up on tiptoe and kissed my cheek, her too-warm lips soft. Then she left, brushing past Martin just hard enough to jostle him into taking a little step to keep his balance.

Martin nodded to me and walked out too. After a minute I followed them, long enough to see them getting into a cab on the street outside.

We.

"Hell's bells," I muttered, and stalked back inside my house. I slammed the door behind me, lit a candle, stomped into my little bathroom, and turned on the shower. The water was only a couple degrees short of becoming sleet, but I stripped and got in anyway, simmering with several varieties of frustration.

We.

We, we, we. Which implied she and someone else together. Someone who was not me. Was she? Susan, with the Pedantic Avenger there? That didn't track. I mean, hell's bells, the guy was just so dull. Boring. Blasé.

And maybe stable.

Face it, Harry. Interesting you might be. Exciting you might be. Stable you ain't.

I pushed my head under the freezing water and left it there. Susan hadn't said they were together. Neither had he. I mean, that wouldn't be why she had broken off the kiss. She had a really good reason to do that, after all.

But then again, it wasn't like we were together. She'd been gone for better than a year.

A lot can change in a year.

Her mouth hadn't. Or her hands. Or the curve of her body. Or the smoldering sensuality of her eyes. Or the soft sounds she made as she arched against me, her body begging me to—

I looked down at myself, sighed, and turned the water to its coldest setting.

I came out of the shower shriveled and turning blue, dried off, and got into bed.

I had just managed to get the covers warm so that I could stop shivering when my phone rang.

I swore sulfurously, got out of bed into the freezing air, snatched up the phone, and growled, "What." Then, on the off chance it was Susan, I forced some calm into my voice and said, "I mean, hello?"

"Sorry to wake you, Harry," said Karrin Murphy, the head of Chicago PD's Special Investigations division. SI routinely handled any crime that fell between the cracks of the other departments, as well as being handed the really smelly cases no one else wanted. As a result, they wound up looking into all kinds of things that weren't easily explained. Their job was to make sure that things were taken care of, and that everything typed up neatly into the final report.

Murphy called me in as a consultant from time to time, when she had something weird that she didn't know how to handle. We'd been working together for a while, and Murphy had gotten to where she and SI could handle your average, everyday supernatural riffraff. But from time to time, she ran into something that stumped her. My phone number is on her quick dial.

"Murph," I said. "What's up?"

"Unofficial business," she said. "I'd like your take on something."

"Unofficial means not paid, I guess," I said.

"You up for any pro bono work?" She paused and then said, "This could be important to me."

What the hell. My night had pretty much been shot anyway. "Where do you want me?"

"Cook County Morgue," Murphy said. "I want to show you a corpse."

Chapter Five

They don't make morgues with windows. In fact, if the geography allows for it, they hardly ever make morgues above the ground. I guess it's partly because it must be easier to refrigerate a bunch of coffin-sized chambers in a room insulated by the earth. But that can't be all there is to it. Under the earth means a lot more than relative altitude. It's where dead things fit. Graves are under the earth. So are Hell, Gehenna, Hades, and a dozen other reported afterlives.

Maybe it says something about people. Maybe for us, under the earth is a subtle and profound statement. Maybe ground level provides us with a kind of symbolic boundary marker, an artificial construct that helps us remember that we are alive. Maybe it helps us push death's shadow back from our lives.

I live in a basement apartment and like it. What does that say about me?

Probably that I overanalyze things.

"You look pensive," Murphy said. We walked down an empty hospital corridor toward the Cook County Morgue. We'd had to go the long way around so that I could avoid any areas with important medical equipment. My leather duster whispered around my legs as I walked. My blasting rod thumped against my leg rhythmically, where I'd tied it to the inside of the duster. I'd traded in my slacks for blue jeans and my dress shoes for hiking boots.

Murphy didn't look like a monster-hunting Valkyrie. Murphy looked like someone's kid sister. She was five nothing, a hundred and nothing, and was built like an athlete, all springy muscle. Her blond hair hung down over her blue eyes, and was cut close in back. She wore nicer clothes than usual—a maroon blouse with a grey pantsuit—and she had on more makeup than was her habit. She looked every inch the professional businesswoman.

That said, Murphy was a monster-hunting Valkyrie. She was the only person I'd ever heard of who had killed one with a chainsaw.

"I said you look pensive, Harry," she repeated, a little louder.

I shook my head and told Murphy, "I don't like hospitals."

She nodded. "Morgues spook me. Morgues and dogs."

"Dogs?" I asked.

"Not like beagles or cocker spaniels or anything. Just big dogs."

I nodded. "I like dogs. They give Mister something to snack on."

Murphy gave me a smile. "I've seen you spooked. It doesn't make you look like that."

"What do I look like?" I asked.

Murphy pursed her lips, as though considering her words. "You look worried. And frustrated. And guilty. You know, romance things."

I gave her a wry glance, and then nodded. "Susan's in town."

Murphy whistled. "Wow. She's . . . okay?"

"Yeah. As much as she can be."

"Then why do you look like you just swallowed something that was still wriggling?"

I shrugged. "She's in town to quit her job. And she was with someone."

"A *guy*?" Murphy asked.

"Yeah."

She frowned. "With him, or *with* him?"

I shook my head. "Just with him, I think. I don't know."

"She's quitting her job?"

"Guess so. We're going to talk, I think."

"She said so?"

"Said she'd get in touch and we'd talk."

Murphy's eyes narrowed, and she said, "Ah. One of those."

"Eh?" I said, and eyed her.

She lifted her hands, palms out. "None of my business."

"Hell's bells, Murph."

She sighed and didn't look up at me, and didn't speak for a few steps. Finally she said, "You don't set up a guy for a good talk, Harry."

I stared at her profile, and then scowled down at my feet for a while. No one said anything.

We got to the morgue. Murphy pushed a button on the wall and said, "It's Murphy," at a speaker next to the door. A second later, the door buzzed and clicked. I swung open the door and held it for Murphy. She gave me an even look before she went through. Murphy does not respond well to chivalry.

The morgue was like others I'd seen, cold, clean, and brightly lit with fluorescent lights. Metal refrigerator doors lined one wall. An occupied autopsy table sat in the middle of the room, and a white sheet covered its subject. A rolling medical cart sat next to the autopsy table, another by a cheap office-furniture desk.

Polka music, heavy on accordion and clarinet, *oompah*ed cheerfully through the room from a little stereo on the desk. At the desk sat a small man with a wild shock of black hair. He was dressed in medical scrubs and green bunny slippers, complete with floppy ears. He had a pen clenched in one hand, and scribbled furiously at a stack of forms.

When we came in, he held up a hand toward us, and finished his scribbling with a flourish, before hopping up with a broad smile. "Karrin!" he said. "Wow, you're looking nice tonight. What's the occasion?"

"Municipal brass are tromping around," Murphy said. "So we're all supposed to wear our Sunday clothes and smile a lot."

"Bastards," the little guy said cheerfully. He shot me a glance. "You aren't supposed to be spending money on psychic consultants, either, I bet. You must be Harry Dresden."

"That's what it says on my underwear," I agreed.

He grinned. "Great coat, love it."

"Harry," Murphy said, "this is Waldo Butters. Assistant medical examiner."

Butters shook my hand, then turned to walk to the autopsy table. He snapped on some rubber gloves and a surgical mask. "Pleased to meet you, Mister Dresden," he said over his shoulder. "Seems like every time you're working with SI my job gets really interesting."

Murphy chucked me on the arm with one fist, and followed Butters. I followed her.

"Masks on that tray to your left. Stay a couple of feet back from the table, and for God's sake, don't throw up on my floor." We put on masks and Butters threw back the sheet.

I'd seen corpses before. Hell's bells, I'd created some. I'd seen what was left of people who had been burned alive, savaged to death by animals, and who had died when their hearts exploded out of their chests, courtesy of black magic.

But I hadn't ever seen anything quite like this. I shoved the thought to the back of my head, and tried to focus purely upon taking in details. It wouldn't do to think too much, looking at this. Thinking too much would lead me to messing up Butters's floor.

The victim had been a man, maybe a little over six feet tall, thin build. His chest looked like twenty pounds of raw hamburger. Fine grid marks stretched vertically from his collarbones to his belly, and horizontally across the width of his body. The cuts were spaced maybe a sixteenth of an inch apart, and the grid pattern slashed into the flesh looked nearly flawless. The cuts were deep ones, and I had the unsettling impression that I could have brushed my hand across the surface of that ruined body and sent chunks of flesh pattering to the floor. The Y-incision of the autopsy had been closed, at least. Its lines marred the precision of the grid of incisions.

The next thing I noticed were the corpse's arms. Or rather, the missing bits of them. His left arm had been hacked off two or three inches above the wrist. The flesh around it gaped, and a shard of black-crusted bone poked out from it. His right arm had been severed just beneath the elbow, with similar hideous results.

My belly twitched and I felt myself taking one of those pre-vomit breaths. I closed my eyes for a second and forced the impending reaction down. *Don't think, Harry. Look. See what there is to see. That isn't a man anymore. It's just a shell. Throwing up won't bring him back.*

I opened my eyes again, tore my gaze from his mutilated chest and hands, and forced myself to study the corpse's features.

I couldn't.

His head had been hacked off, too.

I stared at the ragged stump of his neck. The head just wasn't there. Even though that's where heads *go*. Ditto his hands. A man should have a head. Should have hands. They shouldn't simply be *gone*.

The impression it left on me was unsettling—simply and profoundly wrong. Inside me, some little voice started screaming and running away. I stared down at the corpse, my stomach threatening insurrection again. I stared at his missing head, but aloud all I said was, "Gee. Wonder what killed him."

"What *didn't* kill him," Butters said. "I can tell you this much. It wasn't blood loss."

I frowned at Butters. "What do you mean?"

Butters lifted one of the corpse's arms and pointed down at dark mottling in the dead grey flesh, just where the corpse's back met the table. "See that?" he asked. "Lividity. If this guy had bled out, from his wrists or his neck either one, I don't think there'd be enough blood left in the body to show this much. His heart would have just kept on pumping it out of his body until he died."

I grunted. "If not one of the wounds, then what was it?"

"My guess?" Butters said. "Plague."

I blinked and looked at him.

"Plague," he said again. "Or more accurately plagues. His insides looked like models for a textbook on infection. Not all the tests have come back yet, but so far every one I've done has returned positive. Everything from bubonic plague to strep throat. And there are symptoms I've found in him that don't match any disease I've ever heard of."

"You're telling me he died of disease?" I asked.

"Diseases. Plural. And get this. I think one of them was smallpox."

"I thought smallpox was extinct," Murphy said.

"Pretty much. They have some in vaults, probably some in some bioweapon research facilities, but that's it."

I stared at Butters for a second. "And we're standing here next to his plague-ridden body why?"

"Relax," Butters said. "The really nasty stuff wasn't airborne. I disinfected the corpse pretty well. Wear your mask and don't touch it, you should be fine."

"What about the smallpox?" I said.

Butters's voice turned wry. "You're vaccinated."

"This is dangerous, though, isn't it? Having the body out like this?"

"Yeah," Butters said, his voice frank. "But County is full, and the only thing that's going to happen if I report an occurrence of free-range smallpox is another evaluation."

Murphy shot me a warning look and stepped a very little bit between me and Butters. "You got a time of death?"

Butters shrugged. "Maybe forty-eight hours ago, tops. All of those diseases seemed to sprout up at exactly the same time. I make cause of death as either shock or a massive failure and necrosis of several major organs, plus tissue damage from an outrageously high fever. It's anyone's guess as to which one gets the blue ribbon. Lungs, kidneys, heart, liver, spleen—"

"We get the point," Murphy said.

"Let me finish. It's like every disease the guy had ever had contact with all got together and planned when to hit him. It just isn't possible. He probably had more germs in him than blood cells."

I frowned. "And then someone Ginsued him after he died?"

Butters nodded. "Partly. Though the cuts on his chest weren't postmortem. They had filled with blood. Tortured before he died, maybe."

"Ugh," I said. "Why?"

Murphy regarded the corpse without any emotion showing in her cool blue eyes. "Whoever cut him up must have taken the arms and hands to make it hard to identify him after he died. That's the only logical reason I can think of."

"Same here," said Butters.

I frowned down at the table. "Why prevent identification of the corpse if it had died of disease?" Butters began to lower the arm slowly and I saw something as he did. "Wait, hold it."

He looked up at me. I pressed closer to the table and had Butters lift the arm again. I had almost missed it against the rotted tone of the dead man's flesh—a tattoo, maybe an inch square, located on the inside of the corpse's biceps. It wasn't fancy. Faded green ink in the shape of a symbolic open eye, not too different from the CBS network logo.

"See there?" I asked. Murphy and Butters peered at the tattoo.

"Do you recognize it, Harry?" Murphy asked.

I shook my head. "Almost looks old Egyptian, but with fewer lines. Hey, Butters, do you have a piece of paper?"

"Better," Butters said. He got an old instant camera off the bottom tray of one of the medical carts, and snapped several shots of the tattoo. He passed one of them over to Murphy, who waved it around a little while the image developed. I got another.

"Okay," I said, thinking out loud. "Guy dies of a zillion diseases he somehow contracted all at once. How long do you think it took?"

Butters shrugged. "No idea. I mean, the odds against him getting all of those at once like that are beyond astronomical."

"Days?" I asked.

"If I had to guess," Butters said, "I'd say more like hours. Maybe less."

"Okay," I said. "And during those hours, someone uses a knife on him and turns his chest into tuna cubes. Then when they're done, they take his hands and his head and dump the body. Where was it found?"

"Under an overpass on the expressway," Murphy said. "Like this, naked."

I shook my head. "SI got handed this one?"

Murphy's face flickered with annoyance. "Yeah. Homicide dumped it on us to take some high-profile case all the municipal folk are hot about."

I took a step back from the corpse, frowning, putting things together. I figured odds were pretty good that there weren't all that many people running around the world torturing victims by carving their skin into graph paper before murdering them. At least I hoped there weren't all that many.

Murphy peered at me, her expression serious. "What. Harry, do you know something?"

I glanced from Murphy to Butters and then back again.

Butters raised both his hands and headed for the doors, stripping his gloves and dumping them in a container splattered with red biohazard signs. "You guys stay here and Mulder it out. I have to go down the hall anyway. Back in five minutes."

I watched him go and said, after the door swung shut, "Bunny slippers and polka music."

"Don't knock it," Murphy said. "He's good at his job. Maybe too good."

"What's that mean?"

She walked away from the autopsy table, and I followed her. Murphy said, "Butters was the one who handled the bodies after the fire at the Velvet Room."

The one I'd started. "Oh?"

"Mmm-hmm. His original report stated that some of the remains recovered from the scene were humanoid, but definitely not human."

"Yeah," I said. "Red vampires."

Murphy nodded. "But you can't just stick that in a report without people getting their panties in a bunch. Butters wound up doing a three-month stint at a mental hospital for observation. When he came out, they tried to fire him, but his lawyer convinced them that they couldn't. So instead he lost all his seniority and got stuck on the night shift. But he knows there's weirdness out there. He calls me when he gets some of it."

"Seems nice enough. Except for the polka."

Murphy smiled again and said, "What do you know?"

"Nothing I can tell you," I said. "I agreed to keep the information confidential."

Murphy peered up at me for a moment. Once upon a time, that comment might have sent her into a fit of stubborn confrontation. But I guess times had changed. "All right," she said. "Are you holding back anything that might get someone hurt?"

I shook my head. "It's too early to tell."

Murphy nodded, her lips pressed together. She appeared to weigh things for a moment before saying, "You know what you're doing."

"Thanks."

She shrugged. "I expect you to tell me if it turns into something I should know."

"Okay," I said, staring at her profile. Murphy had done something I knew she didn't do very often. She'd extended her trust. I'd expected her to threaten and demand. I could have handled that. This was almost worse. Guilt gnawed on my insides. I'd agreed not to divulge anything, but I hated doing that to Murphy. She'd gone out on a limb for me too many times.

But what if I didn't tell her anything? What if I just pointed her toward information she'd find sooner or later in any case?

"Look, Murph. I specifically agreed to confidentiality for this client. But . . . if I were going to talk to you, I'd tell you to check out the murder of a Frenchman named LaRouche with Interpol."

Murphy blinked and then looked up at me. "Interpol?"

I nodded. "If I were going to talk."

"Right," she said. "If you'd said anything. You tight-lipped bastard."

One corner of my mouth tugged up into a grin. "Meanwhile, I'll see if I can't find out anything about that tattoo."

She nodded. "You figure we're dealing with another sorcerer type?"

I shrugged. "Maybe. But if you give someone a disease with magic, it's usually so that you make it look like they *haven't* been murdered. Natural causes. This kind of mishmash . . . I don't know. Maybe it's something a demon would do."

"A real demon? Like *Exorcist* demon?"

I shook my head. "Those are the Fallen. The former angels. Not the same thing."

"Why not?"

"Demons are just intelligent beings from somewhere in the Nevernever. Mostly they don't care about the mortal world, if they notice it at all. The ones who do are usually the hungry types, or the mean types that someone calls up to do thug work. Like that thing Leonid Kravos had called up."

Murphy shivered. "I remember. And the Fallen?"

"They're very interested in our world. But they aren't free to act, like demons are."

"Why not?"

I shrugged. "Depends on who you talk to. I've heard everything from advanced magical resonance theory to 'because God said so.' One of the Fallen couldn't do this unless it had permission to."

"Right. And how many people would give permission to be infected and then tortured to death," Murphy said.

"Yeah, exactly."

She shook her head. "Going to be a busy week. Half a dozen professional hitters for the outfit are in town. The county morgue is doing double business. City Hall is telling us to bend over backward for some bigwig from Europe or somewhere. And now some kind of plague monster is leaving unidentifiable, mutilated corpses on the side of the road."

"That's why they pay you the big bucks, Murph."

Murphy snorted. Butters came back in, and I made my goodbyes. My eyes were getting heavy and I had aches in places where I hadn't known I had places. Sleep sounded like a great idea, and with so many things going on, the smart option was to get lots of rest in order to be as capably paranoid as possible.

I walked the long route back out of the hospital, but found a hall blocked by a patient on some kind of life-support machinery being moved on a gurney from one room to another. I wound up heading out through the empty cafeteria, into an alley not far from the emergency room exit.

A cold chill started at the base of my spine and slithered up over my neck. I stopped and looked around me, reaching for my blasting rod. I extended my magical senses as best I could, tasting the air to see what had given me the shivers.

I found nothing, and the eerie sensation eased away. I started down the alley, toward a parking garage half a block from the hospital, and tried to look in every direction at once as I went. I passed a little old homeless man, hobbling along heavily on a thick wooden cane. A while farther on, I passed a tall young black man, dressed in an old overcoat and tattered and too-small suit, clutching an open bottle of vodka in one heavy-knuckled hand. He glowered at me, and I moved on past him. Chicago nightlife.

I kept on moving toward my car, and heard footsteps growing closer, behind me. I told myself not to be too jumpy. Maybe it was just some other frightened, endangered, paranoid, sleep-deprived consultant who had been called to the morgue in the middle of the night.

Okay. Maybe not.

The steady tread of the footsteps behind me shifted, becoming louder and unsteady. I spun to face the person following me, raising the blasting rod in my right hand as I did.

I turned around in time to see a bear, a freaking grizzly bear, fall to all four feet and charge. I had already begun preparing a magical strike with the rod, and the tip burst into incandescent light. Shadows fell harshly back from the scarlet fire of the rod, and I saw the details of the thing coming at me.

It wasn't a bear. Not unless a bear can have six legs and a pair of curling ram's horns wrapping around the sides of its head. Not unless bears can somehow get an extra pair of eyes, right over the first set, one pair glowing with faint orange light and one with green. Not unless bears have started getting luminous tattoos of swirling runes on their foreheads and started sprouting twin rows of serrated, slime-coated teeth.

It came charging toward me, several hundred pounds of angry-looking monster, and I did the only thing any reasonable wizard could have done.

I turned around and ran like hell.

Chapter Six

I'd learned something in several years of professional wizarding. Never walk into a fight when the bad guys are the ones who set it up. Wizards can call down lightning from the heavens, rip apart the earth beneath their enemy's feet, blow them into a neighboring time zone with gale winds, and a million other things even less pleasant—but not if we don't plan things out in advance.

And we're not all that much tougher than regular folks. I mean, if some nasty creature tears my head off my shoulders, I'll die. I might be able to lay out some serious magical pounding when I need to, but I'd made the mistake of tangling with a few things that had prepared to go up against me, and it hadn't been pretty.

This bear-thing, whatever the hell it was, had followed me. Hence, it had probably picked its time and place. I could have stood and blasted away at it, but in the close quarters of the alley, if it was able to shrug off my blasts, it would tear me apart before I could try Plan B. So I ran.

One other thing I'd learned. Wheezy wizards aren't all that good at running. That's why I'd been practicing. I took off at a dead sprint and fairly flew down the alley, my duster flapping behind me.

The bear-thing snarled as it came after me, and I could hear it slowly gaining ground. The mouth of the alley loomed into sight and I ran as hard as I could for it. Once I was in the open with room to dodge and put obstacles between me and the creature, I might be able to take a shot at it.

The creature evidently realized that, because it let out a vicious, spitting growl and then leapt. I heard it gather itself for the leap, and turned my head enough to see it out of the corner of my eye. It flew at my back. I threw myself down, sliding and rolling over the asphalt. The creature soared over me, to land at the mouth of the alley, a good twenty feet ahead. I skidded to a stop and went running back down the alley, a growing sense of fear and desperation giving my feet a set of chicken-yellow wings.

I ran for maybe ten seconds, gritting my teeth as the creature took up the pursuit again. I couldn't keep up a full sprint forever. Unless I thought of something else, I was going to have to turn and take my chances.

I all but flattened the tall young black man I'd seen earlier when I leapt over a moldering pile of cardboard boxes. He let out a startled noise, and I answered it with a low curse. "Come on!" I said, grabbing his arm. "Move, move, move!"

He looked past me and his eyes widened. I looked back and saw the four glowing eyes of the bear-creature coming at us. I hauled him into motion, and he picked up speed and started running with me.

We ran for a few seconds more before the little old derelict I'd seen earlier came limping along on his cane. He looked up, and the dim light from the distant street glinted on a pair of spectacles.

"Augh," I shouted. I shoved my running partner past me, toward the old man, and snarled, "Get him out of here. Both of you run!"

I whirled to face the bear-creature, and swept my blasting rod to point right at it. I ran some force of will down into the energy channels in the rod and with a snarled, *"Fuego!"* sent a lance of raw fire whipping through the air.

The blast slammed into the bear-creature's chest, and it hunched its shoulders, turning its head to one side. Its forward charge faltered, and it slid to a stop, crashing against a weathered old metal trash can.

"What do you know," I muttered. "It worked." I stepped forward and unleashed another blast at the creature, hoping to either melt it to bits or drive it away. The bear-thing snarled and turned a hateful, murderous gaze at me with its four eyes.

The soulgaze began almost instantly.

When a wizard looks into someone's eyes, he sees more than just what color they are. Eyes are windows to the soul. When I make eye contact for too long, or too intently, I get to peek in through the windows. You can't hide what you are from a wizard's soulgaze. And he can't hide from you. You both see each other for what you are, within, and it's with a clarity so intense that it burns itself into your head.

Looking on someone's soul is something you never forget.

No matter how badly you might want to.

I felt a whirling, gyrating sensation and fell forward; into the bear-thing's eyes. The glowing sigil on its forehead became a blaze of silver light the size of a stadium scoreboard set against a roundish cliffside of dark green and black marble. I expected to see something hideous, but I guess you can't judge a monster by the slime on its scales. What I saw instead was a man of lean middle years dressed in rags. His hair was long and straight, wispy grey that fell down to his chest. He stood in a posture of agony, his wiry body stretched out in an arch, with his hands held up and apart, his legs stretched out. I followed the lines of his arms back and up and saw why he stood that way.

He'd been crucified.

The man's back rested against the cliff, the great glowing sigil stretching out above him. His arms were pulled back at an agonizing angle, and were sunk to the elbow in the green-black marble of the cliff. His knees were bent, his feet sunk into the stone as well. He hung there, the pressure of all his weight on his shoulders and legs. It must have been agonizing.

The crucified man laughed at me, his eyes glowing a shade of sickly green, and screamed, "As if it will help you! Nothing! You're nothing!"

Pain laced his voice, making it shrill. Agony contorted the lines of his body, veins standing out sharply against straining muscle.

"Stars and stones," I whispered. Creatures like this bear-thing did not have souls to gaze upon. That meant that regardless of appearances to the contrary, this thing was a mortal. It—no, *he*—was a human being. "What the hell is this?"

The man screamed again, this time all rage and anguish, void of words. I lifted a hand and stepped forward, my first instinct to help him.

Before I got close, the ground began to shake. The cliff face rumbled and slits of seething orange light appeared, and then widened, until I faced the second set of eyes, eyes the size of subway tunnels, opening on the great marble cliff. I stumbled several steps back, and that cliff face proved to be exactly that—a face, cold and beautiful and harsh around that fiery gaze.

The quaking in the earth increased, and a voice louder than a Metallica concert spoke, the raw sense of the words, the vicious anger and hate behind them hitting me far more heavily than mere volume.

GET OUT.

The sheer force of presence behind that voice seized me and threw me violently back, away from the tortured man at the cliff-side and out of the soulgaze. The mental connection snapped like dry spaghetti, and the same force that had thrown my mind away from the soul-gaze sent my physical body flying back through the air. I hit an old cardboard box filled with empty bottles and heard glass shattering beneath me. The heavy leather duster held, and no broken shards buried themselves in my back.

For a second or two, I just lay on my back, stunned. My thoughts were a hectic whirlpool I couldn't calm or control. I stared up at the city's light pollution against the low clouds, until some tiny voice in me started screaming that I was in danger. I shoved myself to my knees, just as the bear-creature smacked a trash can aside with one of its paws and started toward me.

My head was still ringing with the aftereffects of the soulgaze and the psychic assault that had broken the connection. I lifted my blasting rod, summoned up every bit of will I could scrape to-gether out of the confusion, and spat a word that sent another lance of flame toward the bear-creature.

This time the blast didn't even slow it down. The set of orange eyes flared with a sudden luminance, and my fire splashed against an unseen barrier, dispersing around the creature in sheets of scar-let. It let out a screaming roar and lumbered toward me.

I tried to get up, stumbled, and fell at the feet of the little old homeless guy, who leaned on his cane and stared at the creature. I had a dim impression of his features—Asian, a short white beard around his chin, heavy white eyebrows, and corrective glasses that made his eyes look the size of an owl's.

"Run, dammit!" I shouted at him. I tried to lead by example, but my balance was still whirling and I couldn't get off the ground.

The old man did not turn to run. He took off his glasses and pushed them at me. "Hold, please."

Then he took a deliberate step forward with his cane, placing himself between me and the bear-creature.

The creature hurled itself at him with a bellow, rearing up on its hindmost legs. It plunged down at the white-haired man, jaws gaping, and I couldn't do anything but watch it happen.

The little man took two steps to one side, pirouetting like a dancer. The end of his wooden cane lashed out and struck the creature's jaws with a crunching impact. Bits of broken yellow teeth flew from the creature's mouth. The little man continued his turn and evaded its claws by maybe an inch. He wound up behind the creature, and it turned to follow him, huge jaws snapping in rage.

The man darted back, staying just ahead of the thing's jaws, and in a blur of sudden light on metal he drew from his cane a long blade, the classic single-edged, chisel-pointed katana. The steel flashed at the creature's eyes, but it ducked low enough that the scything blade only whipped the top couple of inches from one of its ears.

The creature screamed, entirely out of proportion with the injury, a yowl that almost sounded human. It lurched back, shaking its head, a fine spray of blood sprinkling from its wounded ear.

At this point, I noticed three things.

One. The creature was paying me no attention whatsoever. Yippee ki yay. My head still spun wildly, and if it had come for me, I didn't think I could have done anything about it.

Two. The old man's sword was not reflecting light. It was emitting it. The water-patterned steel of the blade glowed with a steady silver flame that slowly grew brighter.

Three. I could feel the humming power of the sword, even from several yards away. It throbbed with a steady, deep strength, as quiet and unshakable as the earth itself.

In my entire life, I'd seen only one sword imbued with that much power.

But I knew that there were a couple more.

"Oi!" shouted the little old man, his English heavily accented. "Ursiel! Let him go! You have no power here!"

The bear-creature—Ursiel, I presumed—focused its four-eyed gaze on the little man and did something unsettling. It spoke. Its voice came out quiet, smooth, melodious, words somehow slithering out through the bear's jaws and throat. "Shiro. Look at yourself, little fool. You are an old man. You were at the peak of your strength when last we met. You cannot defeat me now."

Shiro narrowed his eyes, his sword gripped in one hand, the length of wooden sheath held in the other. "Did you come here to talk?"

Ursiel's head tilted to one side, and then the smooth voice murmured, "No. Indeed I did not."

It whirled, whipping its head toward me, and lunged. As it did, there was a rustle of cloth and then an old overcoat spun through the air, spreading like a fisherman's net. It fell over Ursiel's face, and the demon drew up short with a frustrated howl. It reached up and tore the coat from its head.

While it did, the tall young black man stepped between Ursiel and me. As I watched, he drew a long, heavy saber from the scabbard at his hip. The sword hummed with the same power as Shiro's, though in a slight variation, a different note within the same chord. Silver light flared from the blade's steel, and behind the demon, Shiro's blade answered it with more of its own radiance. The young man looked back at me, and I caught a glimpse of dark, intense eyes before he faced the demon, and said in a rumbling basso, words flavored with a thick Russian accent, "Ursiel. Let him go. You have no power here."

Ursiel hissed, the orange eyes blazing brighter by the moment. "Sanya. Traitor. Do you really think any of us fears even one of the Three, in your pathetic hands? So be it. I will take you all."

Sanya spread his empty hand to one side of his body in mocking invitation, and said nothing.

Ursiel roared and flew at Sanya. The big man extended the saber, and the weapon took Ursiel high on one shoulder, plunging through muscle and sinew. Sanya braced himself as the demon's body hit him, and though the impact drove his feet back across six inches of concrete, he held it up and away from me.

Shiro let out a ringing cry I wouldn't have believed a little old man could make, and Ursiel screamed, thrashing and flailing. Sanya shouted something in what sounded like Russian, and drove forward with both hands on the hilt of the impaling saber, overbearing Ursiel and sending the demon sprawling onto his back. Sanya followed, staying close, and I saw him throw his weight onto the demon as he twisted the hilt of the saber thrust through it.

He'd been too aggressive. Ursiel's paw hit him squarely upon one shoulder, and I heard the snap of breaking bone. The blow threw the young man away from the demon, and he rolled across the ground and into a wall, an explosive breath of pain forced from him as he hit.

Ursiel recovered its feet, tore the saber from its shoulder with a jerk of its jaws, and went after Sanya, but the white-haired old man menaced its flank, forcing it away from the wounded man and, incidentally, from me. For a few seconds, the old man and the demon circled each other. Then the demon lashed out at Shiro, a flurry of slashes with its claws.

The old man ducked them, retreating, his sword flickering and cutting. Twice, he left cuts on the demon's paws, but though it screamed in rage, it only seemed to grow less intimidated, more angry. The old man's breathing grew visibly labored.

"Age," Ursiel's voice purred amidst its attack. "Death comes, old man. Its hand is on your heart now. And your life has been spent in vain."

"Let him go!" spat the old man between breaths.

Ursiel laughed again and the green pair of eyes glowed brighter. Another voice, this one not at all beautiful, the words twisted and snarling, said, "Stupid preacher. Time to die like the Egyptian did."

Shiro's expression changed, from stolid, controlled ferocity to something much sadder, much more resolved. He faced the demon for a moment, panting, and then nodded. "So be it."

The demon drove forward, and the old man gave ground, slowly forced into a corner of the alley. He seemed to be doing pretty well, until one close swipe of the demon's claws caught the glowing silver blade near its hilt, and sent it spinning away. The old man gasped and pressed back against the corner, panting, holding his right hand against the left side of his chest.

"So it ends, Knight," purred the smooth, demon-voice of Ursiel.

"Hai," the old man agreed quietly. He looked up above him, at a fire escape platform ten feet off the ground.

A shadowed figure dropped over the rail of the platform, steel rasping as it did. There was a low thrum of power, a flash of silver, and the hiss of a blade cutting the air. The shadowy figure landed in a crouch beside the creature.

The demon Ursiel jerked once, body stiffening. There was a thump.

Then its body toppled slowly over to one side, leaving its monstrous head lying on the alley floor. The light died from its four eyes.

The third Knight rose away from the demon's corpse. Tall and broad-shouldered, his close-cut hair dark and feathered with silver, Michael Carpenter snapped the blade of his broad sword, *amoracchius,* to one side, clearing droplets of blood from it. He put it back into its sheath, staring down at the fallen demon, and shook his head.

Shiro straightened, his breathing quick but controlled, and went to Michael's side. He gripped the larger man's shoulder and said, "It had to be done."

Michael nodded. The smaller Knight recovered the second sword, cleared the blade, and returned it to its wooden sheath.

Not far from me, the third Knight, the young Russian, pushed himself up from the ground. One of his arms dangled uselessly, but he offered the other to me. I took his hand and rose on wobbly legs.

"You are well?" he asked, his voice quiet.

"Peachy," I responded, wobbling. He arched an eyebrow at me, then shrugged and went to recover his blade from the alley floor.

The aftereffects of the soulgaze had finally begun to fade, and the simple shock and confusion began to give way to a redundant terror. I hadn't been careful enough. One of the bad guys had caught me off guard, and without intervention I would have been killed to death. It wouldn't have been anything quick and painless, either. Without Michael and his two companions, the demon Ursiel would have torn me limb from literal limb, and I wouldn't have been able to do a damned thing about it.

I had never encountered a psychic presence of such raw magnitude as upon the great stone cliff face. Not up close and personal like that, anyway. The first shot I'd taken at him had surprised and annoyed him, but he had been ready for the second blast and swatted aside my magical fire like an insect. Whatever Ursiel had been, he had been operating on a completely different order of magnitude than a mere punk of a mortal wizard like me. My psychic defenses aren't bad, but they had been crushed like a beer can under a bulldozer. That, more than anything, scared the snot out of me. I had tried my psychic strength against more than a few bad guys, and I had never felt so badly outclassed. Oh, I knew there were things out there stronger than me, sure.

But none of them had ever jumped me in a dark alley.

I shook, and found a wall to lean on until my head cleared a little, and then walked stiffly over to Michael. Bits of broken glass fell from folds in my duster.

Michael glanced up as I came over to him. "Harry," he said.

"It isn't that I'm not glad to see you," I said. "But you couldn't have jumped down and beheaded the monster about two minutes sooner?"

Michael was usually pretty good about taking a joke. This time he didn't even smile. "No. I'm sorry."

I frowned at him. "How did you find me? How did you know?"

"Good advice."

Which could have been anything from spotting my car nearby to being told by an angelic chorus. The Knights of the Cross always seemed to turn up in bad places when they were badly needed. Sometimes coincidence seemed to go to incredible lengths to see to it that they were in the right place at the right time. I didn't think I wanted to know. I nodded at the demon's fallen body and said, "What the hell was that thing?"

"He wasn't a thing, Harry," Michael said. He continued staring down at the remains of the demon, and just about then they started shimmering. It only took a few seconds for the demon to dissolve into the form of the man I'd seen in the soulgaze—thin, grey-haired, dressed in rags. Except that in the soulgaze, his head hadn't been lying three feet away like that. I didn't think a severed head should have held an expression, but it did, one of absolute terror, his mouth locked open in a silent scream. The sigil I'd seen on the cliff face stood out on his forehead like a fresh scab, dark and ugly.

There was a glitter of orange-red light, the sigil vanished, and something clinked on the asphalt. A silver coin a little smaller than a quarter rolled away from the man's head, bounced against my foot, and then settled onto the ground. A second later, the body let out a hissing, sighing sound, and began to run with streaks of green-black goo. The body just deflated in on itself, noxious fumes and a spreading puddle of disgusting slime the only things remaining.

"That's it," I said, staring down and trying to keep myself from visibly trembling. "The weirdness has just gone off the end of my meter. I'm going home and going to bed." I bent to recover the coin before the slime engulfed it.

The old man snapped his cane at my wrist, growling, "No."

It stung. I jerked my hand back, shaking my fingers, and scowled at him. "Stars and stones, Michael, who *is* this guy?"

Michael drew a square of white cloth from his pocket and unfolded it. "Shiro Yoshimo. He was my teacher when I became a Knight of the Cross."

The old man grunted at me. I nodded at the wounded man and asked, "How about him?"

The tall black man glanced up at me as the old Knight began examining his arm. He looked me up and down without any sign of approval, glowered, and said, "Sanya."

"The newest of our Order," Michael added. He shook out the cloth, revealing two pairs of crosses embroidered in silver thread upon it. Michael knelt down and picked up the coin through the cloth, turned it over, then folded the cloth completely around the silver.

I frowned down at the coin as he did. One side bore some ancient portrait, maybe of a man's profile. The opposite side had some other design that was hidden under a stain in the shape of a rune—the one I'd seen on the demon Ursiel's forehead.

"What's that?" I asked.

"Shiro was protecting you," Michael said, rather than answering the question. Michael looked over at Shiro, who stood with the towering Sanya, and asked, "How is he?"

"Broken arm," the old man reported. "We should get off the street."

"Agreed," rumbled Sanya. The older Knight fashioned a makeshift sling from the shredded overcoat, and the tall young man slipped his arm into it without a sound of complaint.

"You'd better come with us, Harry," Michael said. "Father Forthill can get you a cot."

"Whoa, whoa," I said. "You never answered my question. *What* was *that*?"

Michael frowned at me and said, "It's a long story, and there's little time."

I folded my arms. "Make time. I'm not going anywhere until I know what the hell is going on here."

The little old Knight snorted and said, "Hell. That is what is going on." He opened his hand to me and said, "Please give them back."

I stared at him for a second, until I remembered his spectacles. I handed them to him, and he put them on, making his eyes goggle out hugely again.

"Wait a minute," I said to Michael. "This thing was one of the Fallen?"

Michael nodded, and a chill went through me.

"That's impossible," I said. "The Fallen can't do . . . things like *that*." I gestured at the puddle of slime. "They aren't allowed."

"Some are," Michael said, his voice quiet. "Please believe me. You are in great danger. I know what you've been hired to find, and so do they."

Shiro stalked down to the end of the alley and swept his gaze around. "Oi. Michael, we must go."

"If he will not come, he will not come," Sanya said. He glared at me, then followed Shiro.

"Michael," I began.

"Listen to me," Michael said. He held up the folded white cloth. "There are more where this one came from, Harry. Twenty-nine of them. And we think they're after you."

Chapter Seven

I followed Michael's white pickup truck in the Blue Beetle to Saint Mary of the Angels Cathedral. It's a big, big church, a city landmark. If there's anything you like in the way of gothic architecture, you can find it somewhere on Saint Mary's. We parked near the back of the cathedral, and went to the delivery entrance, a plain oak door framed by lovingly tended rose vines.

Michael knocked at the door, and I heard the sound of multiple bolts being undone before the door opened.

Father Anthony Forthill opened the door. He was in his late fifties, balding, and carried a comfortable weight of years. He wore black slacks and a black shirt, the stark white square of his clerical collar sharply delineated. He was taller than Shiro, but a lot shorter than everyone else there, and beneath his glasses his eyes looked strained.

"Success?" he asked Michael.

"In part," Michael responded. He held up the folded cloth and said, "Put this in the cask, please. And we'll need to splint an arm."

Forthill winced, and accepted the folded cloth with the kind of ginger reverence paid only to explosives and samples of lethal viruses. "Right away. Good evening, Mister Dresden. Come in, all of you."

"Father," I answered. "You look like my day so far."

Forthill tried to smile at me, then padded away down a long hallway. Michael led us deeper into the church, up a flight of stairs to a storage room whose boxes had been stacked to the ceiling to make room for a number of folding cots, blocking the view of any windows. A mismatched pair of old lamps lit the room in soft gold.

"I'll get food, something to drink," Michael said quietly. He headed back out of the room. "And I need to call Charity. Sanya, you'd better sit down until we can see to your arm."

"I'll be fine," Sanya said. "I will help with food."

Shiro snorted and said, "Sit, boy." He headed for the door, catching up to Michael, and said, "Call your wife. I will do the rest." The two left together, their voices lowering to bare murmurs as they entered the hall.

Sanya glowered at the door for a moment and then settled down on one of the bunks. He looked around at the room for a moment, and then said, "You use the forces of magic, I take it."

I folded my arms and leaned against the wall. "What gave it away?"

He bared his teeth, white against his dark skin. "How long have you been a Wiccan?"

"A what?"

"A pagan. A witch."

"I'm not a witch," I said, glancing out the door. "I'm a wizard."

Sanya frowned. "What is the difference?"

"Wizard has a Z."

He looked at me blankly.

"No one appreciates me," I muttered. "Wicca is a religion. It's a little more fluid than most, but it's still a religion."

"And?"

"And I'm not really big on religion. I do magic, sure, but it's like . . . being a mechanic. Or an engineer. There are forces that behave a certain way. If you know what you're doing, you can get them to work for you, and you don't really need a god or a goddess or a whatever to get involved."

Sanya's expression became surprised. "You are not a religious man, then."

"I wouldn't burden any decent system of faith by participating in it."

The tall Russian regarded me for a moment and then nodded slowly. "I feel the same way."

I felt my eyebrow arch, Spock-like. "That's a joke, right?"

He shook his head. "It is not. I have been an atheist since childhood."

"You've got to be kidding me. You're a Knight of the Cross."

"*Da,*" he said.

"So if you're not religious, you risk your life to help other people because . . . ?"

"Because it must be done," he answered without hesitation. "For the good of the people, some must place themselves in harm's way. Some must pledge their courage and their lives to protect the community."

"Just a minute," I said. "You became a Knight of the Cross because you were a *communist*?"

Sanya's face twisted with revulsion. "Certainly not. Trotsky. Very different."

I stopped myself from bursting out in laughter. But it was a near thing. "How did you get your sword?"

He moved his good hand to rest on the hilt of the blade, where it lay beside him on the cot. "*Esperacchius*. Michael gave it to me."

"Since when has Michael gone running off to Russia?"

"Not that Michael," Sanya said. He pointed a finger up. "That Michael."

I stared at him for a minute and then said, "So. You get handed a holy sword by an archangel, told to go fight the forces of evil, and you somehow remain an atheist. Is that what you're saying?"

Sanya's scowl returned.

"Doesn't that strike you as monumentally stupid?"

His glare darkened for maybe a minute before he took a deep breath and nodded. "Perhaps some could argue that I am agnostic."

"Agnostic?"

"One who does not commit himself to the certain belief in a divine power," he said.

"I know what it means," I said. "What shocks me is that you think it applies to you. You've *met* more than one divine power. Hell, one of them broke your arm not half an hour ago."

"Many things can break an arm. You yourself said that you do not need a god or goddess to define your beliefs about the supernatural."

"Yeah, but I'm not agnostic. Just nonpartisan. Theological Switzerland, that's me."

Sanya said, "Semantics. I do not understand your point."

I took a deep breath, still holding back the threat of giggles, and said, "Sanya. My point is that you have got to be more than a little thick to stand where you are, having seen what you've seen, and claim that you aren't sure whether or not there's a God."

He lifted his chin and said, "Not necessarily. It is possible that I am mad, and all of this is a hallucination."

That's when I started laughing. I just couldn't help it. I was too tired and too stressed to do anything else. I laughed and enjoyed it thoroughly while Sanya sat on his cot and scowled at me, careful not to move his wounded arm.

Shiro appeared at the door, bearing a platter of sandwiches and deli vegetables. He blinked through his owlish glasses at Sanya and then at me. He said something to Sanya in what I took to be Russian. The younger Knight transferred his scowl to Shiro, but nodded his head in a gesture deep enough to be part bow, before he rose, claimed two sandwiches in one large hand, and walked out.

Shiro waited until Sanya was gone before he set the platter down on a card table. My stomach went berserk at the sight of the sandwiches. Heavy exertion coupled with insane fear does that to me. Shiro gestured at the plate and pulled up a couple of folding chairs. I sat down, nabbed a sandwich of my own, and started eating. Turkey and cheese. Heaven.

The old Knight took a sandwich of his own, and ate with what appeared to be a similar appetite. We munched for a while in contented silence before he said, "Sanya told you about his beliefs."

I felt the corners of my mouth start to twinge as another smile threatened. "Yeah."

Shiro let out a pleased snort. "Sanya is a good man."

"I just don't get why he'd be recruited as a Knight of the Cross."

Shiro looked at me over the glasses, chewing. After a while, he said, "Man sees faces. Sees skin. Flags. Membership lists. Files." He took another large bite, ate it, and said, "God sees hearts."

"If you say so," I said.

He didn't answer. Right about the time I finished my sandwich, Shiro said, "You are looking for the Shroud."

"That's confidential," I said.

"If you say so," he said, using my own inflection on the words. The wrinkles at the corners of his eyes deepened. "Why?"

"Why what?"

"Why are you looking for it?" he asked, chewing.

"If I am—and I'm not saying that I am—I'm doing it because I've been hired to look for it."

"Your job," he said.

"Yeah."

"You do it for money," he said.

"Yeah."

"Hmph," he said, and pushed his glasses up with his pinky. "Do you love money then, Mister Dresden?"

I picked up a napkin from one side of the platter, and wiped my mouth. "I used to think I loved it. But now I realize that it's just dependency."

Shiro let out an explosive bark of laughter, and rose, chortling. "Sandwich okay?"

"Super."

Michael came in a few minutes later, his face troubled. There wasn't a clock in the room, but it had to have been well after midnight. I supposed if I had called Charity Carpenter that late, I'd be troubled after the conversation, too. She was ferocious where her husband's safety was concerned—especially when she heard that I was around. Okay, admittedly Michael had gotten pretty thoroughly battered whenever he came along on a case with me, but all the same I didn't think it was fair of her. It wasn't like I did it on purpose.

"Charity wasn't happy?" I asked.

Michael shook his head. "She's worried. Is there a sandwich left?"

There were a couple. Michael took one and I took a second one, just to keep him company. While we ate, Shiro got out his sword and a cleaning kit, and started wiping down the blade with a soft cloth and some kind of oil.

"Harry," Michael said finally. "I have to ask you for something. It's very difficult. And it's something that under normal circumstances I wouldn't even consider doing."

"Name it," I said between chews. At the time, I meant it literally. Michael had risked his life for me more than once. His family had been endangered the last time around, and I knew him well enough to know that he wouldn't ask something unreasonable. "Just name it. I owe you."

Michael nodded. Then looked at me steadily and said, "Get out of this business, Harry. Get out of town for a few days. Or stay home. But get out of it, please."

I blinked at him. "You mean, you don't want my help?"

"I want your safety," Michael said. "You are in great danger."

"You're kidding me," I said. "Michael, I know how to handle myself. You should know that by now."

"Handle yourself," Michael said. "Like you did tonight? Harry, if we hadn't been there—"

"What?" I snapped. "I'd have been dead. It isn't like it isn't going to happen sooner or later. There are enough bad guys after me that one of them is eventually going to get lucky. So what else is new."

"You don't understand," Michael said.

"I understand all right," I said. "One more wacky B-horror-movie reject tried to kill me. It's happened before. It'll probably happen again."

Shiro said, without looking up from his sword, "Ursiel did not come to kill you, Mister Dresden."

I considered that in another pregnant silence. The lamps buzzed a little. Shiro's cleaning cloth whispered over the steel of his sword.

I watched Michael's face and asked, "Why was he there then? I'd have put down money that it was a demon, but it was just a shapechange. There was a mortal inside it. Who was he?"

Michael's gaze never wavered. "His name was Rasmussen. Ursiel took him in eighteen forty-nine, on his way to California."

"I saw him, Michael. I looked in his eyes."

Michael winced. "I didn't know that."

"He was a prisoner in his own soul, Michael. Something was holding him. Something big. Ursiel, I guess. He's one of the Fallen, isn't he?"

Michael nodded.

"How the hell does that happen? I thought the Fallen aren't allowed to take away free will."

"They aren't," Michael said. "But they are allowed to tempt. And the Denarians have more to offer than most."

"Denarians?" I asked.

"The Order of the Blackened Denarius," Michael said. "They see an opportunity in this matter. A chance to do great harm."

"Silver coins." I took a deep breath. "Like the one you wrapped up in blessed cloth. Thirty pieces of silver, eh?"

He nodded. "Whoever touches the coins is tainted by the Fallen within. Tempted. Given power. The Fallen leads the mortal deeper and deeper into its influence. Never forcing them. Just offering. Until eventually they have surrendered enough of themselves and—"

"The thing gets control of them," I finished.

Michael nodded. "Like Rasmussen. We try to help them. Sometimes the person realizes what is happening. Wants to escape their influence. When we face them, we try to wear the demon down. Give the person taken the chance to escape."

"That's why you kept talking to it. Until its voice changed. But Rasmussen didn't want to be free, did he?"

Michael shook his head.

"Believe it or not, Michael, I've been tempted once or twice. I can handle it."

"No," Michael said. "You can't. Against the Denarians, few mortals can. The Fallen know our weaknesses. Our flaws. How to undermine. Even warned and aware of them, they have destroyed men and women for thousands of years."

"I said I'll be fine," I growled.

Shiro grunted. "Pride before fall."

I gave him a sour glance.

Michael leaned forward and said, "Harry, please. I know that your life has not been an easy one. You're a good man. But you are as vulnerable as anyone. These enemies don't want you dead." He looked down at his hands. "They want *you*."

Which scared me. Really scared me. Maybe because it seemed to disturb Michael so much, and very little disturbs him. Maybe because I had seen Rasmussen, and would always be able to see him there, trapped, wildly laughing.

Or maybe it was because part of me wondered if it would be so impossible to find a way to use the power the coin obviously offered. If it had made some random schmuck on the way to pan for gold into a killing machine that it took all three Knights of the Cross to handle, what could someone like me do with it?

Beat the living snot out of Duke Paolo Ortega. That's for sure.

I blinked, refocusing my eyes. Michael watched me, his expression pained, and I knew that he'd guessed at my thoughts. I closed my eyes, shame making my stomach uneasy.

"You're in danger, Harry," Michael said. "Leave the case alone."

"If I was in so much danger," I responded, "why did Father Vincent come and hire me?"

"Forthill asked him not to," Michael said. "Father Vincent . . . disagrees with Forthill on how supernatural matters are to be handled."

I stood up and said, "Michael, I'm tired. I'm really damned tired."

"Harry," Michael chided me.

"Darned," I mumbled. "Darned tired. Darn me unto heck." I headed for the door and said, "I'm heading home to get some sleep. I'll think about it."

Michael stood up, and Shiro with him, both of them facing me. "Harry," Michael said. "You are my friend. You've saved my life. I've named a child for you. But stay out of this business. For my sake, if not for your own."

"And if I don't?" I asked.

"Then I'll have protect you from yourself. In the name of God, Harry, please don't push this."

I turned and left without saying good-bye.

In this corner, one missing Shroud, one impossibly and thoroughly dead corpse, one dedicated and deadly vampire warlord, three holy knights, twenty-nine fallen angels, and a partridge in a pear tree.

And in the opposite corner, one tired, bruised, underpaid professional wizard, threatened by his allies and about to get dumped by his would-be girlfriend for John Q. Humdrum.

Oh, yeah.

Definitely bedtime.

Chapter Eight

⋘⟶ ⟵⋙

I fumed and brooded all the way back to my apartment, the Beetle's engine sputtering nervously the whole time. Mister was sitting at the top of the steps, and let out a plaintive meow as I shut and locked up my car. Though I kept my blasting rod and shield bracelet ready in case any vanilla goons were waiting around with more silenced guns, I was fairly confident no preternasties were hanging around in ambush. Mister tended to make lots of noise and then leave whenever supernatural danger was around.

Which just goes to show that my cat has considerably more sense than me.

Mister slammed his shoulder against my legs, and didn't quite manage to trip me into falling down the stairs. I didn't waste any time getting inside and locked up behind me.

I lit a candle, got out some cat food and fresh water for Mister's bowls, and spent a couple minutes pacing back and forth. I glanced at my bed and wrote it off as a useless idea. I was too worked up to sleep, even tired as I was. I was already chin deep in alligators and sinking fast.

"Right, then, Harry," I mumbled. "Might as well do some work."

I grabbed a heavy, warm robe off its hook, shoved aside one of my rugs, and opened the trapdoor leading down to the subbasement. A folding ladder-staircase led down to the damp stone chamber beneath, where I kept my lab, and I padded down it, my robe's hem dragging against the wooden steps.

I started lighting candles. My lab, barring a brief bout of insanity, generally reflects the state of my own mind—cluttered, messy, unorganized, but basically functional. The room isn't large. Three worktables line three of the walls in a U shape, and a fourth table runs down the center of the U, leaving a narrow walkway around it. Wire utility shelves line the walls above the tables. Piled on the shelves and tables are a vast array of magical ingredients, plus that sort of miscellaneous domestic clutter that in households of more substance always winds up in a big drawer in the kitchen. Books, notebooks, journals, and papers line the shelves, together with containers and boxes and pouches full of all sorts of herbs, roots, and magical ingredients, from a bottle of snake hisses to a vial of milk-thistle extract.

At the far end of the room there was a patch of floor kept completely clear of all clutter. A copper ring set into the stone of the floor, my summoning circle, resided there. Experience had shown me that you never can tell when you might need a ritual circle to defend yourself from magical attack, or for its other most obvious use—keeping a denizen of the Nevernever a temporary prisoner.

One of the shelves had less on it than the others. At either end rested a candleholder, long since overrun with many colors of melted wax until they were nothing but mounds, like a honeybee Vesuvius. Books, mostly paperback romances, and various small and feminine articles took up the rest of the shelf, but for where a bleached human skull sat in the middle. I picked up a pencil and rapped it against the shelf. "Bob. Bob, wake up. Work to be done."

Twin points of orange and gold light kindled in the shadows of the skull's eye sockets, and grew brighter as I went about the room lighting half a dozen candles and a kerosene lamp. The skull rattled a little, and then said, "It's only a few hours from dawn, and you're just starting up? What gives?"

I started getting out beakers and vials and a small alcohol burner. "More trouble," I said. "It's been one hell of a day." I told Bob the Skull about the television studio, the vampire's challenge, the hit man, the missing Shroud, and the plague-filled corpse.

"Wow. You don't do things halfway, do you, Harry?"

"Advise now; critique later. I'm going to look into things and whip up a potion or two, and you're going to help."

"Right," Bob said. "Where do you want to start?"

"With Ortega. Where is my copy of the Accords?"

"Cardboard box." Bob said. "Third shelf, on the bottom row, behind the pickling jars."

I found the box and pawed through it until I had found a vellum scroll tied shut with a white ribbon. I opened it and peered down at the handwritten calligraphy. It started off with the word *Insomuch,* and the syntax got more opaque from there.

"I can't make heads or tails of this," I said. "Where's the section about duels?"

"Fifth paragraph from the end. You want the Cliff's Notes version?"

I rolled the scroll shut again. "Hit me."

"It's based on Code Duello," Bob said. "Well, technically it's based on much older rules that eventually inspired the Code Duello, but that's just chickens and eggs. Ortega is the challenger, and you're the challenged."

"I know that. I get to pick the weapons and the ground, right?"

"Wrong," Bob said. "You pick the weapons, but he gets to choose the time and location."

"Damn," I muttered. "I was going to take high noon out in a park somewhere. But I guess I can just say that we'll duel with magic."

"If it's one of the available choices. It almost always is."

"Who decides?"

"The vampires and the Council will pick from a list of neutral emissaries. The emissary decides."

I nodded. "So if I don't have it as an option I'm screwed, right? I mean, magic, wizard, kind of my bag."

Bob said. "Yeah, but be careful. It's got to be a weapon that he can use. If you pick one he can't, he can refuse it, and force you to take your second choice."

"Meaning what?"

"Meaning that regardless of what happens, if he doesn't want to fight you in magic, he won't have to. Ortega didn't get to be a warlord without thinking things through, Harry. Odds are that he has a good idea what you can do and has planned accordingly. What do you know about him?"

"Not much. Presumably he's tough."

Bob's eyelights stared at me for a minute. "Well, Napoléon, I'm sure he'll never overcome that kind of tactical genius."

I flicked my pencil at the skull in annoyance. It bounced off a nose hole. "Get to the point."

"The point is that you'd be better off taking something you can predict."

"I'm better off not fighting to begin with," I said. "Do I need to get a second?"

"You both do," Bob said. "The seconds will work out the

terms of the duel. His should be getting in touch with yours at some point."

"Uh. I don't have one."

Bob's skull turned a bit on its shelf and banged its forehead gently into the brick wall a few times. "Then get one, dolt. Obviously."

I got another pencil and a pad of yellow lined paper and wrote *To do* across the top, and *Ask Michael about duel* underneath it. "Okay. And I want you to find out whatever you can about Ortega before dawn."

"Check," Bob said. "I have your permission to come out?"

"Not yet. There's more."

Bob's eyelights rolled. "Of course there's more. My job sucks."

I got out a jug of distilled water and a can of Coke. I opened the can, took a sip, and said, "That corpse Murphy showed me. Plague curse?"

"Probably," Bob agreed. "But if it was really that many diseases, it was a big one."

"How big?"

"Bigger than that spell the Shadowman was using to tear hearts out a few years ago."

I whistled. "And he was running it off of thunderstorms and ceremonial rites, too. What would it take to power a curse that strong?"

"Curses aren't really my thing," Bob hedged. "But a lot. Like maybe tapping into a sorcerous ley line, or a human sacrifice."

I sipped more Coke, and shook my head. "Someone is playing some serious hardball then."

Bob mused, "Maybe the Wardens used it to get nasty on a Red Court agent."

"They wouldn't," I said. "They wouldn't use magic like that. Even if technically it was the diseases that killed the guy, it's too damn close to breaking the First Law."

"Who else would have that kind of power?" Bob asked me.

I turned to a fresh page and sketched out a rough version of the tattoo on the corpse. I held it up to show it to Bob. "Someone who didn't like this, maybe."

"Eye of Thoth," Bob supplied. "That the tattoo on the corpse?"

"Yeah. Was this guy in someone's secret club?"

"Maybe. The eye is a pretty popular occult symbol though, so you can't rule out the possibility that he was an independent."

"Okay," I said. "So who uses it?"

"Plenty of groups. Brotherhoods connected to the White Council, historic societies, a couple of fringe groups of occult scholars, personality cults, television psychics, comic book heroes—"

"I get the point," I said. I turned to a fresh page and from razor-sharp memory sketched out the symbol I'd seen on the demon Ursiel's forehead. "Do you recognize this?"

Bob's eyelights widened. "Are you insane? Harry, tear that paper up. Burn it."

I frowned. "Bob, wait a minute—"

"Do it now!"

The skull's voice was frightened, and I get nervous when Bob gets frightened. Not much can scare Bob out of his usual wiseass-commentator state of mind. I tore up the paper. "I guess you recognize it."

"Yeah. And I'm not having anything to do with that bunch."

"I didn't hear that, Bob. I need information on them. They're in town, they've taken a shot at me, and I'm betting they're after the Shroud."

"Let them have it," Bob said. "Seriously. You've got no idea the kind of power this group has."

"Fallen, I know," I said. "Order of the Blackened Denarius. But they have to play by the rules, right?"

"Harry, it isn't just the Fallen. The people they've taken are nearly as bad. They're assassins, poisoners, warriors, sorcerers—"

"Sorcerers?"

"The coins make them effectively immortal. Some of the Order have had a thousand years to practice, and maybe more. That much time, even modest talents can grow teeth. Never mind everything experience would have taught them, everything they could have found to make themselves stronger over the years. Even without infernal superpowers, they'd be badass."

I frowned, and tore the bits of paper into smaller bits. "Badass enough to manage that curse?"

"There's no question that they'd have the skill. Maybe enough that they wouldn't need as big a power source."

"Great," I said, and rubbed at my eyes. "All right, then. Big-leaguers all around. I want you to track down the Shroud."

"No can do," Bob said.

"Give me a break. How many pieces of two-thousand-year-old linen are in town?"

"That's not the point, Harry. The Shroud is . . ." Bob seemed to struggle to find words. "It doesn't exist on the same wavelength as me. It's out of my jurisdiction."

"What are you talking about?"

"I'm a spirit of intellect, Harry. Of reason, logic. The Shroud isn't about logic. It's an artifact of faith."

"What?" I demanded. "That doesn't make any sense."

"You don't know everything, Harry," Bob said. "You don't even know a lot. I can't touch this. I can't come anywhere near it. And if I even try, I'll be crossing boundaries I shouldn't. I'm not going up against angels, Dresden, Fallen, or otherwise."

I sighed, and lifted my hands. "Fine, fine. Is there someone I can talk to?"

Bob was quiet for a moment before he said, "Maybe. Ulsharavas."

"Ulsha-who?"

"Ulsharavas. She's an ally of the *loa,* an oracle spirit. There's details about halfway through your copy of *Dumont's Guide to Divinationators.*"

"How are her prices?"

"Reasonable," Bob said. "You've got everything you need for the calling. She isn't usually malicious."

"Isn't usually?"

"The *loa* are basically good guys, but they all have their darker aspects, too. Ulsharavas is a pretty gentle guide, but she's been harsh before. Don't let your guard down."

"I won't," I said, and frowned. "One more thing. Swing by Marcone's place and see if there's anything interesting there. You don't have to go all David Niven; just take a look around."

"You think Marcone's involved in this one?"

"His thugs already took a poke at me. I might as well find out whatever I can. I give you permission to leave in pursuit of that information, Bob. Get back before dawn. Oh, do we still have that recipe for the antivenom to vampire spit?"

A cloud of orange lights flowed out of the skull, across the table, and then up the stairs. Bob's voice, oddly modulated, floated back to me. "Red notebook. Don't forget to light the ward-flame while I'm gone."

"Yeah, yeah," I muttered. I gave Bob a minute to clear my wards, then got down a three-candle holder with green, yellow, and red candles on it. I lit the green one and set the candleholder aside. I got out *Dumont's Guide* and read over the entry for Ulsharavas. It looked pretty simple, though you couldn't be too careful whenever you called something in from the Nevernever.

I took a couple of minutes to gather what I'd need. The oracle spirit couldn't put together a body for herself, not even a nebulous cloud of light, like Bob could. She required a homunculus to manifest in the mortal world. Dumont recommended a newly dead corpse, but as the only one I was likely to find was my own, I needed a substitute. I found it in another box and plopped it down in the center of my summoning circle.

I added a cup of whiskey and a freshly opened tin of Prince Albert's chewing tobacco to the circle, the required down payment to convince Ulsharavas to show up. It was the last of my whiskey and the last of the tins of tobacco, so I added *Get more scotch and Prince Albert in a can* to my to-do list, and stuck it in my pocket.

I spent a couple of minutes sweeping the floor around the circle, so that I wouldn't kick a stray hair or bit of paper across the circle and flub it up. After a brief deliberation I chalked down another circle outside the copper one. Then I took a moment to go over the guide a last time, and to clear my head of distractions.

I took a deep breath and gathered in my strength. Then I focused, reached down, and touched the copper circle, willing a tiny jolt of power into it. The summoning circle closed. I felt it as a tingling prickle on the back of my neck and a faint warmth on the skin of my face. I repeated the process with the chalk circle, adding a second layer, and then knelt down by the circle, lifting both hands palms-up.

"Ulsharavas," I murmured, willing energy into the words. My voice shook oddly, skittering around tones in what seemed a random fashion. "Ulsharavas. Ulsharavas. One lost in ignorance seeks you. One darkened by the lack of knowledge seeks your light. Come, guardian of memory, sentinel of the yet to come. Accept this offering and join me here."

At the conclusion of the ritual words, I released the power I'd been holding, sending it coursing from me into the circle, and through it to seek out the oracle spirit in the Nevernever.

The response came immediately. A sudden swirl of light appeared within the copper circle, and briefly made the barrier around it visible as a curved plane of blue sparkles. The light drizzled down over the homunculus, and a moment later it twitched, then sat up.

"Welcome, oracle," I said. "Bob the Skull thought you might be of some help."

The homunculus sat up and stretched out pudgy arms. Then it blinked, looked at its arms, and rose to stare down at itself. It looked up at me with one eyebrow raised, and asked, in a tiny voice, "A Cabbage Patch doll? You expect me to help you while wearing *this*?"

It was a cute doll. Blond ringlets fell to her plush shoulders, and she wore a pink-and-blue calico dress, complete with matching ribbons and little black shoes. "Uh, yeah. Sorry," I said. "I didn't have anything else with two arms and two legs, and I'm pressed for time."

Ulsharavas the Cabbage Patch doll sighed and sat down in the circle, legs straight out like a teddy bear's. She struggled to pick up the comparatively large cup of whiskey, and drank it down. It looked like she was taking a pull from a rain barrel, but she downed the whiskey in one shot. I don't know where it went, given that the doll didn't actually have a mouth or a stomach, but none of it spilled onto the floor. That done, she thrust a tiny fist into the tobacco and stuffed a wad of it into her mouth.

"So," she said, between chews. "You want to know about the Shroud, and the people who stole it."

I lifted my eyebrows. "Uh. Yeah, actually. You're pretty good."

"There are two problems."

I frowned. "Okay. What are they?"

Ulsharavas peered at me and said, "First. I don't work for *bokkor*."

"I'm not a *bokkor*," I protested.

"You aren't a *houngun*. You aren't a *mambo*. That makes you a sorcerer."

"Wizard," I said. "I'm with the White Council."

The doll tilted her head. "You're stained," she said. "I can feel black magic on you."

"It's a long story," I said. "But mostly it isn't mine."

"Some of it is."

I frowned at the doll and then nodded. "Yeah. I've made a bad call or two."

"But honest," Ulsharavas noted. "Well enough. Second is my price."

"What did you have in mind?"

The doll spat to one side, flecks of tobacco landing on the

floor. "An honest answer to one question. Answer me and I will tell you what you seek."

"Yeah, right," I said. "You could just ask me for my Name. I've heard that one before."

"I didn't say you'd have to answer in full," the doll said. "I certainly do not wish to threaten you. But what you would answer, you must answer honestly."

I thought about it for a minute before I said, "All right. Done."

Ulsharavas scooped up more tobacco and started chomping. "Answer only this. Why do you do what you do?"

I blinked at her. "You mean tonight?"

"I mean always," she answered. "Why are you a wizard? Why do you present yourself openly? Why do you help other mortals as you do?"

"Uh," I said. I stood up and paced over to my table. "What else would I do?"

"Precisely," the doll said, and spat. "You could be doing many other things. You could be seeking a purpose in life in other careers. You could be sequestered and studying. You could be using your skills for material gain and living in wealth. Even in your profession as an investigator, you could do more to avoid confrontation than you do. But instead you consign yourself to a poor home, a dingy office, and the danger of facing all manner of mortal and supernatural foe. Why?"

I leaned back against my table, folded my arms, and frowned at the doll. "What the hell kind of question is that?"

"An important one," she said. "And one that you agreed to answer honestly."

"Well," I said. "I guess I wanted to do something to help people. Something I was good at."

"Is that why?" she asked.

I chewed over the thought for a moment. Why *had* I started doing this stuff? I mean, it seemed like every few months I was running up against situations that had the potential to horribly kill me. Most wizards never had the kind of problems I did. They stayed at home, minded their own business, and generally speaking went on about their lives. They did not challenge other supernatural forces. They didn't declare themselves to the public at large. They didn't get into trouble for sticking their noses in other people's business, whether or not they'd been paid to do so. They didn't start wars, get challenged to duels with vampire patriots, or get the windows shot out of their cars.

So why did I do it? Was it some kind of masochistic death wish? Maybe a psychological dysfunction of some sort?

Why?

"I don't know," I said, finally. "I guess I never thought about it all that much."

The doll watched me with unnerving intensity for a full minute before nodding. "Don't you think you should?"

I scowled down at my shoes, and didn't answer.

Ulsharavas took one last fistful of tobacco, and sat back down in her original position, settling her calico dress primly about her. "The Shroud and the thieves you seek have rented a small vessel docked in the harbor. It is a pleasure craft called the *Etranger*."

I nodded and exhaled through my nose. "All right then. Thank you for your help."

She lifted a tiny hand. "One thing more, wizard. You must know why the Knights of the White God wish you to stay away from the Shroud."

I arched an eyebrow. "Why?"

"They received part of a prophecy. A prophecy that told them that should you seek the Shroud, you will most assuredly perish."

"Only part of a prophecy?" I asked.

"Yes. Their Adversary concealed some of it from them."

I shook my head. "Why are you telling me this?"

"Because," Ulsharavas said. "You must hear the second half of the prophecy in order to restore the balance."

"Uh. Okay."

The doll nodded and fixed me with that unsettling, unblinking stare. "Should you seek the Shroud, Harry Dresden, you will most assuredly perish."

"All right," I said. "So what happens if I don't?"

The doll lay down on her back, and wisps of light began flowing back out of her, back from whence Ulsharavas had come. Her voice came to me quietly, as if from a great distance. "If you do not, they all die. And this city with them."

Chapter Nine

I hate cryptic warnings. I know, the whole cryptic-remark concept is part and parcel of the wizard gig, but it doesn't suit my style. I mean, what *good* is a warning like that? All three Knights and the population of Chicago would die if I didn't get involved—and my number would be up if I did. That sounded like the worst kind of self-fulfilling crap.

There's a case to be made for prophecy; don't get me wrong. Mortals, even wizards, all exist at a finite point in the flow of time. Or, to make it simple, if time is a river, then you and I are like pebbles in it. We exist in one spot at a time, occasionally jostled back and forth by the currents. Spirits don't always have the same kind of existence. Some of them are more like a long thread than a stone—their presence tenuous, but rippling upstream and down as a part of their existence, experiencing more of the stream than the pebble.

That's how oracle spirits know about the future and the past. They're living in them both at the same time they're delivering mysterious messages to you. That's why they only give brief warnings, or mysterious dreams or prophetic knock-knock jokes, or however they drop their clues. If they tell you too much, it will change the future that they're experiencing, so they have to give out the advice with a light touch.

I know. It makes my head hurt too.

I don't put much stock in prophecy. As extensive and aware as these spirits might be, they aren't all-knowing. And as nutty as people are, I don't buy that any spirit is going to be able to keep an absolute lock on every possible temporal outcome.

Maybe-genuine prophecies aside, I could hardly drop the case now. In the first place, I'd been paid up front, and I didn't have the kind of financial breathing space I would need to be able to turn down the money and pay my bills at the same time.

In the second place, the risk of imminent death just didn't hit me the same way it used to. It wasn't that it didn't scare me. It did, in that kind of horrible, uncertain way that left me with nothing to focus my fears upon. But I've beaten risks before. I could do it again.

You want to know another reason I didn't back off? I don't like getting pushed around. I don't like threats. As well-intentioned and polite and caring as Michael's threat had been, it still made me want to punch someone in the nose. The oracle's prophecy had been another threat, of sorts, and I don't let spirits from the Nevernever determine what I'm going to do, either.

Finally, if the prophecy was right, Michael and his brother Knights could be in danger, and they had saved my skinny wizard's ass not long ago. I could help them. They might be heaven-on-wheels when it came to taking on bad guys in a fight, but they weren't investigators. They couldn't run these thieves down the way I could. It was just a question of making them see reason. Once I'd convinced them that the prophecy they'd received wasn't wholly correct, everything would be fine.

Yeah, right.

I shoved those thoughts aside, and checked the clock. I wanted to move on Ulsharavas's tip as soon as possible, but I was beat and likely to make mistakes. With all the bad guys running around town, there was no sense in going out there into the dark, exhausted and unprepared. I'd wait for the potions to be ready and Bob to come back from his mission, at least. Sunlight would cut down on the risk as well, since Red Court vampires got incinerated by it—and I doubted these Denarian fruitcakes would get along with it either.

Thus prioritized, I checked my notes, and started putting together a couple of potions that would offer me a few hours of protection from the narcotic venom of the Red Court. The potions were simple ones. Brewing any kind of potion required a base liquid, and then several other ingredients meant to bind the magic put into the potion to the desired effect. One ingredient was linked to each of the five senses, then one to the mind and one to the spirit.

In this case, I wanted something that would offset the venomous saliva of the Red Court vampires, a narcotic that rendered those exposed to it passively euphoric. I needed a potion that would ruin the pleasurable sensations of the poison.

I used stale coffee as my base ingredient. To that I added hairs from a skunk, for scent. A small square of sandpaper for touch. I tossed in a small photo of Meat Loaf, cut from a magazine, for sight. A rooster's crow I'd stored in a small quartz crystal went in for hearing, and a powdered aspirin for taste. I cut the surgeon general's warning label from a pack of cigarettes and chopped it fine to add in for the mind, and then lit a stick of the incense I sometimes used while meditating and wafted some of the smoke into the two bottles for the spirit. Once the potions were bubbling over a burner, I drew in my wearied will and released power into the mixes, suffusing them with energy. They fizzed and frothed with gratifying enthusiasm.

I let them simmer for a while, then took them from the fire and emptied them into a pair of small sports-drink bottles. After that, I slumped on a stool and waited for Bob to come home.

I must have nodded off, because when my phone rang, I jerked myself up straight and nearly fell off my stool. I clambered up the ladder and picked up the phone.

"Dresden."

"Hoss," said a weather-beaten voice on the other end. Ebenezar McCoy, a sometime teacher of mine, sounded businesslike. "Did I wake you up?"

"No, sir," I said. "I was up anyway. Working on a case."

"You sound tired as a coal-mine mule."

"Been up all night."

"Uh-huh," Ebenezar said. "Hoss, I just called to let you know not to worry about this duel nonsense. We're going to slap it down."

By "we," Ebenezar meant the Senior Council members. Seven of the most experienced wizards on the White Council held positions of particular authority, especially during times of crisis, when quick decisions were needed. Ebenezar had turned down his chance at a seat on the Senior Council for nearly fifty years. He took it only recently to block a potentially fatal political attack directed against yours truly by some of the more conservative (read, fanatic) members of the White Council.

"Slap it down? No, don't do that."

"What?" Ebenezar said. "You *want* to fight this duel? Did you fall and hit your head, boy?"

I rubbed at my eyes. "Tell me about it. I'll work out something to give me a shot at winning."

"Sounds like your wagon's already pretty full to be letting this vampire push you."

"He knew where to push," I said. "Ortega brought a bunch of goons into town. Vampires and straight hit men, too. He says that if I don't face him he's going to have a bunch of people I know killed."

Ebenezar spat something in what I presumed was Gaelic. "You'd better tell me what happened, then."

I told Ebenezar all about my encounter with Ortega. "Oh, and a contact of mine says that the Red Court is divided over the issue. There are lots of them who don't want the war to end."

"Of course they don't," Ebenezar said. "That fool of a Merlin won't let us take the offensive. He thinks his fancy wards will make them give up."

"How are they working out?" I asked.

"Well enough for now," Ebenezar admitted. "One major attack has been pushed back by the wards. No more Council members have been killed in attacks on their homes, though the Red Court's allies are putting pressure on ours, and a few Wardens have died on intelligence-gathering missions. But it isn't going to last. You can't win a war sitting behind a wall and hoping the enemy decides to leave."

"What do you think we should do?"

"Officially," Ebenezar said, "we follow the Merlin's lead. More than anything, now, we need to stay together."

"What about unofficially?"

"Think about it," Ebenezar snorted. "If we just sit here, the vampires are going to take apart or drive away our allies and then we'll have to take them all on alone. Look, Hoss. Are you sure about this duel?"

"Hell no," I said. "I just didn't see much choice. I'll figure out something. If I win, it might be worth it to the Council. Neutral territory for meeting and negotiating could come in handy."

Ebenezar sighed. "Aye. The Merlin will think the same thing." He was quiet for a moment before he said, "Not much like the days on the farm, is it, Hoss?"

"Not much," I agreed.

"Do you remember that telescope we set up in the loft?"

Ebenezar had taught me what I knew of astronomy, on long, dark summer evenings in the Ozark hills, hay doors to the barn's loft open, stars overhead shining in the country darkness by the millions. "I remember. That asteroid we discovered that turned out to be an old Russian satellite."

"Asteroid Dresden was a better name than Kosmos Five." He chuckled and added, as an afterthought, "Do you remember whatever happened to that telescope and such? I kept meaning to ask you but I never got around to it."

"We packed it in that steamer trunk in the horse stall."

"With the observation logs?"

"Yeah," I said.

"Oh, that's right," Ebenezar said. "Obliged."

"Sure."

"Hoss, we'll agree to the duel if that's what you want. But be careful."

"I don't plan to roll over and die," I said. "But if something should happen to me . . ." I coughed. "Well, if it does, there are some papers in my lab. You'll know how to find them. Some people I'd like to make sure are protected."

"Of course," Ebenezar said. "But I'm likely to carry on cranky if I have to drive all the way up to Chicago twice in as many years."

"Hate for that to happen."

"Luck, Hoss."

"Thanks."

I hung up the phone, rubbed tiredly at my eyes, and stomped back down to the lab. Ebenezar hadn't come out and said it, but the offer had been there, behind the old man's talk of days gone by. He'd been offering me sanctuary at his farm. It wasn't that I didn't like Chicago, but the offer was a tempting one. After a couple of rough years slugging it out with various bad guys, a quiet year or two on the farm near Hog Hollow, Missouri, sounded tempting.

Of course, the safety offered in that image was an illusion. Ebenezar's place was going to be as well protected as any wizard's on earth, and the old man himself could be a terrible foe. But the Red Court of vampires had a big network supporting it and they didn't generally bother to play fair. They'd destroyed a wizard stronghold the previous summer, and if they'd cracked that place they could do it to Ebenezar's Ozark hideaway too. If I went there and they found out about it, it would make the old man's farm too tempting a target to pass by.

Ebenezar knew that as well as I did, but he and I shared a common trait—he doesn't like bullies either. He'd be glad to have me and he'd fight to the death against the Reds if they came. But I didn't want to draw that kind of thing down on him. I was grateful for the old man's support, but I owed him more than that.

Besides, I was almost as well protected here in Chicago. My own wards, defensive screens of magic to protect my apartment, had kept me safe and alive for a couple of years, and the presence of a large mortal population kept the vampires from trying anything completely overt. Wizards and vampires notwithstanding, everyone in the supernatural community knew damned well that plain old vanilla mortals were one of the most dangerous forces on the planet, and went out of their way not to become too noticeable to the population at large.

The population at large, meanwhile, did everything it possibly could to keep from noticing the supernatural, so that worked out. The vampires had taken a poke or two at me since the war began, but it hadn't been anything I couldn't handle, and they didn't want to risk being any more obvious.

Thus, Ortega and his challenge.

So how the hell was I supposed to fight a duel with him without using magic?

My bed called to me, but that thought was enough to keep me from answering. I paced around my living room for a while, trying to think of some kind of weapon that would give me the most advantage. Ortega was stronger, faster, more experienced, and more resistant to injury than me. How the hell was I supposed to pick a weapon to go up against that? I supposed if the duel could be worked into some kind of pizza-eating contest I might have a shot, but somehow I didn't think that the Pizza Spress Hungry Man Special was on the list of approved weaponry.

I checked the clock and frowned. Dawn was only minutes away, and Bob wasn't back yet. Bob was a spirit being, a spirit of intellect from one of the more surreal corners of the Nevernever. He wasn't evil as much as he was magnificently innocent of any kind of morality, but as a spirit, daylight was a threat to him as surely as it was to the vampires of the Red Court. If he got caught out in it, it could kill him.

Dawn was about two minutes off before Bob returned, flowing down the ladder and toward the skull.

Something was wrong.

Bob's manifestation of a candle flame–colored cloud of swirling lights bobbed drunkenly left and right on its way back to the shelf with the skull. Purple globs of glowing plasm dribbled from the cloud in a steady trail, striking the floor, where they winked out into blobs of transparent goo. The cloud flowed into the skull, and after a moment, faint violet flames appeared in the skull's empty eye sockets.

"Ow," Bob said, his voice tired.

"Hell's bells," I muttered. "Bob, you all right?"

"No."

Bob? Monosyllabic? Crap. "Is there anything I can do to help?"

"No," Bob said, faintly. "Rest."

"But—"

"Report," Bob said. "Have to."

Right. He'd been sent out on a mission and he was feeling pressured to finish it. "What happened?"

"Wards," Bob said. "Marcone's."

I felt my mouth fall open. "What?"

"Wards," Bob repeated.

I sat down on my stool. "How the hell did Marcone get wards?"

Bob's tone became a shade contemptuous. "Magic?"

The insult relieved me a little. If he was able to be a wiseass he'd probably be okay. "Could you tell who did the wards?"

"No. Too good."

Damn. A spell had to get up pretty early in the morning to get around Bob. Maybe he'd been hurt worse than I thought. "What about Ortega?"

"Rothchild," Bob said. "Half a dozen vamps with him. Maybe a dozen mortals."

Bob's eyelights flickered and guttered. I couldn't risk losing Bob by pushing him too hard—and spirit or not, he wasn't immortal. He wasn't afraid of bullets or knives, but there were things that could kill him. "Good enough for now," I said. "Tell me the rest later. Get some sleep."

Bob's eyelights flickered out without another word.

I frowned at the skull for a while and then shook my head. I collected my potion bottles, cleaned up the work area, and turned to leave and let Bob get some rest.

I was leaning over the wardflames to blow them out when the green candle hissed and shrank to a pinpoint of light. The yellow candle beside it flared up without warning, brighter than an incandescent lightbulb.

My heart started pounding and nervous fear danced over the back of my neck.

Something was approaching my apartment. That's what it meant when the flame spread from the green to the yellow candle. Warning spells I had threaded out to a couple of blocks from my house had sensed the approach of supernatural hostility.

The yellow candle dimmed, and the red candle exploded into a flame the size of my head.

Stars and stones. The intruder that had triggered the warning system the wardflames were linked to was getting closer; and it was something big. Or else a lot of somethings. They were heading in fast to set off the red candle so quickly, only a few dozen yards from my house.

I dashed up the ladder from the lab and got ready to fight.

Chapter Ten

I got up the ladder in time to hear a car door shut outside my apartment. I'd lost my .357 during a battle between the Faerie Courts hosted on clouds over Lake Michigan the previous midsummer, so I'd moved my .44 from the office to home. It hung on a gun belt on a peg beside the door, just over a wire basket I'd attached to the wall. Holy water, a couple cloves of garlic, vials of salt, and iron filings filled the basket, intended to be door prizes for anything that showed up in an attempt to suck my blood, carry me off to faerieland, or sell me stale cookies.

The door itself was reinforced steel, and could stand up to punishment better than the wall around it. I'd had a demon come a-knocking before, and I didn't want an encore performance. I couldn't afford new furniture, even secondhand.

I belted on the gun, shook out my shield bracelet, and took up my staff and blasting rod. Anything that came through my door would have to contend with my threshold, the aura of protective energy around any home. Most supernatural things didn't do so well with thresholds. After that, they'd have to force their way past my wards—barriers of geometrically aligned energy that would block out physical or magical intrusion, turning that energy back upon its source. A small, gentle push at my wards would result in a similar push against whatever was trying to get in. A swift or heavy push would result in more energy feeding back onto the attacker. Within the wards were sigils of fire and ice, which were designed to deliver bursts of destructive energy about as powerful as your average land mine.

It was a solid and layered defense. With luck, it should be

enough to stop a considerable amount of threat from even reaching my door.

And since I'm such a lucky guy, I took a deep breath, pointed my blasting rod at the door, and waited.

It didn't take long. I expected flashes of magical discharge, demon howls, maybe some kind of pyrotechnics as evil magic clashed against my own defensive spells. Instead I got seven polite knocks.

I peered at the door suspiciously and then asked, "Who's there?"

A low, rough man's voice growled, "The Archive."

What the hell. "The Archive who?"

Evidently the speaker didn't have a sense of humor. "The Archive," the voice repeated firmly. "The Archive has been appointed emissary in this dispute, and is here to speak to Wizard Dresden about the duel."

I frowned at the door. I vaguely remembered mention of an Archive of some sort during the last White Council meeting I'd attended, as a neutral party. At the time, I'd assumed it had been some sort of arcane library. I'd had other things on my mind at the time, and I hadn't been listening too closely. "How do I know who you are?"

There was a rasp of paper on stone, and an envelope slid under my door, one corner poking out. "Documentation, Wizard Dresden," the voice replied. "And a pledge to abide by the laws of hospitality during this visit."

Some of the tension left my shoulders, and I lowered the gun. That was one good thing about dealing with the supernatural community. If something gave you its word, you could trust it. Within reason.

Then again, maybe that was just me. Of all the things I'd encountered, I'd been more of a weasel about keeping my word than any of them. Maybe that's why I was leery about trusting someone else.

I picked up the envelope and unfolded a sheet of plain paper certifying that its bearer had been approved by the White Council to act as emissary in the matter of the duel. I passed my hand over it and muttered a quick charm with the last password I'd gotten from the Wardens, and in response a brief glowing pentacle appeared centered on the paper like a bioluminescent watermark. It was legit.

I folded the paper closed again, but I didn't set my rod and staff aside just yet. I undid the dead bolt, muttered my wards back, and opened the door enough to see outside.

A man stood on my doorstep. He was nearly as tall as me but looked a lot more solid, with shoulders wide enough to make the loose black jacket he wore fit tightly on his upper arms. He wore a navy blue shirt and stood so that I could see the wrinkles caused by the straps of a shoulder rig. A black ball cap reined in dark golden hair that might have fallen to his shoulders. He hadn't shaved in a few days, and had a short, white scar below his mouth that highlighted the cleft in his chin. His eyes were grey-blue and empty of any expression in a way I had seldom seen. Not like he was hiding what he felt. More like there was simply nothing there.

"Dresden?" he asked.

"Yeah." I eyed him up and down. "You don't look very Archive-esque."

He lifted his eyebrows, a mildly interested expression. "I'm Kincaid. You're wearing a gun."

"Only when company comes over."

"I haven't seen any of the Council's people carrying a gun. Good for you." He turned and waved his hand. "This shouldn't take long."

I glanced past him. "What do you mean?"

A second later, a little girl started down my stairs, one hand carefully on the guide rail. She was adorable, maybe seven years old, her blond hair still baby-fine and straight, clipped neatly at her shoulders and held back with a hairband. She wore a plain little corduroy dress with a white blouse and shiny black shoes, and her coat was a puffy down-filled jacket that seemed like a bit of overkill for the weather.

I looked from the kid to Kincaid and said, "You can't be bringing a child into this."

"Sure I can," Kincaid said.

"What, couldn't you find a baby-sitter?"

The child stopped a couple of steps up so that her face was even with my own and said, her voice serious and marked with a faint British accent, "He *is* my baby-sitter."

I felt my eyebrows shoot up.

"Or more accurately my driver," she said. "Are you going to let us in? I prefer not to remain outdoors."

I stared at the kid for a second. "Aren't you a little short for a librarian?"

"I am not a librarian," the child said. "I am the Archive."

"Hang on a minute," I said. "What do you—"

"I am the Archive," the child said, her voice steady and assured. "I assume that your wards detected my presence. They seemed functional."

"You?" I said. "You've got to be kidding." I extended my senses gingerly toward her. The air around her fairly hummed with power, different from what I would expect around another wizard, but strong all the same, a quiet and dangerous buzz like that around high-tension power lines.

I had to suppress a sudden rush of apprehension from showing on my face. The girl had power. She had a hell of a lot of power. Enough to make me wonder if my wards would be enough to stop her if she decided to come through them. Enough to make me think of little Billy Mumy as the omnipotent brat on that old episode of *The Twilight Zone*.

She regarded me with implacable blue eyes I suddenly did not want to take the chance of looking into. "I can explain it to you, wizard," she said. "But not out here. I have neither an interest nor an inclination to do you any harm. Perhaps the opposite."

I frowned at her. "Promise?"

"Promise," the child said solemnly.

"Cross your heart and hope to die?"

She drew an X over her puffy jacket with one index finger. "You don't know how much."

Kincaid took a couple of steps up and glanced warily around the street. "Make up your mind, Dresden. I'm not keeping her out here for long."

"What about him?" I asked the Archive, and nodded toward Kincaid. "Can he be trusted?"

"Kincaid?" the girl asked, her voice whimsical. "Can you be trusted?"

"You're paid up through April," the man replied, his eyes still scanning the street. "After that I might get a better offer."

"There," the girl said to me. "Kincaid can be trusted until April. He's an ethical man, in his way." She shivered and put her hands into the pockets of her puffy coat. She hunched up her shoulders and watched my face.

Generally speaking, my instincts about people (who weren't women who might potentially end up doing adult things with me) were pretty good. I trusted the Archive's promise. Besides, she was darling and looked like she was starting to get cold. "Fine," I said. "Come inside."

I stepped back and opened the door. The Archive came in and told Kincaid, "Wait with the car. Come fetch me in ten minutes."

Kincaid frowned at her, and then me. "You sure?"

"Quite." The Archive stepped in past me, and started taking off her coat. "Ten minutes. I want to head back before rush hour begins."

Kincaid fixed his empty eyes on me and said, "Be nice to the little girl, wizard. I've handled your kind before."

"I get more threats before nine a.m. than most people get all day," I responded, and shut the door on him. Purely for effect, I locked it too.

Me, petty? Surely not.

I lit a couple of candles in order to get a little more light into the living room and stirred up the fire, adding more wood to it as soon as the embers were glowing. While I did, the Archive took off her coat, folded it neatly over the arm of one of my lumpy comfy chairs, and sat down, back straight, hands folded in her lap. Her little black shoes waved back and forth above the floor.

I frowned at her. It's not like I don't like kids or anything, but I hadn't had much experience with them. Now I had one sitting there wanting to talk to me about a duel. How the hell did a child, no matter how large her vocabulary, manage to get appointed an emissary?

"So, uh. What's your name?"

She said, "The Archive."

"Yeah, I got that part. But I meant your name. What people call you."

"The Archive," she repeated. "I do not have a familiar name. I am the Archive, and have always been the Archive."

"You're not human," I said.

"Incorrect. I am a seven-year-old human child."

"With no name? Everybody has a name," I said. "I'm can't go around calling you the Archive."

The girl tilted her head to one side, arching a pale gold eyebrow. "Then what would you call me?"

"Ivy," I said at once.

"Why Ivy?" she asked.

"You're the Archive, right? Arch-ive. Arch-ivy. Ivy."

The girl pursed her lips. "Ivy," she said, and then nodded slowly. "Ivy. Very well." She regarded me for a moment and then said, "Go ahead and ask the question, wizard. We might as well get it out of the way."

"Who are you?" I asked. "Why are you called the Archive?"

Ivy nodded. "The thorough explanation is too complex to convey to you here. But in short, I am the living memory of mankind."

"What do you mean, the living memory?"

"I am the sum of human knowledge, passed down from generation to generation, mother to daughter. Culture, science, philosophy, lore, tradition. I hold the accumulated memories of a thousand generations of mankind. I take in all that is written and spoken. I study. I learn. That is my purpose, to procure and preserve knowledge."

"So you're saying that if it's been written down, you know it?"

"I know it. I understand it."

I sat down slowly on the couch, and stared at her. Hell's bells. It was almost too much to comprehend. Knowledge is power, and if Ivy was telling me the truth, she knew more than anyone alive. "How did you get this gig?"

"My mother passed it on to me," she replied. "As I was born, just as she received it when she was born."

"And your mother lets a mercenary drive you around?"

"Certainly not. My mother is dead, wizard." She frowned. "Not dead, technically. But all that she knew and was came into me. She became an empty cup. A persistent vegetative state." Her eyes grew a little wistful, distant. "She's free of it. But she certainly isn't alive in the most vital sense."

"I'm sorry," I said.

"I wouldn't know why. I know my mother. And all before her." She put a finger to her temple. "It's all in here."

"You know how to use magic?" I asked.

"I prefer calculus."

"But you can do it."

"Yes."

Yikes. If the reaction of my wards was any indication, it meant that she was at least as strong as any Wizard of the White Council. Probably stronger. But if that was true . . .

"If you know that much," I said, "if you are that powerful, why did you hire a bodyguard to bring you here?"

"My feet don't reach the pedals."

I felt like smacking myself on the forehead. "Oh, right."

Ivy nodded. "In preparation for the duel, I will need some information. Namely, where I might contact your second and what weapon you prefer for the duel."

"I don't have a second yet."

Ivy arched an eyebrow. "Then you have until sundown this evening to gain one. Otherwise the match, and your life, will be forfeit."

"Forfeit? Uh, how would the forfeit be collected?"

The little girl stared at me for a silent moment. Then she said, "I'll do it."

I swallowed, a cold chill rippling over me. I believed her. I believed that she could, and I believed that she would. "Um. Okay. Look, I haven't exactly chosen a weapon yet, either. If I—"

"Simply choose one, Mister Dresden. Will, skill, energy, or flesh."

"Wait," I said. "I thought I got to pick swords or guns or something."

Ivy shook her head. "Read your copy of the Accords. I choose what is available, and I choose the ancient ways. You may match wills with your opponent to gauge which of you is the most determined. You may match your skill at arms against his, each of you with weaponry of your individual choosing. You may wield energy forces against each other. Or you may challenge him to unarmed combat." She considered. "I would advise against the last."

"Thanks," I muttered. "I'll take magic. Energy."

"You realize, of course, that he will decline in that venue and you will be forced to choose another."

I sighed. "Yeah. But until he does, I don't have to pick another one, right?"

"Indeed," Ivy acknowledged.

There was a knock on the door, and I got up to open it. Kincaid nodded to me, then leaned in and said, "Ten minutes."

"Thank you, Kincaid," Ivy said. She rose, drew a business card from her pocket, and passed it to me. "Have your second call this number."

I took the card and nodded. "I will."

Just then, Mister emerged from my bedroom and lazily arched his back. Then he padded over to me and rubbed his shoulder against my shin by way of greeting.

Ivy blinked and looked down at Mister, and her child's face was suddenly suffused with a pure and uncomplicated joy. She said, "Kitty!" and immediately knelt down to pet Mister. Mister apparently liked her. He started purring louder, and walked around Ivy, rubbing up against her while she petted him and spoke to him quietly.

Hell's bells. It was adorable. She was just a kid.

A kid who knew more than any mortal alive. A kid with a scary amount of magical power. A kid who would kill me if I didn't show up to the duel. But still a kid.

I glanced up at Kincaid, who stood frowning down at Ivy fawning all over Mister. He shook his head and muttered, "Now, that's just creepy."

Chapter Eleven

❧❦

Ivy seemed reluctant to leave off petting Mister, but she and Kincaid left without further conversation. I shut the door after them and leaned on it, listening with my eyes closed until they'd gone. I didn't feel as tired as I should have. Probably because I had a wealth of experience that suggested I would get a lot more worn out before I got a real chance to rest.

Mister rubbed up against my legs until I'd leaned down to pet him, after which he promptly walked over to his food bowl, ignoring me altogether. I grabbed a Coke from the icebox while he ate, absently pouring a bit onto a saucer and leaving it on the floor by Mister. By the time I'd finished it, I'd made up my mind about what I had to do next.

Make phone calls.

I called the number Vincent had left for me first. I expected to reach an answering service, but to my surprise Vincent's voice, tense and anxious, said, "Yes?"

"It's Harry Dresden," I said. "I wanted to check in with you."

"Ah, yes, just a moment," Vincent said. I heard him say something, caught a bit of conversation in the background, and then heard him walking and a door shut behind him. "The police," he said. "I've been working with them throughout the evening."

"Any luck?" I asked.

"God only knows," Vincent said. "But from my perspective, it seems the only thing accomplished is deciding which department is going to handle the investigation."

"Homicide?" I guessed.

Vincent's tired voice became dry. "Yes. Though the mind boggles at the chain of logic that led to it."

"Election year. City management is politicking," I said. "But once you start dealing with the actual police personnel, you should be all right. There are good people in every department."

"One hopes. Have you found anything?"

"I've got a lead. I don't know how good. The thieves might be on a small craft in the harbor. I'm heading down there presently."

"Very well," Vincent said.

"If the lead is good, do you want me to call CPD?"

"I'd rather you contacted me first," Vincent said. "I am still uncertain of how much trust to place in the local police. I cannot help but think it must have been the reason the thieves fled here— that they possessed some contact or advantage with the local authorities. I'd like as much time as possible to decide whom to trust."

I frowned and thought about Marcone's flunkies taking a shot at me. Chicago PD had an unfair reputation for corruption, thanks in part to the widespread mob activity during Prohibition. It was inaccurate, but people were people, and people aren't immune to being bought. Marcone had attained police-only information with disturbing speed before. "Might be smart. I'll check it out and let you know. Shouldn't be more than an hour or two."

"Very good. Thank you, Mister Dresden. Is there anything else?"

"Yeah," I said. "I should have thought of this last night. Do you have any pieces of the Shroud?"

"Pieces?" Vincent asked.

"Scraps or threads. I know that many samples were analyzed back in the seventies. Do you have access to any of those pieces?"

"Very possibly. Why?"

I had to remind myself that Vincent seemed to be largely a nonbeliever in the supernatural, so I couldn't come out and say that I wanted to use thaumaturgy to track down the Shroud. "To confirm identification when I find it. I don't want to get foxed with a decoy."

"Of course. I'll make a call," Vincent said. "Get a sample FedExed here. Thank you, Mister Dresden."

I said good-bye, hung up, and stared at the phone for a minute. Then I took a deep breath and dialed Michael's number.

Even though the sky was barely light with morning, the phone rang only once before a woman's voice said, "Hello?"

This was my nightmare. "Oh. Uh, hello, Charity. It's Harry Dresden."

"Hi!" the voice said brightly. "This isn't Charity though."

So maybe it wasn't my nightmare. It was my nightmare's oldest daughter. "Molly?" I asked. "Wow, you sound all grown-up now."

She laughed. "Yeah, the breast fairy came to visit and everything. Did you want to talk to my mom?"

Some might find it significant that it took me a second to realize she wasn't being literal about the faerie. Sometimes I hate my life. "Well, um. Is your dad around?"

"So you *don't* want to talk to Mom, check," she said. "He's working on the addition. Let me get him."

She set the phone down and I heard footsteps walking away. In the background, I could hear recorded children's voices singing, the rattle of plates and forks, and people talking. Then there was a rustling sound, and a thump as the handset on the other end must have fallen to the floor. Then I heard the sound of heavy, squishy breathing.

"Harry," sighed another voice from what must have been the same room. She sounded much like Molly but less cheerful. "No, no, honey, don't play with the phone. Give that to me, please." The phone rattled some more, the woman said, "Thank you, sweetie," and then she picked up the phone and said, "Hello? Anyone there?"

For a second I was tempted to remain silent, or possibly try to imitate a recording of the operator, but I steeled myself against that. I didn't want to let myself get rattled. I was pretty sure that Charity could smell fear, even over the phone. It could trigger an attack. "Hello, Charity. It's Harry Dresden. I was calling to speak to Michael."

There was a second of silence during which I couldn't help but imagine the way Michael's wife's eyes must have narrowed. "I suppose it was inevitable," she said. "Naturally if there is a situation so dangerous as to require all three of the Knights, you come crawling out of whatever hole you live in."

"Actually, this is sort of unrelated."

"I assumed it was. Your idiocy tends to strike at the worst possible place and time."

"Oh, come on, Charity, that's not fair."

Growing anger made her voice clearer and sharper, if no louder. "No? At the one time in the last year that Michael most needs to be focused on his duty, to be alert and careful, you arrive to distract him."

Anger warred with guilt for dominance of my reaction. "I'm trying to help."

"He has scars from the last time you helped, Mister Dresden."

I felt like slamming the receiver against the wall until it broke, but I restrained myself again. I couldn't stop the anger from making my words bite, though. "You're never going to give me an inch, are you?"

"You don't deserve an inch."

I said, "Is that why you named your son after me?"

"That was Michael," Charity said. "I was still on drugs, and the paperwork was done when I woke up."

I kept my voice calm. Mostly. "Look, Charity. I'm real sorry you feel the way you do, but I need to talk to Michael. Is he there or not?"

The line clicked as someone else picked up another extension and Molly said, "Sorry, Harry, but my dad isn't here. Sanya says he went out to pick up some doughnuts."

"Molly," Charity said, her voice hard. "It's a school day. Don't dawdle."

"Uh-oh," Molly said. "I swear, it's like she's telepathic or something."

I could almost hear Charity grinding her teeth. "That isn't funny, Molly. Get off the line."

Molly sighed and said, "Surrender, Dorothy," before she hung up. I choked on a sudden laugh, and tried to turn it into a series of coughs for Charity's benefit.

From the tone of her voice, she hadn't been fooled. "I'll give him a message."

I hesitated. Maybe I should ask to wait for him to return. There wasn't any love lost between Charity and myself, and if she didn't pass word along to Michael, or if she delayed before telling him, it could mean my death. Michael and the other Knights were busy with their pursuit of the Shroud, and God only knew if I'd be able to get in touch with him again today. On the other hand, I had neither the time nor the attention to spare to sit there butting heads with Charity until Michael returned.

Charity had been unreservedly hostile to me for as long as I had known her. She loved her husband ferociously, and feared for his safety—especially when he worked with me. In my head, I knew that her antagonism wasn't wholly without basis. Michael had been busted up several times when teamed up with me. During the last such outing, a bad guy gunning for me had nearly killed Charity and her unborn child, little Harry. Now she worried about the consequences that might be visited on her other children as well.

I knew that. But it still hurt.

I had to make a decision—to trust her or not. I decided to do it. Charity might not like me, but she was no coward and no liar. She knew Michael would want her to tell him.

"Well, Mister Dresden?" Charity asked.

"Just let him know that I need to talk to him."

"Regarding?"

For a second, I debated passing Michael my tip on the Shroud. But Michael believed that I was going to get killed if I got involved. He took protecting his friends seriously, and if he knew that I was poking around he might be inclined to knock me unconscious and lock me in a closet now and apologize later. I decided against it.

"Tell him that I need a second by sundown tonight or bad things will happen."

"To who?" Charity asked.

"Me."

She paused, then said, "I'll give him your message."

And then she hung up on me.

I hung up the phone, frowning. "That pause wasn't significant," I told Mister. "It doesn't mean that she was chewing over the thought of intentionally getting me killed in order to protect her husband and children."

Mister regarded me with that mystic-distance focus in his feline eyes. Or maybe that was the look he got when his brain waves flatlined. Either way, it was neither helpful nor reassuring.

"I'm not worried," I said. "Not one bit."

Mister's tail twitched.

I shook my head, got my stuff together, and headed out to investigate the lead at the harbor.

Chapter Twelve

<del>⋙ ⋘</del>

When I first came to Chicago I thought of a harbor as a giant bowl of ocean with ships and boats in the foreground and the faded outline of the buildings on the far side in the background. I had always imagined political subversives dressed up as tribal natives and a huge hit in the profit margin of the East India Company.

Burnham Harbor looked like the parking lot of an oceangoing Wal-Mart. It might have been able to hold a football field or three. White wharves stretched out over the water with pleasure boats and small fishing vessels in rows within a placid oval of water. The scent of the lake was one part dead fish, one part algae-coated rock, and one part motor oil. I parked in the lot up the hill from the harbor, got out, and made sure I had my equipment with me. I wore my force ring on my right hand and my shield bracelet on my left wrist, and my blasting rod thumped against my leg where I had tied it to the inside of my leather duster. I'd added a can of self-defense spray to my arsenal, and I slipped it into my pants pocket. I would rather have had my gun, but toting it around in my pocket was a felony. The pepper spray wasn't.

I locked up the car and felt a sudden, slithering pressure on my back—my instincts' way of screaming that someone was watching me. I kept my head down, my hands in my pockets, and walked toward the harbor. I didn't rubberneck around, but I tried to get a look at everything while moving only my eyes.

I didn't see anyone, but I couldn't shake the impression that I was being observed. I doubted it was anyone from the Red Court. The morning hadn't reached full brightness yet, but it was still light enough to parboil a vampire. That didn't rule out any number of other flavors of assassin, though. And it was possible that if the thieves were here, they were keeping an eye on everyone coming and going.

All I could do was walk steadily and hope that whoever was watching me wasn't one of Marcone's thugs, a vampire groupie or a rent-a-gun aiming a rifle at my back from several hundred yards away.

I found the *Etranger* in a few minutes, moored at a slip not far from the entrance. It was a pretty little ship, a white pleasure boat roomy enough to house a comfortable cabin. The *Etranger* wasn't new, but she looked neat and well cared for. A Canadian flag hung from a little stand on the ship's afterdeck. I moved on past the ship at a steady pace and Listened as I did.

Listening is a trick I'd picked up when I was a kid. Not many people have worked out the trick of it, blocking out all other sound in order to better hear one sound in particular—such as distant voices. It isn't as much about magic, I think, as it is focus and discipline. But the magic helps.

"Unacceptable," said a quiet, female voice in the *Etranger*'s cabin. It was marked with a gentle accent, both Spanish and British. "The job entailed a great deal more expense than was originally estimated. I'm raising the price to reflect this, nothing more." There was a short pause, and then the woman said, "Would you like an invoice for your tax return then? I told you the quote was only an estimate. It happens." Another pause, and then the woman said, "Excellent. As scheduled, then."

I stared out at the lake, just taking in the view, and strained to hear anything else. Evidently the conversation was over. I checked around, but there weren't any people in sight moving around the harbor on a February weekday morning. I took a breath to steady myself, and moved closer to the ship.

I caught a glimpse of motion through a window in the cabin, and heard a chirping sound. A cell phone rested on a counter beside a pad of hotel stationary. A woman appeared in the window dressed in a long gown of dark silk, and picked up the cell phone. She answered it without speaking and a moment later said, "I'm sorry. You've the wrong number."

I watched as she put the phone down and casually let the nightgown slide to the floor. I watched a little more. I wasn't being a peeping Tom. This was professional. I noted that she had some intriguing curves. See? Professionalism in action.

She opened a door, and a bit of steam wafted out, the sound of the water growing louder. She stepped in and closed the door again, leaving the cabin empty.

I had an opportunity. I'd seen only one woman, and not well enough to positively identify her as either Anna Valmont or Francisca Garcia, the two remaining Churchmice. I hadn't seen the Shroud hanging from a laundry line or anything. Even so, I had the feeling I'd come to the right place. My gut told me to trust my spiritual informer.

I made my decision and stepped up a short gangplank onto the *Etranger*.

I had to move fast. The woman on the ship might not be a fan of long showers. All I needed to do was get inside, see if I could find anything that might verify the presence of the Shroud, and get out again. If I moved quickly enough, I could get in and out without anyone the wiser.

I went down the stairs to the cabin with as much stealth as I could manage. The stairs didn't creak. I had to duck my head a bit when I stepped into the cabin. I stayed close to the door and checked around, listening to the patter of the water from the shower. The room wasn't large and didn't offer a bonanza of places to hide. A double bed took up nearly a quarter of the space in the room. A tiny washing machine and dryer were stacked one on another in a corner, a basket of laundry stowed atop them. A counter and kitchenette with a couple of small refrigerators used up most of the rest.

I frowned. Two fridges? I checked them out. The first was stocked with perishables and beer. The second was a fake, and opened onto a cabinet containing a heavy metal strongbox. Bingo.

The shower kept running. I reached out to pick up the strongbox, but a thought struck me. The Churchmice may have gotten themselves into a lot of trouble, but they'd evidently been good enough to avoid Interpol for a number of years. The hiding place for the strongbox was too clumsy, too obvious. I shut the fake fridge and looked around the room. I was starting to get nervous. I couldn't have much time left to find the Shroud and get out.

Of course. I took a couple of long steps to the washer and dryer and grabbed the laundry basket. I found it under several clean, fluffy towels, an opaque plastic package a little larger than a folded shirt. I touched it with my left hand. A tingling sensation pulsed against my palm, and the hairs along my arm rose up straight.

"Damn, I'm good," I muttered. I picked up the Shroud and turned to go.

A woman stood behind me, dressed in black fatigue pants, a heavy jacket, and battered combat boots. Her peroxide-blond hair was cut very short, but it did nothing to detract from the appeal of her features. She was elegantly pretty and pleasant to look at.

The gun she had pointed at my nose wasn't pretty, though. It was an ugly old .38 revolver, a cheap Saturday-night special.

I was careful not to move. Even a cheap gun can kill you, and I doubted I could raise a shield in time to do me any good. She'd taken me off guard. I'd never heard her coming, never sensed her presence.

"Damn, I'm good," the woman echoed, her accent high British, a touch of amusement in her voice. "Put the package down."

I held it out to her. "Here."

I wouldn't have tried for the gun, but if she stepped closer to me it might show that she was an amateur. She wasn't, and remained standing out of grab range. "On the counter, if you please."

"What if I don't?" I said.

She smiled without humor. "In that case, I'll have a dreary day of chores dismembering the body and cleaning up the blood. I'll leave it up to you."

I put the package on the counter. "Far be it from me to inconvenience a lady."

"What a dear boy you are," she said. "That's a very nice coat. Take it off. Slowly, if you please."

I slipped out of the coat and let it fall to the floor. "You tricked me onto the boat," I said. "That second phone call was you, telling your partner to draw me in."

"The shocking thing is that you fell for it," the woman said. She kept giving directions and she knew what she was doing. I leaned forward and put my hands against the wall while she patted me down. She found the pepper spray and took it, along with my wallet. She made me sit down on the floor on my hands while she took my coat and stepped back.

"A stick," she said, looking at my blasting rod. "How very pre-neolithic of you."

Aha. A professional she might be, but she was a straight. She didn't believe in the supernatural. I wasn't sure if that was going to help or hurt. It might mean that she would be a little less eager to shoot me. People who know what a wizard can do get really nervous if they think the wizard is about to try a spell. On the other hand, it meant that I didn't have either the support of the rest of the Council or the threat of my own retribution to use as leverage. I decided it was best to act like a normal for the time being.

The blonde laid my coat on the counter and said, "Clear."

The door to the bathroom opened, and the woman I'd heard before came out. She now wore a knit fabric dress the color of dark wine, and a couple of combs held her hair back from her face. She wouldn't stand out in a crowd but she wasn't unattractive. "He's not Gaston," she said, frowning at me.

"No," said the blonde. "He was here for the merchandise. He was just about to leave with it."

The dark-haired woman nodded and asked me, "Who are you?"

"Dresden," I said. "I'm a private investigator, Ms. Garcia."

Francisca Garcia's features froze, and she traded a look with the gun-wielding blond. "How did you know my name?"

"My client told me. You and Ms. Valmont could be in a lot of trouble."

Anna Valmont kicked the wall and spat, "Bollocks." She glared at me, gun steady on me despite her outburst. "Are you working with Interpol?"

"Rome."

Anna looked at Francisca and said, "We should scrub this sale. It's falling apart."

"Not yet," Francisca said.

"There's no point in waiting."

"I'm not leaving yet," the dark-haired woman said, her eyes hard. "Not until he gets here."

"He isn't coming," Anna said. "You know he isn't."

"Who?" I asked.

Francisca said, "Gaston."

I didn't say anything. Evidently Francisca could read faces well enough that I didn't have to. She stared at me for a moment and then closed her eyes, the blood draining from her face. "Oh. Oh, *Dio*."

"How?" Anna said. The gun never wavered. "How did it happen?"

"Murder," I said quietly. "And someone set it up to point the police at Chicago."

"Who would have done that?"

"Some bad people after the Shroud. Killers."

"Terrorists?"

"Not that playful," I said. "As long as you have the Shroud, your lives are in danger. If you come with me, I can get you to some people who will protect you."

Francisca shook her head and blinked her eyes a couple of times. "You mean the police."

I meant the Knights, but I knew darn well what their stance would be on what to do with the thieves once any supernatural peril was past. "Yeah."

Anna swallowed and looked at her partner. Something around her eyes softened with concern, with sympathy. The two of them weren't solely partners in crime. They were friends. Anna's voice softened as she said, "Cisca, we have to move. If this one found us, others may not be far behind."

The dark-haired woman nodded, her eyes not focused on anything. "Yes. I'll get ready." She rose and stepped across the cabin to the washing machine. She drew out a pair of gym bags and put them on the counter, over the package. Then she slipped into some shoes.

Anna watched for a moment and then said to me, "Now. We can't have you running to the police to tell them everything. I wonder what to do with you, Mister Dresden. It really does make a great deal of sense to kill you."

"Messy, remember? You'd have that dreary day," I pointed out.

That got a bit of a smile from her. "Ah, yes. I'd forgotten." She reached into her pocket and drew out a pair of steel handcuffs. They were police quality, not the naughty fun kind. She tossed them to me underhand. I caught them. "Put one on your wrist," she said. I did. "There's a ring on that bulkhead. Put the other through it and lock the cuffs."

I hesitated, watching Francisca slip into a coat, her expression still blank. I licked my lips and said, "You don't know how much danger you two are in, Ms. Valmont. You really don't. Please let me help you."

"I think not. We're professionals, Mister Dresden. Thieves we might be, but we do have a work ethic."

"You didn't see what they did to Gaston LaRouche," I said. "How bad it was."

"When isn't death bad? The bulkhead, Mister Dresden."

"But—"

Anna lifted the gun.

I grimaced and lifted the cuffs to a steel ring protruding from the wall beside the stairs.

As a result, I was looking up them to the ship's deck when the second Denarian in twelve hours came hurtling down the stairway straight toward me.

Chapter Thirteen

I only saw it coming out of the corner of my eye, and I barely had time to register the movement and lunge as far as I could to one side. The demon went by me in a blur of rustling, metallic whispers, carrying the scent of lake water and dried blood. Neither of the Churchmice screamed, though whether this was intention or a by-product of surprise I couldn't tell.

The demon was more or less human, generally speaking, and disturbingly female. The lines of curvy hips swept down to legs that were oddly hinged, back-jointed like a lion's. She had skin of metallic green scales, and her arms ended in four-fingered, metallic-clawed hands. Like the demon form of Ursiel, she had two sets of eyes, one luminescent green, one glowing cherry red, and a luminous sigil burned at the center of her forehead.

Her hair was long. I mean like fifteen feet long, and looked like the demented love child of Medusa and Doctor Octopus. It had seemingly been cut in one-inch strips from half a mile of sheet metal. It writhed around her like a cloud of living serpents, metallic strands thrusting into the walls and the floor of the ship, supporting her weight like a dozen additional limbs.

Anna recovered from the surprise first. She already had a gun out and ready, but she hadn't been trained in how to use it in real combat. She pointed the gun more or less at the Denarian and emptied it at her in the space of a panicked breath. Since I was a couple of feet behind the demon, I flopped to one side as best I could, stayed low, and prayed to avoid becoming collateral damage.

The demon flinched once, maybe taking a hit, before it shrieked and twisted its shoulders and neck. A dozen metallic ribbons of writhing hair lashed across the room. One of them hit the gun itself, and metal shrieked as the demon tendril slashed clean through the gun's barrel. Half a dozen more whipped toward Anna's face, but the blond thief had reflexes fast enough to get her mostly out of the way. A tendril wrapped around Anna's ankle, jerked, and sent the woman sprawling to the floor, while another lashed across her belly like a scalpel, cutting through her jacket and sprinkling the cabin with fine drops of blood.

Francisca stared at the thing for a second, her eyes huge and surrounded by white. Then she jerked open a drawer in the tiny galley, pulled out a heavy cutting knife, and lunged at the Denarian, blade flickering. It bit into the demon's arm and drew a furious shriek that did not sound at all human from her throat. The Denarian spun, silvery blood glistening on her scaly skin, and ripped one claw in a sweeping arch. The demon's claws sliced into Francisca's forearm, drawing blood. The knife tumbled to the ground. Francisca cried out and reeled back, into one of the walls.

The Denarian, eyes burning, whipped her head in a circle, the motion boneless, unnerving. Too many tendrils for me to count lanced across the room and slammed into Francisca Garcia's belly, thrusting like knives. She let out a choking gasp, and stared down at her wounds as several more tendrils thrust through her. They made a thunking sound as they hit the wooden wall of the cabin.

The demon laughed. It was a quick, breathless, excited laugh, the kind you expect from a nervous teenage girl. Her face twisted into a feral smile, showing a mouthful of metallic-seeming teeth, and both sets of eyes glowed brightly.

Francisca whispered, "Oh, my Gaston." Then her head bowed, dark hair falling about her face in a veil, and her body relaxed. The demon shivered and the tendril-blades whipped out of her, the last foot or so of each soaked in scarlet. The tendrils lashed about in a sort of mad excitement, and more droplets of blood appeared everywhere. Francisca slumped down to the floor, blood beginning to soak her dress, and fell limply onto her side.

Then the Denarian's two sets of eyes turned to me, and a swarm of razor-edged tendrils of her hair came whipping toward me.

I had already begun to ready my shield, but when I saw Francisca fall a surge of fury went coursing through me, filling me from toes to teeth with scarlet rage. The shield came together before me in a quarter-dome of blazing crimson energy, and the writhing tendrils slammed against it in a dozen flashes of white

light. The Denarian shrieked, jerking back, and the attacking tendrils went sailing back across the cabin with their ends scorched
and blackened.

I looked around wildly for my blasting rod, but it wasn't
where Anna had left it when she took it from me. The pepper
spray was, though. I grabbed it and faced the Denarian in time to
see her raise her clawed hand. A shimmer in the air around her fingers threw off a prismatic flash of color, and with a flash of light
from the upper set of eyes, the demoness drove her fist at my
shield.

She hit the shield hard, and she was incredibly strong. The
blow drove me back against a wall, and when the heat-shimmer of
power touched my scarlet shield, it fractured into shards of light
that went flying around the cabin like the sparks from a campfire.
I tried to get to one side, away from the demon's vicious strength,
but she snarled and strands of hair punched into the hull on either
side of me, caging me. The Denarian reached for me with her
claws.

I shouted a panicked battle cry and gave her the pepper spray
full in the face, right into both sets of eyes.

The demoness screamed again, twisting her face away, ruining
the tendril-cage, the human eyes squeezing shut over a sudden
flood of tears. The glowing demon-eyes did not even blink, and a
sweep of the Denarian's arm fetched me a backhanded blow that
sent me sprawling and made me see stars.

I got back to my feet, terrified at the notion of being caught
helpless on the ground. The Denarian seemed able to blow off my
magic with a bit of effort, and she was deadly in these confined
quarters. I didn't think I could get up the stairs without her tearing
me apart. Which meant I had to find another way to get the demon away.

The Denarian swiped a clawed hand at her eyes and snarled in
mangled, throaty English, "You will pay for that."

I looked up to see that Anna had dragged herself across the
floor to the fallen Francisca, and knelt over her, shielding the other
woman from the Denarian with her body. Her face was white with
pain, or shock, or both—but she shot me a glance and then jerked
her head toward the far side of the cabin.

I followed her gaze and got her drift. As the Denarian recovered and blinked watery, murderous eyes at me, I lunged toward
the far side of the room and shouted, "Get it out of the fridge!
They must not have it!"

The Denarian spat out what I took to be an oath, and I felt that lionlike foot land in the middle of my back, flattening me to the floor, claws digging into my skin. She stepped over me, past me, and her tendrils tore open the real fridge, taking the door from its hinges before slithering inside and knocking everything within to the floor. She hadn't quite finished with the first fridge before her hair had gone on to tear open the dummy fridge, and dragged out the steel strongbox.

While the Denarian did that, I looked wildly around the cabin, and spotted my blasting rod on the floor. I rolled, my back burning with pain, and grabbed the blasting rod. Calling up fire within the tiny cabin was a bad idea—but waiting around for the Denarian to murder me with her hairdo was even worse.

She stood up with the strongbox just as I began channeling energy into the blasting rod. Its carved runes began to burn with golden radiance and the tip of the rod suddenly gleamed with red light and wavered with hot-air shimmer.

The Denarian crouched, demonic limbs too long, feminine shape disturbingly attractive, red light gleaming on her metallic-green scales. Her hair writhed in a hissing mass, striking sparks as one edge rasped against another. Violent lust burned in both sets of eyes for a second, and then she turned away. Her hair tore the cabin's ceiling apart like papier-mâché, and using her hair, an arm, and one long leg, she swarmed out of the ship's cabin. I heard a splash as she hit the water, taking the strongbox with her.

"What was that?" stammered Anna Valmont, clutching Francisca's limp form to her. "What the bloody hell was that?"

I didn't drop the blasting rod or look away from the hole in the roof, because I didn't think the Denarian was the sort to leave a lot of people alive behind her. The end of the blasting rod was wavering drunkenly. "How is she?"

I watched the hole in the ceiling for several shaking breaths until Anna said, her voice barely audible, "She's gone."

A stabbing feeling went through my belly, sharp and hot. Maybe I'm some kind of Neanderthal for thinking so, but it hurt me. A minute ago, Francisca Garcia had been talking, planning, grieving, breathing. Living. She'd been killed by violence, and I couldn't stand the thought of things like that happening to a woman. It wouldn't have been any less wrong had it happened to a man, but in my gut it wasn't the same. "Dammit," I whispered. "How are you? Can you walk?"

Before she could answer, the ship lurched and leaned to one

side. There was a wrenching, snapping roar and the rushing sound of water. Icy cold ran over my ankles and began to rise.

"The hull's breached," Anna said. "We're taking on water."

I headed for the stairway, blasting rod up, to make sure it was clear. "Can you get out?"

Light exploded behind my eyes and I dropped to my hands and knees at the bottom of the stairway. Anna had slugged me with something. A second burst of light and pain drove my head far enough down to splash some cold water against my forehead. I dimly saw Anna's foot kick my blasting rod away from me. Then she picked up the Shroud in its package from the counter, and tore off the top sheet of the hotel memo pad. I saw that she had blood on her jacket, soaked through, and staining her fatigue pants down to the top of her left leg. She grabbed my coat, wincing, and one of the duffel bags. She put my leather duster on, covering the blood. The water had filled the cabin almost to the tops of her combat boots.

I tried to get my wits together, but something was keeping me from doing much besides focusing my eyes. I knew that I needed to leave, but I couldn't get the message from my head to my arms and legs.

Anna Valmont stepped past me and went up the stairs. She stopped about halfway up, spat out another curse, and came back down them enough to reach down and splash cold water into my face. The shock jump-started something in my body, and I coughed, my head spinning, and started to move again. I'd been too drunk to stand up a time or two, but even then I'd been more capable than I was at that moment.

The blond thief grabbed my arm and half hauled me up a couple of stairs, her face twisted in pain. I desperately held on to that momentum, struggling up another stair even after she stopped pulling.

She kept going up the stairs and didn't look back as she said, "I'm only doing this because I like your coat, Dresden. Don't come near me again."

Then she padded up out of the cabin and disappeared with the Shroud.

My head had started to throb and swell, but it was clearing rapidly also. But evidently I wasn't all that bright even when fully conscious, because I staggered back down into the ship's cabin. Francisca Garcia's corpse had fallen onto its side, glassy eyes staring, mouth slightly open. One of her cheeks had been half-covered by water. There were still the tracks of tears on the other one. The water around her was a cloudy, brownish pink.

My stomach heaved and the anger that came with it nearly sent me to the floor again. Instead, I sloshed through the freezing water to the counter. I picked up the cell phone there, and the blank memo pad. I hesitated over Francisca. She didn't deserve to have her body swallowed by the lake like a discarded beer bottle.

My balance wobbled again. The water had begun to rise more quickly. It covered my shins already, and I couldn't feel my feet for the cold. I tried to lift her body, but the effort brought a surge of pain to my head and I almost threw up.

I settled the body back down, unable to even curse coherently, and made do with gently closing her eyes with one hand. It was all I could do for her. The police would find her, of course, probably within a few hours.

And if I didn't get moving, they'd find me too. I couldn't afford to spend a night in the pokey while I was interrogated, charged and awaiting bail, but what else was new. I'd get in touch with Murphy as soon as I could.

I folded my arms against the growing cold, hugging the memo pad and cell phone to my chest, and slogged out of the bloody water of the *Etranger*'s cabin and onto the deck. I had to make a short jump up to the dock. A couple of people were on the sidewalk above the little harbor, staring down, and I saw a couple of folks out on the decks of their ships, also staring.

I ducked my head, thought inconspicuous thoughts, and hurried away before my morning could get any worse.

Chapter Fourteen

I've been clouted in the head a few times in my day. The bump Anna Valmont had given me was smaller than some, but my head pounded all the way home. At least my stomach settled down before I started throwing up all over myself. I shambled in, washed down a couple of Tylenol with a can of Coke, and folded some ice into a towel. I sat down by the phone, put the ice pack against the back of my head, and called Father Vincent.

The phone rang once. "Yes?"

"It's in town," I said. "The two Churchmice had it on a boat in Burnham Harbor."

Vincent's voice gained an edge of tension. "You have it?"

"Uh," I said. "Not strictly speaking, no. Something went wrong."

"What happened?" he demanded, his voice growing more frustrated, angrier. "Why didn't you call me?"

"A third party made a grab for it, and what do you think I'm doing right now? I had a shot to recover the thing. I took it. I missed."

"And the Shroud was taken from the thieves?"

"Thief, singular. Chicago PD is probably recovering the body of her partner right now."

"They turned on each other?"

"Not even. A new player killed Garcia. Valmont duped the third party into taking a decoy. Then she grabbed the real McCoy and ran."

"And you didn't see fit to follow her?"

My head pounded steadily. "She ran really fast."

Vincent was silent for a moment before he said, "So the Shroud is lost to us once more."

"For now," I said. "I might have another lead."

"You know where it has gone?"

I took in a deep breath and tried to sound patient. "Not yet. That's why it's called a lead and not a solution. I need that sample of the Shroud."

"To be frank, Mister Dresden, I did bring a few threads with me from the Vatican, but . . ."

"Great. Get one of them to my office and drop it off with security downstairs. They'll hold it for me until I can pick it up. I'll call you as soon as I have anything more definite."

"But—"

I hung up on Vincent, and felt a twinge of vindictive satisfaction. " 'You didn't see fit to follow her,' " I muttered to Mister, doing my best to imitate Vincent's accent. "I gotcher didn't see fit to follow her. White-collar jerk. How about I ring your bell a few times, and then you can go say Mass or something."

Mister gave me a look as if to say that I shouldn't say such things about paying clients. I glared at him to let him know that I was well aware of it, got up, went into my bedroom, and rummaged in my closet until I found a stick of charcoal and a clipboard. Then I lit several candles on the end table next to my big comfy chair and settled down with the memo pad I'd taken from the *Etranger*. I brushed the stick of charcoal over it as carefully as I could, and hoped that Francisca Garcia hadn't been using a felt tip.

She hadn't. Faint white letters began to appear amidst the charcoal on the paper. It read *Marriott* on the first line and *2345* on the second.

I frowned down at the pad. Marriott. One of the hotels? It could have been someone's last name, too. Or maybe some kind of French word. *No, don't make it more complicated than it has to be, Harry*. It probably meant the hotel. The number appeared to be military time for a quarter to midnight. Maybe even a room number.

I glared at the note. It didn't tell me enough. Even though I may have had the time and place, I didn't know where and when.

I looked at the cell phone I'd taken. I knew as much about cell phones as I did about gastrointestinal surgery. There were no markings on the case, not even a brand name. The phone was off, but I didn't dare turn it on. It would probably stop working. Hell, it would probably explode. I would need to ask Murphy to see what she could find out when I talked to her.

My head kept pounding and my eyes itched with weariness. I needed rest. The lack of sleep was making me sloppy. I shouldn't have chanced going onto the ship in the first place, and I should have been more careful about watching my back. I'd had a gut instinct someone was watching me, but I had been too tired, too impatient, and I'd nearly gotten myself shot, impaled, concussed, and drowned as a result.

I headed into the bedroom, set my alarm clock for a couple hours after noon, and flopped down on my bed. It felt obscenely good.

Naturally it didn't last.

The phone rang and I gave serious thought to blasting it into orbit, where it could hang around with Asteroid Dresden. I stomped back into the living room, picked up the phone, and snarled, "What."

"Oh, uh," said a somewhat nervous voice on the other end. "This is Waldo Butters. I was calling to speak to Harry Dresden."

I moderated my voice to a mere snarl. "Oh. Hey."

"I woke you up, huh?"

"Some."

"Yeah, late nights suck. Look, there's something odd going on and I thought maybe I could ask you something."

"Sure."

"Sullen monosyllabism, a sure sign of sleep deprivation."

"Eh."

"Now descending into formless vocalization. My time is short." Butters cleared his throat and said, "The germs are gone."

"Germs?" I asked.

"In the samples I took from that body. I ran all the checks again just to be sure, and better than half of them turned up negative. Nothing. Zip, zero."

"Ungh," I said.

"Okay, then, Caveman Og. Where germs go?"

"Sunrise," I said. "Poof."

Butter's voice sounded bewildered. "Vampire germs?"

"The tiny capes are a dead giveaway," I said. I started pulling my train of thought into motion at last. "Not vampire germs. Constructs. See, at sunrise it's like the whole magical world gets reset to zero. New beginnings. Most spells don't hold together through even one sunrise. And it takes a lot to make them last through two or three."

"Magic germs?" Butters asked. "Are you telling me I've got magic germs?"

"Magic germs," I confirmed. "Someone called them up with magic."

"Like an actual magic spell?"

"Usually you call nasty hurtful spells a curse. But by tomorrow or the next day, those other samples will probably have zeroed out too."

"Are they still infectious?"

"Assume they are. They're good as real until the energy that holds them together falls apart."

"Christ. You're serious. It's for real."

"Well, yeah."

"Is there a book or a Cliff's Notes or something on this stuff?"

I actually smiled that time. "Just me. Anything else?"

"Not much. I swept the body for genetic remains but got nothing. The cuts on the corpse were made with either a surgical scalpel or some other kind of small, fine blade. Maybe a utility knife."

"I've seen cuts like that before, yeah."

"Here's the best part. The same blade evidently took off the hands and head. The cuts are cleaner than a surgeon could manage on an operating table. Three single cuts. The heat from it half cauterized parts of the wounds. So what kind of tool can cut fine, precise lines and cleave through bones too?"

"Sword?"

"Have to be one hell of a sharp sword."

"There's a few around like that. Any luck identifying the victim?"

"None. Sorry."

"'S okay."

"You want to know if anything changes?"

"Yeah. Or if you see anyone else come in like that guy."

"God forbid, will do. You find anything on that tattoo?"

"Called the Eye of Thoth," I said. "Trying to narrow down exactly who uses it around here. Oh, give Murphy a call. Let her know about those samples."

"Already did. She's the one who told me to keep you in the loop. I think she was heading toward sleep too. Would she want me to wake her up to talk to you?"

I talked through a yawn. "Nah, it can wait. Thanks for the call, Butters."

"No trouble," he said. "Sleep is god. Go worship."

I grunted, hung up the phone, and didn't get to take the second step toward my bed when someone knocked at the door.

"I need one of those trapdoors," I muttered to Mister. "I could push a button and people would fall screaming down a wacky slide thing and land in mud somewhere."

Mister was far too mature to dignify that with a response, so I kept a hand near my gift rack as I opened the door a crack and peeked out.

Susan tilted her head sideways and gave me a small smile. She was wearing jeans, an old tee, a heavy grey fleece jacket, and sunglasses. "Hi," she said.

"Hi."

"You know, it's hard to tell through the door, but your eyes look sunken and bloodshot. Did you sleep last night?"

"What is this thing you speak of, 'sleep'?"

Susan sighed and shook her head. "Mind if I come in?"

I stepped back and opened the door wider. "No scolding."

Susan came in and folded her arms. "Always so cold in here in the winter."

I had a couple suggestions on how to warm up, but I didn't say them out loud. Maybe I didn't want to see her response to them. I thought about what Murphy had said about setting up a talk. I got some more wood and stirred up the fireplace. "Want me to make some tea or something?"

She shook her head. "No."

Susan never turned down a cup of hot tea. I tried, but I couldn't keep a hard edge out of my voice. "Just going to dump me and run, then. Drive-by dumping."

"Harry, that isn't fair," Susan said. I could hear the hurt in her voice, but only barely. I raked harder at the fire, making sparks fly up, though flames were already licking the new wood. "This isn't easy for anyone."

My mouth kept running without checking in with my brain. My heart maybe, but not my brain. I shot her a look over my shoulder and said, "Except for Captain Mediocrity, I guess."

She raised both eyebrows. "Do you mean Martin?"

"Isn't that what this is about?" A spark flipped out of the fire and landed on my hand, stinging. I yelped and pulled my hand away. I closed the heavy mesh curtain over the fire and put the poker away. "And before you say anything, I know damn well I'm being insane. And possessive. I know that we were quits before you left town. It's been more than a year, and it's been hard on you. It's only natural for you to find someone. It's irrational and childish for me to be upset, and I don't care."

"Harry—" she began.

"And it's not as if you haven't been thinking about it," I continued. Somewhere I knew that I'd start choking on my foot if I kept shoving it in my mouth. "You kissed me. You *kissed* me, Susan. I know you. You meant it."

"This isn't—"

"I'll bet you don't kiss Snoozy Martin like that."

Susan rolled her eyes and walked to me. She sat down on the lintel of my little fireplace while I knelt before it. She cupped my cheek in one hand. She was warm. It felt good. I was too tired to control my reaction to the simple, gentle touch, and I looked back at the fire.

"Harry," she said. "You're right. I don't kiss Martin like that."

I pulled my cheek away, but she put her fingers on my chin and tugged my face back toward her. "I don't kiss him at all. I'm not involved with Martin."

I blinked. "You're not?"

She drew an invisible X over her heart with her index finger.

"Oh," I said. I felt my shoulders ease up a little.

Susan laughed. "Was that really worrying you, Harry? That I was leaving you for another man?"

"I don't know. I guess."

"God, you are a dolt sometimes." She smiled at me, but I could see the sadness in it. "It always shocked me how you could understand so many things and be such a complete idiot about so many others."

"Practice," I said. She looked down at me for a while, with that same sad smile, and I understood. "It doesn't change anything, does it?"

"Martin?"

"Yeah."

She nodded. "It doesn't change anything."

I swallowed a sudden frog in my throat. "You want it to be over."

"I don't *want* it," she said quickly. "But I think it's necessary. For both of us."

"You came back here to tell me that?"

Susan shook her head. "I don't have my mind set. I think it wouldn't be fair to do that without talking to you about it. We both have to make this decision."

I growled and looked back at the fire. "Would be a lot simpler if you just gave me the Dear John speech and left."

"Simpler," she said. "Easier. But not fair and not right."

I didn't say anything.

"I've changed," Susan said. "Not just the vampire thing. There's a lot that's been happening in my life. A lot of things that I didn't know."

"Like what?"

"How dangerous the world is, for one," she said. "I wound up in Peru, but I went all over South America, Central America. I couldn't have imagined what things are like there. Harry, the Red Court is *everywhere*. There are whole villages out in the country supporting groups of them. Like cattle bred for the lord of the manor. The vampires feed on everyone. Addict them all." Her voice hardened. "Even the children."

My stomach twitched unpleasantly. "I hadn't ever heard that."

"Not many know."

I mopped a hand over my face. "God. Kids."

"I want to help. To do something. I've found where I can help down there, Harry. A job. I'm going to take it."

Something in my chest hurt, a literal pain. "I thought this was our decision."

"I'm coming to that," she said.

I nodded. "Okay."

She slipped to the floor next to me and said, "You could come with me."

Go with her. Leave Chicago. Leave Murphy, the Alphas, Michael. Leave a horde of problems—many of them ones I'd created for myself. I thought of packing up and heading out. Maybe fighting the good fight. Being loved again, held again. God, I wanted that.

But people would get hurt. Friends. Others who might be in my kind of danger and have no one to turn to.

I looked into Susan's eyes and saw hope there for just a moment. Then understanding. She smiled, but it was somehow sadder than ever. "Susan—" I said.

She pressed a finger to my lips and blinked back tears. "I know."

And then I understood. She knew because she was feeling the same way.

There are things you can't walk away from. Not if you want to live with yourself afterward.

"Now do you understand?" she asked.

I nodded, but my voice came out rough. "Wouldn't be fair. Not to either of us," I said. "Not being together. Both of us hurting."

Susan leaned her shoulder against mine and nodded. I put my arm around her.

"Maybe someday things will change," I said.

"Maybe someday," she agreed. "I love you. I never stopped loving you, Harry."

"Yeah," I said. I choked on the end of the word, and the fire went blurry. "I love you too. Dammit." We sat there and warmed up in front of the fire for a couple of minutes before I said, "When are you leaving?"

"Tomorrow," she said.

"With Martin?"

She nodded. "He's a coworker. He's helping me move, watching my back. I have to put everything in order here. Pack some things from the apartment."

"What kind of work?"

"Pretty much the same kind. Investigate and report. Only I report to a boss instead of to readers." She sighed and said, "I'm not supposed to tell you anything else about it."

"Hell's bells," I muttered. "Will I be able to reach you?"

She nodded. "I'll set up a drop. You can write. I'd like that."

"Yeah. Stay in touch."

Long minutes after that, Susan said, "You're on a case again, aren't you?"

"Does it show?"

She leaned a little away from me, and I drew my arm back. "I smelled it," she said, and stood up to add wood to the fire. "There's blood on you."

"Yeah," I said. "A woman was killed about five feet away from me."

"Vampires?" Susan asked.

I shook my head. "Some kind of demon."

"Are you okay?"

"Peachy."

"That's funny, because you look like hell," Susan said.

"I said no scolding."

She almost smiled. "You'd be smart to get some sleep."

"True, but I'm not all that bright," I said. Besides, I didn't have a prayer of falling asleep now, after talking to her.

"Ah," she said. "Is there anything I can do to help?"

"Don't think so."

"You need rest."

I waved a hand at the stationery pad. "I will. I just have to run down a lead first."

Susan folded her arms, facing me directly. "So do it after you get some rest."

"There probably isn't time."

Susan frowned and picked up the pad. "Marriott. The hotel?"

"Dunno. Likely."

"What are you looking for?"

I sighed, too tired to stick to my confidentiality guns very closely. "Stolen artifact. I think the note is probably about a site for the sale."

"Who is the buyer?"

I shrugged.

"Lots of legwork, then."

"Yeah."

Susan nodded. "Let me look into this. You get some sleep."

"It's probably better if you don't—"

She waved a hand, cutting me off. "I want to help. Let me do this for you."

I opened my mouth and closed it again. I guess I could relate. I knew how much I'd wanted to help her. I couldn't. It had been tough to handle. It would have been a relief to me to have done her some good, no matter how small it was.

"All right," I said. "But just the phone work. Okay?"

"Okay." She copied down the word and the number on a sheet she tore from the bottom of the memo pad and turned toward the door.

"Susan?" I said.

She paused without turning to look back at me.

"Do you want to get dinner or something? Before you go, I mean. I want to, uh, you know."

"Say good-bye," she said quietly.

"Yeah."

"All right."

She left. I sat in my apartment, in front of the fire, and breathed in the scent of her perfume. I felt cold, lonely, and tired.

I felt like a hollowed-out husk. I felt as if I had failed her. Failed to protect her to begin with, failed to cure her after the vampires had changed her.

Change. Maybe that's what this was really about. Susan had changed. She'd grown. She was more relaxed than I remembered, more confident. There had always been a sense of purpose to her, but now it seemed deeper, somehow. She'd found a place for herself, somewhere where she felt she could do some good.

Maybe I should have gone with her after all.

But no. Part of the change was that she felt hungrier now, too. More quietly sensual, as if every sight and sound and touch in the room was occupying most of her attention. She'd smelled drops of blood on my clothing and it had excited her enough to make her move away from me.

Another change. She had an instinctive hunger for my blood. And she could throw vampires twenty feet through the air. She sure as hell wouldn't have any trouble tearing my throat out in an intimate moment if her control slipped.

I washed my face mechanically, showered in my unheated shower, and went shivering to my bed. The routine hadn't helped me. It only delayed me from facing the harshest truth of my relationship with Susan.

She had left Chicago.

Probably for good.

That was going to hurt like hell in the morning.

Chapter Fifteen

⋙ ∞ ⋘

I had bad dreams.

They were the usual fare. Flames devoured someone who screamed my name. A pretty girl spread her arms, eyes closed, and fell slowly backward as dozens of fine cuts opened all over her skin. The air became a fine pink spray. I turned from it, into a kiss with Susan, who drew me down and tore out my throat with her teeth.

A woman who seemed familiar but whom I did not recognize shook her head and drew her hand from left to right. The dream-scenery faded to black in the wake of her motion. She turned to me, dark eyes intent and said, "You need to rest."

Mickey Mouse woke me up, my alarm jangling noisily, his little hand on two and the big hand on twelve. I wanted to smack the clock for waking me up, but I reined in the impulse. I'm not against a little creative violence now and then, but you have to draw the line somewhere. I wouldn't sleep in the same room with a person who would smack Mickey Mouse.

I got up, got dressed, left a message for Murphy, another for Michael, fed Mister, and hit the road.

Michael's house did not blend in with most of the other homes in his neighborhood west of Wrigley Field. It had a white picket fence. It had elegant window dressings. It had a tidy front lawn that was always green, even in the midst of a blazing Chicago summer. It had a few shady trees, a lot of well-kept shrubberies, and if I had found a couple of deer grazing on the lawn or drinking from the birdbath, it wouldn't have surprised me.

I got out of the Beetle, holding my blasting rod loosely in my right hand. I opened the gate, and a few jingle bells hanging on a string tinkled happily. The gate swung shut on a lazy spring behind me. I knocked on the front door and waited, but no one answered. I frowned. Michael's house had never been empty before. Charity had at least a couple kids who weren't old enough to be in school yet, including the poor little guy they'd named after me. Harry Carpenter. How cruel is that?

I frowned at the cloud-hazed sun. Weren't the older kids getting out of school shortly? Charity had some kind of maternal obsession with never allowing her kids to come home to an empty house.

Someone should have been there.

I got a sick, twisty feeling in the pit of my stomach.

I knocked again, put my ear against the door, and Listened. I could hear the slow tick of the old grandfather clock in the front room. The heater cycled on for a moment, and the vents inside whispered. There were a few sounds when a bit of breeze touched the house, the creaks of old and comfortable wood.

Nothing else.

I tried the front door. It was locked. I stepped back off the porch, and followed the narrow driveway to the back of the property.

If the front of the Carpenter home would have qualified for *Better Homes and Gardens,* the back would have been fit for a Craftsman commercial. The large tree centered on the back lawn cast lots of shade in the summer, but with the leaves gone I could see the fortresslike tree house Michael had built for his kids in it. It had finished walls, an actual window, and guardrails anywhere anyone could possibly have thought about falling. The tree house had a porch that overlooked the yard. Hell, I didn't have a porch. It's an unfair world.

A big section of the yard had been bitten off by an addition connected to the back of the house. The foundation had been laid, and there were wooden beams framing what would eventually be walls. Heavy contractor's plastic had been stapled to the wooden studs to keep the wind off the addition. The separate garage was closed, and a peek in the window showed me that it was pretty well filled with lumber and other construction materials.

"No cars," I muttered. "Maybe they went to McDonald's. Or church. Do they have church at three in the afternoon?"

I turned around to go back to the Beetle. I'd leave a Michael a note. My stomach fluttered. If I didn't get a second for the duel, it was likely to be a bad evening. Maybe I should ask Bob to be my second. Or maybe Mister. No one dares to mess with Mister.

Something rattled against the metal gutters running the length of the back of the house.

I jumped like a spooked horse and scrambled away from the house, toward the garage at the back of the yard so that I could get a look at the roof. Given that in the past day or so no less than three different parties had taken a poke at me, I felt totally justified in being on edge.

I got to the back of the yard, but couldn't see the whole roof from there, so I clambered up into the branches, then took a six-foot ladder up to the main platform of the tree house. From there, I could see that the roof was empty.

I heard brisk, somewhat heavy footsteps below me, and beyond the fence at the back of the little yard. I froze in place in the tree house, Listening.

The heavy footsteps padded up to the fence at the back of the yard, and I heard the scrape of chain link dragging against dry leaves and other late-winter detritus. I heard a muted grunt of effort and a long exhalation. Then the footsteps came to the base of the tree.

Leather scraped against a wooden step, and the tree shivered almost imperceptibly. Someone was climbing up.

I looked around me but the ladder was the only way down, unless I felt like jumping. It couldn't have been more than nine or ten feet down. Odds were I could land more or less in one piece. But if I misjudged the jump I could sprain an ankle or break a leg, which would make running away both impractical and embarrassing. Jumping would have to be a last resort.

I gathered in my will and settled my grip on my blasting rod, pointing it directly at where the ladder met the platform. The tip of the blasting rod glowed with a pinpoint of bright red energy.

Blond hair and the top half of a girl's angelic young face appeared at the top of the ladder. There was a quiet gasp and her blue eyes widened. "Holy crap."

I jerked the tip of the blasting rod up and away from the girl, releasing the gathered energy. "Molly?"

The rest of the girl's face appeared as she climbed on up the ladder. "Wow, is that an acetylene torch or something?"

I blinked and peered more closely at Molly. "Is that an earring in your eyebrow?"

The girl clapped her fingers over her right eyebrow.

"And your *nose*?"

Molly shot a furtive look over her shoulder at the house, and scrambled the rest of the way up to the tree house. As tall as her mother, Molly was all coltish legs and long arms. She wore a typical private-school uniform of skirt, blouse, and sweater—but it looked like she'd been attacked by a lech with razor blades where fingers should have been.

The skirt was essentially slashed to ribbons, and underneath it she wore black tights, also torn to nigh indecency. Her shirt and sweater had apparently endured the Blitz, but the bright red satin bra that peeked out from beneath looked new. She had on too much makeup. Not as bad as most kids too old to play tag but too young to drive, but it was there. She wore a ring of fine gold wire through one pale gold eyebrow, and a golden stud protruded from one side of her nose.

I worked hard not to smile. Smiling would have implied that I found her outfit amusing. She was young enough to be hurt by that kind of opinion, and I had a vague memory of being that ridiculous at one time. Let he who hath never worn parachute pants cast the first stone.

Molly clambered in and tossed a bulging backpack down on the wooden floor. "You lurk in tree houses a lot, Mister Dresden?"

"I'm looking for your dad."

Molly wrinkled up her nose, then started removing the stud from it. I didn't want to watch. "I don't want to tell you how to investigate stuff, but generally speaking you won't find him in tree houses."

"I came over, but no one answered the door when I knocked. Is that normal?"

Molly took out the eyebrow ring, dumped the backpack out onto the floorboards, and started sorting out a long skirt with a floral print, a T-shirt, and a sweater. "It is on errands day. Mom loads up the sandcrawler with all the little snot-nosed Jawas and goes all over town."

"Oh. Do you know when she's due back?"

"Anytime," Molly said. She hopped into the skirt, and wriggled out of the tattered skirt and tights in that mystifyingly modest way that girls always seem to manage to acquire sometime in their teens. The shirt and pink sweater went on next, and the ripped up sweater and, to my discomfort, the bright red bra came out from under the conservative clothes and got tucked back into the backpack.

I turned my back on the girl as well as I could in the limited space. The link of handcuff Anna Valmont had slapped onto my wrist chafed and pinched. I scratched at it irritably. You'd think I'd been cuffed enough times that I should have gotten myself a key by now.

Molly took a wet-wipe from somewhere and started peeling the makeup from her face. "Hey," she asked a minute later. "What's wrong?"

I grunted and waved my wrist vaguely, swinging the cuff around.

"Hey, neat," Molly said. "Are you on the lam? Is that why you're hiding in a tree house, so the cops won't find you?"

"No," I said. "It's kind of a long story."

"Ohhhh," Molly said wisely. "Those are fun-time handcuffs, not bad-time handcuffs. I gotcha."

"No!" I protested. "And how the hell would you know about fun-time handcuffs anyway? You're like ten."

She snorted. "Fourteen."

"Whatever, too young."

"Internet," she said sagely. "Expanding the frontiers of adolescent knowledge."

"God, I'm old."

Molly clucked and dipped into the backpack again. She grabbed my wrist firmly, shook out a ring of small keys, and started trying them in the lock of the cuffs. "So give me the juicy details," she said. "You can say 'bleep' instead of the fun words if you want."

I blinked. "Where the bleep did you get a bunch of cuff keys?"

She looked up at me and narrowed her eyes. "Think about this one. Do you *really* want to know?"

I sighed. "No. Probably not."

"Cool," she said, and turned her attention back to the handcuffs. "So stop dodging the issue. What's up with you and Susan?"

"Why do you want to know?"

"I like romance. Plus I heard Mom say that you two were a pretty hot item."

"Your mom said that?"

Molly shrugged. "Sorta. As much as she ever would. She used words like 'fornication' and 'sin' and 'infantile depravity' and 'moral bankruptcy.' So are you?"

"Morally bankrupt?"

"A hot item with Susan."

I shrugged and said, "Not anymore."

"Don't move your wrist." Molly fiddled with one key for a moment before discarding it. "What happened?"

"A lot," I said. "It's complicated."

"Oh," Molly said. The cuffs clicked and loosened and she beamed up at me. "There."

"Thanks." I rubbed my sore wrist and put the cuffs in my coat pocket.

Molly bent over and picked up a piece of paper. She read it and said, "Ask Michael about duel? Whiskey and tobacco?"

"It's a shopping list."

Molly frowned. "Oh." She was quiet for a moment and then asked, "So was it the vampire thing?"

I blinked at the girl again. "Was there a PBS special or something? Is there some kind of unauthorized biography of my life?"

"I snuck downstairs so I could listen to Dad tell Mom what had happened."

"Do you eavesdrop on every private conversation you can?"

She rolled her eyes and sat down on the edge of the platform, her shoes waving in the air. "No one says anything interesting in a public conversation, do they? Why did you guys split up?"

I sat down next to her. "Like I said. It was complicated."

"Complicated how?"

I shrugged. "Her condition gives her . . . an impulse-control problem," I said. "She told me that strong emotions and uh, other feelings, are dangerous for her. She could lose control and hurt someone."

"Oh," Molly said, and scrunched up her nose again. "So you can't make a play for her or—"

"Bad things could happen. And then she'd be a full vampire."

"But you both want to be together?" Molly asked.

"Yeah."

She frowned. "God, that's sad. You want to be with her but the sex part—"

I shuddered. "Ewg. You are far too young to say that word."

The girl's eyes shone. "What word? Sex?"

I put my hands over my ears. "Gah."

Molly grinned and enunciated. "But the *bleep* part would make her lose control."

I coughed uncomfortably, lowering my hands. "Basically. Yeah."

"Why don't you tie her up?"

I stared at the kid for a second.

She lifted her eyebrows expectantly.

"What?" I stammered.

"It's only practical," Molly stated firmly. "And hey, you've already got the handcuffs. If she can't move while the two of you are bleeping, she can't drink your blood, right?"

I stood up and started climbing down the ladder. "This conversation has become way too bleeping disturbing."

Molly laughed at me and followed me back to the ground. She unlocked the back door with another key, presumably from the same ring, and that was when Charity's light blue minivan turned into the driveway. Molly opened the door, darted into the house, and returned without her backpack. The minivan ground to a halt and the engine died.

Charity got out of the van, frowning at me and at Molly in more or less equal proportions. She wore jeans, hiking boots, and a heavy jacket. She was a tall woman, only an inch or so under six feet, and carried herself with an assurance that conveyed a sense of ready strength. Her face had the remote beauty of a marble statue, and her long blond hair was knotted behind her head.

Without being told, Molly went to the rolling side panel door, opened it, and reached inside, unloading children from safety seats, while Charity went to the rear of the van and opened the rear doors. "Mister Dresden," she said. "Lend a hand."

I frowned. "Uh. I'm sort of in a hurry. I was hoping to find Michael here."

Charity took a twenty-four-pack of Coke from the van in one arm and a couple of bulging paper grocery sacks in the other. She marched over to me and shoved them at my chest. I had to fumble to catch them, and my blasting rod clattered to the ground.

Charity waited until I had the sacks before heading for the van again. "Put them on the table in the kitchen."

"But—" I said.

She walked past me toward the house. "I have ice cream melting, meat thawing, and a baby about to wake up hungry. Put them on the table, and we'll talk."

I sighed and looked glumly at the groceries. They were heavy enough to make my arms burn a little. Which probably isn't saying much. I don't spend much time working out.

Molly appeared from the van, lowering a tiny, tow-headed girl to the driveway. She was wearing a pink dress with a clashing orange sweater and bright purple shoes and a red coat. She walked up to me and said, words edged with babyish syllables, "My name is Amanda. I'm five and a half and my daddy says I'm a princess."

"I'm Harry, Your Highness," I said.

She frowned and said, "There's already a Harry. You can be Bill." With that, she broke into a flouncing skip and followed her mother into the house.

"Well, I'm glad that's settled," I muttered. Molly lowered an even smaller blond girl to the driveway. This one was dressed in blue overalls with a pink shirt and a pink coat. She held a plush dolly in one arm and a battered-looking pink blanket in the other. Upon seeing me, she retreated a couple of steps and hid around the corner of the van. She leaned out to look at me once, and then hid again.

"I've got him," said an accented male voice.

Molly hopped out of the van, grabbed a grocery bag from the back, and said, "Come on, Hope." The little girl followed her big sister like a duckling while Molly went into the house, but Hope glanced back at me shyly three or four times on the way.

Shiro emerged from the van carrying a baby seat. The little old knight carried the walking stick that concealed his sword on a strap over one wide shoulder, and his scarred hands held the chair carefully. A boy, probably not yet two years old, slept in it.

"Little Harry?" I asked.

"Yes, Bill," Shiro said. His eyes sparkled behind his glasses.

I frowned and said, "Good-looking kid."

"Dresden!" snapped Charity's voice from the house. "You're holding the ice cream."

I scowled and told Shiro, "Guess we'd better get in."

Shiro nodded wisely. I took the groceries into the Carpenters' big kitchen and put them on the table. For the next five minutes, Shiro and Molly helped me carry in enough groceries to feed a Mongol horde.

After all the perishables got put away, Charity fixed a bottle of formula and passed it off to Molly, who took it, the diaper bag, and the sleeping boy into another room. Charity waited until she had left, then shut the door. "Very well," she said, still putting groceries away. "I haven't spoken to Michael since you called this morning. I left a message with his cell phone voice mail."

"Where is he?" I asked.

Shiro laid his cane on the table and sat down. "Mister Dresden, we have asked you not to get involved in this business."

"That isn't why I'm here," I said. "I just need to talk to him."

"Why are you looking for him?" Shiro asked.

"I'm dueling a vampire under the Accords. I need a second before sundown or I get disqualified. Permanently."

Shiro frowned. "Red Court?"

"Yeah. Some guy named Ortega."

"Heard of him," Shiro said. "Some kind of war leader."

I nodded. "That's the rumor. That's why I'm here. I had hoped Michael would be willing to help."

Shiro stroked a thumb over the smooth old wood of his cane. "We received word of Denarian activity near St. Louis. He and Sanya went to investigate."

"When will they get back?"

Shiro shook his head. "I do not know."

I looked at the clock and bit my lip. "Christ."

Charity walked by with an armload of groceries and glared at me.

I lifted my hands. "Sorry. I'm a little tense."

Shiro studied me for a moment, and then asked, "Would Michael help him?"

Charity's voice drifted out of the cavernous walk-in pantry. "My husband is sometimes an idiot."

Shiro nodded and said, "Then I will assist you in his stead, Mister Dresden."

"You'll what?" I asked.

"I will be your second in the duel."

"You don't have to do that," I said. "I mean, I'll figure out something."

Shiro lifted an eyebrow. "Have the weapons been set for the duel?"

"Uh, not yet," I said.

"Then where is the meeting with the emissary and your opponent's second?"

I fished out the card I'd gotten from the Archive. "I don't know. I was told to have my second call this number."

Shiro took the card and rose without another word, heading for the phone in the next room.

I put my hand on his arm and said, "You don't need to take any chances. You don't really know me."

"Michael does. That is enough for me."

The old Knight's support was a relief, but I felt guilty, somehow, for accepting it. Too many people had been hurt on my behalf in the past. Michael and I had faced trouble together before, looked out for each other before. Somehow, it made it easier for me to go to him and ask for help. Accepting the same thing from a stranger, Knight of the Cross or not, grated on my conscience. Or maybe on my pride.

But what choice did I have?

I sighed and nodded. "I just don't want to drag someone else into more trouble with me."

Charity muttered, "Let me think. Where have I heard that before?"

Shiro smiled at her, the expression both paternal and amused, and said, "I'll make the call."

I waited while Shiro made a call from the room that served as the family study and the office for Michael's contracting business. Charity stayed in the kitchen and wrestled a huge Crock-Pot onto the counter. She got out a ton of vegetables, stew meat, and a spice rack and set to chopping things up without a word to me.

I watched her quietly. She moved with the kind of precision you see only in someone who is so versed at what they are doing that they are already thinking of the steps coming twenty minutes in the future. I thought she took her knife to the carrots a little more violently than she needed to. She started preparing another meal somewhere in the middle of making the stew, this one chicken and rice and other healthy things I rarely saw in three dimensions.

I fidgeted for a bit, until I stood up, washed my hands in the sink, and started cutting vegetables.

Charity frowned at me for a moment. She didn't say anything. But she got a few more veggies out and put them down next to me, then collected what had been cut so far and pitched them into the Crock-Pot. A couple of minutes later she sighed, opened a can of Coke, and put it on the counter next to me.

"I worry about him," she said.

I nodded, and focused on cucumbers.

"I don't even know when he'll be home tonight."

"Good thing you have a Crock-Pot," I said.

"I don't know what I would do without him. What the children would do. I'd feel so lost."

What the hell. An ounce of well-intentioned but irrational reassurance didn't cost anything. I took a sip of the Coke. "He'll be all right. He can handle himself. And he has Shiro and Sanya with him."

"He's been hurt three times, you know."

"Three?" I asked.

"Three. With you. Every time."

"So it's my fault." My turn to chop vegetables like teenagers in a slasher movie. "I see."

I couldn't see her face but her voice was, more than anything else, tired. "It isn't about blame. Or whose fault it is. All that matters is that when you're around, my husband, my children's father, gets hurt."

The knife slipped and I cut off a neat little slice of skin on my index finger. "Ow," I snarled. I slapped the cold water on in the sink and put my finger under it. You can't tell, with cuts like that, how bad they're going to be until you see how much you're leaking. Charity passed me a paper towel, and I examined the cut for a minute before wrapping the towel around it. It wasn't bad, though it hurt like hell. I watched my blood stain the paper towel for a minute and then I asked, "Why didn't you get rid of me, then?"

I looked up to see Charity frowning at me. There were dark circles under her eyes that I hadn't noticed before. "What do you mean?"

"Just now," I said. "When Shiro asked you if Michael would help me. You could have said no."

"But he would have helped you in an instant. You know that."

"Shiro didn't."

Her expression became confused. "I don't understand."

"You could have lied."

Her face registered comprehension, and some fire came back into her eyes. "I don't like you, Mister Dresden. I certainly don't care enough for you to abandon beliefs I hold dear, to use you as an excuse to cheapen myself, or to betray what my husband stands for." She stepped to a cabinet and got out a small, neat medical kit. Without another word, she took my hand and the paper towel and opened the kit.

"So you're taking care of me?" I asked.

"I don't expect you to understand. Whether or not I can personally stand you, it has no bearing on what choices I make. Michael is your friend. He would risk his life for you. It would break his heart if you came to grief, and I will not allow that to happen."

She fell silent and doctored the cut with the same brisk, confident motions she'd used for cooking. I hear that they make disinfectants that don't hurt these days.

But Charity used iodine.

Chapter Sixteen

Shiro came out of the office and showed me an address written on a piece of paper. "We meet them tonight at eight."

"After sundown," I noted. "I know the place. I'll pick you up here?"

"Yes. I will need a little time to prepare."

"Me too. Around seven." I told them good-bye and headed for the door. Charity didn't answer me but Shiro did. I got into my car. More kids came pelting into the house as I did, two boys and a girl. The smaller of the two boys stopped to peer at my car, but Charity appeared in the door and chivied him inside. She frowned at me until I coaxed the Blue Beetle to life and pulled out.

Driving home left me with too much time to think. This duel with Ortega was something I had no way to prepare for. Ortega was a warlord of the Red Court. He'd probably fought duels before. Which meant that he'd killed people before. Hell, maybe even wizards. I'd squared off against various toughs but that had been free-for-all fighting. I had been able to find ways to cheat, by and large. In a one-on-one duel, I wasn't going to be able to fall back on cleverness, to take advantage of whatever I could find in my environment.

This was going to be a straight fight, and if Ortega was better than me, he'd kill me. Simple as that. The fear was simple, too. Simple and undeniable.

I swallowed, and my knuckles turned white. I tried to relax my fingers but they wouldn't. They were too afraid to let go of the wheel. Stupid fingers.

I got back to my apartment, pried my fingers off the steering wheel, and found my door halfway open. I ducked to one side, in case someone had a gun pointed up the narrow stairway down to my apartment door, and drew out my blasting rod.

"Harry?" called a quiet, female voice from my apartment. "Harry, is that you?"

I lowered the blasting rod. "Murph?"

"Get inside," Murphy said. I looked down the stairway and saw her appear in the doorway, her face pale. "Hurry."

I came down the stairs warily, feeling out my wards as I did. They were intact, and I relaxed a little. I had given Murphy a personalized talisman that would let her through my defenses, and it would only have worked for her.

I slipped into my apartment. Murphy shut the door behind me and locked it. She'd started a fire in the fireplace and had one of my old kerosene lamps lit. I went to the fireplace and warmed up my hands, watching Murphy in silence. She stood with her back and shoulders rigid for a moment, before she came over to stand beside me, facing the fire. Her lips were held into a tense, neutral line. "We should talk."

"People keep saying that to me," I muttered.

"You promised me you'd call me in when you had something."

"Whoa, there, hang on. Who said I had anything?"

"There is a corpse on a pleasure ship in Burnham Harbor and several eyewitnesses who describe a tall, dark-haired man leaving the scene and getting into a multicolored Volkswagen Beetle."

"Wait a second—"

"There's been a *murder*, Dresden. I don't care how sacred client confidentiality is to you. People are dying."

Frustration made me clench my teeth. "I was going to tell you about it. It's been a really busy day."

"Too busy to talk to the police about a murder you may have witnessed?" Murphy said. "That is considered aiding and abetting a first-degree murder in some places. Like courts of law."

"This again," I muttered. My fingers clenched into fists. "I remember how this one goes. You slug me in the jaw and arrest me."

"I damn well should."

"Hell's bells, Murph!"

"Relax." She sighed. "If that was what I had in mind you'd be in the car already."

My anger evaporated. "Oh." After a moment, I asked, "Then why are you here?"

Murphy scowled. "I'm on vacation."

"You're what?"

Murphy's jaw twitched. Her words sounded a little odd, since she kept her teeth ground together while she talked. "I've been taken off the case. And when I protested I was told that I could either be on vacation or collecting unemployment."

Holy crap. The muckety-mucks at CPD had ordered Murphy off a case? But why?

Murphy answered the question I hadn't asked yet. "Because when Butters looked at the victim from the harbor, he determined that the weapon used to kill her and the one used on that victim you saw last night were the same."

I blinked. "What?"

"Same weapon," Murphy said. "Butters seemed pretty confident about it."

I turned that over in my head a few times, trying to shake out the kinks in the chains of logic. "I need a beer. You?"

"Yeah."

I went over to the pantry and grabbed a couple of brown bottles. I used an old bottle opener to take off the lids and took the drinks back to Murphy. She took her bottle in hand and eyed it suspiciously. "It's warm."

"It's the new recipe. Mac would kill me if he heard I served his brown cold." I took a pull from my bottle. The ale had a rich, full flavor, a little nutty, and it left a pleasant aftertaste lingering in the mouth. Make what jokes you will about trendy microbrews. Mac knew his stuff.

Murphy made a face. "Ugh. Too much taste."

"Wimpy American," I said.

Murphy almost smiled. "Homicide got wind that there was a link between the killing in Italy, the one here by the airport, and the one this morning. So they pulled strings and hogged the whole thing."

"How did they find out?"

"Rudolph," Murphy spat. "There's no way to prove anything but I'll bet you the little weasel heard me on the phone with Butters and ran straight over there to tell them."

"Isn't there anything you can do?"

"Officially, yes. But in real life people are going to start accidentally losing reports and forms and requests if I try to file them. And when I tried to apply some pressure of my own, I got put down hard." She took another angry drink. "I could lose my job."

"That both sucks and blows, Murph."

"Tell me about it." She frowned and looked up at my eyes briefly. "Harry. I want you to back off on this case. For your own sake. That's why I came over here."

I frowned. "Wait a minute. You mean people are threatening *you* with *me*? That's a switch."

"Don't joke about it," Murphy said. "Harry, you've got a history with the department, and not everyone thinks well of you."

"You mean Rudolph."

"Not just Rudolph. There are plenty of people who don't want to believe you're for real. Besides that, you were near the scene of and may have witnessed a felony. They could put you away."

Obviously my life was too easy already. I swigged more beer. "Murph, cop, crook, or creature, it doesn't matter. I don't back off because some bully doesn't like what I do."

"I'm not a bully, Harry. I'm your friend."

I winced. "And you're asking me."

She nodded. "Pretty please. With sugar."

"With sugar. Hell, Murph." I took a drink and squinted at her. "How much do you know about what's going on?"

"I had some of the files taken away before I could read them." She glanced up at me. "But I can read between the lines."

"Okay," I said. "This might take a little explaining."

"You aren't backing off, are you?"

"It isn't an option."

"Stop there then," Murphy said. "The less you tell me, the less I can testify to."

Testify? Hell. There should be some kind of rule about being forced to dodge several kinds of legal land mines at the same time. "This isn't a friendly situation," I said. "If straight cops go into it like it's normal business, they're going to get killed. I'd be really worried even if it were SI."

"Okay," Murphy said. She didn't look happy. She drank her beer in a long pull and set the bottle on my mantel.

I put my hand on her shoulder. She didn't snap it off at the wrist. "Murph. This looks bad already. I have a hunch it could get worse, fast. I have to."

"I know," she said. "I wish I could help."

"Did you get the information on that cell phone?"

"No," she said. But as she said it, she passed me a folded piece of paper. I unfolded it with my fingers and read Murphy's print-ing: *Quebec Nationale, Inc, owner. No phone number. Address a P.O. box. Dead end.*

A dummy company, probably, I thought. The Churchmice could have it set up to do a lot of the buying and selling for them. Maybe dead Gaston had been from Quebec instead of France.

"Got it. Thanks, Murph."

"I don't know what you're talking about," Murphy said. She picked up her jacket from where she'd tossed it on my couch and shrugged into it. "There's no APB out for you yet, Harry, but I'd be discreet if I were you."

"Discreet. That's me."

"I'm serious."

"Serious, yep."

"Dammit, Harry." But she smiled when she said it.

"You probably don't want me to call you if I need help."

She nodded. "Hell, no. That would be illegal. Keep your nose clean, walk the straight and narrow."

"Okay."

Murphy paused and asked, "I don't think I've seen you with-out that coat outside of summer. Where's your duster?"

I grimaced. "Missing in action."

"Oh. You talk to Susan?"

I said, "Yeah."

I felt Murphy's eyes on my face. She got it without being told. "Oh," she said again. "Sorry, Harry."

"Thanks."

"See you." She opened my door, kept her hand near her gun, and then warily padded on out.

I shut my door after her and leaned against it. Murphy was worried. She wouldn't have come to me in person if she weren't. And she'd been extra careful with the legal stuff. Were things that dicey in the CPD?

Murphy was the first head of Special Investigations not to get her rear bounced onto the street after a token week or three of un-solvable cases. Generally speaking, when the administration wanted someone off the force, they'd get promoted to running SI. Or at least working in it. Every cop there had some kind of failing that had landed them what everyone else considered to be a cruddy assignment. It had, by and large, created a strong sense of camaraderie among the SI officers, a bond only made tighter by the way they occasionally faced off with one kind of nightmarish creature or another.

SI cops had taken down several half-assed dark spellslingers, half a dozen vampires, seven or eight ravening trolls, and a demon that had manifested itself out of a mound of compost-heated garbage behind a pawnshop in Chinatown. SI could handle itself pretty well because they played careful, they worked together, and they understood that there were unnatural beings that sometimes had to be dealt with in ways not strictly in accordance with police procedure. Oh, and because they had a hired wizard to advise them about bad guys, of course. I liked to think that I had contributed too.

But I guess every bucket of fruit has something go rotten sooner or later. In SI the stinker was Detective Rudolph. Rudy was young, good-looking, clean-cut, and had slept with the wrong councilman's daughter. He had applied some industrial-strength denial to his experiences with SI despite freak encounters with monsters, magic, and human kindness. He had clung to a steadfast belief that everything was normal, and the realm of the paranormal was all make-believe.

Rudy didn't like me. Rudy didn't like Murphy. If the kid had sabotaged Murphy's investigation in order to curry favor with the folks in Homicide, maybe he was angling to get out of SI.

And maybe he'd lose a bunch of teeth the next time he walked through a quiet parking garage. I doubted Murphy would take that kind of backstabbing with good grace. I spent a moment indulging myself in a pleasant fantasy in which Murphy pounded Rudy's head against the door of her office at SI's home building until the cheap wood had a Rudolph-shaped dent in it. I enjoyed the thought way too much.

I gathered up a few things from around my apartment, including the antivenom potions Bob had helped me with. I checked on Bob while I was in the lab, and got a sleepy and incoherent response that I understood to mean that he needed more rest. I let him, went back upstairs, and called my answering service.

I had a message from Susan, a phone number. I called it, and a second later she answered. "Harry?"

"You've become clairvoyant. If you can do a foreign accent you could get a hot line."

"Like, sure, as if," Susan drawled ditzily.

"California isn't foreign," I said.

"You'd be surprised. How did things go?"

"Okay, I guess," I said. "I got a second."

"Michael?" she asked.

"Shiro."

"Who?"

"He's like Michael but shorter and older."

"Oh, uh. Good. I did the legwork."

I thought of some work I'd seen Susan's legs do before. But I only said, "And?"

"And the downtown Marriott is hosting an art gala this very night, including a gallery sale and a fund-raiser auction for charity."

I whistled. "Wow. So lots of art and money moving around, changing hands, being shipped hither and yon."

"Hither maybe, but I don't think UPS does yon," Susan said. "Seems like a good place to sell a hot article or three. And it's all sponsored by the Chicago Historical and Art Society."

"Who?"

"A very small and very elite club for the upper crust. Gentleman Johnny Marcone is chairman of its board of directors."

"Sounds like smuggling country all right," I said. "How do I get in?"

"You put up a five-thousand-dollar-per-plate donation to charity."

"Five *thousand*," I said. "I don't think I've ever had that much all in one place at one time."

"Then you might try option two."

"Which is?"

Susan's voice took on a note of satisfaction. "You go with a reporter from the *Midwest Arcane* on her last assignment for her editor. I talked to Trish and got two tickets that had originally been given to a reporter on the *Tribune*."

"I'm impressed," I said.

"It gets better. I got us formal wear. The gala begins at nine."

"Us? Uh, Susan. I don't want to sound like an ass, but do you remember the last time you wanted to come on an investigation with me?"

"This time I'm the one with the tickets," she said. "Are you coming with me or not?"

I thought about it for a minute but didn't see any way around it. There wasn't time for a long argument, either. "I'm in. I have to meet the Reds at McAnnally's at eight."

"Meet you there with your tux. Eight-thirty?"

"Yeah. Thank you."

"Sure," she said quietly. "Glad I could help."

Silence stretched long enough to become painful for both of us. I finally broke it at the same time as Susan. "Well, I'd better—"

"Well, I'd better let you go," Susan said. "I have to hurry to get all of this done."

"All right," I said. "Be careful."

"Stones and glass houses, Harry. See you this evening."

We hung up, and I made sure I was ready to go.

Then I went to pick up my second, and work out the terms to a duel I was increasingly certain I had little chance of surviving.

Chapter Seventeen

I put on an old fleece-lined denim jacket and went by my office. The night security guy gave me a little trouble, but I eventually browbeat him into opening the safe in the office to retrieve my envelope from Father Vincent. I opened it and found a plastic case the size of a playing card, like the kind coin collectors use to frame paper money. In the exact center of the case was a single, dirty white thread about two inches long. The sample from the Shroud.

It wasn't much to work with. I could use the thread to create a channel to the rest of the Shroud, but nothing was certain. The thread had presumably been absent from the rest of the Shroud for going on thirty years. Not only that, but it had presumably been handled by various scientists or clergy, and it was possible that they had left enough of a psychic residue on the thread to cloud a seeking spell.

On top of all that, the thread was tiny. I would have to be extremely careful if I used a spell to go hunting the Shroud, or the forces in it would overload the thread in the same way that enough electrical current will overload the filament in a lightbulb. I'm not so great with delicate spell work. I've got plenty of power, but fine control of it could be a problem. By necessity, I would have to use a very gentle spell, and that would put severe limits on the range of it.

The spell would be a metal detector, rather than a radar dish, but it was a whole lot better than nothing. I hit the door.

Rather than inflicting another Charity encounter upon myself, I pulled the Beetle up to the curb in front of Michael's house and honked the horn. A moment later, Shiro appeared. The little old man had shaved the white down from his head, and where he didn't have liver spots, the skin shone. He wore some kind of loose-fitting black pants that looked a lot like the ones I'd seen Murphy wear at one of her aikido tournaments. He also wore a black shirt and a white gi jacket with a scarlet cross on either side of his chest. A belt of red silk held the jacket closed, and he wore his sword through it, still in its wooden cane-sheath. He opened the door, slipped into the Beetle, and held his sword across his lap.

I got going, and neither of us said anything for a while. My knuckles were getting white again, so I started talking. "So you've done one of these duels before?"

"Hai," he said, nodding. "Many times."

"Why?"

Shiro shrugged. "Many reasons. Protect someone. Force something to leave an area in peace. Fight without involving others."

"To the death?"

Shiro nodded. "Many times."

"Guess you're pretty good at it then," I said.

Shiro smiled a little, eyes wrinkling even more. "Always someone better."

"You ever dueled a vampire?"

"Hai. Jade Court. Black Court."

"Jade Court?" I said. "I've never heard that there was such a thing."

"Southeast Asia, China, Japan. Very secretive. But they respect the Accords."

"Have you dueled any of the Denarians?"

He frowned out the window. "Twice. But they do not honor agreements. Treachery both times."

I thought that over for a while before I said, "I'm going for energy. If he won't take it, we'll do will."

Shiro glanced aside at me and nodded. "But there is a better choice."

"What?"

"Don't fight. Can't lose a fight you don't have."

I felt a snort coming on but I held it back. "I'm sort of locked into it now."

"Both parties want to quit, duel over," Shiro said. "I will be talking to Ortega's second. Ortega will be there. Smart for you try to talk him out of it."

"I don't think he'll do it."

"Maybe. Maybe not. Not fighting always smarter."

"Says the militant Knight of the Cross and his holy blade?"

"I hate fighting."

I glanced at him for a second, then said, "You don't usually hear that from someone good at it."

Shiro smiled. "Fighting is never good. But sometimes necessary."

I blew out a deep breath. "Yeah. I guess I know what you mean."

The rest of the ride to McAnnally's was quiet. In the streetlights, my knuckles looked the same color as the rest of my hands.

McAnnally's is a tavern. Not a bar, not a pub, but an actual, Old World–style tavern. When I went in, I stepped down three steps to the hardwood floor and looked around the place. The bar has thirteen stools at it. There were thirteen columns of dark wood, each one hand-carved with swirling leaves and images of beings of tale and fantasy. Thirteen tables had been spaced out around the room in an irregular pattern, and like the columns and bar stools, they had been intentionally placed that way in order to deflect and scatter random magical energies. It cut down on the accidents from grumpy wizards and clueless kids just discovering their power. Several ceiling fans whirled lazily, and were low enough that I always felt a bit nervous about one of them whirling into my eyebrows. The place smells of wood smoke, old whiskey barrels, fresh bread, and roasting meat. I like it.

Mac stood behind the bar. I didn't know much about Mac. He was tall, medium build, bald, and somewhere between thirty and sixty. He had large and facile hands and thick wrists. All I've ever seen him wear is dark pants with a loose white shirt and an apron that somehow remained free of splatters of grease, spilled drinks, and the various other things he prepared for customers.

Mac caught my eye when I came in and nodded to my left. I looked. A sign on the wall said, ACCORDED NEUTRAL GROUND. I looked back at Mac. He drew a shotgun out from behind the bar so that I could see it and said, "Got it?"

"No problem," I answered.

"Good."

The room was otherwise empty, though normally there would be a couple of dozen members of the local magical scene. Not full-fledged wizards or anything, but there were plenty of people with a dab of magical talent. Then there were a couple of different Wiccan groups, the occasional changeling, scholars of the arcane, a gang of do-gooder werewolves, members of secret societies, and who knew what else. Mac must have put out the word that a meeting was happening here. No one sane wants to be anywhere close to what could be a fight between a White Council member and a Red Court warlord. I knew I was sane because I didn't want to be there, either.

I walked over to the bar and said, "Beer." Mac grunted and plopped down a bottle of brown. I pushed some bills at him but he shook his head.

Shiro stood at the bar next to me, facing the opposite way. Mac put a bottle down beside him. Shiro twisted off the cap with one hand, took a modest sip, and set the bottle back down. Then he glanced at it thoughtfully, picked it up, and took a slower sip. *"Yosh."*

Mac grunted, "Thanks."

Shiro said something in what I guessed was Japanese. Mac answered monosyllabically. A man of many talents and few syllables is Mac.

I killed time with a couple more sips and the door opened.

Kincaid walked in, in the same outfit I'd seen that morning, but without the baseball cap. His dark blond hair was instead pulled back into an unruly tail. He nodded at Mac and asked, "All set?"

"Ungh," said Mac.

Kincaid prowled the room, looking under tables and behind columns, and checked the rest rooms and behind the counter as well. Mac said nothing, but I had the impression that he felt the precaution to be useless. Kincaid went to a corner table, nudging other tables back from it a bit, and put three chairs around it. He drew a gun out of a shoulder rig and set it on the table, then took a seat.

"Hi," I said toward him. "Nice to see you, too. Where's Ivy?"

"Past her bedtime," Kincaid said without smiling. "I'm her proxy."

"Oh," I said. "She has a bedtime?"

Kincaid checked his watch. "She believes very strongly in an early bedtime for children."

"Heh, heh, eh-heh." I don't fake amused chuckles well. "So where's Ortega?"

"Saw him parking outside," Kincaid said.

The door opened and Ortega entered. He wore a casual black blazer with matching slacks and a shirt of scarlet silk. He hadn't worn a coat despite the cold. His skin was darker than I remembered it. Maybe he'd fed recently. He carried himself with a relaxed, patient quality as he entered and surveyed the room.

He bowed slightly at the waist toward Mac, who nodded back. The vampire's eyes landed on Shiro and narrowed. Shiro said nothing and did not move. Ortega then regarded me with an unreadable expression and gave me a very slight nod. It seemed polite to nod back to him, so I did. Ortega did the same to Kincaid, who returned it with a lazy wave of one hand.

"Where is your second?" Kincaid asked.

Ortega grimaced. "Primping."

He hadn't finished the word before a young man slapped the door open and stepped jauntily into the tavern. He was wearing tight, white leather pants, a black fishnet shirt, and a white leather jacket. His hair was dark and hung to his shoulders in an unruly mane. He had a male model's face, smoky grey eyes, and thick, dark eyelashes. I knew him. Thomas Raith, a White Court vampire.

"Thomas," I said by way of greeting.

"Evening, Harry," he answered. "What happened to your duster?"

"There was a woman."

"I see," Thomas said. "Pity. It was the only thing you owned that gave me hope that there might be a feeble flicker of style in you."

"You should talk. That outfit you're wearing is treading dangerously close to the Elvis zone."

"Young, sleek Elvis ain't bad," Thomas said.

"I meant old, fat Elvis. Possibly Michael Jackson."

The pale man put a hand to his heart. "That hurts, Harry."

"Yeah, I've had a rough day too."

"Gentlemen," Kincaid said, a note of impatience in his voice. "Shall we begin?"

I nodded. So did Ortega. Kincaid introduced everyone and produced a document that stated he was working for the Archive. It was written in crayon. I drank some more beer. After that, Kincaid invited Shiro and Thomas to join him at the corner table. I went back to the bar, and a moment later, Ortega followed me. He sat down with a couple of empty stools between us, while Kincaid, Thomas, and Shiro spoke quietly in the background.

I finished my bottle and set it down with a thump. Mac turned around to get me another. I shook my head. "Don't bother. I've got enough on my tab already."

Ortega put a twenty down on the bar and said, "I'll cover it. Another for me as well."

I started to make a wiseass remark about how buying me a beer would surely make up for threatening my life and the lives of those I cared about, but I bit it back. Shiro had been right about fighting. You can't lose a fight you don't show up to. So I took the beer Mac brought me and said, "Thanks, Ortega."

He nodded, and took a sip. His eyes lit up a bit, and he took a second, slower one. "It's good."

Mac grunted.

"I thought you guys drank blood," I said.

"It's all we really need," Ortega said.

"Then why do you have anything else?"

Ortega held up the bottle. "Life is more than mere survival. All you need is the water, after all. Why drink beer?"

"You ever tasted the water in this town?"

He almost smiled. "Touché."

I turned the plain brown bottle around in my fingers. "I don't want this," I said.

"The duel?"

I nodded.

Ortega leaned an elbow on the bar and considered me. "Neither do I. This isn't personal. It isn't something I want."

"So don't do it," I said. "We could both walk."

"And the war would go on."

"It's been going on for nearly two years," I said. "It's mostly been cat and mouse, a couple of raids, fights in back alleys. It's like the Cold War, only with fewer Republicans."

Ortega frowned, and watched Mac cleaning the grill behind the bar. "It can get worse, Mister Dresden. It can get a great deal worse. And if the conflict escalates, it will threaten the balance of power throughout the worlds of flesh and spirit alike. Imagine the destruction, the loss of life that could ensue."

"So why not contribute to the peace effort? Starting with this duel. Maybe we could get some beads and some fringe and make signs that say 'Make blood not war' or something."

This time, Ortega did smile. It was a weary expression on him. "It's too late for that," he said. "Your blood is all that will satisfy many of my peers."

"I can donate," I said. "Let's say once every two months. You provide cookies and orange juice."

Ortega leaned toward me, the smile fading. "Wizard. You murdered a noble of our Court."

I got angry. My voice gained heat. "The only reason—"

Ortega cut me off, lifting his hand. "I do not say that your reasons were not valid. But the fact of the matter is that you appeared in her home as a guest and representative of the Council. And you attacked and eventually killed both Bianca and those under her protection."

"Killing me won't bring her back," I said.

"But it will slake the thirst for vengeance that plagues many of my kinsmen. When you are no more, they will be willing to at least attempt a peaceful resolution."

"Dammit," I muttered, and fiddled with the bottle.

"Though . . ." Ortega murmured. His eyes became distant for a moment. "There might be another way."

"What other way?"

"Yield," Ortega said. "Yield to the duel and let me take you into custody. If you are willing to work with me, I could place you under my protection."

"Work with you," I said. My stomach flip-flopped. "You mean become like you."

"It is an alternative to death," Ortega said, his expression earnest. "My kinsmen may not like it, but they could not argue against it. For taking Bianca's life, you could replace it with your own."

"As one of you."

Ortega nodded. "As one of us." He was quiet for a moment, then said, "You could bring Miss Rodriguez with you. Be together. She would not be a threat to you, were you both my vassals." He put his beer down. "I think you will find that we are much alike, Dresden. We're just playing for different teams."

I rubbed at my mouth. My instinctive reaction to Ortega's offer was one of revulsion. The Red Court vampires don't look like most would think. They looked like giant, hairless bats with slick, rubbery skin. They could cover themselves with a flesh mask in order to look human, but I'd seen what was underneath the mask.

I'd been exposed to it. Thoroughly. I still had nightmares.

I opened my eyes. "Let me ask you a question."

"Very well."

"Do you live in a manor?"

"Casaverde," Ortega responded. "It's in Honduras. There is a village nearby."

"Uh-huh," I said. "So you feed on the villagers."

"Carefully. I provide them with supplies, medical attention, other necessities."

"Sounds reasonable," I said.

"It's beneficial to both of us. The villagers know that."

"Yeah, they probably do." I finished off the bottle. "Do you feed on children?"

Ortega frowned at me. "What do you mean?"

I didn't bother to hide the anger in my voice. "Do. You. Feed. On. Children."

"It's the safest way. The more the feeding is spread among many, the less dangerous it is for all of them."

"You're wrong. We're different." I stood up. "You hurt kids. We're done."

Ortega's voice sharpened. "Dresden. Do not lightly discard my offer."

"The offer to make me into a blood-drinking monster in eternal slavery to you? Why would I want to do that?"

"It is the only way to keep your life," Ortega said.

I felt the anger coalescing into rage. My upper lip curled away from my teeth, baring them in a snarl. "I thought life is more than mere survival."

Ortega's expression changed. It was only for a second, but in that moment I saw furious rage, arrogant pride, and violent blood-lust on his face. He regained his calm quickly, but traces of the hidden emotions thickened his accent.

"So be it. I will kill you, wizard."

He sounded convincing. It scared me. I turned and walked to the door. "I'll be outside," I said to no one in particular, and stepped out into the late-February cold.

That way, I'd have an excuse to be trembling.

Chapter Eighteen

I didn't have long to wait. The door opened behind me, and Kincaid emerged. He didn't say a word to me, just got into a rented sedan and left. Ortega came next. A car swung in off the street, and he opened the passenger door. He paused and looked back at me.

"I have a measure of respect for your principles and skills, Dresden. But this situation is of your own making, and I cannot allow it to continue. I'm sorry."

I watched him get in the car, and I didn't offer him any reply. Hell, he hadn't said a word that was untrue. Ortega had a genuine ax to grind and people—well, fellow monsters—to protect. And thus far, the Dresden-versus-vampires scoreboard read a whole bunch to zero.

If a vampire had done that to the White Council, I wonder if we would have reacted with as much reason and calm.

The taillights of Ortega's car hadn't yet gotten out of sight when Thomas emerged from the tavern and swaggered casually over to me. Thomas was a shade under six feet tall, which put him at half a head shorter than me. He was better-looking though, and despite my earlier comments about his outfit, he was one of those men who made anything look good. The fishnet shirt he wore cast patterns of shadow over the pale skin beneath it, adding to the lines of muscle on his stomach.

My stomach had muscles, but not so many that you could see them rippling. I'd have looked pathetic in a shirt like that.

"That was simple enough," Thomas said. He drew a pair of black leather driving gloves from his jacket pocket and started tugging them on. "Though I take it this duel isn't the only game in town at the moment."

"Why would you say that?" I asked.

"I've had a pro hitter following me ever since I landed yesterday. The itch between my shoulder blades got annoying."

I glanced around. "Is he here now?"

Thomas's eyes glittered. "No. I introduced him to my sisters."

The White Court were the most human of the vampires and in some ways the weakest. They fed on psychic energies, on pure life force rather than on blood. Most often, they would seduce those they fed upon, drawing life from them through physical contact during the act. If a couple of Thomas's sisters had met the hired gun tailing Thomas, the assassin probably wasn't going to be a problem to anyone. Ever. My eye twitched.

"The gunman was probably Ortega's," I said. "He hired some goons to take out people I knew if I didn't agree to this duel."

"That explains it, then," Thomas said. "Ortega really doesn't like me much. Must be the unsavory company I've kept in the past."

"Gee, thanks. How the hell did you end up his second?"

"It's my father's idea of a joke," Thomas said. "Ortega asked him to be his second. Show of solidarity between the Red and White Courts. Instead, Daddy dearest found the most annoying and insulting member of the family he possibly could to stand in."

"You," I said.

"C'est moi," Thomas confirmed with a little bow. "One would almost think Father was trying to get me killed."

I felt one side of my mouth tug up into a smile. "Nice father figure. Him and Bill Cosby. How's Justine?"

Thomas grimaced. "She's in Aruba is how she is. Which is where I was until one of pappa Raith's goons dragged me back up here."

"What did you two decide on for the duel?"

Thomas shook his head. "Can't tell you. Shiro is supposed to do that. I mean, technically I'm at war with you."

I grimaced and stared after Ortega's vanished car. "Yeah."

Thomas was quiet for a second, then said, "He means to kill you."

"I know."

"He's dangerous, Harry. Smart. My father is afraid of him."

"I could like him," I said. "It's sort of refreshing to have someone trying to kill me right to my face, instead of throwing me a bunch of curveballs and shooting me in the back. It's almost nice to have a fair fight."

"Sure. Theoretically."

"Theoretically?"

Thomas shrugged. "Ortega's been alive for about six hundred years. It isn't something you do by playing nice."

"From what I've heard, the Archive will object to any monkey business."

"It's only cheating if he gets caught."

I frowned at him and said, "Are you saying someone is planning to avoid getting caught?"

Thomas put his hands in his jacket pockets. "I'm not saying anything. I wouldn't mind seeing you kick his ass, but I'm sure as hell not going to do something that would attract attention to me."

"You intend to participate without being involved. That's clever."

Thomas rolled his eyes. "I won't throw a banana peel under you. But don't expect any help from me, either. I'm just making sure it's a fair fight and then I'm back at my beach house." He drew car keys from his pocket and headed for the parking lot. "Good luck."

"Thomas," I said to his back. "Thanks for the heads-up."

He paused.

I asked, "Why do it?"

The vampire glanced over his shoulder at me and smiled. "Life would be unbearably dull if we had answers to all our questions." He walked out to a white sports car and slipped into it. A second later, loud, screaming metal music started from the car's stereo, the engine roared, and Thomas drove off.

I checked my watch. Ten more minutes until Susan arrived. Shiro emerged from McAnnally's and put on his glasses. Once he spotted me, he walked over and took the glasses off again. "Ortega refused to cancel the duel?"

"He made me an offer I couldn't excuse," I said.

Shiro grunted. "Duel is wills. Tomorrow, just after sundown. Wrigley Field."

"A stadium? Why don't we put it on pay-per-view while we're at it." I glowered at the street and checked my watch again. "I'm meeting someone in a minute. I'll give you the keys to my car. I can pick it up from Michael's tomorrow."

"No need," Shiro said. "Mac called me a cab."

"Okay." I pocketed my keys.

Shiro stood quietly for a moment, lips pursed thoughtfully, before he said, "Ortega means to kill you."

"Yes. Yes, he does," I said. I managed not to grind my teeth as I said it. "Everyone is saying that like I didn't know it already."

"But you do not know *how*." I frowned and looked down at Shiro. His shaved head gleamed under a nearby streetlight. "The war is not your fault."

"I know that," I said, but my voice lacked conviction.

"No," Shiro said. "It *truly* is not your fault."

"What do you mean?"

"The Red Court has been quietly building its resources for years," he said. "How else were they ready to start their attacks in Europe only days after you defeated Bianca?"

I frowned at him.

Shiro drew a cigar from inside his jacket and bit off the end. He spat it to one side. "You were not the cause of the war. You were merely the excuse. The Reds would have attacked when they were ready."

"No," I said. "That's not how it is. I mean, damn near everyone I've spoken to on the Council—"

Shiro snorted. He struck a match and puffed on the cigar a few times while he lit it. "The Council. Arrogant. As if nothing significant could happen unless a wizard did it."

For someone who wasn't on the White Council, Shiro seemed to have its general attitude pretty well surrounded. "If the Red Court wanted a war, why is Ortega trying to stop it?"

"Premature," Shiro said. "Needed more time to be completely prepared. The advantage of surprise is gone. He wishes to strike once and be certain it is a lethal stroke."

I watched the little old man for a minute. "Everyone's got advice tonight. Why are you giving it?"

"Because in some ways you are every bit as arrogant as the Council, though you do not realize it. You blame yourself for what happened to Susan. You want to blame yourself for more."

"So what if I do?"

Shiro turned me and faced me squarely. I avoided meeting his eyes. "Duels are a test of fire. They are fought in the will. The heart. If you do not find your balance, Ortega will not need to kill you. You will do so for him."

"I guess you were a psychoanalyst before you were a sword-swinging vigilante against evil."

Shiro puffed on the cheroot. "Either way, been alive longer than you. See more than you."

"Like what?"

"Like this vampire warlord. How he manipulates you. He is not what he seems to be."

"Really? I've never seen that one before," I said. "Someone not what they appear to be. How ever will I adjust."

Shiro shrugged. "He is centuries old. He is not from the same world. The world Ortega lived in was savage. Brutal. Men like him destroyed entire civilizations for gold and glory. And for hundreds of years since then, he has fought rival vampires, demons, and enemies of his kind. If he approaches you through formal, civilized channels, it is because he thinks it is the best way to kill you. Regardless of what happens in the duel, he intends to see you dead by any means necessary. Maybe before. Maybe after. But dead."

Shiro didn't put any particular emphasis on the words. He didn't need to. They were enough to scare me without any added dramatics. I glowered at his cigar and said, "Those things will kill you."

The old man smiled again. "Not tonight."

"I'd think a good Christian boy wouldn't be puffing down the cigars."

"Technicality," Shiro said.

"The cigars?"

"My Christianity," Shiro said. "When I was a boy, I liked Elvis. Had a chance to see him in concert when we moved to California. It was a big revival meeting. There was Elvis and then a speaker and my English was not so good. He invited people backstage to meet the king. Thought he meant Elvis, so I go backstage." He sighed. "Found out later I had become a Baptist."

I barked out a laugh. "You're kidding."

"No. But it was done, so I tried not to be too bad at being Baptist." He rested a hand on the handle of his sword. "Then came into this. Made the whole thing more simple. I serve."

"Serve who?"

"Heaven. Or the divine in nature. The memory of my fathers past. My fellow man. Myself. All pieces of the same thing. Do you know the story of the blind men and the elephant?"

"Have you heard the one about the bear that walks into a bar?" I responded.

"I think that is a no," Shiro said. "Three blind men were shown an elephant. They touched it with their hands to determine what the creature was. The first man felt the trunk, and claimed that an elephant was like a snake. The second man touched its leg and claimed that an elephant was like a tree. The third man touched its tail, and claimed that the elephant was like a slender rope."

I nodded. "Oh. I get it. All of them were right. All of them were wrong. They couldn't get the whole picture."

Shiro nodded. "Precisely. I am just another blind man. I do not get the whole picture of what transpires in all places. I am blind and limited. I would be a fool to think myself wise. And so, not knowing what the universe means, I can only try to be responsible with the knowledge, the strength, and the time given to me. I must be true to my heart."

"Sometimes that isn't good enough," I said.

He tilted his head and looked up at me. "How do you know?"

A cab swerved in from the street and rattled to a stop. Shiro stepped over to it and nodded to me. "Will be at Michael's if you need me. Be watchful."

I nodded at him. "Thank you."

Shiro said, "Thank me after." Then he got into the cab and left.

Mac closed up shop a minute later, and put on a dark fedora on his way out. He nodded at me on the way to his Trans Am, and said nothing. I found a shadowy spot to linger in as Mac left, and kept an eye on the street. I'd hate for someone to drive by and shoot me with a plain old gun. Embarrassing.

A long, dark limo pulled into the parking lot. A uniformed driver got out and opened the door nearest to me. A pair of long, honey-brown legs slid out of the limo on top of black stiletto heels. Susan glided out of the car, managing grace despite the shoes, which probably qualified her for superhuman status all by itself. A sleeveless sheath of shimmering black cloth clung to her, an evening gown slit high on one side. Dark gloves covered her arms to the elbow, and her hair had been done up in a pile on top of her head, held in place with a couple of gleaming black chopsticks.

My tongue dropped out of my mouth and flopped onto my shoes. Well, not literally, but if I'd been a cartoon my eyeballs would have been about six feet long.

Susan had read my face and apparently enjoyed my reaction. "How much, good-looking?"

I looked down at my rumpled clothing. "I think I'm a tad underdressed."

"One tuxedo, coming up," Susan said.

The driver opened the trunk and drew out a hanger covered

with a dry-cleaning bag. When he turned around with it, I realized that the driver was Martin. All he'd done to disguise himself was don an archetypical uniform and I hadn't even recognized him until second glance. I guess sometimes it's handy to be bland.

"Is it my size?" I asked, taking the tux when Martin passed it to me.

"I had to guess," Susan said, lowering her eyelids in a sultry expression. "But it wasn't like I didn't know my way around."

Martin's face might have flickered with disapproval. My heart sped up a bit. "All right then," I said. "Let's get moving. I'll dress on the way."

"Do I get to look?" Susan asked.

"It'll cost you extra," I said. Martin opened the door for Susan and I slid in after her. I filled her in on what I'd found out about the Shroud and those after it. "I should be able to find the thing if we get close."

"You think there will be any more of these Denarians there?"

"Probably," I said. "If anything gets ugly, we'll take the best part of valor, pronto. These guys play hardball."

Susan nodded agreement. "Sounds like the thieves aren't exactly shy about waving guns, either."

"And we'll have Marcone around too. Whither he goeth, there too goeth armed thugs and homicide investigations."

Susan smiled. It was a new expression to me—a small, quiet, fierce little smile that showed her teeth. It looked natural on her. "You're all about fun, aren't you, Harry?"

"I am the Bruce Lee of fun," I concurred. "Give me some space here."

Susan slid over as far as she could to give me room to climb into the tux. I tried not to mar it too badly in the limited space. Susan glanced at me with a faint frown.

"What?" I asked her.

"You're wrinkling it."

"This isn't as easy as I'm making it look," I responded.

"If you weren't staring at my legs, maybe it wouldn't be such a challenge."

"I wasn't staring," I lied.

Susan smiled at me as the car cruised through downtown and I did my best to dress like Roger Moore. Her expression became thoughtful after a moment, and she said, "Hey."

"What?"

"What happened to your leather coat?"

Chapter Nineteen

The downtown Marriott was huge, brilliantly lit, and busy as an anthill. Several blue-and-whites were parked nearby, and a couple of officers were helping to direct traffic in front of the hotel. I could see maybe twenty limos on the street and pulling through the archway in front of the hotel doors, and every one of them looked bigger and nicer than ours. Valets rushed around to park the cars of guests who had driven themselves. There were a dozen men in red jackets standing around with bored expressions that some might mistake for inattention. Hotel security.

Martin pulled up to the entryway and said, "I'll wait for you out here." He passed a palm-sized cell phone to Susan. She slipped it into a black clutch. "If you get into trouble, speed-dial one."

At that point, a valet opened the door on my side, and I slipped out of the car. My rental tux felt a little awkward. The shoes were long enough for me but they were an inch and a half too wide. I shrugged my jacket into place, straightened the cummerbund, and offered a hand to Susan. She slid out of the car with a brilliant smile, and straightened my tie.

"Smile," she said quietly. "Everyone here is worried about image. If you walk in scowling like that we won't blend in."

I smiled in what I thought was a camouflaging manner. Susan regarded the expression critically, nodded, and slipped her arm through mine. We walked in under the cover our smiles provided. One of the security guards stopped us inside the door, and Susan presented the tickets to him. He waved us through.

"First thing to do is find some stairs," I said from behind my smile. "The loading docks will be near the kitchens, and they're below us. That's where they'll be bringing in the art stuff."

Susan held her course toward the stairs. "Not yet," she said. "If we snoop around the second we get in the door someone is likely to notice. We should mingle until the auction is running. People will be distracted then."

"If we wait, the whole thing could go down while we hobnob."

"Maybe," Susan said. "But odds are that Anna Valmont and the buyer are both thinking the same thing."

"When does the auction start?"

"Eleven."

"Assuming the note means that the sale is at eleven forty-five, that doesn't give us much time to look around. This place is huge."

We got onto an escalator and Susan arched an eyebrow at me. "Do you have any better ideas?"

"Not yet," I said. I caught a glimpse of myself in a polished brass column. I didn't look half-bad. There's a reason the tux has weathered a century virtually unchanged. You don't fix what isn't broken. Tuxedos make anyone look good, and I was a living testament to it. "Think they will have anything to eat? I'm starving."

"Just keep the shirt clean," Susan muttered.

"No problem. I can wipe my fingers on the cummerbund."

"I can't take you anywhere," Susan said. She leaned a little against me, and it felt nice. I felt nice, generally speaking. I cleaned up pretty well, it would seem, and I had a lovely woman—no, I had *Susan* on my arm, looking lovely. It was a small silver lining compared to the troubled clouds I'd been floundering through, but it was something, and it lasted all the way up the escalator. I take the good moments wherever I can get them.

We followed the flow of formally dressed men and women up another escalator or three to a cavernous ballroom. Chandeliers hung from the ceiling and tables laden with expensive-looking snacks and ice sculptures all but overflowed onto the floor. A group of musicians played on the far side of the ballroom. They didn't seem to be stretching themselves with some relaxed and classy jazz. Couples who also weren't stretching themselves danced together on a floor the size of a basketball court.

The room wasn't crammed with people, but there were a couple of hundred there already, and more coming in behind us. Polite but insincere chatter filled the space, accompanied by equally insincere smiles and laughter. There were a number of city officials whom I recognized in the immediate area, plus a couple of professional musicians and at least one motion-picture actor.

A waiter in a white jacket offered us a tray of champagne glasses, and I promptly appropriated a pair of them, passing the first to Susan. She lifted the glass to her mouth but didn't drink. The champagne smelled good. I took a sip, and it tasted good. I'm not a terribly impressive drinker, so I stopped after the first sip. Chugging down champagne on an empty stomach would probably prove inconvenient if it turned out I needed to do any quick thinking. Or quick leaving. Or quick anything.

Susan said hello to an older couple, and stopped for introductions. I kept my duck blind of a smile in place, and mouthed appropriately polite phrases in the right spots. My cheeks had already started hurting. We repeated that for half an hour or so, while the band played a bunch of low-key dance music. Susan knew a lot of people. She'd been a reporter in Chicago for five or six years before she'd had to leave town, but she had evidently managed to ingratiate herself to more people than I would have guessed. You go, Susan.

"Food," I said, after a stooped older man kissed Susan's cheek and walked away. "Feed me, Seymour."

"It's always the brain stem with you," she murmured. But she guided us over to the refreshment tables so that I could pick up a tiny sandwich. I didn't wolf the thing down in one bite, which was just as well, since it had a toothpick through it to hold it together. But the sandwich didn't last long.

"At least chew with your mouth closed," Susan said.

I took a second sandwich. "Can't help it. I got all kinds of joie de vivre, baby."

"And smile."

"Chew *and* smile? At the same time? Do I look like Jackie Chan?"

She had a retort but it died after a syllable. I felt her hand tighten on my arm. I briefly debated wolfing the second sandwich, just to get it out of the way, but I took the more sophisticated option instead. I put it in my jacket pocket for later, and turned to follow Susan's gaze.

I looked just in time to meet the gaze of Gentleman Johnny Marcone. He was a man of slightly above average height and unassuming build. He had handsome but unremarkable features. Central casting would have placed him as the genial next-door neighbor. He didn't have the usual boater's tan, it being February and all, but the crow's-feet at the corners of his pale green eyes remained. He looked a lot like the fictional public image he projected—that of a normal, respectable businessman, an American tale of middle class made good.

That said, Marcone scared me more than any single human being I'd ever met. I'd seen him produce a knife from his sleeve faster than a hyperstrong psychotic could swing a tire iron at him. He'd thrown another knife through a rope while spinning in circles as he hung upside down in the dark, later the same night. Marcone may have been human, but he wasn't normal. He'd taken control of Chicago's organized crime during a free-for-all gang war, and he'd run it ever since despite the efforts of both everyday and supernatural threats. He'd done it by being deadlier than anything that came after him. Of all the people in the room, Marcone was the only one I could see who wasn't wearing a fake smile. It didn't look like he was particularly troubled by the fact, either.

"Mister Dresden," he said. "And Miss Rodriguez, I believe. I didn't realize you were an art collector."

"I am the foremost collector of velvet Elvii in the city of Chicago," I said at once.

"Elvii?" Marcone inquired.

"The plural could be Elvises, I guess," I said. "But if I say that too often, I start muttering to myself and calling things 'my precious,' so I usually go with the Latin plural."

Marcone did smile that time. It was a cool expression. Tigers with full stomachs wear smiles like Marcone's when they're watching baby deer play. "Ah. I hope you can find something to suit your tastes tonight."

"I'm easy," I said. "Any old rag will do."

Marcone narrowed his eyes. There was a short, pointed silence while he met my gaze. He could do that. I'd gotten into a soulgaze with him in the past. It was one of the reasons he scared me. "In that case, I would advise you to exercise caution in your acquisitions."

"Cautious, that's me," I said. "You sure you wouldn't rather make this simple?"

"In deference to your limitations, I almost would," Marcone said. "But I'm afraid I'm not quite sure what you're talking about."

I felt my eyes narrow and I took a step forward. Susan's hand pressed against my arm, silently urging restraint. I lowered my voice to something between Marcone and myself. "Tell you what. Let's start with one of your monkeys trying to punch my ticket in a parking garage. From there, we can move along to the part where I come up with a suitable reply."

I didn't expect what happened next.

Marcone blinked.

It wasn't a huge giveaway. At a card table, only a couple of the players would have seen it. But I was right in his face, and I knew him and I saw it. My words startled Marcone, and for half a second it showed. He covered it, bringing out a businessman's smile that was a lot better than my fake smile, and clapped a hand gently to my arm. "Don't try me in public, Dresden. You can't afford to do it. I can't afford to let you."

A shadow fell over Marcone, and I looked up to see Hendricks hulk into view behind him. Hendricks was still huge, still red-headed, still looked vaguely like a defensive lineman a little too awkward to make it from college to pro ball. His tux was nicer than mine. I wondered if he was wearing body armor under it again.

Cujo Hendricks had a date. He had a blond date. He had a gorgeous, leggy, blue-eyed, elegant, tall, Nordic angel of a date. She was wearing a white gown, and silver flashed at her throat, on each wrist, and on one ankle. I'd seen bikinis in issues of *Sports Illustrated* that might have felt too plain to be worn by Hendricks's date.

She spoke, and her voice was a throaty purr. "Mister Marcone. Is there a problem?"

Marcone arched an eyebrow. "Is there, Mister Dresden?"

I probably would have said something stupid, but Susan's nails dug into my forearm through my jacket. "No trouble," Susan said. "I don't believe we've met."

"No," said the blonde, with a faint roll of her eyes. "We haven't."

"Mister Dresden, Miss Rodriguez, I believe you both know Mister Hendricks. And this is Miss Gard."

"Ah," I said. "She's an employee, I take it?"

Miss Gard smiled. Professional smiles all around tonight, it would seem. "I'm from the Monoc Foundation," she said. "I'm a consultant."

"Regarding what, one wonders," said Susan. She definitely had the sharpest smile of those present.

"Security," Gard said, unruffled. She focused on me. "I help make sure that thieves, spies, and poor wandering spirits don't wind up all over the lawn."

And I got it. Whoever Miss Gard was, it seemed fairly likely that she was responsible for the wards that had torn Bob up so badly. My head of righteous fury died out, replaced by caution. Marcone had been concerned about my talents. He'd started taking steps to balance things, and Marcone wasn't one to show his hand early, which meant that he was already prepared for trouble of one kind or another with me. He was ready to fight me.

Marcone read my features and said, "Neither one of us wants any unpleasantness, Dresden." His eyes became flat and hard. "If you want to talk, call my office tomorrow. In the meantime, I suggest you search for your classic renditions of Elvis elsewhere."

"I'll take it under advisement," I answered. Marcone shook his head and walked away to do his own mingling, which seemed to consist mainly of shaking hands, and nodding in the appropriate spots. Hendricks and the Amazonian Gard shadowed Marcone, never far away.

"What a charmer you are," Susan murmured.

I grunted.

"Such diplomacy."

"Me and Kissinger." I scowled after Marcone and said, "I don't like this."

"Why not?"

"Because he's up to something. He set up magical defenses around his house."

"Like he was expecting trouble," Susan said.

"Yeah."

"You think he's the buyer for the Shroud?"

"Would make a lot of sense," I said. "He's got enough contacts and money to do it. The buy is apparently going down here at his gala." I scanned the room as I spoke. "He doesn't do anything without planning it out to his advantage. He's probably got friends in hotel security. It would give him all kinds of freedom to meet Valmont where no one was watching."

I spotted Marcone as he found a spot near a wall and lifted a tiny cell phone to his ear. He spoke into it, his eyes hard, and he had the look of a man who wasn't listening, only giving orders. I tried to Listen in on what he was saying, but between the band, the ballroom, and the chatter of voices I wasn't able to make anything out.

"But why?" Susan asked. "He's got the means and the resources but what reason would he have to buy the Shroud?"

"Hell if I know."

Susan nodded. "He certainly isn't happy to see you here."

"Yeah. Something unsettled him, gave him a nasty surprise. Did you see his face?"

Susan shook her head. "What do you mean?"

"A reaction, during the conversation. I'm sure I saw it. He got caught flat-footed when I was talking to him, and he didn't like it."

"You rattled him?"

"Maybe," I said.

"Enough to push him into moving early?" Susan's dark eyes had also picked out Marcone, who snapped the cell phone closed and headed for one of the service doors with Gard and Hendricks behind him. Marcone paused to speak to a red-jacketed security guard and glanced in our direction.

"Looks like we'd better get moving," I said. "I need a minute to use the spell on this thread sample and lead us to the Shroud."

"Why haven't you done that already?"

"Limited range," I said. "And the spell won't last long. We need to be close."

"How close?" Susan asked.

"Maybe a hundred feet."

Marcone left the room, and the security guard lifted his radio to his mouth.

"Crap," I said.

"Relax," Susan said, though her own voice sounded tight. "These are the upper crust of Chicago. The security guards won't want to make a scene."

"Right," I said, and started for the door.

"Slowly," Susan said, her smile in place again. "Don't rush."

I tried not to rush, despite the security guard closing in behind us. I saw red jackets moving in my peripheral vision as well. We kept up the slow, graceful walk of people wandering around a party, and Susan smiled enough for both of us. We got as far as the doors before another red jacket appeared in the doors in front of us, cutting us off.

I recognized the man—the gunman outside the television studio, the one who had nearly ventilated Father Vincent and me in the parking garage. His eyes widened in recognition and his hand moved toward his jacket, where a gun would be inside a shoulder holster. The body language was clear: *Come along quietly or get shot.*

I looked around us, but other than the partygoers, the dance floor, and the other security guards, nothing really seemed to present itself as an option. Then the band struck up something a little faster with a syncopated Latin beat, and several of the younger couples who hadn't been dancing previously moved out onto the floor.

"Come on," I said, and guided Susan with me.

"What are you doing?" she asked.

"Buying some time to get across the room to those other doors," I said. I turned to her, put one hand on her waist and took her other hand in mine, and led off onto the dance floor with an uncomplicated two-step. "Just follow."

I looked back to her to see her mouth open in shock. "You told me you couldn't dance."

"Not like in clubs and stuff," I said. She followed me well enough to let me do a little dip and step into a restrained hustle. "I don't do so well with rock and roll. Ballroom is something else."

Susan laughed, her dark eyes shining, even as she watched the crowd around us for more red jackets. "Between this and the tux, you're threatening to become classy. Where did you learn?"

I kept us moving down the dance floor, rolling Susan out to the length of our arms and then drawing her in again. "When I first came to Chicago, I had a bunch of jobs until I hooked up with Nick Christian at Ragged Angel Investigations. One of them was as a dance partner with a senior-citizen organization."

"You learned from little old ladies?"

"Tough to tango with someone with lumbago," I said. "It requires great skill." I spun Susan again, this time bringing her back to me with her back to my chest, one hand still on her hip with the other holding her arm out. There was a subtle electricity in touching her, her waist slender and supple under my hand. Her hair smelled of cinnamon, and her dress left quite a bit of her back naked to view. It was distracting as hell, and when she glanced over her shoulder at me, her eyes were growing heated. She felt it too.

I swallowed. *Focus, Harry.* "See those doors behind the food tables?"

Susan nodded.

I checked over my shoulder. The security guards had been slowed down by the press of the crowd, and we had beaten them to the other side of the room. "That's where we're going. We need to ditch these guys and find Valmont before Marcone gets to her."

"Won't security just follow us through the kitchen?"

"Not if Vanilla Martin diverts their attention before we leave the floor."

Susan's eyes glittered and she kept dancing with me, drawing the tiny cell phone from her clutch. "You have a devious mind."

"Call me crazy but I'd rather not have Marcone's goons walk us out." A little luck came our way, and the band moved to a somewhat slower number. Susan was able to stay closer to me, half concealing her cell phone. I heard the phone dialing numbers, and I tried to still my thoughts and feelings. It hadn't worked for long at the Larry Fowler studio, but if I could rein in my emotions, Susan should at least be able to make a call.

It worked. She spoke quietly into the phone for all of three or four seconds, then clicked it closed and put it away. "Two minutes," she said.

Damn. Martin was good. I could pick out a couple of security guards at the main doors. Marcone's dark-haired hitter was closer. He had trouble making his way politely through the crowd, and we had managed to gain a small lead on him as we danced.

"Do we have a signal or anything?"

"I think we wait for something distracting to happen," Susan said.

"Like what?"

The sudden shriek of braking tires cut through the band music. There was a loud crunch, and the sound of plate glass breaking, along with shrieks from the hotel lobby below. The band stopped in confusion, and people crowded toward the exit to see what was happening.

"Like that," Susan said. We had to swim upstream, so to speak, but it didn't look like anyone was bothering to look at us. I caught a glimpse of Marcone's hitter, heading out toward the ruckus. The ass had his gun in his hand, despite any possible field of fire he might have picked being filled with rich and influential socialites. At least he was holding the weapon low and against his leg.

The staff were just as interested in the disturbance as anyone else, and we were able to duck back into the service hallway without comment from anyone. Susan took a quick look around and said, "Elevator?"

"Stairs if they have them. If someone shoots at us on stairs, we can scream and flail around a lot more." I spotted a fire alarm diagram on the wall and traced my finger over it. "Here, down the hall and left."

Susan stepped out of her shoes while I did that. It left her a lot shorter, but her feet were silent on the utilitarian carpet. We went down the hall, found the stairs, and started down them. We went down three flights, which put us at ground level again, I guessed. I opened the door from the stairwell and took a look around. A dingy little elevator opened, and a couple of guys in the food-stained white of kitchen hands went walking down the hallway, peering ahead and chattering. I heard a siren or two wailing outside.

"I'll say this for Martin," I muttered. "When he distracts, he distracts."

"He has a strong work ethic," Susan agreed.

"Keep an eye out," I said, and stepped back from the door. Susan's gaze flicked around the stairwell and over the hallway while I stepped back to kneel on the ground, drawing out what I would need for my seeking spell.

I pulled out a black Magic Marker and drew a smooth circle on the tiled landing, all the way around me. The marker squealed as I did, and as I closed the circle I willed it shut. A gentle barrier, something I couldn't see but could easily feel closed around me, screening out disruptive forces so that I could work my spell.

"Is that a permanent marker?" Susan asked.

"Thus do I strike a blow for anarchy whenever the mood takes me," I muttered. "Just a minute." I took out the sample from Father Vincent and a windup plastic duck.

Which isn't as goofy as it sounds. Stay with me.

I touched the thread to the duck's bill, then wound the duck up. I muttered a low chant, mostly nonsense syllables, and focused on what I wanted. I set the duck down on the floor, but instead of beginning to waddle, it instead waited, completely still. I had to use a rubber band to attach the tiny thread to the duck's bill. It was too short to tie on. I focused, brushing aside any thoughts besides those I needed for the spell, and let the gathered magic go with a whispered, "Seek, seek, seek."

The power poured out of me, leaving me a bit short of breath. The little yellow duck quivered and then lurched into motion, spinning about in an aimless circle. I nodded once, reached out a hand, and with an effort of will to support the gesture, I broke the circle. The screen vanished as quickly as it had arrived, and the little yellow duck quacked and marched toward the door.

I glanced up at Susan. Her dark and lovely eyes watched the duck with what could charitably be termed extreme skepticism.

I scowled at her. "Don't say it."

"I didn't say anything."

"Well, don't."

She fought down a smile. "I won't."

I opened the door. The duck waddled out into the hallway, quacked, and turned to the left. I stepped out, picked the duck up, and said, "It's close. Let's move. We just check the duck at intersections."

"Does the duck know about stairs?"

"More or less. Come on; I don't know how long the spell will last."

I led the way. I'm not the world's mightiest athlete, but I exercise a bit, I have really long legs, and I can walk faster than some run. The duck led us down a pair of long hallways to a door with an EMPLOYEES ONLY sign on it.

I opened the door, peeked in, and reported in a whisper, "Big laundry room."

Footsteps sounded behind us, coming down another hallway. Susan looked at me with wide eyes. I pushed into the room, Susan close behind me. I closed the door almost all the way, holding it from closing completely so that the lock wouldn't click and give us away.

The footsteps came closer, a couple sets of them, and two shapes went quickly by, passing close to the cracked doorway.

"Hendricks and Gard," I murmured to Susan.

"How do you know?" she whispered back.

"Smelled the blonde's perfume." I counted silently to ten and opened the door, looking out. The hallway was clear. I closed the door and turned on the lights. The room was fairly large, with several commercial washing machines ranked against one wall. A bank of dryers faced them on the opposite side of the room, and in between were several long counters that held stacks and stacks of folded white sheets and towels. I put the duck on the floor, and it waddled off down the row of counters. "This is how they had it hidden on the yacht. Concealed among laundry."

"And those professional-thief types tend to be so predictable?" Susan asked.

I frowned and put the duck on the floor. "Watch the door."

The duck waddled at once over to the far side of the room, and bumped into some hanging laundry. I pulled the hanging sheets to one side, and found a large ventilation grate behind them. I knelt down, running my fingers and eyes over the edges of the grate, and found a pair of holes where screws had been. A quick tug on the grate had it off the wall, revealing a vent maybe three feet square. I stuck my head in and found a ventilation shaft running between the walls. The duck waddled in and took a determined right.

"Air duct," I said. I twisted out of the tuxedo jacket and absently ripped off the tie from around my neck. I stepped out of the clumsy shoes and rolled up my shirtsleeves, baring my shield bracelet to view. "Be right back."

"Harry," Susan began, her voice worried.

"I saw *Alien*. I'm not Tom Skerritt." I winked at Susan, picked up the duck, and entered the air duct, moving as quietly as I could.

Evidently, it was very quiet. The duct ran straight, grates opening into utility rooms every fifteen or twenty feet. I had gone past three of the grates when I heard voices.

"This isn't according to the deal," came Marcone's voice. It had the scratchy edges of a radio transmission to it.

Anna Valmont's smooth British accent answered it from the other side of the next grate. "Neither was an early rendezvous. I don't like it when a buyer changes the plan."

A radio clicked. Marcone's voice came through it, smooth and calm. "I assure you that I have no interest in breaking faith with your organization. It isn't good business."

"When I have confirmation of the transfer of funds, you'll get the article. Not a second before."

"My factor in Zurich—"

"Do you think I'm an idiot? This job has already cost us more than any of us bargained for. Clear off the bloody radio and contact me when you have something worth saying or I'll destroy the bloody thing and leave."

"Wait," Marcone said. There was tension in his voice. "You can't—"

"Can't I?" Valmont answered. "Don't fuck with me, Yank. And add another million to the bill for telling me my job. I'm calling off the deal if the money isn't there in ten minutes. Out."

I came up to the grate and found it sitting not quite squarely in its frame. Valmont must have entered the hotel and moved around through the air shafts. I peered out through the grate. Valmont had set up in a storage room of some kind. The only light in the room was a dim green shimmer that rose up from what must have been a palmtop computer. Valmont muttered something to herself beneath her breath, her eyes on the screen. She was wearing a lot of tight-fitting black clothing and a black baseball cap. She wasn't wearing my coat, dammit, but I guess I couldn't have expected to find everything wrapped up in a nice package.

I checked the duck, setting it down facing toward me. It immediately walked in a little circle and pointed toward Anna Valmont.

The thief paced the room like a restless cat, eyes on the palmtop. My eyes adjusted to the dimness over the course of a few minutes of waiting, and I saw that Valmont was pacing back and forth around a tube with a carrying strap. The tube wasn't more than five or six feet from me.

I watched Valmont pace until her expression and steps froze, eyes locking hard on the palmtop. "Great Jupiter's balls," she said quietly. "He paid it."

Now or never. I put my hands on the grate and pushed it as gently as I could. It slid soundlessly from the wall and I set it to one side. Valmont was focused entirely on her little computer. If the prospect of payment distracted Valmont for a moment more, I'd be able to slip away with the Shroud, which would be very James Bond of me. Hopefully the tuxedo would help out with that. I needed only a few seconds to creep out, nip the Shroud, and get back into the vents.

I almost died when Valmont's radio crackled again and Marcone's voice said, "There. As agreed, plus your additional fee. Will that be sufficient?"

"Quite. You will find your merchandise in a storage closet in the basement."

Marcone's voice gained an edge. "Please be more specific."

I slipped out of the vents, thinking silent thoughts. A long stretch put my fingertips on the tube's carrying strap.

"If you wish," Valmont replied. "The article is in a locked room, in a courier's tube. The tube itself is outfitted with an incendiary. A radio transmitter in my possession has the capacity to disarm or to trigger the device. Once I am safely on my way from the city, I will disarm the device and notify you via telephone. Until that time, I suggest you do not try to open it."

I jerked my fingers away from the tube.

"Again you have altered our agreement," Marcone said. He said it in a voice as smooth and cold as the inside wall of a refrigerator.

"It does seem to be a seller's market."

"There are very few people able to speak about taking advantage of me."

Valmont let out a quiet, bitter little laugh. "Come, now. This is nothing more than an entirely reasonable piece of insurance," Valmont said. "Be a good boy and your precious cloth is in no danger. Attempt to betray me, and you'll have nothing."

"And if the authorities find you on their own?" Marcone asked.

"You'll need a broom and a dustpan when you come for the article. I should think you would be wise to do whatever you can to clear the path for me." She turned the radio off.

I bit my lip, thinking furiously. Even if I took the Shroud now, Marcone would be upset when he didn't get his hands on it. If he didn't have Valmont killed, he'd at least tip off the police to her. Valmont, in turn, would destroy the Shroud. If I took it, I would have to move fast to get the Shroud away from the device. I couldn't count on simply blowing the device out with magic. It was as likely to malfunction and explode as it was to just go dead.

I would need the transmitter too, and there was only one way to get it.

I stepped up behind Valmont and pressed the bill of the plastic duck against her spine. "Don't move," I said. "I'll shoot."

She stiffened. "Dresden?"

"Let me see your hands," I said. She held them up, the green light of the palmtop showing columns of numbers. "Where's the transmitter?"

"What transmitter?"

I pushed the duck against her a little harder. "I've had a long day too, Miss Valmont. The one you just told Marcone about."

She let out a small sound of discomfort. "If you take it, Marcone will kill me."

"Yeah, he takes his image seriously. You'd be smart to come with me and get protection from the authorities. Now where is the transmitter?"

Her shoulders slumped and she bowed her head forward for a moment. I felt a twinge of guilt. She had planned on being here with friends. They'd been killed. She was a young woman, alone in a strange land, and regardless of what happened, she wasn't likely to come out of this situation ahead of the game. And here I was holding a duck to her back. I felt like a bully.

"My left jacket pocket," Valmont said, her tone quiet. I reminded myself that I was a professional and reached into her pocket to get the transmitter.

She clobbered me.

One second, I was holding the duck to her back and reaching into her pocket. The next, I was falling to the ground with a bruise shaped like one of her elbows forming on my jaw. The light from the palmtop clicked out. A small red-tinted flashlight came on, and Valmont kicked the duck out of my hand. The beam of the flashlight followed the duck for a silent second, and then she laughed.

"A duck," she said. She dipped a hand into her pocket and came out with a small silver semiautomatic. "I was fairly certain you wouldn't shoot, but that goes a step beyond ridiculous."

I've got to get a concealed-carry permit. "You won't shoot either," I said, and started to get up. "So you might as well put the gun d—"

She pointed the gun at my leg and pulled the trigger. Pain flashed through my leg and I let out an involuntary shout. I grabbed at my thigh as the red flashlight settled on me.

I pawed at my leg. I had a couple of smallish cuts, but I hadn't been shot. The bullet had hit the concrete floor next to me and gouged a bite out of the concrete. A flying chip or two must have cut my leg.

"Terribly sorry," Valmont said. "Were you saying something?"

"Nothing important," I responded.

"Ah," Valmont said. "Well, it would be bad etiquette to leave a corpse here for my buyer to clean up, so it seems as though I'll be hand-delivering to Marcone after all. We can't have you running off with what everyone is so excited over."

"Marcone is the least of your worries," I said.

"No, actually, he's quite prominent among them."

"Marcone isn't going to sprout horns and claws and start tearing you apart," I said. "Or at least, I don't think he is. There's another group after that Shroud. Like the thing from the ship this morning."

I couldn't see her face from the other end of the red flashlight, but her voice sounded a little shaky. "What was it?"

"A demon."

"A real demon?" There was a strained tone in her voice, as though she couldn't decide whether to laugh or sob. I'd heard it before. "You expect me to believe it was a literal demon?"

"Yeah."

"And you're some sort of angel, I suppose."

"Hell, no," I said. "I'm just working for them. Sort of. Look, I know people who can protect you from those things. People who won't hurt you. They'll help."

"I don't need help," Valmont said. "They're dead, they're both dead. Gaston, Francisca. My friends. Whoever these people, these *things* are, they can't hurt me any more."

The locked door of the storeroom screamed as something tore it off its hinges and out into the hall. The hallway lights poured in through the gap in a blinding flood, and I had to shield my eyes against them for a second.

I could see dim shapes, shadows in front of the light. One was lean and crouched, with shadowy tendrils of razor-edged hair slithering around it in a writhing cloud. One was sinuous and strong-looking, like a man who had traded its legs in on the scaled body of an enormous snake. Between them stood a shape that looked human, like a man in an overcoat, his hands in his pockets—but the shadows the shape cast writhed and boiled madly, making the lights flicker and swim in a nauseating fashion.

"Cannot hurt you any more," said the central shape in a quietly amused, male voice. "No matter how many times I hear that one, it's always a fresh challenge."

Chapter Twenty

⬥⟫∞⟪⬥

My eyes adjusted enough to make out some details. The demonic female with the Joan Jett hair, two sets of eyes, a glowing sigil, and vicious claws was the same Denarian who had attacked at the harbor that morning. The second demonic being was covered in dark grey scales flecked with bits of rust red. From shoulders to waist, he looked more or less human. From the neck up and the waist down, he looked like some kind of flattened serpent. No legs. Coils slithered out behind him, scales rasping over the floor. He too had the double pair of eyes, one set golden and serpentine, the other, inside the first, glowing faintly blue-green, matching the pulsing symbol of the same light that seemed to dance in the gleam of the scales of the snake's head.

One little, two little, three little Denarians, or so I judged the last of them. Of the three, he was the only one that looked human. He wore a tan trench coat, casually open. His clothes were tailor-fit to him and looked expensive. A slender grey tie hung loosely around his throat. He was a man of medium height and build, with short, dark hair streaked through with an off-center blaze of silver. His expression was mild, amused, and his dark eyes were half-closed and sleepy-looking. He spoke English with a faint British accent. "Well, well. What have we here? Our bold thief and her—"

I got the impression that he would have been glad to begin one of those trademark bantering conversations all the urbane bad guys seem to be such big fans of, but before he could finish the sentence Anna Valmont turned with her little pistol and shot him three times in the chest. I saw him jerk and twist. Blood abruptly stained his shirt and coat. She'd hit the heart or an artery.

The man blinked and stared at Valmont in shock, as more red spread over his shirt. He opened his coat a bit, and looked down at the spreading scarlet. I noted that the tie he wore wasn't a tie, as such. It looked like a piece of old grey rope, and though he wore it as apparent ornamentation, it was tied in a hangman's noose.

"I do not appreciate being interrupted," the man said in a sharp and ugly tone. "I hadn't even gotten around to the introductions. There are proprieties to observe, young woman."

A girl after my own heart, Anna Valmont had a quick reply. She shot him some more.

He wasn't five feet away. The blond thief aimed for the center of mass and didn't miss him once. The man folded his arms as bullets hit him, tearing new wounds that bled freely. He rolled his eyes after the fourth shot, and made a rolling "move this along" gesture with his left hand until Valmont's gun clicked empty, the slide open.

"Where was I," he said.

"Proprieties," purred the feminine demon with the wild hair. The word came out a little mangled, due to the heavy canines that dimpled her lips as she spoke. "Proprieties, Father."

"There seems little point," the man said. "Thief, you have stolen something I have an interest in. Give it to me at once and you are free to go your own way. Refuse me, and I will become annoyed with you."

Anna Valmont's upper lip had beaded with sweat, and she looked from her empty gun to the man in the trench coat with wide, wild eyes, frozen in confusion and obvious terror.

The gunshots would bring people running. I needed to buy a little time. I leaned up, fished a hand into Valmont's jacket pocket, and drew out a small box of black plastic that looked vaguely like a remote control to a VCR. I held up the transmitter, put my thumb on it as if I knew what I was doing, and said to the man in the trench coat, "Hey, Bogart. You and the wonder twins back off or the bedsheet gets it."

The man lifted his eyebrows. "Excuse me?"

I waggled the remote. "Click. Boom. No more Shroud."

The snakeman hissed, body twisting in restless, lithe motion, and the demon-girl parted her lips in a snarl. The man between them stared at me for a moment, his eyes flat and empty, before he said, "You're bluffing."

"Like the bedsheet matters to me," I said.

The man stared at me without moving. But his shadow did. It writhed and undulated, and the motion made me feel vaguely carsick. His eyes went from me to Valmont to the courier's message tube on the floor. "A remote detonator, I take it. You do realize you are standing next to the device?"

I realized it. I had no idea how big the incendiary was. But that was all right, since I had no idea which button to push to set it off, either. "Yup."

"You would kill yourself rather than surrender the Shroud?"

"Rather than letting *you* kill me."

"Who said I would kill anyone?"

I glared at him and at the demon-girl and said, "Francisca Garcia mentioned it."

The man's shadow boiled but he watched me with flat, calculating eyes. "Perhaps we can reach an arrangement."

"Which would be?"

He drew a heavy-caliber handgun from his pocket and pointed it at Anna Valmont. "Give me the remote and I won't kill this young woman."

"The demon groupie headman uses a gun? You've got to be kidding me," I said.

"Call me Nicodemus." He glanced at the revolver. "Trendy, I know, but one can only watch so many dismemberments before they become predictable." He pointed the gun at the terror-stricken Valmont and said, "Shall I count to three?"

I threw on a puppet's Transylvanian accent. "Count as high as you vant, but you von't get one, one detonator, ah, ah, ah."

"One," Nicodemus said.

"Do you expect me to hand it over on reflex or something?"

"You've done such things repeatedly when there was a woman in danger, Harry Dresden. Two."

This Nicodemus knew me. And he'd picked a pressure tactic that wasn't going to take long, however it turned out, so he knew I was stalling for time. Crap. I wasn't going to be able to bluff him. "Hold on," I said.

He thumbed back the hammer of the revolver and aimed at Valmont's head. "Thr—"

So much for cleverness. "All right," I snapped, and I tossed the remote to him underhand. "Here you go."

Nicodemus lowered the gun, turning to catch the remote in his left hand. I waited until his eyes flicked from Valmont to the remote.

And then I pulled up every bit of power I could muster in that instant, hurled my right hand forward, and snarled, *"Fuego!"*

Fire rose up from the floor in a wave as wide as the doorway and rolled forward in a surge of superheated air. It expanded as it lashed out, and slammed into Nicodemus's bloodied chest. The force of it threw him back across the hallway and into the wall on the opposite side. He didn't quite go through the wall, but only because there must have been a stud lined up with his spine. The drywall crumpled in from his shoulders to his hips, and his head snapped back in a whiplash of impact. It almost seemed that his shadow was thrown back with him, slapping wetly against the wall around him like blobs of tar.

The snakeman moved with blinding speed, slithering to one side of the blast. The demon-girl shrieked, and her bladed tresses gathered together in an effort to shield her as the fire and concussion threw her back and away from the door.

The heat was unbearable, an oven-hot flash that sucked the air from my lungs. Backwash from the explosion drove me back across the floor, rolling until I hit the wall myself. I cowered and shielded my face as the scarlet flames went out, replaced with a sudden cloud of ugly black smoke. My ears rang, and I couldn't hear anything but the hammering of my own heart.

The fire spell had been something I wouldn't have done if I'd had an option. That's why I had made a blasting rod. Down-and-dirty fast magic was difficult, dangerous, and likely to run out of control. The blasting rod helped me focus that kind of magic, contain it. It helped me avoid explosions that left heat burns on my lungs.

I fumbled around in the blinding smoke, unable to breathe and unable to see. I found a feminine wrist with one hand, followed it up to a shoulder, and found Anna Valmont. I hauled on her with one hand, found the courier's tube with the other, and crawled for the ventilation duct, hauling them both behind me.

There was air in the ventilation shaft, and Valmont coughed and stirred as I dragged her into it. Enough of the storage room had caught on fire that I had light enough to see. One of Valmont's eyebrows was gone, and one side of her face was red and blistered. I screamed, "Move!" at her as loudly as I could. Her eyes blinked with dull comprehension as I pushed her past me and toward the opening in the laundry room, and she started moving stiffly in front of me.

Valmont didn't crawl as quickly as I wanted her to, but then she wasn't the one closest to the fire and the monsters. My heart hammered in my ears and the shaft felt oppressively small. I knew that the demonic forms of the Denarians were tougher than either me or Anna Valmont. Unless I'd gotten lethally lucky, they'd recover from the blast, and it wouldn't be long before they came after us. If we couldn't shake them or get into a car, and fast, they'd catch us, plain and simple. I shoved at Valmont, growing more frantic as my imagination turned up images of whipping tendrils cutting my legs to shreds, or venomous serpent fangs sinking into my calves as scaled hands dragged me backward by my ankles.

Valmont tumbled out of the air shaft and into the laundry room. I followed her closely enough to make me think of a program I'd seen about howler monkey mating habits. My ears were starting to get their act together, and I heard the high, buzzing ring of a fire alarm in the hallway outside.

"Harry?" Susan said. She looked between Valmont and me and helped the woman to her feet. "What's happening?"

I got to my feet and choked out, "We need to be gone. Right now."

Susan nodded at me, and then shoved me. Hard. I went stumbling sideways and into the wall of drying machines, slamming my shoulder and head. I looked back to see the demon-girl's hair pureeing its way out of the vents, and then the rest of the Denarian came out, scales, claws and all, rolling to all fours with dizzying grace.

Fast as the Denarian was, Susan was faster. The demon-girl came up with those rich lips split into a snarl, and Susan drove her heel right into them. She kicked hard enough that something crunched, and the demon-girl screamed in surprise and pain.

"Susan!" I shouted. "Look—"

I was going to say "out" but there wasn't time. Half a dozen bunches of tendrils drove at Susan like spears.

Susan dodged them. All of them. She had to fling herself across the room to the washing machines to do it, and the Denarian regained her balance and pursued. More blades drove toward Susan, but she ducked to one side, one hand ripping open the door to one of the washing machines. Susan slammed the door down on the demon-girl's hair, and without missing a beat kicked the Denarian's reverse-jointed knee in sideways.

The demon-girl shrieked in pain, struggling. I knew she was strong enough to pull free of the washing machine before long, but for the moment she was trapped. Susan reached up and tore a fold-down ironing board from where it was mounted on a nearby wall. Then she spun around and slammed it edge-on into the Denarian. Susan hit her three times, in the wounded leg, the small of the back, and the back of the neck. The Denarian shrieked at the first two blows and then collapsed into a limp heap at the third.

Susan stared down at the demon-girl for a moment, dark eyes hard and hot. The ironing board's metal frame was now bent and twisted from the force of the blows Susan had dealt with it. Susan took a deep breath and then tossed the ironing board to one side, straightened her hair with one hand, and commented, "Bitch."

"Wow," I said.

"Are you all right, Harry?" Susan asked. She wasn't looking at me.

"Yeah," I said. "Wow."

Susan walked over to the counter, where she'd left her clutch. She opened it, got the phone, and said, "I'll have Martin pick us up at the exit."

I shook myself into motion and helped draw Anna Valmont to her feet. "What exit?"

Susan pointed wordlessly at a fire-escape diagram on the wall, still not looking at me. She spoke maybe a dozen quiet words into the phone and then folded it shut. "He's coming. They're evacuating the hotel. We'll need to—"

I felt a surge of magical energies. The air around Susan grew darker and then coalesced into a cloud of shadows. Within a heartbeat, the cloud deepened, then solidified into a writhing tangle of snakes of all sizes and colors wrapped all around Susan. The air suddenly filled with the sound of hissing and buzzing rattles. I saw the snakes begin to strike, fangs flashing. Susan let out a scream.

I turned to the doorway and saw the snakeman Denarian standing in it. One not-quite-human hand was held out toward Susan. His serpent mouth was rolling out hissing sounds, and I could feel the thrumming tension in the air between the Denarian's outstretched hand and Susan.

Rage flooded over me, and I barely stopped myself from throwing out another blast of raw spellfire at the snakeman. With that much rage behind it, I'd probably have killed everyone in the room. Instead, I reached out to the air in the hallway beyond the Denarian and pulled it all toward him, the words, *"Ventas servitas!"* thundering off my lips.

A column of wind hit the snakeman from behind, lifted him from the floor, and flung him across the room. He slammed into the wall of washing machines, driving a foot-and-a-half-deep dent in one of them, and let out a wailing, hissing whistle of what I hoped was surprise and pain.

Susan flung herself onto the ground, rolling, tearing at snakes, flinging them away. I could see flashes of her honey-brown skin and saw the black dress tearing. Droplets of red blood appeared on the floor near her, on her skin, and on the discarded snakes, but they were hanging on. She was tearing herself apart in her panic to remove the snakes.

I closed my eyes for a second that felt a year long, and gathered together enough will to attempt to disrupt the Denarian's spell. I formed the counterspell in my head, and hoped to God that I didn't misjudge how much power I'd need to undo it. Too little and the spell might actually get stronger, like steel forged in a flame. Too much, and the counterspell could unleash the power of both spells in a random, destructive flash of energies. I focused my will on the cloak of serpents over Susan and lashed out at them with my power, letting loose the counterspell with a snarled, *"Entropus!"*

The counterspell worked. The serpents writhed and thrashed around for a second, and then imploded, vanishing, leaving behind nothing but a coating of clear, glistening slime in their place.

Susan scrambled away, still gasping, still bleeding. Her skin shone, wet and slick with the residue of the conjured serpents. Rivulets of blood laced her arms and one leg, and thick black bruises banded the skin of one arm, one leg, her throat, and one side of her face.

I stared for a second. The darkness on her skin wasn't bruising. It gained shape, as I watched, resolving itself from vague discoloration to the dark, sharp lines of a tattoo. I watched the tattoo come into being over her skin, all curves and points, Maori-style. It began on her cheek under one eye and wound down around her face, around the back of her neck, and on down over one collarbone and into the neckline of her evening gown. It emerged again winding down along her left arm and left leg, finishing at the back of her hand and over the bridge of her left foot. She hauled herself to her feet, panting and shaking, the swirling designs lending a savage aspect to her appearance. She stared at me for a moment, her eyes dark and enlarged, the irises too big to be human. They filled with tears that didn't fall, and she looked away.

The snakeman recovered enough to slither his way vertical again, looking around. He focused yellow snake eyes on Susan and let out a surprised wheeze. "Fellowship," he rasped, the word a hiss. "Fellowship here." The Denarian looked around and spotted the courier's tube still hanging by its strap from my shoulder. Its tail lashed about and the Denarian darted toward me.

I slipped to one side, keeping a table between us, and shouted, "Susan!"

The snakeman struck the table with one arm and broke it in half. Then he came at me over the pieces—until Susan ripped a dryer out of the wall and threw it at his head.

The Denarian saw it coming and dodged at the last second, but the dryer clipped him and sent him sprawling. He hissed again, and slithered away from both of us, shooting into the air shaft and out of sight.

I panted and watched the vent for a second, but he didn't reappear. Then I hauled the still-stunned Valmont toward the door and asked Susan, "Fellowship?"

Her lips pressed together, and she averted her too-large eyes. "Not now."

I ground my teeth in frustration and worry, but she was right. The smoke was getting thicker, and we had no way of knowing if tall, green, and scaly would be reappearing. I pulled Valmont along with me, made sure I still had the Shroud, and followed Susan out the door. She ran along barefoot without breaking stride, and between the pain in my lungs and the blond thief's torpor, I could barely keep up with her.

We went up a flight of stairs and Susan opened a door on a pair of gorillas in red security blazers. They tried to stop us. Susan threw a right and a left cross, and we walked over them on our way out. I kind of felt bad for them. Getting punched out by a dame was not going to pad their goon résumés.

We left the building through a side door, and the dark limo was waiting, Martin standing beside it. I could hear sirens, people shouting, the blaring horns of fire vehicles trying to get to the hotel.

Martin took one look at Susan and stiffened. Then he hurried over to us.

"Take her," I rasped. Martin picked up Valmont and carried her to the limo like a sleepy child. I followed him. Martin put the blond thief in and got behind the wheel. Susan slipped in after her, and I slung the tube off my shoulder to get in behind her.

Something grabbed me from behind, wrapping around my waist like a soft, squishy rope. I slapped at the car door, but I managed only to slam it shut as I was hauled back off my feet. I landed on the ground near the fire door.

"Harry!" Susan shouted.

"Go!" I gasped. I looked at Martin, behind the wheel of the limo. I grabbed the Shroud and tried to throw it at the car, but something pinned my arm down before I could. "Get out! Get help!"

"No!" Susan screamed, and tried for the door.

Martin was faster. I heard locks click shut on the limo. Then the engine roared, and the car screamed into the street and away.

I tried to run. Something tangled my feet and I couldn't even get off the ground. I turned to find Nicodemus standing over me, the hangman's noose the only thing he wore that wasn't soaked with blood. His shadow, his freaking *shadow* was wrapped around my waist, my legs, my hands, and it moved and wriggled like something alive. I reached for my magic, but the grasping shadow-coils grew suddenly cold, colder than ice or frosted steel, and my power crumbled to frozen powder beneath it.

One of the shadow-coils took the courier's tube from my numbed hands, curling through the air to hand it to Nicodemus. "Excellent," he said. "I have the Shroud. And I have you, Harry Dresden."

"What do you want?" I rasped.

"Just to talk," Nicodemus assured me. "I want to have a polite conversation with you."

"Blow me."

His eyes darkened with cold anger, and he drew out the heavy revolver.

Great, Harry, I thought. *That's what you get for trying to be a hero. You get to eat a six-pack of nine-millimeter bon-bons.*

But Nicodemus didn't shoot me.

He clubbed me over the head with the butt of the gun.

Light flashed in my eyes, and I started to fall. I was out before my cheek hit the ground.

Chapter Twenty-one

The cold woke me.

I came to my senses in complete darkness, under a stream of freezing water. My head hurt enough to make the wound on my leg feel pleasant by comparison. My wrists and shoulders hurt even more. My neck felt stiff, and it took me a second to realize that I was vertical, my hands bound together over my head. My feet were tied too. My muscles started jumping and twitching under the cold water and I tried to get out from under it. The ropes prevented me. The cold started cutting into me. It hurt a lot.

I tried to get loose, working my limbs methodically, testing the ropes, trying to free my hands. I couldn't tell if I was making any progress. Thanks to the cold, I couldn't even feel my wrists, and it was too dark to see.

I got more scared by the moment. If I couldn't work my hands free, I might have to risk using magic to scorch the ropes. Hell, I was cold enough that the thought of burning myself had a certain appeal. But when I started trying to reach out for the power to manage it, it slithered away from me. Then I understood. Running water. Running water grounds magical energies, and every time I tried to get something together the water washed it away.

The cold grew more intense, more painful. I couldn't escape it. I panicked, thrashing wildly, dull pain flaring in my bound limbs, and fading away into numbness under the cold. I screamed a few times, I think. I remember choking on water while I tried.

I didn't have much energy. After a few minutes, I hung panting and hurting and too tired to struggle any more, the water only getting colder, bound limbs screaming.

I hurt, but I figured the pain couldn't possibly get any worse.

A few hours went by and showed me how wrong I was.

A door opened and firelight stabbed at my eyes. I would have flinched if I had been able to move that much. A couple of large, blocky men came through the door carrying actual flaming torches. The light let me see the room. The wall beside the door was finished stone, but the walls all around me were a mishmash of fallen rubble and ancient brick, and one was made of curved concrete—some kind of piping for the city's water system, I supposed. The ceiling was all rough earth, some stone, some roots. Water poured down from somewhere, over me, and vanished down a groove worn in the floor.

They had taken me to Undertown, a network of caves, ruined buildings, tunnels, and ancient construction that underlay the city of Chicago. Undertown was dark, damp, cold, full of various creatures that shunned sunlight and human company, and might have been radioactive. The tunnels where the Manhattan Project had been housed were just the start of Undertown. The people who knew of its existence didn't come down here—not even wizards like me—unless matters were desperate.

No one knew their way around down here. And no one would be coming to find me.

"Been working out pretty hard," I muttered to the two men, my voice a croak. "One of you guys got a cold beer? Maybe a freeze pop?"

They didn't so much as look at me. One man took up a position on the wall to my left. The other took the wall to my right.

"I should have cleaned up, I know," I told them. "If I'd realized I was having company I'd have taken a shower. Mopped the floor."

No answer. No expression on their faces. No nothing.

"Tough room," I said.

"You'll have to forgive them," said Nicodemus. He came through the door and into the torchlight, freshly dressed, shaved, and showered. He wore pajama pants, slippers, and a smoking jacket of Hugh Hefner vintage. The grey noose still circled his throat. "I like to encourage discretion in my employees, and I have very high standards. Sometimes it makes them seem standoffish."

"You don't let your goons talk?" I asked.

He removed a pipe from his pocket, along with a small tin of Prince Albert tobacco. "I remove their tongues."

"I guess your human resources department isn't exactly under siege, is it," I said.

He tamped tobacco into his pipe and smiled. "You'd be surprised. I offer an excellent dental plan."

"You're going to need it when the formal-wear police knock your teeth out. This is a rented tux."

His dark eyes glittered with something ugly. "Little Maggie's youngest. You've grown up to be a man of considerable strengths."

I stared at him for a long second, shivering and startled into silence. My mother's name was Margaret.

And I was her youngest? As far as I knew, I had been an only child. But I knew precious little of my parents. My mother died giving birth to me. My father had suffered an aneurism when I had been about six years old. I had a picture of my father on a piece of yellowed newspaper I kept in a photo album. It showed him performing at a children's benefit dinner in a small town in Ohio. I had a Polaroid instant picture showing my father and my mother, her stomach round with pregancy, standing in front of the Lincoln Memorial. I wore my mother's pentacle amulet around my neck. It was scarred and dented, but that's to be expected when you run around using it to kill werewolves.

They were the only concrete things I had left of my parents. I'd heard stories before, that my mother hadn't run with a very pleasant crowd. Nothing of substance, just inferences made from passing comments. I'd had a demon tell me that my parents had been murdered, and the same creature had hinted that I might have relatives. I'd shied away from the whole concept, deciding that the demon had been a dirty liar.

And given that Nicodemus and Chauncy worked for the same organization, I probably couldn't trust the Denarian either. He was probably lying. Probably.

But what if he wasn't?

Keep him talking, I decided. *Fish for information.* It wasn't like I had a lot to lose, and knowledge was power. I might find out something that would give me some kind of edge.

Nicodemus lit the pipe with a match and puffed on it a few times, watching my face with a little smile on his lips. He read me, easily. I avoided looking at his eyes.

"Harry—may I call you Harry?"

"Would it matter if I told you no?"

"It would tell me something about you," he said. "I'd like to get to know you, and I would rather not make this a trip to the dentist if I can avoid it."

I glared at him, shivering under the freezing water, the bump on my head pounding, and my limbs aching beneath the ropes. "I've got to ask—just what kind of freaking dentist do you *go* to? Ortho de Sade? Smokin' Joe Mengele, DDS?"

Nicodemus puffed on the pipe and regarded my bonds. Another expressionless man came in, this one older, thin, with thick grey hair. He pushed a room-service cart. He unfolded a small table and set it up over to one side, where the water wouldn't splash on it. Nicodemus toyed with the bowl of his pipe. "Dresden, may I be frank with you?"

I figured the cart would open up to show an array of hardware intended to frighten me with its potential torture applications. "If it's okay with Frank, I guess I don't mind."

Nicodemus watched the valet set out three folding chairs and cover the table with a white cloth. "You have faced a great many dangerous beings. But by and large, they have been idiots. I try to avoid that whenever I am able, and that is why you are bound and held under running water."

"You're afraid of me," I said.

"Boy, you've destroyed three rival practitioners of the Arts, a noble of the vampire Courts, and even one of the Faerie Queens. They underestimated you as well as your allies. I don't. I suppose you could think of your current position as a compliment."

"Yeah," I muttered, shaking freezing water out of my eyes. "You're way too kind."

Nicodemus smiled. The valet opened the cart and something far more diabolical than torture hardware was there. It was breakfast. The old valet started setting out food on the table. Hash browns. Some cheese. Some biscuits, bacon, sausages, pancakes, toast, fruit. And coffee, dear God. Hot coffee. The smell hit my stomach, and even frozen as it was it started crawling around on the inside of my abdomen, trying to figure out how to get away and get some food.

Nicodemus sat down, and the valet poured him some coffee. I guess pouring his own was beneath him. "I did try to keep you out of this affair."

"Yeah. You seem like such a sweet guy. You're the one who edited the prophecy Ulsharavas told me about?"

"You've no idea how difficult it is to waylay an angelic messenger."

"Uh-huh," I said. "So why'd you do it?"

Nicodemus was not too important to add his own cream, no sugar. His spoon clinked on the cup. "I have a fond memory or two of your mother. It cost me little to attempt it. So why not?"

"That's the second time you've mentioned her," I said.

"Yes. I respected her. Which is quite unusual for me."

"You respected her so much you snatched me and brought me here. I see."

Nicodemus waved his hand. "It worked out that way. I needed someone of a certain metaphysical mass. You interfered in my business, you were convenient, and you fit the recipe."

Recipe? "What recipe?"

He sipped at his coffee and closed his eyes in enjoyment. The bastard. "I take it that this is the portion of the conversation where I reveal my plans to you?"

"What have you got to lose?"

"And apparently you expect me to tell you of any vulnerabilities I might have as well. I am wounded by the lack of professional respect this implies."

I ground my teeth. "Chicken."

He picked up a piece of bacon and nibbled at it. "It is enough for you to know that one of two things will happen."

"Oh, yeah?" Master of repartee, that's me.

"Indeed. Either you will be freed and sit down to enjoy a nice breakfast . . ." He picked up a slightly curved and sharp-looking knife from the table. "Or I will cut your throat as soon as I finish eating."

He said it scary—without any melodrama to it at all. Matter-of-fact. The way most people say that they need to take out the trash. "Ye olde 'join up or die' ultimatum," I said. "Gee, no matter how many times I get it, that one never goes out of style."

"Your history indicates that you are too dangerous to leave alive, I'm afraid—and I am on a schedule," Nicodemus said.

A schedule? He was working against a time limit, then. "I'm really inconvenient that way. Don't take it personal."

"I don't," he assured me. "This isn't easy for either of us. I'd use some sort of psychological technique on you, but I haven't gotten caught up on some of the more recent developments." He took a piece of toast and buttered it. "Then again, I suppose not many psychologists can drive chariots, so perhaps it balances out."

The door opened again, and a young woman came into the room. She had long, sleep-tousled dark hair, dark eyes, and a face a little too lean to be conventionally pretty. She wore a kimono of red silk belted loosely, so that gaps appeared as she moved. She evidently didn't have anything on underneath it. Like I said, Undertown is cold.

The girl yawned and stretched lazily, watching me as she did. She too spoke with an odd, vaguely British accent. "Good morning."

"And you, little one. Harry Dresden, I don't believe you've been introduced to my daughter, Deirdre."

I eyed the girl, who seemed vaguely familiar. "We haven't met."

"Yes, we have," Deirdre said, reaching out to pluck a strawberry from the breakfast table. She took a slow bite from it, lips sealed around the fruit. "At the harbor."

"Ah. Madame Medusa, I presume."

Deirdre sighed. "I've never heard that one before. It's so amusing. May I kill him, Father?"

"Not just yet," Nicodemus said. "But if it comes to that, he's mine."

Deirdre nodded sleepily. "Have I missed breakfast?"

Nicodemus smiled at her. "Not at all. Give us a kiss."

She slid onto his lap and did. With tongue. Yuck. After a moment she rose, and Nicodemus held one of the chairs out for her as she sat down. He reseated himself and said, "There are three chairs here, Dresden. Are you sure you wouldn't like to take breakfast with us?"

I started to tell him what he could do with his third chair, but the smell of food stopped me. I suddenly felt desperately, painfully hungry. The water got colder. "What did you have in mind?"

Nicodemus nodded to one of the goons. The man walked over to me, drawing a jewelry box out of his pocket. He opened it, offering it out to me.

I mimed a gasp. "But this is so sudden."

The goon glared. Nicodemus smiled. Inside the jewelry box was an ancient silver coin, like the one I'd seen in the alley behind the hospital. The tarnish on the coin was in the shape of another sigil.

"You like me. You really like me," I said without enthusiasm. "You want me to join up?"

"You needn't if you do not wish to," Nicodemus said. "I just want you to hear our side of things before you make up your mind to die needlessly. Accept the coin. Have some breakfast with us. We can talk. After that, if you don't want to have anything to do with me, you may leave."

"You'd just let me go. Sure."

"If you accept the coin, I doubt I'd be able to stop you."

"So what says I wouldn't turn around and use it against you?"

"Nothing," Nicodemus said. "But I am a great believer in the benevolence of human nature."

Like hell he was. "Do you actually think you could convince me to join up with you?"

"Yes," he said. "I know you."

"Do not."

"Do too," he replied. "I know more about you than you do yourself."

"Such as?"

"Such as why you chose this kind of life for yourself. To appoint yourself protector of mortal kind, and to make yourself the enemy of any who would do them harm. To live outcast from your own kind, laughed at and mocked by most mortals. Living in a hovel, barely scraping by. Spurning wealth and fame. Why do you do it?"

"I'm a disciple of the Tao of Peter Parker, obviously," I said.

I guess Nicodemus was a DC Comics fan, because he didn't get it. "It is all you will allow yourself, and I know why."

"All right. Why?"

"Because you are ruled by fear. You are afraid, Dresden."

I said, "Of what?"

"Of what you could be if you ever let yourself stray from the right-hand path," Nicodemus said. "Of the power you could use. You've thought about what it might be like to bend the world to your will. The things you could have. The people. Some part of you has considered and found joy in the idea of using your abilities to take what you wish. And you are afraid of that joy. So you drive yourself toward martyrdom instead."

I started to deny his words. But I couldn't. He was right, or at least not wholly wrong. My voice came out subdued. "Everyone has thoughts like that sometimes."

"No," Nicodemus said, "they don't. Most people never consider such actions. It never crosses their minds. The average mortal would have no sure way of taking that kind of power. But for you, it's different. You may pretend you are like them. But you are not."

"That's not true," I replied.

"Of course it is," Nicodemus said. "You might not like to admit it, but that makes it no less true. It's denial. There are a number of ways you express it in your life. You don't want to see what you are, so you have very few pictures of yourself. No mirrors, either."

I ground my teeth. "I'm not different in any way that matters.

I'm not any better than anyone else. We all put our pants on one leg at a time."

"Granted," Nicodemus said. "But a century from now, your mortal associates will be rotting in the earth, whereas, barring amputation or radical shifts in fashion, you will still be putting your pants on one leg at a time. All these allies and friends you have made will be withered and gone, while you are just beginning to come into your full strength. You look like a mortal, Dresden. But make no mistake. You aren't one."

"Oh, shut up."

"You are different. You are a freak. In a city of millions, you are all but alone."

"Which explains my dating life," I said, but I couldn't put much zing in the words. Something in my throat felt heavy.

Nicodemus had the valet pour coffee for Deirdre, but he spooned sugar into it himself. "You're afraid, but you don't have to be. You're above them, Dresden. There's an entire world waiting for you. Uncounted paths you could take. Allies who would stand with you over the years. Who would accept you instead of scorning you. You could discover what happened to your parents. Avenge them. Find your family. Find a place where you truly belonged."

He'd chosen to use words that struck hard on the oldest wound in me, a child's pain that had never fully healed. It hurt to hear those words. It stirred up a senseless old hope, a yearning. It made me feel lost. Empty.

Alone.

"Harry," Nicodemus said, his voice almost compassionate. "I used to be much as you are now. You are trapped. You are lying to yourself. You pretend to be like any other mortal because you are too terrified to admit that you aren't."

I didn't have an answer for that. The silver coin gleamed, still offered out to me.

Nicodemus laid one hand on the knife again. "I'm afraid I must ask you for an immediate decision."

Deirdre looked at the knife and then at me, eyes hot. She licked some spilled sugar off the rim of her coffee cup, and remained silent.

What if I did take the coin? If Nicodemus was on the level, I could at least live to fight another day. I had no doubts that Nicodemus would kill me, as he had Gaston LaRouche, Francisca Garcia, and that poor bastard Butters had cut into. There was nothing stopping him, and with the water still running over me, I doubted that even my death curse would be at one hundred percent.

I couldn't stop myself from imagining what it would feel like to bleed to death, there under the cold water. A hot, burning line on my throat. Dizziness and cold. Weakness fading into warmth that became perfect, endless darkness. Death.

God help me, I didn't want to die.

But I'd seen the poor bastard Ursiel had enslaved and driven mad. What he'd suffered was worse than death. And chances were that if I took the coin, the demon that came with it might coerce or corrupt me into the same thing. I'm not a saint. I'm not even particularly sterling, morally speaking. I've had dark urges before. I've been fascinated by them. Attracted to them. And more than once, I've given in to them.

It was a weakness that the demon in the ancient coin could exploit. I wasn't immune to temptation. The demon, the Fallen, would drown me in it. It's what the Fallen do.

I made my decision.

Nicodemus watched me, eyes steady, his knife hand perfectly still.

"Lead us not into temptation," I said. "But deliver us from evil. Isn't that how it goes?"

Deirdre licked her lips. The goon shut the box and stepped back.

"Are you certain, Dresden?" Nicodemus said in a quiet voice. "This is your very last chance."

I slumped weakly. There didn't seem to be much of a point to bravado anymore. I'd made the call, and that was that. "I'm certain. Fuck off, Nick."

Nicodemus stared at me impassively for a moment. Then he stood up with the knife and said, "I suppose I've had enough breakfast."

Chapter Twenty-two

Nicodemus walked over to me, his expression somewhat distracted. I realized with a chill that he looked like a man planning his activities for the day. To Nicodemus, I wasn't a person anymore. I was an item on his checklist, a note in his appointment book. He would feel no differently about cutting my throat than he would about putting down a check mark.

When he got within arm's reach, I couldn't stop myself from trying to get away from him. I thrashed at the ropes, hanging on to the desperate hope that one of them might break and give me a chance to fight, to run, to live. The ropes didn't break. I didn't get loose. Nicodemus watched me until I'd exhausted myself again.

Then he took a handful of my hair and pulled my chin up and back, twisting my head to my right. I tried to stop him, but I was immobilized and exhausted.

"Be still," he said. "I'll make it clean."

"Do you want the bowl, Father?" Deirdre asked.

Nicodemus's expression flickered with annoyance. His voice came out tight and impatient. "Where is my mind today? Porter, bring it to me."

The grey-haired valet opened the door and left the room.

A heartbeat later there was a wheezing grunt, and Porter flew back through the doorway and landed on his back. He let out a pained croak and curled into a fetal position.

Nicodemus sighed, turning. "Bother. What now?"

Nicodemus had looked bored when Anna Valmont emptied her gun into him. When I'd blasted a Nicodemus-shaped dent in the drywall of the hotel, he'd come through it without a ruffled hair.

But when he saw the valet laying on the ground before the open door, Nicodemus's face went pale, his eyes widened, and he took a pair of quick steps to stand behind me, his knife at my throat. Even his shadow recoiled, rolling back away from the open door.

"The Jap," Nicodemus snarled. "Kill him."

There was a second of startled silence, and then the goons went for their guns. The one nearest the door didn't get his weapon out of its holster. Shiro, still in the outfit he'd worn at McAnnally's, came through the opening in a flash of black and white and red, his cane in his hand. He drove the end of the cane into Goon A's neck, and the thug dropped to the ground.

Goon B got his gun out and pointed it at Shiro. The old man bobbed to his left and then smoothly rolled right. The gun went off, and sparks flew up from two of the walls as the bullet ricocheted. Shiro drew *Fidelacchius* clear of its wooden sheath as he spun closer to the goon, the movement so fast that the sword looked like a blurred sheet of shining steel. Goon B's gun went flying through the air, his shooting hand still gripping it. The man stared at the stump at the end of his arm as blood gouted from it, and Shiro spun again, one heel rising to chin level. The kick broke something in the wounded goon's jaw, and the man collapsed to the damp floor.

Shiro had taken out three men in half as many seconds, and he hadn't stopped moving. *Fidelacchius* flashed again, and the chair beneath Deirdre collapsed, spilling her onto the floor. The old man promptly stepped on her wealth of dark hair, whirled the sword, and brought its tip down to rest against the back of Deirdre's neck.

The room became almost completely silent. Shiro kept his blade to Deirdre's neck, and Nicodemus did the same to mine. The little old man didn't look like the same person I'd talked to. Not that he had physically changed, so much as that the sheer presence of him was different—his features hard as stone, weathering the years only to grow stronger. When he had moved, it had been with a dancer's grace, speed, and skill. His eyes flashed with a silent strength that had been concealed before, and his hands and forearms were corded with muscle. The sword's blade gleamed red with blood and torchlight.

Nicodemus's shadow edged a bit farther back from the old man.

I think the freezing water was blending in with my sudden surge of hope and making me a little loopy. I found myself drunkenly singing, "Speed of lightning! Roar of thunder! Fighting all who rob or plunder! Underdog!"

"Be quiet," Nicodemus said.

"You sure?" I asked. "'Cause I could do Mighty Mouse if you'd rather. Underdog had this whole substance-use issue anyway." Nicodemus pressed the knife a bit harder, but my mouth was on autopilot. "That looked fast. I mean, I'm not much of a fencer, but that old man looked amazingly quick to me. Did he look that quick to you? Bet that sword could go right through you and you wouldn't even realize it until your face fell on your feet."

I heard Nicodemus's teeth grind.

"Harry," Shiro said quietly. "Please."

I shut up, and stood there with a knife at my throat, shivering, aching, and hoping.

"The wizard is mine," Nicodemus said. "He's through. You know that. He chose to be a part of this."

"Yes," Shiro said.

"You cannot take him from me."

Shiro glanced pointedly at the goons lying on the floor, and then at the captive he held pinned down. "Maybe yes. Maybe no."

"Take your chances with it and the wizard dies. You've no claim of redemption here."

Shiro was quiet for a moment. "Then we trade."

Nicodemus laughed. "My daughter for the wizard? No. I've plans for him, and his death will serve me as well now as later. Harm her, and I kill him now."

Shiro regarded the Denarian steadily. "I did not mean your daughter."

I suddenly got a sick feeling in my stomach.

I almost heard Nicodemus's smile. "Very clever, old man. You knew I'd not pass the opportunity by."

"I know you," Shiro said.

"Then you should know that your offer isn't enough," Nicodemus said. "Not by half."

Shiro's face did not show any surprise. "Name it."

Nicodemus's voice dropped lower. "Swear to me that you will make no effort to escape. That you will summon no aid. That you will not release yourself quietly."

"And let you keep me for years? No. But I will give you this day. Twenty-four hours. It is enough."

I shook my head at Shiro. "Don't do this. I knew what I was doing. Michael will need your—"

Nicodemus delivered a swift jab to my right kidney and I lost my breath. "Be silent," he said. He focused his attention on Shiro and inclined his head slowly. "Twenty-four hours. Agreed."

Shiro mirrored the gesture. "Now. Let him go."

"Very well," Nicodemus said. "As soon as you release my daughter and lay down your sword, the wizard will go free. I swear it."

The old knight only smiled. "I know the value of your promises. And you know the value of mine."

I felt an eager tension in my captor. He leaned forward and said, "Swear it."

"I do," Shiro said. And as he did, he placed his palm lightly along the base of his sword's blade. He lifted it to show a straight cut on his hand, already dribbling blood. "Set him free. I will take his place as you demand."

Nicodemus's shadow writhed and boiled on the ground at my feet, bits of it lashing hungrily toward Shiro. The Denarian let out a harsh laugh, and the knife left my neck. He made a couple of quick movements, cutting the rope holding my wrists.

Without the support of my bonds, I fell. My body screamed in pain. It hurt so much that I didn't notice him cutting my feet free until it was done. I didn't make any noise. Partly because I was too proud to let Nicodemus know how bad I felt. Partly because I didn't have enough breath to whimper anyway.

"Harry," Shiro said. "Get up."

I tried. My legs and feet were numb.

Shiro's voice changed, carrying a quiet note of authority and command. "Get up."

I did it, barely. The wound on my leg felt hot and painful, and the muscle around it twitched and clenched involuntarily.

"Foolishness," Nicodemus commented.

"Courage," Shiro said. "Harry, come over here. Get behind me."

I managed to lurch to Shiro's side. The old man never looked away from Nicodemus. My head spun a bit and I almost lost my balance. My legs felt like dead wood from the knees down, and my back had started cramping. I ground my teeth and said, "I don't know how far I can walk."

"You must," Shiro said. He knelt down by Deirdre, rested his knee on her spine, and wrapped one arm around her throat. She began to move, but the old man applied pressure, and Deirdre went still again with a whimper of discomfort. That done, Shiro gave *Fidelacchius* a flick, and the beads of blood upon it sprinkled against one wall. He sheathed the blade in a liquid movement, drew the cane-sheath from his belt, and then passed the hilt of the sword back toward me. "Take it."

"Uh," I said. "I don't have a real good record with handling these things."

"Take it."

"Michael and Sanya might not be too happy with me if I do."

Shiro was quiet for a moment before he said, "They will understand. Take it now."

I swallowed and did. The wooden hilt of the sword felt too warm for the room, and I could sense a buzz of energy emanating from it in rippling waves. I made sure I had a good grip on it.

Shiro said quietly, "They will come for you. Go. Second right. Ladder up."

Nicodemus watched me as I fell back through the doorway into the dimness of the hall beyond it. I stared at Shiro for a moment. He knelt on the floor, still holding Deirdre's neck at the breaking point, his eyes on Nicodemus. From the back, I could see the wrinkled skin on the back of his neck, the age spots on his freshly shaved scalp. Nicodemus's shadow had grown to the size of a movie screen, and it covered the back wall and part of the floor, twitching and writhing slowly closer to Shiro.

I turned and headed down the tunnel as quickly as I could. Behind me, I heard Nicodemus say, "Keep your word, Japan. Release my daughter."

I looked back. Shiro released the girl and stood up. She flung herself away from him, and as she did Nicodemus's shadow rolled forward like an ocean wave and crashed over the old Knight. One moment, he was there. The next, the room where he stood went totally black, filled with the rasping, seething mass of Nicodemus's demon shadow.

"Kill the wizard," Nicodemus snarled. "Get the sword."

Deirdre let out wild, primal scream from somewhere inside the darkness. I heard ripping, tearing sounds. I heard popping noises that might have been bones breaking or joints being dislocated. Then I heard the steely, slithery rasp of Deirdre's hairdo, and half a dozen metallic strands whipped toward me from the darkness.

I shuffled back, and the blades fell short of me. I turned around and started hobbling away. I didn't want to leave Shiro there, but if I'd stayed, I only would have died with him. My shame dug at me like a knife.

More blades emerged from the dark, presumably while

Deirdre was still transforming into her demonic aspect. It couldn't be long before she finished and came flashing down the hallway after me. If I couldn't get myself clear, I'd be done for.

So once again I ran like hell. And hated myself for doing it.

Chapter Twenty-three

The shrieks died off more quickly than I would have thought, and I did my best to keep moving in a straight line. It was mostly dark. I was aware of a couple of doorways passing on my left, and I stumbled along until I found the second one on my right. I took it, and found a ladder that led up some kind of pipe or shaft, with a light shining down from about seven hundred miles above.

I got a couple of rungs off the floor when something hit me at knee level, grabbed my legs, and twisted. I fell off the ladder, the cane clattering onto the floor. I had a brief impression of a man's face, and then my attacker let out a wordless snarl and hit me hard on my left eye.

I ducked and rolled with the punch. The good news was that it didn't tear my face off or anything, which meant that the person throwing the punch was probably another mortal. The bad news was that he was built more heavily than me and probably had a lot more muscle. He piled atop me, trying to grasp my throat.

I hunched my shoulders and ducked my head as much as I could, and kept him from squeezing my head off. He threw another punch at me, but it's tough to throw a good punch when you're rolling around on the floor in the dark. He missed, and I started fighting dirty. I reached up and raked my nails across his eyes. I got one of them and he yelled, flinching away.

I managed to wriggle out from under him, giving him a hard shove that added to the momentum of the flinch. He fell, rolled, and started to rise.

I kicked him in the head with my rented formal shoes. My shoe went flying off, which I was pretty sure never happened to

James Bond. The goon faltered, wobbling, so I kicked him with the other foot. He was tough. He started coming back from that one too. I bent over and slammed my fist down sledgehammer style at the back of his neck, several times. I was shouting as I did it, and the edges of my vision burned with a film of red.

The rabbit punches dropped him, and he fell limp to the ground.

"Son of a bitch." I panted, feeling around until I found Shiro's cane. "I didn't get my ass kicked."

"Good day to get that lottery ticket," Susan said. She came down the last several feet of ladder, dressed again in the black leather pants, the dark coat. She checked to make sure the goon wasn't faking it. Where's Shiro?"

I shook my head. "He isn't coming."

Susan took a breath and then nodded. "Can you climb?"

"Think so," I said, eyeing the ladder. I held out the cane. "Take this for me?"

Susan reached out to take the blade. There was a flicker of silver static and she hissed, jerking her fingers back. "What the hell is that?"

"Magic sword."

"Well, it sucks," Susan said. "Go ahead; I'll come up behind you."

I fumbled around with the cane, slipping it as best I could through the tux's cummerbund. I started up the ladder and once again Deirdre shrieked, this time her voice wholly demonic, echoing weirdly through the stone corridors.

"Wasn't that—" Susan asked, shaking her fingers.

"Yeah. Climb," I said. "Climb fast."

The action and adrenaline had done something to thaw me out, or at least it felt that way. My fingers tingled, but they were functional, and I gained speed as I climbed. "How'd you find me?"

"Shiro," Susan responded. "We went to Michael's house for help. He seemed to know where to go. Like instinct."

"I saw Michael do that once," I said, panting. "He told me he knew how to find where he was needed. How long is this freaking ladder?"

"Another twenty or thirty feet," Susan said. "Comes out in the basement of an empty building south of the Loop. Martin's waiting with the car."

"Why did that guy talk about a Fellowship when he saw you back at the auction?" I asked. "What Fellowship?"

"It's a long story."

"Condense it."

"Later."

"But—"

I didn't get to protest any further, because I slipped and nearly fell when I reached the top of the ladder. I recovered my balance and scrambled up into a completely dark room. I looked back over my shoulder and saw Susan outlined, a dim shadow against a faint green-gold light.

"What's that light?" I asked.

"Eyes," Susan said. Her voice was a little thready. "Coming up. Move over."

I did. Susan slid onto the floor as the green-gold light grew brighter, and I heard the steely rasping sound of Deirdre's hair moving below. Susan turned and drew something from her jacket pocket. There was a clinking, clicking sound. Then she whispered, "One, one thousand, two, one thousand, three, one thousand, four, one thousand," and dropped something down the ladder.

She turned to me, and I felt her fingers cover my eyes, pushing me away from the ladder. I got it then, and leaned away from the shaft the ladder had come up just before there was a hellishly loud noise and a flash of light, scarlet through Susan's fingertips.

My ears rang and my balance wavered. Susan helped me to my feet and started moving out through the darkness, her steps swift and certain. From the shaft, I could dimly hear the demon-girl shrieking in fury. I asked, "Was that a grenade?"

"Just a stunner," Susan said. "Lots of light and noise."

"And you had it in your pocket," I said.

"No. Martin did. I borrowed it."

I tripped over something faintly yielding in the darkness, a limp form. "Whoa, what is that?"

"I don't know. Some kind of guard animal. Shiro killed it."

My next step squished in something damp and faintly warm that soaked through my sock. "Perfect."

Susan slammed a door open onto nighttime Chicago, and I could see again. We left the building behind us and went down a flight of concrete steps to the sidewalk. I didn't recognize the neighborhood offhand, but it wasn't a good one. It had that wary, hard-core feel that made *The Jungle* seem like *Mary Poppins* by comparison. There was dim light in the sky—evidently dawn was not far away.

Susan looked up and down the street and cursed quietly. "Where is he?"

I turned and looked at Susan. The dark swirls and spikes of her tattoo still stood out dark against her skin. Her face looked leaner than I remembered.

Another shrieking scream came from inside the building. "This is a really bad time for him to be late," I said.

"I know," she said, flexing her fingers. "Harry, I don't know if I can handle that demon bitch if she comes at us again." She looked down at her own hand, where the dark tattoos swirled and curved. "I'm almost out."

"Out?" I asked. "Of what?"

Her lip lifted into a quiet snarl and she swept dark eyes up and down the street. "Control."

"Oooooookay," I said. "We can't just stand here. We need to move."

Just then, an engine growled, and a dark green rental sedan came screeching around the corner of the block. It swerved across to the wrong side of the street and came up on the curb before sliding to a stop.

Martin threw open the back door. There was a cut on his left temple and a streak of blood had dried dark on his jaw. Tattoos like Susan's, but thicker, framed one eye and the left side of his face. "They're behind me," he said. "Hurry."

He didn't have to tell either of us twice. Susan shoved me into the back of the car and piled in after me. Martin had the car moving again before she'd shut the door, and I looked back to see another sedan after us. Before we'd gone a block, a second car slid in behind the first, and the two accelerated, coming after us.

"Dammit," Martin said, glaring at his rearview mirror. "What did you do to these people, Dresden?"

"I turned down their recruiting officer," I said.

Martin nodded, and snapped the car around a corner. "I'd say they don't handle rejection well. Where's the old man?"

"Gone."

He exhaled through his nose. "These idiots are going to land us all in jail if this keeps up. How bad do they want you?"

"More than most."

Martin nodded. "Do you have a safe house?"

"My place. I've got some emergency wards I can set off. They could keep out a mail-order record club." I bobbed my eyebrows at Susan. "For a while, anyway."

Martin juked the car around another corner. "It isn't far. You can jump out. We'll draw them off."

"He can't," Susan objected. "He can barely move. He's been hurt, and he could go into shock. He isn't like us, Martin."

Martin frowned. "What did you have in mind?"

"I'll go with him."

He stared up at the rearview mirror for a moment, at Susan. "It's a bad idea."

"I know."

"It's dangerous."

"I *know*," she said, voice tight. "There's no choice, and no time to argue."

Martin turned his eyes back to the road and said, "Are you sure?"

"Yeah."

"God be with you both, then. Sixty seconds."

"Wait a minute," I said. "What are you both—"

Martin screeched around another corner and roared ahead at top speed. I bounced off the door on my side and flattened my cheek against the window. I recognized my neighborhood as I did. I glanced at the speedometer of the car and wished I hadn't.

Susan reached across me to open the door and said, "We get out here."

I stared at her and then motioned vaguely at the door.

She met my eyes and that same hard, delighted smile spread over her lips. "Trust me. This is kid stuff."

"Cartoons are kid stuff. Petting zoos are kid stuff. Jumping out of a car is *insane*."

"You did it before," she accused me. "The lycanthropes."

"That was different."

"Yes. You left me in the car." Susan crawled across my lap, which appreciated her. Especially in the tight leather pants. My eyes agreed with my lap wholeheartedly. Especially about the tight leather pants. Susan then crouched, one foot on the floorboards, one hand on the door, and offered her other hand to me. "Come on."

Susan had changed in the last year. Or maybe she hadn't. She had always been good at what she did. She'd just altered her focus to something other than reporting. She could take on demonic murderers in hand-to-hand combat now, rip home appliances from the wall and throw them with one hand, and use grenades in the dark. If she said she could jump out of a speeding car and keep us both from dying, I believed her. *What the hell,* I thought. It wasn't like I hadn't done this before—albeit at a fifth the speed.

But there was something deeper than that, something darker that Susan's vulpine smile had stirred inside of me. Some wild, reckless, primal piece of me had always loved the danger, the adrenaline, had always loved testing myself against the various and sundry would-be lethalities that crossed my paths. There was an ecstasy in the knife edge of the struggle, a vital energy that couldn't be found anywhere else, and part of me (a stupid, insane, but undeniably powerful part) missed it when it was gone.

That wildness rose up in me, and gave me a smile that matched Susan's.

I took her hand, and a second later we leapt from the car. I heard myself laughing like a madman as we did.

Chapter Twenty-four

⋘⋙

As we went out the door, Susan pulled me hard against her. On general policy, I approved. She got one arm around the back of my head, shielding the base of my skull and the top of my neck. We hit the ground with Susan on the bottom, bounced up a bit, rolling, and hit the ground again. The impacts were jolting, but I was on the bottom only once. The rest of the time, the impact was something I felt only through my contact with Susan.

We wound up on the tiny patch of grass two doors down from my boardinghouse, in front of some cheap converted apartments. Several seconds later, the two pursuing cars went roaring by after Martin and his rented sedan. I kept my head down until they had passed, and then looked at Susan.

I was on top. Susan panted quietly beneath me. One of her legs was bent at the knee, half holding my thigh between hers. Her dark eyes glittered, and I felt her hips twitch in the kind of motion that brought a number of evenings (and mornings, and afternoons, and late nights) to mind.

I wanted to kiss her. A lot. I held off. "You all right?" I asked.

"You never complained," she answered. Her voice was a little breathless. "Nothing too bad. You? Anything hurt?"

"My ego," I said. "You're embarrassing me with the super-strength and whatnot." I rose, took her hand, and drew her to her feet. "How's a guy supposed to assert his masculinity?"

"You're a big boy. You'll think of something."

I looked around and nodded. "I think we'd better get off the street, pronto."

"Is running and hiding assertively masculine?" We started for my apartment. "The part where we don't die is."

She nodded. "That's practical, but I'm not sure it's masculine."

"Shut up."

"There you go," Susan said.

We went only a couple of steps before I felt the spell coming. It started as a low shiver on the back of my neck, and my eyes twitched almost of their own accord up to the roof of the apartment house we were walking by. I saw a couple of bricks from one of the chimneys fall free of their mortar. I grabbed Susan's collar and sidestepped, pulling her with me. The bricks shattered into shards and red powder on the sidewalk a step from Susan's feet.

Susan tensed and looked up. "What was that?"

"An entropy curse," I muttered.

"A what?"

I looked around, struggling to sense where the next surge of magic might come from. "Sort of a bad-luck spell. A really, *really* bad-luck spell. Preferred magic for getting rid of someone who annoys you."

"Who is doing it?"

"My guess? Snakeboy. He seems to have some talent, and he could have gotten some of my blood to target me with." I felt another gathering surge of energy to my right, and my eyes went to the power lines running overhead. "Oh, hell. Run."

Susan and I broke into a sprint. As we did, I heard one of the power lines snap, cables squealing. The longer end of loose cable flew toward us, trailing a cloud of blue and white sparks. It hit the ground somewhere behind us.

My clothes hadn't yet dried out from Nicodemus's guest accommodations. If it had been raining, the downed power line might have killed me. As it was, I felt a vibrating, clenching tingle wash over my legs. I almost fell, but managed to get a few more paces away from the sputtering line and regained control of my legs.

I felt another magical strike building, bringing a gust of wind with it, but before I could zero in on it Susan shouldered me to one side. I fell to the ground just as I heard a loud cracking sound. A branch as thick as my thigh slammed to the ground. I looked up to see a strip of bare white bark showing along the trunk of the old tree behind my boardinghouse.

Susan helped drag me to my feet and we ran the rest of the way to my apartment door. Even as we did, I felt another strike building, stronger than the last. I fumbled open the lock while thunder rumbled through the predawn grey, and we got inside.

I could still feel the curse growing and reaching for me. It was a strong one, and I wasn't sure that either my apartment's threshold or my standard wards would be able to keep it out. I slammed the door closed behind me, locked it. The room fell into darkness as I reached for the basket beside the door. There was a waxy lump the size of my fist in it, and I lifted it and slammed it hard against the door, across the crack between the door and the jamb. I found the wick standing out from the wax, focused on it, and drew in my will. I murmured, *"Flickum bicus,"* and released the magic, and the wick suddenly glowed with a pure white flame.

Around the room at precisely the same moment, two dozen other candles of white and butter-colored wax also lit with a gentle flicker of white fire. As they did, I felt a sudden thrum of my own magic, prepared months before, raise into a rampart around my home. The curse pulsed again, somewhere outside, and hammered against the barrier, but my protection held. The malevolent energy shattered against it.

"Boo-ya, snakeboy," I muttered, letting out a tense breath. "Stick that in your scaly ass and smoke it."

"The action-hero one-liner doesn't count if you mix metaphors," Susan said, panting.

"Looks like no Harry Dresden action figures for me," I answered.

"Did you get him?"

"Slammed the door on his curse," I answered. "We should be safe for a while."

Susan looked around her at all the lit candles, getting her breath back. I saw her expression soften, and turn a little sad. We'd eaten a lot of dinners here, by candlelight. We'd done a lot of things that way. I studied her features while she stood lost in thought. The tattoos changed her, I decided. They changed the proportions and lines of her face. They lent her features a sort of exotic remoteness, an alien beauty.

"Thirsty?" I asked. She shot me a look with a hint of frustration in it. I lifted my hands. "Sorry. I didn't think."

She nodded, turning a little away from me. "I know. Sorry."

"Coke?"

"Yeah."

I limped to the icebox, which was going to need more ice before long. I didn't have the leftover energy to freeze the water again by magic. I grabbed two cans of Coca-Cola, opened them both, and took one to Susan. She took a long guzzle and I joined her.

"You're limping," she said when she was done.

I looked down at my feet. "Only one shoe. It makes me lop-sided."

"You're hurt," she said. Her eyes were fastened on my leg. "Bleeding."

"It isn't too bad. I'll clean it up in a minute."

Susan's eyes never wavered, but they got darker. Her voice grew quieter. "Do you need help?"

I turned a bit warily so that she couldn't see the injured leg. She shivered and made an evident effort to look away. The tattoos on her face were lighter now—not fainter, but changing in colors. "I'm sorry. Harry, I'm sorry, but I'd better go."

"You can't," I said.

Her voice remained very quiet, very toneless. "You don't get it. I'll explain everything to you in a little while. I promise. But I have to leave."

I cleared my throat. "Um. No, you don't get it. You can't. Cannot. Literally."

"What?"

"The defenses I put up have two sides and they don't have an off switch. We literally, physically can't leave until they go down."

Susan looked up at me and then folded her arms, staring at her Coke can. "Crud," she said. "How long?"

I shook my head. "I built them to run for about eight hours. Sunrise is going to degrade it a little though. Maybe four hours, five at the most."

"Five hours," she said under her breath. "Oh, God."

"What's wrong?"

She waved a hand vaguely. "I've been . . . been using some of the power. To be faster. Stronger. If I'm calm, it doesn't get stirred up. But I haven't been calm. It's built up inside of me. Water on a dam. It wants to break free, to get loose."

I licked my lips. If Susan lost control of herself, there was no place to run. "What can I do to help?"

She shook her head, refusing to look up at me. "I don't know. Let me have some quiet. Try to relax." Something cold and hungry flickered in her eyes. "Get your leg cleaned up. I can smell it. It's . . . distracting."

"See if you can build the fire," I said, and slipped into my room, closing the door behind me. I went into the bathroom and closed that door too. My first-aid kit had its own spot on one of the shelves. I downed a couple of Tylenol, slipped out of the remains of my rented tux, and cleaned up the cut on my leg. It was a shallow cut, but a good four inches long, and it had bled messily. I used disinfectant soap with cold water to wash it out, then slathered it in an antibacterial gel before laying several plastic bandages over the injury, to hold it closed. It didn't hurt. Or at least I didn't pick it out from the background of aches and pains my body was telling me about.

Shivering again, I climbed into some sweats, a T-shirt, and a flannel bathrobe. I looked around in my closet, at a couple of the other things I'd made for a rainy day. I took one of the potions I'd brewed, the ones to counter the venom of the Red Court, and put it in my pocket. I missed my shield bracelet.

I opened the door to the living room and Susan was standing six inches away, her eyes black with no white to them, the designs on her skin flushed a dark maroon.

"I can still smell your blood," she whispered. "I think you need to find a way to hold me back, Harry. And you need to do it now."

Chapter Twenty-five

❦❦

I didn't have much left in me in the way of magic. I wouldn't until I got a chance to rest and recuperate from what Nicodemus had done to me. I might have been able to manage a spell that would hold a normal person, but not a hungry vampire. And that was what Susan was. She'd gained strength in more senses than the merely physical, and that never happened without granting a certain amount of magical defense, even if in nothing but the naked will to fight. Snakeboy's serpent-cloud had been one of the nastier spells I'd seen, and it had only slowed Susan down.

If she came at me, and it looked like she might, I wouldn't be able to stop her.

My motto, after the past couple of years, was to be prepared. I had something that I knew could restrain her—assuming I could get past her and to the drawer where I kept it.

"Susan," I said quietly. "Susan, I need you to stay with me. Talk to me."

"Don't want to talk," she said. Her eyelids lowered and she inhaled slowly. "I don't want it to smell so good. Your blood. Your fear. But it does."

"The Fellowship," I said. I struggled to rein in my emotions. For her sake, I couldn't afford to feel afraid. I edged a little toward her. "Let's sit down. You can tell me about the Fellowship."

For a second, I thought she wouldn't give way, but she did. "Fellowship," she said. "The Fellowship of Saint Giles."

"Saint Giles," I said. "The patron of lepers."

"And other outcasts. Like me. They're all like me."

"You mean infected?"

"Infected. Half-turned. Half-human. Half-dead. There are a lot of ways to say it."

"Uh-huh," I said. "So what's their deal?"

"The Fellowship tries to help people the Red Court has harmed. Work against the Red Court. Expose them whenever they can."

"Find a cure?"

"There is no cure."

I put my hand on her arm and guided her toward my couch. She moved with a dreamy deliberation. "So the tattoos are what? Your membership card?"

"A binding," she said. "A spell cut into my skin. To help me hold the darkness inside. To warn me when it is rising."

"What do you mean, warn you?"

She looked down at her design-covered hand, then showed it to me. The tattoos there and on her face were slowly growing brighter, and had turned a shade of medium scarlet. "To warn me when I'm about to lose control. Red, red, red. Danger, danger, danger."

The first night she'd arrived, when she'd been tussling with something outside, she'd stayed in the shadows for the first several moments inside, her face turned away. She'd been hiding the tattoos. "Here," I said quietly. "Sit down."

She sat on the couch and met my eyes. "Harry," she whispered. "It hurts. It hurts to fight it. I'm tired of holding on. I don't know how long I can."

I knelt down to be on eye level with her. "Do you trust me?"

"With my heart. With my life."

"Close your eyes," I said.

She did.

I got up and walked slowly to the kitchen drawer. I didn't move quickly. You don't move quickly away from something that is thinking about making you food. It sets them off. Whatever had been placed inside her was growing—I could feel that, see it, hear it in her voice.

I was in danger. But it didn't matter, because so was she.

I usually keep a gun in the kitchen drawer. At the time, I had a gun and a short length of silver-and-white rope in there. I picked up the rope and walked back over to her.

"Susan," I said quietly. "Give me your hands."

She opened her eyes and looked at the soft, fine rope. "That won't hold me."

"I made it in case an ogre I pissed off came visiting. Give me your hands."

She was silent for a moment. Then she shrugged out of her jacket, and held her hands out, wrists up.

I tossed the rope at her and whispered, *"Manacus."*

I'd enchanted the rope six months before, but I'd done it right. It took barely a whisper of power to set the rope into motion. It whipped into the air, silver threads flashing, and bound itself around her wrists in neat loops.

Susan reacted instantly, going completely tense. I saw her set herself and strain against the ropes. I waited, watching for a full half a minute before she started shaking and stopped trying to break them. She let out a shaking breath, her head bowed, hair fallen around her face. I started to move toward her, when she stood up, legs spread enough to brace herself firmly, and tried again, lifting her arms.

I licked my lips, watching. I didn't think she'd break the ropes, but I'd underestimated people before. Her face, her too-black eyes scared me. She strained against the ropes again, the movement drawing her shirt up, showing me her smooth brown stomach, the winding swirls and barbs of her tattoo red and stark against her skin. There were dark bruises over her ribs, and patches of skin that had been scraped raw. She hadn't come away from our tumble from Martin's car without being hurt, after all.

After a minute more, she hissed out a breath and sat down, hair a tumbled mess around her face. I could feel her eyes on me more than I could actually see them. They didn't feel like Susan's eyes anymore. The tattoos stood out against her skin, red as blood. I backed off, again deliberately, calmly, and got the first aid kit out of the bathroom.

When I came back out, she flung herself at me in blinding speed and utter silence. I'd been expecting as much, and snapped, *"Forzare!"*

The silver rope flashed with a glitter of blue light and darted toward the ceiling. Her wrists went with it and she was pulled completely from the floor. Her feet swung up, and she twisted, again in silence, fighting the bonds on her. She didn't get free, and I let her swing there until her legs had settled again, her toes barely touching the floor.

She let out a quiet sob and whispered, "I'm sorry. Harry, I can't stop it."

"It's okay. I've got you." I stepped closer to examine the injuries on her midsection and winced. "God. You got torn up."

"I hate this. I'm so sorry."

It hurt me to hear her voice. There was enough pain in it for both of us. "Shhhh," I said. "Let me take care of you."

She fell quiet then, though I could sense flashes of that feral hunger in her. I got a bowl of water, a cloth, and set to cleaning up the scrapes as best I could. She quivered once in a while. Once she let out a pained groan. The bruises went all the way up her back, and she had another patch of abraded skin on her neck. I put my hand on her head and pushed forward. She bowed her head and let it hang forward while I tended to the wound.

While I did, the quality of the tension changed. I could smell her hair, her skin, their scent like candle smoke and cinnamon. I became suddenly, intensely aware of the curve of her back, her hips. She leaned back a little toward me, bringing her body into contact with mine, the heat of her something that could have singed me. Her breathing changed, growing faster, heavier. She turned her head, enough to look at me over her shoulder. Her eyes burned, and her tongue flickered over her lips.

"Need you," she whispered.

I swallowed. "Susan. I think maybe that—"

"Don't think," she said. Her hips brushed against the front of my sweats, and I was abruptly so hard that it hurt. "Don't think. Touch me."

Somewhere, I knew it wasn't the best of ideas. But I laid the fingers of one hand on the curve of her waist, wrapping them slowly to her heated skin. Soft smoothness caressed my hand. There was a pleasure in it, a primal, possessive pleasure in touching her. I ran my palm and spread fingers over her flank, her belly, in slow and light circles. She arched at the caress, her eyes closing, and whispered, "Yes," over and over again. "Yes."

I let the washcloth fall from my other hand and reached up to touch her hair. More softness, rich texture, dark hairs gliding between my fingers. I felt a second of gathering tension in her and then she whipped her head around, teeth bared, reaching for my hand. I should have drawn my hand away. Instead, I tightened my fingers in her hair and pulled back, forcing her chin up and keeping her from reaching me.

I expected anger from her, but instead her body became pliant again, moving against me with a more willing abandon. A languid smile spread over her lips, and faded away to an openmouthed gasp as I slid my other hand up, beneath the cotton shirt, and ran my fingertips lightly over her breasts. She gasped, and at the sound all of my recent worry, fear, anger, pain—it all faded away, burned to ash by a sudden fire of raw need. To feel her under my hand again, to have the scent of her filling my head—I'd dreamed of it on too many cold and lonely nights.

It wasn't the smart thing to do. It was the only thing.

I slid both hands around her body, teasing her breasts, loving the way their tips hardened to rounded points beneath my fingers. She tried to turn on me again, but I jerked her back hard against me, my mouth pressing against the side of her throat, keeping her from turning her head. It only excited her more.

"Need," she whispered, panting. "Need you. Don't stop."

I wasn't sure I could have. I couldn't get enough of the taste of her onto my lips. Impatient, I shoved her shirt up, over her breasts, to the top of her back, and spent a slow and delicious moment following the line of her spine with my lips and tongue, tasting her skin, testing its texture with my teeth. Some part of me struggled to remember to be gentle. Another part didn't give a damn. *Feel. Taste. Indulge.*

My teeth left small marks here and there on her skin, and I remember thinking that they looked intriguing beside the curling scarlet designs that swept in a spiral around her body. The dark leather of her pants blocked my mouth, a sudden ugliness beneath my lips, and I straightened with a snarl to get it out of my way.

For the record, tight leather pants don't come off easily. Berserk lust is likely not the best frame of mind for removing them. I didn't let that stop me. She gasped when I started taking them off, started squirming and wriggling, trying to help me. Mostly, it just drove me insane as she brushed against me, as I watched her move in sinuous, delicious need. Her panting gasps all had a quiet vocalization to them now, a sound that both spoke of her need and urged me on.

I got the pants down over her hips. There wasn't anything else beneath them. I shivered and paused to spend another moment savoring her with my hands, my mouth, placing delicate kisses around the scrapes, biting at unmarred skin to elicit more desperate movements, louder moans. The scent of her was driving me insane.

"Now," she whispered, a frenzied edge to her voice. "Now."

But I didn't hurry. I don't know how long I stood there, kissing, touching, driving her cries into higher and more desperate pitches. All I knew was that something I'd wanted, needed, longed for had come to me again. At that moment there was nothing on earth, in heaven or hell, that meant more to me.

She looked over her shoulder at me, eyes black and burning with hunger. She tried for my hand again, driven beyond words now. I had to control her head again, fingers knotted into her hair while my free hand got the interfering clothes out of the way. She let out mewling sounds of raw need, until I pulled her hips back against me, feeling my way, and in a rush of fire and silk felt my hardness press into her.

Her eyes flew open wide, out of focus, and she cried out, moving against me, meeting my motion with her own. I had a fleeting thought of slowing down. I didn't. Neither of us wanted that. I took her that way, my mouth on her ear, her throat, one hand in her hair, her hands stretched out over her, body straining back to meet mine.

God, she was beautiful.

She screamed and started shuddering, and it was all I could do not to explode. I fought away the inevitable for a little time more. Susan sagged down after a moment, until with my hands, with my mouth, with the thrusts of my body, I kindled the quiet moans once again to cries of need. She screamed again, the motions of her body swift, liquid, desperate, and there wasn't any way I could keep her from driving me over the brink with her.

Our cries mingled together as we intertwined. The strain of muscles and bodies and hungers overwhelmed me.

Pleasure like fire consumed us both and burned my thoughts to ash.

Time drifted by and did not touch us.

When I recovered my senses, I found myself on the floor. Susan lay on her stomach beneath me, her still-bound arms laid out above her head. Not much time had passed. Both of us were still short of breath. I shivered, and felt myself still inside her. I didn't remember releasing the spell that held the bonds up to the ceiling, but I must have done it. I moved my head to kiss her shoulder, her cheek, very softly.

Her eyes blinked slowly open, human again, though her pupils were dilated until they all but hid the dark brown of her irises. She didn't focus them. She smiled and made a soft sound, somewhere between a moan and a cat's purr. I stared at her for a moment, until I realized that the designs on her face had gone dark again, and had begun to fade away. As I watched over the next few moments, they vanished completely.

"I love you," she whispered.

"I love you."

"Wanted that."

"Me too," I said.

"Dangerous. Harry, you could have been hurt. I might have—"

I leaned down and kissed the corner of her mouth, silencing her. "You didn't. It's okay."

She shivered, but nodded. "So tired."

I felt like nothing more than dropping off to sleep, but instead I got to my feet. Susan let out a soft sound, half pleasure and half protest. I gathered her up and put her on the couch. I touched the rope, willing it to release her, and it slid away from her skin, coiling itself into neat loops in my hand. I pulled a blanket from the back of the couch and folded it over her. "Sleep," I said. "Get some rest."

"You should—"

"I will. Promise. But . . . I don't think it would be a good idea to go to sleep near you."

Susan nodded wearily. "You're right. I'm sorry."

"It's okay," I said.

"Should call Martin."

"The phone won't call out," I said. "Not until the defenses go down."

I didn't think her voice sounded particularly disappointed as she snuggled down a bit more onto my couch. "Oh," she said. "We'll have to wait it out then."

"Yeah," I said. I stroked her hair. "Susan—"

She touched my hand with hers, and closed her eyes. "It's all right. I told you, I'd never be able to separate the hungers with you. It . . . it was a release. Took some of the pressure off me. I wanted it. Needed it."

"Did I hurt you?"

She made a purring sound without opening her eyes. "Maybe a little. I didn't mind."

I shivered and said, "You're okay?"

She nodded slowly. "As I can be. Get some rest, Harry."

"Yeah," I said. I touched her hair again, and then shuffled into my bedroom. I didn't shut the door. I put my pillows at the foot of my bed, so that I could see the couch when I lay down. I watched her face, graced by pale candlelight, until my eyes closed.

She was so lovely.

I wished that she were with me.

Chapter Twenty-six

I opened my eyes a while later, and saw Susan standing in the living room, her eyes closed. She was crouched, her hands held before her as if grasping an invisible basketball. As I watched, she moved, arms and legs gliding through gentle, circular motions. Tai chi. It was a meditative form of exercise that had originally come from martial arts. Lots of people who practiced tai chi didn't realize that the movements they followed were beautiful, slow-motion renditions of bone-breaking throws and joint locks.

I had a feeling Susan knew. She wore her T-shirt and a pair of my running shorts. She moved with the graceful simplicity of a natural talent honed by training.

A turn showed me her face, her expression set in peaceful concentration. I spent a minute watching her in silence, cataloging my own aches and pains.

She suddenly smiled, without opening her eyes, and said, "Don't start drooling, Harry."

"My house. I can drool as much as I want."

"What was that rope you used?" she asked, still going through her routine. "I've broken handcuffs before. Magic?"

Shoptalk. I had hoped for some other kind of discussion. Or maybe I'd been nervous about it. Work talk held a certain appeal for me, too. It was safe. "Faerie make," I said. "Has hair from a unicorn's mane woven through it."

"Really?"

I shrugged. "That's what Fix said. I imagine he knows."

"Would be handy to have around if the Denarians showed up again, don't you think?"

"Not unless they came here," I told her. "It's set to this place. Take it out of here and it wouldn't work."

"Why not?"

"Because I'm not that good yet," I said. "It's easy to make something that works at home. Takes a lot more know-how than I have to take an enchantment on the road." I got out of bed and got moving. The clock said that it wasn't yet ten in the morning. I hopped in and out of the shower, dressed, slapped a comb through my hair, and decided that the rakish, unshaven look was in.

By the time I got back out into the living room, Susan was dressed in the leather pants again and only four or five candles were still lit. The defensive barriers were winding down. "What happened after Martin took off from the hotel?" I asked.

Susan slouched into a chair. "I tried to get him to stop. He wouldn't. We fought about it and he put a gun in my face."

I choked. "He *what*?"

"To be fair, I wasn't being very rational."

"Hell's bells."

"Martin didn't want to, but I convinced him to go to Michael's place. I figured if anyone could get you out of a mess with the Denarians it would be him."

"Seems reasonable to me," I said. I debated between coffee and cola. The Coke won by virtue of convenience. Susan nodded at me before I could get the question out of my mouth, and I got her one too. "What about Anna Valmont?"

"She was in shock. Charity put her to bed."

"Did you call the police?"

Susan shook her head. "I thought she might have known something that would help. We wouldn't be able to find out what it was if she was angry and locked away."

"What did Michael have to say about it?"

"He wasn't there," Susan said. "Shiro was. Charity said that Michael and someone named Sanya hadn't come back from St. Louis and hadn't called."

I frowned and passed over the second can to her. "That doesn't sound like him."

"I know. They were worried." She frowned. "Or Charity was. I don't think Shiro was worried at all. It was almost as though he'd been expecting all of it. He was still dressed in the samurai clothes and he opened the front door before I could knock."

"Michael's done that kind of thing before. Fringe benefit of his job, maybe."

Susan shook her head. "God works in mysterious ways?"

I shrugged. "Maybe so. Did Shiro say anything?"

"He just told Martin where to turn left or right and where to park. Then he told me to give him two minutes' lead and to get ready to get you back to the car. He just . . . smiled a little, the whole time. It would have been a little spooky on anyone else. He seemed content. Maybe he just had a good poker face."

I toyed with my can. "Has. He has a good poker face."

Susan arched an eyebrow. "I don't understand."

"I don't think he's dead. Not yet. He . . . he agreed to give himself over to the Denarians in exchange for them letting me go. The head Denarian guy, said his name was Nicodemus, made Shiro promise to not to fight back or escape for twenty-four hours."

"That doesn't sound good."

I shivered. "Yeah. I figure they're archenemies. When Shiro offered himself, Nicodemus looked like a kid on Christmas morning."

Susan sipped at her drink. "How bad are these people?"

I thought of Nicodemus and his knife. Of the sheer helplessness I'd felt as he drew my head back, baring my throat. I thought of sliced and diced corpses. "Bad."

Susan regarded me quietly for a moment, while I stared at my drink.

"Harry," she said finally. "You going to open that or just look at it?"

I shook my head and popped the tab on the can. My wrists felt sore, and the skin around them had been pretty thoroughly abraded. Evidently Nicodemus preferred regular old ropes to special unicorn-mane custom jobs. "Sorry. Got a lot to think about."

"Yeah," she said, her own voice softening. "What's our next move?"

I checked the candles. Three to go. "Barrier will go down in maybe twenty minutes. We'll call a cab, pick up the Beetle at McAnnally's, and head to Michael's place."

"What if the Denarians are waiting outside for us?"

I picked up my blasting rod from the stand in the corner by the door and twirled it around in my fingers. "They'll have to find their own cab."

"And then?"

I picked up my staff and leaned it against the wall by the door. "We tell Michael and Sanya what happened."

"Assuming they're back."

"Uh-huh." I opened the kitchen drawer and got out my gun and its holster. "After that, I ask the nice Denarians to let Shiro go."

Susan nodded. "We ask?"

I flipped open the cylinder on the gun and loaded it. "I'll say pretty please," I said, and snapped the cylinder shut again.

Susan's eyes flashed. "Count me in." She watched me while I put on a shoulder rig and slipped the gun into it. "Harry," she said. "I don't want to break up the righteous-vengeance vibe, but there are a couple of questions that are really bothering me."

"Why do the Denarians want the Shroud, and what are they going to do with it," I said.

"Yeah."

I got an old squall jacket out of my room and slid it on. It felt wrong. I hadn't worn anything but my old canvas duster or the newer leather one Susan had given me for the past several years. I checked the candles, and they had all gone out. I laid my hand on the wall, feeling for the defenses. There was a faint echo of them left, but nothing of substance, so I went back out into the living room and called for a cab. "We're good to go. I think I've got an idea of what they're doing, but I can't be sure."

She straightened my jacket collar absently. "Very sloppy of you. Didn't you get the meglomaniacal bragfest from this Nicodemus?"

"He must have read that Evil Overlord list."

"Sounds like someone who intends to get things done."

He sure as hell had. "He let a couple things slip. I think we can get ahead of him."

She shook her head. "Harry, when I went down there with Shiro, I didn't see much. But I heard their voices through the tunnels. There was . . ." She closed her eyes for a moment, her expression one of faint nausea. "It's hard for me to explain. Their voices gave me a strong impression. Shiro sounded like . . . I don't know. A trumpet. Clear and strong. The other one . . . his voice stank. It was rotted. Corrupt."

I didn't understand what would have made Susan say that. Maybe it was something that the vampires had done to her. Maybe it was something she'd learned between tai chi classes. Maybe it was just pure intuition. But I knew what she was talking about. There was a sense to Nicodemus, of something quiet and still and dangerous—of something patient and vile and malicious beyond the scope of mortal understanding. He scared the hell out of me.

"I know what you mean. Nicodemus isn't another misguided idealist, or some greedy bastard out to make money," I said. "He's different."

Susan nodded. "Evil."

"And he plays hardball." I wasn't sure if I was asking Susan or myself, but I said, "You ready?"

She got her jacket on. I went to the door and she followed.

"The one bad thing about the duster," she mused. "I could never see your butt."

"I never noticed."

"If you went around noticing your own ass I'd worry about you, Harry."

I looked over my shoulder at her, smiling. She smiled back.

It didn't last long. Both of our smiles turned a little sad.

"Susan," I said.

She put two fingertips to my lips. "Don't."

"Dammit, Susan. Last night—"

"Shouldn't have happened," she said. Her voice sounded tired, but her eyes stayed steady on mine. "It doesn't—"

"—change anything," I finished. I sounded bitter, even to me.

She took her hand away and buttoned up the dark leather jacket.

"Right," I said. I should have stuck to shoptalk. I opened the door and looked outside. "Cab's here. Let's get to work."

Chapter Twenty-seven

I grabbed my staff, blasting rod, and Shiro's cane, and made a note to get myself a freaking golf bag. We took the cab to McAnnally's. The Blue Beetle was still in the nearby lot, and it hadn't been stolen, vaporized, or otherwise mishandled.

"What happened to your back window?" Susan asked.

"One of Marcone's goons winged a few shots at me outside the *Larry Fowler* studio."

Susan's mouth twitched. "You went on *Larry Fowler* again?"

"I don't want to talk about it."

"Uh-huh. And what about the hood?"

"Little holes are from Marcone's thug. Big dent was a chlorofiend," I said.

"A what?"

"Plant monster."

"Oh. Why don't you just say 'plant monster'?"

"I have my pride."

"Your poor car."

I got out my keys, but Susan put her hand on mine, and walked a circle around the car. She crouched down and looked beneath it a couple of times, then said, "Okay."

I got in. "Thank you, double oh seven, but no one bombs a Volkswagen. They're too cute."

Susan got in the passenger door and said, "Cute confetti if you aren't careful, Harry."

I grunted, revved up the car, and puttered to Michael's place.

The morning was cold and clear. Winter hadn't yet given up its grip on the Great Lakes, and where Lake Michigan went, Chicago went too. Susan got out and looked around the front lawn, frowning from behind black sunglasses. "How does he manage to make this place so nice, run his own business, and fight demons on the side?"

"He probably watches a lot of those home-and-garden shows," I said.

She frowned. "The grass is green. It's February and his grass is green. Doesn't that strike you as strange?"

"Sod works in mysterious ways."

She made a disgusted sound, and then followed me up the walk to the door.

I knocked. A moment later Father Forthill said, "Who's there?"

"Donny and Marie," I responded. "Salt-N-Pepa asked us to fill in for them."

He opened the door, smiling from behind his gold-rimmed glasses. He was the same short, stocky, balding old Forthill, but he looked strained and tired. The lines of his face had grown deeper than I remembered. "Hello, Harry."

"Father," I said. "You know Susan?"

He looked at her thoughtfully. "By reputation," he said. "Come in, come in."

We did, and as I came in, Forthill set a Louisville Slugger baseball bat down in the corner. I raised my eyebrows, traded a look with Susan, and then put my staff and Shiro's cane beside the bat. We followed Forthill into the kitchen.

"Where's Charity?" I asked.

"Taking the children to her mother's house," Forthill said. "She should be back soon."

I let out a breath of relief. "Anna Valmont?"

"Guest room. Sleeping."

"I need to call Martin," Susan said. "Excuse me." She stepped aside into the small study.

"Coffee, doughnut?" Father Forthill asked.

I sat down at the table. "Father, you've never been closer to converting me."

He laughed. "The Fantastic Forthill, saving souls one Danish at a time." He produced the nectar of the gods themselves in Dunkin Donuts paper sacks and Styrofoam cups, taking some for himself as well. "I've always admired your ability to make jokes when faced with adversity. Matters are grave."

"I sort of noticed," I said through a mouthful of glazed doughnut. "Where's Michael?"

"He and Sanya went to St. Louis to investigate possible Denarian activity. They were both arrested by the local police."

"They what? What for?"

"No charges were filed," Forthill said. "They were arrested, held for twenty-four hours, and released."

"Sand trap," I said. "Someone wanted them out of the way."

Forthill nodded. "So it would seem. I spoke to them about two hours ago. They're on their way back now and should be here soon."

"Then as soon as they get here, we have to go get Shiro back."

Forthill frowned and nodded. "What happened to you last night?"

I told him the short version—all about the art auction and the Denarians, but I elided over the details afterward, which were none of his chaste business. And which would have embarrassed me to tell. I'm not particularly religious, but come on, the man was a priest.

When I finished, Forthill took off his glasses and stared hard at me. He had eyes the color of robin's eggs, and they could be disturbingly intense. "Nicodemus," he said quietly. "Are you *sure* that is what he called himself?"

"Yeah."

"Without a doubt?"

"Yeah. We had a nice chat."

Forthill folded his hands and exhaled slowly. "Mother of God. Harry, could you describe him for me?"

I did, while the old priest listened. "Oh, and he was always wearing a rope around his neck. Not like a ship's hawser, a thin rope, like clothesline. I thought it was a string tie at first."

Forthill's fingers reached up to touch the crucifix at his throat. "Tied in a noose?"

"Yeah."

"What did you think of him?" he asked.

I looked down at my half-eaten doughnut. "He scared the hell out of me. He's . . . bad, I guess. Wrong."

"The word you are looking for is 'evil,' Harry."

I shrugged, ate the rest of the doughut, and didn't argue.

"Nicodemus is an ancient foe of the Knights of the Cross," Forthill said quietly. "Our information about him is limited. He has made it a point to find and destroy our archives every other century or so, so we cannot be sure who he is or how long he has been alive. He may even have walked the earth when the Savior was crucified."

"Didn't look a day over five hundred," I mumbled. "How come some Knight hasn't gone and parted his hair for him?"

"They've tried," Forthill said.

"He's gotten away?"

Forthill's eyes and voice stayed steady. "He's killed them. He's killed all of them. More than a hundred Knights. More than a thousand priests, nuns, monks. Three thousand men, women, children. And those are only the ones listed in the pages recovered from the destroyed archives. Only two Knights have ever faced him and survived."

I had a flash of insight. "Shiro is one of them. That's why Nicodemus was willing to trade me for him."

Forthill nodded and closed his eyes for a moment. "Likely. Though the Denarians grow in power by inflicting pain and suffering on others. They become better able to use the strength the Fallen give them. And they gain the most from hurting those meant to counter them."

"He's torturing Shiro," I said.

Forthill put his hand on mine for a moment, his voice quiet, calming. "We must have faith. We may be in time to help him."

"I thought the whole point of the Knights was to deal out justice," I said. "The Fists of God and all that. So why is it that Nicodemus can slaughter them wholesale?"

"For much the same reason any man can kill another," Forthill said. "He is intelligent. Cautious. Skilled. Ruthless. Like his patron fallen angel."

I guessed at the name. "Badassiel?"

Forthill almost smiled. "Anduriel. He was a captain of Lucifer's, after the Fall. Anduriel leads the thirty Fallen who inhabit the coins. Nicodemus wasn't seduced into Anduriel's domination. It's a partnership. Nicodemus works with Fallen as a near-equal and of his free will. No one of the priesthood, of any of the Knightly Orders, of the Knights of the Cross, has so much as scratched him."

"The noose," I guessed. "The rope. It's like the Shroud, isn't it? It has power."

Forthill nodded. "We think so, yes. The same rope the betrayer used in Jerusalem."

"How many Denarians are working with him? I take it that they probably don't get along with each other."

"You are correct, thank God. Nicodemus rarely has more than five or six other Denarians working with him, according to our information. Usually, he keeps three others nearby."

"Snakeboy, demon-girl, and Ursiel."

"Yes."

"How many coins are running around the world?"

"Only nine are accounted for at this time. Ten, with Ursiel's coin."

"So Nicodemus could theoretically have nineteen other Fallen working with him. Plus a side order of goons."

"Goons?"

"Goons. Normal hired hands, they looked like."

"Ah. They aren't normal," Forthill said. "From what we have been able to tell, they are almost a small nation unto themselves. Fanatics. Their service is hereditary, passed on from father to son, mother to daughter."

"This gets better and better," I said.

"Harry," Forthill said. "I know of no tactful way to ask this, so I will simply ask. Did he give you one of the coins?"

"He tried," I said. "I turned him down."

Forthill's eyes stayed on my face for a moment before he let out a breath. "I see. Do you remember the sigil upon it?"

I grunted in affirmation, picked up a chocolate-covered jelly, and drew the symbol in the chocolate with a forefinger.

Forthill tilted his head, frowning. "Lasciel," he murmured.

"Lasciel?" I said. It came out muffled, since I was licking chocolate off my finger.

"The Seducer," Forthill murmured. He smeared his finger over the chocolate, erasing the sigil. "Lasciel is also called the Web-weaver and the Temptress," he said, between licks. "Though it seems odd that Nicodemus would want to free her. Typically, she does not follow Anduriel's lead."

"A rebel angel among rebel angels?"

"Perhaps," Forthill said. "It is something better not discussed, for now."

Susan stepped out of the little office, a wireless phone to her ear. "All right," she said to the phone, and walked past us, jerking one hand at us to tell us to follow her. Father Forthill lifted his eyebrows, and we went out to the Carpenter family's living room.

It was a fairly huge room divided into several clumps of furniture. The television was in the smallest clump, and still looked about three sizes too small. Susan marched over to it, flicked it on, and flipped through stations.

She stopped on a local station, a news report, that showed a helicopter angle of a building being consumed by a raging fire. About a dozen yellow-and-red fire trucks circled around it, but it was obvious that they were only containing the fire. The building was lost.

"What's this?" Forthill asked.

"Dammit," I snarled, and turned away from the television, pacing.

"It's the building Shiro took us to last night," Susan said. "The Denarians were in some tunnels beneath it."

"Not anymore," I snapped. "They've left and covered their tracks. Hell, they've had what? Six hours? They could be a couple of states away by now."

"Nicodemus," Forthill said. "It's his style."

"We'll find them," Susan said quietly.

"How?" I asked.

She pressed her lips together and turned away from me. She spoke quietly into the phone. I couldn't hear what she said, but it had that end-of-conversation tone to it. She turned the handset off a moment later. "What can we do?"

"I can go to the underworld," I said. "Call up some answers from there. But I can't do it until the sun sets."

Forthill said quietly, "You mustn't do that. It's far too dangerous. None of the Knights would want—"

I slashed my hand through the air, cutting him off. "We need information or Shiro is going to die. Not only that, but if we don't run down Nicodemus, he gets to do whatever badness he's getting ready to do with the Shroud. If I have to go to Downbelow for answers, then that's where I go."

"What about Michael?" Susan asked. "Couldn't he find Shiro the way Shiro found Harry?"

Forthill shook his head. "Not necessarily. It isn't something he can control. At times, the Knights are given that kind of discernment, but they can't call it up at will."

I checked my watch, figuring up distances. "Michael and Sanya should be back here in what? An hour or so?"

"Barring further difficulties," Forthill said.

"Fine. We'll see if the side of the angels wants to pitch in. If they don't, I'm calling Chauncy up as soon as the sun goes down." I took the phone from Susan and walked out of the room.

"Where are you going?" Susan asked.

"To talk to Anna Valmont. And after that, I'm going to call my client. On the off chance I survive, I want to look like I at least tried to be professional."

Charity kept a guest room that had slowly been engulfed in a jungle of fabric. Clear boxes full of the stuff in every imaginable color stood stacked against one wall, and a small sewing machine sat on a table, barely visible among neatly folded stacks of more. More boxes of fabric had been stacked into a rampart around a single bed, which was occupied by a lump buried underneath several quilts.

I turned on a small lamp on the sewing table and hoped that the room wouldn't burst into flame. "Anna. Wake up."

The lump made a mumbling sound and stirred before settling again.

I turned the phone on and let the dial tone sound in the room's silence. "I know you're awake, Miss Valmont. And you know that I saved your ass back at the Marriott. So if you don't sit up and talk to me right now, I'm calling the cops to come pick you up."

She didn't move. I punched in a number and let the phone start to ring.

"Bastard," she muttered. With the British accent, it came out *bah-stuhd*. She sat up, her expression wary, holding the covers to her front. Her shoulders were bare. "Very well. What do you want?"

"My coat, for starters," I said. "But since I doubt you're palming it, I'll settle for the name of your buyer."

She stared at me for a moment before she said, "If I tell you that, it could kill me."

"If you don't, I'm turning you over to the police."

She shrugged. "Which, while unpleasant, won't kill me. Besides, you intend to turn me over in any case."

I scowled at her. "I saved your life. Twice."

"I am aware of that," she said. She stared through me for a moment before she said, "It's so hard to believe. Even though it happened to me. It seems . . . mad. Like a dream."

"You aren't crazy," I said. "Or at least, you aren't hallucinating or anything."

She half laughed. "I know. Cisca is dead. Gaston is dead. It happened to them. My friends." Her voice broke, and she started blinking very quickly. "I just wanted to finish it. So that they didn't die for nothing at all. I owed it to them."

I sighed. "Look, I'll make this easy for you. Was it Marcone?"

She shrugged without focusing her eyes. "We went through an intermediary, so I can't be sure."

"But was it Marcone?"

Valmont nodded. "If I had to guess, I would say it was. The buyer was someone with a great deal of money and local influence."

"Does he know that you know?"

"One doesn't mention to the buyer that you know who he is when he is taking precautions to prevent it. It's impolite."

"If you know anything about Marcone, you know that he isn't going to pay you off and let you walk away without delivering," I said.

She rubbed at her eyes. "I'll offer to return it."

"Good idea. Assuming he doesn't kill you before you finish offering."

She glared at me for a second, angry and crying. "What do you want from me?"

I picked up a box of tissues from behind a bunch of yellow cotton on the table and offered it to her. "Information. I want to know everything. It's possible you've heard or seen something that might help me recover the Shroud. Help me out, and I might be able to buy you some time to leave town."

She took the box and blotted her eyes on a tissue. "How do I know you will deliver on that promise?"

"Earth to Larceny Spice, come in Larceny Spice. I've saved your life twice. I think you can safely assume goodwill."

She looked down, biting her lip. "I . . . I don't know."

"This is a limited-time offer."

She drew in a shaking breath. "All right. All right, let me clean up a little. Get dressed. I'll tell you what I know."

"Fine," I said. "Come on. There's a shower in the bathroom at the end of the hall. I'll get you towels and stuff."

"Is this your house?"

"Friends'. But I've stayed here before."

She nodded and fished around until she came up with the black shirt she'd been wearing the night before. She slipped into it and rose. She had long, pretty, and bruised legs, and as she stepped onto her right leg she let out a pained cry and fell forward. I caught her before she could hit the ground, and she leaned into me, lifting her right foot from the floor.

"Bloody hell," she wheezed. "I must have twisted my ankle last night." She shot me a hard-eyed glance. "Hands."

I jerked my hand off something pleasantly smooth and firm. "Sorry. Accident. Can you manage?"

She shook her head, balanced on one leg. "I don't think so. Lend me your arm a moment."

I helped her hobble down the hall and into the bathroom. I dug some more towels out of the linen closet, then passed them into her through a mostly closed door. She locked it behind her and started the shower.

I shook my head and went back down the hall, dialing Father Vincent's phone number. On the fifth ring, he answered, his voice sounding tired and strained. "Vincent."

"It's Harry Dresden," I said. "I know where the Shroud came into Chicago and who was buying. It got intercepted by a third party and they have it now."

"You're certain?" Vincent demanded.

"Yeah."

"Do you know where it is?"

"Not exactly, but I'm going to find out. I should know by this evening, maybe sooner."

"Why will it take until this evening?" Vincent asked.

"Well, uh. It's a little hard to explain," I said.

"Perhaps the police should handle the rest of the investigation."

"I'd advise against it."

"Why?"

"I have some information that indicates your mistrust may not have been misplaced."

"Oh," Vincent said. His voice sounded worried. "I think we should meet and talk, Mister Dresden. I'd rather not discuss this over the phone. Two o'clock, at the room we spoke in last?"

"I can probably do that," I said.

"Until then," said Vincent, and hung up.

I paced back into the living room and found Susan sitting and reading the morning paper with coffee and a doughnut. One of the sliding glass doors that had previously led to the back patio was open, and on the other side was a lot of bare wood and plastic—the addition Michael was building. The rasping of a saw came through the open door.

I stepped out and found Father Forthill at work. He'd taken off his coat and collar. He had a short-sleeved black shirt underneath. He wore leather work gloves and safety glasses. He finished sawing a beam, and blew dust off the cut before rising. "How is Father Vincent?"

"Sounds tired," I said. "I'm going to talk to him later, assuming we don't have something going on first."

"I worry for him," Forthill said. He held up the beam to the top of what would eventually be a window. "Here, hold this for me."

I did. Forthill started driving in a few nails, clenching several in his teeth. "And Miss Valmont?"

"Taking a shower. She's going to cooperate with us."

Forthill frowned, taking a nail from his lips. "I really wouldn't have expected that from her, from the sense I had of her."

"It's my charming personality," I said. "The ladies can't resist."

"Mmmm," Forthill said, around the nails.

"It's the only decent thing to do. And her back is against a wall, right?"

Forthill drove the nail in and frowned. He looked at me.

I looked back at him for a moment and then said, "I'll just go check on her."

I got about halfway across the living room before I heard a car door shut, immediately followed by a car engine. I ran to the front door and threw it open just in time to see the shattered rear window of the Blue Beetle zipping down the street and out of sight.

I fumbled at my pockets and groaned. My keys were missing. "Son of a *bitch*," I snarled. I punched the door frame in sheer frustration. I didn't punch it very hard. I was angry, not looking to break my own knuckles. "The old stumble and bump and I *fell* for it."

Susan stepped up beside me and sighed. "Harry, you idiot. You're a good man. But an idiot where women are concerned."

"First my coat and now my car. That's freaking gratitude for you."

Susan nodded. "No good deed goes unpunished."

I stared at her. "Are you laughing at me?"

She faced me from behind a perfectly straight face. But her voice sounded a little choked. "No."

"You *are*."

Her face turned pink and she shook her head.

"Laughing at my pain."

She turned and walked back to the living room and picked up her paper. She sat down and held it up so that I couldn't see her face. Choked sounds came out from behind the paper.

I stalked back out to the addition, growling. Forthill looked back at me, his eyebrows raised.

"Give me something to break. Or hit really hard," I told him.

His eyes sparkled. "You'll hurt yourself. Here, hold this for me."

I lifted another cut board into place, while Forthill reached up to hammer it in. As he did, the sleeve of his shirt tugged up, and showed me a pair of green lines.

"Wait," I said, and snapped my hand over to his arm. The board slipped out of my other hand and bonked me on the head on the way down. I scowled at it, wincing, but tugged the sleeve up.

Forthill had a tattoo on the inside of his right arm.

An Eye of Thoth.

"What is this?" I demanded.

Forthill looked around and tugged his sleeve back down. "A tattoo."

"Duh, a tattoo. I know that. What does it mean?"

"It's something I had done when I was younger," he answered. "An organization I belonged to."

I tried to calm down but my voice still sounded harsh. "What organization?"

Forthill blinked mildly at me. "I don't understand why you are so upset, Harry—"

"*What* organization?"

He continued to look confused. "Just several of us who took our orders together. We were barely more than boys, really. And we'd . . . well. We'd happened on to some of the stranger events of our day. And records of others. A vampire had killed two people in town, and we stopped it together. No one believed us, of course."

"Of course," I said. "What about the tattoo?"

Forthill pursed his lips, thoughtful. "I haven't thought about it in so long. Well, the next morning we went out and got the tattoos. We swore an oath to be always watchful against the forces of darkness, to help one another whenever we could."

"Then what?"

"After the hangovers faded, we went a very good distance out of our way to make sure none of the senior clergy saw them," Forthill responded, smiling faintly. "We were young."

"And then?"

"And then no other supernatural events presented themselves over the next few years and the five of us drifted apart. Until I heard from Vittorio—from Father Vincent last week, I hadn't spoken to any of them in years."

"Wait. Vincent has a tattoo like this?"

"I suppose he could have had it removed. He might be the sort to do that."

"What about the others in the group?"

"Passed away over the last several years," Forthill said. He stripped off one of the work gloves and regarded his weathered hand. "Back then, I don't think any of us thought we would ever live to be so old."

The wheels spun in my head, and I got it. I understood what was happening, and why. On pure intuition I stalked to the front of the house, gathering up my things on the way. Father Forthill followed me. "Harry?"

I walked past Susan, who set her paper aside and stood up to follow me. "Harry?"

I got to the front door and jerked it open.

The engine of Michael's white pickup rattled to a halt as I did, and he and Sanya got out of the truck. They looked a little rumpled and unshaven, but fine. Michael blinked at me and asked, "Harry? I think I just saw a woman driving your car toward the highway. What's going on?"

"Get anything you need for a fight," I said. "We're going."

Chapter Twenty-eight

When Father Vincent answered my knock, I kicked the door into his face as hard as I could. He fell back with a grunt of surprise. I came into the room with Father Forthill's Louisville Slugger in my hands, and jabbed the broad end of the bat into Vincent's throat.

The old priest made a sick croaking sound and clutched at his neck on the way to the floor.

I didn't let it stop there. I kicked him in the ribs twice, and when he rolled over, trying to get away from me, I stomped down on the back of his neck, drew my gun, and shoved it against his skull.

"Dio," Vincent whimpered, panting. *"Dio,* wait! Please, don't hurt me!"

"I don't have time to play pretend," I said. "Drop the act."

"Please, Mister Dresden, I don't know what you mean." He coughed, panting, and I saw droplets of scarlet dripping onto the carpet. I'd bloodied his nose, or maybe his lip. He turned his head a tiny bit, eyes wide with panic. "Please, don't do anything to me. I don't know what you want, but I'm sure that we can talk about it."

I drew back the hammer on the revolver and said, "I'm sure that we can't."

His face went white. "No, wait!"

"I'm getting tired of playing pretend. Three."

"But I don't know—" He choked, and I heard him trying not to retch. "You have to tell me—"

"Two," I said. "I'm not going to elaborate about the other number."

"You can't! You can't!"

"One," I said, and pulled the trigger.

In the instant between the word and the deed, Vincent changed. A sheath of green scales appeared over his skin, and his legs twined together into a serpent's long and sinuous body. The eyes went last, changing to vertically slit yellow orbs while a second set of glowing green eyes opened above the first.

The trigger came down on an empty chamber. Click.

The snake twisted to bite me, but I was already getting out of the way. Michael came through the door, his unshaven face set in grim determination, *Amoracchius* blazing with its own white light. The snakeman whirled to face Michael with a hiss. Michael tried for a clean horizontal cut, but the snakeman ducked under it and went for the door in a streak of gleaming green scales.

When the snakeman went out the door, Sanya brought a four-foot length of two-by-six down on its head. The blow drove the snakeman's chin flat to the ground. It twitched a couple of times and then lay still.

"You were right," Michael noted. He slipped the sword away into its sheath.

"Better get him back inside before some maid sees him," I said.

Michael nodded, grabbed the snakeman's tail, and hauled him back into the hotel room.

Sanya looked in, nodded, and set the end of the length of heavy board down with a certain amount of satisfaction. I realized he'd used the thing with one arm. Good grief. I needed to get to the gym. "Good," the big Russian said. "Let me put this back in the truck, and I will join you."

A few minutes later, the snakeman woke up in the corner of the hotel room with me, Michael, and Sanya standing over him. His tongue flickered out and in a few times, and his two sets of eyes darted around the room.

"What did I miss?" it hissed. The last word came out with an extra large helping of S sounds.

"A tattoo," I said. "Father Vincent had a tattoo on the inside of his right arm."

"There was no tattoo," the snakeman insisted.

"Maybe it was covered with all the blood. You made a stupid mistake. It's understandable. Most criminals aren't all that bright, so you were working uphill from the get-go."

The snakeman hissed, shifting its scales restlessly, a cobralike hood flaring around its neck and shoulders.

Michael drew *Amoracchius*. Sanya did the same with *Esperacchius*. The two blades threw pure white light over the snakeman, and he subsided, flinching back from them. "What do you want?"

"To talk," I said. "See, the way it works is that I ask you questions. You answer them. And as long as you do we'll all be happy."

"And if I don't?" the snakeman hissed.

"I get a new pair of boots."

The snake's scales and coils twined around on one another, rasping. Its eyes remained on the two Knights. "Ask."

"Here's what I figure happened. Somehow, your glee club heard that the Churchmice were being hired to find and take the Shroud. You thought you'd just nip it from them on their way out of town, but you missed. You caught Gaston LaRouche, but he didn't have the Shroud. So you tortured him until he told you everything."

"And after he told us everything," the snakeman said. "Nicodemus was indulging his little bitch."

"I think it's sweet to see a father and daughter doing things together. So you found out what LaRouche knew, killed him, and left his body where it would be found, pointed at where the Shroud was going. You figured you'd let the mortal authorities do the work of finding them for you, and take the Shroud when they did."

"Drudge work. Unworthy of us."

"You're gonna hurt my feelings, snakeboy. You found out who the Church was sending over. Then you grabbed poor Father Vincent at the airport. You took his place."

"Any infant could reason as much," the Denarian hissed.

I pulled up a chair and sat. "Here's where it gets interesting. Because you decided to hire me on. Why?"

"Why do you think?"

"To keep tabs on the Knights," I said. "Or to distract them by making them try to keep me out of the search. Or maybe you thought I could really turn up the Shroud for you. Probably all three. No sense doing things for one reason when you can fit in a few ulterior motives for free. You even gave me a sample of the Shroud to make it more likely I'd find it." I leaned back in the chair. "That's where I started seeing something wrong. I talked to Marcone about his new thug gunning for me, and he blinked."

"I don't know what you are talking about," the snakeman said.

"Marcone was the buyer."

A cold laugh slithered out of the snakeman's mouth. "A mortal. Nothing more."

"Yeah, well, the mortal figured out that Father Vincent had been replaced, and he sent an assassin to kill you. The new guy wasn't shooting at me outside of Fowler's studio. He was after you."

"Impossible," the snakeman said.

"Pride goeth, legs. Marcone wasn't born yesterday."

"I am sure you have pleased yourself with your cleverness, wizard."

"It gets better," I said brightly. "See, Nicodemus didn't let much drop, other than that he was on a deadline and he needed someone savvy to the supernatural. His daughter did, though. She asked if he didn't want a silver bowl. That's a ceremonial bowl, and if I was guessing, I'd say it was meant to be used to catch lifeblood. Fuel a ritual."

The snakeman's tail lashed around restlessly.

"I think Father Vincent was a warm-up. A test for the ritual. I think he came over here with two samples from the Shroud, and you used one of them as the focus for the plague curse that killed him. Once you knew it would work, you went after the Shroud itself."

"You know nothing, wizard," said the snakeman. The glowing sigil on his forehead throbbed in time with the extra set of eyes. "You are pathetic."

"You're hurting my feelings. Don't make me get the baseball bat," I said. "Nicodemus covered his tracks this morning by burning down the building you'd been in. I suppose he sent you to cover everything up nice and neat with the cops and with me. I think he's got something in mind, and I think it's tonight. So why not make this a comparatively pleasant discussion and tell me all about it."

"Do you think that you frighten me, wizard?" said the Denarian. "I was destroying men more powerful than you before this pathetic nation was born."

"Where is Nicodemus and what is he doing with the Shroud? I'll give you a hint. It's got something to do with a plague curse."

"I have served Nicodemus since—"

"Since my last dental appointment, I get it," I said. "But let me point something out to you. Nicodemus isn't here." I held my palms out to either side of me, Vanna White–style. "These two gentlemen are very much here. And very much angry."

Sanya stared at the Denarian, the saber in his hand swishing back and forth a little. He growled. It was enough to make me want to edge away from him.

"Look," I told him. "We're going to find Nicodemus and push his face in. We're going to shut down whatever he's got in mind, and we're going to get Shiro back. And you're going to tell us what we need to know."

"Or?"

Michael said, in a very quiet voice, "I end you."

The snakeman stared at me for a very long time. Then he started to rasp and shake. It took me a minute to realize that he was laughing at me. Snakes weren't really meant for laughter. It didn't sit well on a serpentine body.

"You cannot threaten me," he said. "There is nothing you can do to me."

"I see a couple of holy swords here that make me think otherwise."

"No," the Denarian said. He reached up to his forehead and clawed at the sigil there, as if trying to peel off his own skin. The symbol flashed, and then faded, along with the second set of eyes. The whole of him rippled, scales abruptly melting away. For a second, the features of Father Vincent emerged from beneath the scales. Then they too faded away, replaced by a man's pinched and hardened features. He was dark of skin, maybe Moorish, and he wasn't big. Five feet and a little change, and not more than one-fifty. Average height, several centuries ago.

The man lowered his hand and let a slightly tarnished silver coin roll across the floor to Michael's feet. "My name is Quintus Cassius, and I have long been slave to the will of the demon Saluriel." His dark eyes glittered with malice, and his tone dripped with sarcasm. "I beg you for mercy and the chance to mend my ways. How ever can I thank you, Sir Knight, for saving me from that torment."

Shit. He was playing the morality card. I shot a glance at Michael.

The big man frowned at snakeboy Cassius, but didn't miss a beat in drawing out a white handkerchief embroidered with a silver cross, and folding the coin up in it. Michael and Sanya exchanged a long look, and then both of them put away their swords.

"Uh, guys. What the hell are you doing? Dangerous demon murderer here, remember?"

"Harry," Michael said. "We can't. Not if he's surrendered the coin and asked mercy."

"*What?*" I demanded. "That's *stupid*."

"Of course it is," Cassius said. Glee danced in his voice. "They know that I am not sincere. They know I will turn on them at the first opportunity. That I will obtain one of the other coins and return to what I have done for centuries."

I stood up, angry enough that the chair fell over. "Michael, if you turn the other cheek on this bastard he'll tear it off your face. You're supposed to be the freaking Fist of God."

"No, I'm not, Harry," Michael said. "The purpose of the Knights is not to destroy those who serve evil."

"Indeed not," Cassius said. Somehow, there was more of a hiss in his voice now than when he'd been a snake. "They're here to save us."

"To *save* them?" I stared at Michael. "Is he kidding?"

Michael shook his head. "No one else can face the Denarians, Harry. No one else can challenge the Fallen. This moment might be the only chance Cassius has to turn aside from what he has chosen. To change his path."

"Great. I'm all for changing his path. Let's change it to a direct line to the bottom of Lake Michigan."

Michael's expression was pained. "The Knights are here to protect freedom. To give those who are under the oppression of dark forces the chance to win free of them. I cannot sit in judgment on this man's soul, Harry Dresden. Not for you. Not for anyone. All I can do is remain faithful to my calling. Give him the chance to see hope for his future. To show him the love and compassion any human being should show another. The rest is out of my hands."

I watched Cassius's face while Michael spoke. His expression changed. It became harder. More brittle. And bitter. What Michael said had touched him. I didn't believe for a second that it had touched Cassius enough to change his mind. But it touched him enough to drive him toward fury.

I turned to Michael and said, "Do you really think that thing is going to start sipping of the milk of human kindness?"

"No," Michael said. "But that doesn't change my purpose. He has surrendered his coin, and the influence of it. The rest is not for Sanya or me to decide. It is Cassius's choice."

"You've seen these things," I snarled, stalking over to face Michael. "I've seen the corpses they've left. They would have killed me, Susan, you—hell, all of us—without blinking an eye. God only knows what they have in mind with that curse they're putting together."

"All power has its limits, Harry." He shook his head. "This is the limit of mine."

Without really thinking about it, I shoved his shoulder. "They might already have *killed* Shiro. And you're going to let this bastard walk?"

Michael caught my arm in one hand and twisted. Michael is strong. I had to rise up onto my toes to relieve the pressure he put on my elbow, and he shoved me back from him, his eyes hard and cold and angry as hell.

"I know that," he said in that same deadly quiet voice. "I know they've hurt him. That they're going to kill him. Just as Shiro knew that Nicodemus would betray his promise to set you free. It's one of the things that makes us different than they are, Harry. The blood on their hands does not make it right to bloody my own. My choices are measured against my own soul. Not against the stains on theirs." He looked at Cassius, and the Denarian flinched away from the silent flame in Michael's expression. "It is not for me to judge his soul. No matter how much I might want to."

"Hell's bells," I muttered. "No wonder Nicodemus has killed so many Knights, if you're all as idiotic as this."

"Harry—" Michael began.

I interrupted him. "Look at him, Michael. He isn't a victim. He's a freaking collaborator. That poor bastard Rasmussen might have been dragooned into working with the Denarians, but Cassius does it because he wants to do it."

"There's no way for you to be sure of that, Harry," Sanya said.

"Why are you giving him a fair chance? Which of them has *ever* turned away from their coins?"

Sanya put his dark hand on my shoulder and said, "I did."

I looked back at him, frowning.

"I was of their number," Sanya said. "I was less experienced. Foolish. Proud. I did not set out to be a monster, but that much power corrupts. Shiro faced the Fallen I had allowed in. He exposed its lies. And I made a better choice."

"Traitor," said Cassius, his voice cold. "We handed you the world. Power. Glory. Everything you could have wanted."

Sanya faced the man and said, "What I wanted you could never give me. I had to find it for myself." He extended a hand. "Cassius, you can leave them just as I did. Help us, please. And let us help you."

Cassius leaned back, as though Sanya's hand might burn him, and hissed, "I will eat your eyes."

"We can't leave him here," I said. "He'll shoot us in the back. He'll try to kill us."

"Maybe," Michael said quietly, and didn't move.

I wanted to be angry with Sanya and Michael. But I couldn't. I'm only human. I'd flirted with dark powers before. Made stupid deals. Bad choices. I'd been given a chance to work free of them, or I'd have been dead long ago.

I understood what Michael and Sanya were saying and doing. I understood why. I didn't like it, but I couldn't really gainsay it without making a hypocrite of myself. There but for the lack of a demon-infested coin went I.

Cassius started wheezing and laughing his dry, contemptuous laugh. "Run along," he said. "Run along. I'll think over your words. Reexamine my life. Walk the straight and narrow."

"Let's go," Michael said quietly.

"We can't leave him," I insisted.

"The police aren't going to have anything on him, Harry. We're not going to kill him. We're finished here. Have faith. We'll find an answer somehow."

Cassius laughed at Michael's back as he walked out. Sanya followed him, lingering to look back over his shoulder at me.

"Fools," Cassius murmured, rising. "Weak fools."

I picked up the bat again and turned to the door. "You're wrong," I said to Cassius.

"Weak," Cassius repeated. "The old man was screaming after only an hour, you know. Nicodemus started with his back. Lashed him with chains. Then Deirdre played with him."

I gave Cassius a hard look over my shoulder.

He was sneering, lip lifted from his teeth. "Deirdre likes to break fingers and toes. I wish I'd been able to stay longer. I only got to pull out his toenails." His smile widened, eyes gleaming. "The woman, the Fellowship woman. She is yours?"

I felt my lip lift away from my teeth.

Cassius's eyes gleamed. "She bled prettily, didn't she? The next time I catch her, you won't be there to disrupt my conjuration. I'll let the snakes eat her. Bite by bite."

I stared at him.

Cassius smiled again. "But there is mercy for me, is there not? Forgiveness. Indeed, God is great."

I turned away from him again and said, very quietly, "People like you always mistake compassion for weakness. Michael and Sanya aren't weak. Fortunately for you, they're good men."

Cassius laughed at me.

"Unfortunately for you, I'm not."

I spun around, swinging the bat as hard as I could, and broke Cassius's right kneecap.

He screamed in shock and sudden surprise, and went down. Odd crackling sounds came from the joint.

I swung again and broke his right ankle.

Cassius screamed.

I broke his left knee for him too. And his left ankle. He was thrashing around and screaming a lot, so it took me maybe a dozen swings.

"Stop!" he managed to gasp. "Stop, stop, stop!"

I kicked him in the mouth to shut him up, stomped his right forearm to the floor, and crushed his hand with another half dozen swings.

I pinned his left arm down the same way, and put the bat on my shoulder. "Listen to me, you worthless piece of shit. You aren't a victim. You chose to be one of them. You've been serving dark forces your whole life. Freddie Mercury would say Beelzebub has a devil put aside for you."

"What do you think you're doing?" He gasped. "You can't . . . you won't . . ."

I leaned down and twisted his false priest's collar, half choking him. "The Knights are good men. I'm not. And I won't lose a second's sleep over killing you." I shook him with each word, hard enough to rattle his bloodied teeth. "Where. Is. Nicodemus."

Cassius broke, sobbing. His bladder had let go at some point, and the room smelled like urine. He choked and spat out blood and a broken tooth. "I'll tell." He gasped. "Please, don't."

I let his collar go and straightened. "Where?"

"I don't know," he said, cowering away from my eyes. "He didn't tell me. Meeting him tonight. Was going to meet him tonight. Eight."

"Meet him where?"

"Airport," Cassius said. He started throwing up. I kept his arm pinned, so it mostly went all over himself. "I don't know exactly where."

"What is he doing?"

"The curse. He's going to unleash the curse. Use the Shroud. The old man's blood. He has to be moving when he completes the ritual."

"Why?"

"Curse is a contagion. He has to spread it as far as he can. More exposure to it. Make himself stronger. A-apocalypse."

I took my foot off of his arm and smashed the motel's phone to pieces with the bat. I found his cell phone and crushed it, too. Then I reached into my pocket and dropped a quarter on the floor near him. "There's a pay phone on the other side of the parking lot, past a patch of broken glass. You'd better get yourself an ambulance." I turned and walked to the door without looking back. "If I see you again—ever—I'll kill you."

Michael and Sanya waited for me outside the door. Sanya's face held a certain amount of satisfaction. Michael's expression was grave, worried, his eyes on mine.

"It had to be done," I said to Michael. My voice sounded cold. "He's alive. It's more than he deserves."

"Perhaps," Michael said. "But what you did, Harry. It was wrong."

A part of me felt sick. Another part felt satisfied. I wasn't sure which of them was bigger. "You heard what he said about Shiro. About Susan."

Michael's eyes darkened, and he nodded. "It doesn't make it right."

"No. It doesn't." I met his eyes. "Think God'll forgive me?"

Michael was quiet for a moment, and then his expression softened. He clasped my shoulder and said, "God is always merciful."

"What you did for him was actually quite generous," Sanya said philosophically. "Relatively speaking. He might be hurt, but he is, after all, alive. He'll have a nice, long while to reconsider his choices."

"Uh-huh," I said. "I'm a giver. Did it for his own good."

Sanya nodded gravely. "Good intentions."

Michael nodded. "Who are we to judge you?" His eyes flashed, and he asked Sanya, "Did you see the snake's face, right when Harry turned with the bat?"

Sanya smiled and started whistling as we walked through the parking lot.

We piled into the truck. "Drop me off at my place," I said. "I need to pick up a couple things. Make some phone calls."

"The duel?" Michael asked. "Harry, are you sure you don't want me to—"

"Leave it to me," I said. "You've already got something on your plate. I can handle things. I'll meet you at the airport afterward and help you find Shiro."

"If you live," Sanya said.

"Yes. Thank you, Comrade Obvious."

The Russian grinned. "Was that a quarter you gave Cassius?"

"Yeah."

"For the phone?"

"Yeah."

Michael noted, "Phone calls cost more than that now."

I slouched back and allowed myself a small smile. "Yeah. I know."

Sanya and Michael burst out laughing. Michael pounded on the steering wheel.

I didn't join them, but I enjoyed their laughter while I could. The February sun was already sinking fast toward the horizon.

Chapter Twenty-nine

◆◇◆◇◆

Back at my apartment, I called Murphy on her personal cell phone. I used simple sentences and told her everything.

"Dear God," Murphy said. Can I summarize or what? "They can infect the city with this curse thing?"

"Looks like," I said.

"How can I help?"

"We've got to keep them from getting it into the air. They won't be on public transportation. Find out if any chartered planes are taking off between seven and eight-thirty. Helicopters too."

"Hang on," Murphy said. I heard computer keys clicking, Murphy saying something to someone, a police radio. A moment later she said, voice tense, "There's trouble."

"Yeah?"

"There are a pair of detectives heading out to arrest you. Looks like Homicide wants you for questioning. There's no warrant listed."

"Crap." I took a deep breath. "Rudolph?"

"Brownnosing rat," Murphy muttered. "Harry, they're almost to your place. You've only got a few minutes."

"Can you decoy them? Get some manpower to the airport?"

"I don't know," Murphy said. "I'm supposed to be a mile from this case. And it isn't as though I can announce that terrorists are about to use a biological weapon on the city."

"Use Rudolph," I said. "Tell him off the record that I said the Shroud is leaving town on a chartered flight from the airport. Let him take the heat for it if they don't find anything."

Murphy let out a harsh little laugh. "There are times when you can be a clever man, Harry. It takes me by surprise."

"Why, thank you."

"What else can I do?"

I told her.

"You're kidding."

"No. We may need the manpower, and SI is out of this one."

"Just when I had hope for your intelligence, too."

"You'll do it?"

"Yeah. Can't promise anything, but I'll do it. Get moving. They're less than five minutes away."

"Gone. Thank you, Murph."

I hung up the phone, opened my closet, and dug into a couple of old cardboard boxes I kept at the back until I found my old canvas duster. It was battered and torn in a couple of places, but it was clean. It didn't have the same reassuring weight as the leather duster, but it did more to hide my gun than my jacket. And it made me look cool. Well, maybe cooler, anyway.

I grabbed my things, locked up my place behind me, and got into Martin's rental car. Martin wasn't in it. Susan sat behind the wheel. "Hurry," I said. She nodded and pulled out.

A few minutes later, no one had pulled us over. "I take it Martin isn't helping."

Susan shook her head. "No. He said he had other duties that took precedence. He said that I did, too."

"What did you say?"

"That he was a narrow-minded, hidebound, anachronistic, egotistical bastard."

"No wonder he likes you."

Susan smiled a little and said, "The Fellowship is his life. He serves a cause."

"What is it to you?" I asked.

Susan remained silent for a long time as we drove across town. "How did it go?"

"We caught the impostor. He told us where the bad guys would be later tonight."

"What did you do with him?"

I told her.

She looked at me for a while and then said, "Are you all right?"

"Fine."

"You don't look fine."

"It's done."

"But are you all right?"

I shrugged. "I don't know. I'm glad you didn't see it."

Susan asked, "Oh? Why?"

"You're a girl. Beating up bad guys is a boy thing."

"Chauvinist pig," Susan said.

"Yeah. I get it from Murphy. She's a bad influence."

We hit the first traffic sign directing us toward the stadium, and Susan asked, "Do you really think you can win?"

"Yeah. Hell, Ortega is only the third or fourth most disturbing thing I've tangled with today."

"But even if you do win, what does it change?"

"Me getting killed now. That way, I get to be killed later tonight instead."

Susan laughed. There was nothing happy in it. "You don't deserve a life like this."

I squinted my eyes and made my voice gravelly. "Deserve's got nothin'—"

"So help me God, if you quote Clint Eastwood at me, I'm wrapping this car around a telephone pole."

"Do you feel lucky, punk?" I smiled and turned my left hand palm up.

I felt her hand settle lightly on mine a moment later, and she said, "A girl's got to draw the line somewhere."

We rode the rest of the way to the stadium in silence, holding hands.

I hadn't ever been to Wrigley when it was empty. That wasn't really the point of a stadium. You went there to be among about a bajillion people and see something happen. This time, with acres and acres of unoccupied asphalt, the stadium at its center looked huge and somehow more skeletal than when it was filled with vehicles and cheering thousands. The wind sighed through the stadium, gusting, whistling, and moaning. Twilight had fallen, and the unlit street lamps cast spidery shadows over the lots. Darkness gaped in the arches and doorways of the stadium, empty as the eyes of a skull.

"Thank God that isn't too creepy or anything," I muttered.

"What now?" Susan asked.

Another car pulled in behind us. I recognized it from McAnnally's the night before. The car pulled up maybe fifty feet away and rolled to a stop. Ortega got out, and leaned down to say something to the driver, a man with a dark complexion and amber-tone glasses. There were two more men in the backseat, though I couldn't see much of them. I was betting they were all Red Court.

"Let's not look scared," I said, and got out of the car.

I didn't look at Ortega, but drew out my staff with me, planted it on the ground, and stared at the stadium. The wind caught my coat, and blew it back enough to show the gun on my hip now and again. I'd traded in my sweats for dark jeans and a black silk shirt. The Mongols or somebody wore silk shirts because they would catch arrows as they entered wounds, and enable them to pull barbed arrowheads out without ripping their innards apart. I wasn't planning on getting shot with barbed arrows, but weirder things have happened.

Susan got out and walked up to stand beside me. She stared at the stadium too, and the wind blew her hair back the same way it did my coat. "Very nice," she murmured, hardly moving her mouth. "That's a good look on you. Ortega's driver is about to wet his pants."

"You say the nicest things to me."

We just stood there for a couple of minutes, until I heard a deep, rhythmic rumbling—one of those annoyingly loud bass stereos in some moron's car. The rumbling got louder; then there was a squealing of tires taking a tight turn, and Thomas pulled into the lot in a different white sports car than I'd seen him in the night before. The music got louder as he sped across the lot and parked his car diagonally across the lines I'd unconsciously re-spected when I'd parked. He killed the stereo and got out, a small cloud of smoke emerging with him. It wasn't cigarette smoke.

"Paolo!" Thomas caroled. He wore tight blue jeans and a black T-shirt with a *Buffy the Vampire Slayer* logo. The laces to one of his combat boots were untied, and he carried a bottle of scotch in his hand. He pulled from it cheerfully and wove a drunken line to Ortega. Thomas offered out the bottle, his balance wobbling. "Have a swig?"

Ortega slapped the bottle from Thomas's hand. It shattered on the ground.

"Shpoilshport," Thomas slurred, wavering. "Hola, Harry! Hola, Susan!" He waved at us, and all but fell down. "I was going to offer you some too, but that plan's been blown all to hell now."

"Maybe another time," Susan said.

A blue light appeared in one of the tunnels from the stadium. A moment later, a vehicle somewhere between a compact car and a golf cart rolled into the parking lot, a whirling blue bubble light flashing on its roof. With the quiet hum of electric motors, it zipped over to us and stopped. Kincaid sat behind the steering wheel and nodded to the rear of the vehicle. "In. We're set up inside."

We walked over to the security cart. Ortega started to get on, but I held up my hand to him. "Ladies first," I said quietly, and gave Susan my hand as she got on. I followed her. Ortega and Thomas followed. Thomas had put on a pair of headphones and was bobbing his chin in a vague fashion that was probably supposed to be in rhythm.

Kincaid started up the cart and called over his shoulder, "Where is the old man?"

"Gone," I said. I jerked a thumb at Susan. "Had to go to the bench."

Kincaid looked from me to Susan and shrugged. "Nice bench."

He drove us through several passages in the stadium, somehow finding his way despite the fact that no lights were on, and I could barely see. Eventually we rolled out onto the field from one of the bullpens. The stadium was dark but for where three spotlights basted the pitcher's mound and first and third base in pools of light. Kincaid drove to the pitcher's mound, stopped, and said, "Everyone out."

We did. Kincaid parked the cart over home plate, then padded through the shadows to the visiting team's dugout. "They're here," he said quietly.

The Archive emerged from the dugout, carrying a small, carved wooden box before her. She wore a dark dress with no frills or ruffles, and a grey cape held closed with a silver brooch. She was still little, still adorable, but something in her bearing left no illusions about the difference in her apparent age and her knowledge and capability.

She walked to the pitcher's mound, not looking at anyone, her focus on the box she carried. She set it down, very carefully, and then lifted the lid from the top of the box and stepped back.

A wave of nauseating cold flooded out when she opened the box. It went past me, through me. I was the only one there to react to it. Susan put her hand on my arm, kept her eyes on Ortega and Thomas, and asked, "Harry?"

My last meal had been a drive-through taco on the way back from the meeting with Cassius, but it was trying to leave. I kept it down and forced the sickening cold away from me with an effort of will. The sensation lessened. "Fine," I said. "I'm fine."

The Archive looked up at me, child features solemn. "You know what is inside the box?"

"I think so. I've never actually seen it."

"Seen what?" Thomas asked.

Instead of answering, the Archive drew a small box out of her pocket. She opened the box and delicately plucked out an insect as long as her own fingers—a brown scorpion—by its tail. She looked around to make sure she had everyone's attention. She did. Then she dropped the scorpion into the box.

There was an instant, immediate sound, somewhere between a wildcat's scream and the sizzle of bacon hitting a hot skillet. Something that looked vaguely like a cloud of ink in clear water floated up out of the box. It was about the size of a baby's head. Dozens of shadowy tendrils held the scorpion, drawing it up into the air along with the inky cloud. Dark violet flickers of flame played over the insect's shell for all of two or three seconds—and then it simply crumbled, carapace falling away in flakes and dust.

The cloudy mass rose up to a height of about five feet, before the Archive murmured a word. It stopped in place, bobbing gently, holding there.

"Damn," Thomas said, he took the earphones out. Music with many electric guitars sounded tinnily from them. "And this is what?"

"Mordite," I said quietly. "Deathstone."

"Yes," the Archive said.

Ortega drew in a slow breath, and nodded in understanding.

"Deathstone, huh?" Thomas said. "It sort of looks like someone spray-painted a soap bubble. And gave it tentacles."

"It isn't a soap bubble," I said. "There's a solid piece inside. The energies it carries in it are what create that shroud effect around it."

Thomas poked a finger at it. "What does it do?"

I caught his wrist before he could touch it, and pushed his hand away. "It kills. Hence the name *deathstone*, you half-wit."

"Oh," Thomas said, nodding with drunken sagacity. "It looked cool when it gacked that little thing, but so what? It's a bug zapper."

"If you disrespect this thing it's going to get you killed," I said. "It would kill anything living exactly the same way. Anything. It's not from our world."

"It's extraterrestrial?" asked Susan.

"You do not understand, Miss Rodriguez," Ortega said quietly.

"Mordite is not from this galaxy or this universe. It is not of our reality."

I had reservations about Ortega's presence on the home-team roster, but I nodded. "It's from Outside. It's . . . congealed antilife. A chip of this stuff makes nuclear waste look like secondhand smoke. Being near it draws the life off you bit by bit. If you touch it, it kills you. Period."

"Precisely," said the Archive. She stepped forward to look at both Ortega and me. "An enchantment binds the particle in place. It is also sensitive to applied will. The duelists will face each other, the mordite between them. Will it toward your opponent. He with the greatest force of will controls the mordite. The duel will end when it has devoured one of you."

Gulp.

The Archive continued. "Seconds will observe from first and third bases, facing their duelist's opponent. Mister Kincaid will ensure that no undue interference is perpetrated by either second. I have instructed him to do so with extreme prejudice."

Thomas wobbled a little and eyed the Archive. "Eh?"

The girl faced him and said, "He'll kill you if you interfere."

"Oh," Thomas said cheerfully. "Gotcha, punkin."

Ortega glared at Thomas and made a disgusted sound. Thomas found something else to look at and backed a prudent step away.

"I will monitor both duelists to ensure that no energies are employed on their behalf. I, too, will resolve any infractions with extreme prejudice. Do you understand?"

Ortega nodded. I said, "Yeah."

"Are there any questions, gentlemen?" the Archive asked.

I shook my head. Ortega did too.

"Each of you may make a brief statement," said the Archive.

Ortega drew a band of black and silver beads from his pocket. Without making an effort, I could feel the defensive energies bound up within them. He regarded me with casual mistrust as he bound the bracelet to his left side and said, "This can end in only one way."

In answer, I fished one of the antivenom potions from my pocket, popped the top, and slugged it down. I burped and said, "Excuse me."

"You've really got class, Dresden," Susan said.

"Class oozes out my every orifice," I agreed. I passed her my staff and rod. "Hold these for me."

"Seconds, please retire to your positions," said the Archive.

Susan put her hand on my arm, fingers clenching tight for a second. I reached up and touched her hand. She let go and backed away to third base.

Thomas offered to high-five Ortega. Ortega glared. Thomas smiled a Colgate smile and swaggered over to first base. He drew a silver flask of something from his hip pocket on the way, and took a sip.

The Archive looked back and forth between me and Ortega. She was standing on the pitcher's mound, next to the floating glob of chilling energy, so she was a shade taller than Ortega and a shade shorter than me. Her face was solemn, even grim. It didn't sit well on a child who should have been getting up for school in the morning.

"Are you both resolved to this duel?"

"I am," Ortega said.

"Uh-huh." I nodded.

The Archive nodded. "Gentlemen. Present your right hands, please."

Ortega lifted his right arm, palm faced toward me. I mirrored him. The Archive gestured, and the mordite sphere floated up until it hovered precisely halfway between Ortega and me. Tension gathered against my palm, an invisible and silent pressure. It felt vaguely like holding my hand against a recirculating outlet in a swimming pool—it was a tenuous thing, that felt like it might easily slide to one side.

If it did, I'd get to see the mordite up close and personal. My heart skittered over a couple of beats, and I took a deep breath, trying to focus and ready myself. If I was Ortega, I'd want to open up with everything I had in the first heartbeat of the contest and end it almost before it began. I took a couple of deep breaths and narrowed my focus, my thoughts, until the pressure against my hand and the deadly darkness a few feet away from it were all that existed.

"Begin," said the Archive. She backed quickly toward home plate.

Ortega let out a shout, a battle cry, his body dipping slightly, hips twisting, shoving his hand forward like a man trying to close a vault door with one arm. His will flooded toward me, wild and strong, and the pressure of it drove me back onto my heels. The mordite sphere zipped across three of the four feet between it and me.

Ortega's will was strong. Really, really strong. I tried to divert it, to overcome it and stop the sphere. For a panicked second I had nothing. The sphere kept drifting closer to me. A foot. Ten inches. Six inches. Small tendrils of inky darkness drifted out from the cloud around the mordite, reaching out blindly toward my fingers.

I gritted my teeth, hardened my will, and stopped the thing five inches from my hand. I tried to mount up some momentum of my own, but Ortega held strong against me.

"Don't draw this out, boy," Ortega said through clenched teeth. "Your death will save lives. Even if you kill me, my vassals at Casaverde are sworn to hunt you down. You and everyone you know and love."

The sphere came a bit closer. "You said you wouldn't harm them if I agreed to the duel," I growled.

"I lied," Ortega said. "I came here to kill you and end this war. Anything else is immaterial."

"You bastard."

"Stop fighting it, Dresden. Make it painless for yourself. If you kill me, they will be executed. By surrendering, you preserve them. Your Miss Rodriguez. The policewoman. The investigator you apprenticed under. The owner of that bar. The Knight and his family. The old man in the Ozarks. The wolf-children at the university. All of them."

I snarled, "Buddy, you just said the wrong thing."

I let the anger Ortega's words had ignited flood down through my arm. A cloud of scarlet sparks erupted against the mordite sphere, and it started creeping the other way.

Ortega's face became strained, his breathing heavier. He didn't waste any effort on words now. His eyes darkened until they were entirely black and inhuman. There were ripples, here and there, under the surface of his skin—the flesh mask that contained the vaguely batlike monster those of the Red Court really were. The monstrous Ortega, the true Ortega, stirred underneath the false human shell. And he was afraid.

The sphere crept closer. Ortega renewed his efforts with another war cry. But the sphere made it to the midway point, and got closer to him.

"Fool," Ortega said in a gasp.

"Murderer," I said, and shoved the sphere another foot closer to him.

His jaw clenched harder, the muscles in his face bulging. "You'll destroy us all."

"Starting with you." The sphere darted a little nearer.

"You are a selfish, self-righteous madman."

"You murder and enslave children," I said. I shoved the mordite sphere to within a foot of him. "You threaten the people I love." I shoved it closer still. "How does it feel, Ortega. Being too weak to protect yourself. How does it feel to know you are about to die?"

In answer, a slow smile crept over his face. His shoulders moved a little, and I saw that one of his arms hung limply at his side, like an empty sleeve. A small bulge appeared just to one side of his stomach, like a gun being held in an overcoat pocket.

I stared at it in shock. He'd pulled his real arm out of the flesh mask. He was holding a gun on me.

"How does it feel?" Ortega asked, voice very quiet. "Why don't you tell me?"

Chapter Thirty

"You can't," I said. I shot a glance toward home plate, but the Archive apparently hadn't noticed anything amiss. My will wavered, and the mordite sphere bobbed back and forth. "They'll hear the shot. They'll kill you."

"Quite possibly," he agreed. "As I said, I am prepared to accept that."

His words chilled me, and the mordite sphere darted at my head. I caught it a couple of feet from me and held it, but just barely.

"I told you, Dresden. There's only one way this can end. I would have preferred an honorable demise for you, but any death will do."

I stared at the hidden gun.

A dot of bright scarlet light appeared on Ortega's chest, and tracked slowly up.

My expression must have changed, because Ortega glanced down too. The bright pinpoint of the laser sight settled over his heart and became still.

Ortega's eyes widened and his expression twisted into fury.

A lot of things happened at once.

There was a hissing sound, a thump, and a big section of Ortega's chest dented in. Scarlet sprayed out behind him. An instant later, a booming sound much deeper than the crack of a rifle echoed around the stadium.

Ortega let out a screech that went off the high end of the scale. Fire erupted from the hidden gun, burning through Ortega's flesh mask and shirt to reveal the muzzle of a small-caliber revolver clenched in an inhuman black hand. The bullet Ortega had taken had half twisted him, and he missed. I thought hanging around to let him try again was a bad idea, so I threw myself to one side and gave the mordite sphere another shove.

Ortega dodged the mordite, and even wounded, he was fast. A bright red dot appeared on his thigh for half a second, and with another *hiss-thump-boom*, the unseen gunman hit him again. I heard the bones of Ortega's leg break.

Susan threw my staff and rod to me and leapt for Ortega, grabbing his free arm and twisting as if to throw him. Instead, the vampire writhed weirdly, and she wound up tearing the flesh mask from him, peeling it away like a banana skin to reveal the slime-slick, flabby-bodied creature beneath it—the true Ortega. He still held the gun though, and he turned to shoot at me again.

I screamed, *"Ventas servitas!"* at the top of my lungs, throwing my will at dirt of the pitcher's mound. It whirled up into a miniature cyclone of fine brown soil, forcing the vampire to turn its head and shield its eyes. The second shot went wild as well, and I scrambled to get my blasting rod.

The flying dirt slowed her down, but Susan still went for Ortega's gun hand. It was a mistake. Even with only one leg to support him, Ortega screeched again, twisted, and flung Susan from the pitcher's mound into the third row of seats behind first base. She hit with bone-breaking force and dropped out of sight.

Sudden screeches filled the air, and I looked up to see as many as a dozen of the Red Court, revealed in their true forms, coming into the stadium. Some climbed over the walls, some jumped in from the upper levels, and some came bursting out of private boxes in showers of exploding glass.

I spun toward Ortega, lifting my blasting rod, rammed my will through it, and shouted, *"Fuego!"* A jet of flame as thick as my arm roared at him, but one of the incoming vampires hit him at the shoulder, dragging him out of the line of fire. The newcomer was set alight though, greasy skin going up like a bonfire, and it screamed hideously as it burned.

I sensed movement behind me, and turned to find Kincaid dashing across the ground. He scooped up the Archive and raced for one of the dugouts. One of the Red Court vamps got in his way. Kincaid's arm blurred, a semiautomatic appearing in it, and without missing a step he put two shots neatly between the vampire's eyes. The vampire started to fall, and as he went by it, Kincaid pumped another half dozen shots into its belly, which erupted in a messy shower of scarlet, and left the vampire screaming and thrashing weakly on the ground.

"Harry, look out!" Thomas screamed.

I didn't look out. I figured on the worst and leapt forward. I heard a vampire hiss as it missed me, and it came rushing up behind me. I turned and unleashed another gout of fire from my blasting rod, but missed. The vampire closed on me, spraying venomous saliva into my face.

I'd been hit with vampire venom before, and the stuff worked fast, particularly in large amounts. But I'd taken the potion to block it, and all this did was make me itch. I used the time while the vampire sprayed me to prepare another blast, and unleashed the strike with the rod pressed against the vamp's flabby body. It scorched a wound in the vampire's belly the size of my fist and blew a two-foot hole in the creature's back. The vampire went into weak spasms, and I kicked it off me, rising.

Seven or eight vampires were within fifty feet of me, and coming fast. Thomas sprinted toward me, a knife gleaming in his hand, and hit one of the vamps from behind. He cut open the vampire's belly with a single slice, and the creature collapsed to the ground. "Harry, get out!"

"No!" I shouted. "Get Susan out of here!"

Thomas gritted his teeth, but changed course. He leapt up onto the first-base dugout and hopped neatly over the rail into the stands.

No help there, and there wasn't time to look for options. I crouched and concentrated, chanting, "Defendre, defendre," in a steady litany. It was difficult to do without my shield bracelet to focus it, but I brought up all the defensive energy I could manage in a dome around me.

The vampires hit it, slamming against it in mindless, shrieking rage. Any one of them could have flipped my car over lengthwise with only a little effort. Their blows against the shield could have crushed concrete. Within seconds, and I knew I was not going to be able to hold the defense in place for long. Once it went down, they were going to literally tear me limb from limb. I gave the shield my all, and felt them slowly breaking it down.

Then there was a roar, and a flash of brilliant light. A jet of fire streaked over me and took one of the vampires full-on in the head. It burst into flame, screaming and waving its too-thin arms, and went down onto the field, thrashing like a half-crushed bug. My shield collapsed, overloaded, and the bracelet began burning my wrist. I crouched lower.

Another jet of fire went by, incinerating the head of another vampire. All of them stopped, crouching, shrieking in confusion.

Kincaid stood outside the dugout and dropped a smoking shotgun to the ground. He reached into a golf bag next to him, smooth and professional, and drew out another double-barreled shotgun. One of the vampires leapt at him, but Kincaid was too fast. He pulled the trigger, and the shotgun roared. A jet of flame streaked out and went through the vampire, taking this one in the neck, and continuing to the right-field fence, where it blew a hole the size of my face in the wall. There was a sound behind him, and Kincaid spun to shoot the other barrel at a vampire bounding down through the stands above the third-base dugout. He put the shot right down the vampire's throat, literally, and the creature went up in flames. Kincaid discarded that shotgun as well, and reached for the stock of another in his golf bag.

The other vampires leapt at Kincaid when he turned his back.

They got to deal with the Archive instead.

The child stepped out from behind the golf bag, the tenebrous mordite sphere floating between her hands. She released the sphere and made a single gesture.

The little cloud of darkness blurred toward the vampires and streaked into each in turn at the pace of a busy workman's hammer, *bang-bang-bang*. When the mordite sphere struck them, there was a flash of cold purple light, a swell of darkness, and then the sphere passed on through. It left ash and black bones raining down behind it. I could barely follow the mordite sphere's path, it moved so fast. One second the vampires were all there, and then they were simply gone. Black bones and grey ash littered the ground around me.

Silence fell, and the only thing I could hear was my own ragged breathing and the roaring of my own pulse in my ears. I looked around wildly, but I didn't see Ortega anywhere. The two vampires who had been gutted writhed feebly on the ground. Kincaid drew the last shotgun from the golf bag, and with two more flaming blasts executed them both.

The mordite sphere glided gently back to rest between the Archive's tiny hands, and she stood regarding me for a long and silent moment. There was nothing in her expression. Nothing in her eyes. Nothing. I felt the beginnings of a soulgaze and pulled my face away, fast.

"Who broke the sanctity of the duel first, Kincaid?" asked the Archive.

"Couldn't tell," Kincaid answered. He wasn't so much as breathing hard. "But Dresden was winning."

The Archive stood there a moment more, and then said, "Thank you for letting me pet your kitty, Mister Dresden. And thank you for my name."

That sounded frighteningly like a good-bye, but it was only polite to answer, "You're welcome, Ivy."

The Archive nodded and said, "Kincaid. The box, please."

I looked up to watch Kincaid set the wooden box down on the ground. The Archive sent the mordite sphere gliding slowly down into it, and then closed the lid on the box. "These proceedings are concluded."

I looked around at the bones, dust, and smoldering vampire corpses. "You think?"

The Archive regarded me with neutral eyes and said, "Let's go. It's after my bedtime."

"I'm hungry," Kincaid said, shouldering his golf bag. "We'll hit a drive-through. You can have the cookies."

"Cookies aren't good for me," the Archive said, but she smiled.

Kincaid said, "Dresden, hand me that, will you?"

I looked numbly at the ground where he pointed. One of the shotguns was there. Its barrels were still smoking hot. I picked it up gingerly by the stock and passed it to Kincaid, who wrapped it with the other gun he'd used in some kind of silver-lined blanket. "What the hell are those things?" I asked.

"Incendiary rounds," he said. He passed my dropped staff over to me. "Work real well on the Reds, but they're so hot they warp gun barrels. If you get unlucky, the second shot can blow back into your face, so you have to use throwaway guns."

I nodded thanks and took my staff. "Where can I get some?"

Kincaid grinned. "I know a guy. I'll have him call you. See you, Dresden."

Kincaid and the Archive started out of the stadium. A thought finally made its way through the combat adrenaline and I broke into a sprint toward the first-base dugout. Thomas had simply hopped up onto it. I managed to flop and clamber my way up, then into the stands.

Thomas was already there, on the ground with Susan. He'd taken off her jacket and used it to elevate her feet slightly. It looked as if he'd tilted her head back a little to clear the airway. He looked up and said, "She's unconscious, but she's alive."

I crouched down too, and touched her throat, just to be certain. "How bad is she hurt?"

He shook his head. "No real way to tell."

"We have to get her to a hospital, then," I said, rising.

Thomas caught my arm. "You don't want her waking up, injured and dazed, in a place packed to the roof with weakened prey."

"Then what the hell do we do?"

"Look, if she's not dead, odds are she'll recover." Thomas held up his hand and fished out a ballpoint pen from his pocket. He twisted it and said, "Clear." Then he twisted it again and put it back.

A moment later, Martin came rapidly down the aisle. He somehow made even that look boring, as if he were simply a man wanting to take his seat again before the opening pitch. It was especially impressive since he carried a huge rifle, a military sniper weapon with a telescopic sight and a laser attachment. He set the rifle aside and went over Susan for a moment, feeling here and there, before he said, "She'll be sore."

"You?" I asked. "You were the gunman?"

"Obviously," Martin said. "Why do you think we were in Chicago to begin with?"

"Susan said she was getting her things."

He looked up at me skeptically. "You believed that? I would have thought you knew Susan well enough to know that material things don't hold a lot of interest for her."

"I knew that," I said. "But she said . . ." I trailed off and shook my head.

Martin looked up and said, "We knew Ortega was coming to kill you. We knew that if he succeeded, he might be able to bring the war to a peaceful conclusion, only to begin it again twenty years from now, from a much stronger position. I was sent to make sure Ortega did not kill you, and to eliminate him if I could."

"Did you?"

Martin shook his head. "He had planned for the contingency. Two of his vassals got to him during the fight. They pulled him out. I don't know how badly he was hurt, but it's likely he'll make it back to Casaverde."

"You want the war to keep going. You're hoping the White Council will destroy the Red Court for you."

Martin nodded.

"How did you find out about the duel?"

Martin didn't answer.

I narrowed my eyes and looked at Thomas.

Thomas put on an innocent expression. "Don't look at me. I'm a drunken, chemical-besotted playboy who does nothing but cavort, sleep, and feed. And even if I had the mind to take a bit of vengeance on the Red Court, I wouldn't have the backbone to actually stand up to anyone." He flashed me a radiant smile. "I'm totally harmless."

"I see," I said. I took a deep breath, and regarded Susan's face quietly for a moment. Then I bent down, got into her pockets, and got the keys to the rental car. "Are you leaving now, Martin?"

"Yes. I don't think our presence will be noticed here, but there's no sense in taking chances."

"Take care of her for me," I said.

Martin looked up at me for a second and then said, in a quiet voice, "Everything in my power. You have my word."

I nodded. "Thank you." I stood up and started for the exits, drawing the coat to cover my gun.

"Where are you going?" Thomas called.

"The airport," I answered. "I've got to meet some people about an old man and a bedsheet."

Chapter Thirty-one

❖❖❖

I parked at a rental lot outside O'Hare about five minutes after seven. I got out of the car with my staff and rod in hand. There was only one old light burning on the lot, but the moon had risen huge and bright, and I had no trouble seeing Michael coming. His white truck came crunching to a halt on the gravel in front of me. I walked around to the passenger door. Sanya swung it open for me, then slid over. He was wearing blue denim and a big black cowboy hat.

"Harry," Michael said as I got in. "I was getting worried. You won?"

"Not exactly."

"You lost?"

"Not exactly. I had Ortega on the ropes and he cheated. Both of us cleared the benches. I came out of it in one piece. He came out in a couple of pieces but he got away."

"Is Susan all right?"

"She got thrown about twenty-five yards through the air and hit steel and concrete. She'll be fine." Something tickled my nose, and I sniffed. The sharp odor of metal filled the cab of the truck. "Michael, are you wearing the armor?"

"I am wearing the armor," Michael said. "And the cloak."

"Hello, Michael. We're going to an airport. The kind with metal detectors."

"It's all right, Harry. Things will work out."

"Will it sound like alarms going off when they do?" I glanced at the younger Knight and said, "Sanya isn't wearing armor."

Sanya half turned toward me and pulled his denim jacket

open, revealing a Kevlar vest beneath it. "I am," he said soberly. "Fifteen layers with ceramic plating over critical areas."

"Well, at least you don't look like a Renaissance festival," I said. "This thing might actually protect you, besides making a slightly less medieval fashion statement. Is this the new stuff or the old stuff?"

"New," Sanya said. "Will stop civilian munitions, even some military rounds."

"But not knives or claws," Michael murmured. "Or arrows."

Sanya buttoned his coat back up, frowning. "Yours will not stop bullets."

Michael said, "My faith protects me."

I exchanged a skeptical look with Sanya and said, "Okey-dokey, Michael. Do we have any idea where the bad guys are?"

"The airport," Michael said.

I sat there silently for a second before I said, "Needle, haystack. Where, at the airport?"

Michael shrugged, smiling, and opened his mouth to speak.

I held up my hand. "We must have faith," I said, doing my best to imitate Michael's voice. "How did I guess. Did you bring *Fidelacchius*?"

"In the tool locker," Michael said.

I nodded. "Shiro's going to need it back."

Michael was quiet for a moment before he said, "Yes, of course."

"We're going to save him."

"I pray it is so, Harry."

"We will," I said. I stared out the window as Michael pulled into the airport proper. "It's not too late."

O'Hare is huge. We drove around in crowded parking lots and auto loading zones for nearly half an hour before Michael abruptly slowed the truck down outside the international concourse, his spine and neck straightening as if he'd heard a warning klaxon.

Sanya glanced aside at Michael and said, "What is it?"

"Do you feel that?" Michael asked him.

"Feel what?"

"Close your eyes," Michael said. "Try to still your thoughts."

I muttered, "I sense a great disturbance in the Force."

"You do?" Michael asked, blinking at me.

I sighed and rubbed at the bridge of my nose. Sanya closed his eyes, and a second later his expression twisted in distaste. "Rot," the Russian reported. "Sour milk. Mildew. The air smells greasy."

"There's a Pizza Hut kiosk about fifty feet away," I pointed out, looking through the windows of the concourse. "But maybe it's just a coincidence."

"No," Michael said. "It's Nicodemus. He leaves a kind of stain everywhere he goes. Arrogance. Ambition. Disregard."

"I only smell rotten things," Sanya said.

"You're sensing him too," Michael said. "Your mind is interpreting it differently. He's here." He started pulling forward, but a cab zipped in front of him and stopped. The cabby got out and began unloading an elderly couple's bags.

I muttered to myself and sniffed. I even reached out with my magical senses, trying to detect what Michael had. I felt nothing but the usual—patternless white noise of thousands of lives moving around us.

I opened my eyes, and found myself staring at the back of Detective Rudolph's head. He had on the usual expensive suit, and stood with a spare, well-coiffed man I recognized from the district attorney's office.

I froze for a second. Then I snatched Sanya's black Stetson and pulled it down over my head. I tugged the brim down over my eyes and slouched down as low as I could.

"What is it?" Michael asked.

"Police," I said. I took a more careful look around. I spotted seven uniformed officers and maybe ten other men who wore suits and casual clothes but walked and stood like cops. "I passed word to them that the Shroud might be on the way out of Chicago through here."

"Then why are you hiding?"

"A witness reported me leaving the scene of a murder. If someone identifies me, I'm going to spend the next day or so getting questioned, and that won't help Shiro."

Michael's brow knitted in concern. "True. Do the police know of the Denarians?"

"Probably not. SI isn't on the case. Probably they've been told they're some kind of terrorists and to be considered dangerous."

The cabby in front of us finally finished up, and Michael pulled away from the loading zone and toward the parking lot. "That isn't good enough. We can't have them there."

"As long as the police are around, it will restrict the Denarians' movements. Make them keep their heads down and play nice."

Michael shook his head. "Most supernatural creatures will hesitate before killing a mortal police officer. But Nicodemus won't. He has nothing but contempt for mortal authorities. If we confront him, he *will* kill anyone who attempts to stop him, as well as taking hostages to use against us."

Sanya nodded. "Not to mention that if this plague curse is as formidable as you say, it would be dangerous to those nearby."

"It's worse than that," I said.

Michael rolled the steering wheel toward a parking space. "How so?"

"Forthill told me that the Denarians get a power boost from hurting people, right? Causing mayhem and destruction?"

"Yes," Michael said.

"The curse is only going to last a few days, but while it does it's going to make the Black Death look like chicken pox. That's why he's here. It's one of the busiest international terminals on the planet."

"Mother of God," Michael swore.

Sanya whistled. "Flights from here go directly to every major nation in the world. If the Denarians' plague is easily communicable . . ."

"I think I pretty well summed that up with the Black Death comment, Sanya."

The Russian shrugged. "Sorry. What do we do?"

"We call in a bomb threat. Clear out the people and shut down the planes."

"We need to be inside immediately," Sanya said. "How long would it take the authorities to react?"

"It would only work if I knew who to call to get an immediate reaction."

"Do you?" Sanya asked.

I held out my hand out to Michael. He slapped his cell phone into it. "No," I said. "But I know someone who does."

I called Murphy, trying to remain calm and hoping that the phone didn't explode against my head. When I got the connection, it was cloudy with bursts of static, but I managed to tell her what was going on.

"You're insane, Dresden," Murphy said. "Do you know how incredibly irresponsible—and illegal—it is to falsify a bomb threat?"

"Yeah. Less irresponsible than letting cops and civilians get in these people's way."

Murphy was quiet for a second, and then asked, "How dangerous are they?"

"Worse than the loup-garou," I said.

"I'll make the call."

"Did you get in touch with him?" I asked.

"I think so, yes. Do you need any more muscle?"

"Got plenty," I said. "What I'm short on is time. Please hurry."

"Be careful, Harry."

I hung up the phone and got out of the truck. Michael and Sanya came with me. "Murphy's going to report a bomb threat. The cops will clear everyone out of the building. That will clear out the area for us."

"Leaving the Denarians without anyone to infect, or take hostage," Sanya said.

"That's the idea. After that, they'll call in the bomb squad and backup. We'll have twenty minutes, tops, to take advantage of the confusion."

Michael unlocked the tool locker in the back of the pickup, and drew out Shiro's cane. He tied a strap to it and slung it over his shoulder. While he did, Sanya buckled *Esperacchius* to his hip, then drew a freaking assault rifle out of the tool locker.

"Kalashnikov, isn't it?" I asked. "That's an extremely Chuck Heston look for the Knights of the Cross."

Sanya slapped a magazine into the weapon, chambered a round, and made sure the gun's safety was on. "I consider myself a progressive."

"Too random for my taste," Michael said. "Too easy to hurt the wrong person."

"Maybe," Sanya said. "But the only people inside should be the Denarians, yes?"

"And Shiro," I said.

"I will not shoot Shiro," Sanya assured me.

Michael buckled *Amoracchius* onto his hip. "How much longer will it take?"

The buzzing ring of a fire alarm blared from the concourse, and the police got together. A grizzled detective in a bad suit took charge and started directing suits and uniforms around. People started hurrying out of the concourse.

"Ask and ye shall receive," I said. "Let's circle around. Get in through one of the service entrances."

Sanya slipped the assault rifle into an over-the-shoulder sports bag, but kept one hand on the stock. Michael nodded to me, and I took the lead. We circled around the building until we could see some of the planes. Ground crews were rushing around in confusion, and several guys with orange flashlights were waving them at flight crews, directing the wallowing jets away from the ramps to the concourse.

We had to climb a fence and drop down a ten-foot retaining wall to get behind the concourse, but in the dark and the confusion no one noticed us. I led us through a ground-crew door and through a room that was part garage and part baggage storage. Emergency lights were on and fire alarms still jangled. I passed a section of wall covered with calendar pinup girls, pictures of trucks, and a map of the concourse.

"Whoa, stop," I said. Sanya bumped into my back. I glowered at him, and then peered at the map.

"Here," I said, pointing at a marked door. "We'll come out on this stairway."

"Midway through," Michael noted. "Which way do we go?"

"Split up," Sanya suggested.

Michael and I said, "Bad idea," at precisely the same time.

"Think," I muttered, mostly to myself. "If I were an arrogant psychotic demon-collaborating terrorist out to trigger an apocalypse, where would I be?"

Sanya leaned over to look at the map and said, "The chapel."

"The chapel," said Michael.

"The chapel," I echoed. "Down this hall, up the stairs, and to the left."

We ran down the hall and up the stairs. I pushed open the door and heard a recorded voice telling me to be calm and proceed to the nearest exit. I checked my right before I did my left, and it saved my life.

A man in nondescript business wear stood watching the door and holding a submachine gun. When he saw me, he lifted the weapon, hesitated for a fraction of a second, and started shooting.

The slight pause was enough to let me reverse my direction. A couple of bullets went right through the steel fire door, but I stumbled back into Sanya. The big man caught me and spun, putting his back between me and the incoming bullets. I felt him jerk and heard him grunt once, and then we hit a wall and sank down.

I knew the gunman would be coming. Right then, he was probably circling out to the far wall across from the door. Once he had a clear line of fire down the stairs, he'd move up and gun us down.

I saw his shadow in the crack under the door, and I struggled to regain my feet. Sanya was doing the same thing, and the two of us managed to do little but keep each other down. The gunman came closer, his shadow moving in the little space beneath the door's edge.

Michael stepped over me and Sanya, *Amoracchius* in hand, and shouted as he lunged forward, both hands driving the weight of the sword at the closed steel door. The sword went through the door, sinking almost to the hilt.

An erratic burst of gunfire sounded. Michael drew the sword back out of the door. Blood gleamed wet and scarlet along the length of the weapon's blade. Michael put his back against the wall of the stairwell. The gun barked a couple of times more and fell silent. After a minute, blood seeped under the door in a spreading red puddle.

Sanya and I got untangled and got up. "You're hit."

Michael had already moved and stood behind Sanya. He ran his hands over Sanya's back, grunted, and then held up a small, bright piece of metal, presumably the round. "It hit a strike plate. The vest caught it."

"Progressive." Sanya panted, wincing.

"You're lucky the bullet had to go through a steel door before it got to you," I muttered. I readied a shield and pressed the door slowly open.

The gunman lay on the floor. Michael's thrust had taken him just under the floating ribs, and had to have hit an artery to kill him so quickly. His gun lay in his hand, and his finger was limp on the trigger.

Sanya and Michael slipped out of the stairwell. Sanya had his rifle in hand. They stood lookout while I bent down and pried open the dead gunman's mouth. He didn't have a tongue. "One of Nicodemus's boys," I said quietly.

"Something is wrong," Michael said. Blood dripped from the tip of the sword to the floor. "I don't feel him anymore."

"If you can feel him, can he feel you? Could he know if you were getting close to him?"

Michael shrugged. "It seems likely."

"He's cautious," I said, remembering how Nicodemus had reacted when Shiro came through the door. "He doesn't take chances. He wouldn't wait around to start a fight he wasn't sure he could win. He's running." I stood up and headed for the chapel. "Come on."

Just as I got to the chapel's door, it swung open and two more men came out, both of them slapping clips into submachine guns. One of them didn't look up in time to see me, so I checked him in the forehead with a double-handed thrust of my staff, getting my whole weight behind the blow. His head snapped back and he dropped. The other gunman started to bring his weapon up, but I batted the barrel aside with a sweep of my staff, then snapped the end of it hard into his nose. Before he could recover, Sanya stepped into him and slammed the butt of the Kalashnikov against his head. He fell on top of the first guy, tongueless mouth lolled open.

I stepped over them and into the chapel.

It had been a small, modest room. There were two rows of three pews each, a pulpit, a table, and subdued lighting. There were no specific religious trappings to the place. It was simply a room set aside to accommodate the spiritual needs of worldwide travelers of every belief, creed, and faith.

Any one of them would have felt profaned by what had been done to the room.

The walls had been covered in sigils, somewhat similar to those I had seen on the Denarians so far. They were painted in blood, and still wet. The pulpit had been leaned against the back wall, and the heavy table laid along it, so that it lay at an angle to the floor. On either side of the table was a chair covered in bits of bone, a few candles. On one of the chairs was a carved silver bowl, almost entirely covered in fresh blood. The room smelled sickly sweet, and whatever was in those candles made the air thick, languid, and hazy. Maybe opium. It had probably accounted for the slowed reaction of the second two gunmen. The candles shed muted light over the table's surface.

What was left of Shiro lay on it.

He was on his back, and shirtless. Torn flesh and dark, savage bruises, some of them in the clear outline of chains, lapped around from his back. His hands and feet were grotesquely swollen. They'd been broken so badly and in so many places that they looked more like sausages than human limbs. His belly and chest had been sliced up as I'd seen before, on the real Father Vincent and on Gaston LaRouche's corpse as well.

"There's so much blood," I whispered.

I felt Michael enter the room behind me. He made a soft, choking sound.

I stepped closer to Shiro's remains, noting clinical details. His face had been left more or less untouched. There were several items scattered around him on the floor—ritual implements. Whatever they had intended him for, they'd already done it. There were sores on his skin, fever blisters, I thought, and his throat was swollen. The damage to his skin probably hid many other such marks of pestilence.

"We're too late," Michael said quietly. "Have they already worked the spell?"

"Yeah," I said. I sat down on the first pew.

"Harry?" Michael said.

"There's so much blood," I said. "He wasn't a very big person. You wouldn't think there could be so much blood."

"Harry, there's nothing else we can do here."

"I knew him, and he wasn't very big. You wouldn't think there would be enough for all the painting. The ritual."

"We should go," Michael said.

"And do what? The plague has already started. Odds are we have it. If we carry it out, we only spread it. Nicodemus has the Shroud and he's probably out looking for a full school bus or something. He's gone. We missed."

"Harry," Michael said quietly. "We must—"

Anger and frustration suddenly burned hot and bright behind my eyes. "If you talk to me about faith I'll kill you."

"You don't mean that," Michael said. "I know you too well."

"Shut up, Michael."

He stepped up next to me and leaned Shiro's cane against my knee. Then, without a word, he drew back to the wall and waited.

I picked up the cane and drew the wooden handle of the old man's sword out enough to see five or six inches of clean, gleaming metal. I slapped it shut again, stepped up to Shiro, and composed him as best I could. Then I rested the sword beside him.

When he coughed and wheezed, I almost screamed.

I wouldn't have thought that anyone could survive that much abuse. But Shiro drew in a ragged breath, and blinked open one eye. The other had been put out, and his eyelid looked sunken and strange.

"Hell's bells," I stammered. "Michael!"

Michael and I both rushed down beside him. It took him a moment to focus his eye on us. "Ah, good," he rasped. "Was getting tired waiting for you."

"We've got to get him to a hospital," I said.

The old man twitched his head in a negative gesture. "Too late. Would do no good. The noose. The Barabbus curse."

"What is he talking about?" I asked Michael.

"The noose Nicodemus wears. So long as he bears it, he apparently cannot die. We believe the noose is the one used by Judas," Michael said quietly.

"So what's this Barabbus curse?"

"Just as the Romans put it within the power of the Jews to choose one condemned prisoner each year to be pardoned and given life, the noose allows Nicodemus to mandate a death that cannot be avoided. Barabbus was the prisoner the Jews chose, though Pilate wanted to free the Savior. The curse is named for him."

"And Nicodemus used it on Shiro?"

Shiro twitched his head again, and a faint smile touched his mouth. "No, boy. On you. He was angry that you escaped him despite his treachery."

Hell's bells. The entropy curse that had nearly killed both me, and Susan with me. I stared at Shiro for a second, and then at Michael.

Michael nodded. "We cannot stop the curse," he said. "But we can take the place of its subject, if we choose to do it. That's why we wanted you to stay away, Harry. We were afraid Nicodemus would target you."

I stared at him and then at Shiro. My vision blurred. "It should be me lying there," I said. "Dammit."

"No," Shiro said. "There is much you do not yet understand." He coughed, and pain flashed over his face. "You will. You will." He twitched the arm nearest the sword. "Take it. Take it, boy."

"No," I said. "I'm not like you. Like any of you. I never will be."

"Remember. God sees hearts, boy. And now I see yours. Take it. Hold it in trust until you find the one it belongs to."

I reached out and picked up the cane. "How do I know who to give it to?"

"You will know," Shiro said, his voice becoming thinner. "Trust your heart."

Sanya entered the room and padded over to us. "The police heard the gunfire. There's an assault team getting ready to—" He froze, staring at Shiro.

"Sanya," Shiro said. "This is our parting, friend. I am proud of you."

Sanya swallowed and knelt down by the old man. He kissed Shiro's forehead. Blood stained his lips when he straightened.

"Michael," Shiro said. "The fight is yours now. Be wise."

Michael laid his hand on Shiro's bald head and nodded. The big man was crying, though his face was set in a quiet smile.

"Harry," Shiro whispered. "Nicodemus is afraid of you. Afraid that you saw something. I don't know what."

"He should be afraid," I said.

"No," the old man said. "Don't let him unmake you. You must

find him. Take the Shroud from him. So long as he touches it, the plague grows. If he loses it, it ends."

"We don't know where he is," I said.

"Train," Shiro whispered. "His backup plan. A train to St. Louis."

"How do you know?" Michael asked.

"Told his daughter. They thought I was gone." Shiro focused on me and said, "Stop them."

My throat clenched. I nodded. I managed to half growl, "Thank you."

"You will understand," Shiro said. "Soon."

Then he sighed, like a man who has just laid down a heavy burden. His eye closed.

Shiro died. There was nothing pretty about it. There was no dignity to it. He'd been brutalized and savagely murdered—and he'd allowed it to happen to him in my place.

But when he died, there was a small, contented smile on his face. Maybe the smile of someone who had run his course without wavering from it. Someone who had served something greater than himself. Who had given up his life willingly, if not gladly.

Sanya said, his voice strained, "We cannot remain here."

I stood up and slung the cane on its strap over my shoulder. I felt cold, and shivered. I put a hand to my forehead, and found it clammy and damp. The plague.

"Yeah," I said, and strode out of the room and back toward the blood-spattered stairs. "Clock's running."

Michael and Sanya kept pace. "Where are we going?"

"The airfield," I said. "He's smart. He'll figure it out. He'll be there."

"Who?" Michael asked.

I didn't answer. I led them back down through the garage area and out onto the airfield tarmac. We hurried down along the concourse, and then out onto the open acres of asphalt that led from the concourses to the landing fields. Once we'd gotten out there, I took off my pentacle amulet and held it aloft, focusing on it in order to cause it to begin to shed a distinctive blue light.

"What are you doing?" Sanya asked.

"Signaling," I said.

"Who?"

"Our ride."

It took maybe forty-five seconds before the sound of a helicopter's blades whirled closer to us. The aircraft, a blue-and-white-painted commercial job, zipped down to hover over us before dropping down for a precise if hurried landing.

"Come on," I said, and headed for the craft. The side door opened, and I climbed in with Michael and Sanya close behind me.

Gentleman Johnny Marcone, dressed in dark fatigues, nodded to me and to the two Knights. "Good evening, gentlemen," he said. "Just tell me where to take you."

"Southwest," I said, yelling over the noise of the chopper. "They're going to be on a commercial train heading for St. Louis."

Michael stared at Marcone in shock. "This is the man who ordered the Shroud stolen to begin with," he said. "You don't think he's going to work with us?"

"Sure he will," I said. "If Nicodemus gets away with the Shroud and pulls off this big curse, Marcone's spent all that money for nothing."

"Not to mention that the plague would be bad for business," Marcone added. "I think we can agree to help one another against this Nicodemus. We can discuss the disposition of the Shroud afterward." He turned and thumped the pilot's shoulder a couple of times, and yelled directions. The pilot glanced back at us, and I saw Gard's profile against the flight instruments. Hendricks leaned in from the passenger seat, listening to Marcone, and nodded himself.

"Very well then," Marcone called, leaning back into the cabin. He took a large-caliber hunting rifle down from a rack and settled into a seat, buckling up. "Best strap in, gentlemen. Let's go recover the holy Shroud."

I settled in and told Michael, "Now, if only we had a bit of Wagner to send us on our way."

I saw Gard's reflection in the chopper's front windows look up at my words. Then she flicked a couple of switches, and "Ride of the Valkyries" started thrumming through the helicopter's cabin.

"Yee-haw," I said as my elbows and knees started a nagging ache. "As long as we're going, we might as well go out in style."

DEATH MASKS
571

Chapter Thirty-two

After a few minutes, the ride got bumpy. The chopper started jouncing at random, lurching several feet in any given direction. If I hadn't been strapped in, I probably would have slammed my head against the walls or ceiling.

Marcone put on a headset and spoke into a microphone. He listened to the answer and then shouted to the rest of us, "The ride may be a bit bumpier. The stabilizers are run by the onboard computer, which has failed." He gave me a direct look. "I can only speculate as to why."

I looked around, picked up another headset, put it on, and said, "Blow me."

"Excuse me?" came Gard's somewhat outraged voice over the intercom.

"Not you, blondie. I was talking to Marcone."

Marcone folded his arms in his seat, half smiling. "It's all right, Miss Gard. Compassion dictates that we must make allowances. Mister Dresden is a diplomatically challenged individual. He should be in a shelter for the tactless."

"I'll tell you what you can do with your shelter," I said. "Marcone, I need to speak to you."

Marcone frowned at me, and then nodded. "How much time before we reach the southbound tracks?"

"We're over the first one now," Gard replied. "Three minutes to catch the train."

"Inform me when we reach it. Mister Hendricks, please switch the cabin headphones to channel two."

Hendricks didn't say anything, and it made me wonder why he had bothered with a headset.

"There," came Marcone's voice after a moment. "We're speaking privately."

"Why didn't you tell me?" I said.

"Tell you that I hadn't sent Mister Franklin for you?"

"Yeah."

"Would you have believed me?"

"No."

"Would you have thought I was playing some kind of game with you?"

"Yes."

"Then why waste the time and make you more suspicious? Generally speaking, you are quite perceptive—given enough time. And I know you well enough to know that I do not wish to have you as my enemy."

I glowered at him.

He arched an eyebrow, meeting my gaze without fear or hostility.

"Why do you want the Shroud?"

"That's none of your business."

I scowled. "Actually it is. Literally. Why do you want it?"

"Why do you?"

"Because the Denarians are going to kill a lot of people with it." Marcone shrugged. "That's reason enough for me as well."

"Sure it is."

"It's simple business, Mister Dresden. I can't conduct business with a mound of corpses."

"Why don't I believe you?"

Marcone's teeth flashed. "Because given enough time, you are a perceptive individual."

There was a beep in the headphones, and Gard said, "Fifteen seconds, sir."

"Thank you," Marcone replied. "Dresden, why should these people take the Shroud and this plague of theirs to St. Louis?"

"It's another international airport," I said. "It's the central hub for TWA. And hell, as long as they're there, they could probably go for a swim in the Mississippi."

"Why not simply stay in Chicago?"

I nodded toward Michael and Sanya. "Them. Plus I figure they know that Murphy and SI would give them a hard time. Even the regular cops were out in force looking for them."

He looked speculatively at Michael and Sanya. "I assume you have a means to locate the Shroud if that is the correct train?"

"Yeah," I said. "And here's the deal. You drop us off, and we get the Shroud."

"I'm going with you," Marcone said.

"No, you aren't."

"I can always order Miss Gard to return to O'Hare."

"Where we'll all die of the plague, since we didn't stop the Denarians."

"That may be. Either way, I'm going with you."

I scowled at him, then shook my head and leaned back against the seat, shivering. "You suck. You suck diseased moose wang, Marcone."

Marcone smiled with just his mouth. "How colorful." He looked out the window and said, "My people tell me there are only three trains leaving Chicago for St. Louis this evening. Two freight trains and a passenger train."

"They won't be on the passenger train," I said. "They'd have to ditch weapons and goons, and they won't."

"Even odds that this is the one, then," Marcone said.

The chopper descended until the trees near the tracks were swaying in the downblast. That's the nice part about the Midwest. Go twenty miles from a town hall and there's nothing but lightly settled farm country. I looked out the window and saw a long train rumbling along the tracks.

Michael sat bolt upright and nodded to me.

"This is it," I said to Marcone. "Now what?"

"I bought this helicopter as Coast Guard surplus. It's fitted with a rescue winch. We climb down it onto the train."

"You're joking, right?"

"Nothing worth doing is ever easy, Dresden." Marcone took off the headphones and shouted to Sanya and Michael. Sanya's reaction was about like mine, but Michael only nodded and got unstrapped. Marcone opened a locker and drew out several nylon harnesses. He strapped one on himself and passed out another to each of us. Then he hauled the side door of the helicopter open. Wind filled the cabin. Marcone opened a cabinet, and started drawing a length of cable from it. I looked and saw the winch inside. Marcone looped the cable through a ring outside the door then said, "Who first?"

Michael stepped forward. "Me."

Marcone nodded and clipped the cable onto the harness. A

minute later, Michael hopped out of the helicopter. Marcone flicked a switch near the electric winch, and cable began playing out. Marcone watched intently and then nodded. "He's down."

The winch reeled back in, and Sanya stepped up to the door. It took a couple of minutes, and it felt like the chopper was doing too much lurching around, but Marcone eventually nodded. "Dresden."

My mouth felt dry as Marcone checked my harness and clipped the cable to it. Then he shouted, "Go!"

I didn't want to go but I sure as hell wasn't going to chicken out in front of Marcone. I clutched my staff and rod to me, made sure Shiro's cane was strapped to my back, took a deep breath, and jumped. I swung around a little on the cable, and then felt myself going down.

The downdraft from the chopper all but blinded me, but when I did look around I could see the train beneath me. We were being lowered onto a car just forward of the end of the train, a large metal container with a flat lid. The helicopter had a searchlight pointed at the train, and I could see Michael and Sanya crouching and looking up at me.

I swayed and dangled like a kid's first yo-yo. My legs got clipped by an outgrown tree branch that hit me hard enough to leave bruises. When I got close, Michael and Sanya grabbed me and brought me down in one piece.

Marcone came down, his rifle hanging on his shoulder. I figured Hendricks was operating the winch. The Knights pulled Marcone safely in, and he detached the cable. It swung away and the chopper arched up and away, turning its searchlight out. It took a moment for my eyes to adjust to the brilliant moon, and I stayed crouched so that I could keep my balance.

"Harry," Michael called. "Where now?"

"Head for the engine and look for a boxcar," I told him. "Something it would be easy for them to hop into."

Michael nodded. "Sanya, rear guard."

The big Russian held his rifle like trained military and fell back to the rear of our group, watching behind us. Michael took the lead, one hand on his sword, and moved forward with a predatory grace and purpose.

I glowered at Marcone and said, "I'm not going anywhere with you behind me."

Marcone smiled again, and took his gun off his shoulder. He looked like trained military, too. He fell into line behind Michael.

I pulled my old duster back until it fell behind the handle of my pistol, leaving it clear for a draw. It probably didn't look military. It probably looked more like a spaghetti Western. I moved in behind Marcone, staff in my left hand, rod in my right.

We all moved forward over the rumbling freight cars, just like every Western movie you've ever seen. If I hadn't been feverish and nauseous, it might have been fun.

Michael abruptly crouched and held a closed fist beside his ear. Marcone stopped immediately, crouching, the rifle at his shoulder. Closed fist means stop, check. I crouched too.

Michael turned around to face us, poked a couple of fingers at his eyes, held three fingers up, and pointed at the car ahead of us. I took it to mean that he could see three bad guys up there. Michael beckoned Sanya, and the Russian slipped silently forward. Michael pointed at me and then at the back of the train. I nodded to him, and kept an eye out behind us.

I checked over my shoulder, and saw Michael and Sanya both swing down between the cars and out of sight.

When I faced the rear of the train again, I saw a nightmare running toward me over the cars.

Whatever creation process this thing had undergone, it hadn't been a kind one. Four-legged and lanky, it looked vaguely like a cat. But it didn't have fur. Its skin was leathery, wrinkled and mottled. Its head was somewhere between that of a jaguar and a wild boar. It had both tusks and fangs in its gaping, drooling mouth, and it moved with graceless speed.

I let out a strangled cry, lifting my blasting rod. I pushed power through it, yelled the word, and loosed a flashing bolt of fire at it. The bolt hit the thing in the face just as it gathered itself to leap at me. It let out an unnerving, wailing cry, then convulsed in pain as it jumped and sailed off the side of the car.

The fire blinded me for a moment, leaving a bright green dot over my vision. I heard the next one coming, but I couldn't see it. I dropped down to my stomach and yelled, "Marcone!"

The rifle cracked three times in deliberately spaced reports. I heard the thing squeal, and then saw it as my eyes started to adjust. It lay on top of the car maybe ten feet from me, hindquarters dragging, struggling to haul itself forward with one claw.

Marcone stepped closer, lifted the hunting rifle, and coolly put another shot right between its eyes. The creature twitched, fell, and slid bonelessly over the side of the train.

Marcone peered after it. "What was that?"

"Some kind of guard dog," I said.

"Interesting. Demon?"

I pushed myself to my feet. "Doubt it. Demons are usually a lot tougher."

"Then what was it?"

"How the hell should I know? Never seen anything like it before. Where are Michael and Sanya?"

We went to look. The next car was an empty one with spaced wooden slats and an open top. It looked like something used to haul cattle. There were three men in it, unconscious or dead. Michael climbed the far wall of the cattle car and onto the next car in line.

We climbed down into the car. "Dead?" Marcone asked.

"Napping," Sanya said.

Marcone nodded. "We should finish them. These men are fanatics. If they wake up, they'll attack us without hesitation, armed or not."

I eyed him. "We're not going to murder them in cold blood."

"Is there a particular reason why not?"

"Shut up, Marcone."

"They would show us no such mercy. And if they are allowed to live they will surely be used by the Denarians to cause pain and death. It's their purpose."

"We're not killing them."

Marcone's mouth curled into a bitter smile. "How did I guess." He snapped open a case on his belt and tossed two sets of handcuffs at Sanya. The Russian caught them and cuffed the downed men together, looping one of the sets around a metal strut of the car.

"There," Marcone said. "I suppose we'll just have to take the chance that none of them will chew off his own hand at the wrist and slip free."

"Sanya!" Michael's voice thundered over the noise of the train, and a sudden, brilliant glare of white light leapt up from the top of the next car. Steel chimed on steel.

Sanya shoved his assault rifle at me. I caught it, and he pushed past me to start climbing out of the car. He hauled himself up with his right arm, his injured arm dangling, and heaved himself to the lip of the cattle car. He stood, drew *Esperacchius* in a blaze of more white light, and threw himself to the next car with a rumbling shout.

I let my staff drop and fumbled with the assault rifle, trying to find the safety. Marcone set his hunting rifle aside and said, "You're going to hurt yourself." He took the assault rifle out of my hands, checked a couple of things without needing to look at the weapon, and then slung it over his shoulder as he climbed out of the car. I muttered to myself and went up the wooden slats beside him.

The next car was another metal box. Michael's and Sanya's swords shone like the sun, and I had to shield my eyes against them. They stood side by side with their backs to me, facing the front of the train.

Nicodemus stood against them.

The lord of the Denarians wore a grey silk shirt and black pants. The Shroud had been draped over his body, like a contestant in a beauty pageant. The noose around his neck blew out toward the rear of the train in the wind. He held a sword in his hands, a Japanese katana with a worn hilt. Droplets of blood stained the very tip of the sword. He held the sword at his side, a small smile on his lips, to all appearances relaxed.

Michael checked over his shoulder, and I saw a line of blood on his cheek. "Stay back, Harry."

Nicodemus attacked in the moment Michael's attention was elsewhere. The Denarian's weapon blurred, and Michael barely managed to get *Amoracchius* into a parry. He was thrown off balance and to one knee for a fatal second, but Sanya roared and attacked, whipping his saber through whistling arcs, and driving Nicodemus back. The Russian drove the Denarian toward the far side of the car.

I saw the trap coming and shouted, "Sanya, back off!"

The Russian couldn't stop his forward momentum entirely, but he pivoted and lunged to one side. As he did, steely blades erupted from within the car. The metal of the roof screamed as the blades pierced it, rising to a height of four or five feet in a line, a half breath behind Sanya. Nicodemus turned to pursue the Russian.

Michael got his feet, whipped the heavy blade of *Amoracchius* around, and slashed three times at the roof of the railcar. A triangular section three feet across fell down into the car, and the edges of the metal glowed dull orange with the heat of the parted steel. Michael dropped down through the hole and out of sight.

I lifted up my blasting rod and focused on Nicodemus. He shot a glance at me and flicked his wrist in my direction.

His shadow flashed across the top of the railcar and smashed into me. The shadow wrenched the blasting rod from my grip, dragged it through the air, and then crushed it to splinters.

Sanya let out a cry as a blade tore through the car's roof and one of his legs collapsed. He fell to one knee.

Then brilliant light flared up within the car beneath the combatants, spears of white lancing out through the holes the blades had cut into the metal. I heard Deirdre's demon form shriek in the car beneath us, and the blades harassing Sanya vanished.

Nicodemus snarled. He flung a hand toward me, and his shadow sent the splinters of my blasting rod shrieking toward my face. As they did, Nicodemus attacked Sanya, his sword flickering in the moonlight.

I got my arms up in time to deflect the splinters, but I was helpless to assist Sanya. Nicodemus knocked Sanya's saber out to one side. Sanya rolled, avoiding the stroke that would have taken his head. Doing it left Sanya's wounded arm on the ground, and Nicodemus crushed the heel of his boot down upon it.

Sanya screamed in pain.

Nicodemus raised his sword for the death blow.

Gentleman Johnny Marcone opened up with the Kalashnikov.

Marcone shot in three chattering bursts of fire. The first one tore through Nicodemus's chest and neck, just above the Shroud. The next hit on his arm and shoulder opposite the Shroud, all but tearing it off his torso. The last burst ripped apart his hip and thigh, on the hip opposite the Shroud's drape. Nicodemus's expression blackened with fury, but the bullets had torn half his body to shreds, and he toppled from the car and out of sight.

Below, there was another demonic shriek, and the sound of wrenching metal. The shrieks faded toward the front of the train, and a moment later Michael climbed up the ladder rungs on the side of the boxcar, his sword in its sheath.

I leapt forward and ran to Sanya. He was bleeding a lot from his leg. He had already taken off his belt, and I helped him wrap it around the leg in a makeshift tourniquet.

Marcone stepped up to where Nicodemus had fallen, frowned, and said, "Dammit. He should have dropped in place. Now we'll have to go back for the Shroud."

"No, we won't," I said. "You didn't kill him. You probably just pissed him off."

Michael stepped past Marcone to help Sanya, tearing off a section off his white cloak.

"Do you think so?" Marcone asked. "The damage seemed fairly thorough."

"I don't think he can be killed," I said.

"Interesting. Can he run faster than a train?"

"Probably," I said.

Marcone said to Sanya, "Do you have another clip?"

"Where is Deirdre?" I asked Michael.

He shook his head. "Wounded. She tore her way through the front wall of the car into the next one. Too risky to pursue her alone in close quarters."

I stood up and crawled back over to the cattle car. I clambered down in it to fetch my staff. After a moment of hesitation, I got Marcone's rifle, too, and started back up.

As it turned out, I was mistaken. Nicodemus could not run faster than a train.

He *flew* faster than a train.

He came sailing down out of the sky, his shadow spread like immense bat wings. His sword flashed toward Marcone. Marcone's reflexes could make a striking snake look sluggish, and he dodged and rolled out of the way of the Denarian's sword.

Nicodemus sailed to the next car on the train and landed in a crouch, facing us. A glowing sigil had appeared on his forehead, the sign itself something twisting, nauseating to look upon. His skin was marred and ugly where Marcone's shots had hit him, but it was whole, and getting better by the second. His face twisted in fury and a kind of ecstatic agony, and his shadow flooded forward, over the length of the railcar in front of him and dipping down between his car and ours.

There was a wrenching sound and our car shook. Then the sound of tearing metal, and our car started shuddering.

"He's uncoupled the cars!" I shouted. As I did, Nicodemus's car began drawing away from us, as our own slowed down, the gap between them growing.

"Go!" Sanya shouted. "I'll be all right!"

Michael stood and threw himself over the gap without hesitation. Marcone ditched the assault rifle and sprinted toward the gap. He threw himself over it, arms windmilling, and landed, barely, on the other car's roof.

I got to the top of the car and did the same thing. I imagined missing the other car and landing on the tracks in front of the uncoupled end of the train. Even without an engine, pure momentum would be more than enough to kill me. I dropped Marcone's rifle and gathered my will in my staff. As I leapt, I thrust the staff back behind me and screamed, *"Forzare!"*

The raw force I sent out behind me shoved me forward. Actually, it shoved me too far forward. I landed closer to Nicodemus than either Michael or Marcone, but at least I didn't wind up sprawled at his feet.

Michael stepped up to stand beside me, and a second later Marcone did as well. He had an automatic pistol in either hand.

"The boy isn't very fast, is he, Michael?" said Nicodemus. "You're an adequate opponent, I suppose. Not as experienced as you could be, but it's hard to find someone with more than thirty or forty years of practice, much less twenty centuries. Not as talented as the Japanese, but then not many are."

"Give up the Shroud, Nicodemus," Michael shouted. "It is not yours to take."

"Oh, yes, it is," Nicodemus answered. "You certainly will not be able to stop me. And when I've finished you and the wizard, I'll go back for the boy. Three Knights in a day, as it were."

"He can't make bad puns," I muttered. "That's my shtick."

"At least he didn't overlook you entirely," Marcone answered. "I feel somewhat insulted."

"Hey!" I shouted. "Old Nick, can I ask you a question?"

"Please do, wizard. Once we get to the fighting, there really isn't going to be much opportunity for it."

"Why?" I said.

"Beg pardon?"

"Why?" I asked again. "Why the hell are you doing this? I mean, I get why you stole the Shroud. You needed a big battery. But why a plague?"

"Have you read Revelations?"

"Not in a while," I admitted. "But I just can't buy that you really think you're touching off the Apocalypse."

Nicodemus shook his head. "Dresden, Dresden. The Apocalypse, as you refer to it, isn't an event. At least, it isn't any specific event. One day, I'm sure, there will be an apocalypse that really does bring on the end, but I doubt it will be this event that begins it."

"Then why *do* this?"

Nicodemus studied me for a moment before smiling. "Apocalypse is a frame of mind," he said then. "A belief. A surrender to inevitability. It is despair for the future. It is the death of hope."

Michael said quietly, "And in that kind of environment, there is more suffering. More pain. More desperation. More power to the underworld and their servants."

"Exactly," Nicodemus said. "We have a terrorist group prepared to take credit for this plague. It will likely stir up reprisals, protests, hostilities. All sorts of things."

"One step closer," said Michael. "That's how he sees it. Progress."

"I like to think of it as simple entropy," Nicodemus said. "The real question, to my mind, is why do you stand against me? It is the way of the universe, Knight. Things fall apart. Your resistance to it is pointless."

In answer, Michael drew his sword.

"Ah," said Nicodemus. "Eloquence."

"Stay back," Michael said to me. "Don't distract me."

"Michael—"

"I mean it." He stepped forward to meet Nicodemus.

Nicodemus took his time, sauntering up to meet Michael. He crossed swords with him lightly, then lifted his blade in a salute. Michael did the same.

Nicodemus attacked, and *Amoracchius* flared into brilliant light. The two men met each other and traded a quick exchange of cuts and thrusts. They parted, and then clashed together again, steps carrying each past the other. Both of them emerged from it unscathed.

"Shooting him hardly seems to inconvenience him," Marcone said quietly to me. "I take it that the Knight's sword can harm him?"

"Michael doesn't think so," I said.

Marcone blinked and looked at me. "Then why is he fighting him?"

"Because it needs to be done," I said.

"Do you know what I think?" Marcone said.

"You think we should shoot Nicodemus in the back at the first opportunity and let Michael dismember him."

"Yes."

I drew my gun. "Okay."

Just then Demon-girl Deirdre's glowing eyes appeared several cars ahead of us and came forward at a sprint. I caught a glimpse of her before she jumped onto our car—still all supple scales and hairstyle by the Tasmanian Devil. But in addition she had a sword gripped in one hand.

"Michael!" I shouted. "Behind you!"

Michael turned and dodged to one side, avoiding Deirdre's

first attack. Her hair followed him, lashing at him, tangling around the hilt of his sword.

I acted without thinking. I stripped Shiro's cane from my back, shouted, "Michael!" and threw the cane at him.

Michael didn't so much as turn his head. He reached out, caught the cane, and with a sweep of his arm threw the cane-sheath free of the sword so that *Fidelacchius*'s blade shone with its own light. Without pausing, he swung the second sword and struck Deirdre's tangling hair from his arm, sending her stumbling back.

Nicodemus attacked him, and Michael met him squarely, shouting, *"O Dei! Lava quod est sordium!"* *Cleanse what is unclean, O God.* Michael managed to hold his ground against Nicodemus, their blades ringing. Michael drove Nicodemus to one side and I had a shot at his back. I took it. Beside me, Marcone did the same.

The shots took Nicodemus by surprise and stole his balance. Michael shouted and pressed forward on the offensive, seizing the advantage for the first time. Both shining blades dipped and circled through attack after attack, and Michael drove Nicodemus back step by step.

"Hell's bells, he's going to win," I muttered.

But Nicodemus drew a gun from the back of his belt.

He shoved it against Michael's breastplate and pulled the trigger. Repeatedly. Light and thunder made even the rushing train sound quiet.

Michael fell and did not move.

The light of the two swords went out.

I shouted, "No!" I raised my gun and started shooting again. Marcone joined me.

We didn't do too badly considering we were standing on a moving train and all. But Nicodemus didn't seem to care. He walked toward us through the bullets, jerking and twitching occasionally. He casually kicked the two swords over the side of the train.

I ran dry on bullets, and Nicodemus took the gun from my hand with a stroke of his sword. It hit the top of the boxcar once, then bounced off and into the night. The train thundered down a long, shallow grade toward a bridge. Demon-girl Deirdre leapt over to her father's side on all fours, her face distorted in glee. Tendrils of her hair ran lovingly over Michael's unmoving form.

I drew up my unfocused shield into a regular barrier before me, and said, "Don't even bother offering me a coin."

"I hadn't planned on it," Nicodemus said. "You don't seem like a team player to me." He looked past me and said. "But I've heard about you, Marcone. Are you interested in a job?"

"I was just going to ask you the same thing," Marcone said.

Nicodemus smiled and said, "Bravo, sir. I understand. I'm obliged to kill you, but I understand."

I traded a look with Marcone. I flicked my eyes at the upcoming bridge. He took a deep breath and nodded.

Nicodemus lifted the gun and aimed for my head. His shadow suddenly swept forward, under and around my shield, seizing my left hand. It ripped at my arm hard, pulling me off balance.

Marcone was ready. He let one of his empty guns fall and produced a knife from somewhere on his person. He flicked it at Nicodemus's face.

I went for his gun hand when he flinched. The gun went off. My senses exploded with a flash of light, and I lost the feeling in my left arm. But I trapped his gun arm between my body and my right arm and pried at his fingers.

Marcone went for him with another knife. It swept past my face, missing me. But it hit the Shroud. Marcone cut through it cleanly, seized it, and pulled it off Nicodemus entirely.

I felt the release of energy as the Shroud was removed, a wave of fever-hot magic that swept over me in a sudden, potent surge. When it was gone, my chills and my aching joints were gone with it. The curse had been broken.

"No!" Nicodemus shouted. "Kill him!"

Deirdre leapt at Marcone. Marcone turned and jumped off the train just as it rolled out over the river. He hit the water feet first, still clutching the Shroud, and was lost in the darkness.

I pried the gun from Nicodemus's fingers. He caught me by the hair, jerked my head back, and got his arm around my throat. He started choking me, hissing, "It's going to take days to kill you, Dresden."

He's afraid of you, said Shiro's voice in my mind.

In my memories, I watched Nicodemus edge away from Shiro as the old man entered the room.

The noose made him invulnerable to any lasting harm.

But in a flash of insight, I was willing to bet that the one thing the noose wouldn't protect him against was itself.

I reached back, fumbling until I felt the noose. I pulled on it as hard as I could, and then twisted it, pressing my knuckles hard into Nicodemus's throat.

Nicodemus reacted in sudden and obvious panic, releasing my throat and struggling to get away. I held on for dear life and dragged him off balance. I tried to throw him off the train, letting go of the noose at the last moment. He went over the edge but Deirdre let out a shriek and leapt forward, her tendrils writhing around one of his arms and holding him.

"Kill him," Nicodemus choked. "Kill him now!"

Coughing and wheezing, I picked up Michael's still form as best I could and leapt off the train.

We hit the water together. Michael sank. I wouldn't let go of him. I sank too. I tried to get us out, but I couldn't, and things started to become confusing and black.

I had almost given up trying when I felt something near me in the water. I thought it was a rope and I grabbed it. I was still holding on to Michael as whoever had thrown the rope started pulling me out.

I gasped for breath when my head broke water, and someone helped me drag Michael's body over to the shallows at the side of the river.

It was Marcone. And he hadn't thrown me a rope.

He'd hauled me out with the Shroud.

Chapter Thirty-three

I woke up in the back of Michael's pickup staring up at the stars and the moon and in considerable pain. Sanya sat at the back of the truck, facing me. Michael lay still and unmoving beside me.

"He's awake," Sanya said when he saw me moving.

Murphy's voice came from the front of the truck. "Harry, be still, okay? We don't know how badly you've been shot."

"Okay," I said. "Hi, Murph. It should have torn."

"What?" Murphy asked.

"Shroud. It should have torn like wet tissue. That just makes sense, right?"

"Shhhhh, Harry. Be still and don't talk."

That sounded fine to me. The next time I opened my eyes, I was in the morgue.

This, all by itself, is enough to really ruin your day.

I was lying on the examining table, and Butters, complete with his surgical gown and his tray of autopsy instruments, stood over me.

"I'm not dead!" I sputtered. "I'm not dead!"

Murphy appeared in my field of vision, her hand on my chest. "We know that, Harry. Easy. We've got to get the bullet out of you. We can't take you to the emergency room. They have to report any gunshot wounds."

"I don't know," Butters said. "This X ray is all screwed up. I'm not sure it's showing me where the bullet is. If I don't do this right, I could make things worse."

"You can do it," Murphy said. "The technical stuff always messes up around him."

Things spun around.

Michael stood over me at one point, his hand on my head. "Easy, Harry. It's almost done."

And I thought, *Great. I'm going to require an armed escort to make sure I get to hell.*

When I woke up again, I was in a small bedroom. Stacks and boxes and shelves of fabric filled the place nearly to the ceiling, and I smiled, recognizing it. The Carpenters' guest room.

On the floor next to the bed was Michael's breastplate. There were four neat holes in it where the bullets had gone through. I sat up. My shoulder screamed at me, and I found it covered in bandaging.

There was a sound by the door. A small pair of eyes peeked around the corner, and little Harry Carpenter stared at me with big blue-grey eyes.

"Hi," I said to him.

He dutifully lifted his pudgy fingers and waved them at me.

"I'm Harry," I said.

He frowned thoughtfully and then said, "Hawwy."

"Good enough, kid."

He ran off. A minute later he came back, reaching way up over his head to hold on to his daddy's fingers. Michael came in the room and smiled at me. He was wearing jeans, a clean white T-shirt, and bandages over one arm. The cut on his face was healing, and he looked rested and relaxed. "Good afternoon," he said.

I smiled tiredly at him. "Your faith protects you, eh?"

Michael reached down and turned the breastplate around. There was a cream-colored material lining in the inside of the breastplate, with several deep dents in it. He peeled it back to show me layers and layers of bulletproof fabric backing ceramic strike plates set against the front of the breastplate. "My faith protects me. My Kevlar helps."

I laughed a little. "Charity made you put it in?"

Michael picked up little Harry and put him on his shoulders. "She did it herself. Said she wasn't going to spend all that trouble making the breastplate and then have me get killed with a gun."

"She made the breastplate?" I asked.

Michael nodded. "All of my armor. She used to work on motorcycles."

My shoulder throbbed hard enough to make me miss the next sentence. "Sorry. What did you say?"

"I said you'll need to take your medicine. Can you handle some food first?"

"I'll try."

I had soup. It was exhausting. I took a Vicodin and slept without dreaming.

Over the next couple of days, I managed to piece together what had happened from talking to Michael and, on the second day, to Sanya.

The big Russian had come out of things all right. Marcone, after getting me and Michael out of the water, had called Murphy and told her where to find us. She had already been on the way, and got there in only a couple of minutes.

The crew of the train, it turned out, had been killed. The three goons that had been trussed up on the train had bitten down on suicide pills and were dead when the cops found them. Murphy had taken us all to Butters instead of to the emergency room, since once my gunshot wound was reported, Rudolph and company could have made my life hell.

"I must be out of my mind," Murphy told me when she visited. "I swear, Dresden, if this comes back to bite me in the ass, I'm taking it out on your hide."

"We're fighting the good fight, Murph," I said.

She rolled her eyes at me, but said, "I saw the body at the airport concourse, Harry. Did you know him?"

I looked out the window, at Michael's three youngest playing in the yard, watched over by a tolerant Molly. "He was a friend. It could have been me instead."

Murphy shivered. "I'm sorry, Harry. The people who did it. Did they get away from you?"

I looked at her and said, "I got away from them. I don't think I did much more than annoy them."

"What happens when they come back?"

"I don't know," I said.

"Wrong," Murphy said. "The answer to that question is that you don't know exactly but that you will certainly call Murphy from the get-go. You get less busted up when I'm around."

"That's true." I covered her hand with mine and said, "Thanks, Murph."

"You're gonna make me puke, Dresden," she said. "Oh, so you know. Rudolph is out of SI. The assistant DA he was working for liked his toadying style."

"Rudolph the Brownnosed Reindeer," I said.

Murphy grinned. "At least he's not my problem anymore. Internal Affairs has to worry now."

"Rudolph in Internal Affairs. That can't be good."

"One monster at a time."

On the fourth day, Charity inspected my wound and told Michael that I could leave. She never actually spoke to me, which I considered an improvement over most visits. That afternoon, Michael and Sanya came in. Michael was carrying Shiro's battered old cane.

"We got the swords back," Michael said. "This is for you."

"You'll have a better idea what to do with that than me," I told him.

"Shiro wanted you to have it," Michael said. "Oh, and you got some mail."

"I what?"

Michael offered me an envelope and the cane as a unit. I took them both, and frowned at the envelope. The lettering was in black calligraphy, and flowed beautifully across the envelope.

"To Harry Dresden. And it's your address, Michael. Postmarked two weeks ago."

Michael shrugged.

I opened the envelope and found two pages inside. One was a copy of a medical report. The other was ornately handwritten, like the envelope. It read:

Dear Mr. Dresden,

By the time you read this letter, I will be dead. I have not been given the details, but I know a few things that will happen over the next few days. I write you now to say what I might not have the chance to in the flesh.

Your path is often a dark one. You do not always have the luxury that we do as Knights of the Cross. We struggle against powers of darkness. We live in black and white, while you must face a world of greys. It is never easy to know the path in such a place.

Trust your heart. You are a decent man. God lives in such hearts.

Enclosed is a medical report. My family is aware of it, though I have not shared it with Michael or Sanya. It is my hope that it will give you a measure of comfort in the face of my choice. Do not waste tears on me. I love my work. We all must die. There is no better way to do so than in the pursuit of something you love.

Walk in mercy and truth,

Shiro

I read over the medical report, blinking at several tears.

"What is it?" Sanya asked.

"It's from Shiro," I said. "He was dying."

Michael frowned at me.

I held up the medical report. "Cancer. Terminal. He knew it when he came here."

Michael took it and let out a long breath. "Now I understand."

"I don't."

Michael passed the report to Sanya and smiled. "Shiro must have known that we would need you to stop the Denarians. It's why he traded himself for your freedom. And why he accepted the curse in your place."

"Why?"

Michael shrugged. "You were the one we needed. You had all of the information. You were the one who realized Cassius was masquerading as Father Vincent. You had contacts within the local authorities to give you access to more information, to help us when we needed the concourse emptied. You were the one who could call in Marcone for his help."

"I'm not sure that says anything good about me," I said, glowering.

"It says that you were the right man in the right place and at the right time," Michael said. "What of the Shroud? Does Marcone have it?"

"I think so."

"How should we handle it?"

"We don't. I do."

Michael regarded me for a moment, then said, "All right." He stood up and then said, "Oh. The dry cleaners called. They said they're going to charge you a late fee if you don't swing by and pick up your laundry today. I'm running out for groceries. I can take you."

"I don't have anything that goes to a dry cleaners," I muttered. But I went with Michael.

The dry cleaners had my leather duster. It had been cleaned up and covered with a protective treatment. In the pockets were the keys to the Blue Beetle, along with a bill to a parking garage. On the back of the bill, written in flowing letters, were the words *thank you*.

So I guess Anna Valmont wasn't all that horrible a person after all.

But then, I've always been a sucker for a pretty face.

When I got back to my house, I found a postcard with a picture of Rio and no return address with my mail. There was a number on the back. I called the number, and after a few rings, Susan asked, "Harry?"

"Harry," I said.

"Are you all right?"

"Shot," I said. "It'll heal."

"Did you beat Nicodemus?"

"I got away from him," I said. "We stopped the plague. But he killed Shiro."

"Oh," she said quietly. "I'm sorry."

"I got my coat back. And my car. Not a total loss." I started opening mail as I spoke.

Susan asked, "What about the Shroud?"

"Jury's not out yet. Marcone got involved."

"What happened?" she said.

"He saved my life," I said. "Michael's too. He didn't have to do it."

"Wow."

"Yeah. Sometimes it feels like the older I get, the more confused everything is."

Susan coughed. "Harry. I'm sorry I wasn't around. By the time I was conscious, we were already over Central America."

"It's okay," I said.

"I didn't know what Martin had in mind," she said. "Honestly. I wanted to talk to you and to Trish and pick up a few of my things. I thought Martin was only coming along to help. I didn't know that he had come here to kill Ortega. He used me to cover his movements."

"It's okay."

"It isn't okay. And I'm sorry."

I opened an envelope, read it, and blurted, "Oh, you're *kidding* me."

"What?"

"I just opened a letter. It's from Larry Fowler's lawyer. The jerk is *suing* me for trashing his car and his studio."

"He can't prove that," Susan said. "Can he?"

"Whether or not he can, this is going to cost me a fortune in legal fees. Smarmy, mealymouthed jerk."

"Then I hate to add more bad news. Ortega is back in Casaverde, recovering. He's called in all his strongest knights and let it be widely known that he's coming to kill you personally."

"I'll cross that bridge when I come to it. Did you see the subtle humor there? Vampires, cross? God, I'm funny."

Susan said something in Spanish, not into the phone, and sighed. "Damn. I have to go."

"Saving nuns and orphans?" I asked.

"Leaping tall buildings in a single bound. I should probably put on some underwear."

That brought a smile to my face. "You joke around a lot more than you used to," I said. "I like it."

I could picture the sad smile on her face as she spoke. "I'm dealing with a lot of scary things," she said. "I think you have to react to them. And you either laugh at them or you go insane. Or you become like Martin. Shut off from everything and everyone. Trying not to feel."

"So you joke," I said.

"I learned it from you."

"I should open a school."

"Maybe so," she said. "I love you, Harry. I wish things were different."

My throat got tight. "Me too."

"I'll get you a drop address. If you ever need my help, get in touch."

"Only if I need your help?" I asked.

She exhaled slowly and said, "Yeah."

I tried to say, "Okay," but my throat was too tight to speak.

"Good-bye, Harry," Susan said.

I whispered, "Good-bye."

And that was the end of that.

I woke up to a ringing telephone the next day. "Hoss," Ebenezar said. "You should watch the news today." He hung up on me.

I went down to a nearby diner for breakfast, and asked the waitress to turn on the news. She did.

". . . extraordinary event reminiscent of the science-fiction horror stories around the turn of the millennium, what appeared to be an asteroid fell from space and impacted just outside the village of Casaverde in Honduras." The screen flickered to an aerial shot of an enormous, smoking hole in the ground, and a half-mile-wide circle of trees that had been blasted flat. Just past the circle of destruction stood a poor-looking village. "However, information coming in from agencies around the world indicates that the so-called meteor was in actuality a deactivated Soviet communications satellite which decayed in orbit and fell to earth. No estimates of the number of deaths or injuries in this tragic freak accident have yet reached authorities, but it seems unlikely that anyone in the manor house could possibly have survived the impact."

I sat slowly back, pursing my lips. I decided that maybe I wasn't sorry Asteroid Dresden turned out to be an old Soviet satellite after all. And I made a mental note to myself never to get on Ebenezar's bad side.

The next day I tracked down Marcone. It wasn't easy. I had to call in a couple of favors in the spirit world to get a beacon-spell going on him, and he knew all the tricks for losing a tail. I had to borrow Michael's truck so that I could have a prayer of following him inconspicuously. The Beetle may be way sexy, but subtle it ain't.

He changed cars twice and somehow called into effect the magical equivalent of a destructive electromagnetic pulse that scrambled my beacon-spell. Only quick thinking and some inspired thaumaturgy combined with my investigative skills let me stay with him.

He drove right on into the evening, to a private hospital in Wisconsin. It was a long-term-care and therapeutic facility. He pulled in, dressed in casual clothes and wearing a baseball cap, which alone generated enough cognitive dissonance to make me start drooling. He pulled a backpack out of the car and went inside. I gave him a little bit of a lead and then followed him with my beacon. I stayed outside, peering in windows at lit hallways, keeping pace and watching.

Marcone stopped at a room and went inside. I stood at the window, keeping track of him. The paper tag on the door from the hall read DOE, JANE in big, permanent marker letters that were faded with age. There was a single bed in the room, and there was a girl on it.

She wasn't old. I'd place her in her late teens or early twenties. She was so thin it was hard to tell. She wasn't on life support, but her bedcovers were flawlessly unwrinkled. Combined with her emaciated appearance, I was guessing she was in a coma, whoever she was.

Marcone drew up a chair beside the bed. He pulled out a teddy bear and slipped it into the crook of the girl's arm. He got out a book. Then he started reading to her, out loud. He sat there reading to her for an hour, before he slipped a bookmark into place and put the book back into the backpack.

Then he reached into the pack and pulled out the Shroud. He peeled down the outermost blanket on her bed, and carefully laid the Shroud over the girl, folding its ends in a bit to keep it from spilling out. Then he covered it up with the blanket and sat down in the chair again, his head bowed. I hadn't ever pictured John Marcone praying. But I saw him forming the word *please,* over and over.

He waited for another hour. Then, his face sunken and tired, he rose and kissed the girl on the head. He put the teddy bear back into the backpack, got up, and left the room.

I went to his car and sat down on the hood.

Marcone stopped in his tracks and stared at me when he saw me. I just sat there. He padded warily over to his car and said, voice quiet, "How did you find me?"

"Wasn't easy," I said.

"Is anyone else with you?"

"No."

I saw the wheels spinning in his head. I saw him panic a little. I saw him consider killing me. I saw him force himself to slow down and decide against any rash action. He nodded once, and said, "What do you want?"

"The Shroud."

"No," he said. There was a hint of frustration to his voice. "I just got it here."

"I saw," I said. "Who is the girl?"

His eyes went flat, and he said nothing.

"Okay, Marcone," I said. "You can give me the Shroud or you can explain it to the police when they come out here to search this place."

"You can't," he said, his voice quiet. "You can't do that to her. She'd be in danger."

My eyes widened. "She's yours?"

"I'll kill you," he said in that same soft voice. "If you so much as breathe in her direction, I'll kill you, Dresden. Myself."

I believed him.

"What's wrong with her?" I asked.

"Persistent vegetative state," he said. "Coma."

"You wanted it to heal her," I said quietly. "That's why you had it stolen."

"Yes."

"I don't think it works like that," I said. "It isn't as simple as plugging in a light."

"But it might work," he said.

I shrugged. "Maybe."

"I'll take it," he said. "It's all I have."

I looked back toward the window and was quiet for a minute. I made up my mind and said, "Three days."

He frowned. "What?"

"Three days," I said. "Three's a magic number. And supposedly that's how long Christ was wrapped in it. In three days, three sunrises, you should know whether it's going to help or not."

"And then?"

"Then the Shroud is returned in a plain brown wrapper to Father Forthill at Saint Mary of the Angels," I said. "No note. No nothing. Just returned."

"And if I don't, you'll expose her."

I shook my head and stood up. "No. I won't do that. I'll take it up with you."

He stared at me for a long moment before his expression softened. "All right."

I left him there.

When I'd first met Marcone, he'd tricked me into a soulgaze. Though I hadn't known the specifics, I knew then that he had a secret—one that gave him the incredible amount of will and inner strength needed to run one of the nation's largest criminal empires. He had something that drove him to be remorseless, practical, deadly.

Now I knew what that secret was.

Marcone was still a black hat. The pain and suffering of the criminal state he ruled accounted for an untold amount of human misery. Maybe he'd been doing it for a noble reason. I could understand that. But it didn't change anything. Marcone's good intentions could have paved a new lane on the road to hell.

But dammit, I couldn't hate him anymore. I couldn't hate him because I wasn't sure that I wouldn't have made the same choice in his place.

Hate was simpler, but the world ain't a simple place. It would have been easier to hate Marcone.

I just couldn't do it.

A few days later, Michael threw a cookout as a farewell celebration for Sanya, who was heading back to Europe now that the Shroud had been returned to Father Forthill. I was invited, so I showed up and ate about a hundred and fifty grilled hamburgers. When I was done with them, I went into the house, but stopped to glance into the sitting room by the front door.

Sanya sat in a recliner, his expression puzzled, blinking at the phone. "Again," he said.

Molly sat cross-legged on the couch near him with a phone book in her lap and my shopping list she'd picked up in the tree house laid flat over one half of it. Her expression was serious, but her eyes were sparkling as she drew a red line through another entry in the phone book. "How strange," she said, and read off another number.

Sanya started dialing. "Hello?" he said a moment later. "Hello, sir. Could you please tell me if you have Prince Albert in a can—" He blinked again, mystified, and reported to Molly, "They hung up *again*."

"*Weird,*" Molly said, and winked at me.

I left before I started choking on the laugh I had to hold back, and went out into the front yard. Little Harry was there by himself, playing in the grass in sight of his sister, inside.

"Heya, kid," I said. "You shouldn't be out here all by yourself. People will accuse you of being a reclusive madman. Next thing you know, you'll be wandering around saying, 'Woahse-bud.' "

I heard a clinking sound. Something shining landed in the grass by little Harry, and he immediately pushed himself to his feet, wobbled, then headed for it.

I panicked abruptly and lunged out ahead of him, slapping my hand down over a polished silver coin before the child could squat down to pick it up. I felt a prickling jolt shoot up my arm, and had the sudden, intangible impression that someone nearby was waking up from a nap and stretching.

I looked up to see a car on the street, driver-side window rolled down.

Nicodemus sat at the wheel, relaxed and smiling. "Be seeing you, Dresden."

He drove away. I took my shaking hand from the coin.

Lasciel's blackened sigil lay before my eyes. I heard a door open, and on pure instinct palmed the coin and slipped it in my pocket. I looked back to find Sanya frowning and looking up and down the street. His nostrils flared a few times, and he paced over to stand near me. He sniffed a few more times and then peered down at the baby. "Aha," he rumbled. "Someone is stinky." He swooped the kid up in his arms, making him squeal and laugh. "You mind if I steal your playmate for a minute, Harry?"

"Go ahead," I said. "I need to get going anyway."

Sanya nodded and grinned at me, offering his hand. I shook it. "It has been a pleasure to work with you," Sanya said. "Perhaps we will see each other again."

The coin felt cool and heavy in my pocket. "Yeah. Maybe so."

I left the cookout without saying good-bye, and headed home. I heard something the whole time, something whispering almost inaudibly. I drowned it out with loud and off-key singing, and got to work.

Ten hours later, I put down the excavating pick and glowered at the two-foot hole I had chipped in my lab's concrete floor. The whispering in my head had segued into "Sympathy for the Devil" by the Stones.

"Harry," whispered a gentle voice.

I dropped the coin into the hole. I slipped a steel ring about three inches across around it. I muttered to myself and willed energy into the ring. The whispering abruptly cut off.

I dumped two buckets of cement into the hole and smoothed it until it was level with the rest of my floor. After that, I hurried out of the lab and shut the door behind me.

Mister came over to demand attention. I settled on the couch, and he jumped up to sprawl on his back over my legs. I petted him and stared at Shiro's cane, resting in the corner.

"He said that I must live in a world of greys. To trust my heart." I rubbed Mister's favorite spot, behind his right ear, and he purred in approval. Mister, at least for the moment, agreed that my heart was in the right place. But it's possible he wasn't being objective.

After a while, I picked up Shiro's cane and stared down at the smooth old wood. *Fidelacchius*'s power whispered against my fingertips. There was a single Japanese character carved into the sheath. When I asked Bob, he told me that it read, simply, *Faith*.

It isn't good to hold on too hard to the past. You can't spend your whole life looking back. Not even when you can't see what lies ahead. All you can do is keep on keeping on, and try to believe that tomorrow will be what it should be—even if it isn't what you expected.

I took Susan's picture down. I put the postcards in a brown envelope. I picked up the jewel box that held the dinky engagement ring I'd offered her, and that she'd turned down. Then I put them all away in my closet.

I laid the old man's cane on my fireplace mantel.

Maybe some things just aren't meant to go together. Things like oil and water. Orange juice and toothpaste.

Me and Susan.

But tomorrow was another day.

A martial arts enthusiast whose résumé includes a long list of skills rendered obsolete at least two hundred years ago, **Jim Butcher** turned to writing as a career because anything else probably would have driven him insane. He lives in Independence, Missouri, with his wife, his son, and a ferocious guard dog.